MARK TWAIN

MARK TWAIN

HUCK FINN; PUDD'NHEAD WILSON;
NO. 44, THE MYSTERIOUS STRANGER;
AND OTHER WRITINGS

THE LIBRARY OF AMERICA

Volume compilation, notes, and chronology copyright © 1982, 1992, 2000
by Literary Classics of the United States, Inc., New York, N.Y.
All rights reserved.
No part of this book may be reproduced commercially
by offset-lithographic or equivalent copying devices without
the permission of the publisher.

No. 44, The Mysterious Stranger © 1969 by the Mark Twain
Foundation. "Selected Tales and Sketches" © 1979, 1981 by
the Mark Twain Foundation. Published by arrangement with
the University of California Press and Robert H. Hirst,
General Editor of the Mark Twain Project.

Distributed in the United States
by Penguin Putnam Inc.
and in Canada by Penguin Books Canada Ltd.

Library of Congress Catalog Number: 99–057964
For cataloging information, see end of *Notes* section.
ISBN 1–883011–88–4

First Library of America College Edition
Spring 2000

Manufactured in the United States of America

This volume includes works originally published in the
following Library of America volumes:

Mississippi Writings, edited by Guy Cardwell

Collected Tales Sketches, Speeches, & Essays (2 vols.),
edited by Louis J. Budd

Contents

ADVENTURES OF HUCKLEBERRY FINN

NOTICE.

Persons attempting to find a motive in this narrative will be prosecuted; persons attempting to find a moral in it will be banished; persons attempting to find a plot in it will be shot.

BY ORDER OF THE AUTHOR
Per G. G., Chief of Ordnance.

EXPLANATORY.

In this book a number of dialects are used, to wit: the Missouri negro dialect; the extremest form of the back-woods South-Western dialect; the ordinary "Pike-County" dialect; and four modified varieties of this last. The shadings have not been done in a hap-hazard fashion, or by guess-work; but pains-takingly, and with the trustworthy guidance and support of personal familiarity with these several forms of speech.

I make this explanation for the reason that without it many readers would suppose that all these characters were trying to talk alike and not succeeding.

The Author.

Contents

I

YOU DON'T KNOW about me, without you have read a book by the name of "The Adventures of Tom Sawyer," but that ain't no matter. That book was made by Mr. Mark Twain, and he told the truth, mainly. There was things which he stretched, but mainly he told the truth. That is nothing. I never seen anybody but lied, one time or another, without it was Aunt Polly, or the widow, or maybe Mary. Aunt Polly—Tom's Aunt Polly, she is—and Mary, and the Widow Douglas, is all told about in that book—which is mostly a true book; with some stretchers, as I said before.

Now the way that the book winds up, is this: Tom and me found the money that the robbers hid in the cave, and it made us rich. We got six thousand dollars apiece—all gold. It was an awful sight of money when it was piled up. Well, Judge Thatcher, he took it and put it out at interest, and it fetched us a dollar a day apiece, all the year round—more than a body could tell what to do with. The Widow Douglas, she took me for her son, and allowed she would sivilize me; but it was rough living in the house all the time, considering how dismal regular and decent the widow was in all her ways; and so when I couldn't stand it no longer, I lit out. I got into my old rags, and my sugar-hogshead again, and was free and satisfied. But Tom Sawyer, he hunted me up and said he was going to start a band of robbers, and I might join if I would go back to the widow and be respectable. So I went back.

The widow she cried over me, and called me a poor lost lamb, and she called me a lot of other names, too, but she never meant no harm by it. She put me in them new clothes again, and I couldn't do nothing but sweat and sweat, and feel all cramped up. Well, then, the old thing commenced again. The widow rung a bell for supper, and you had to come to time. When you got to the table you couldn't go right to eating, but you had to wait for the widow to tuck down her head and grumble a little over the victuals, though there warn't really anything the matter with them. That is, nothing only everything was cooked by itself. In a barrel of odds and ends it is different; things get mixed up, and the juice kind of swaps around, and the things go better.

After supper she got out her book and learned me about Moses and the Bulrushers; and I was in a sweat to find out all about him; but by-and-by she let it out that Moses had been dead a considerable long time; so then I didn't care no more about him; because I don't take no stock in dead people.

Pretty soon I wanted to smoke, and asked the widow to let me. But she wouldn't. She said it was a mean practice and wasn't clean, and I must try to not do it any more. That is just the way with some people. They get down on a thing when they don't know nothing about it. Here she was a bothering about Moses, which was no kin to her, and no use to anybody, being gone, you see, yet finding a power of fault with me for doing a thing that had some good in it. And she took snuff too; of course that was all right, because she done it herself.

Her sister, Miss Watson, a tolerable slim old maid, with goggles on, had just come to live with her, and took a set at me now, with a spelling-book. She worked me middling hard for about an hour, and then the widow made her ease up. I couldn't stood it much longer. Then for an hour it was deadly dull, and I was fidgety. Miss Watson would say, "Dont put your feet up there, Huckleberry;" and "dont scrunch up like that, Huckleberry—set up straight;" and pretty soon she would say, "Don't gap and stretch like that, Huckleberry—why don't you try to behave?" Then she told me all about the bad place, and I said I wished I was there. She got mad, then, but I didn't mean no harm. All I wanted was to go somewheres; all I wanted was a change, I warn't particular. She said it was wicked to say what I said; said she wouldn't say it for the whole world; *she* was going to live so as to go to the good place. Well, I couldn't see no advantage in going where she was going, so I made up my mind I wouldn't try for it. But I never said so, because it would only make trouble, and wouldn't do no good.

Now she had got a start, and she went on and told me all about the good place. She said all a body would have to do there was to go around all day long with a harp and sing,

forever and ever. So I didn't think much of it. But I never
said so. I asked her if she reckoned Tom Sawyer would go
there, and, she said, not by a considerable sight. I was glad
about that, because I wanted him and me to be together.

Miss Watson she kept pecking at me, and it got tiresome
and lonesome. By-and-by they fetched the niggers in and had
prayers, and then everybody was off to bed. I went up to my
room with a piece of candle and put it on the table. Then I
set down in a chair by the window and tried to think of
something cheerful, but it warn't no use. I felt so lonesome I
most wished I was dead. The stars was shining, and the leaves
rustled in the woods ever so mournful; and I heard an owl,
away off, who-whooing about somebody that was dead, and
a whippowill and a dog crying about somebody that was
going to die; and the wind was trying to whisper something
to me and I couldn't make out what it was, and so it made
the cold shivers run over me. Then away out in the woods I
heard that kind of a sound that a ghost makes when it wants
to tell about something that's on its mind and can't make
itself understood, and so can't rest easy in its grave and has to
go about that way every night grieving. I got so down-
hearted and scared, I did wish I had some company. Pretty
soon a spider went crawling up my shoulder, and I flipped it
off and it lit in the candle; and before I could budge it was
all shriveled up. I didn't need anybody to tell me that that
was an awful bad sign and would fetch me some bad luck, so
I was scared and most shook the clothes off of me. I got up
and turned around in my tracks three times and crossed my
breast every time; and then I tied up a little lock of my hair
with a thread to keep witches away. But I hadn't no confidence. You do that when you've lost a horse-shoe that you've
found, instead of nailing it up over the door, but I hadn't
ever heard anybody say it was any way to keep off bad luck
when you'd killed a spider.

I set down again, a shaking all over, and got out my pipe
for a smoke; for the house was all as still as death, now, and
so the widow wouldn't know. Well, after a long time I heard
the clock away off in the town go boom—boom—boom—
twelve licks—and all still again—stiller than ever. Pretty soon
I heard a twig snap, down in the dark amongst the trees—

something was a stirring. I set still and listened. Directly I
could just barely hear a "*me-yow! me-yow!*" down there. That
was good! Says I, "*me-yow! me-yow!*" as soft as I could, and
then I put out the light and scrambled out of the window
onto the shed. Then I slipped down to the ground and
crawled in amongst the trees, and sure enough there was Tom
Sawyer waiting for me.

II

WE WENT TIP-TOEING along a path amongst the trees back towards the end of the widow's garden, stooping down so as the branches wouldn't scrape our heads. When we was passing by the kitchen I fell over a root and made a noise. We scrouched down and laid still. Miss Watson's big nigger, named Jim, was setting in the kitchen door; we could see him pretty clear, because there was a light behind him. He got up and stretched his neck out about a minute, listening. Then he says,

"Who dah?"

He listened some more; then he come tip-toeing down and stood right between us; we could a touched him, nearly. Well, likely it was minutes and minutes that there warn't a sound, and we all there so close together. There was a place on my ankle that got to itching; but I dasn't scratch it; and then my ear begun to itch; and next my back, right between my shoulders. Seemed like I'd die if I couldn't scratch. Well, I've noticed that thing plenty of times since. If you are with the quality, or at a funeral, or trying to go to sleep when you ain't sleepy—if you are anywheres where it won't do for you to scratch, why you will itch all over in upwards of a thousand places. Pretty soon Jim says:

"Say—who is you? Whar is you? Dog my cats ef I didn' hear sumf'n. Well, I knows what I's gwyne to do. I's gwyne to set down here and listen tell I hears it agin."

So he set down on the ground betwixt me and Tom. He leaned his back up against a tree, and stretched his legs out till one of them most touched one of mine. My nose begun to itch. It itched till the tears come into my eyes. But I dasn't scratch. Then it begun to itch on the inside. Next I got to itching underneath. I didn't know how I was going to set still. This miserableness went on as much as six or seven minutes; but it seemed a sight longer than that. I was itching in eleven different places now. I reckoned I couldn't stand it more'n a minute longer, but I set my teeth hard and got ready to try. Just then Jim begun to breathe heavy; next he begun to snore—and then I was pretty soon comfortable again.

Tom he made a sign to me—kind of a little noise with his mouth—and we went creeping away on our hands and knees. When we was ten foot off, Tom whispered to me and wanted to tie Jim to the tree for fun; but I said no; he might wake and make a disturbance, and then they'd find out I warn't in. Then Tom said he hadn't got candles enough, and he would slip in the kitchen and get some more. I didn't want him to try. I said Jim might wake up and come. But Tom wanted to resk it; so we slid in there and got three candles, and Tom laid five cents on the table for pay. Then we got out, and I was in a sweat to get away; but nothing would do Tom but he must crawl to where Jim was, on his hands and knees, and play something on him. I waited, and it seemed a good while, everything was so still and lonesome.

As soon as Tom was back, we cut along the path, around the garden fence, and by-and-by fetched up on the steep top of the hill the other side of the house. Tom said he slipped Jim's hat off of his head and hung it on a limb right over him, and Jim stirred a little, but he didn't wake. Afterwards Jim said the witches bewitched him and put him in a trance, and rode him all over the State, and then set him under the trees again and hung his hat on a limb to show who done it. And next time Jim told it he said they rode him down to New Orleans; and after that, every time he told it he spread it more and more, till by-and-by he said they rode him all over the world, and tired him most to death, and his back was all over saddle-boils. Jim was monstrous proud about it, and he got so he wouldn't hardly notice the other niggers. Niggers would come miles to hear Jim tell about it, and he was more looked up to than any nigger in that country. Strange niggers would stand with their mouths open and look him all over, same as if he was a wonder. Niggers is always talking about witches in the dark by the kitchen fire; but whenever one was talking and letting on to know all about such things, Jim would happen in and say, "Hm! What you know 'bout witches?" and that nigger was corked up and had to take a back seat. Jim always kept that five-center piece around his neck with a string and said it was a charm the devil give to him with his own hands and told him he could cure anybody with it and fetch witches whenever he wanted to, just by saying something to it; but he never told what it was he said to it. Niggers would come from all around there and give Jim anything they had, just for a sight of that five-center piece; but they wouldn't touch it, because the devil had had his hands on it. Jim was most ruined, for a servant, because he got so stuck up on account of having seen the devil and been rode by witches.

Well, when Tom and me got to the edge of the hill-top, we looked away down into the village and could see three or four lights twinkling, where there was sick folks, may be; and the stars over us was sparkling ever so fine; and down by the village was the river, a whole mile broad, and awful still and grand. We went down the hill and found Jo Harper, and Ben Rogers, and two or three more of the boys, hid in the old tanyard. So we unhitched a skiff and pulled down the river two mile and a half, to the big scar on the hillside, and went ashore.

We went to a clump of bushes, and Tom made everybody swear to keep the secret, and then showed them a hole in the hill, right in the thickest part of the bushes. Then we lit the candles and crawled in on our hands and knees. We went about two hundred yards, and then the cave opened up. Tom poked about amongst the passages and pretty soon ducked under a wall where you wouldn't a noticed that there was a hole. We went along a narrow place and got into a kind of room, all damp and sweaty and cold, and there we stopped. Tom says:

"Now we'll start this band of robbers and call it Tom Sawyer's Gang. Everybody that wants to join has got to take an oath, and write his name in blood."

Everybody was willing. So Tom got out a sheet of paper that he had wrote the oath on, and read it. It swore every boy to stick to the band, and never tell any of the secrets; and if anybody done anything to any boy in the band, whichever boy was ordered to kill that person and his family must do it, and he mustn't eat and he mustn't sleep till he had killed them and hacked a cross in their breasts, which was the sign of the band. And nobody that didn't belong to the band could use that mark, and if he did he must be sued; and if he done it again he must be killed. And if anybody that belonged to the band told the secrets, he must have his throat cut, and then have his carcass burnt up and the ashes scattered all around, and his name blotted off of the list with blood and never mentioned again by the gang, but have a curse put on it and be forgot, forever.

Everybody said it was a real beautiful oath, and asked Tom if he got it out of his own head. He said, some of it, but the rest was out of pirate books, and robber books, and every gang that was high-toned had it.

Some thought it would be good to kill the *families* of boys that told the secrets. Tom said it was a good idea, so he took a pencil and wrote it in. Then Ben Rogers says:

"Here's Huck Finn, he hain't got no family—what you going to do 'bout him?"

"Well, hain't he got a father?" says Tom Sawyer.

"Yes, he's got a father, but you can't never find him, these days. He used to lay drunk with the hogs in the tanyard, but he hain't been seen in these parts for a year or more."

They talked it over, and they was going to rule me out, because they said every boy must have a family or somebody to kill, or else it wouldn't be fair and square for the others. Well, nobody could think of anything to do—everybody was stumped, and set still. I was most ready to cry; but all at once I thought of a way, and so I offered them Miss Watson— they could kill her. Everybody said:

"Oh, she'll do, she'll do. That's all right. Huck can come in."

Then they all stuck a pin in their fingers to get blood to sign with, and I made my mark on the paper.

"Now," says Ben Rogers, "what's the line of business of this Gang?"

"Nothing only robbery and murder," Tom said.

"But who are we going to rob? houses—or cattle—or——"

"Stuff! stealing cattle and such things ain't robbery, it's burglary," says Tom Sawyer. "We ain't burglars. That ain't no sort of style. We are highwaymen. We stop stages and carriages on the road, with masks on, and kill the people and take their watches and money."

"Must we always kill the people?"

"Oh, certainly. It's best. Some authorities think different, but mostly it's considered best to kill them. Except some that you bring to the cave here and keep them till they're ransomed."

"Ransomed? What's that?"

"I don't know. But that's what they do. I've seen it in books; and so of course that's what we've got to do."

"But how can we do it if we don't know what it is?"

"Why blame it all, we've *got* to do it. Don't I tell you it's in the books? Do you want to go to doing different from what's in the books, and get things all muddled up?"

"Oh, that's all very fine to *say*, Tom Sawyer, but how in the nation are these fellows going to be ransomed if we don't know how to do it to them? that's the thing *I* want to get at. Now what do you *reckon* it is?"

"Well I don't know. But per'aps if we keep them till they're ransomed, it means that we keep them till they're dead."

"Now, that's something *like*. That'll answer. Why couldn't you said that before? We'll keep them till they're ransomed to death—and a bothersome lot they'll be, too, eating up everything and always trying to get loose."

"How you talk, Ben Rogers. How can they get loose when there's a guard over them, ready to shoot them down if they move a peg?"

"A guard. Well, that *is* good. So somebody's got to set up all night and never get any sleep, just so as to watch them. I think that's foolishness. Why can't a body take a club and ransom them as soon as they get here?"

"Because it ain't in the books so—that's why. Now Ben Rogers, do you want to do things regular, or don't you?— that's the idea. Don't you reckon that the people that made the books knows what's the correct thing to do? Do you reckon *you* can learn 'em anything? Not by a good deal. No, sir, we'll just go on and ransom them in the regular way."

"All right. I don't mind; but I say it's a fool way, anyhow. Say—do we kill the women, too?"

"Well, Ben Rogers, if I was as ignorant as you I wouldn't let on. Kill the women? No—nobody ever saw anything in the books like that. You fetch them to the cave, and you're always as polite as pie to them; and by-and-by they fall in love with you and never want to go home any more."

"Well, if that's the way, I'm agreed, but I don't take no stock in it. Mighty soon we'll have the cave so cluttered up with women, and fellows waiting to be ransomed, that there won't be no place for the robbers. But go ahead, I ain't got nothing to say."

Little Tommy Barnes was asleep, now, and when they waked him up he was scared, and cried, and said he wanted to go home to his ma, and didn't want to be a robber any more.

So they all made fun of him, and called him cry-baby, and that made him mad, and he said he would go straight and tell all the secrets. But Tom give him five cents to keep quiet, and said we would all go home and meet next week and rob somebody and kill some people.

Ben Rogers said he couldn't get out much, only Sundays, and so he wanted to begin next Sunday; but all the boys said it would be wicked to do it on Sunday, and that settled the thing. They agreed to get together and fix a day as soon as they could, and then we elected Tom Sawyer first captain and Jo Harper second captain of the Gang, and so started home.

I clumb up the shed and crept into my window just before day was breaking. My new clothes was all greased up and clayey, and I was dog-tired.

III

WELL, I got a good going-over in the morning, from old Miss Watson, on account of my clothes; but the widow she didn't scold, but only cleaned off the grease and clay and looked so sorry that I thought I would behave a while if I could. Then Miss Watson she took me in the closet and prayed, but nothing come of it. She told me to pray every day, and whatever I asked for I would get it. But it warn't so. I tried it. Once I got a fish-line, but no hooks. It warn't any good to me without hooks. I tried for the hooks three or four times, but somehow I couldn't make it work. By-and-by, one day, I asked Miss Watson to try for me, but she said I was a fool. She never told me why, and I couldn't make it out no way.

I set down, one time, back in the woods, and had a long think about it. I says to myself, if a body can get anything they pray for, why don't Deacon Winn get back the money he lost on pork? Why can't the widow get back her silver snuff-box that was stole? Why can't Miss Watson fat up? No, says I to myself, there ain't nothing in it. I went and told the widow about it, and she said the thing a body could get by praying for it was "spiritual gifts." This was too many for me, but she told me what she meant—I must help other people, and do everything I could for other people, and look out for them all the time, and never think about myself. This was including Miss Watson, as I took it. I went out in the woods and turned it over in my mind a long time, but I couldn't see no advantage about it—except for the other people—so at last I reckoned I wouldn't worry about it any more, but just let it go. Sometimes the widow would take me one side and talk about Providence in a way to make a body's mouth water; but maybe next day Miss Watson would take hold and knock it all down again. I judged I could see that there was two Providences, and a poor chap would stand considerable show with the widow's Providence, but if Miss Watson's got him there warn't no help for him any more. I thought it all out, and reckoned I would belong to the widow's, if he wanted me, though I couldn't make out how he was agoing to be any better off then than what he was before, seeing I was so ignorant and so kind of low-down and ornery.

Pap he hadn't been seen for more than a year, and that was comfortable for me; I didn't want to see him no more. He used to always whale me when he was sober and could get his hands on me; though I used to take to the woods most of the time when he was around. Well, about this time he was found in the river drowned, about twelve mile above town, so people said. They judged it was him, anyway; said this drowned man was just his size, and was ragged, and had uncommon long hair—which was all like pap—but they couldn't make nothing out of the face, because it had been in the water so long it warn't much like a face at all. They said he was floating on his back in the water. They took him and buried him on the bank. But I warn't comfortable long, because I happened to think of something. I knowed mighty well that a drownded man don't float on his back, but on his face. So I knowed, then, that this warn't pap, but a woman dressed up in a man's clothes. So I was uncomfortable again. I judged the old man would turn up again by-and-by, though I wished he wouldn't.

We played robber now and then about a month, and then I resigned. All the boys did. We hadn't robbed nobody, we hadn't killed any people, but only just pretended. We used to hop out of the woods and go charging down on hog-drovers and women in carts taking garden stuff to market, but we never hived any of them. Tom Sawyer called the hogs "ingots," and he called the turnips and stuff "julery" and we would go to the cave and pow-wow over what we had done and how many people we had killed and marked. But I couldn't see no profit in it. One time Tom sent a boy to run about town with a blazing stick, which he called a slogan (which was the sign for the Gang to get together), and then he said he had got secret news by his spies that next day a whole parcel of Spanish merchants and rich A-rabs was going to camp in Cave Hollow with two hundred elephants, and six hundred camels, and over a thousand "sumter" mules, all loaded down with di'monds, and they didn't have only a guard of four hundred soldiers, and so we would lay in ambuscade, as he called it, and kill the lot and scoop the things. He said we must slick up our swords and guns, and get ready. He never could go after even a turnip-cart but he must have the swords and guns all scoured up for it; though they was only lath and broom-sticks, and you might scour at them till you rotted and then they warn't worth a mouthful of ashes more than what they was before. I didn't believe we could lick such a crowd of Spaniards and A-rabs, but I wanted to see the camels and elephants, so I was on hand next day, Saturday, in the ambuscade; and when we got the word, we rushed out of the woods and down the hill. But there warn't no Spaniards and A-rabs, and there warn't no camels nor no elephants. It warn't anything but a Sunday-school picnic, and only a primer-class at that. We busted it up, and chased the children up the hollow; but we never got anything but some doughnuts and jam, though Ben Rogers got a rag doll, and Jo Harper got a hymn-book and a tract; and then the teacher charged in and made us drop everything and cut. I didn't see no di'monds, and I told Tom Sawyer so. He said there was loads of them there, anyway; and he said there was A-rabs there, too, and elephants and things. I said, why couldn't we see them, then? He said if I warn't so ignorant, but had read a book called "Don Quixote," I would know without asking. He said it was all done by enchantment. He said there was hundreds of soldiers there, and elephants and treasure, and so on, but we had enemies which he called magicians, and they had turned the whole thing into an infant Sunday school, just out of spite. I said, all right, then the thing for us to do was to go for the magicians. Tom Sawyer said I was a numskull.

"Why," says he, "a magician could call up a lot of genies, and they would hash you up like nothing before you could say Jack Robinson. They are as tall as a tree and as big around as a church."

"Well," I says, "s'pose we got some genies to help *us*— can't we lick the other crowd then?"

"How you going to get them?"

"I don't know. How do *they* get them?"

"Why they rub an old tin lamp or an iron ring, and then the genies come tearing in, with the thunder and lightning a-ripping around and the smoke a-rolling, and everything

they're told to do they up and do it. They don't think nothing of pulling a shot tower up by the roots, and belting a
Sunday-school superintendent over the head with it—or any
other man."

"Who makes them tear around so?"

"Why, whoever rubs the lamp or the ring. They belong to
whoever rubs the lamp or the ring, and they've got to do
whatever he says. If he tells them to build a palace forty miles
long, out of di'monds, and fill it full of chewing gum, or
whatever you want, and fetch an emperor's daughter from
China for you to marry, they've got to do it—and they've
got to do it before sun-up next morning, too. And more—
they've got to waltz that palace around over the country
wherever you want it, you understand."

"Well," says I, "I think they are a pack of flatheads for not
keeping the palace themselves 'stead of fooling them away
like that. And what's more—if I was one of them I would see
a man in Jericho before I would drop my business and come
to him for the rubbing of an old tin lamp."

"How you talk, Huck Finn. Why, you'd *have* to come
when he rubbed it, whether you wanted to or not."

"What, and I as high as a tree and as big as a church? All
right, then; I *would* come; but I lay I'd make that man climb
the highest tree there was in the country."

"Shucks, it ain't no use to talk to you, Huck Finn. You
don't seem to know anything, somehow—perfect sap-head."

I thought all this over for two or three days, and then I
reckoned I would see if there was anything in it. I got an old
tin lamp and an iron ring and went out in the woods and
rubbed and rubbed till I sweat like an Injun, calculating to
build a palace and sell it; but it warn't no use, none of the
genies come. So then I judged that all that stuff was only just
one of Tom Sawyer's lies. I reckoned he believed in the Arabs
and the elephants, but as for me I think different. It had all
the marks of a Sunday school.

IV

WELL, three or four months run along, and it was well into the winter, now. I had been to school most all the time, and could spell, and read, and write just a little, and could say the multiplication table up to six times seven is thirty-five, and I don't reckon I could ever get any further than that if I was to live forever. I don't take no stock in mathematics, anyway.

At first I hated the school, but by-and-by I got so I could stand it. Whenever I got uncommon tired I played hookey, and the hiding I got next day done me good and cheered me up. So the longer I went to school the easier it got to be. I was getting sort of used to the widow's ways, too, and they warn't so raspy on me. Living in a house, and sleeping in a bed, pulled on me pretty tight, mostly, but before the cold weather I used to slide out and sleep in the woods, sometimes, and so that was a rest to me. I liked the old ways best, but I was getting so I liked the new ones, too, a little bit. The widow said I was coming along slow but sure, and doing very satisfactory. She said she warn't ashamed of me.

One morning I happened to turn over the salt-cellar at breakfast. I reached for some of it as quick as I could, to throw over my left shoulder and keep off the bad luck, but Miss Watson was in ahead of me, and crossed me off. She says, "Take your hands away, Huckleberry—what a mess you are always making." The widow put in a good word for me, but that warn't going to keep off the bad luck, I knowed that well enough. I started out, after breakfast, feeling worried and shaky, and wondering where it was going to fall on me, and what it was going to be. There is ways to keep off some kinds of bad luck, but this wasn't one of them kind; so I never tried to do anything, but just poked along low-spirited and on the watch-out.

I went down the front garden and clumb over the stile, where you go through the high board fence. There was an inch of new snow on the ground, and I seen somebody's tracks. They had come up from the quarry and stood around the stile a while, and then went on around the garden fence. It was funny they hadn't come in, after standing around so. I couldn't make it out. It was very curious, somehow. I was going to follow around, but I stooped down to look at the tracks first. I didn't notice anything at first, but next I did. There was a cross in the left boot-heel made with big nails, to keep off the devil.

I was up in a second and shinning down the hill. I looked over my shoulder every now and then, but I didn't see nobody. I was at Judge Thatcher's as quick as I could get there. He said:

"Why, my boy, you are all out of breath. Did you come for your interest?"

"No sir," I says; "is there some for me?"

"Oh, yes, a half-yearly is in, last night. Over a hundred and fifty dollars. Quite a fortune for you. You better let me invest it along with your six thousand, because if you take it you'll spend it."

"No sir," I says, "I don't want to spend it. I don't want it at all—nor the six thousand, nuther. I want you to take it; I want to give it to you—the six thousand and all."

He looked surprised. He couldn't seem to make it out. He says:

"Why, what can you mean, my boy?"

I says, "Don't you ask me no questions about it, please. You'll take it—won't you?"

He says:

"Well I'm puzzled. Is something the matter?"

"Please take it," says I, "and don't ask me nothing—then I won't have to tell no lies."

He studied a while, and then he says:

"Oho-o. I think I see. You want to *sell* all your property to me—not give it. That's the correct idea."

Then he wrote something on a paper and read it over, and says:

"There—you see it says 'for a consideration.' That means I have bought it of you and paid you for it. Here's a dollar for you. Now, you sign it."

So I signed it, and left.

*   *   *

Miss Watson's nigger, Jim, had a hair-ball as big as your fist, which had been took out of the fourth stomach of an ox, and he used to do magic with it. He said there was a spirit inside of it, and it knowed everything. So I went to him that night and told him pap was here again, for I found his tracks in the snow. What I wanted to know, was, what he was going to do, and was he going to stay? Jim got out his hair-ball, and said something over it, and then he held it up and dropped it on the floor. It fell pretty solid, and only rolled about an inch. Jim tried it again, and then another time, and it acted just the same. Jim got down on his knees and put his ear against it and listened. But it warn't no use; he said it wouldn't talk. He said sometimes it wouldn't talk without money. I told him I had an old slick counterfeit quarter that warn't no good because the brass showed through the silver a little, and it wouldn't pass nohow, even if the brass didn't show, because it was so slick it felt greasy, and so that would tell on it every time. (I reckoned I wouldn't say nothing about the dollar I got from the judge.) I said it was pretty bad money, but maybe the hair-ball would take it, because maybe it wouldn't know the difference. Jim smelt it, and bit it, and rubbed it, and said he would manage so the hair-ball would think it was good. He said he would split open a raw Irish potato and stick the quarter in between and keep it there all night, and next morning you couldn't see no brass, and it wouldn't feel greasy no more, and so anybody in town would take it in a minute, let alone a hair-ball. Well, I knowed a potato would do that, before, but I had forgot it.

Jim put the quarter under the hair-ball and got down and listened again. This time he said the hair-ball was all right. He said it would tell my whole fortune if I wanted it to. I says, go on. So the hair-ball talked to Jim, and Jim told it to me. He says:

"Yo' ole father doan' know, yit, what he's a-gwyne to do. Sometimes he spec he'll go 'way, en den agin he spec he'll stay. De bes' way is to res' easy en let de ole man take his own way. Dey's two angels hoverin' roun' 'bout him. One uv 'em is white en shiny, en 'tother one is black. De white one gits him to go right, a little while, den de black one sail in en bust it all up. A body can't tell, yit, which one gwyne to fetch him at de las'. But you is all right. You gwyne to have considable trouble in yo' life, en considable joy. Sometimes you gwyne to git hurt, en sometimes you gwyne to git sick; but every time you's gwyne to git well agin. Dey's two gals flyin' 'bout you in yo' life. One uv 'em's light en 'tother one is dark. One is rich en 'tother is po'. You's gwyne to marry de po' one fust en de rich one by-en-by. You wants to keep 'way fum de water as much as you kin, en don't run no resk, 'kase it's down in de bills dat you's gwyne to git hung."

When I lit my candle and went up to my room that night, there set pap, his own self!

V

I HAD shut the door to. Then I turned around, and there he was. I used to be scared of him all the time, he tanned me so much. I reckoned I was scared now, too; but in a minute I see I was mistaken. That is, after the first jolt, as you may say, when my breath sort of hitched—he being so unexpected; but right away after, I see I warn't scared of him worth bothering about.

He was most fifty, and he looked it. His hair was long and tangled and greasy, and hung down, and you could see his eyes shining through like he was behind vines. It was all black, no gray; so was his long, mixed-up whiskers. There warn't no color in his face, where his face showed; it was white; not like another man's white, but a white to make a body sick, a white to make a body's flesh crawl—a tree-toad white, a fish-belly white. As for his clothes—just rags, that was all. He had one ankle resting on 'tother knee; the boot on that foot was busted, and two of his toes stuck through, and he worked them now and then. His hat was laying on the floor; an old black slouch with the top caved in, like a lid.

I stood a-looking at him; he set there a-looking at me, with his chair tilted back a little. I set the candle down. I noticed the window was up; so he had clumb in by the shed. He kept a-looking me all over. By-and-by he says:

"Starchy clothes—very. You think you're a good deal of a big-bug, *don't* you?"

"Maybe I am, maybe I ain't," I says.

"Don't you give me none o' your lip," says he. "You've put on considerble many frills since I been away. I'll take you down a peg before I get done with you. You're educated, too, they say; can read and write. You think you're better'n your father, now, don't you, because he can't? *I'll* take it out of you. Who told you you might meddle with such hifalut'n foolishness, hey?—who told you you could?"

"The widow. She told me."

"The widow, hey?—and who told the widow she could put in her shovel about a thing that ain't none of her business?"

"Nobody never told her."

"Well, I'll learn her how to meddle. And looky here—you drop that school, you hear? I'll learn people to bring up a boy to put on airs over his own father and let on to be better'n what *he* is. You lemme catch you fooling around that school again, you hear? Your mother couldn't read, and she couldn't write, nuther, before she died. None of the family couldn't, before *they* died. *I* can't; and here you're a-swelling yourself up like this. I ain't the man to stand it—you hear? Say—lemme hear you read."

I took up a book and begun something about General Washington and the wars. When I'd read about a half a minute, he fetched the book a whack with his hand and knocked it across the house. He says:

"It's so. You can do it. I had my doubts when you told me. Now looky here; you stop that putting on frills. I won't have it. I'll lay for you, my smarty; and if I catch you about that school I'll tan you good. First you know you'll get religion, too. I never see such a son."

He took up a little blue and yaller picture of some cows and a boy, and says:

"What's this?"

"It's something they give me for learning my lessons good."

He tore it up, and says—

"I'll give you something better—I'll give you a cowhide."

He set there a-mumbling and a-growling a minute, and then he says—

"*Ain't* you a sweet-scented dandy, though? A bed; and bedclothes; and a look'n-glass; and a piece of carpet on the floor—and your own father got to sleep with the hogs in the tanyard. I never see such a son. I bet I'll take some o' these frills out o' you before I'm done with you. Why there ain't no end to your airs—they say you're rich. Hey?—how's that?"

"They lie—that's how."

"Looky here—mind how you talk to me; I'm a-standing about all I can stand, now—so don't gimme no sass. I've been in town two days, and I hain't heard nothing but about you bein' rich. I heard about it away down the river, too.

That's why I come. You git me that money to-morrow—I want it."

"I hain't got no money."

"It's a lie. Judge Thatcher's got it. You git it. I want it."

"I hain't got no money, I tell you. You ask Judge Thatcher; he'll tell you the same."

"All right. I'll ask him; and I'll make him pungle, too, or I'll know the reason why. Say—how much you got in your pocket? I want it."

"I hain't got only a dollar, and I want that to——"

"It don't make no difference what you want it for—you just shell it out."

He took it and bit it to see if it was good, and then he said he was going down town to get some whisky; said he hadn't had a drink all day. When he had got out on the shed, he put his head in again, and cussed me for putting on frills and trying to be better than him; and when I reckoned he was gone, he come back and put his head in again, and told me to mind about that school, because he was going to lay for me and lick me if I didn't drop that.

Next day he was drunk, and he went to Judge Thatcher's and bullyragged him and tried to make him give up the money, but he couldn't, and then he swore he'd make the law force him.

The judge and the widow went to law to get the court to take me away from him and let one of them be my guardian; but it was a new judge that had just come, and he didn't know the old man; so he said courts mustn't interfere and separate families if they could help it; said he'd druther not take a child away from its father. So Judge Thatcher and the widow had to quit on the business.

That pleased the old man till he couldn't rest. He said he'd cowhide me till I was black and blue if I didn't raise some money for him. I borrowed three dollars from Judge Thatcher, and pap took it and got drunk and went a-blowing around and cussing and whooping and carrying on; and he kept it up all over town, with a tin pan, till most midnight; then they jailed him, and next day they had him before court, and jailed him again for a week. But he said *he* was satisfied; said he was boss of his son, and he'd make it warm for *him*.

When he got out the new judge said he was agoing to make a man of him. So he took him to his own house, and dressed him up clean and nice, and had him to breakfast and dinner and supper with the family, and was just old pie to him, so to speak. And after supper he talked to him about temperance and such things till the old man cried, and said he'd been a fool, and fooled away his life; but now he was agoing to turn over a new leaf and be a man nobody wouldn't be ashamed of, and he hoped the judge would help him and not look down on him. The judge said he could hug him for them words; so *he* cried, and his wife she cried again; pap said he'd been a man that had always been misunderstood before, and the judge said he believed it. The old man said that what a man wanted that was down, was sympathy; and the judge said it was so; so they cried again. And when it was bed-time, the old man rose up and held out his hand, and says:

"Look at it gentlemen, and ladies all; take ahold of it; shake it. There's a hand that was the hand of a hog; but it ain't so no more; it's the hand of a man that's started in on a new life, and 'll die before he'll go back. You mark them words— don't forget I said them. It's a clean hand now; shake it— don't be afeard."

So they shook it, one after the other, all around, and cried. The judge's wife she kissed it. Then the old man he signed a pledge—made his mark. The judge said it was the holiest time on record, or something like that. Then they tucked the old man into a beautiful room, which was the spare room, and in the night sometime he got powerful thirsty and clumb out onto the porch-roof and slid down a stanchion and traded his new coat for a jug of forty-rod, and clumb back again and had a good old time; and towards daylight he crawled out again, drunk as a fiddler, and rolled off the porch and broke his left arm in two places and was most froze to death when somebody found him after sun-up. And when they come to look at that spare room, they had to take soundings before they could navigate it.

The judge he felt kind of sore. He said he reckoned a body could reform the ole man with a shot-gun, maybe, but he didn't know no other way.

VI

WELL, pretty soon the old man was up and around again, and then he went for Judge Thatcher in the courts to make him give up that money, and he went for me, too, for not stopping school. He catched me a couple of times and thrashed me, but I went to school just the same, and dodged him or out-run him most of the time. I didn't want to go to school much, before, but I reckoned I'd go now to spite pap. That law trial was a slow business; appeared like they warn't ever going to get started on it; so every now and then I'd borrow two or three dollars off of the judge for him, to keep from getting a cowhiding. Every time he got money he got drunk; and every time he got drunk he raised Cain around town; and every time he raised Cain he got jailed. He was just suited—this kind of thing was right in his line.

He got to hanging around the widow's too much, and so she told him at last, that if he didn't quit using around there she would make trouble for him. Well, *wasn't* he mad? He said he would show who was Huck Finn's boss. So he watched out for me one day in the spring, and catched me, and took me up the river about three mile, in a skiff, and crossed over to the Illinois shore where it was woody and there warn't no houses but an old log hut in a place where the timber was so thick you couldn't find it if you didn't know where it was.

He kept me with him all the time, and I never got a chance to run off. We lived in that old cabin, and he always locked the door and put the key under his head, nights. He had a gun which he had stole, I reckon, and we fished and hunted, and that was what we lived on. Every little while he locked me in and went down to the store, three miles, to the ferry, and traded fish and game for whisky and fetched it home and got drunk and had a good time, and licked me. The widow she found out where I was, by-and-by, and she sent a man over to try to get hold of me, but pap drove him off with the gun, and it warn't long after that till I was used to being where I was, and liked it, all but the cowhide part.

It was kind of lazy and jolly, laying off comfortable all day, smoking and fishing, and no books nor study. Two months or more run along, and my clothes got to be all rags and dirt, and I didn't see how I'd ever got to like it so well at the widow's, where you had to wash, and eat on a plate, and comb up, and go to bed and get up regular, and be forever bothering over a book and have old Miss Watson pecking at you all the time. I didn't want to go back no more. I had stopped cussing, because the widow didn't like it; but now I took to it again because pap hadn't no objections. It was pretty good times up in the woods there, take it all around.

But by-and-by pap got too handy with his hick'ry, and I couldn't stand it. I was all over welts. He got to going away so much, too, and locking me in. Once he locked me in and was gone three days. It was dreadful lonesome. I judged he had got drowned and I wasn't ever going to get out any more. I was scared. I made up my mind I would fix up some way to leave there. I had tried to get out of that cabin many a time, but I couldn't find no way. There warn't a window to it big enough for a dog to get through. I couldn't get up the chimbly, it was too narrow. The door was thick solid oak slabs. Pap was pretty careful not to leave a knife or anything in the cabin when he was away; I reckon I had hunted the place over as much as a hundred times; well, I was 'most all the time at it, because it was about the only way to put in the time. But this time I found something at last; I found an old rusty wood-saw without any handle; it was laid in between a rafter and the clapboards of the roof. I greased it up and went to work. There was an old horse-blanket nailed against the logs at the far end of the cabin behind the table, to keep the wind from blowing through the chinks and putting the candle out. I got under the table and raised the blanket and went to work to saw a section of the big bottom log out, big enough to let me through. Well, it was a good long job, but I was getting towards the end of it when I heard pap's gun in the woods. I got rid of the signs of my work, and dropped the blanket and hid my saw, and pretty soon pap come in.

Pap warn't in a good humor—so he was his natural self. He said he was down to town, and everything was going wrong. His lawyer said he reckoned he would win his lawsuit and get the money, if they ever got started on the trial; but then there was ways to put it off a long time, and Judge Thatcher knowed how to do it. And he said people allowed there'd be another trial to get me away from him and give me to the widow for my guardian, and they guessed it would win, this time. This shook me up considerable, because I didn't want to go back to the widow's any more and be so cramped up and sivilized, as they called it. Then the old man got to cussing, and cussed everything and everybody he could think of, and then cussed them all over again to make sure he hadn't skipped any, and after that he polished off with a kind of a general cuss all round, including a considerable parcel of people which he didn't know the names of, and so called them what's-his-name, when he got to them, and went right along with his cussing.

He said he would like to see the widow get me. He said he would watch out, and if they tried to come any such game on him he knowed of a place six or seven mile off, to stow me in, where they might hunt till they dropped and they couldn't find me. That made me pretty uneasy again, but only for a minute; I reckoned I wouldn't stay on hand till he got that chance.

The old man made me go to the skiff and fetch the things he had got. There was a fifty-pound sack of corn meal, and a side of bacon, ammunition, and a four-gallon jug of whisky, and an old book and two newspapers for wadding, besides some tow. I toted up a load, and went back and set down on the bow of the skiff to rest. I thought it all over, and I reckoned I would walk off with the gun and some lines, and take to the woods when I run away. I guessed I wouldn't stay in one place, but just tramp right across the country, mostly night times, and hunt and fish to keep alive, and so get so far away that the old man nor the widow couldn't ever find me any more. I judged I would saw out and leave that night if pap got drunk enough, and I reckoned he would. I got so full of it I didn't notice how long I was staying, till the old man hollered and asked me whether I was asleep or drownded.

I got the things all up to the cabin, and then it was about dark. While I was cooking supper the old man took a swig or two and got sort of warmed up, and went to ripping again.

He had been drunk over in town, and laid in the gutter all night, and he was a sight to look at. A body would a thought he was Adam, he was just all mud. Whenever his liquor begun to work, he most always went for the govment. This time he says:

"Call this a govment! why, just look at it and see what it's like. Here's the law a-standing ready to take a man's son away from him—a man's own son, which he has had all the trouble and all the anxiety and all the expense of raising. Yes, just as that man has got that son raised at last, and ready to go to work and begin to do suthin' for *him* and give him a rest, the law up and goes for him. And they call *that* govment! That ain't all, nuther. The law backs that old Judge Thatcher up and helps him to keep me out o' my property. Here's what the law does. The law takes a man worth six thousand dollars and upards, and jams him into an old trap of a cabin like this, and lets him go round in clothes that ain't fitten for a hog. They call that govment! A man can't get his rights in a govment like this. Sometimes I've a mighty notion to just leave the country for good and all. Yes, and I *told* 'em so; I told old Thatcher so to his face. Lots of 'em heard me, and can tell what I said. Says I, for two cents I'd leave the blamed country and never come anear it agin. Them's the very words. I says, look at my hat—if you call it a hat—but the lid raises up and the rest of it goes down till it's below my chin, and then it ain't rightly a hat at all, but more like my head was shoved up through a jint o' stove-pipe. Look at it, says I— such a hat for me to wear—one of the wealthiest men in this town, if I could git my rights.

"Oh, yes, this is a wonderful govment, wonderful. Why, looky here. There was a free nigger there, from Ohio; a mulatter, most as white as a white man. He had the whitest shirt on you ever see, too, and the shiniest hat; and there ain't a man in that town that's got as fine clothes as what he had; and he had a gold watch and chain, and a silver-headed cane—the awfulest old gray-headed nabob in the State. And what do you think? they said he was a p'fessor in a college, and could talk all kinds of languages, and knowed everything. And that ain't the wust. They said he could *vote*, when he was at home. Well, that let me out. Thinks I, what is the country

a-coming to? It was 'lection day, and I was just about to go
and vote, myself, if I warn't too drunk to get there; but when
they told me there was a State in this country where they'd
let that nigger vote, I drawed out. I says I'll never vote agin.
Them's the very words I said; they all heard me; and the
country may rot for all me—I'll never vote agin as long as I
live. And to see the cool way of that nigger—why, he
wouldn't a give me the road if I hadn't shoved him out o' the
way. I says to the people, why ain't this nigger put up at
auction and sold?—that's what I want to know. And what
do you reckon they said? Why, they said he couldn't be sold
till he'd been in the State six months, and he hadn't been
there that long yet. There, now—that's a specimen. They call
that a govment that can't sell a free nigger till he's been in the
State six months. Here's a govment that calls itself a govment,
and lets on to be a govment, and thinks it is a govment, and
yet's got to set stock-still for six whole months before it can
take ahold of a prowling, thieving, infernal, white-shirted free
nigger, and——"

Pap was agoing on so, he never noticed where his old limber legs was taking him to, so he went head over heels over
the tub of salt pork, and barked both shins, and the rest of
his speech was all the hottest kind of language—mostly hove
at the nigger and the govment, though he give the tub some,
too, all along, here and there. He hopped around the cabin
considerable, first on one leg and then on the other, holding
first one shin and then the other one, and at last he let out
with his left foot all of a sudden and fetched the tub a rattling
kick. But it warn't good judgment, because that was the boot
that had a couple of his toes leaking out of the front end of
it; so now he raised a howl that fairly made a body's hair
raise, and down he went in the dirt, and rolled there, and
held his toes; and the cussing he done then laid over anything
he had ever done previous. He said so his own self, afterwards. He had heard old Sowberry Hagan in his best days,
and he said it laid over him, too; but I reckon that was sort
of piling it on, maybe.

After supper pap took the jug, and said he had enough
whisky there for two drunks and one delirium tremens. That
was always his word. I judged he would be blind drunk in

about an hour, and then I would steal the key, or saw myself out, one or 'tother. He drank, and drank, and tumbled down on his blankets, by-and-by; but luck didn't run my way. He didn't go sound asleep, but was uneasy. He groaned, and moaned, and thrashed around this way and that, for a long time. At last I got so sleepy I couldn't keep my eyes open, all I could do, and so before I knowed what I was about I was sound asleep, and the candle burning.

I don't know how long I was asleep, but all of a sudden there was an awful scream and I was up. There was pap, looking wild and skipping around every which way and yelling about snakes. He said they was crawling up his legs; and then he would give a jump and scream, and say one had bit him on the cheek—but I couldn't see no snakes. He started and run round and round the cabin, hollering "take him off! take him off! he's biting me on the neck!" I never see a man look so wild in the eyes. Pretty soon he was all fagged out, and fell down panting; then he rolled over and over, wonderful fast, kicking things every which way, and striking and grabbing at the air with his hands, and screaming, and saying there was devils ahold of him. He wore out, by-and-by, and laid still a while, moaning. Then he laid stiller, and didn't make a sound. I could hear the owls and the wolves, away off in the woods, and it seemed terrible still. He was laying over by the corner. By-and-by he raised up, part way, and listened, with his head to one side. He says very low:

"Tramp—tramp—tramp; that's the dead; tramp—tramp —tramp; they're coming after me; but I won't go— Oh, they're here! don't touch me—don't! hands off—they're cold; let go— Oh, let a poor devil alone!"

Then he went down on all fours and crawled off begging them to let him alone, and he rolled himself up in his blanket and wallowed in under the old pine table, still a-begging; and then he went to crying. I could hear him through the blanket.

By-and-by he rolled out and jumped up on his feet looking wild, and he see me and went for me. He chased me round and round the place, with a clasp-knife, calling me the Angel of Death and saying he would kill me and then I couldn't come for him no more. I begged, and told him I was only Huck, but he laughed *such* a screechy laugh, and roared and cussed, and kept on chasing me up. Once when I turned short and dodged under his arm he made a grab and got me by the jacket between my shoulders, and I thought I was gone; but I slid out of the jacket quick as lightning, and saved myself. Pretty soon he was all tired out, and dropped down with his back against the door, and said he would rest a minute and then kill me. He put his knife under him, and said he would sleep and get strong, and then he would see who was who.

So he dozed off, pretty soon. By-and-by I got the old split-bottom chair and clumb up, as easy as I could, not to make any noise, and got down the gun. I slipped the ramrod down it to make sure it was loaded, and then I laid it across the turnip barrel, pointing towards pap, and set down behind it to wait for him to stir. And how slow and still the time did drag along.

VII

"GIT UP! what you 'bout!"

I opened my eyes and looked around, trying to make out where I was. It was after sun-up, and I had been sound asleep. Pap was standing over me, looking sour—and sick, too. He says—

"What you doin' with this gun?"

I judged he didn't know nothing about what he had been doing, so I says:

"Somebody tried to get in, so I was laying for him."

"Why didn't you roust me out?"

"Well I tried to, but I couldn't; I couldn't budge you."

"Well, all right. Don't stand there palavering all day, but out with you and see if there's a fish on the lines for breakfast. I'll be along in a minute."

He unlocked the door and I cleared out, up the river bank. I noticed some pieces of limbs and such things floating down, and a sprinkling of bark; so I knowed the river had begun to rise. I reckoned I would have great times, now, if I was over at the town. The June rise used to be always luck for me; because as soon as that rise begins, here comes cord-wood floating down, and pieces of log rafts—sometimes a dozen logs together; so all you have to do is to catch them and sell them to the wood yards and the sawmill.

I went along up the bank with one eye out for pap and 'tother one out for what the rise might fetch along. Well, all at once, here comes a canoe; just a beauty, too, about thirteen or fourteen foot long, riding high like a duck. I shot head first off of the bank, like a frog, clothes and all on, and struck out for the canoe. I just expected there'd be somebody laying down in it, because people often done that to fool folks, and when a chap had pulled a skiff out most to it they'd raise up and laugh at him. But it warn't so this time. It was a drift-canoe, sure enough, and I clumb in and paddled her ashore. Thinks I, the old man will be glad when he sees this—she's worth ten dollars. But when I got to shore pap wasn't in sight yet, and as I was running her into a little creek like a gully, all hung over with vines and willows, I struck another idea; I judged I'd hide her good, and then, stead of taking to the woods when I run off, I'd go down the river about fifty mile and camp in one place for good, and not have such a rough time tramping on foot.

It was pretty close to the shanty, and I thought I heard the old man coming, all the time; but I got her hid; and then I out and looked around a bunch of willows, and there was the old man down the path apiece just drawing a bead on a bird with his gun. So he hadn't seen anything.

When he got along, I was hard at it taking up a "trot" line. He abused me a little for being so slow, but I told him I fell in the river and that was what made me so long. I knowed he would see I was wet, and then he would be asking questions. We got five cat-fish off of the lines and went home.

While we laid off, after breakfast, to sleep up, both of us being about wore out, I got to thinking that if I could fix up some way to keep pap and the widow from trying to follow me, it would be a certainer thing than trusting to luck to get far enough off before they missed me; you see, all kinds of things might happen. Well, I didn't see no way for a while, but by-and-by pap raised up a minute, to drink another barrel of water, and he says:

"Another time a man comes a-prowling round here, you roust me out, you hear? That man warn't here for no good. I'd a shot him. Next time, you roust me out, you hear?"

Then he dropped down and went to sleep again—but what he had been saying give me the very idea I wanted. I says to myself, I can fix it now so nobody won't think of following me.

About twelve o'clock we turned out and went along up the bank. The river was coming up pretty fast, and lots of drift-wood going by on the rise. By-and-by, along comes part of a log raft—nine logs fast together. We went out with the skiff and towed it ashore. Then we had dinner. Anybody but pap would a waited and seen the day through, so as to catch more stuff; but that warn't pap's style. Nine logs was enough for one time; he must shove right over to town and sell. So he locked me in and took the skiff and started off towing the raft about half-past three. I judged he wouldn't come back that

night. I waited till I reckoned he had got a good start, then
I out with my saw and went to work on that log again. Before he was 'tother side of the river I was out of the hole; him
and his raft was just a speck on the water away off yonder.

I took the sack of corn meal and took it to where the canoe
was hid, and shoved the vines and branches apart and put it
in; then I done the same with the side of bacon; then the
whisky jug; I took all the coffee and sugar there was, and all
the ammunition; I took the wadding; I took the bucket and
gourd, I took a dipper and a tin cup, and my old saw and
two blankets, and the skillet and the coffee-pot. I took fish-
lines and matches and other things—everything that was
worth a cent. I cleaned out the place. I wanted an axe, but
there wasn't any, only the one out at the wood pile, and I
knowed why I was going to leave that. I fetched out the gun,
and now I was done.

I had wore the ground a good deal, crawling out of the
hole and dragging out so many things. So I fixed that as good
as I could from the outside by scattering dust on the place,
which covered up the smoothness and the sawdust. Then I
fixed the piece of log back into its place, and put two rocks
under it and one against it to hold it there,—for it was bent
up at that place, and didn't quite touch ground. If you stood
four or five foot away and didn't know it was sawed, you
wouldn't ever notice it; and besides, this was the back of the
cabin and it warn't likely anybody would go fooling around
there.

It was all grass clear to the canoe; so I hadn't left a track.
I followed around to see. I stood on the bank and looked out
over the river. All safe. So I took the gun and went up a piece
into the woods and was hunting around for some birds, when
I see a wild pig; hogs soon went wild in them bottoms after
they had got away from the prairie farms. I shot this fellow
and took him into camp.

I took the axe and smashed in the door—I beat it and
hacked it considerable, a-doing it. I fetched the pig in and
took him back nearly to the table and hacked into his throat
with the ax, and laid him down on the ground to bleed—I
say ground, because it *was* ground—hard packed, and no
boards. Well, next I took an old sack and put a lot of big

rocks in it,—all I could drag—and I started it from the pig and dragged it to the door and through the woods down to the river and dumped it in, and down it sunk, out of sight. You could easy see that something had been dragged over the ground. I did wish Tom Sawyer was there. I knowed he would take an interest in this kind of business, and throw in the fancy touches. Nobody could spread himself like Tom Sawyer in such a thing as that.

Well, last I pulled out some of my hair, and bloodied the ax good, and stuck it on the back side, and slung the ax in the corner. Then I took up the pig and held him to my breast with my jacket (so he couldn't drip) till I got a good piece below the house and then dumped him into the river. Now I thought of something else. So I went and got the bag of meal and my old saw out of the canoe and fetched them to the house. I took the bag to where it used to stand, and ripped a hole in the bottom of it with the saw, for there warn't no knives and forks on the place—pap done everything with his clasp-knife, about the cooking. Then I carried the sack about a hundred yards across the grass and through the willows east of the house, to a shallow lake that was five mile wide and full of rushes—and ducks too, you might say, in the season. There was a slough or a creek leading out of it on the other side, that went miles away, I don't know where, but it didn't go to the river. The meal sifted out and made a little track all the way to the lake. I dropped pap's whetstone there too, so as to look like it had been done by accident. Then I tied up the rip in the meal sack with a string, so it wouldn't leak no more, and took it and my saw to the canoe again.

It was about dark, now; so I dropped the canoe down the river under some willows that hung over the bank, and waited for the moon to rise. I made fast to a willow; then I took a bite to eat, and by-and-by laid down in the canoe to smoke a pipe and lay out a plan. I says to myself, they'll follow the track of that sackful of rocks to the shore and then drag the river for me. And they'll follow that meal track to the lake and go browsing down the creek that leads out of it to find the robbers that killed me and took the things. They won't ever hunt the river for anything but my dead carcass.

They'll soon get tired of that, and won't bother no more about me. All right; I can stop anywhere I want to. Jackson's Island is good enough for me; I know that island pretty well, and nobody ever comes there. And then I can paddle over to town, nights, and slink around and pick up things I want. Jackson's Island's the place.

I was pretty tired, and the first thing I knowed, I was asleep. When I woke up I didn't know where I was, for a minute. I set up and looked around, a little scared. Then I remembered. The river looked miles and miles across. The moon was so bright I could a counted the drift logs that went a slipping along, black and still, hundred of yards out from shore. Everything was dead quiet, and it looked late, and *smelt* late. You know what I mean—I don't know the words to put it in.

I took a good gap and a stretch, and was just going to unhitch and start, when I heard a sound away over the water. I listened. Pretty soon I made it out. It was that dull kind of a regular sound that comes from oars working in rowlocks when it's a still night. I peeped out through the willow branches, and there it was—a skiff, away across the water. I couldn't tell how many was in it. It kept a-coming, and when it was abreast of me I see there warn't but one man in it. Thinks I, maybe it's pap, though I warn't expecting him. He dropped below me, with the current, and by-and-by he come a-swinging up shore in the easy water, and he went by so close I could a reached out the gun and touched him. Well, it *was* pap, sure enough—and sober, too, by the way he laid to his oars.

I didn't lose no time. The next minute I was a-spinning down stream soft but quick in the shade of the bank. I made two mile and a half, and then struck out a quarter of a mile or more towards the middle of the river, because pretty soon I would be passing the ferry landing and people might see me and hail me. I got out amongst the drift-wood and then laid down in the bottom of the canoe and let her float. I laid there and had a good rest and a smoke out of my pipe, looking away into the sky, not a cloud in it. The sky looks ever so deep when you lay down on your back in the moonshine; I never knowed it before. And how far a body can hear on the water such nights! I heard people talking at the ferry landing. I heard what they said, too, every word of it. One man said it was getting towards the long days and the short nights, now. 'Tother one said *this* warn't one of the short ones, he reckoned—and then they laughed, and he said it over again and they laughed again; then they waked up another fellow and told him, and laughed, but he didn't laugh; he ripped out something brisk and said let him alone. The first fellow said he 'lowed to tell it to his old woman—she would think it was pretty good; but he said that warn't nothing to some things he had said in his time. I heard one man say it was nearly three o'clock, and he hoped daylight wouldn't wait more than about a week longer. After that, the talk got further and further away, and I couldn't make out the words any more, but I could hear the mumble; and now and then a laugh, too, but it seemed a long ways off.

I was away below the ferry now. I rose up and there was Jackson's Island, about two mile and a half down stream, heavy-timbered and standing up out of the middle of the river, big and dark and solid, like a steamboat without any lights. There warn't any signs of the bar at the head—it was all under water, now.

It didn't take me long to get there. I shot past the head at a ripping rate, the current was so swift, and then I got into the dead water and landed on the side towards the Illinois shore. I run the canoe into a deep dent in the bank that I knowed about; I had to part the willow branches to get in; and when I made fast nobody could a seen the canoe from the outside.

I went up and set down on a log at the head of the island and looked out on the big river and the black driftwood, and away over to the town, three mile away, where there was three or four lights twinkling. A monstrous big lumber raft was about a mile up stream, coming along down, with a lantern in the middle of it. I watched it come creeping down, and when it was most abreast of where I stood I heard a man say, "Stern oars, there! heave her head to stabboard!" I heard that just as plain as if the man was by my side.

There was a little gray in the sky, now; so I stepped into the woods and laid down for a nap before breakfast.

VIII

THE SUN was up so high when I waked, that I judged it
was after eight o'clock. I laid there in the grass and the
cool shade, thinking about things and feeling rested and
ruther comfortable and satisfied. I could see the sun out at
one or two holes, but mostly it was big trees all about, and
gloomy in there amongst them. There was freckled places on
the ground where the light sifted down through the leaves,
and the freckled places swapped about a little, showing there
was a little breeze up there. A couple of squirrels set on a
limb and jabbered at me very friendly.

I was powerful lazy and comfortable—didn't want to get
up and cook breakfast. Well, I was dozing off again, when I
thinks I hears a deep sound of "boom!" away up the river. I
rouses up and rests on my elbow and listens; pretty soon I
hears it again. I hopped up and went and looked out at a hole
in the leaves, and I see a bunch of smoke laying on the water
a long ways up—about abreast the ferry. And there was the
ferry-boat full of people, floating along down. I knowed what
was the matter, now. "Boom!" I see the white smoke squirt
out of the ferry-boat's side. You see, they was firing cannon
over the water, trying to make my carcass come to the top.

I was pretty hungry, but it warn't going to do for me to
start a fire, because they might see the smoke. So I set there
and watched the cannon-smoke and listened to the boom.
The river was a mile wide, there, and it always looks pretty
on a summer morning—so I was having a good enough time
seeing them hunt for my remainders, if I only had a bite to
eat. Well, then I happened to think how they always put
quicksilver in loaves of bread and float them off because they
always go right to the drownded carcass and stop there. So
says I, I'll keep a lookout, and if any of them's floating
around after me, I'll give them a show. I changed to the Illinois edge of the island to see what luck I could have, and I
warn't disappointed. A big double loaf come along, and I
most got it, with a long stick, but my foot slipped and she
floated out further. Of course I was where the current set in

44

the closest to the shore—I knowed enough for that. But by-and-by along comes another one, and this time I won. I took out the plug and shook out the little dab of quicksilver, and set my teeth in. It was "baker's bread"—what the quality eat—none of your low-down corn-pone.

I got a good place amongst the leaves, and set there on a log, munching the bread and watching the ferry-boat, and very well satisfied. And then something struck me. I says, now I reckon the widow or the parson or somebody prayed that this bread would find me, and here it has gone and done it. So there ain't no doubt but there is something in that thing. That is, there's something in it when a body like the widow or the person prays, but it don't work for me, and I reckon it don't work for only just the right kind.

I lit a pipe and had a good long smoke and went on watching. The ferry-boat was floating with the current, and I allowed I'd have a chance to see who was aboard when she come along, because she would come in close, where the bread did. When she'd got pretty well along down towards me, I put out my pipe and went to where I fished out the bread, and laid down behind a log on the bank in a little open place. Where the log forked I could peep through.

By-and-by she come along, and she drifted in so close that they could a run out a plank and walked ashore. Most everybody was on the boat. Pap, and Judge Thatcher, and Bessie Thatcher, and Jo Harper, and Tom Sawyer, and his old Aunt Polly, and Sid and Mary, and plenty more. Everybody was talking about the murder, but the captain broke in and says:

"Look sharp, now; the current sets in the closest here, and maybe he's washed ashore and got tangled amongst the brush at the water's edge. I hope so, anyway."

I didn't hope so. They all crowded up and leaned over the rails, nearly in my face, and kept still, watching with all their might. I could see them first-rate, but they couldn't see me. Then the captain sung out:

"Stand away!" and the cannon let off such a blast right before me that it made me deef with the noise and pretty near blind with the smoke, and I judged I was gone. If they'd a had some bullets in, I reckon they'd a got the corpse they was after. Well, I see I warn't hurt, thanks to goodness. The boat floated on and went out of sight around the shoulder of the island. I could hear the booming, now and then, further and further off, and by-and-by after an hour, I didn't hear it no more. The island was three mile long. I judged they had got to the foot, and was giving it up. But they didn't yet a while. They turned around the foot of the island and started up the channel on the Missouri side, under steam, and booming once in a while as they went. I crossed over to that side and watched them. When they got abreast the head of the island they quit shooting and dropped over to the Missouri shore and went home to the town.

I knowed I was all right now. Nobody else would come a-hunting after me. I got my traps out of the canoe and made me a nice camp in the thick woods. I made a kind of a tent out of my blankets to put my things under so the rain couldn't get at them. I catched a cat-fish and haggled him open with my saw, and towards sundown I started my camp fire and had supper. Then I set out a line to catch some fish for breakfast.

When it was dark I set by my camp fire smoking, and feeling pretty satisfied; but by-and-by it got sort of lonesome, and so I went and set on the bank and listened to the currents washing along, and counted the stars and drift-logs and rafts that come down, and then went to bed; there ain't no better way to put in time when you are lonesome; you can't stay so, you soon get over it.

And so for three days and nights. No difference—just the same thing. But the next day I went exploring around down through the island. I was boss of it; it all belonged to me, so to say, and I wanted to know all about it; but mainly I wanted to put in the time. I found plenty strawberries, ripe and prime; and green summer-grapes, and green razberries; and the green blackberries was just beginning to show. They would all come handy by-and-by, I judged.

Well, I went fooling along in the deep woods till I judged I warn't far from the foot of the island. I had my gun along, but I hadn't shot nothing; it was for protection; thought I would kill some game nigh home. About this time I mighty near stepped on a good sized snake, and it went sliding off through the grass and flowers, and I after it, trying to get a shot at it. I clipped along, and all of a sudden I bounded right on to the ashes of a camp fire that was still smoking.

My heart jumped up amongst my lungs. I never waited for to look further, but uncocked my gun and went sneaking back on my tip-toes as fast as ever I could. Every now and then I stopped a second, amongst the thick leaves, and listened; but my breath come so hard I couldn't hear nothing else. I slunk along another piece further, then listened again; and so on, and so on; if I see a stump, I took it for a man; if I trod on a stick and broke it, it made me feel like a person had cut one of my breaths in two and I only got half, and the short half, too.

When I got to camp I warn't feeling very brash, there warn't much sand in my craw; but I says, this ain't no time to be fooling around. So I got all my traps into my canoe again so as to have them out of sight, and I put out the fire and scattered the ashes around to look like an old last year's camp, and then clumb a tree.

I reckon I was up in the tree two hours; but I didn't see nothing, I didn't hear nothing—I only *thought* I heard and seen as much as a thousand things. Well, I couldn't stay up there forever; so at last I got down, but I kept in the thick woods and on the lookout all the time. All I could get to eat was berries and what was left over from breakfast.

By the time it was night I was pretty hungry. So when it was good and dark, I slid out from shore before moonrise and paddled over to the Illinois bank—about a quarter of a mile. I went out in the woods and cooked a supper, and I had about made up my mind I would stay there all night, when I hear a *plunkety-plunk, plunkety-plunk*, and says to myself, horses coming; and next I hear people's voices. I got everything into the canoe as quick as I could, and then went creeping through the woods to see what I could find out. I hadn't got far when I hear a man say:

"We better camp here, if we can find a good place; the horses is about beat out. Let's look around."

I didn't wait, but shoved out and paddled away easy. I tied up in the old place, and reckoned I would sleep in the canoe.

I didn't sleep much. I couldn't, somehow, for thinking. And every time I waked up I thought somebody had me by the neck. So the sleep didn't do me no good. By-and-by I says to myself, I can't live this way; I'm agoing to find out who it is that's here on the island with me; I'll find it out or bust. Well, I felt better, right off.

So I took my paddle and slid out from shore just a step or two, and then let the canoe drop along down amongst the shadows. The moon was shining, and outside of the shadows it made it most as light as day. I poked along well onto an hour, everything still as rocks and sound asleep. Well by this time I was most down to the foot of the island. A little ripply, cool breeze begun to blow, and that was as good as saying the night was about done. I give her a turn with the paddle and brung her nose to shore; then I got my gun and slipped out and into the edge of the woods. I set down there on a log and looked out through the leaves. I see the moon go off watch and the darkness begin to blanket the river. But in a little while I see a pale streak over the tree-tops, and knowed the day was coming. So I took my gun and slipped off to-wards where I had run across that camp fire, stopping every minute or two to listen. But I hadn't no luck, somehow; I couldn't seem to find the place. But by-and-by, sure enough, I catched a glimpse of fire, away through the trees. I went for it, cautious and slow. By-and-by I was close enough to have a look, and there laid a man on the ground. It most give me the fan-tods. He had a blanket around his head, and his head was nearly in the fire. I set there behind a clump of bushes, in about six foot of him, and kept my eyes on him steady. It was getting gray daylight, now. Pretty soon he gapped, and stretched himself, and hove off the blanket, and it was Miss Watson's Jim! I bet I was glad to see him. I says:

"Hello, Jim!" and skipped out.

He bounced up and stared at me wild. Then he drops down on his knees, and puts his hands together and says:

"Doan' hurt me—don't! I hain't ever done no harm to a ghos'. I awluz liked dead people, en done all I could for 'em. You go en git in de river agin, whah you b'longs, en doan' do nuffin to Ole Jim, 'at 'uz awluz yo' fren'."

Well, I warn't long making him understand I warn't dead.

I was ever so glad to see Jim. I warn't lonesome, now. I told him I warn't afraid of *him* telling the people where I was. I talked along, but he only set there and looked at me; never said nothing. Then I says:

"It's good daylight. Le's get breakfast. Make up your camp fire good."

"What's de use er makin' up de camp fire to cook strawbries en sich truck? But you got a gun, hain't you? Den we kin git sumfn better den strawbries."

"Strawberries and such truck," I says. "Is that what you live on?"

"I couldn' git nuffn else," he says.

"Why, how long you been on the island, Jim?"

"I come heah de night arter you's killed."

"What, all that time?"

"Yes-indeedy."

"And ain't you had nothing but that kind of rubbage to eat?"

"No, sah—nuffn else."

"Well, you must be most starved, ain't you?"

"I reck'n I could eat a hoss. I think I could. How long you ben on de islan'?"

"Since the night I got killed."

"No! W'y, what has you lived on? But you got a gun. Oh, yes, you got a gun. Dat's good. Now you kill sumfn en I'll make up de fire."

So we went over to where the canoe was, and while he built a fire in a grassy open place amongst the trees, I fetched meal and bacon and coffee, and coffee-pot and frying-pan, and sugar and tin cups, and the nigger was set back considerable, because he reckoned it was all done with witchcraft. I catched a good big cat-fish, too, and Jim cleaned him with his knife, and fried him.

When breakfast was ready, we lolled on the grass and eat it smoking hot. Jim laid it in with all his might, for he was most about starved. Then when we had got pretty well stuffed, we laid off and lazied.

By-and-by Jim says:

"But looky here, Huck, who wuz it dat 'uz killed in dat shanty, ef it warn't you?"

Then I told him the whole thing, and he said it was smart. He said Tom Sawyer couldn't get up no better plan than what I had. Then I says:

"How do you come to be here, Jim, and how'd you get here?"

He looked pretty uneasy, and didn't say nothing for a minute. Then he says:

"Maybe I better not tell."

"Why, Jim?"

"Well, dey's reasons. But you wouldn' tell on me ef I 'uz to tell you, would you, Huck?"

"Blamed if I would, Jim."

"Well, I b'lieve you, Huck. I—I *run off*."

"Jim!"

"But mind, you said you wouldn't tell—you know you said you wouldn't tell, Huck."

"Well, I did. I said I wouldn't, and I'll stick to it. Honest *injun* I will. People would call me a low down Ablitionist and despise me for keeping mum—but that don't make no difference. I ain't agoing to tell, and I ain't agoing back there anyways. So now, le's know all about it."

"Well, you see, it 'uz dis way. Ole Missus—dat's Miss Watson—she pecks on me all de time, en treats me pooty rough, but she awluz said she wouldn' sell me down to Orleans. But I noticed dey wuz a nigger trader roun' de place considable, lately, en I begin to git oneasy. Well, one night I creeps to de do', pooty late, en de do' warn't quite shet, en I hear ole missus tell de widder she gwyne to sell me down to Orleans, but she didn' want to, but she could git eight hund'd dollars for me, en it 'uz sich a big stack o' money she couldn' resis'. De widder she try to git her to say she wouldn' do it, but I never waited to hear de res'. I lit out mighty quick, I tell you.

"I tuck out en shin down de hill en 'spec to steal a skift 'long de sho' som'ers 'bove de town, but dey wuz people a-stirrin' yit, so I hid in de ole tumble-down cooper shop on de bank to wait for everybody to go 'way. Well, I wuz dah all night. Dey wuz somebody roun' all de time. 'Long 'bout six in de mawnin', skifts begin to go by, en 'bout eight er nine every skift dat went 'long wuz talkin' 'bout how yo' pap come over to de town en say you's killed. Dese las' skifts wuz full o' ladies en genlmen agoin' over for to see de place. Sometimes dey'd pull up at de sho' en take a res' b'fo' dey started acrost, so by de talk I got to know all 'bout de killin'. I 'uz powerful sorry you's killed, Huck, but I ain't no mo', now.

"I laid dah under de shavins all day. I 'uz hungry, but I warn't afeared; bekase I knowed ole missus en de widder wuz goin' to start to de camp-meetn' right arter breakfas' en be gone all day, en dey knows I goes off wid de cattle 'bout daylight, so dey wouldn' 'spec to see me roun' de place, en so dey wouldn' miss me tell arter dark in de evenin'. De yuther servants wouldn' miss me, kase dey'd shin out en take holiday, soon as de ole folks 'uz out'n de way.

"Well, when it come dark I tuck out up de river road, en went 'bout two mile er more to whah dey warn't no houses. I'd made up my mine 'bout what I's agwyne to do. You see ef I kep' on tryin' to git away afoot, de dogs 'ud track me; ef I stole a skift to cross over, dey'd miss dat skift, you see, en dey'd know 'bout what I'd lan' on de yuther side en whah to pick up my track. So I says, a raff is what I's arter; it doan' *make* no track.

"I see a light a-comin' roun' de p'int, bymeby, so I wade' in en shove' a log ahead o' me, en swum more'n half-way acrost de river, en got in 'mongst de drift-wood, en kep' my head down low, en kinder swum agin de current tell de raff come along. Den I swum to de stern uv it, en tuck aholt. It clouded up en 'uz pooty dark for a little while. So I clumb up en laid down on de planks. De men 'uz all 'way yonder in de middle, whah de lantern wuz. De river wuz arisin' en dey wuz a good current; so I reck'n'd 'at by fo' in de mawnin' I'd be twenty-five mile down de river, en den I'd slip in, jis' b'fo' daylight, en swim asho' en take to de woods on de Illinoi side.

"But I didn' have no luck. When we 'uz mos' down to de head er de islan', a man begin to come aft wid de lantern. I see it warn't no use fer to wait, so I slid overboad, en struck out fer de islan'. Well, I had a notion I could lan' mos' anywhers, but I couldn't—bank too bluff. I 'uz mos' to de foot

er de islan' b'fo' I foun' a good place. I went into de woods
en jedged I wouldn' fool wid raffs no mo', long as dey move
de lantern roun' so. I had my pipe en a plug er dog-leg, en
some matches in my cap, en dey warn't wet, so I 'uz all right."

"And so you ain't had no meat nor bread to eat all this
time? Why didn't you get mud-turkles?"

"How you gwyne to git'm? You can't slip up on um en
grab um; en how's a body gwyne to hit um wid a rock? How
could a body do it in de night? en I warn't gwyne to show
myself on de bank in de daytime."

"Well, that's so. You've had to keep in the woods all the
time, of course. Did you hear 'em shooting the cannon?"

"Oh, yes. I knowed dey was arter you. I see um go by
heah; watched um thoo de bushes."

Some young birds come along, flying a yard or two at a
time and lighting. Jim said it was a sign it was going to rain.
He said it was a sign when young chickens flew that way, and
so he reckoned it was the same way when young birds done
it. I was going to catch some of them, but Jim wouldn't let
me. He said it was death. He said his father laid mighty sick
once, and some of them catched a bird, and his old granny
said his father would die, and he did.

And Jim said you musn't count the things you are going to
cook for dinner, because that would bring bad luck. The same
if you shook the table-cloth after sundown. And he said if a
man owned a bee-hive, and that man died, the bees must be
told about it before sun-up next morning, or else the bees
would all weaken down and quit work and die. Jim said bees
wouldn't sting idiots; but I didn't believe that, because I had
tried them lots of times myself, and they wouldn't sting me.

I had heard about some of these things before, but not all
of them. Jim knowed all kinds of signs. He said he knowed
most everything. I said it looked to me like all the signs was
about bad luck, and so I asked him if there warn't any good-
luck signs. He says:

"Mighty few—an' *dey* ain' no use to a body. What you
want to know when good luck's a-comin' for? want to keep
it off?" And he said: "Ef you's got hairy arms en a hairy
breas', it's a sign dat you's agwyne to be rich. Well, dey's
some use in a sign like dat, 'kase it's so fur ahead. You see,

maybe you's got to be po' a long time fust, en so you might git discourage' en kill yo'sef 'f you did n' know by de sign dat you gwyne to be rich bymeby."

"Have you got hairy arms and a hairy breast, Jim?"

"What's de use to ax dat question? don' you see I has?"

"Well, are you rich?"

"No, but I ben rich wunst, and gwyne to be rich agin. Wunst I had foteen dollars, but I tuck to specalat'n', en got busted out."

"What did you speculate in, Jim?"

"Well, fust I tackled stock."

"What kind of stock?"

"Why, live stock. Cattle, you know. I put ten dollars in a cow. But I ain' gwyne to resk no mo' money in stock. De cow up 'n' died on my han's."

"So you lost the ten dollars."

"No, I didn' lose it all. I on'y los' 'bout nine of it. I sole de hide en taller for a dollar en ten cents."

"You had five dollars and ten cents left. Did you speculate any more?"

"Yes. You know dat one-laigged nigger dat b'longs to old Misto Bradish? well, he sot up a bank, en say anybody dat put in a dollar would git fo' dollars mo' at de en' er de year. Well, all de niggers went in, but dey didn' have much. I wuz de on'y one dat had much. So I stuck out for mo' dan fo' dollars, en I said 'f I didn' git it I'd start a bank mysef. Well o' course dat nigger want' to keep me out er de business, bekase he say dey warn't business 'nough for two banks, so he say I could put in my five dollars en he pay me thirty-five at de en' er de year.

"So I done it. Den I reck'n'd I'd inves' de thirty-five dollars right off en keep things a-movin'. Dey wuz a nigger name' Bob, dat had ketched a wood-flat, en his marster didn' know it; en I bought it off'n him en told him to take de thirty-five dollars when de en' er de year come; but somebody stole de wood-flat dat night, en nex' day de one-laigged nigger say de bank 's busted. So dey didn' none uv us git no money."

"What did you do with the ten cents, Jim?"

"Well, I 'uz gwyne to spen' it, but I had a dream, en de dream tole me to give it to a nigger name' Balum—Balum's

Ass dey call him for short, he's one er dem chuckle-heads, you know. But he's lucky, dey say, en I see I warn't lucky. De dream say let Balum inves' de ten cents en he'd make a raise for me. Well, Balum he tuck de money, en when he wuz in church he hear de preacher say dat whoever give to de po' len' to de Lord, en boun' to git his money back a hund'd times. So Balum he tuck en give de ten cents to de po,' en laid low to see what wuz gwyne to come of it."

"Well, what did come of it, Jim?"

"Nuffn' never come of it. I couldn' manage to k'leck dat money no way; en Balum he couldn'. I ain' gwyne to len' no mo' money 'dout I see de security. Boun' to git yo' money back a hund'd times, de preacher says! Ef I could git de ten *cents* back, I'd call it squah, en be glad er de chanst."

"Well, it's all right, anyway, Jim, long as you're going to be rich again some time or other."

"Yes—en I's rich now, come to look at it. I owns mysef, en I's wuth eight hund'd dollars. I wisht I had de money, I wouldn' want no mo'."

IX

I WANTED to go and look at a place right about the middle
of the island, that I'd found when I was exploring; so we
started, and soon got to it, because the island was only three
miles long and a quarter of a mile wide.

This place was a tolerable long steep hill or ridge, about
forty foot high. We had a rough time getting to the top, the
sides was so steep and the bushes so thick. We tramped and
clumb around all over it, and by-and-by found a good big
cavern in the rock, most up to the top on the side towards
Illinois. The cavern was as big as two or three rooms bunched
together, and Jim could stand up straight in it. It was cool in
there. Jim was for putting our traps in there, right away, but
I said we didn't want to be climbing up and down there all
the time.

Jim said if we had the canoe hid in a good place, and had
all the traps in the cavern, we could rush there if anybody was
to come to the island, and they would never find us without
dogs. And besides, he said them little birds had said it was
going to rain, and did I want the things to get wet?

So we went back and got the canoe and paddled up abreast
the cavern, and lugged all the traps up there. Then we hunted
up a place close by to hide the canoe in, amongst the thick
willows. We took some fish off of the lines and set them
again, and begun to get ready for dinner.

The door of the cavern was big enough to roll a hogshead
in, and on one side of the door the floor stuck out a little bit
and was flat and a good place to build a fire on. So we built
it there and cooked dinner.

We spread the blankets inside for a carpet, and eat our dinner in there. We put all the other things handy at the back of
the cavern. Pretty soon it darkened up and begun to thunder
and lighten; so the birds was right about it. Directly it begun
to rain, and it rained like all fury, too, and I never see the
wind blow so. It was one of these regular summer storms. It
would get so dark that it looked all blue-black outside, and
lovely; and the rain would thrash along by so thick that the

trees off a little ways looked dim and spider-webby; and here
would come a blast of wind that would bend the trees down
and turn up the pale underside of the leaves; and then a perfect ripper of a gust would follow along and set the branches
to tossing their arms as if they was just wild; and next, when
it was just about the bluest and blackest—*fst!* it was as bright
as glory and you'd have a little glimpse of tree-tops a-plung-
ing about, away off yonder in the storm, hundreds of yards
further than you could see before; dark as sin again in a second, and now you'd hear the thunder let go with an awful
crash and then go rumbling, grumbling, tumbling down the
sky towards the under side of the world, like rolling empty
barrels down stairs, where it's long stairs and they bounce a
good deal, you know.

"Jim, this is nice," I says. "I wouldn't want to be nowhere
else but here. Pass me along another hunk of fish and some
hot corn-bread."

"Well, you wouldn't a ben here, 'f it hadn't a ben for Jim.
You'd a ben down dah in de woods widout any dinner, en
gittn' mos' drownded, too, dat you would, honey. Chickens
knows when its gwyne to rain, en so do de birds, chile."

The river went on raising and raising for ten or twelve
days, till at last it was over the banks. The water was three or
four foot deep on the island in the low places and on the
Illinois bottom. On that side it was a good many miles wide;
but on the Missouri side it was the same old distance across—
a half a mile—because the Missouri shore was just a wall of
high bluffs.

Daytimes we paddled all over the island in the canoe. It
was mighty cool and shady in the deep woods even if the sun
was blazing outside. We went winding in and out amongst
the trees; and sometimes the vines hung so thick we had to
back away and go some other way. Well, on every old bro-
ken-down tree, you could see rabbits, and snakes, and such
things; and when the island had been overflowed a day or
two, they got so tame, on account of being hungry, that you
could paddle right up and put your hand on them if you
wanted to; but not the snakes and turtles—they would slide
off in the water. The ridge our cavern was in, was full of
them. We could a had pets enough if we'd wanted them.

One night we catched a little section of a lumber raft—nice pine planks. It was twelve foot wide and about fifteen or sixteen foot long, and the top stood above water six or seven inches, a solid level floor. We could see saw-logs go by in the daylight, sometimes, but we let them go; we didn't show ourselves in daylight.

Another night, when we was up at the head of the island, just before daylight, here comes a frame house down, on the west side. She was a two-story, and tilted over, considerable. We paddled out and got aboard—clumb in at an up-stairs window. But it was too dark to see yet, so we made the canoe fast and set in her to wait for daylight.

The light begun to come before we got to the foot of the island. Then we looked in at the window. We could make out a bed, and a table, and two old chairs, and lots of things around about on the floor; and there was clothes hanging against the wall. There was something laying on the floor in the far corner that looked like a man. So Jim says:

"Hello, you!"

But it didn't budge. So I hollered again, and then Jim says:

"De man ain't asleep—he's dead. You hold still—I'll go en see."

He went and bent down and looked, and says:

"It's a dead man. Yes, indeedy; naked, too. He's been shot in de back. I reck'n he's been dead two er three days. Come in, Huck, but doan' look at his face—it's too gashly."

I didn't look at him at all. Jim throwed some old rags over him, but he needn't done it; I didn't want to see him. There was heaps of old greasy cards scattered around over the floor, and old whisky bottles, and a couple of masks made out of black cloth; and all over the walls was the ignorantest kind of words and pictures, made with charcoal. There was two old dirty calico dresses, and a sun-bonnet, and some women's under-clothes, hanging against the wall, and some men's clothing, too. We put the lot into the canoe; it might come good. There was a boy's old speckled straw hat on the floor; I took that too. And there was a bottle that had had milk in it; and it had a rag stopper for a baby to suck. We would a took the bottle, but it was broke. There was a seedy old chest, and an old hair trunk with the hinges broke. They stood open, but there warn't nothing left in them that was any account. The way things was scattered about, we reckoned the people left in a hurry and warn't fixed so as to carry off most of their stuff.

We got an old tin lantern, and a butcher knife without any handle, and a bran-new Barlow knife worth two bits in any store, and a lot of tallow candles, and a tin candlestick, and a gourd, and a tin cup, and a ratty old bed-quilt off the bed, and a reticule with needles and pins and beeswax and buttons and thread and all such truck in it, and a hatchet and some nails, and a fish-line as thick as my little finger, with some monstrous hooks on it, and a roll of buckskin, and a leather dog-collar, and a horse-shoe, and some vials of medicine that didn't have no label on them; and just as we was leaving I found a tolerable good curry-comb, and Jim he found a ratty old fiddle-bow, and a wooden leg. The straps was broke off of it, but barring that, it was a good enough leg, though it was too long for me and not long enough for Jim, and we couldn't find the other one, though we hunted all around.

And so, take it all around, we made a good haul. When we was ready to shove off, we was a quarter of a mile below the island, and it was pretty broad day; so I made Jim lay down in the canoe and cover up with the quilt, because if he set up, people could tell he was a nigger a good ways off. I paddled over to the Illinois shore, and drifted down most a half a mile doing it. I crept up the dead water under the bank, and hadn't no accidents and didn't see nobody. We got home all safe.

X

AFTER BREAKFAST I wanted to talk about the dead man and guess out how he come to be killed, but Jim didn't want to. He said it would fetch bad luck; and besides, he said, he might come and ha'nt us; he said a man that warn't buried was more likely to go a-ha'nting around than one that was planted and comfortable. That sounded pretty reasonable, so I didn't say no more; but I couldn't keep from studying over it and wishing I knowed who shot the man, and what they done it for.

We rummaged the clothes we'd got, and found eight dollars in silver sewed up in the lining of an old blanket overcoat. Jim said he reckoned the people in that house stole the coat, because if they'd a knowed the money was there they wouldn't a left it. I said I reckoned they killed him, too; but Jim didn't want to talk about that. I says:

"Now you think it's bad luck; but what did you say when I fetched in the snake-skin that I found on the top of the ridge day before yesterday? You said it was the worst bad luck in the world to touch a snake-skin with my hands. Well, here's your bad luck! We've raked in all this truck and eight dollars besides. I wish we could have some bad luck like this every day, Jim."

"Never you mind, honey, never you mind. Don't you git too peart. It's a-comin'. Mind I tell you, it's a-comin'."

It did come, too. It was a Tuesday that we had that talk. Well, after dinner Friday, we was laying around in the grass at the upper end of the ridge, and got out of tobacco. I went to the cavern to get some, and found a rattlesnake in there. I killed him, and curled him up on the foot of Jim's blanket, ever so natural, thinking there'd be some fun when Jim found him there. Well, by night I forgot all about the snake, and when Jim flung himself down on the blanket while I struck a light, the snake's mate was there, and bit him.

He jumped up yelling, and the first thing the light showed was the varmint curled up and ready for another spring. I laid him out in a second with a stick, and Jim grabbed pap's whisky jug and begun to pour it down.

He was barefooted, and the snake bit him right on the heel. That all comes of my being such a fool as to not remember that wherever you leave a dead snake its mate always comes there and curls around it. Jim told me to chop off the snake's head and throw it away, and then skin the body and roast a piece of it. I done it, and he eat it and said it would help cure him. He made me take off the rattles and tie them around his wrist, too. He said that that would help. Then I slid out quiet and throwed the snakes clear away amongst the bushes; for I warn't going to let Jim find out it was all my fault, not if I could help it.

Jim sucked and sucked at the jug, and now and then he got out of his head and pitched around and yelled; but every time he come to himself he went to sucking at the jug again. His foot swelled up pretty big, and so did his leg; but by-and-by the drunk begun to come, and so I judged he was all right; but I'd druther been bit with a snake than pap's whisky.

Jim was laid up for four days and nights. Then the swelling was all gone and he was around again. I made up my mind I wouldn't ever take aholt of a snake-skin again with my hands, now that I see what had come of it. Jim said he reckoned I would believe him next time. And he said that handling a snake-skin was such awful bad luck that maybe we hadn't got to the end of it yet. He said he druther see the new moon over his left shoulder as much as a thousand times than take up a snake-skin in his hand. Well, I was getting to feel that way myself, though I've always reckoned that looking at the new moon over your left shoulder is one of the carelessest and foolishest things a body can do. Old Hank Bunker done it once, and bragged about it; and in less than two years he got drunk and fell off of the shot tower and spread himself out so that he was just a kind of a layer, as you may say; and they slid him edgeways between two barn doors for a coffin, and buried him so, so they say, but I didn't see it. Pap told me. But anyway, it all come of looking at the moon that way, like a fool.

Well, the days went along, and the river went down between its banks again; and about the first thing we done was to bait one of the big hooks with a skinned rabbit and set it and catch a cat-fish that was as big as a man, being six foot two inches long, and weighed over two hundred pounds. We couldn't handle him, of course; he would a flung us into Illinois. We just set there and watched him rip and tear around till he drownded. We found a brass button in his stomach, and a round ball, and lots of rubbage. We split the ball open with the hatchet, and there was a spool in it. Jim said he'd had it there a long time, to coat it over so and make a ball of it. It was as big a fish as was ever catched in the Mississippi, I reckon. Jim said he hadn't ever seen a bigger one. He would a been worth a good deal over at the village. They peddle out such a fish as that by the pound in the market house there; everybody buys some of him; his meat's as white as snow and makes a good fry.

Next morning I said it was getting slow and dull, and I wanted to get a stirring up, some way. I said I reckoned I would slip over the river and find out what was going on. Jim liked that notion; but he said I must go in the dark and look sharp. Then he studied it over and said, couldn't I put on some of them old things and dress up like a girl? That was a good notion, too. So we shortened up one of the calico gowns and I turned up my trowser-legs to my knees and got into it. Jim hitched it behind with the hooks, and it was a fair fit. I put on the sun-bonnet and tied it under my chin, and then for a body to look in and see my face was like looking down a joint of stove-pipe. Jim said nobody would know me, even in the daytime, hardly. I practiced around all day to get the hang of the things, and by-and-by I could do pretty well in them, only Jim said I didn't walk like a girl; and he said I must quit pulling up my gown to get at my britches pocket. I took notice, and done better.

I started up the Illinois shore in the canoe just after dark.

I started across to the town from a little below the ferry landing, and the drift of the current fetched me in at the bottom of the town. I tied up and started along the bank. There was a light burning in a little shanty that hadn't been lived in for a long time, and I wondered who had took up quarters there. I slipped up and peeped in at the window. There was a woman about forty year old in there, knitting by a candle that was on a pine table. I didn't know her face; she was a stranger, for you couldn't start a face in that town that I didn't know. Now this was lucky, because I was weakening; I was getting afraid I had come; people might know my voice and find me out. But if this woman had been in such a little town two days she could tell me all I wanted to know; so I knocked at the door, and made up my mind I wouldn't forget I was a girl.

XI

"COME IN," says the woman, and I did. She says:
"Take a cheer."

I done it. She looked me all over with her little shiny eyes, and says:

"What might your name be?"

"Sarah Williams."

"Where 'bouts do you live? In this neighborhood?"

"No'm. In Hookerville, seven mile below. I've walked all the way and I'm all tired out."

"Hungry, too, I reckon. I'll find you something."

"No'm, I ain't hungry. I was so hungry I had to stop two mile below here at a farm; so I ain't hungry no more. It's what makes me so late. My mother's down sick, and out of money and everything, and I come to tell my uncle Abner Moore. He lives at the upper end of the town, she says. I hain't ever been here before. Do you know him?"

"No; but I don't know everybody yet. I haven't lived here quite two weeks. It's a considerable ways to the upper end of the town. You better stay here all night. Take off your bonnet."

"No," I says, "I'll rest a while, I reckon, and go on. I ain't afeard of the dark."

She said she wouldn't let me go by myself, but her husband would be in by-and-by, maybe in a hour and a half, and she'd send him along with me. Then she got to talking about her husband, and about her relations up the river, and her relations down the river, and about how much better off they used to was, and how they didn't know but they'd made a mistake coming to our town, instead of letting well alone—and so on and so on, till I was afeard I had made a mistake coming to her to find out what was going on in the town; but by-and-by she dropped onto pap and the murder, and then I was pretty willing to let her clatter right along. She told about me and Tom Sawyer finding the six thousand dollars (only she got it ten) and all about pap and what a hard lot he was, and what a hard lot I

was, and at last she got down to where I was murdered. I
says:

"Who done it? We've heard considerable about these
goings on, down in Hookerville, but we don't know who
'twas that killed Huck Finn."

"Well, I reckon there's a right smart chance of people *here*
that 'd like to know who killed him. Some thinks old Finn
done it himself."

"No—is that so?"

"Most everybody thought it at first. He'll never know how
nigh he come to getting lynched. But before night they
changed around and judged it was done by a runaway nigger
named Jim."

"Why *he*——"

I stopped. I reckoned I better keep still. She run on, and
never noticed I had put in at all.

"The nigger run off the very night Huck Finn was killed.
So there's a reward out for him—three hundred dollars. And
there's a reward out for old Finn too—two hundred dollars.
You see, he come to town the morning after the murder, and
told about it, and was out with 'em on the ferry-boat hunt,
and right away after he up and left. Before night they wanted
to lynch him, but he was gone, you see. Well, next day they
found out the nigger was gone; they found out he hadn't ben
seen sence ten o'clock the night the murder was done. So
then they put it on him, you see, and while they was full of
it, next day back comes old Finn and went boo-hooing to
Judge Thatcher to get money to hunt for the nigger all over
Illinois with. The judge give him some, and that evening he
got drunk and was around till after midnight with a couple of
mighty hard looking strangers, and then went off with them.
Well, he hain't come back sence, and they ain't looking for
him back till this thing blows over a little, for people thinks
now that he killed his boy and fixed things so folks would
think robbers done it, and then he'd get Huck's money without
having to bother a long time with a lawsuit. People do say he
warn't any too good to do it. Oh, he's sly, I reckon. If he don't
come back for a year, he'll be all right. You can't prove anything
on him, you know; everything will be quieted down then, and
he'll walk into Huck's money as easy as nothing."

"Yes, I reckon so, 'm. I don't see nothing in the way of it. Has everybody quit thinking the nigger done it?"

"Oh, no, not everybody. A good many thinks he done it. But they'll get the nigger pretty soon, now, and maybe they can scare it out of him."

"Why, are they after him yet?"

"Well, you're innocent, ain't you! Does three hundred dollars lay round every day for people to pick up? Some folks thinks the nigger ain't far from here. I'm one of them—but I hain't talked it around. A few days ago I was talking with an old couple that lives next door in the log shanty, and they happened to say hardly anybody ever goes to that island over yonder that they call Jackson's Island. Don't anybody live there? says I. No, nobody, says they. I didn't say any more, but I done some thinking. I was pretty near certain I'd seen smoke over there, about the head of the island, a day or two before that, so I says to myself, like as not that nigger's hiding over there; anyway, says I, it's worth the trouble to give the place a hunt. I hain't seen any smoke sence, so I reckon maybe he's gone, if it was him; but husband's going over to see—him and another man. He was gone up the river; but he got back to-day and I told him as soon as he got here two hours ago."

I had got so uneasy I couldn't set still. I had to do something with my hands; so I took up a needle off of the table and went to threading it. My hands shook, and I was making a bad job of it. When the woman stopped talking, I looked up, and she was looking at me pretty curious, and smiling a little. I put down the needle and thread and let on to be interested—and I was, too—and says:

"Three hundred dollars is a power of money. I wish my mother could get it. Is your husband going over there to-night?"

"Oh, yes. He went up town with the man I was telling you of, to get a boat and see if they could borrow another gun. They'll go over after midnight."

"Couldn't they see better if they was to wait till daytime?"

"Yes. And couldn't the nigger see better, too? After midnight he'll likely be asleep, and they can slip around through

the woods and hunt up his camp fire all the better for the
dark, if he's got one."

"I didn't think of that."

The woman kept looking at me pretty curious, and I didn't
feel a bit comfortable. Pretty soon she says:

"What did you say your name was, honey?"

"M—Mary Williams."

Somehow it didn't seem to me that I said it was Mary before, so I didn't look up; seemed to me I said it was Sarah;
so I felt sort of cornered, and was afeared maybe I was looking it, too. I wished the woman would say something more;
the longer she set still, the uneasier I was. But now she says:

"Honey, I thought you said it was Sarah when you first
come in?"

"Oh, yes'm, I did. Sarah Mary Williams. Sarah's my first
name. Some calls me Sarah, some calls me Mary."

"Oh, that's the way of it?"

"Yes'm."

I was feeling better, then, but I wished I was out of there,
anyway. I couldn't look up yet.

Well, the woman fell to talking about how hard times was,
and how poor they had to live, and how the rats was as free
as if they owned the place, and so forth, and so on, and then
I got easy again. She was right about the rats. You'd see one
stick his nose out of a hole in the corner every little while.
She said she had to have things handy to throw at them when
she was alone, or they wouldn't give her no peace. She
showed me a bar of lead, twisted up into a knot, and said she
was a good shot with it generly, but she'd wrenched her arm
a day or two ago, and didn't know whether she could throw
true, now. But she watched for a chance, and directly she
banged away at a rat, but she missed him wide, and said
"Ouch!" it hurt her arm so. Then she told me to try for the
next one. I wanted to be getting away before the old man got
back, but of course I didn't let on. I got the thing, and the
first rat that showed his nose I let drive, and if he'd a stayed
where he was he'd a been a tolerable sick rat. She said that
that was first-rate, and she reckoned I would hive the next
one. She went and got the lump of lead and fetched it back

and brought along a hank of yarn, which she wanted me to help her with. I held up my two hands and she put the hank over them and went on talking about her and her husband's matters. But she broke off to say:

"Keep your eye on the rats. You better have the lead in your lap, handy."

So she dropped the lump into my lap, just at that moment, and I clapped my legs together on it and she went on talking. But only about a minute. Then she took off the hank and looked me straight in the face, but very pleasant, and says:

"Come, now—what's your real name?"

"Wh-what, mum?"

"What's your real name? Is it Bill, or Tom, or Bob?—or what is it?"

I reckon I shook like a leaf, and I didn't know hardly what to do. But I says:

"Please to don't poke fun at a poor girl like me, mum. If I'm in the way, here, I'll——"

"No, you won't. Set down and stay where you are. I ain't going to hurt you, and I ain't going to tell on you, nuther. You just tell me your secret, and trust me. I'll keep it; and what's more, I'll help you. So'll my old man, if you want him to. You see, you're a runaway 'prentice—that's all. It ain't anything. There ain't any harm in it. You've been treated bad, and you made up your mind to cut. Bless you, child, I wouldn't tell on you. Tell me all about it, now—that's a good boy."

So I said it wouldn't be no use to try to play it any longer, and I would just make a clean breast and tell her everything, but she mustn't go back on her promise. Then I told her my father and mother was dead, and the law had bound me out to a mean old farmer in the country thirty mile back from the river, and he treated me so bad I couldn't stand it no longer; he went away to be gone a couple of days, and so I took my chance and stole some of his daughter's old clothes, and cleared out, and I had been three nights coming the thirty miles; I traveled nights, and hid day-times and slept, and the bag of bread and meat I carried from home lasted me all the

way and I had a plenty. I said I believed my uncle Abner
Moore would take care of me, and so that was why I struck
out for this town of Goshen.

"Goshen, child? This ain't Goshen. This is St. Petersburg.
Goshen's ten mile further up the river. Who told you this was
Goshen?"

"Why, a man I met at day-break this morning, just as I was
going to turn into the woods for my regular sleep. He told
me when the roads forked I must take the right hand, and
five mile would fetch me to Goshen."

"He was drunk I reckon. He told you just exactly wrong."

"Well, he did act like he was drunk, but it ain't no matter
now. I got to be moving along. I'll fetch Goshen before daylight."

"Hold on a minute. I'll put you up a snack to eat. You
might want it."

So she put me up a snack, and says:

"Say—when a cow's laying down, which end of her gets
up first? Answer up prompt, now—don't stop to study over
it. Which end gets up first?"

"The hind end, mum."

"Well, then, a horse?"

"The for'rard end, mum."

"Which side of a tree does the most moss grow on?"

"North side."

"If fifteen cows is browsing on a hillside, how many of
them eats with their heads pointed the same direction?"

"The whole fifteen, mum."

"Well, I reckon you *have* lived in the country. I thought
maybe you was trying to hocus me again. What's your real
name, now?"

"George Peters, mum."

"Well, try to remember it, George. Don't forget and tell
me it's Elexander before you go, and then get out by saying
it's George-Elexander when I catch you. And don't go about
women in that old calico. You do a girl tolerable poor, but
you might fool men, maybe. Bless you, child, when you set
out to thread a needle, don't hold the thread still and fetch
the needle up to it; hold the needle still and poke the thread
at it—that's the way a woman most always does; but a man

always does 'tother way. And when you throw at a rat or anything, hitch yourself up a tip-toe, and fetch your hand up over your head as awkard as you can, and miss your rat about six or seven foot. Throw stiff-armed from the shoulder, like there was a pivot there for it to turn on—like a girl; not from the wrist and elbow, with your arm out to one side, like a boy. And mind you, when a girl tries to catch anything in her lap, she throws her knees apart; she don't clap them together, the way you did when you catched the lump of lead. Why, I spotted you for a boy when you was threading the needle; and I contrived the other things just to make certain. Now trot along to your uncle, Sarah Mary Williams George Elexander Peters, and if you get into trouble you send word to Mrs. Judith Loftus, which is me, and I'll do what I can to get you out of it. Keep the river road, all the way, and next time you tramp, take shoes and socks with you. The river road's a rocky one, and your feet 'll be in a condition when you get to Goshen, I reckon."

I went up the bank about fifty yards, and then I doubled on my tracks and slipped back to where my canoe was, a good piece below the house. I jumped in and was off in a hurry. I went up stream far enough to make the head of the island, and then started across. I took off the sun-bonnet, for I didn't want no blinders on, then. When I was about the middle, I hear the clock begin to strike; so I stops and listens; the sound come faint over the water, but clear—eleven. When I struck the head of the island I never waited to blow, though I was most winded, but I shoved right into the timber where my old camp used to be, and started a good fire there on a high-and-dry spot.

Then I jumped in the canoe and dug out for our place a mile and a half below, as hard as I could go. I landed, and slopped through the timber and up the ridge and into the cavern. There Jim laid, sound asleep on the ground. I roused him out and says:

"Git up and hump yourself, Jim! There ain't a minute to lose. They're after us!"

Jim never asked no questions, he never said a word; but the way he worked for the next half an hour showed about how he was scared. By that time everything we had in the world was on our raft and she was ready to be shoved out from the willow cove where she was hid. We put out the camp fire at the cavern the first thing, and didn't show a candle outside after that.

I took the canoe out from shore a little piece and took a look, but if there was a boat around I couldn't see it, for stars and shadows ain't good to see by. Then we got out the raft and slipped along down in the shade, past the foot of the island dead still, never saying a word.

XII

I T MUST a been close onto one o'clock when we got below
the island at last, and the raft did seem to go mighty slow.
If a boat was to come along, we was going to take to the
canoe and break for the Illinois shore; and it was well a boat
didn't come, for we hadn't ever thought to put the gun into
the canoe, or a fishing-line or anything to eat. We was in
ruther too much of a sweat to think of so many things. It
warn't good judgment to put *everything* on the raft.

If the men went to the island, I just expect they found the
camp fire I built, and watched it all night for Jim to come.
Anyways, they stayed away from us, and if my building the
fire never fooled them it warn't no fault of mine. I played it
as low-down on them as I could.

When the first streak of day begun to show, we tied up to
a tow-head in a big bend on the Illinois side, and hacked off
cotton-wood branches with the hatchet and covered up the
raft with them so she looked like there had been a cave-in in
the bank there. A tow-head is a sand-bar that has cotton-
woods on it as thick as harrow-teeth.

We had mountains on the Missouri shore and heavy timber
on the Illinois side, and the channel was down the Missouri
shore at that place, so we warn't afraid of anybody running
across us. We laid there all day and watched the rafts and
steamboats spin down the Missouri shore, and up-bound
steamboats fight the big river in the middle. I told Jim all
about the time I had jabbering with that woman; and Jim
said she was a smart one, and if she was to start after us herself *she* wouldn't set down and watch a camp fire—no, sir,
she'd fetch a dog. Well, then, I said, why couldn't she tell her
husband to fetch a dog? Jim said he bet she did think of it by
the time the men was ready to start, and he believed they
must a gone up town to get a dog and so they lost all that
time, or else we wouldn't be here on a tow-head sixteen or
seventeen mile below the village—no, indeedy, we would be
in that same old town again. So I said I didn't care what was
the reason they didn't get us, as long as they didn't.

When it was beginning to come on dark, we poked our heads out of the cottonwood thicket and looked up, and down, and across; nothing in sight; so Jim took up some of the top planks of the raft and built a snug wigwam to get under in blazing weather and rainy, and to keep the things dry. Jim made a floor for the wigwam, and raised it a foot or more above the level of the raft, so now the blankets and all the traps was out of the reach of steamboat waves. Right in the middle of the wigwam we made a layer of dirt about five or six inches deep with a frame around it for to hold it to its place; this was to build a fire on in sloppy weather or chilly; the wigwam would keep it from being seen. We made an extra steering oar, too, because one of the others might get broke, on a snag or something. We fixed up a short forked stick to hang the old lantern on; because we must always light the lantern whenever we see a steamboat coming down stream, to keep from getting run over; but we wouldn't have to light it for up-stream boats unless we see we was in what they call a "crossing;" for the river was pretty high yet, very low banks being still a little under water; so up-bound boats didn't always run the channel, but hunted easy water.

This second night we run between seven and eight hours, with a current that was making over four mile an hour. We catched fish, and talked, and we took a swim now and then to keep off sleepiness. It was kind of solemn, drifting down the big still river, laying on our backs looking up at the stars, and we didn't ever feel like talking loud, and it warn't often that we laughed, only a little kind of a low chuckle. We had mighty good weather, as a general thing, and nothing ever happened to us at all, that night, nor the next, nor the next.

Every night we passed towns, some of them away up on black hillsides, nothing but just a shiny bed of lights, not a house could you see. The fifth night we passed St. Louis, and it was like the whole world lit up. In St. Petersburg they used to say there was twenty or thirty thousand people in St. Louis, but I never believed it till I see that wonderful spread of lights at two o'clock that still night. There warn't a sound there; everybody was asleep.

Every night, now, I used to slip ashore, towards ten o'clock, at some little village, and buy ten or fifteen cents' worth of meal or bacon or other stuff to eat; and sometimes I lifted a chicken that warn't roosting comfortable, and took him along. Pap always said, take a chicken when you get a chance, because if you don't want him yourself you can easy find somebody that does, and a good deed ain't ever forgot. I never see pap when he didn't want the chicken himself, but that is what he used to say, anyway.

Mornings, before daylight, I slipped into corn fields and borrowed a watermelon, or a mushmelon, or a punkin, or some new corn, or things of that kind. Pap always said it warn't no harm to borrow things, if you was meaning to pay them back, sometime; but the widow said it warn't anything but a soft name for stealing, and no decent body would do it. Jim said he reckoned the widow was partly right and pap was partly right; so the best way would be for us to pick out two or three things from the list and say we wouldn't borrow them any more—then he reckoned it wouldn't be no harm to borrow the others. So we talked it over all one night, drifting along down the river, trying to make up our minds whether to drop the watermelons, or the cantelopes, or the mushmelons, or what. But towards daylight we got it all settled satisfactory, and concluded to drop crabapples and p'simmons. We warn't feeling just right, before that, but it was all comfortable now. I was glad the way it come out, too, because crabapples ain't ever good, and the p'simmons wouldn't be ripe for two or three months yet.

We shot a water-fowl, now and then, that got up too early in the morning or didn't go to bed early enough in the evening. Take it all around, we lived pretty high.

The fifth night below St. Louis we had a big storm after midnight, with a power of thunder and lightning, and the rain poured down in a solid sheet. We stayed in the wigwam and let the raft take care of itself. When the lightning glared out we could see a big straight river ahead, and high rocky bluffs on both sides. By-and-by says I, "Hel-lo, Jim, looky yonder!" It was a steamboat that had killed herself on a rock. We was drifting straight down for her. The lightning showed her very distinct. She was leaning over, with part of her upper deck above water, and you could see every little chimbly-guy clean and clear, and a chair by the big bell, with an old slouch hat hanging on the back of it when the flashes come.

Well, it being away in the night, and stormy, and all so mysterious-like, I felt just the way any other boy would a felt when I see that wreck laying there so mournful and lonesome in the middle of the river. I wanted to get aboard of her and slink around a little, and see what there was there. So I says:

"Le's land on her, Jim."

But Jim was dead against it, at first. He says:

"I doan' want to go fool'n 'long er no wrack. We's doin' blame' well, en we better let blame' well alone, as de good book says. Like as not dey's a watchman on dat wrack."

"Watchman your grandmother," I says; "there ain't nothing to watch but the texas and the pilot-house; and do you reckon anybody's going to resk his life for a texas and a pilot-house such a night as this, when it's likely to break up and wash off down the river any minute?" Jim couldn't say nothing to that, so he didn't try. "And besides," I says, "we might borrow something worth having, out of the captain's stateroom. Seegars, *I* bet you—and cost five cents apiece, solid cash. Steamboat captains is always rich, and get sixty dollars a month, and *they* don't care a cent what a thing costs, you know, long as they want it. Stick a candle in your pocket; I can't rest, Jim, till we give her a rummaging. Do you reckon Tom Sawyer would ever go by this thing? Not for pie, he wouldn't. He'd call it an adventure—that's what he'd call it; and he'd land on that wreck if it was his last act. And wouldn't he throw style into it?—wouldn't he spread himself, nor nothing? Why, you'd think it was Christopher C'lumbus discovering Kingdom-Come. I wish Tom Sawyer *was* here."

Jim he grumbled a little, but give in. He said we mustn't talk any more than we could help, and then talk mighty low. The lightning showed us the wreck again, just in time, and we fetched the starboard derrick, and made fast there.

The deck was high out, here. We went sneaking down the slope of it to labboard, in the dark, towards the texas, feeling our way slow with our feet, and spreading our hands out to fend off the guys, for it was so dark we couldn't see no sign of them. Pretty soon we struck the forward end of the sky-

light, and clumb onto it; and the next step fetched us in front
of the captain's door, which was open, and by Jimminy, away
down through the texas-hall we see a light! and all in the
same second we seem to hear low voices in yonder!

Jim whispered and said he was feeling powerful sick, and
told me to come along. I says, all right; and was going to
start for the raft; but just then I heard a voice wail out and
say:

"Oh, please don't, boys; I swear I won't ever tell!"

Another voice said, pretty loud:

"It's a lie, Jim Turner. You've acted this way before. You
always want more'n your share of the truck, and you've always got it, too, because you've swore 't if you didn't you'd
tell. But this time you've said it jest one time too many.
You're the meanest, treacherousest hound in this country."

By this time Jim was gone for the raft. I was just a-biling
with curiosity; and I says to myself, Tom Sawyer wouldn't
back out now, and so I won't either; I'm agoing to see what's
going on here. So I dropped on my hands and knees, in the
little passage, and crept aft in the dark, till there warn't but
about one stateroom betwixt me and the cross-hall of the
texas. Then, in there I see a man stretched on the floor and
tied hand and foot, and two men standing over him, and one
of them had a dim lantern in his hand, and the other one had
a pistol. This one kept pointing the pistol at the man's head
on the floor and saying—

"I'd *like* to! And I orter, too, a mean skunk!"

The man on the floor would shrivel up, and say: "Oh,
please don't. Bill—I hain't ever goin' to tell."

And every time he said that, the man with the lantern
would laugh, and say:

"'Deed you *ain't*! You never said no truer thing 'n that,
you bet you." And once he said: "Hear him beg! and yit if
we hadn't got the best of him and tied him, he'd a killed us
both. And what *for*? Jist for noth'n. Jist because we stood on
our *rights*—that's what for. But I lay you ain't agoin' to
threaten nobody any more, Jim Turner. Put *up* that pistol,
Bill."

Bill says:

"I don't want to, Jake Packard. I'm for killin' him—and

didn't he kill old Hatfield jist the same way—and don't he deserve it?"

"But I don't *want* him killed, and I've got my reasons for it."

"Bless yo' heart for them words, Jake Packard! I'll never forgit you, long's I live!" says the man on the floor, sort of blubbering.

Packard didn't take no notice of that, but hung up his lantern on a nail, and started towards where I was, there in the dark, and motioned Bill to come. I crawfished as fast as I could, about two yards, but the boat slanted so that I couldn't make very good time; so to keep from getting run over and catched I crawled into a stateroom on the upper side. The man come a-pawing along in the dark, and when Packard got to my stateroom, he says:

"Here—come in here."

And in he come, and Bill after him. But before they got in, I was up in the upper berth, cornered, and sorry I come. Then they stood there, with their hands on the ledge of the berth, and talked. I couldn't see them, but I could tell where they was, by the whisky they'd been having. I was glad I didn't drink whisky; but it wouldn't made much difference, anyway, because most of the time they couldn't a treed me because I didn't breathe. I was too scared. And besides, a body *couldn't* breathe, and hear such talk. They talked low and earnest. Bill wanted to kill Turner. He says:

"He's said he'll tell, and he will. If we was to give both our shares to him *now*, it wouldn't make no difference after the row, and the way we've served him. Shore's you're born, he'll turn State's evidence; now you hear *me*. I'm for putting him out of his troubles."

"So'm I," says Packard, very quiet.

"Blame it, I'd sorter begun to think you wasn't. Well, then, that's all right. Les' go and do it."

"Hold on a minute; I hain't had my say yit. You listen to me. Shooting's good, but there's quieter ways if the thing's *got* to be done. But what *I* say, is this; it ain't good sense to go court'n around after a halter, if you can git at what you're up to in some way that's jist as good and at the same time don't bring you into no resks. Ain't that so?"

"You bet it is. But how you goin' to manage it this time?"

"Well, my idea is this: we'll rustle around and gether up whatever pickins we've overlooked in the staterooms, and shove for shore and hide the truck. Then we'll wait. Now I say it ain't agoin' to be more 'n two hours befo' this wrack breaks up and washes off down the river. See? He'll be drownded, and won't have nobody to blame for it but his own self. I reckon that's a considerble sight better'n killin' of him. I'm unfavorable to killin' a man as long as you can git around it; it ain't good sense, it ain't good morals. Ain't I right?"

"Yes—I reck'n you are. But s'pose she *don't* break up and wash off?"

"Well, we can wait the two hours, anyway, and see, can't we?"

"All right, then; come along."

So they started, and I lit out, all in a cold sweat, and scrambled forward. It was dark as pitch there; but I said in a kind of a coarse whisper, "Jim!" and he answered up, right at my elbow, with a sort of a moan, and I says:

"Quick, Jim, it ain't no time for fooling around and moaning; there's a gang of murderers in yonder, and if we don't hunt up their boat and set her drifting down the river so these fellows can't get away from the wreck, there's one of 'em going to be in a bad fix. But if we find their boat we can put *all* of 'em in a bad fix—for the Sheriff 'll get 'em. Quick—hurry! I'll hunt the labboard side, you hunt the stabboard. You start at the raft, and——"

"Oh, my lordy, lordy! *Raf'*? Dey ain' no raf' no mo', she done broke loose en gone!—'en here we is!"

XIII

WELL, I catched my breath and most fainted. Shut up on a wreck with such a gang as that! But it warn't no time to be sentimentering. We'd *got* to find that boat, now—had to have it for ourselves. So we went a-quaking and shaking down the stabboard side, and slow work it was, too—seemed a week before we got to the stern. No sign of a boat. Jim said he didn't believe he could go any further—so scared he hadn't hardly any strength left, he said. But I said come on, if we get left on this wreck, we are in a fix, sure. So on we prowled, again. We struck for the stern of the texas, and found it, and then scrabbled along forwards on the skylight, hanging on from shutter to shutter, for the edge of the skylight was in the water. When we got pretty close to the cross-hall door, there was the skiff, sure enough! I could just barely see her. I felt ever so thankful. In another second I would a been aboard of her; but just then the door opened. One of the men stuck his head out, only about a couple of foot from me, and I thought I was gone; but he jerked it in again, and says:

"Heave that blame lantern out o' sight, Bill!"

He flung a bag of something into the boat, and then got in himself, and set down. It was Packard. Then Bill *he* come out and got in. Packard says, in a low voice:

"All ready—shove off!"

I couldn't hardly hang onto the shutters, I was so weak. But Bill says:

"Hold on—'d you go through him?"

"No. Didn't you?"

"No. So he's got his share o' the cash, yet."

"Well, then, come along—no use to take truck and leave money."

"Say—won't he suspicion what we're up to?"

"Maybe he won't. But we got to have it anyway. Come along."

So they got out and went in.

The door slammed to, because it was on the careened side; and in a half second I was in the boat, and Jim come a tumbling after me. I out with my knife and cut the rope, and away we went!

We didn't touch an oar, and we didn't speak nor whisper, nor hardly even breathe. We went gliding swift along, dead silent, past the tip of the paddle-box, and past the stern; then in a second or two more we was a hundred yards below the wreck, and the darkness soaked her up, every last sign of her, and we was safe, and knowed it.

When we was three or four hundred yards down stream, we see the lantern show like a little spark at the texas door, for a second, and we knowed by that that the rascals had missed their boat, and was beginning to understand that they was in just as much trouble, now, as Jim Turner was.

Then Jim manned the oars, and we took out after our raft. Now was the first time that I begun to worry about the men—I reckon I hadn't had time to before. I begun to think how dreadful it was, even for murderers, to be in such a fix. I says to myself, there ain't no telling but I might come to be a murderer myself, yet, and then how would I like it? So says I to Jim:

"The first light we see, we'll land a hundred yards below it or above it, in a place where it's a good hiding-place for you and the skiff, and then I'll go and fix up some kind of a yarn, and get somebody to go for that gang and get them out of their scrape, so they can be hung when their time comes."

But that idea was a failure; for pretty soon it begun to storm again, and this time worse than ever. The rain poured down, and never a light showed; everybody in bed, I reckon. We boomed along down the river, watching for lights and watching for our raft. After a long time the rain let up, but the clouds staid, and the lightning kept whimpering, and by-and-by a flash showed us a black thing ahead, floating, and we made for it.

It was the raft, and mighty glad was we to get aboard of it again. We seen a light, now, away down to the right, on shore. So I said I would go for it. The skiff was half full of plunder which that gang had stole, there on the wreck. We hustled it onto the raft in a pile, and I told Jim to float along down, and show a light when he judged he had gone about two mile, and keep it burning till I come; then I manned my oars and shoved for the light. As I got down towards it, three or four more showed—up on a hillside. It was a village. I closed in above the shore-light, and laid on my oars and floated. As I went by, I see it was a lantern hanging on the jackstaff of a double-hull ferry-boat. I skimmed around for the watchman, a-wondering whereabouts he slept: and by-and-by I found him roosting on the bitts, forward, with his head down between his knees. I give his shoulder two or three little shoves, and begun to cry.

He stirred up, in a kind of a startlish way; but when he see it was only me, he took a good gap and stretch, and then he says:

"Hello, what's up? Don't cry, bub. What's the trouble?"

I says:

"Pap, and mam, and sis, and——"

Then I broke down. He says:

"Oh, dang it, now, *don't* take on so, we all has to have our troubles and this'n 'll come out all right. What's the matter with 'em?"

"They're—they're—are you the watchman of the boat?"

"Yes," he says, kind of pretty-well-satisfied like. "I'm the captain and the owner, and the mate, and the pilot, and watchman, and head deck-hand; and sometimes I'm the freight and passengers. I ain't as rich as old Jim Hornback, and I can't be so blame' generous and good to Tom, Dick and Harry as what he is, and slam around money the way he does; but I've told him a many a time 't I wouldn't trade places with him; for, says I, a sailor's life's the life for me, and I'm derned if *I'd* live two mile out o' town, where there ain't nothing ever goin' on, not for all his spondulicks and as much more on top of it. Says I——"

I broke in and says:

"They're in an awful peck of trouble, and——"

"*Who* is?"

"Why, pap, and mam, and sis, and Miss Hooker; and if you'd take your ferry-boat and go up there——"

"Up where? Where are they?"

"On the wreck."

"What wreck?"

"Why, there ain't but one."

"What, you don't mean the *Walter Scott?*"

"Yes."

"Good land! what are they doin' *there*, for gracious sakes?"

"Well, they didn't go there a-purpose."

"I bet they didn't! Why, great goodness, there ain't no chance for 'em if they don't git off mighty quick! Why, how in the nation did they ever git into such a scrape?"

"Easy enough. Miss Hooker was a-visiting, up there to the town——"

"Yes, Booth's Landing—go on."

"She was a-visiting, there at Booth's Landing, and just in the edge of the evening she started over with her nigger woman in the horse-ferry, to stay all night at her friend's house, Miss What-you-may-call-her, I disremember her name, and they lost their steering-oar, and swung around and went a-floating down, stern-first, about two mile, and saddle-baggsed on the wreck, and the ferry man and the nigger woman and the horses was all lost, but Miss Hooker she made a grab and got aboard the wreck. Well, about an hour after dark, we come along down in our trading-scow, and it was so dark we didn't notice the wreck till we was right on it; and so *we* saddle-baggsed; but all of us was saved but Bill Whipple—and oh, he *was* the best cretur!—I most wish't it had been me, I do."

"My George! It's the beatenest thing I ever struck. And *then* what did you all do?"

"Well, we hollered and took on, but it's so wide there, we couldn't make nobody hear. So pap said somebody got to get ashore and get help somehow. I was the only one that could swim, so I made a dash for it, and Miss Hooker she said if I didn't strike help sooner, come here and hunt up her uncle, and he'd fix the thing. I made the land about a mile below, and been fooling along ever since, trying to get people to do something, but they said, 'What, in such a night and such a current? there ain't no sense in it; go for the steam-ferry.' Now if you'll go, and——"

"By Jackson, I'd *like* to, and blame it I don't know but I will; but who in the dingnation's agoin' to *pay* for it? Do you reckon your pap——"

"Why *that's* all right. Miss Hooker she told me, *particular*, that her uncle Hornback——"

"Great guns! is *he* her uncle? Looky here, you break for that light over yonder-way, and turn out west when you git there, and about a quarter of a mile out you'll come to the tavern; tell 'em to dart you out to Jim Hornback's and he'll foot the bill. And don't you fool around any, because he'll want to know the news. Tell him I'll have his niece all safe before he can get to town. Hump yourself, now; I'm agoing up around the corner here, to roust out my engineer."

I struck for the light, but as soon as he turned the corner I went back and got into my skiff and bailed her out and then pulled up shore in the easy water about six hundred yards, and tucked myself in among some woodboats; for I couldn't rest easy till I could see the ferry-boat start. But take it all around, I was feeling ruther comfortable on accounts of taking all this trouble for that gang, for not many would a done it. I wished the widow knowed about it. I judged she would be proud of me for helping these rapscallions, because rapscallions and dead beats is the kind the widow and good people takes the most interest in.

Well, before long, here comes the wreck, dim and dusky, sliding along down! A kind of cold shiver went through me, and then I struck out for her. She was very deep, and I see in a minute there warn't much chance for anybody being alive in her. I pulled all around her and hollered a little, but there wasn't any answer; all dead still. I felt a little bit heavy-hearted about the gang, but not much, for I reckoned if they could stand it, I could.

Then here comes the ferry-boat; so I shoved for the middle of the river on a long down-stream slant; and when I judged I was out of eye-reach, I laid on my oars, and looked back and see her go and smell around the wreck for Miss Hooker's remainders, because the captain would know her uncle Hornback would want them; and then pretty soon the ferry-boat give it up and went for shore, and I laid into my work and went a-booming down the river.

It did seem a powerful long time before Jim's light showed up; and when it did show, it looked like it was a thousand mile off. By the time I got there the sky was beginning to get a little gray in the east; so we struck for an island, and hid the raft, and sunk the skiff, and turned in and slept like dead people.

XIV

B Y-AND-BY, when we got up, we turned over the truck the
gang had stole off of the wreck, and found boots, and
blankets, and clothes, and all sorts of other things, and a lot
of books, and a spyglass, and three boxes of seegars. We
hadn't ever been this rich before, in neither of our lives. The
seegars was prime. We laid off all the afternoon in the woods
talking, and me reading the books, and having a general good
time. I told Jim all about what happened inside the wreck,
and at the ferry-boat; and I said these kinds of things was
adventures; but he said he didn't want no more adventures.
He said that when I went in the texas and he crawled back to
get on the raft and found her gone, he nearly died; because
he judged it was all up with *him*, anyway it could be fixed;
for if he didn't get saved he would get drownded; and if he
did get saved, whoever saved him would send him back home
so as to get the reward, and then Miss Watson would sell him
South, sure. Well, he was right; he was most always right; he
had an uncommon level head, for a nigger.

I read considerable to Jim about kings, and dukes, and
earls, and such, and how gaudy they dressed, and how much
style they put on, and called each other your majesty, and
your grace, and your lordship, and so on, 'stead of mister;
and Jim's eyes bugged out, and he was interested. He says:

"I didn' know dey was so many un um. I hain't hearn 'bout
none un um, skasely, but ole King Sollermun, onless you
counts dem kings dat's in a pack er k'yards. How much do a
king git?"

"Get?" I says; "why, they get a thousand dollars a month
if they want it; they can have just as much as they want;
everything belongs to them."

"*Ain'* dat gay? En what dey got to do, Huck?"

"*They* don't do nothing! Why how you talk. They just set
around."

"No—is dat so?"

"Of course it is. They just set around. Except maybe when
there 's a war; then they go to the war. But other times they

just lazy around; or go hawking—just hawking and sp—
Sh!—d' you hear a noise?"

We skipped out and looked; but it warn't nothing but the
flutter of a steamboat's wheel, away down coming around the
point; so we come back.

"Yes," says I, "and other times, when things is dull, they
fuss with the parlyment; and if everybody don't go just so he
whacks their heads off. But mostly they hang round the
harem."

"Roun' de which?"

"Harem."

"What's de harem?"

"The place where he keep his wives. Don't you know about
the harem? Solomon had one; he had about a million wives."

"Why, yes, dat's so; I—I'd done forgot it. A harem's a
bo'd'n-house, I reck'n. Mos' likely dey has rackety times in de
nussery. En I reck'n de wives quarrels considable; en dat
'crease de racket. Yit dey say Sollermun de wises' man dat
ever live'. I doan' take no stock in dat. Bekase why: would a
wise man want to live in de mids' er sich a blimblammin' all
de time? No—'deed he wouldn't. A wise man 'ud take en
buil' a biler-factry; en den he could shet *down* de biler-factry
when he want to res'."

"Well, but he *was* the wisest man, anyway; because the
widow she told me so, her own self."

"I doan k'yer what de widder say, he *warn't* no wise man,
nuther. He had some er de dad-fetchedes' ways I ever see.
Does you know 'bout dat chile dat he 'uz gwyne to chop in
two?"

"Yes, the widow told me all about it."

"*Well*, den! Warn' dat de beatenes' notion in de worl'? You
jes' take en look at it a minute. Dah's de stump, dah—dat's
one er de women; heah's you—dat's de yuther one; I's Sollermun; en dish-yer dollar bill's de chile. Bofe un you claims
it. What does I do? Does I shin aroun' mongs' de neighbors
en fine out which un you de bill *do* b'long to, en han' it over
to de right one, all safe en soun', de way dat anybody dat had
any gumption would? No—I take en whack de bill in *two*, en
give half un it to you, en de yuther half to de yuther woman.

Dat's de way Sollermun was gwyne to do wid de chile. Now
I want to ast you: what's de use er dat half a bill?—can't buy
noth'n wid it. En what use is a half a chile? I would'n give a
dern for a million un um."

"But hang it, Jim, you've clean missed the point—blame it,
you've missed it a thousand mile."

"Who? Me? Go 'long. Doan' talk to *me* 'bout yo' pints. I
reck'n I knows sense when I sees it; en dey ain' no sense in
sich doin's as dat. De 'spute warn't 'bout a half a chile, de
'spute was 'bout a whole chile; en de man dat think he kin
settle a 'spute 'bout a whole chile wid a half a chile, doan'
know enough to come in out'n de rain. Doan' talk to me
'bout Sollermun, Huck, I knows him by de back."

"But I tell you you don't get the point."

"Blame de pint! I reck'n I knows what I knows. En mine
you, de *real* pint is down furder—it's down deeper. It lays
in de way Sollermun was raised. You take a man dat's got
on'y one er two chillen; is dat man gwyne to be waseful o'
chillen? No, he ain't; he can't 'ford it. *He* know how to
value 'em. But you take a man dat's got 'bout five million
chillen runnin' roun' de house, en it's diffunt. *He* as soon
chop a chile in two as a cat. Dey's plenty mo'. A chile er
two, mo' er less, warn't no consekens to Sollermun, dad
fetch him!"

I never see such a nigger. If he got a notion in his head
once, there warn't no getting it out again. He was the most
down on Solomon of any nigger I ever see. So I went to
talking about other kings, and let Solomon slide. I told about
Louis Sixteenth that got his head cut off in France long time
ago; and about his little boy the dolphin, that would a been
a king, but they took and shut him up in jail, and some say
he died there.

"Po' little chap."

"But some says he got out and got away, and come to
America."

"Dat's good! But he'll be pooty lonesome—dey ain' no
kings here, is dey, Huck?"

"No."

"Den he cain't git no situation. What he gwyne to do?"

"Well, I don't know. Some of them gets on the police, and some of them learns people how to talk French."

"Why, Huck, doan' de French people talk de same way we does?"

"*No*, Jim; you couldn't understand a word they said—not a single word."

"Well, now, I be ding-busted! How do dat come?"

"*I* don't know; but it's so. I got some of their jabber out of a book. Spose a man was to come to you and say *Polly-voo-franzy*—what would you think?"

"I wouldn' think nuff'n; I'd take en bust him over de head. Dat is, if he warn't white. I wouldn't 'low no nigger to call me dat."

"Shucks, it ain't calling you anything. It's only saying do you know how to talk French."

"Well, den, why couldn't he *say* it?"

"Why, he *is* a-saying it. That's a Frenchman's *way* of saying it."

"Well, it's a blame' ridicklous way, en I doan' want to hear no mo' 'bout it. Dey ain' no sense in it."

"Looky here, Jim; does a cat talk like we do?"

"No, a cat don't."

"Well, does a cow?"

"No, a cow don't, nuther."

"Does a cat talk like a cow, or a cow talk like a cat?"

"No, dey don't."

"It's natural and right for 'em to talk different from each other, ain't it?"

"'Course."

"And ain't it natural and right for a cat and a cow to talk different from *us*?"

"Why, mos' sholy it is."

"Well, then, why ain't it natural and right for a *Frenchman* to talk different from us? You answer me that."

"Is a cat a man, Huck?"

"No."

"Well, den, dey ain't no sense in a cat talkin' like a man. Is a cow a man?—er is a cow a cat?"

"No, she ain't either of them."

"Well, den, she ain' got no business to talk like either one er the yuther of 'em. Is a Frenchman a man?"

"Yes."

"*Well*, den! Dad blame it, why doan' he *talk* like a man? You answer me *dat*!"

I see it warn't no use wasting words—you can't learn a nigger to argue. So I quit.

XV

WE JUDGED that three nights more would fetch us to Cairo, at the bottom of Illinois, where the Ohio River comes in, and that was what we was after. We would sell the raft and get on a steamboat and go way up the Ohio amongst the free States, and then be out of trouble.

Well, the second night a fog begun to come on, and we made for a tow-head to tie to, for it wouldn't do to try to run in fog; but when I paddled ahead in the canoe, with the line, to make fast, there warn't anything but little saplings to tie to. I passed the line around one of them right on the edge of the cut bank, but there was a stiff current, and the raft come booming down so lively she tore it out by the roots and away she went. I see the fog closing down, and it made me so sick and scared I couldn't budge for most a half a minute it seemed to me—and then there warn't no raft in sight; you couldn't see twenty yards. I jumped into the canoe and run back to the stern and grabbed the paddle and set her back a stroke. But she didn't come. I was in such a hurry I hadn't untied her. I got up and tried to untie her, but I was so excited my hands shook so I couldn't hardly do anything with them.

As soon as I got started I took out after the raft, hot and heavy, right down the tow-head. That was all right as far as it went, but the tow-head warn't sixty yards long, and the minute I flew by the foot of it I shot out into the solid white fog, and hadn't no more idea which way I was going than a dead man.

Thinks I, it won't do to paddle; first I know I'll run into the bank or a tow-head or something; I got to set still and float, and yet it's mighty fidgety business to have to hold your hands still at such a time. I whooped and listened. Away down there, somewheres, I hears a small whoop, and up comes my spirits. I went tearing after it, listening sharp to hear it again. The next time it come, I see I warn't heading for it but heading away to the right of it. And the next time, I was heading away to the left of it—and not gaining on it much, either, for I was flying around, this way and that and 'tother, but it was going straight ahead all the time.

I did wish the fool would think to beat a tin pan, and beat it all the time, but he never did, and it was the still places between the whoops that was making the trouble for me. Well, I fought along, and directly I hears the whoop *behind* me. I was tangled good, now. That was somebody else's whoop, or else I was turned around.

I throwed the paddle down. I heard the whoop again; it was behind me yet, but in a different place; it kept coming, and kept changing its place, and I kept answering, till by-and-by it was in front of me again and I knowed the current had swung the canoe's head down stream and I was all right, if that was Jim and not some other raftsman hollering. I couldn't tell nothing about voices in a fog, for nothing don't look natural nor sound natural in a fog.

The whooping went on, and in about a minute I come a booming down on a cut bank with smoky ghosts of big trees on it, and the current throwed me off to the left and shot by, amongst a lot of snags that fairly roared, the current was tearing by them so swift.

In another second or two it was solid white and still again. I set perfectly still, then, listening to my heart thump, and I reckon I didn't draw a breath while it thumped a hundred.

I just give up, then. I knowed what the matter was. That cut bank was an island, and Jim had gone down 'tother side of it. It warn't no tow-head, that you could float by in ten minutes. It had the big timber of a regular island; it might be five or six mile long and more than a half a mile wide.

I kept quiet, with my ears cocked, about fifteen minutes, I reckon. I was floating along, of course, four or five mile an hour; but you don't ever think of that. No, you *feel* like you are laying dead still on the water; and if a little glimpse of a snag slips by, you don't think to yourself how fast *you're* going, but you catch your breath and think, my! how that snag's tearing along. If you think it ain't dismal and lonesome out in a fog that way, by yourself, in the night, you try it once—you'll see.

Next, for about a half an hour, I whoops now and then; at last I hears the answer a long ways off, and tries to follow it, but I couldn't do it, and directly I judged I'd got into a nest of tow-heads, for I had little dim glimpses of them on both sides of me, sometimes just a narrow channel between; and some that I couldn't see, I knowed was there, because I'd hear the wash of the current against the old dead brush and trash that hung over the banks. Well, I warn't long losing the whoops, down amongst the tow-heads; and I only tried to chase them a little while, anyway, because it was worse than chasing a Jack-o-lantern. You never knowed a sound dodge around so, and swap places so quick and so much.

I had to claw away from the bank pretty lively, four or five times, to keep from knocking the islands out of the river; and so I judged the raft must be butting into the bank every now and then, or else it would get further ahead and clear out of hearing—it was floating a little faster than what I was.

Well, I seemed to be in the open river again, by-and-by, but I couldn't hear no sign of a whoop nowheres. I reckoned Jim had fetched up on a snag, maybe, and it was all up with him. I was good and tired, so I laid down in the canoe and said I wouldn't bother no more. I didn't want to go to sleep, of course; but I was so sleepy I couldn't help it; so I thought I would take just one little cat-nap.

But I reckon it was more than a cat-nap, for when I waked up the stars was shining bright, the fog was all gone, and I was spinning down a big bend stern first. First I didn't know where I was; I thought I was dreaming; and when things begun to come back to me, they seemed to come up dim out of last week.

It was a monstrous big river here, with the tallest and the thickest kind of timber on both banks; just a solid wall, as well as I could see, by the stars. I looked away down stream, and seen a black speck on the water. I took out after it; but when I got to it it warn't nothing but a couple of saw-logs made fast together. Then I see another speck, and chased that; then another, and this time I was right. It was the raft.

When I got to it Jim was setting there with his head down between his knees, asleep, with his right arm hanging over the steering oar. The other oar was smashed off, and the raft was littered up with leaves and branches and dirt. So she'd had a rough time.

I made fast and laid down under Jim's nose on the raft, and begun to gap, and stretch my fists out against Jim, and says:

"Hello, Jim, have I been asleep? Why didn't you stir me up?"

"Goodness gracious, is dat you, Huck? En you ain' dead— you ain' drownded—you's back agin? It's too good for true, honey, it's too good for true. Lemme look at you, chile, lemme feel o' you. No, you ain' dead! you's back agin, 'live en soun', jis de same ole Huck—de same ole Huck, thanks to goodness!"

"What's the matter with you, Jim? You been a drinking?"

"Drinkin'? Has I ben a drinkin'? Has I had a chance to be a drinkin'?"

"Well, then, what makes you talk so wild?"

"How does I talk wild?"

"*How?* why, hain't you been talking about my coming back, and all that stuff, as if I'd been gone away?"

"Huck—Huck Finn, you look me in de eye; look me in de eye. *Hain't* you ben gone away?"

"Gone away? Why, what in the nation do you mean? *I* hain't been gone anywheres. Where would I go to?"

"Well, looky here, boss, dey's sumf'n wrong, dey is. Is I *me*, or who *is* I? Is I heah, or whah *is* I? Now dat's what I wants to know?"

"Well, I think you're here, plain enough, but I think you're a tangle-headed old fool, Jim."

"I is, is I? Well you answer me dis. Didn't you tote out de line in de canoe, fer to make fas' to de tow-head?"

"No, I didn't. What tow-head? I hain't seen no tow-head."

"You hain't seen no tow-head? Looky here—didn't de line pull loose en de raf' go a hummin' down de river, en leave you en de canoe behine in de fog?"

"What fog?"

"Why *de* fog. De fog dat's ben aroun' all night. En didn't you whoop, en didn't I whoop, tell we got mix' up in de islands en one un us got los' en 'tother one was jis' as good as los', 'kase he didn' know whah he wuz? En didn't I bust up agin a lot er dem islands en have a turrible time en mos' git drownded? Now ain' dat so, boss—ain't it so? You answer me dat."

"Well, this is too many for me, Jim. I hain't seen no fog, nor no islands, nor no troubles, nor nothing. I been setting here talking with you all night till you went to sleep about ten minutes ago, and I reckon I done the same. You couldn't a got drunk in that time, so of course you've been dreaming."

"Dad fetch it, how is I gwyne to dream all dat in ten minutes?"

"Well, hang it all, you did dream it, because there didn't any of it happen."

"But Huck, it's all jis' as plain to me as——"

"It don't make no difference how plain it is, there ain't nothing in it. I know, because I've been here all the time."

Jim didn't say nothing for about five minutes, but set there studying over it. Then he says:

"Well, den, I reck'n I did dream it, Huck; but dog my cats ef it ain't de powerfullest dream I ever see. En I hain't ever had no dream b'fo' dat's tired me like dis one."

"Oh, well, that's all right, because a dream does tire a body like everything, sometimes. But this one was a staving dream—tell me all about it, Jim."

So Jim went to work and told me the whole thing right through, just as it happened, only he painted it up considerable. Then he said he must start in and "'terpret" it, because it was sent for a warning. He said the first tow-head stood for a man that would try to do us some good, but the current was another man that would get us away from him. The whoops was warnings that would come to us every now and then, and if we didn't try hard to make out to understand them they'd just take us into bad luck, 'stead of keeping us out of it. The lot of tow-heads was troubles we was going to get into with quarrelsome people and all kinds of mean folks, but if we minded our business and didn't talk back and aggravate them, we would pull through and get out of the fog and into the big clear river, which was the free States, and wouldn't have no more trouble.

It had clouded up pretty dark just after I got onto the raft, but it was clearing up again, now.

"Oh, well, that's all interpreted well enough, as far as it goes, Jim," I says; "but what does *these* things stand for?"

It was the leaves and rubbish on the raft, and the smashed oar. You could see them first rate, now.

Jim looked at the trash, and then looked at me, and back at the trash again. He had got the dream fixed so strong in his head that he couldn't seem to shake it loose and get the facts back into its place again, right away. But when he did get the thing straightened around, he looked at me steady, without ever smiling, and says:

"What do dey stan' for? I's gwyne to tell you. When I got all wore out wid work, en wid de callin' for you, en went to sleep, my heart wuz mos' broke bekase you wuz los', en I didn' k'yer no mo' what become er me en de raf'. En when I wake up en fine you back agin', all safe en soun', de tears come en I could a got down on my knees en kiss' yo' foot I's so thankful. En all you wuz thinkin 'bout wuz how you could make a fool uv ole Jim wid a lie. Dat truck dah is *trash*; en trash is what people is dat puts dirt on de head er dey fren's en makes 'em ashamed."

Then he got up slow, and walked to the wigwam, and went in there, without saying anything but that. But that was enough. It made me feel so mean I could almost kissed *his* foot to get him to take it back.

It was fifteen minutes before I could work myself up to go and humble myself to a nigger—but I done it, and I warn't ever sorry for it afterwards, neither. I didn't do him no more mean tricks, and I wouldn't done that one if I'd a knowed it would make him feel that way.

XVI

WE SLEPT most all day, and started out at night, a little ways behind a monstrous long raft that was as long going by as a procession. She had four long sweeps at each end, so we judged she carried as many as thirty men, likely. She had five big wigwams aboard, wide apart, and an open camp fire in the middle, and a tall flag-pole at each end. There was a power of style about her. It *amounted* to something being a raftsman on such a craft as that.

We went drifting down into a big bend, and the night clouded up and got hot. The river was very wide, and was walled with solid timber on both sides; you couldn't see a break in it hardly ever, or a light. We talked about Cairo, and wondered whether we would know it when we got to it. I said likely we wouldn't, because I had heard say there warn't but about a dozen houses there, and if they didn't happen to have them lit up, how was we going to know we was passing a town? Jim said if the two big rivers joined together there, that would show. But I said maybe we might think we was passing the foot of an island and coming into the same old river again. That disturbed Jim—and me too. So the question was, what to do? I said, paddle ashore the first time a light showed, and tell them pap was behind, coming along with a trading-scow, and was a green hand at the business, and wanted to know how far it was to Cairo. Jim thought it was a good idea, so we took a smoke on it and waited.

There warn't nothing to do, now, but to look out sharp for the town, and not pass it without seeing it. He said he'd be mighty sure to see it, because he'd be a free man the minute he seen it, but if he missed it he'd be in the slave country again and no more show for freedom. Every little while he jumps up and says:

"Dah she is!"

But it warn't. It was Jack-o-lanterns, or lightning-bugs; so he set down again, and went to watching, same as before. Jim said it made him all over trembly and feverish to be so close to freedom. Well, I can tell you it made me all over trembly and feverish, too, to hear him, because I begun to get it through my head that he *was* most free—and who was to blame for it? Why, *me*. I couldn't get that out of my conscience, no how nor no way. It got to troubling me so I couldn't rest; I couldn't stay still in one place. It hadn't ever come home to me before, what this thing was that I was doing. But now it did; and it staid with me, and scorched me more and more. I tried to make out to myself that *I* warn't to blame, because *I* didn't run Jim off from his rightful owner; but it warn't no use, conscience up and says, every time, "But you knowed he was running for his freedom, and you could a paddled ashore and told somebody." That was so—I couldn't get around that, noway. That was where it pinched. Conscience says to me, "What had poor Miss Watson done to you, that you could see her nigger go off right under your eyes and never say one single word? What did that poor old woman do to you, that you could treat her so mean? Why, she tried to learn you your book, she tried to learn you your manners, she tried to be good to you every way she knowed how. *That's* what she done."

I got to feeling so mean and so miserable I most wished I was dead. I fidgeted up and down the raft, abusing myself to myself, and Jim was fidgeting up and down past me. We neither of us could keep still. Every time he danced around and says, "Dah's Cairo!" it went through me like a shot, and I thought if it *was* Cairo I reckoned I would die of miserableness.

Jim talked out loud all the time while I was talking to myself. He was saying how the first thing he would do when he got to a free State he would go to saving up money and never spend a single cent, and when he got enough he would buy his wife, which was owned on a farm close to where Miss Watson lived; and then they would both work to buy the two children, and if their master wouldn't sell them, they'd get an Ab'litionist to go and steal them.

It most froze me to hear such talk. He wouldn't ever dared to talk such talk in his life before. Just see what a difference it made in him the minute he judged he was about free. It was according to the old saying, "give a nigger an inch and he'll take an ell." Thinks I, this is what comes of my not thinking. Here was this nigger which I had as good as helped to run away, coming right out flat-footed and saying he would steal his children—children that belonged to a man I didn't even know; a man that hadn't ever done me no harm.

I was sorry to hear Jim say that, it was such a lowering of him. My conscience got to stirring me up hotter than ever, until at last I says to it, "Let up on me—it ain't too late, yet—I'll paddle ashore at the first light, and tell." I felt easy, and happy, and light as a feather, right off. All my troubles was gone. I went to looking out sharp for a light, and sort of singing to myself. By-and-by one showed. Jim sings out:

"We's safe, Huck, we's safe! Jump up and crack yo' heels, dat's de good ole Cairo at las', I jis knows it!"

I says:

"I'll take the canoe and go see, Jim. It mightn't be, you know."

He jumped and got the canoe ready, and put his old coat in the bottom for me to set on, and give me the paddle; and as I shoved off, he says:

"Pooty soon I'll be a-shout'n for joy, en I'll say, it's all on accounts o' Huck; I's a free man, en I couldn't ever ben free ef it hadn' ben for Huck; Huck done it. Jim won't ever forgit you, Huck; you's de bes' fren' Jim's ever had; en you's de *only* fren' ole Jim's got now."

I was paddling off, all in a sweat to tell on him; but when he says this, it seemed to kind of take the tuck all out of me. I went along slow then, and I warn't right down certain whether I was glad I started or whether I warn't. When I was fifty yards off, Jim says:

"Dah you goes, de ole true Huck; de on'y white genlman dat ever kep' his promise to ole Jim."

Well, I just felt sick. But I says, I *got* to do it—I can't get *out* of it. Right then, along comes a skiff with two men in it, with guns, and they stopped and I stopped. One of them says:

"What's that, yonder?"

"A piece of a raft," I says.

"Do you belong on it?"

"Yes, sir."

"Any men on it?"

"Only one, sir."

"Well, there's five niggers run off to-night, up yonder above the head of the bend. Is your man white or black?"

I didn't answer up prompt. I tried to, but the words wouldn't come. I tried, for a second or two, to brace up and out with it, but I warn't man enough—hadn't the spunk of a rabbit. I see I was weakening; so I just give up trying, and up and says—

"He's white."

"I reckon we'll go and see for ourselves."

"I wish you would," says I, "because it's pap that's there, and maybe you'd help me tow the raft ashore where the light is. He's sick—and so is mam and Mary Ann."

"Oh, the devil! we're in a hurry, boy. But I s'pose we've got to. Come—buckle to your paddle, and let's get along."

I buckled to my paddle and they laid to their oars. When we had made a stroke or two, I says:

"Pap'll be mighty much obleeged to you, I can tell you. Everybody goes away when I want them to help me tow the raft ashore, and I can't do it by myself."

"Well, that's infernal mean. Odd, too. Say, boy, what's the matter with your father?"

"It's the—a—the—well, it ain't anything, much."

They stopped pulling. It warn't but a mighty little ways to the raft, now. One says:

"Boy, that's a lie. What *is* the matter with your pap? Answer up square, now, and it'll be the better for you."

"I will, sir, I will, honest—but don't leave us, please. It's the—the—gentlemen, if you'll only pull ahead, and let me heave you the head-line, you won't have to come a-near the raft—please do."

"Set her back, John, set her back!" says one. They backed water. "Keep away, boy—keep to looard. Confound it, I just expect the wind has blowed it to us. Your pap's got the small-pox, and you know it precious well. Why didn't you come out and say so? Do you want to spread it all over?"

"Well," says I, a-blubbering, "I've told everybody before, and then they just went away and left us."

"Poor devil, there's something in that. We are right down sorry for you, but we—well, hang it, we don't want the small-pox, you see. Look here, I'll tell you what to do. Don't you try to land by yourself, or you'll smash everything to pieces. You float along down about twenty miles and you'll come to a town on the left-hand side of the river. It will be long after sun-up, then, and when you ask for help, you tell them your folks are all down with chills and fever. Don't be a fool again, and let people guess what is the matter. Now we're trying to do you a kindness; so you just put twenty miles between us, that's a good boy. It wouldn't do any good to land yonder where the light is—it's only a wood-yard. Say—I reckon your father's poor, and I'm bound to say he's in pretty hard luck. Here—I'll put a twenty dollar gold piece on this board, and you get it when it floats by. I feel mighty mean to leave you, but my kingdom! it won't do to fool with small-pox, don't you see?"

"Hold on, Parker," says the other man, "here's a twenty to put on the board for me. Good-bye, boy, you do as Mr. Parker told you, and you'll be all right."

"That's so, my boy—good-bye, good-bye. If you see any runaway niggers, you get help and nab them, and you can make some money by it."

"Good-bye, sir," says I, "I won't let no runaway niggers get by me if I can help it."

They went off, and I got aboard the raft, feeling bad and low, because I knowed very well I had done wrong, and I see it warn't no use for me to try to learn to do right; a body that don't get *started* right when he's little, ain't got no show—when the pinch comes there ain't nothing to back him up and keep him to his work, and so he gets beat. Then I thought a minute, and says to myself, hold on,—s'pose you'd a done right and give Jim up; would you felt better than what you do now? No, says I, I'd feel bad—I'd feel just the same way I do now. Well, then, says I, what's the use you learning to do right, when it's troublesome to do right and ain't no trouble to do wrong, and the wages is just the same? I was stuck. I couldn't answer that. So I reckoned I wouldn't bother no more about it, but after this always do whichever come handiest at the time.

I went into the wigwam; Jim warn't there. I looked all around; he warn't anywhere. I says:

"Jim!"

"Here I is, Huck. Is dey out o' sight yit? Don't talk loud."

He was in the river, under the stern oar, with just his nose out. I told him they was out of sight, so he come aboard. He says:

"I was a-listenin' to all de talk, en I slips into de river en was gwyne to shove for sho' if dey come aboard. Den I was gwyne to swim to de raf' agin when dey was gone. But lawsy, how you did fool 'em, Huck! Dat *wuz* de smartes' dodge! I tell you, chile, I 'speck it save' ole Jim—ole Jim ain't gwyne to forgit you for dat, honey."

Then we talked about the money. It was a pretty good raise, twenty dollars apiece. Jim said we could take deck passage on a steamboat now, and the money would last us as far as we wanted to go in the free States. He said twenty mile more warn't far for the raft to go, but he wished we was already there.

Towards daybreak we tied up, and Jim was mighty particular about hiding the raft good. Then he worked all day fixing things in bundles, and getting all ready to quit rafting.

That night about ten we hove in sight of the lights of a town away down in a left-hand bend.

I went off in the canoe, to ask about it. Pretty soon I found a man out in the river with a skiff, setting a trot-line. I ranged up and says:

"Mister, is that town Cairo?"

"Cairo? no. You must be a blame' fool."

"What town is it, mister?"

"If you want to know, go and find out. If you stay here botherin' around me for about a half a minute longer, you'll get something you won't want."

I paddled to the raft. Jim was awful disappointed, but I said never mind, Cairo would be the next place, I reckoned.

We passed another town before daylight, and I was going out again; but it was high ground, so I didn't go. No high ground about Cairo, Jim said. I had forgot it. We laid up for the day, on a tow-head tolerable close to the left-hand bank. I begun to suspicion something. So did Jim. I says:

"Maybe we went by Cairo in the fog that night."

He says:

"Doan' less' talk about it, Huck. Po' niggers can't have no luck. I awluz 'spected dat rattle-snake skin warn't done wid it's work."

"I wish I'd never seen that snake-skin, Jim—I do wish I'd never laid eyes on it."

"It ain't yo' fault, Huck; you didn' know. Don't you blame yo'self 'bout it."

When it was daylight, here was the clear Ohio water in shore, sure enough, and outside was the old regular Muddy! So it was all up with Cairo.

We talked it all over. It wouldn't do to take to the shore; we couldn't take the raft up the stream, of course. There warn't no way but to wait for dark, and start back in the canoe and take the chances. So we slept all day amongst the cotton-wood thicket, so as to be fresh for the work, and when we went back to the raft about dark the canoe was gone!

We didn't say a word for a good while. There warn't anything to say. We both knowed well enough it was some more work of the rattle-snake skin; so what was the use to talk about it? It would only look like we was finding fault, and that would be bound to fetch more bad luck—and keep on fetching it, too, till we knowed enough to keep still.

By-and-by we talked about what we better do, and found there warn't no way but just to go along down with the raft till we got a chance to buy a canoe to go back in. We warn't going to borrow it when there warn't anybody around, the way pap would do, for that might set people after us.

So we shoved out, after dark, on the raft.

Anybody that don't believe yet, that it's foolishness to handle a snake-skin, after all that that snake-skin done for us, will believe it now, if they read on and see what more it done for us.

The place to buy canoes is off of rafts laying up at shore. But we didn't see no rafts laying up; so we went along during three hours and more. Well, the night got gray, and ruther thick, which is the next meanest thing to fog. You can't tell the shape of the river, and you can't see no distance. It got to be very late and still, and then along comes a steamboat up the river. We lit the lantern, and judged she would see it. Up-stream boats didn't generly come close to us; they go out and follow the bars and hunt for easy water under the reefs; but nights like this they bull right up the channel against the whole river.

We could hear her pounding along, but we didn't see her good till she was close. She aimed right for us. Often they do that and try to see how close they can come without touch-ing; sometimes the wheel bites off a sweep, and then the pilot sticks his head out and laughs, and thinks he's mighty smart. Well, here she comes, and we said she was going to try to shave us; but she didn't seem to be sheering off a bit. She was a big one, and she was coming in a hurry, too, looking like a black cloud with rows of glow-worms around it; but all of a sudden she bulged out, big and scary, with a long row of wide-open furnace doors shining like red-hot teeth, and her monstrous bows and guards hanging right over us. There was a yell at us, and a jingling of bells to stop the engines, a pow-wow of cussing, and whistling of steam—and as Jim went overboard on one side and I on the other, she come smashing straight through the raft.

I dived—and I aimed to find the bottom, too, for a thirty-foot wheel had got to go over me, and I wanted it to have plenty of room. I could always stay under water a minute; this time I reckon I staid under water a minute and a half. Then I bounced for the top in a hurry, for I was nearly bust-ing. I popped out to my arm-pits and blowed the water out of my nose, and puffed a bit. Of course there was a booming current; and of course that boat started her engines again ten seconds after she stopped them, for they never cared much for raftsmen; so now she was churning along up the river, out of sight in the thick weather, though I could hear her.

I sung out for Jim about a dozen times, but I didn't get any answer; so I grabbed a plank that touched me while I was "treading water," and struck out for shore, shoving it ahead of me. But I made out to see that the drift of the current was towards the left-hand shore, which meant that I was in a crossing; so I changed off and went that way.

It was one of these long, slanting, two-mile crossings; so I was a good long time in getting over. I made a safe landing, and clum up the bank. I couldn't see but a little ways, but I went poking along over rough ground for a quarter of a mile or more, and then I run across a big old-fashioned double log house before I noticed it. I was going to rush by and get away, but a lot of dogs jumped out and went to howling and barking at me, and I knowed better than to move another peg.

XVII

IN ABOUT HALF A MINUTE somebody spoke out of a window, without putting his head out, and says:

"Be done, boys! Who's there?"

I says:

"It's me."

"Who's me?"

"George Jackson, sir."

"What do you want?"

"I don't want nothing, sir. I only want to go along by, but the dogs won't let me."

"What are you prowling around here this time of night, for—hey?"

"I warn't prowling around, sir; I fell overboard off of the steamboat."

"Oh, you did, did you? Strike a light there, somebody. What did you say your name was?"

"George Jackson, sir. I'm only a boy."

"Look here; if you're telling the truth, you needn't be afraid—nobody 'll hurt you. But don't try to budge; stand right where you are. Rouse out Bob and Tom, some of you, and fetch the guns. George Jackson, is there anybody with you?"

"No, sir, nobody."

I heard the people stirring around in the house, now, and see a light. The man sung out:

"Snatch that light away, Betsy, you old fool—ain't you got any sense? Put it on the floor behind the front door. Bob, if you and Tom are ready, take your places."

"All ready."

"Now, George Jackson, do you know the Shepherdsons?"

"No, sir—I never heard of them."

"Well, that may be so, and it mayn't. Now, all ready. Step forward, George Jackson. And mind, don't you hurry—come mighty slow. If there's anybody with you, let him keep back—if he shows himself he'll be shot. Come along, now.

Come slow; push the door open, yourself—just enough to squeeze in, d' you hear?"

I didn't hurry, I couldn't if I'd a wanted to. I took one slow step at a time, and there warn't a sound, only I thought I could hear my heart. The dogs were as still as the humans, but they followed a little behind me. When I got to the three log door-steps, I heard them unlocking and unbarring and unbolting. I put my hand on the door and pushed it a little and a little more, till somebody said, "There, that's enough—put your head in." I done it, but I judged they would take it off.

The candle was on the floor, and there they all was, looking at me, and me at them, for about a quarter of a minute. Three big men with guns pointed at me, which made me wince, I tell you; the oldest, gray and about sixty, the other two thirty or more—all of them fine and handsome—and the sweetest old gray-headed lady, and back of her two young women which I couldn't see right well. The old gentleman says:

"There—I reckon it's all right. Come in."

As soon as I was in, the old gentleman he locked the door and barred it and bolted it, and told the young men to come in with their guns, and they all went in a big parlor that had a new rag carpet on the floor, and got together in a corner that was out of range of the front windows—there warn't none on the side. They held the candle, and took a good look at me, and all said, "Why *he* ain't a Shepherdson—no, there ain't any Shepherdson about him." Then the old man said he hoped I wouldn't mind being searched for arms, because he didn't mean no harm by it—it was only to make sure. So he didn't pry into my pockets, but only felt outside with his hands, and said it was all right. He told me to make myself easy and at home, and tell all about myself; but the old lady says:

"Why bless you, Saul, the poor thing's as wet as he can be; and don't you reckon it may be he's hungry?"

"True for you, Rachel—I forgot."

So the old lady says:

"Betsy" (this was a nigger woman), "you fly around and get him something to eat, as quick as you can, poor thing; and one of you girls go and wake up Buck and tell him— Oh, here he is himself. Buck, take this little stranger and get the wet clothes off from him and dress him up in some of yours that's dry."

Buck looked about as old as me—thirteen or fourteen or along there, though he was a little bigger than me. He hadn't on anything but a shirt, and he was very frowsy-headed. He come in gaping and digging one fist into his eyes, and he was dragging a gun along with the other one. He says:

"Ain't they no Shepherdsons around?"

They said, no, 'twas a false alarm.

"Well," he says, "if they'd a ben some, I reckon I'd a got one."

They all laughed, and Bob says:

"Why, Buck, they might have scalped us all, you've been so slow in coming."

"Well, nobody come after me, and it ain't right. I'm always kep' down; I don't get no show."

"Never mind, Buck, my boy," says the old man, "you'll have show enough, all in good time, don't you fret about that. Go 'long with you now, and do as your mother told you."

When we got up stairs to his room, he got me a coarse shirt and a roundabout and pants of his, and I put them on. While I was at it he asked me what my name was, but before I could tell him, he started to telling me about a blue jay and a young rabbit he had catched in the woods day before yesterday, and he asked me where Moses was when the candle went out. I said I didn't know; I hadn't heard about it before, no way.

"Well, guess," he says.

"How'm I going to guess," says I, "when I never heard tell about it before?"

"But you can guess, can't you? It's just as easy."

"*Which* candle?" I says.

"Why, any candle," he says.

"I don't know where he was," says I; "where was he?"

"Why he was in the *dark*! That's where he was!"

"Well, if you knowed where he was, what did you ask me for?"

"Why, blame it, it's a riddle, don't you see? Say, how long are you going to stay here? You got to stay always. We can

just have booming times—they don't have no school now.
Do you own a dog? I've got a dog—and he'll go in the river
and bring out chips that you throw in. Do you like to comb
up, Sundays, and all that kind of foolishness? You bet I don't,
but ma she makes me. Confound these ole britches, I reckon
I'd better put 'em on, but I'd ruther not, it's so warm. Are
you all ready? All right—come along, old hoss."

Cold corn-pone, cold corn-beef, butter and butter-milk—
that is what they had for me down there, and there ain't nothing better that ever I've come across yet. Buck and his ma and
all of them smoked cob pipes, except the nigger woman,
which was gone, and the two young women. They all smoked
and talked, and I eat and talked. The young women had quilts
around them, and their hair down their backs. They all asked
me questions, and I told them how pap and me and all the
family was living on a little farm down at the bottom of Arkansaw, and my sister Mary Ann run off and got married and
never was heard of no more, and Bill went to hunt them
and he warn't heard of no more, and Tom and Mort died,
and then there warn't nobody but just me and pap left, and
he was just trimmed down to nothing, on account of his troubles; so when he died I took what there was left, because the
farm didn't belong to us, and started up the river, deck passage, and fell overboard; and that was how I come to be here.
So they said I could have a home there as long as I wanted
it. Then it was most daylight, and everybody went to bed,
and I went to bed with Buck, and when I waked up in the
morning, drat it all, I had forgot what my name was. So I
laid there about an hour trying to think, and when Buck
waked up, I says:

"Can you spell, Buck?"

"Yes," he says.

"I bet you can't spell my name," says I.

"I bet you what you dare I can," says he.

"All right," says I, "go ahead."

"G-o-r-g-e J-a-x-o-n—there now," he says.

"Well," says I, "you done it, but I didn't think you could.
It ain't no slouch of a name to spell—right off without
studying."

I set it down, private, because somebody might want *me* to

spell it, next, and so I wanted to be handy with it and rattle it off like I was used to it.

It was a mighty nice family, and a mighty nice house, too. I hadn't seen no house out in the country before that was so nice and had so much style. It didn't have an iron latch on the front door, nor a wooden one with a buckskin string, but a brass knob to turn, the same as houses in a town. There warn't no bed in the parlor, not a sign of a bed; but heaps of parlors in towns has beds in them. There was a big fireplace that was bricked on the bottom, and the bricks was kept clean and red by pouring water on them and scrubbing them with another brick; sometimes they washed them over with red water-paint that they call Spanish-brown, same as they do in town. They had big brass dog-irons that could hold up a saw-log. There was a clock on the middle of the mantel-piece, with a picture of a town painted on the bottom half of the glass front, and a round place in the middle of it for the sun, and you could see the pendulum swing behind it. It was beautiful to hear that clock tick; and sometimes when one of these peddlers had been along and scoured her up and got her in good shape, she would start in and strike a hundred and fifty before she got tuckered out. They wouldn't took any money for her.

Well, there was a big outlandish parrot on each side of the clock, made out of something like chalk, and painted up gaudy. By one of the parrots was a cat made of crockery, and a crockery dog by the other; and when you pressed down on them they squeaked, but didn't open their mouths nor look different nor interested. They squeaked through underneath. There was a couple of big wild-turkey-wing fans spread out behind those things. On a table in the middle of the room was a kind of a lovely crockery basket that had apples and oranges and peaches and grapes piled up in it which was much redder and yellower and prettier than real ones is, but they warn't real because you could see where pieces had got chipped off and showed the white chalk or whatever it was, underneath.

This table had a cover made out of beautiful oil-cloth, with a red and blue spread-eagle painted on it, and a painted border all around. It come all the way from Philadelphia, they said. There was some books too, piled up perfectly exact, on each corner of the table. One was a big family Bible, full of pictures. One was "Pilgrim's Progress," about a man that left his family it didn't say why. I read considerable in it now and then. The statements was interesting, but tough. Another was "Friendship's Offering," full of beautiful stuff and poetry; but I didn't read the poetry. Another was Henry Clay's Speeches, and another was Dr. Gunn's Family Medicine, which told you all about what to do if a body was sick or dead. There was a Hymn Book, and a lot of other books. And there was nice split-bottom chairs, and perfectly sound, too—not bagged down in the middle and busted, like an old basket.

They had pictures hung on the walls—mainly Washingtons and Lafayettes, and battles, and Highland Marys, and one called "Signing the Declaration." There was some that they called crayons, which one of the daughters which was dead made her own self when she was only fifteen years old. They was different from any pictures I ever see before; blacker, mostly, than is common. One was a woman in a slim black dress, belted small under the arm-pits, with bulges like a cabbage in the middle of the sleeves, and a large black scoop-shovel bonnet with a black veil, and white slim ankles crossed about with black tape, and very wee black slippers, like a chisel, and she was leaning pensive on a tombstone on her right elbow, under a weeping willow, and her other hand hanging down her side holding a white handkerchief and a reticule, and underneath the picture it said "Shall I Never See Thee More Alas." Another one was a young lady with her hair all combed up straight to the top of her head, and knotted there in front of a comb like a chair-back, and she was crying into a handkerchief and had a dead bird laying on its back in her other hand with its heels up, and underneath the picture it said "I Shall Never Hear Thy Sweet Chirrup More Alas." There was one where a young lady was at a window looking up at the moon, and tears running down her cheeks; and she had an open letter in one hand with black sealing-wax showing on one edge of it, and she was mashing a locket with a chain to it against her mouth, and underneath the picture it said "And Art Thou Gone Yes Thou Art Gone Alas." These was all nice pictures, I reckon, but I didn't somehow seem to take to them, because if ever I was down a little, they always give me the fan-tods. Everybody was sorry she died, because she had laid out a lot more of these pictures to do, and a body could see by what she had done what they had lost. But I reckoned, that with her disposition, she was having a better time in the graveyard. She was at work on what they said was her greatest picture when she took sick, and every day and every night it was her prayer to be allowed to live till she got it done, but she never got the chance. It was a picture of a young woman in a long white gown, standing on the rail of a bridge all ready to jump off, with her hair all down her back, and looking up to the moon, with the tears running down her face, and she had two arms folded across her breast, and two arms stretched out in front, and two more reaching up towards the moon—and the idea was, to see which pair would look best and then scratch out all the other arms; but, as I was saying, she died before she got her mind made up, and now they kept this picture over the head of the bed in her room, and every time her birthday come they hung flowers on it. Other times it was hid with a little curtain. The young woman in the picture had a kind of a nice sweet face, but there was so many arms it made her look too spidery, seemed to me.

This young girl kept a scrap-book when she was alive, and used to paste obituaries and accidents and cases of patient suffering in it out of the *Presbyterian Observer*, and write poetry after them out of her own head. It was very good poetry. This is what she wrote about a boy by the name of Stephen Dowling Bots that fell down a well and was drownded:

ODE TO STEPHEN DOWLING BOTS, DEC'D.

And did young Stephen sicken,
    And did young Stephen die?
And did the sad hearts thicken,
    And did the mourners cry?

No; such was not the fate of
    Young Stephen Dowling Bots;
Though sad hearts round him thickened,
    'Twas not from sickness' shots.

No whooping-cough did rack his frame,
 Nor measles drear, with spots;
Not these impaired the sacred name
 Of Stephen Dowling Bots.

Despised love struck not with woe
 That head of curly knots,
Nor stomach troubles laid him low,
 Young Stephen Dowling Bots.

O no. Then list with tearful eye,
 Whilst I his fate do tell.
His soul did from this cold world fly,
 By falling down a well.

They got him out and emptied him;
 Alas it was too late;
His spirit was gone for to sport aloft
 In the realms of the good and great.

If Emmeline Grangerford could make poetry like that before she was fourteen, there ain't no telling what she could a
done by-and-by. Buck said she could rattle off poetry like
nothing. She didn't ever have to stop to think. He said she
would slap down a line, and if she couldn't find anything to
rhyme with it she would just scratch it out and slap down
another one, and go ahead. She warn't particular, she could
write about anything you choose to give her to write about,
just so it was sadful. Every time a man died, or a woman
died, or a child died, she would be on hand with her "tribute"
before he was cold. She called them tributes. The neighbors
said it was the doctor first, then Emmeline, then the undertaker—the undertaker never got in ahead of Emmeline but
once, and then she hung fire on a rhyme for the dead person's
name, which was Whistler. She warn't ever the same, after
that; she never complained, but she kind of pined away and
did not live long. Poor thing, many's the time I made myself
go up to the little room that used to be hers and get out her
poor old scrap-book and read in it when her pictures had
been aggravating me and I had soured on her a little. I liked

all that family, dead ones and all, and warn't going to let anything come between us. Poor Emmeline made poetry about all the dead people when she was alive, and it didn't seem right that there warn't nobody to make some about her, now she was gone; so I tried to sweat out a verse or two myself, but I couldn't seem to make it go, somehow. They kept Emmeline's room trim and nice and all the things fixed in it just the way she liked to have them when she was alive, and nobody ever slept there. The old lady took care of the room herself, though there was plenty of niggers, and she sewed there a good deal and read her Bible there, mostly.

Well, as I was saying about the parlor, there was beautiful curtains on the windows: white, with pictures painted on them, of castles with vines all down the walls, and cattle coming down to drink. There was a little old piano, too, that had tin pans in it, I reckon, and nothing was ever so lovely as to hear the young ladies sing, "The Last Link is Broken" and play "The Battle of Prague" on it. The walls of all the rooms was plastered, and most had carpets on the floors, and the whole house was whitewashed on the outside.

It was a double house, and the big open place betwixt them was roofed and floored, and sometimes the table was set there in the middle of the day, and it was a cool, comfortable place. Nothing couldn't be better. And warn't the cooking good, and just bushels of it too!

XVIII

OL. GRANGERFORD was a gentleman, you see. He was a
gentleman all over; and so was his family. He was well
born, as the saying is, and that's worth as much in a man as
it is in a horse, so the Widow Douglas said, and nobody ever
denied that she was of the first aristocracy in our town; and
pap he always said it, too, though he warn't no more quality
than a mud-cat, himself. Col. Grangerford was very tall and
very slim, and had a darkish-paly complexion, not a sign of
red in it anywheres; he was clean-shaved every morning, all
over his thin face, and he had the thinnest kind of lips, and
the thinnest kind of nostrils, and a high nose, and heavy eyebrows, and the blackest kind of eyes, sunk so deep back that
they seemed like they was looking out of caverns at you, as
you may say. His forehead was high, and his hair was black
and straight, and hung to his shoulders. His hands was long
and thin, and every day of his life he put on a clean shirt and
a full suit from head to foot made out of linen so white it
hurt your eyes to look at it; and on Sundays he wore a blue
tail-coat with brass buttons on it. He carried a mahogany
cane with a silver head to it. There warn't no frivolishness
about him, not a bit, and he warn't ever loud. He was as kind
as he could be—you could feel that, you know, and so you
had confidence. Sometimes he smiled, and it was good to see;
but when he straightened himself up like a liberty-pole, and
the lightning begun to flicker out from under his eyebrows
you wanted to climb a tree first, and find out what the matter
was afterwards. He didn't ever have to tell anybody to mind
their manners—everybody was always good mannered where
he was. Everybody loved to have him around, too; he was
sunshine most always—I mean he made it seem like good
weather. When he turned into a cloud-bank it was awful dark
for a half a minute and that was enough; there wouldn't nothing go wrong again for a week.

When him and the old lady come down in the morning, all
the family got up out of their chairs and give them good-day,
and didn't set down again till they had set down. Then Tom

and Bob went to the sideboard where the decanters was, and mixed a glass of bitters and handed it to him, and he held it in his hand and waited till Tom's and Bob's was mixed, and then they bowed and said "Our duty to you, sir, and madam;" and *they* bowed the least bit in the world and said thank you, and so they drank, all three, and Bob and Tom poured a spoonful of water on the sugar and the mite of whisky or apple brandy in the bottom of their tumblers, and give it to me and Buck, and we drank to the old people too.

Bob was the oldest, and Tom next. Tall, beautiful men with very broad shoulders and brown faces, and long black hair and black eyes. They dressed in white linen from head to foot, like the old gentleman, and wore broad Panama hats.

Then there was Miss Charlotte, she was twenty-five, and tall and proud and grand, but as good as she could be, when she warn't stirred up; but when she was, she had a look that would make you wilt in your tracks, like her father. She was beautiful.

So was her sister, Miss Sophia, but it was a different kind. She was gentle and sweet, like a dove, and she was only twenty.

Each person had their own nigger to wait on them—Buck, too. My nigger had a monstrous easy time, because I warn't used to having anybody do anything for me, but Buck's was on the jump most of the time.

This was all there was of the family, now; but there used to be more—three sons; they got killed; and Emmeline that died.

The old gentleman owned a lot of farms, and over a hundred niggers. Sometimes a stack of people would come there, horseback, from ten or fifteen mile around, and stay five or six days, and have such junketings round about and on the river, and dances and picnics in the woods, day-times, and balls at the house, nights. These people was mostly kin-folks of the family. The men brought their guns with them. It was a handsome lot of quality, I tell you.

There was another clan of aristocracy around there—five or six families—mostly of the name of Shepherdson. They was as high-toned, and well born, and rich and grand, as the tribe of Grangerfords. The Shepherdsons and the Grangerfords used the same steamboat landing, which was about two mile above our house; so sometimes when I went up there with a lot of our folks I used to see a lot of the Shepherdsons there, on their fine horses.

One day Buck and me was away out in the woods, hunting, and heard a horse coming. We was crossing the road. Buck says:

"Quick! Jump for the woods!"

We done it, and then peeped down the woods through the leaves. Pretty soon a splendid young man come galloping down the road, setting his horse easy and looking like a soldier. He had his gun across his pommel. I had seen him before. It was young Harney Shepherdson. I heard Buck's gun go off at my ear, and Harney's hat tumbled off from his head. He grabbed his gun and rode straight to the place where we was hid. But we didn't wait. We started through the woods on a run. The woods warn't thick, so I looked over my shoulder, to dodge the bullet, and twice I seen Harney cover Buck with his gun; and then he rode away the way he come—to get his hat, I reckon, but I couldn't see. We never stopped running till we got home. The old gentleman's eyes blazed a minute—'twas pleasure, mainly, I judged—then his face sort of smoothed down, and he says, kind of gentle:

"I don't like that shooting from behind a bush. Why didn't you step into the road, my boy?"

"The Shepherdsons don't, father. They always take advantage."

Miss Charlotte she held her head up like a queen while Buck was telling his tale, and her nostrils spread and her eyes snapped. The two young men looked dark, but never said nothing. Miss Sophia she turned pale, but the color come back when she found the man warn't hurt.

Soon as I could get Buck down by the corn-cribs under the trees by ourselves, I says:

"Did you want to kill him, Buck?"

"Well, I bet I did."

"What did he do to you?"

"Him? He never done nothing to me."

"Well, then, what did you want to kill him for?"

"Why nothing—only it's on account of the feud."

"What's a feud?"

"Why, where was you raised? Don't you know what a feud is?"

"Never heard of it before—tell me about it."

"Well," says Buck, "a feud is this way. A man has a quarrel with another man, and kills him; then that other man's brother kills *him*; then the other brothers, on both sides, goes for one another; then the *cousins* chip in—and by-and-by everybody's killed off, and there ain't no more feud. But it's kind of slow, and takes a long time."

"Has this one been going on long, Buck?"

"Well I should *reckon*! it started thirty year ago, or som'ers along there. There was trouble 'bout something and then a lawsuit to settle it; and the suit went agin one of the men, and so he up and shot the man that won the suit—which he would naturally do, of course. Anybody would."

"What was the trouble about, Buck?—land?"

"I reckon maybe—I don't know."

"Well, who done the shooting?—was it a Grangerford or a Shepherdson?"

"Laws, how do *I* know? it was so long ago."

"Don't anybody know?"

"Oh, yes, pa knows, I reckon, and some of the other old folks; but they don't know, now, what the row was about in the first place."

"Has there been many killed, Buck?"

"Yes—right smart chance of funerals. But they don't always kill. Pa's got a few buck-shot in him; but he don't mind it 'cuz he don't weigh much anyway. Bob's been carved up some with a bowie, and Tom's been hurt once or twice."

"Has anybody been killed this year, Buck?"

"Yes, we got one and they got one. 'Bout three months ago, my cousin Bud, fourteen year old, was riding through the woods, on t'other side of the river, and didn't have no weapon with him, which was blame' foolishness, and in a lonesome place he hears a horse a-coming behind him, and sees old Baldy Shepherdson a-linkin' after him with his gun in his hand and his white hair a-flying in the wind; and 'stead of jumping off and taking to the brush, Bud 'lowed he could outrun him; so they had it, nip and tuck, for five mile or

more, the old man a-gaining all the time; so at last Bud seen
it warn't any use, so he stopped and faced around so as to
have the bullet holes in front, you know, and the old man he
rode up and shot him down. But he didn't git much chance
to enjoy his luck, for inside of a week our folks laid *him* out."

"I reckon that old man was a coward, Buck."

"I reckon he *warn't* a coward. Not by a blame' sight. There
ain't a coward amongst them Shepherdsons—not a one. And
there ain't no cowards amongst the Grangerfords, either.
Why, that old man kep' up his end in a fight one day, for a
half an hour, against three Grangerfords, and come out winner. They was all a-horseback; he lit off of his horse and got
behind a little wood-pile, and kep' his horse before him to
stop the bullets; but the Grangerfords staid on their horses
and capered around the old man, and peppered away at him,
and he peppered away at them. Him and his horse both went
home pretty leaky and crippled, but the Grangerfords had to
be *fetched* home—and one of 'em was dead, and another died
the next day. No, sir, if a body's out hunting for cowards, he
don't want to fool away any time amongst them Shepherdsons, becuz they don't breed any of that *kind*."

Next Sunday we all went to church, about three mile, everybody a-horseback. The men took their guns along, so did
Buck, and kept them between their knees or stood them
handy against the wall. The Shepherdsons done the same. It
was pretty ornery preaching—all about brotherly love, and
such-like tiresomeness; but everybody said it was a good sermon, and they all talked it over going home, and had such a
powerful lot to say about faith, and good works, and free
grace, and preforeordestination, and I don't know what all,
that it did seem to me to be one of the roughest Sundays I
had run across yet.

About an hour after dinner everybody was dozing around,
some in their chairs and some in their rooms, and it got to be
pretty dull. Buck and a dog was stretched out on the grass in
the sun, sound asleep. I went up to our room, and judged I
would take a nap myself. I found that sweet Miss Sophia
standing in her door, which was next to ours, and she took
me in her room and shut the door very soft, and asked me if
I liked her, and I said I did; and she asked me if I would do

something for her and not tell anybody, and I said I would. Then she said she'd forgot her Testament, and left it in the seat at church, between two other books and would I slip out quiet and go there and fetch it to her, and not say nothing to nobody. I said I would. So I slid out and slipped off up the road, and there warn't anybody at the church, except maybe a hog or two, for there warn't any lock on the door, and hogs likes a puncheon floor in summer-time because it's cool. If you notice, most folks don't go to church only when they've got to; but a hog is different.

Says I to myself something's up—it ain't natural for a girl to be in such a sweat about a Testament; so I give it a shake, and out drops a little piece of paper with "*Half-past two*" wrote on it with a pencil. I ransacked it, but couldn't find anything else. I couldn't make anything out of that, so I put the paper in the book again, and when I got home and up stairs, there was Miss Sophia in her door waiting for me. She pulled me in and shut the door; then she looked in the Testament till she found the paper, and as soon as she read it she looked glad; and before a body could think, she grabbed me and give me a squeeze, and said I was the best boy in the world, and not to tell anybody. She was mighty red in the face, for a minute, and her eyes lighted up and it made her powerful pretty. I was a good deal astonished, but when I got my breath I asked her what the paper was about, and she asked me if I had read it, and I said no, and she asked me if I could read writing, and I told her "no, only coarse-hand," and then she said the paper warn't anything but a book-mark to keep her place, and I might go and play now.

I went off down to the river, studying over this thing, and pretty soon I noticed that my nigger was following along behind. When we was out of sight of the house, he looked back and around a second, and then comes a-running, and says:

"Mars Jawge, if you'll come down into de swamp, I'll show you a whole stack o' water-moccasins."

Thinks I, that's mighty curious; he said that yesterday. He oughter know a body don't love water-moccasins enough to go around hunting for them. What is he up to anyway? So I says—

"All right, trot ahead."

I followed a half a mile, then he struck out over the swamp and waded ankle deep as much as another half mile. We come to a little flat piece of land which was dry and very thick with trees and bushes and vines, and he says—

"You shove right in dah, jist a few steps, Mars Jawge, dah's whah dey is. I's seed 'm befo', I don't k'yer to see 'em no mo'."

Then he slopped right along and went away, and pretty soon the trees hid him. I poked into the place a-ways, and come to a little open patch as big as a bedroom, all hung around with vines, and found a man laying there asleep—and by jings it was my old Jim!

I waked him up, and I reckoned it was going to be a grand surprise to him to see me again, but it warn't. He nearly cried, he was so glad, but he warn't surprised. Said he swum along behind me, that night, and heard me yell every time, but dasn't answer, because he didn't want nobody to pick *him* up, and take him into slavery again. Says he—

"I got hurt a little, en couldn't swim fas', so I wuz a considable ways behind you, towards de las'; when you landed I reck'ned I could ketch up wid you on de lan' 'dout havin' to shout at you, but when I see dat house I begin to go slow. I 'uz off too fur to hear what dey say to you—I wuz 'fraid o' de dogs—but when it 'uz all quiet agin, I knowed you's in de house, so I struck out for de woods to wait for day. Early in de mawnin' some er de niggers come along, gwyne to de fields, en dey tuck me en showed me dis place, whah de dogs can't track me on accounts o' de water, en dey brings me truck to eat every night, en tells me how you's gitt'n along."

"Why didn't you tell my Jack to fetch me here sooner, Jim?"

"Well, 'twarn't no use to 'sturb you, Huck, tell we could do sumfn—but we's all right, now. I ben a-buyin' pots en pans en vittles, as I got a chanst, en a patchin' up de raf', nights, when——"

"*What* raft, Jim?"

"Our ole raf'."

"You mean to say our old raft warn't smashed all to flinders?"

"No, she warn't. She was tore up a good deal—one en' of

her was—but dey warn't no great harm done, on'y our traps was mos' all los'. Ef we hadn' dive' so deep en swum so fur under water, en de night hadn' ben so dark, en we warn't so sk'yerd, en ben sich punkin-heads, as de sayin' is, we'd a seed de raf'. But it's jis' as well we didn't, 'kase now she's all fixed up agin mos' as good as new, en we's got a new lot o' stuff, too, in de place o' what 'uz los'."

"Why, how did you get hold of the raft again, Jim—did you catch her?"

"How I gwyne to ketch her, en I out in de woods? No, some er de niggers foun' her ketched on a snag, along heah in de ben', en dey hid her in a crick, 'mongst de willows, en dey wuz so much jawin' 'bout which un 'um she b'long to de mos', dat I come to heah 'bout it pooty soon, so I ups en settles de trouble by tellin' 'um she don't b'long to none uv um, but to you en me; en I ast 'm if dey gwyne to grab a young white genlman's propaty, en git a hid'n for it? Den I gin 'm ten cents apiece, en dey 'uz mighty well satisfied, en wisht some mo' raf's 'ud come along en make 'm rich agin. Dey's mighty good to me, dese niggers is, en whatever I wants 'm to do fur me, I doan' have to ast 'm twice, honey. Dat Jack's a good nigger, en pooty smart."

"Yes, he is. He ain't ever told me you was here; told me to come, and he'd show me a lot of water-moccasins. If anything happens, *he* ain't mixed up in it. He can say he never seen us together, and it'll be the truth."

I don't want to talk much about the next day. I reckon I'll cut it pretty short. I waked up about dawn, and was agoing to turn over and go to sleep again, when I noticed how still it was—didn't seem to be anybody stirring. That warn't usual. Next I noticed that Buck was up and gone. Well, I gets up, a-wondering, and goes down stairs—nobody around; everything as still as a mouse. Just the same outside; thinks I, what does it mean? Down by the wood-pile I comes across my Jack, and says:

"What's it all about?"

Says he:

"Don't you know, Mars Jawge?"

"No," says I, "I don't."

"Well, den, Miss Sophia's run off! 'deed she has. She run

off in de night, sometime—nobody don't know jis' when—
run off to git married to dat young Harney Shepherdson, you
know—leastways, so dey 'spec. De fambly foun' it out, 'bout
half an hour ago—maybe a little mo'—en' I *tell* you dey
warn't no time los'. Sich another hurryin' up guns en hosses
you never see! De women folks has gone for to stir up de
relations, en ole Mars Saul en de boys tuck dey guns en rode
up de river road for to try to ketch dat young man en kill him
'fo' he kin git acrost de river wid Miss Sophia. I reck'n dey's
gwyne to be mighty rough times."

"Buck went off 'thout waking me up."

"Well I reck'n he *did*! Dey warn't gwyne to mix you up in
it. Mars Buck he loaded up his gun en 'lowed he's gwyne to
fetch home a Shepherdson or bust. Well, dey'll be plenty un
'm dah, I reck'n, en you bet you he'll fetch one ef he gits a
chanst."

I took up the river road as hard as I could put. By-and-by
I begin to hear guns a good ways off. When I come in sight
of the log store and the wood-pile where the steamboats
lands, I worked along under the trees and brush till I got to
a good place, and then I clumb up into the forks of a cotton-
wood that was out of reach, and watched. There was a wood-
rank four foot high, a little ways in front of the tree, and first
I was going to hide behind that; but maybe it was luckier I
didn't.

There was four or five men cavorting around on their
horses in the open place before the log store, cussing and
yelling, and trying to get at a couple of young chaps that was
behind the wood-rank alongside of the steamboat landing—
but they couldn't come it. Every time one of them showed
himself on the river side of the wood-pile he got shot at. The
two boys was squatting back to back behind the pile, so they
could watch both ways.

By-and-by the men stopped cavorting around and yelling.
They started riding towards the store; then up gets one of the
boys, draws a steady bead over the wood-rank, and drops one
of them out of his saddle. All the men jumped off of their
horses and grabbed the hurt one and started to carry him to
the store; and that minute the two boys started on the run.
They got half-way to the tree I was in before the men noticed.

Then the men see them, and jumped on their horses and took out after them. They gained on the boys, but it didn't do no good, the boys had too good a start; they got to the wood-pile that was in front of my tree, and slipped in behind it, and so they had the bulge on the men again. One of the boys was Buck, and the other was a slim young chap about nineteen years old.

The men ripped around awhile, and then rode away. As soon as they was out of sight, I sung out to Buck and told him. He didn't know what to make of my voice coming out of the tree, at first. He was awful surprised. He told me to watch out sharp and let him know when the men come in sight again; said they was up to some devilment or other—wouldn't be gone long. I wished I was out of that tree, but I dasn't come down. Buck begun to cry and rip, and 'lowed that him and his cousin Joe (that was the other young chap) would make up for this day, yet. He said his father and his two brothers was killed, and two or three of the enemy. Said the Shepherdsons laid for them, in ambush. Buck said his father and brothers ought to waited for their relations—the Shepherdsons was too strong for them. I asked him what was become of young Harney and Miss Sophia. He said they'd got across the river and was safe. I was glad of that; but the way Buck did take on because he didn't manage to kill Harney that day he shot at him—I hain't ever heard anything like it.

All of a sudden, bang! bang! bang! goes three or four guns—the men had slipped around through the woods and come in from behind without their horses! The boys jumped for the river—both of them hurt—and as they swum down the current the men run along the bank shooting at them and singing out, "Kill them, kill them!" It made me so sick I most fell out of the tree. I ain't agoing to tell *all* that happened—it would make me sick again if I was to do that. I wished I hadn't ever come ashore that night, to see such things. I ain't ever going to get shut of them—lots of times I dream about them.

I staid in the tree till it begun to get dark, afraid to come down. Sometimes I heard guns away off in the woods; and twice I seen little gangs of men gallop past the log store with

guns; so I reckoned the trouble was still agoing on. I was
mighty down-hearted; so I made up my mind I wouldn't ever
go anear that house again, because I reckoned I was to blame,
somehow. I judged that that piece of paper meant that Miss
Sophia was to meet Harney somewheres at half-past two and
run off; and I judged I ought to told her father about that
paper and the curious way she acted, and then maybe he
would a locked her up and this awful mess wouldn't ever happened.

When I got down out of the tree, I crept along down the
river bank a piece, and found the two bodies laying in the
edge of the water, and tugged at them till I got them ashore;
then I covered up their faces, and got away as quick as I
could. I cried a little when I was covering up Buck's face, for
he was mighty good to me.

It was just dark, now. I never went near the house, but
struck through the woods and made for the swamp. Jim
warn't on his island, so I tramped off in a hurry for the crick,
and crowded through the willows, red-hot to jump aboard
and get out of that awful country—the raft was gone! My
souls, but I was scared! I couldn't get my breath for most a
minute. Then I raised a yell. A voice not twenty-five foot
from me, says—

"Good lan'! is dat you, honey? Doan' make no noise."

It was Jim's voice—nothing ever sounded so good before.
I run along the bank a piece and got aboard, and Jim he
grabbed me and hugged me, he was so glad to see me. He
says—

"Laws bless you, chile, I 'uz right down sho' you's dead
agin. Jack's been heah, he say he reck'n you's ben shot, kase
you didn' come home no mo'; so I's jes' dis minute a startin'
de raf' down towards de mouf er de crick, so's to be all ready
for to shove out en leave soon as Jack comes agin en tells me
for certain you *is* dead. Lawsy, I's mighty glad to git you back
agin, honey."

I says—

"All right—that's mighty good; they won't find me, and
they'll think I've been killed, and floated down the river—
there's something up there that'll help them to think so—so

don't you lose no time, Jim, but just shove off for the big
water as fast as ever you can."

I never felt easy till the raft was two mile below there and
out in the middle of the Mississippi. Then we hung up our
signal lantern, and judged that we was free and safe once
more. I hadn't had a bite to eat since yesterday; so Jim he got
out some corn-dodgers and buttermilk, and pork and cabbage, and greens—there ain't nothing in the world so good,
when it's cooked right—and whilst I eat my supper we
talked, and had a good time. I was powerful glad to get away
from the feuds, and so was Jim to get away from the swamp.
We said there warn't no home like a raft, after all. Other
places do seem so cramped up and smothery, but a raft don't.
You feel mighty free and easy and comfortable on a raft.

XIX

TWO OR THREE DAYS and nights went by; I reckon I
might say they swum by, they slid along so quiet and
smooth and lovely. Here is the way we put in the time. It
was a monstrous big river down there—sometimes a mile
and a half wide; we run nights, and laid up and hid day-
times; soon as night was most gone, we stopped navigating
and tied up—nearly always in the dead water under a tow-
head; and then cut young cotton-woods and willows and hid
the raft with them. Then we set out the lines. Next we slid
into the river and had a swim, so as to freshen up and cool
off; then we set down on the sandy bottom where the water
was about knee deep, and watched the daylight come. Not a
sound, anywheres—perfectly still—just like the whole world
was asleep, only sometimes the bull-frogs a-cluttering, maybe.
The first thing to see, looking away over the water, was a
kind of dull line—that was the woods on t'other side—you
couldn't make nothing else out; then a pale place in the sky;
then more paleness, spreading around; then the river softened
up, away off, and warn't black any more, but gray; you could
see little dark spots drifting along, ever so far away—trading
scows, and such things; and long black streaks—rafts; sometimes you could hear a sweep screaking; or jumbled up
voices, it was so still, and sounds come so far; and by-and-by
you could see a streak on the water which you know by the
look of the streak that there's a snag there in a swift current
which breaks on it and makes that streak look that way; and
you see the mist curl up off of the water, and the east reddens
up, and the river, and you make out a log cabin in the edge
of the woods, away on the bank on t'other side of the river,
being a wood-yard, likely, and piled by them cheats so you
can throw a dog through it anywheres; then the nice breeze
springs up, and comes fanning you from over there, so cool
and fresh, and sweet to smell, on account of the woods
and the flowers; but sometimes not that way, because
they've left dead fish laying around, gars, and such, and
they do get pretty rank; and next you've got the full day,

and everything smiling in the sun, and the song-birds just going it!

A little smoke couldn't be noticed, now, so we would take some fish off of the lines, and cook up a hot breakfast. And afterwards we would watch the lonesomeness of the river, and kind of lazy along, and by-and-by lazy off to sleep. Wake up, by-and-by, and look to see what done it, and maybe see a steamboat, coughing along up stream, so far off towards the other side you couldn't tell nothing about her only whether she was stern-wheel or side-wheel; then for about an hour there wouldn't be nothing to hear nor nothing to see—just solid lonesomeness. Next you'd see a raft sliding by, away off yonder, and maybe a galoot on it chopping, because they're most always doing it on a raft; you'd see the ax flash, and come down—you don't hear nothing; you see that ax go up again, and by the time it's above the man's head, then you hear the *k'chunk!*—it had took all that time to come over the water. So we would put in the day, lazying around, listening to the stillness. Once there was a thick fog, and the rafts and things that went by was beating tin pans so the steamboats wouldn't run over them. A scow or a raft went by so close we could hear them talking and cussing and laughing—heard them plain; but we couldn't see no sign of them; it made you feel crawly, it was like spirits carrying on that way in the air. Jim said he believed it was spirits; but I says:

"No, spirits wouldn't say, 'dern the dern fog.'"

Soon as it was night, out we shoved; when we got her out to about the middle, we let her alone, and let her float wherever the current wanted her to; then we lit the pipes, and dangled our legs in the water and talked about all kinds of things—we was always naked, day and night, whenever the mosquitoes would let us—the new clothes Buck's folks made for me was too good to be comfortable, and besides I didn't go much on clothes, nohow.

Sometimes we'd have that whole river all to ourselves for the longest time. Yonder was the banks and the islands, across the water; and maybe a spark—which was a candle in a cabin window—and sometimes on the water you could see a spark or two—on a raft or a scow, you know; and maybe you could hear a fiddle or a song coming over from one of them crafts. It's lovely to live on a raft. We had the sky, up there, all speckled with stars, and we used to lay on our backs and look up at them, and discuss about whether they was made, or only just happened—Jim he allowed they was made, but I allowed they happened; I judged it would have took too long to *make* so many. Jim said the moon could a *laid* them; well, that looked kind of reasonable, so I didn't say nothing against it, because I've seen a frog lay most as many, so of course it could be done. We used to watch the stars that fell, too, and see them streak down. Jim allowed they'd got spoiled and was hove out of the nest.

Once or twice of a night we would see a steamboat slipping along in the dark, and now and then she would belch a whole world of sparks up out of her chimbleys, and they would rain down in the river and look awful pretty; then she would turn a corner and her lights would wink out and her pow-wow shut off and leave the river still again; and by-and-by her waves would get to us, a long time after she was gone, and joggle the raft a bit, and after that you wouldn't hear nothing for you couldn't tell how long, except maybe frogs or something.

After midnight the people on shore went to bed, and then for two or three hours the shores was black—no more sparks in the cabin windows. These sparks was our clock—the first one that showed again meant morning was coming, so we hunted a place to hide and tie up, right away.

One morning about day-break, I found a canoe and crossed over a chute to the main shore—it was only two hundred yards—and paddled about a mile up a crick amongst the cypress woods, to see if I couldn't get some berries. Just as I was passing a place where a kind of a cow-path crossed the crick, here comes a couple of men tearing up the path as tight as they could foot it. I thought I was a goner, for whenever anybody was after anybody I judged it was *me*—or maybe Jim. I was about to dig out from there in a hurry, but they was pretty close to me then, and sung out and begged me to save their lives—said they hadn't been doing nothing, and was being chased for it—said there was men and dogs a-coming. They wanted to jump right in, but I says—

"Don't you do it. I don't hear the dogs and horses yet; you've got time to crowd through the brush and get up the crick a little ways; then you take to the water and wade down to me and get in—that'll throw the dogs off the scent."

They done it, and soon as they was aboard I lit out for our tow-head, and in about five or ten minutes we heard the dogs and the men away off, shouting. We heard them come along towards the crick, but couldn't see them; they seemed to stop and fool around a while; then, as we got further and further away all the time, we couldn't hardly hear them at all; by the time we had left a mile of woods behind us and struck the river, everything was quiet, and we paddled over to the tow-head and hid in the cotton-woods and was safe.

One of these fellows was about seventy, or upwards, and had a bald head and very gray whiskers. He had an old battered-up slouch hat on, and a greasy blue woolen shirt, and ragged old blue jeans britches stuffed into his boot tops, and home-knit galluses—no, he only had one. He had an old long-tailed blue jeans coat with slick brass buttons, flung over his arm, and both of them had big fat ratty-looking carpet-bags.

The other fellow was about thirty and dressed about as ornery. After breakfast we all laid off and talked, and the first thing that come out was that these chaps didn't know one another.

"What got you into trouble?" says the baldhead to t'other chap.

"Well, I'd been selling an article to take the tartar off the teeth—and it does take it off, too, and generly the enamel along with it—but I staid about one night longer than I ought to, and was just in the act of sliding out when I ran across you on the trail this side of town, and you told me they were coming, and begged me to help you to get off. So I told you I was expecting trouble myself and would scatter out *with* you. That's the whole yarn—what's yourn?"

"Well, I'd ben a-runnin' a little temperance revival thar, 'bout a week, and was the pet of the women-folks, big and little, for I was makin' it mighty warm for the rummies, I *tell* you, and takin' as much as five or six dollars a night—ten cents a head, children and niggers free—and business a growin' all the time; when somehow or another a little report got around, last night, that I had a way of puttin' in my time with a private jug, on the sly. A nigger rousted me out this mornin', and told me the people was getherin' on the quiet, with their dogs and horses, and they'd be along pretty soon and give me 'bout half an hour's start, and then run me down, if they could; and if they got me they'd tar and feather me and ride me on a rail, sure. I didn't wait for no break-fast—I warn't hungry."

"Old man," says the young one, "I reckon we might double-team it together; what do you think?"

"I ain't undisposed. What's your line—mainly?"

"Jour printer, by trade; do a little in patent medicines; theatre-actor—tragedy, you know; take a turn at mesmerism and phrenology when there's a chance; teach singing-geogra-phy school for a change; sling a lecture, sometimes—oh, I do lots of things—most anything that comes handy, so it ain't work. What's your lay?"

"I've done considerble in the doctoring way in my time. Layin' on o' hands is my best holt—for cancer, and paralysis, and sich things; and I k'n tell a fortune pretty good, when I've got somebody along to find out the facts for me. Preachin's my line, too; and workin' camp-meetin's; and mis-sionaryin' around."

Nobody never said anything for a while; then the young man hove a sigh and says—

"Alas!"

"What 're you alassin' about?" says the baldhead.

"To think I should have lived to be leading such a life, and be degraded down into such company." And he begun to wipe the corner of his eye with a rag.

"Dern your skin, ain't the company good enough for you?" says the baldhead, pretty pert and uppish.

"Yes, it *is* good enough for me; it's as good as I deserve; for who fetched me so low, when I was so high? *I* did myself. I don't blame *you*, gentlemen—far from it; I don't blame any-body. I deserve it all. Let the cold world do its worst; one thing I know—there's a grave somewhere for me. The world may go on just as it's always done, and take everything from me—loved ones, property, everything—but it can't take that. Some day I'll lie down in it and forget it all, and my poor broken heart will be at rest." He went on a-wiping.

"Drot your pore broken heart," says the baldhead; "what are you heaving your pore broken heart at *us* f'r? *We* hain't done nothing."

"No, I know you haven't. I ain't blaming you, gentlemen. I brought myself down—yes, I did it myself. It's right I should suffer—perfectly right—I don't make any moan."

"Brought you down from whar? Whar was you brought down from?"

"Ah, you would not believe me; the world never believes—let it pass—'tis no matter. The secret of my birth——"

"The secret of your birth? Do you mean to say——"

"Gentlemen," says the young man, very solemn, "I will reveal it to you, for I feel I may have confidence in you. By rights I am a duke!"

Jim's eyes bugged out when he heard that; and I reckon mine did, too. Then the baldhead says: "No! you can't mean it?"

"Yes. My great-grandfather, eldest son of the Duke of Bridgewater, fled to this country about the end of the last century, to breathe the pure air of freedom; married here, and died, leaving a son, his own father dying about the same time. The second son of the late duke seized the title and estates—the infant real duke was ignored. I am the lineal descendant of that infant—I am the rightful Duke of Bridgewater; and here am I, forlorn, torn from my high estate, hunted of men, despised by the cold world, ragged, worn, heart-broken, and degraded to the companionship of felons on a raft!"

Jim pitied him ever so much, and so did I. We tried to comfort him, but he said it warn't much use, he couldn't be much comforted; said if we was a mind to acknowledge him, that would do him more good than most anything else; so we said we would, if he would tell us how. He said we ought to bow, when we spoke to him, and say "Your Grace," or "My Lord," or "Your Lordship"—and he wouldn't mind it if we called him plain "Bridgewater," which he said was a title, anyway, and not a name; and one of us ought to wait on him at dinner, and do any little thing for him he wanted done.

Well, that was all easy, so we done it. All through dinner Jim stood around and waited on him, and says, "Will yo'

Grace have some o' dis, or some o' dat?" and so on, and a body could see it was mighty pleasing to him.

But the old man got pretty silent, by-and-by—didn't have much to say, and didn't look pretty comfortable over all that petting that was going on around that duke. He seemed to have something on his mind. So, along in the afternoon, he says:

"Looky here, Bilgewater," he says, "I'm nation sorry for you, but you ain't the only person that's had troubles like that."

"No?"

"No, you ain't. You ain't the only person that's ben snaked down wrongfully out'n a high place."

"Alas!"

"No, you ain't the only person that's had a secret of his birth." And by jings, *he* begins to cry.

"Hold! What do you mean?"

"Bilgewater, kin I trust you?" says the old man, still sort of sobbing.

"To the bitter death!" He took the old man by the hand and squeezed it, and says, "The secret of your being: speak!"

"Bilgewater, I am the late Dauphin!"

You bet you Jim and me stared, this time. Then the duke says:

"You are what?"

"Yes, my friend, it is too true—your eyes is lookin' at this very moment on the pore disappeared Dauphin, Looy the Seventeen, son of Looy the Sixteen and Marry Antonette."

"You! At your age! No! You mean you're the late Charlemagne; you must be six or seven hundred years old, at the very least."

"Trouble has done it, Bilgewater, trouble has done it; trouble has brung these gray hairs and this premature balditude. Yes, gentlemen, you see before you, in blue jeans and misery, the wanderin', exiled, trampled-on and sufferin' rightful King of France."

Well, he cried and took on so, that me and Jim didn't know hardly what to do, we was so sorry—and so glad and proud we'd got him with us, too. So we set in, like we done before with the duke, and tried to comfort *him*. But he said it warn't no use, nothing but to be dead and done with it all could do him any good; though he said it often made him feel easier and better for a while if people treated him according to his rights, and got down on one knee to speak to him, and always called him "Your Majesty," and waited on him first at meals, and didn't set down in his presence till he asked them. So Jim and me set to majestying him, and doing this and that and t'other for him, and standing up till he told us we might set down. This done him heaps of good, and so he got cheerful and comfortable. But the duke kind of soured on him, and didn't look a bit satisfied with the way things was going; still, the king acted real friendly towards him, and said the duke's great-grandfather and all the other Dukes of Bilgewater was a good deal thought of by *his* father and was allowed to come to the palace considerable; but the duke staid huffy a good while, till by-and-by the king says:

"Like as not we got to be together a blamed long time, on this h-yer raft, Bilgewater, and so what's the use o' your bein' sour? It'll only make things oncomfortable. It ain't my fault I warn't born a duke, it ain't your fault you warn't born a king—so what's the use to worry? Make the best o' things the way you find 'em, says I—that's my motto. This ain't no bad thing that we've struck here—plenty grub and an easy life—come, give us your hand, Duke, and less all be friends."

The duke done it, and Jim and me was pretty glad to see it. It took away all the uncomfortableness, and we felt mighty good over it, because it would a been a miserable business to have any unfriendliness on the raft; for what you want, above all things, on a raft, is for everybody to be satisfied, and feel right and kind towards the others.

It didn't take me long to make up my mind that these liars warn't no kings nor dukes, at all, but just low-down humbugs and frauds. But I never said nothing, never let on; kept it to myself; it's the best way; then you don't have no quarrels, and don't get into no trouble. If they wanted us to call them kings and dukes, I hadn't no objections, 'long as it would keep peace in the family; and it warn't no use to tell Jim, so I didn't tell him. If I never learnt nothing else out of pap, I learnt that the best way to get along with his kind of people is to let them have their own way.

XX

THEY ASKED us considerable many questions; wanted to know what we covered up the raft that way for, and laid by in the day-time instead of running—was Jim a runaway nigger? Says I—

"Goodness sakes, would a runaway nigger run *south*?"

No, they allowed he wouldn't. I had to account for things some way, so I says:

"My folks was living in Pike County, in Missouri, where I was born, and they all died off but me and pa and my brother Ike. Pa, he 'lowed he'd break up and go down and live with Uncle Ben, who's got a little one-horse place on the river, forty-four mile below Orleans. Pa was pretty poor, and had some debts; so when he'd squared up there warn't nothing left but sixteen dollars and our nigger, Jim. That warn't enough to take us fourteen hundred mile, deck passage nor no other way. Well, when the river rose, pa had a streak of luck one day; he ketched this piece of a raft; so we reckoned we'd go down to Orleans on it. Pa's luck didn't hold out; a steamboat run over the forrard corner of the raft, one night, and we all went overboard and dove under the wheel; Jim and me come up, all right, but pa was drunk, and Ike was only four years old, so they never come up no more. Well, for the next day or two we had considerable trouble, because people was always coming out in skiffs and trying to take Jim away from me, saying they believed he was a runaway nigger. We don't run day-times no more, now; nights they don't bother us."

The duke says—

"Leave me alone to cipher out a way so we can run in the day-time if we want to. I'll think the thing over—I'll invent a plan that'll fix it. We'll let it alone for to-day, because of course we don't want to go by that town yonder in daylight—it mightn't be healthy."

Towards night it begun to darken up and look like rain; the heat lightning was squirting around, low down in the sky, and the leaves was beginning to shiver—it was going to be pretty ugly, it was easy to see that. So the duke and the king went to overhauling our wigwam, to see what the beds was like. My bed was a straw tick—better than Jim's, which was a corn-shuck tick; there's always cobs around about in a shuck tick, and they poke into you and hurt; and when you roll over, the dry shucks sound like you was rolling over in a pile of dead leaves; it makes such a rustling that you wake up. Well, the duke allowed he would take my bed; but the king allowed he wouldn't. He says—

"I should a reckoned the difference in rank would a sejested to you that a corn-shuck bed warn't just fitten for me to sleep on. Your Grace'll take the shuck bed yourself."

Jim and me was in a sweat again, for a minute, being afraid there was going to be some more trouble amongst them; so we was pretty glad when the duke says—

" 'Tis my fate to be always ground into the mire under the iron heel of oppression. Misfortune has broken my once haughty spirit; I yield, I submit; 'tis my fate. I am alone in the world—let me suffer; I can bear it."

We got away as soon as it was good and dark. The king told us to stand well out towards the middle of the river, and not show a light till we got a long ways below the town. We come in sight of the little bunch of lights by-and-by—that was the town, you know—and slid by, about a half a mile out, all right. When we was three-quarters of a mile below, we hoisted up our signal lantern; and about ten o'clock it come on to rain and blow and thunder and lighten like everything; so the king told us to both stay on watch till the weather got better; then him and the duke crawled into the wigwam and turned in for the night. It was my watch below, till twelve, but I wouldn't a turned in, anyway, if I'd had a bed; because a body don't see such a storm as that every day in the week, not by a long sight. My souls, how the wind did scream along! And every second or two there'd come a glare that lit up the white-caps for a half a mile around, and you'd see the islands looking dusty through the rain, and the trees thrashing around in the wind; then comes a *h-wack!*—bum! bum! bumble-umble-um-bum-bum-bum-bum—and the thunder would go rumbling and grumbling away, and quit—and then *rip* comes another flash and another sockdolager. The waves most washed me off the raft, sometimes, but I hadn't any clothes on, and didn't mind. We didn't have no trouble about snags; the lightning was glaring and flittering around so constant that we could see them plenty soon enough to throw her head this way or that and miss them.

I had the middle watch, you know, but I was pretty sleepy by that time, so Jim he said he would stand the first half of it for me; he was always mighty good, that way, Jim was. I crawled into the wigwam, but the king and the duke had their legs sprawled around so there warn't no show for me; so I laid outside—I didn't mind the rain, because it was warm, and the waves warn't running so high, now. About two they come up again, though, and Jim was going to call me, but he changed his mind because he reckoned they warn't high enough yet to do any harm; but he was mistaken about that, for pretty soon all of a sudden along comes a regular ripper, and washed me overboard. It most killed Jim a-laughing. He was the easiest nigger to laugh that ever was, anyway.

I took the watch, and Jim he laid down and snored away; and by-and-by the storm let up for good and all; and the first cabin-light that showed, I rousted him out and we slid the raft into hiding-quarters for the day.

The king got out an old ratty deck of cards, after breakfast, and him and the duke played seven-up a while, five cents a game. Then they got tired of it, and allowed they would "lay out a campaign," as they called it. The duke went down into his carpet-bag and fetched up a lot of little printed bills, and read them out loud. One bill said "The celebrated Dr. Armand de Montalban of Paris," would "lecture on the Science of Phrenology" at such and such a place, on the blank day of blank, at ten cents admission, and "furnish charts of character at twenty-five cents apiece." The duke said that was *him*. In another bill he was the "world renowned Shaksperean trage-dian, Garrick the Younger, of Drury Lane, London." In other bills he had a lot of other names and done other wonderful things, like finding water and gold with a "divining rod," "dissipating witch-spells," and so on. By-and-by he says—

"But the histrionic muse is the darling. Have you ever trod the boards, Royalty?"

"No," says the king.

"You shall, then, before you're three days older, Fallen Grandeur," says the duke. "The first good town we come to, we'll hire a hall and do the sword-fight in Richard III. and the balcony scene in Romeo and Juliet. How does that strike you?"

"I'm in, up to the hub, for anything that will pay, Bilgewater, but you see I don't know nothing about play-actn', and hain't ever seen much of it. I was too small when pap used to have 'em at the palace. Do you reckon you can learn me?"

"Easy!"

"All right. I'm jist a-freezn' for something fresh, anyway. Less commence, right away."

So the duke he told him all about who Romeo was, and who Juliet was, and said he was used to being Romeo, so the king could be Juliet.

"But if Juliet's such a young gal, Duke, my peeled head and my white whiskers is goin' to look oncommon odd on her, maybe."

"No, don't you worry—these country jakes won't ever think of that. Besides, you know, you'll be in costume, and that makes all the difference in the world; Juliet's in a balcony, enjoying the moonlight before she goes to bed, and she's got on her night-gown and her ruffled night-cap. Here are the costumes for the parts."

He got out two or three curtain-calico suits, which he said was meedyevil armor for Richard III. and t'other chap, and a long white cotton night-shirt and a ruffled night-cap to match. The king was satisfied; so the duke got out his book and read the parts over in the most splendid spread-eagle way, prancing around and acting at the same time, to show how it had got to be done; then he give the book to the king and told him to get his part by heart.

There was a little one-horse town about three mile down the bend, and after dinner the duke said he had ciphered out his idea about how to run in daylight without it being dangersome for Jim; so he allowed he would go down to the town and fix that thing. The king allowed he would go too, and see if he couldn't strike something. We was out of coffee, so Jim said I better go along with them in the canoe and get some.

When we got there, there warn't nobody stirring; streets empty, and perfectly dead and still, like Sunday. We found a sick nigger sunning himself in a back yard, and he said everybody that warn't too young or too sick or too old, was gone to camp-meeting, about two mile back in the woods. The king got the directions, and allowed he'd go and work that camp-meeting for all it was worth, and I might go, too.

The duke said what he was after was a printing office. We found it; a little bit of a concern, up over a carpenter shop—carpenters and printers all gone to the meeting, and no doors locked. It was a dirty, littered-up place, and had ink marks, and handbills with pictures of horses and runaway niggers on them, all over the walls. The duke shed his coat and said he was all right, now. So me and the king lit out for the camp-meeting.

We got there in about a half an hour, fairly dripping, for it was a most awful hot day. There was as much as a thousand people there, from twenty mile around. The woods was full of teams and wagons, hitched everywheres, feeding out of the wagon troughs and stomping to keep off the flies. There was sheds made out of poles and roofed over with branches, where they had lemonade and gingerbread to sell, and piles of watermelons and green corn and such-like truck.

The preaching was going on under the same kinds of sheds, only they was bigger and held crowds of people. The benches was made out of outside slabs of logs, with holes bored in the round side to drive sticks into for legs. They didn't have no backs. The preachers had high platforms to stand on, at one end of the sheds. The women had on sun-bonnets; and some had linsey-woolsey frocks, some gingham ones, and a few of the young ones had on calico. Some of the young men was barefooted, and some of the children didn't have on any clothes but just a tow-linen shirt. Some of the old women was knitting, and some of the young folks was courting on the sly.

The first shed we come to, the preacher was lining out a hymn. He lined out two lines, everybody sung it, and it was kind of grand to hear it, there was so many of them and they done it in such a rousing way; then he lined out two more for them to sing—and so on. The people woke up more and more, and sung louder and louder; and towards the end, some begun to groan, and some begun to shout. Then the preacher begun to preach; and begun in earnest, too; and went weaving first to one side of the platform and then the other, and then a leaning down over the front of it, with his arms and his body going all the time, and shouting his words out with all his might; and every now and then he would hold up his Bible and spread it open, and kind of pass it around this way and that, shouting, "It's the brazen serpent in the wilderness! Look upon it and live!" And people would shout out, "Glory!—A-a-*men*!" And so he went on, and the people groaning and crying and saying amen:

"Oh, come to the mourners' bench! come, black with sin! (*amen!*) come, sick and sore! (*amen!*) come, lame and halt, and blind! (*amen!*) come, pore and needy, sunk in shame! (*a-a-men!*) come all that's worn, and soiled, and suffering!— come with a broken spirit! come with a contrite heart! come in your rags and sin and dirt! the waters that cleanse is free, the door of heaven stands open—oh, enter in and be at rest!" (*a-a-men! glory, glory hallelujah!*)

And so on. You couldn't make out what the preacher said, any more, on account of the shouting and crying. Folks got up, everywheres in the crowd, and worked their way, just by main strength, to the mourners' bench, with the tears running down their faces; and when all the mourners had got up there to the front benches in a crowd, they sung, and shouted, and flung themselves down on the straw, just crazy and wild.

Well, the first I knowed, the king got agoing; and you could hear him over everybody; and next he went a-charging up on to the platform and the preacher he begged him to speak to the people, and he done it. He told them he was a pirate—been a pirate for thirty years, out in the Indian Ocean, and his crew was thinned out considerable, last spring, in a fight, and he was home now, to take out some fresh men, and thanks to goodness he'd been robbed last night, and put ashore off of a steamboat without a cent, and he was glad of it, it was the blessedest thing that ever hap-

pened to him, because he was a changed man now, and happy
for the first time in his life; and poor as he was, he was going
to start right off and work his way back to the Indian Ocean
and put in the rest of his life trying to turn the pirates into
the true path; for he could do it better than anybody else,
being acquainted with all the pirate crews in that ocean; and
though it would take him a long time to get there, without
money, he would get there anyway, and every time he convinced a pirate he would say to him, "Don't you thank me,
don't you give me no credit, it all belongs to them dear people in Pokeville camp-meeting, natural brothers and benefac-
tors of the race—and that dear preacher there, the truest
friend a pirate ever had!"

And then he busted into tears, and so did everybody. Then
somebody sings out, "Take up a collection for him, take up
a collection!" Well, a half a dozen made a jump to do it, but
somebody sings out, "Let *him* pass the hat around!" Then
everybody said it, the preacher too.

So the king went all through the crowd with his hat, swabbing his eyes, and blessing the people and praising them and
thanking them for being so good to the poor pirates away off
there; and every little while the prettiest kind of girls, with
the tears running down their cheeks, would up and ask him
would he let them kiss him, for to remember him by; and he
always done it; and some of them he hugged and kissed as
many as five or six times—and he was invited to stay a week;
and everybody wanted him to live in their houses, and said
they'd think it was an honor; but he said as this was the last
day of the camp-meeting he couldn't do no good, and besides
he was in a sweat to get to the Indian Ocean right off and go
to work on the pirates.

When we got back to the raft and he come to count up, he
found he had collected eighty-seven dollars and seventy-five
cents. And then he had fetched away a three-gallon jug of
whisky, too, that he found under a wagon when we was starting home through the woods. The king said, take it all
around, it laid over any day he'd ever put in in the missionarying line. He said it warn't no use talking, heathens don't
amount to shucks, alongside of pirates, to work a camp-
meeting with.

The duke was thinking *he'd* been doing pretty well, till the king come to show up, but after that he didn't think so so much. He had set up and printed off two little jobs for farmers, in that printing office—horse bills—and took the money, four dollars. And he had got in ten dollars worth of advertisements for the paper, which he said he would put in for four dollars if they would pay in advance—so they done it. The price of the paper was two dollars a year, but he took in three subscriptions for half a dollar apiece on condition of them paying him in advance; they were going to pay in cordwood and onions, as usual, but he said he had just bought the concern and knocked down the price as low as he could afford it, and was going to run it for cash. He set up a little piece of poetry, which he made, himself, out of his own head—three verses—kind of sweet and saddish—the name of it was, "Yes, crush, cold world, this breaking heart"—and he left that all set up and ready to print in the paper and didn't charge nothing for it. Well, he took in nine dollars and a half, and said he'd done a pretty square day's work for it.

Then he showed us another little job he'd printed and hadn't charged for, because it was for us. It had a picture of a runaway nigger, with a bundle on a stick, over his shoulder, and "$200 reward" under it. The reading was all about Jim, and just described him to a dot. It said he run away from St. Jacques' plantation, forty mile below New Orleans, last winter, and likely went north, and whoever would catch him and send him back, he could have the reward and expenses.

"Now," says the duke, "after to-night we can run in the daytime if we want to. Whenever we see anybody coming, we can tie Jim hand and foot with a rope, and lay him in the wigwam and show this handbill and say we captured him up the river, and were too poor to travel on a steamboat, so we got this little raft on credit from our friends and are going down to get the reward. Handcuffs and chains would look still better on Jim, but it wouldn't go well with the story of us being so poor. Too much like jewelry. Ropes are the correct thing—we must preserve the unities, as we say on the boards."

We all said the duke was pretty smart, and there couldn't

be no trouble about running daytimes. We judged we could make miles enough that night to get out of the reach of the pow-wow we reckoned the duke's work in the printing office was going to make in that little town—then we could boom right along, if we wanted to.

We laid low and kept still, and never shoved out till nearly ten o'clock; then we slid by, pretty wide away from the town, and didn't hoist our lantern till we was clear out of sight of it.

When Jim called me to take the watch at four in the morning, he says—

"Huck, does you reck'n we gwyne to run acrost any mo' kings on dis trip?"

"No," I says, "I reckon not."

"Well," says he, "dat's all right, den. I doan' mine one er two kings, but dat's enough. Dis one's powerful drunk, en de duke ain' much better."

I found Jim had been trying to get him to talk French, so he could hear what it was like; but he said he had been in this country so long, and had so much trouble, he'd forgot it.

XXI

IT WAS AFTER SUN-UP, now, but we went right on, and didn't tie up. The king and the duke turned out, by-and-by, looking pretty rusty; but after they'd jumped overboard and took a swim, it chippered them up a good deal. After breakfast the king he took a seat on a corner of the raft, and pulled off his boots and rolled up his britches, and let his legs dangle in the water, so as to be comfortable, and lit his pipe, and went to getting his Romeo and Juliet by heart. When he had got it pretty good, him and the duke begun to practice it together. The duke had to learn him over and over again, how to say every speech; and he made him sigh, and put his hand on his heart, and after while he said he done it pretty well; "only," he says, "you mustn't bellow out *Romeo!* that way, like a bull—you must say it soft, and sick, and languishy, so—R-o-o-meo! that is the idea; for Juliet's a dear sweet mere child of a girl, you know, and she don't bray like a jackass."

Well, next they got out a couple of long swords that the duke made out of oak laths, and begun to practice the sword-fight—the duke called himself Richard III.; and the way they laid on, and pranced around the raft was grand to see. But by-and-by the king tripped and fell overboard, and after that they took a rest, and had a talk about all kinds of adventures they'd had in other times along the river.

After dinner, the duke says:

"Well, Capet, we'll want to make this a first-class show, you know, so I guess we'll add a little more to it. We want a little something to answer encores with, anyway."

"What's onkores, Bilgewater?"

The duke told him, and then says:

"I'll answer by doing the Highland fling or the sailor's hornpipe; and you—well, let me see—oh, I've got it—you can do Hamlet's soliloquy."

"Hamlet's which?"

"Hamlet's soliloquy, you know; the most celebrated thing in Shakespeare. Ah, it's sublime, sublime! Always fetches the

house. I haven't got it in the book—I've only got one volume—but I reckon I can piece it out from memory. I'll just
walk up and down a minute, and see if I can call it back from
recollection's vaults."

So he went to marching up and down, thinking, and
frowning horrible every now and then; then he would hoist
up his eyebrows; next he would squeeze his hand on his forehead and stagger back and kind of moan; next he would sigh,
and next he'd let on to drop a tear. It was beautiful to see
him. By-and-by he got it. He told us to give attention. Then
he strikes a most noble attitude, with one leg shoved forwards, and his arms stretched away up, and his head tilted
back, looking up at the sky; and then he begins to rip and
rave and grit his teeth; and after that, all through his speech
he howled, and spread around, and swelled up his chest, and
just knocked the spots out of any acting ever *I* see before.
This is the speech—I learned it, easy enough, while he was
learning it to the king:

To be, or not to be; that is the bare bodkin
That makes calamity of so long life;
For who would fardels bear, till Birnam Wood do come to
    Dunsinane,
But that the fear of something after death
Murders the innocent sleep,
Great nature's second course,
And makes us rather sling the arrows of outrageous fortune
Than fly to others that we know not of.
There's the respect must give us pause:
Wake Duncan with thy knocking! I would thou couldst;
For who would bear the whips and scorns of time,
The oppressor's wrong, the proud man's contumely,
The law's delay, and the quietus which his pangs might take,
In the dead waste and middle of the night, when
    churchyards yawn
In customary suits of solemn black,
But that the undiscovered country from whose bourne no
    traveler returns,
Breathes forth contagion on the world,

And thus the native hue of resolution, like the poor cat i' the
    adage,
Is sicklied o'er with care,
And all the clouds that lowered o'er our housetops,
With this regard their currents turn awry,
And lose the name of action.
'Tis a consummation devoutly to be wished. But soft you,
    the fair Ophelia:
Ope not thy ponderous and marble jaws,
But get thee to a nunnery—go!

Well, the old man he liked that speech, and he mighty soon
got it so he could do it first rate. It seemed like he was just
born for it; and when he had his hand in and was excited, it
was perfectly lovely the way he would rip and tear and rair
up behind when he was getting it off.

The first chance we got, the duke he had some show bills
printed; and after that, for two or three days as we floated
along, the raft was a most uncommon lively place, for there
warn't nothing but sword-fighting and rehearsing—as the
duke called it—going on all the time. One morning, when
we was pretty well down the State of Arkansaw, we come in
sight of a little one-horse town in a big bend; so we tied up
about three-quarters of a mile above it, in the mouth of a
crick which was shut in like a tunnel by the cypress trees, and
all of us but Jim took the canoe and went down there to see
if there was any chance in that place for our show.

We struck it mighty lucky; there was going to be a circus
there that afternoon, and the country people was already beginning to come in, in all kinds of old shackly wagons, and
on horses. The circus would leave before night, so our show
would have a pretty good chance. The duke he hired the
court house, and we went around and stuck up our bills.
They read like this:

Shaksperean Revival ! ! !
Wonderful Attraction !
For One Night Only !
The world renowned tragedians,
David Garrick the younger, of Drury Lane Theatre, London,

and
Edmund Kean the elder, of the Royal Haymarket Theatre,
Whitechapel, Pudding Lane, Piccadilly, London, and
the Royal Continental Theatres, in their sublime
Shaksperean Spectacle entitled
The Balcony Scene
in
Romeo and Juliet ! ! !

Romeo. . . . . Mr. Garrick.
Juliet. . . . . Mr. Kean.
Assisted by the whole strength of the company !
New costumes, new scenery, new appointments !
Also:
The thrilling, masterly, and blood-curdling
Broad-sword conflict
In Richard III. ! ! !

Richard III. . . . . Mr. Garrick.
Richmond. . . . . Mr. Kean.
also:
(by special request,)
Hamlet's Immortal Soliloquy ! !
By the Illustrious Kean !
Done by him 300 consecutive nights in Paris!
For One Night Only,
On account of imperative European engagements!
Admission 25 cents; children and servants, 10 cents.

Then we went loafing around the town. The stores and
houses was most all old shackly dried-up frame concerns that
hadn't ever been painted; they was set up three or four foot
above ground on stilts, so as to be out of reach of the water
when the river was overflowed. The houses had little gardens
around them, but they didn't seem to raise hardly anything in
them but jimpson weeds, and sunflowers, and ash-piles, and
old curled-up boots and shoes, and pieces of bottles, and rags,
and played-out tin-ware. The fences was made of different
kinds of boards, nailed on at different times; and they leaned
every which-way, and had gates that didn't generly have but
one hinge—a leather one. Some of the fences had been
whitewashed, some time or another, but the duke said it was

in Clumbus's time, like enough. There was generly hogs in the garden, and people driving them out.

All the stores was along one street. They had white-domestic awnings in front, and the country people hitched their horses to the awning-posts. There was empty dry-goods boxes under the awnings, and loafers roosting on them all day long, whittling them with their Barlow knives; and chawing tobacco, and gaping and yawning and stretching—a mighty ornery lot. They generly had on yellow straw hats most as wide as an umbrella, but didn't wear no coats nor waistcoats; they called one another Bill, and Buck, and Hank, and Joe, and Andy, and talked lazy and drawly, and used considerable many cuss-words. There was as many as one loafer leaning up against every awning-post, and he most always had his hands in his britches pockets, except when he fetched them out to lend a chaw of tobacco or scratch. What a body was hearing amongst them, all the time was—

"Gimme a chaw 'v tobacker, Hank."

"Cain't—I hain't got but one chaw left. Ask Bill."

Maybe Bill he gives him a chaw; maybe he lies and says he ain't got none. Some of them kinds of loafers never has a cent in the world, nor a chaw of tobacco of their own. They get all their chawing by borrowing—they say to a fellow, "I wisht you'd len' me a chaw, Jack, I jist this minute give Ben Thompson the last chaw I had"—which is a lie, pretty much every time; it don't fool nobody but a stranger; but Jack ain't no stranger, so he says—

"*You* give him a chaw, did you? so did your sister's cat's grandmother. You pay me back the chaws you've awready borry'd off'n me, Lafe Buckner, then I'll loan you one or two ton of it, and won't charge you no back intrust, nuther."

"Well, I *did* pay you back some of it wunst."

"Yes, you did—'bout six chaws. You borry'd store tobacker and paid back nigger-head."

Store tobacco is flat black plug, but these fellows mostly chaws the natural leaf twisted. When they borrow a chaw, they don't generly cut it off with a knife, but they set the plug in between their teeth, and gnaw with their teeth and tug at the plug with their hands till they get it in two—then sometimes the one that owns the tobacco looks mournful at it when it's handed back, and says, sarcastic—

"Here, gimme the *chaw*, and you take the *plug*."

All the streets and lanes was just mud, they warn't nothing else *but* mud—mud as black as tar, and nigh about a foot deep in some places; and two or three inches deep in *all* the places. The hogs loafed and grunted around, everywheres. You'd see a muddy sow and a litter of pigs come lazying along the street and whollop herself right down in the way, where folks had to walk around her, and she'd stretch out, and shut her eyes, and wave her ears, whilst the pigs was milking her, and look as happy as if she was on salary. And pretty soon you'd hear a loafer sing out, "Hi! *so* boy! sick him, Tige!" and away the sow would go, squealing most horrible, with a dog or two swinging to each ear, and three or four dozen more a-coming; and then you would see all the loafers get up and watch the thing out of sight, and laugh at the fun and look grateful for the noise. Then they'd settle back again till there was a dog-fight. There couldn't anything wake them up all over, and make them happy all over, like a dog-fight—unless it might be putting turpentine on a stray dog and setting fire to him, or tying a tin pan to his tail and see him run himself to death.

On the river front some of the houses was sticking out over the bank, and they was bowed and bent, and about ready to tumble in. The people had moved out of them. The bank was caved away under one corner of some others, and that corner was hanging over. People lived in them yet, but it was dangersome, because sometimes a strip of land as wide as a house caves in at a time. Sometimes a belt of land a quarter of a mile deep will start in and cave along and cave along till it all caves into the river in one summer. Such a town as that has to be always moving back, and back, and back, because the river's always gnawing at it.

The nearer it got to noon that day, the thicker and thicker was the wagons and horses in the streets, and more coming all the time. Families fetched their dinners with them, from the country, and eat them in the wagons. There was considerable whiskey drinking going on, and I seen three fights. By-and-by somebody sings out—

"Here comes old Boggs!—in from the country for his little old monthly drunk—here he comes, boys!"

All the loafers looked glad—I reckoned they was used to having fun out of Boggs. One of them says—

"Wonder who he's a gwyne to chaw up this time. If he'd a chawed up all the men he's ben a gwyne to chaw up in the last twenty year, he'd have considerble ruputation, now."

Another one says, "I wisht old Boggs 'd threaten me, 'cuz then I'd know I warn't gwyne to die for a thousan' year."

Boggs comes a-tearing along on his horse, whooping and yelling like an Injun, and singing out—

"Cler the track, thar. I'm on the waw-path, and the price uv coffins is a gwyne to raise."

He was drunk, and weaving about in his saddle; he was over fifty year old, and had a very red face. Everybody yelled at him, and laughed at him, and sassed him, and he sassed back, and said he'd attend to them and lay them out in their regular turns, but he couldn't wait now, because he'd come to town to kill old Colonel Sherburn, and his motto was, "meat first, and spoon vittles to top off on."

He see me, and rode up and says—

"Whar'd you come f'm, boy? You prepared to die?"

Then he rode on. I was scared; but a man says—

"He don't mean nothing; he's always a carryin' on like that, when he's drunk. He's the best-naturedest old fool in Arkansaw—never hurt nobody, drunk nor sober."

Boggs rode up before the biggest store in town and bent his head down so he could see under the curtain of the awning, and yells—

"Come out here, Sherburn! Come out and meet the man you've swindled. You're the houn' I'm after, and I'm a gwyne to have you, too!"

And so he went on, calling Sherburn everything he could lay his tongue to, and the whole street packed with people listening and laughing and going on. By-and-by a proud-looking man about fifty-five—and he was a heap best dressed man in that town, too—steps out of the store, and the crowd drops back on each side to let him come. He says to Boggs, mighty ca'm and slow—he says:

"I'm tired of this; but I'll endure it till one o'clock. Till one o'clock, mind—no longer. If you open your mouth against me only once, after that time, you can't travel so far but I will find you."

Then he turns and goes in. The crowd looked mighty sober; nobody stirred, and there warn't no more laughing. Boggs rode off blackguarding Sherburn as loud as he could yell, all down the street; and pretty soon back he comes and stops before the store, still keeping it up. Some men crowded around him and tried to get him to shut up, but he wouldn't; they told him it would be one o'clock in about fifteen minutes, and so he *must* go home—he must go right away. But it didn't do no good. He cussed away, with all his might, and throwed his hat down in the mud and rode over it, and pretty soon away he went a-raging down the street again, with his gray hair a-flying. Everybody that could get a chance at him tried their best to coax him off of his horse so they could lock him up and get him sober; but it warn't no use—up the street he would tear again, and give Sherburn another cussing. By-and-by somebody says—

"Go for his daughter!—quick, go for his daughter; sometimes he'll listen to her. If anybody can persuade him, she can."

So somebody started on a run. I walked down street a ways, and stopped. In about five or ten minutes, here comes Boggs again—but not on his horse. He was a-reeling across the street towards me, bareheaded, with a friend on both sides of him aholt of his arms and hurrying him along. He was quiet, and looked uneasy; and he warn't hanging back any, but was doing some of the hurrying himself. Somebody sings out—

"Boggs!"

I looked over there to see who said it, and it was that Colonel Sherburn. He was standing perfectly still, in the street, and had a pistol raised in his right hand—not aiming it, but holding it out with the barrel tilted up towards the sky. The same second I see a young girl coming on the run, and two men with her. Boggs and the men turned round, to see who called him, and when they see the pistol the men jumped to one side, and the pistol barrel come down slow and steady to a level—both barrels cocked. Boggs throws up both of his

hands, and says, "O Lord, don't shoot!" Bang! goes the first
shot, and he staggers back clawing at the air—bang! goes the
second one, and he tumbles backwards onto the ground,
heavy and solid, with his arms spread out. That young girl
screamed out, and comes rushing, and down she throws herself on her father, crying, and saying, "Oh, he's killed him,
he's killed him!" The crowd closed up around them, and
shouldered and jammed one another, with their necks
stretched, trying to see, and people on the inside trying to
shove them back, and shouting, "Back, back! give him air,
give him air!"

Colonel Sherburn he tossed his pistol onto the ground, and
turned around on his heels and walked off.

They took Boggs to a little drug store, the crowd pressing
around, just the same, and the whole town following, and I
rushed and got a good place at the window, where I was
close to him and could see in. They laid him on the floor, and
put one large Bible under his head, and opened another one
and spread it on his breast—but they tore open his shirt first,
and I seen where one of the bullets went in. He made about
a dozen long gasps, his breast lifting the Bible up when he
drawed in his breath, and letting it down again when he
breathed it out—and after that he laid still; he was dead.
Then they pulled his daughter away from him, screaming and
crying, and took her off. She was about sixteen, and very
sweet and gentle-looking, but awful pale and scared.

Well, pretty soon the whole town was there, squirming and
scrouging and pushing and shoving to get at the window and
have a look, but people that had the places wouldn't give
them up, and folks behind them was saying all the time, "Say,
now, you've looked enough, you fellows; 'taint right and
'taint fair, for you to stay thar all the time, and never give
nobody a chance; other folks has their rights as well as you."

There was considerable jawing back, so I slid out, thinking
maybe there was going to be trouble. The streets was full,
and everybody was excited. Everybody that seen the shooting
was telling how it happened, and there was a big crowd
packed around each one of these fellows, stretching their
necks and listening. One long lanky man, with long hair and
a big white fur stove-pipe hat on the back of his head, and a

crooked-handled cane, marked out the places on the ground where Boggs stood, and where Sherburn stood, and the people following him around from one place to t'other and watching everything he done, and bobbing their heads to show they understood, and stooping a little and resting their hands on their thighs to watch him mark the places on the ground with his cane; and then he stood up straight and stiff where Sherburn had stood, frowning and having his hat-brim down over his eyes, and sung out, "Boggs!" and then fetched his cane down slow to a level, and says "Bang!" staggered backwards, says "Bang!" again, and fell down flat on his back. The people that had seen the thing said he done it perfect; said it was just exactly the way it all happened. Then as much as a dozen people got out their bottles and treated him.

Well, by-and-by somebody said Sherburn ought to be lynched. In about a minute everybody was saying it; so away they went, mad and yelling, and snatching down every clothes-line they come to, to do the hanging with.

XXII

THEY SWARMED up the street towards Sherburn's house, a-whooping and yelling and raging like Injuns, and everything had to clear the way or get run over and tromped to mush, and it was awful to see. Children was heeling it ahead of the mob, screaming and trying to get out of the way; and every window along the road was full of women's heads, and there was nigger boys in every tree, and bucks and wenches looking over every fence; and as soon as the mob would get nearly to them they would break and skaddle back out of reach. Lots of the women and girls was crying and taking on, scared most to death.

They swarmed up in front of Sherburn's palings as thick as they could jam together, and you couldn't hear yourself think for the noise. It was a little twenty-foot yard. Some sung out "Tear down the fence! tear down the fence!" Then there was a racket of ripping and tearing and smashing, and down she goes, and the front wall of the crowd begins to roll in like a wave.

Just then Sherburn steps out on to the roof of his little front porch, with a double-barrel gun in his hand, and takes his stand, perfectly ca'm and deliberate, not saying a word. The racket stopped, and the wave sucked back.

Sherburn never said a word—just stood there, looking down. The stillness was awful creepy and uncomfortable. Sherburn run his eye slow along the crowd; and wherever it struck, the people tried a little to outgaze him, but they couldn't; they dropped their eyes and looked sneaky. Then pretty soon Sherburn sort of laughed; not the pleasant kind, but the kind that makes you feel like when you are eating bread that's got sand in it.

Then he says, slow and scornful:

"The idea of *you* lynching anybody! It's amusing. The idea of you thinking you had pluck enough to lynch a *man*! Because you're brave enough to tar and feather poor friendless cast-out women that come along here, did that make you think you had grit enough to lay your hands on a *man*? Why, a *man's* safe in the hands of ten thousand of your kind—as long as it's day-time and you're not behind him.

"Do I know you? I know you clear through. I was born and raised in the South, and I've lived in the North; so I know the average all around. The average man's a coward. In the North he lets anybody walk over him that wants to, and goes home and prays for a humble spirit to bear it. In the South one man, all by himself, has stopped a stage full of men, in the day-time, and robbed the lot. Your newspapers call you a brave people so much that you think you *are* braver than any other people—whereas you're just *as* brave, and no braver. Why don't your juries hang murderers? Because they're afraid the man's friends will shoot them in the back, in the dark—and it's just what they *would* do.

"So they always acquit; and then a *man* goes in the night, with a hundred masked cowards at his back, and lynches the rascal. Your mistake is, that you didn't bring a man with you; that's one mistake, and the other is that you didn't come in the dark, and fetch your masks. You brought *part* of a man— Buck Harkness, there—and if you hadn't had him to start you, you'd a taken it out in blowing.

"You didn't want to come. The average man don't like trouble and danger. *You* don't like trouble and danger. But if only *half* a man—like Buck Harkness, there—shouts 'Lynch him, lynch him!' you're afraid to back down—afraid you'll be found out to be what you are—*cowards*—and so you raise a yell, and hang yourselves onto that half-a-man's coat tail, and come raging up here, swearing what big things you're going to do. The pitifulest thing out is a mob; that's what an army is—a mob; they don't fight with courage that's born in them, but with courage that's borrowed from their mass, and from their officers. But a mob without any *man* at the head of it, is *beneath* pitifulness. Now the thing for *you* to do, is to droop your tails and go home and crawl in a hole. If any real lynching's going to be done, it will be done in the dark, Southern fashion; and when they come they'll bring their masks, and fetch a *man* along. Now *leave*—and take your half-a-man with you"—tossing his gun up across his left arm and cocking it, when he says this.

The crowd washed back sudden, and then broke all apart

and went tearing off every which way, and Buck Harkness he heeled it after them, looking tolerable cheap. I could a staid, if I'd a wanted to, but I didn't want to.

I went to the circus, and loafed around the back side till the watchman went by, and then dived in under the tent. I had my twenty-dollar gold piece and some other money, but I reckoned I better save it, because there ain't no telling how soon you are going to need it, away from home and amongst strangers, that way. You can't be too careful. I ain't opposed to spending money on circuses, when there ain't no other way, but there ain't no use in *wasting* it on them.

It was a real bully circus. It was the splendidest sight that ever was, when they all come riding in, two and two, a gentleman and lady, side by side, the men just in their drawers and under-shirts, and no shoes nor stirrups, and resting their hands on their thighs, easy and comfortable—there must a' been twenty of them—and every lady with a lovely complexion, and perfectly beautiful, and looking just like a gang of real sure-enough queens, and dressed in clothes that cost millions of dollars, and just littered with diamonds. It was a powerful fine sight; I never see anything so lovely. And then one by one they got up and stood, and went a-weaving around the ring so gentle and wavy and graceful, the men looking ever so tall and airy and straight, with their heads bobbing and skimming along, away up there under the tent-roof, and every lady's rose-leafy dress flapping soft and silky around her hips, and she looking like the most loveliest parasol.

And then faster and faster they went, all of them dancing, first one foot stuck out in the air and then the other, the horses leaning more and more, and the ring-master going round and round the centre-pole, cracking his whip and shouting "hi!—hi!" and the clown cracking jokes behind him; and by-and-by all hands dropped the reins, and every lady put her knuckles on her hips and every gentleman folded his arms, and then how the horses did lean over and hump themselves! And so, one after the other they all skipped off into the ring, and made the sweetest bow I ever see, and then scampered out, and everybody clapped their hands and went just about wild.

Well, all through the circus they done the most astonishing things; and all the time that clown carried on so it most killed the people. The ring-master couldn't ever say a word to him but he was back at him quick as a wink with the funniest things a body ever said; and how he ever *could* think of so many of them, and so sudden and so pat, was what I couldn't noway understand. Why, I couldn't a thought of them in a year. And by-and-by a drunk man tried to get into the ring— said he wanted to ride; said he could ride as well as anybody that ever was. They argued and tried to keep him out, but he wouldn't listen, and the whole show come to a standstill. Then the people begun to holler at him and make fun of him, and that made him mad, and he begun to rip and tear; so that stirred up the people, and a lot of men begun to pile down off of the benches and swarm towards the ring, saying, "Knock him down! throw him out!" and one or two women begun to scream. So, then, the ring-master he made a little speech, and said he hoped there wouldn't be no disturbance, and if the man would promise he wouldn't make no more trouble, he would let him ride, if he thought he could stay on the horse. So everybody laughed and said all right, and the man got on. The minute he was on, the horse begun to rip and tear and jump and cavort around, with two circus men hanging onto his bridle trying to hold him, and the drunk man hanging onto his neck, and his heels flying in the air every jump, and the whole crowd of people standing up shouting and laughing till the tears rolled down. And at last, sure enough, all the circus men could do, the horse broke loose, and away he went like the very nation, round and round the ring, with that sot laying down on him and hanging to his neck, with first one leg hanging most to the ground on one side, and then t'other one on t'other side, and the people just crazy. It warn't funny to me, though; I was all of a tremble to see his danger. But pretty soon he struggled up astraddle and grabbed the bridle, a-reeling this way and that; and the next minute he sprung up and dropped the bridle and stood! and the horse agoing like a house afire too. He just stood up there, a-sailing around as easy and comfortable as if he warn't ever drunk in his life—and then he begun to pull off his clothes and sling them. He shed them so thick they kind of clogged up the air, and altogether he shed seventeen suits. And then, there he was, slim and handsome, and dressed the gaudiest and prettiest you ever saw, and he lit into that horse with his whip and made him fairly hum—and finally skipped off, and made his bow and danced off to the dressing-room, and everybody just a-howling with pleasure and astonishment.

Then the ring-master he see how he had been fooled, and he *was* the sickest ring-master you ever see, I reckon. Why, it was one of his own men! He had got up that joke all out of his own head, and never let on to nobody. Well, I felt sheepish enough, to be took in so, but I wouldn't a been in that ring-master's place, not for a thousand dollars. I don't know; there may be bullier circuses than what that one was, but I never struck them yet. Anyways it was plenty good enough for *me*; and wherever I run across it, it can have all of *my* custom, every time.

Well, that night we had *our* show; but there warn't only about twelve people there; just enough to pay expenses. And they laughed all the time, and that made the duke mad; and everybody left, anyway, before the show was over, but one boy which was asleep. So the duke said these Arkansaw lunkheads couldn't come up to Shakspeare; what they wanted was low comedy—and may be something ruther worse than low comedy, he reckoned. He said he could size their style. So next morning he got some big sheets of wrapping-paper and some black paint, and drawed off some handbills and stuck them up all over the village. The bills said:

AT THE COURT HOUSE!
FOR 3 NIGHTS ONLY!
The World-Renowned Tragedians
DAVID GARRICK THE YOUNGER!
AND
EDMUND KEAN THE ELDER!
Of the London and Continental Theatres,
In their Thrilling Tragedy of
THE KING'S CAMELOPARD
OR
THE ROYAL NONESUCH! ! !
Admission 50 cents.

Then at the bottom was the biggest line of all—which said:

LADIES AND CHILDREN NOT ADMITTED.

"There," says he, "if that line don't fetch them, I dont know Arkansaw!"

XXIII

WELL, all day him and the king was hard at it, rigging up a stage, and a curtain, and a row of candles for footlights; and that night the house was jam full of men in no time. When the place couldn't hold no more, the duke he quit tending door and went around the back way and come onto the stage and stood up before the curtain, and made a little speech, and praised up this tragedy, and said it was the most thrillingest one that ever was; and so he went on a-bragging about the tragedy and about Edmund Kean the Elder, which was to play the main principal part in it; and at last when he'd got everybody's expectations up high enough, he rolled up the curtain, and the next minute the king come a-prancing out on all fours, naked; and he was painted all over, ring-streaked-and-striped, all sorts of colors, as splendid as a rainbow. And—but never mind the rest of his outfit, it was just wild, but it was awful funny. The people most killed themselves laughing; and when the king got done capering, and capered off behind the scenes, they roared and clapped and stormed and haw-hawed till he come back and done it over again; and after that, they made him do it another time. Well, it would a made a cow laugh to see the shines that old idiot cut.

Then the duke he lets the curtain down, and bows to the people, and says the great tragedy will be performed only two nights more, on accounts of pressing London engagements, where the seats is all sold aready for it in Drury Lane; and then he makes them another bow, and says if he has succeeded in pleasing them and instructing them, he will be deeply obleeged if they will mention it to their friends and get them to come and see it.

Twenty people sings out:

"What, is it over? Is that *all?*"

The duke says yes. Then there was a fine time. Everybody sings out "sold," and rose up mad, and was agoing for that stage and them tragedians. But a big fine-looking man jumps up on a bench, and shouts:

"Hold on! Just a word, gentlemen." They stopped to listen. "We are sold—mighty badly sold. But we don't want to be the laughing-stock of this whole town, I reckon, and never hear the last of this thing as long as we live. *No*. What we want, is to go out of here quiet, and talk this show up, and sell the *rest* of the town! Then we'll all be in the same boat. Ain't that sensible?" ("You bet it is!—the jedge is right!" everybody sings out.) "All right, then—not a word about any sell. Go along home, and advise everybody to come and see the tragedy."

Next day you couldn't hear nothing around that town but how splendid that show was. House was jammed again, that night, and we sold this crowd the same way. When me and the king and the duke got home to the raft, we all had a supper; and by-and-by, about midnight, they made Jim and me back her out and float her down the middle of the river and fetch her in and hide her about two mile below town.

The third night the house was crammed again—and they warn't new-comers, this time, but people that was at the show the other two nights. I stood by the duke at the door, and I see that every man that went in had his pockets bulging, or something muffled up under his coat—and I see it warn't no perfumery neither, not by a long sight. I smelt sickly eggs by the barrel, and rotten cabbages, and such things; and if I know the signs of a dead cat being around, and I bet I do, there was sixty-four of them went in. I shoved in there for a minute, but it was too various for me, I couldn't stand it. Well, when the place couldn't hold no more people, the duke he give a fellow a quarter and told him to tend door for him a minute, and then he started around for the stage door, I after him; but the minute we turned the corner and was in the dark, he says:

"Walk fast, now, till you get away from the houses, and then shin for the raft like the dickens was after you!"

I done it, and he done the same. We struck the raft at the same time, and in less than two seconds we was gliding down stream, all dark and still, and edging towards the middle of the river, nobody saying a word. I reckoned the poor king was in for a gaudy time of it with the audience; but nothing of the sort; pretty soon he crawls out from under the wig-wam, and says:

"Well, how'd the old thing pan out this time, Duke?"

He hadn't been up town at all.

We never showed a light till we was about ten mile below that village. Then we lit up and had a supper, and the king and the duke fairly laughed their bones loose over the way they'd served them people. The duke says:

"Greenhorns, flatheads! *I* knew the first house would keep mum and let the rest of the town get roped in; and I knew they'd lay for us the third night, and consider it was *their* turn now. Well, it *is* their turn, and I'd give something to know how much they'd take for it. I *would* just like to know how they're putting in their opportunity. They can turn it into a picnic, if they want to—they brought plenty provisions."

Them rapscallions took in four hundred and sixty-five dollars in that three nights. I never see money hauled in by the wagon-load like that, before.

By-and-by, when they was asleep and snoring, Jim says:

"Don't it 'sprise you, de way dem kings carries on, Huck?"

"No," I says, "it don't."

"Why don't it, Huck?"

"Well, it don't, because it's in the breed. I reckon they're all alike."

"But, Huck, dese kings o' ourn is regular rapscallions; dat's jist what dey is; dey's reglar rapscallions."

"Well, that's what I'm a-saying; all kings is mostly rapscallions, as fur as I can make out."

"Is dat so?"

"You read about them once—you'll see. Look at Henry the Eight; this'n 's a Sunday-School Superintendent to *him*. And look at Charles Second, and Louis Fourteen, and Louis Fifteen, and James Second, and Edward Second, and Richard Third, and forty more; besides all them Saxon heptarchies that used to rip around so in old times and raise Cain. My, you ought to seen old Henry the Eight when he was in bloom. He *was* a blossom. He used to marry a new wife every day, and chop off her head next morning. And he would do it just as indifferent as if he was ordering up eggs. 'Fetch up

Nell Gwynn,' he says. They fetch her up. Next morning,
'Chop off her head!' And they chop it off. 'Fetch up Jane
Shore,' he says; and up she comes. Next morning 'Chop off
her head'—and they chop it off. 'Ring up Fair Rosamun.'
Fair Rosamun answers the bell. Next morning, 'Chop off her
head.' And he made every one of them tell him a tale every
night; and he kept that up till he had hogged a thousand and
one tales that way, and then he put them all in a book, and
called it Domesday Book—which was a good name and
stated the case. You don't know kings, Jim, but I know them;
and this old rip of ourn is one of the cleanest I've struck in
history. Well, Henry he takes a notion he wants to get up
some trouble with this country. How does he go at it—give
notice?—give the country a show? No. All of a sudden he
heaves all the tea in Boston Harbor overboard, and whacks
out a declaration of independence, and dares them to come
on. That was *his* style—he never give anybody a chance. He
had suspicions of his father, the Duke of Wellington. Well,
what did he do?—ask him to show up? No—drownded him
in a butt of mamsey, like a cat. Spose people left money laying around where he was—what did he do? He collared it.
Spose he contracted to do a thing; and you paid him, and
didn't set down there and see that he done it—what did he
do? He always done the other thing. Spose he opened his
mouth—what then? If he didn't shut it up powerful quick,
he'd lose a lie, every time. That's the kind of a bug Henry
was; and if we'd a had him along 'stead of our kings, he'd a
fooled that town a heap worse than ourn done. I don't say
that ourn is lambs, because they ain't, when you come right
down to the cold facts; but they ain't nothing to *that* old
ram, anyway. All I say is, kings is kings, and you got to make
allowances. Take them all around, they're a mighty ornery
lot. It's the way they're raised."

"But dis one do *smell* so like de nation, Huck."

"Well, they all do, Jim. *We* can't help the way a king
smells; history don't tell no way."

"Now de duke, he's a tolerble likely man, in some ways."

"Yes, a duke's different. But not very different. This one's
a middling hard lot, for a duke. When he's drunk, there ain't
no near-sighted man could tell him from a king."

"Well, anyways, I doan' hanker for no mo' un um, Huck. Dese is all I kin stan'."

"It's the way I feel, too, Jim. But we've got them on our hands, and we got to remember what they are, and make allowances. Sometimes I wish we could hear of a country that's out of kings."

What was the use to tell Jim these warn't real kings and dukes? It wouldn't a done no good; and besides, it was just as I said; you couldn't tell them from the real kind.

I went to sleep, and Jim didn't call me when it was my turn. He often done that. When I waked up, just at daybreak, he was setting there with his head down betwixt his knees, moaning and mourning to himself. I didn't take notice, nor let on. I knowed what it was about. He was thinking about his wife and his children, away up yonder, and he was low and homesick; because he hadn't ever been away from home before in his life; and I do believe he cared just as much for his people as white folks does for their'n. It don't seem natural, but I reckon it's so. He was often moaning and mourning that way, nights, when he judged I was asleep, and saying, "Po' little 'Lizabeth! po' little Johnny! its mighty hard; I spec' I ain't ever gwyne to see you no mo', no mo'!" He was a mighty good nigger, Jim was.

But this time I somehow got to talking to him about his wife and young ones; and by-and-by he says:

"What makes me feel so bad dis time, 'uz bekase I hear sumpn over yonder on de bank like a whack, er a slam, while ago, en it mine me er de time I treat my little 'Lizabeth so ornery. She warn't on'y 'bout fo' year ole, en she tuck de sk'yarlet-fever, en had a powful rough spell; but she got well, en one day she was a-stannin' aroun', en I says to her, I says:

"'Shet de do'.'

"She never done it; jis' stood dah, kiner smilin' up at me. It make me mad; en I says agin, mighty loud, I says:

"'Doan' you hear me?—shet de do'!'

"She jis' stood de same way, kiner smilin' up. I was a-bilin'! I says:

"'I lay I _make_ you mine!'

"En wid dat I fetch' her a slap side de head dat sont her a-sprawlin'. Den I went into de yuther room, en 'uz gone 'bout ten minutes; en when I come back, dah was dat do' a-stannin' open *yit*, en dat chile stannin' mos' right in it, a-lookin' down and mournin', en de tears runnin' down. My, but I *wuz* mad, I was agwyne for de chile, but jis' den—it was a do' dat open innerds—jis' den, 'long come de wind en slam it to, behine de chile, ker-*blam!*—en my lan', de chile never move'! My breff mos' hop outer me; en I feel so—so—I doan' know *how* I feel. I crope out, all a-tremblin', en crope aroun' en open de do' easy en slow, en poke my head in behine de chile, sof' en still, en all uv a sudden, I says *pow!* jis' as loud as I could yell. *She never budge!* Oh, Huck, I bust out a-cryin' en grab her up in my arms, en say, 'Oh, de po' little thing! de Lord God Amighty fogive po' ole Jim, kaze he never gwyne to fogive hisself as long's he live!' Oh, she was plumb deef en dumb, Huck, plumb deef en dumb—en I'd ben a-treat'n her so!"

XXIV

NEXT DAY, towards night, we laid up under a little willow tow-head out in the middle, where there was a village on each side of the river, and the duke and the king begun to lay out a plan for working them towns. Jim he spoke to the duke, and said he hoped it wouldn't take but a few hours, because it got mighty heavy and tiresome to him when he had to lay all day in the wigwam tied with the rope. You see, when we left him all alone we had to tie him, because if anybody happened on him all by himself and not tied, it wouldn't look much like he was a runaway nigger, you know. So the duke said it *was* kind of hard to have to lay roped all day, and he'd cipher out some way to get around it.

He was uncommon bright, the duke was, and he soon struck it. He dressed Jim up in King Lear's outfit—it was a long curtain-calico gown, and a white horse-hair wig and whiskers; and then he took his theatre-paint and painted Jim's face and hands and ears and neck all over a dead dull solid blue, like a man that's been drownded nine days. Blamed if he warn't the horriblest looking outrage I ever see. Then the duke took and wrote out a sign on a shingle so—

Sick Arab—but harmless when not out of his head.

And he nailed that shingle to a lath, and stood the lath up four or five foot in front of the wigwam. Jim was satisfied. He said it was a sight better than laying tied a couple of years every day and trembling all over every time there was a sound. The duke told him to make himself free and easy, and if anybody ever come meddling around, he must hop out of the wigwam, and carry on a little, and fetch a howl or two like a wild beast, and he reckoned they would light out and leave him alone. Which was sound enough judgment; but you take the average man, and he wouldn't wait for him to howl. Why, he didn't only look like he was dead, he looked considerable more than that.

These rapscallions wanted to try the Nonesuch again, because there was so much money in it, but they judged it wouldn't be safe, because maybe the news might a worked along down by this time. They couldn't hit no project that suited, exactly; so at last the duke said he reckoned he'd lay off and work his brains an hour or two and see if he couldn't put up something on the Arkansaw village; and the king he allowed he would drop over to t'other village, without any plan, but just trust in Providence to lead him the profitable way—meaning the devil, I reckon. We had all bought store clothes where we stopped last; and now the king put his'n on, and he told me to put mine on. I done it, of course. The king's duds was all black, and he did look real swell and starchy. I never knowed how clothes could change a body before. Why, before, he looked like the orneriest old rip that ever was; but now, when he'd take off his new white beaver and make a bow and do a smile, he looked that grand and good and pious that you'd say he had walked right out of the ark, and maybe was old Leviticus himself. Jim cleaned up the canoe, and I got my paddle ready. There was a big steamboat laying at the shore away up under the point, about three mile above town—been there a couple of hours, taking on freight. Says the king:

"Seein' how I'm dressed, I reckon maybe I better arrive down from St. Louis or Cincinnati, or some other big place. Go for the steamboat, Huckleberry; we'll come down to the village on her."

I didn't have to be ordered twice, to go and take a steamboat ride. I fetched the shore a half a mile above the village, and then went scooting along the bluff bank in the easy water. Pretty soon we come to a nice innocent-looking young country jake setting on a log swabbing the sweat off of his face, for it was powerful warm weather; and he had a couple of big carpet-bags by him.

"Run her nose in shore," says the king. I done it. "Wher' you bound for, young man?"

"For the steamboat; going to Orleans."

"Git aboard," says the king. "Hold on a minute, my servant 'll he'p you with them bags. Jump out and he'p the gentleman, Adolphus"—meaning me, I see.

I done so, and then we all three started on again. The young chap was mighty thankful; said it was tough work toting his baggage such weather. He asked the king where he

was going, and the king told him he'd come down the river
and landed at the other village this morning, and now he was
going up a few mile to see an old friend on a farm up there.
The young fellow says:

"When I first see you, I says to myself, 'It's Mr. Wilks,
sure, and he come mighty near getting here in time.' But then
I says again, 'No, I reckon it ain't him, or else he wouldn't be
paddling up the river.' You *ain't* him, are you?"

"No, my name's Blodgett—Elexander Blodgett—*Reverend*
Elexander Blodgett, I spose I must say, as I'm one o' the
Lord's poor servants. But still I'm jist as able to be sorry for
Mr. Wilks for not arriving in time, all the same, if he's missed
anything by it—which I hope he hasn't."

"Well, he don't miss any property by it, because he'll get
that all right; but he's missed seeing his brother Peter die—
which he mayn't mind, nobody can tell as to that—but his
brother would a give anything in this world to see *him* before
he died; never talked about nothing else all these three weeks;
hadn't seen him since they was boys together—and hadn't
ever seen his brother William at all—that's the deef and
dumb one—William ain't more than thirty or thirty-five. Peter and George was the only ones that come out here; George
was the married brother; him and his wife both died last year.
Harvey and William's the only ones that's left now; and, as
I was saying, they haven't got here in time."

"Did anybody send 'em word?"

"Oh, yes; a month or two ago, when Peter was first took;
because Peter said then that he sorter felt like he warn't going
to get well this time. You see, he was pretty old, and George's
g'yirls was too young to be much company for him, except
Mary Jane the red-headed one; and so he was kinder lonesome after George and his wife died, and didn't seem to care
much to live. He most desperately wanted to see Harvey—
and William too, for that matter—because he was one of
them kind that can't bear to make a will. He left a letter behind for Harvey, and said he'd told in it where his money was
hid, and how he wanted the rest of the property divided up
so George's g'yirls would be all right—for George didn't
leave nothing. And that letter was all they could get him to
put a pen to."

"Why do you reckon Harvey don't come? Wher' does he live?"

"Oh, he lives in England—Sheffield—preaches there—hasn't ever been in this country. He hasn't had any too much time—and besides he mightn't a got the letter at all, you know."

"Too bad, too bad he couldn't a lived to see his brothers, poor soul. You going to Orleans, you say?"

"Yes, but that ain't only a part of it. I'm going in a ship, next Wednesday, for Ryo Janeero, where my uncle lives."

"It's a pretty long journey. But it'll be lovely; I wisht I was agoing. Is Mary Jane the oldest? How old is the others?"

"Mary Jane's nineteen, Susan's fifteen, and Joanna's about fourteen—that's the one that gives herself to good works and has a hare-lip."

"Poor things! to be left alone in the cold world so."

"Well, they could be worse off. Old Peter had friends, and they ain't going to let them come to no harm. There's Hobson, the Babtis' preacher; and Deacon Lot Hovey, and Ben Rucker, and Abner Shackleford, and Levi Bell, the lawyer; and Dr. Robinson, and their wives, and the widow Bartley, and—well, there's a lot of them; but these are the ones that Peter was thickest with, and used to write about sometimes, when he wrote home; so Harvey 'll know where to look for friends when he gets here."

Well, the old man he went on asking questions till he just fairly emptied that young fellow. Blamed if he didn't inquire about everybody and everything in that blessed town, and all about all the Wilkses; and about Peter's business—which was a tanner; and about George's—which was a carpenter; and about Harvey's—which was a dissentering minister; and so on, and so on. Then he says:

"What did you want to walk all the way up to the steamboat for?"

"Because she's a big Orleans boat, and I was afeard she mightn't stop there. When they're deep they won't stop for a hail. A Cincinnati boat will, but this is a St. Louis one."

"Was Peter Wilks well off?"

"Oh, yes, pretty well off. He had houses and land, and it's reckoned he left three or four thousand in cash hid up som'ers."

"When did you say he died?"

"I didn't say, but it was last night."

"Funeral to-morrow, likely?"

"Yes, 'bout the middle of the day."

"Well, it's all terrible sad; but we've all got to go, one time or another. So what we want to do is to be prepared; then we're all right."

"Yes, sir, it's the best way. Ma used to always say that."

When we struck the boat, she was about done loading, and pretty soon she got off. The king never said nothing about going aboard, so I lost my ride, after all. When the boat was gone, the king made me paddle up another mile to a lonesome place, and then he got ashore, and says:

"Now hustle back, right off, and fetch the duke up here, and the new carpet-bags. And if he's gone over to t'other side, go over there and git him. And tell him to git himself up regardless. Shove along, now."

I see what *he* was up to; but I never said nothing, of course. When I got back with the duke, we hid the canoe and then they set down on a log, and the king told him everything, just like the young fellow had said it—every last word of it. And all the time he was a doing it, he tried to talk like an Englishman; and he done it pretty well too, for a slouch. I can't imitate him, and so I ain't agoing to try to; but he really done it pretty good. Then he says:

"How are you on the deef and dumb, Bilgewater?"

The duke said, leave him alone for that; said he had played a deef and dumb person on the histrionic boards. So then they waited for a steamboat.

About the middle of the afternoon a couple of little boats come along, but they didn't come from high enough up the river; but at last there was a big one, and they hailed her. She sent out her yawl, and we went aboard, and she was from Cincinnati; and when they found we only wanted to go four or five mile, they was booming mad, and give us a cussing, and said they wouldn't land us. But the king was ca'm. He says:

"If gentlemen kin afford to pay a dollar a mile apiece, to be took on and put off in a yawl, a steamboat kin afford to carry 'em, can't it?"

So they softened down and said it was all right; and when we got to the village, they yawled us ashore. About two dozen men flocked down, when they see the yawl a coming; and when the king says—

"Kin any of you gentlemen tell me wher' Mr. Peter Wilks lives?" they give a glance at one another, and nodded their heads, as much as to say, "What d' I tell you?" Then one of them says, kind of soft and gentle:

"I'm sorry, sir, but the best we can do is to tell you where he *did* live yesterday evening."

Sudden as winking, the ornery old cretur went all to smash, and fell up against the man, and put his chin on his shoulder, and cried down his back, and says:

"Alas, alas, our poor brother—gone, and we never got to see him; oh, it's too, *too* hard!"

Then he turns around, blubbering, and makes a lot of idiotic signs to the duke on his hands, and blamed if *he* didn't drop a carpet-bag and bust out a-crying. If they warn't the beatenest lot, them two frauds, that ever I struck.

Well, the men gethered around, and sympathized with them, and said all sorts of kind things to them, and carried their carpet-bags up the hill for them, and let them lean on them and cry, and told the king all about his brother's last moments, and the king he told it all over again on his hands to the duke, and both of them took on about that dead tanner like they'd lost the twelve disciples. Well, if ever I struck anything like it, I'm a nigger. It was enough to make a body ashamed of the human race.

XXV

THE NEWS was all over town in two minutes, and you could see the people tearing down on the run, from every which way, some of them putting on their coats as they come. Pretty soon we was in the middle of a crowd, and the noise of the tramping was like a soldier-march. The windows and dooryards was full; and every minute somebody would say, over a fence:

"Is it *them?*"

And somebody trotting along with the gang would answer back and say,

"You bet it is."

When we got to the house, the street in front of it was packed, and the three girls was standing in the door. Mary Jane *was* red-headed, but that don't make no difference, she was most awful beautiful, and her face and her eyes was all lit up like glory, she was so glad her uncles was come. The king he spread his arms, and Mary Jane she jumped for them, and the hare-lip jumped for the duke, and there they *had* it! Everybody most, leastways women, cried for joy to see them meet again at last and have such good times.

Then the king he hunched the duke, private—I see him do it—and then he looked around and see the coffin, over in the corner on two chairs; so then, him and the duke, with a hand across each other's shoulder, and t'other hand to their eyes, walked slow and solemn over there, everybody dropping back to give them room, and all the talk and noise stopping, people saying "Sh!" and all the men taking their hats off and drooping their heads, so you could a heard a pin fall. And when they got there, they bent over and looked in the coffin, and took one sight, and then they bust out a crying so you could a heard them to Orleans, most; and then they put their arms around each other's necks, and hung their chins over each other's shoulders; and then for three minutes, or maybe four, I never see two men leak the way they done. And mind you, everybody was doing the same; and the place was that damp I never see anything like it. Then one of them got on

one side of the coffin, and t'other on t'other side, and they
kneeled down and rested their foreheads on the coffin, and let
on to pray all to theirselves. Well, when it come to that, it
worked the crowd like you never see anything like it, and so
everybody broke down and went to sobbing right out loud—
the poor girls, too; and every woman, nearly, went up to the
girls, without saying a word, and kissed them, solemn, on the
forehead, and then put their hand on their head, and looked
up towards the sky, with the tears running down, and then
busted out and went off sobbing and swabbing, and give the
next woman a show. I never see anything so disgusting.

Well, by-and-by the king he gets up and comes forward a
little, and works himself up and slobbers out a speech, all full
of tears and flapdoodle about its being a sore trial for him
and his poor brother to lose the diseased, and to miss seeing
diseased alive, after the long journey of four thousand mile,
but its a trial that's sweetened and sanctified to us by this dear
sympathy and these holy tears, and so he thanks them out of
his heart and out of his brother's heart, because out of their
mouths they can't, words being too weak and cold, and all
that kind of rot and slush, till it was just sickening; and then
he blubbers out a pious goody-goody Amen, and turns himself loose and goes to crying fit to bust.

And the minute the words was out of his mouth somebody
over in the crowd struck up the doxolojer, and everybody
joined in with all their might, and it just warmed you up and
made you feel as good as church letting out. Music *is* a good
thing; and after all that soul-butter and hogwash, I never see
it freshen up things so, and sound so honest and bully.

Then the king begins to work his jaw again, and says how
him and his nieces would be glad if a few of the main principal friends of the family would take supper here with them
this evening, and help set up with the ashes of the diseased;
and says if his poor brother laying yonder could speak, he
knows who he would name, for they was names that was very
dear to him, and mentioned often in his letters; and so he will
name the same, to-wit, as follows, vizz:—Rev. Mr. Hobson,
and Deacon Lot Hovey, and Mr. Ben Rucker, and Abner
Shackleford, and Levi Bell, and Dr. Robinson, and their
wives, and the widow Bartley.

Rev. Hobson and Dr. Robinson was down to the end of the town, a-hunting together; that is, I mean the doctor was shipping a sick man to t'other world, and the preacher was pinting him right. Lawyer Bell was away up to Louisville on some business. But the rest was on hand, and so they all come and shook hands with the king and thanked him and talked to him; and then they shook hands with the duke, and didn't say nothing but just kept a-smiling and bobbing their heads like a passel of sapheads whilst he made all sorts of signs with his hands and said "Goo-goo—goo-goo-goo," all the time, like a baby that can't talk.

So the king he blatted along, and managed to inquire about pretty much everybody and dog in town, by his name, and mentioned all sorts of little things that happened one time or another in the town, or to George's family, or to Peter; and he always let on that Peter wrote him the things, but that was a lie, he got every blessed one of them out of that young flathead that we canoed up to the steamboat.

Then Mary Jane she fetched the letter her father left behind, and the king he read it out loud and cried over it. It give the dwelling-house and three thousand dollars, gold, to the girls; and it give the tanyard (which was doing a good business), along with some other houses and land (worth about seven thousand), and three thousand dollars in gold to Harvey and William, and told where the six thousand cash was hid, down cellar. So these two frauds said they'd go and fetch it up, and have everything square and above-board; and told me to come with a candle. We shut the cellar door behind us, and when they found the bag they spilt it out on the floor, and it was a lovely sight, all them yaller-boys. My, the way the king's eyes did shine! He slaps the duke on the shoulder, and says:

"Oh, *this* ain't bully, nor noth'n! Oh, no, I reckon not! Why, Biljy, it beats the Nonesuch, *don't* it!"

The duke allowed it did. They pawed the yaller-boys, and sifted them through their fingers and let them jingle down on the floor; and the king says:

"It ain't no use talkin'; bein' brothers to a rich dead man, and representatives of furrin heirs that's got left, is the line for you and me, Bilge. Thish-yer comes of trust'n to Providence. It's the best way, in the long run. I've tried 'em all, and ther' ain't no better way."

Most everybody would a been satisfied with the pile, and took it on trust; but no, they must count it. So they counts it, and it comes out four hundred and fifteen dollars short. Says the king:

"Dern him, I wonder what he done with that four hunderd and fifteen dollars?"

They worried over that a while, and ransacked all around for it. Then the duke says:

"Well, he was a pretty sick man, and likely he made a mistake—I reckon that's the way of it. The best way's to let it go, and keep still about it. We can spare it."

"Oh, shucks, yes, we can *spare* it. I don't k'yer noth'n 'bout that—it's the *count* I'm thinkin' about. We want to be awful square and open and above-board, here, you know. We want to lug this h-yer money up stairs and count it before everybody—then ther' ain't noth'n suspicious. But when the dead man says ther's six thous'n dollars, you know, we don't want to——"

"Hold on," says the duke. "Less make up the deffisit"—and he begun to haul out yaller-boys out of his pocket.

"It's a most amaz'n' good idea, duke—you *have* got a rattlin' clever head on you," says the king. "Blest if the old Nonesuch ain't a heppin' us out agin"—and *he* begun to haul out yaller-jackets and stack them up.

It most busted them, but they made up the six thousand clean and clear.

"Say," says the duke. "I got another idea. Le's go up stairs and count this money, and then take and *give it to the girls.*"

"Good land, duke, lemme hug you! It's the most dazzling idea 'at ever a man struck. You have cert'nly got the most astonishin' head I ever see. Oh, this is the boss dodge, ther' ain't no mistake 'bout it. Let 'em fetch along their suspicions now, if they want to—this'll lay 'em out."

When we got up stairs, everybody gethered around the table, and the king he counted it and stacked it up, three hundred dollars in a pile—twenty elegant little piles. Everybody looked hungry at it, and licked their chops. Then they raked it into the bag again, and I see the king begin to swell himself up for another speech. He says:

"Friends all, my poor brother that lays yonder, has done generous by them that's left behind in the vale of sorrers. He has done generous by these-yer poor little lambs that he loved and sheltered, and that's left fatherless and motherless. Yes, and we that knowed him, knows that he would a done *more* generous by 'em if he hadn't ben afeard o' woundin' his dear William and me. Now, *wouldn't* he? Ther' ain't no question 'bout it, in *my* mind. Well, then—what kind o' brothers would it be, that 'd stand in his way at sech a time? And what kind o' uncles would it be that 'd rob—yes, *rob*—sech poor sweet lambs as these 'at he loved so, at sech a time? If I know William—and I *think* I do—he—well, I'll jest ask him." He turns around and begins to make a lot of signs to the duke with his hands; and the duke he looks at him stupid and leather-headed a while, then all of a sudden he seems to catch his meaning, and jumps for the king, goo-gooing with all his might for joy, and hugs him about fifteen times before he lets up. Then the king says, "I knowed it; I reckon *that* 'll convince anybody the way *he* feels about it. Here, Mary Jane, Susan, Joanner, take the money—take it *all*. It's the gift of him that lays yonder, cold but joyful."

Mary Jane she went for him, Susan and the hare-lip went for the duke, and then such another hugging and kissing I never see yet. And everybody crowded up with the tears in their eyes, and most shook the hands off of them frauds, saying all the time:

"You *dear* good souls!—how *lovely*!—how *could* you!"

Well, then, pretty soon all hands got to talking about the diseased again, and how good he was, and what a loss he was, and all that; and before long a big iron-jawed man worked himself in there from outside, and stood a listening and looking, and not saying anything; and nobody saying anything to him either, because the king was talking and they was all busy listening. The king was saying—in the middle of something he'd started in on—

"—they bein' partickler friends o' the diseased. That's why they're invited here this evenin'; but to-morrow we want *all* to come—everybody; for he respected everybody, he liked everybody, and so it's fitten that his funeral orgies sh'd be public."

And so he went a-mooning on and on, liking to hear himself talk, and every little while he fetched in his funeral orgies again, till the duke he couldn't stand it no more; so he writes on a little scrap of paper, "*obsequies*, you old fool," and folds it up and goes to goo-gooing and reaching it over people's heads to him. The king he reads it, and puts it in his pocket, and says:

"Poor William, afflicted as he is, his *heart's* aluz right. Asks me to invite everybody to come to the funeral—wants me to make 'em all welcome. But he needn't a worried—it was jest what I was at."

Then he weaves along again, perfectly ca'm, and goes to dropping in his funeral orgies again every now and then, just like he done before. And when he done it the third time, he says:

"I say orgies, not because it's the common term, because it ain't—obsequies bein' the common term—but because orgies is the right term. Obsequies ain't used in England no more, now—it's gone out. We say orgies now, in England. Orgies is better, because it means the thing you're after, more exact. It's a word that's made up out'n the Greek *orgo*, outside, open, abroad; and the Hebrew *jeesum*, to plant, cover up; hence in*ter*. So, you see, funeral orgies is an open er public funeral."

He was the *worst* I ever struck. Well, the iron-jawed man he laughed right in his face. Everybody was shocked. Everybody says, "Why *doctor*!" and Abner Shackleford says:

"Why, Robinson, hain't you heard the news? This is Harvey Wilks."

The king he smiled eager, and shoved out his flapper, and says:

"*Is* it my poor brother's dear good friend and physician? I——"

"Keep your hands off of me!" says the doctor. "*You* talk like an Englishman—*don't* you? It's the worse imitation I ever heard. *You* Peter Wilks's brother. You're a fraud, that's what you are!"

Well, how they all took on! They crowded around the doctor, and tried to quiet him down, and tried to explain to him,
and tell him how Harvey'd showed in forty ways that he *was*
Harvey, and knowed everybody by name, and the names of
the very dogs, and begged and *begged* him not to hurt
Harvey's feelings and the poor girls' feelings, and all that; but
it warn't no use, he stormed right along, and said any man
that pretended to be an Englishman and couldn't imitate the
lingo no better than what he did, was a fraud and a liar. The
poor girls was hanging to the king and crying; and all of a
sudden the doctor ups and turns on *them*. He says:

"I was your father's friend, and I'm your friend; and I warn
you *as* a friend, and an honest one, that wants to protect you
and keep you out of harm and trouble, to turn your backs on
that scoundrel, and have nothing to do with him, the ignorant tramp, with his idiotic Greek and Hebrew as he calls it.
He is the thinnest kind of an impostor—has come here with
a lot of empty names and facts which he has picked up somewheres, and you take them for *proofs*, and are helped to fool
yourselves by these foolish friends here, who ought to know
better. Mary Jane Wilks, you know me for your friend, and
for your unselfish friend, too. Now listen to me; turn this
pitiful rascal out—I *beg* you to do it. Will you?"

Mary Jane straightened herself up, and my, but she was
handsome! She says:

"*Here* is my answer." She hove up the bag of money and
put it in the king's hands, and says, "Take this six thousand
dollars, and invest it for me and my sisters any way you want
to, and don't give us no receipt for it."

Then she put her arm around the king on one side, and
Susan and the hare-lip done the same on the other. Everybody clapped their hands and stomped on the floor like a
perfect storm, whilst the king held up his head and smiled
proud. The doctor says:

"All right. I wash *my* hands of the matter. But I warn you
all that a time's coming when you're going to feel sick whenever you think of this day"—and away he went.

"All right, doctor," says the king, kinder mocking him,
"we'll try and get 'em to send for you"—which made them
all laugh, and they said it was a prime good hit.

XXVI

WELL when they was all gone, the king he asks Mary Jane how they was off for spare rooms, and she said she had one spare room, which would do for Uncle William, and she'd give her own room to Uncle Harvey, which was a little bigger, and she would turn into the room with her sisters and sleep on a cot; and up garret was a little cubby, with a pallet in it. The king said the cubby would do for his valley—meaning me.

So Mary Jane took us up, and she showed them their rooms, which was plain but nice. She said she'd have her frocks and a lot of other traps took out of her room if they was in Uncle Harvey's way, but he said they warn't. The frocks was hung along the wall, and before them was a curtain made out of calico that hung down to the floor. There was an old hair trunk in one corner, and a guitar box in another, and all sorts of little knick-knacks and jim-cracks around, like girls brisken up a room with. The king said it was all the more homely and more pleasanter for these fixings, and so don't disturb them. The duke's room was pretty small, but plenty good enough, and so was my cubby.

That night they had a big supper, and all them men and women was there, and I stood behind the king and the duke's chairs and waited on them, and the niggers waited on the rest. Mary Jane she set at the head of the table, with Susan along side of her, and said how bad the biscuits was, and how mean the preserves was, and how ornery and tough the fried chickens was—and all that kind of rot, the way women always do for to force out compliments; and the people all knowed everything was tip-top, and said so—said "How *do* you get biscuits to brown so nice?" and "Where, for the land's sake *did* you get these amaz'n pickles?" and all that kind of humbug talky-talk, just the way people always does at a supper, you know.

And when it was all done, me and the hare-lip had supper in the kitchen off of the leavings, whilst the others was helping the niggers clean up the things. The hare-lip she got to pumping me about England, and blest if I didn't think the ice was getting mighty thin, sometimes. She says:

"Did you ever see the king?"

"Who? William Fourth? Well, I bet I have—he goes to our church." I knowed he was dead years ago, but I never let on. So when I says he goes to our church, she says:

"What—regular?"

"Yes—regular. His pew's right over opposite ourn—on 'tother side the pulpit."

"I thought he lived in London?"

"Well, he does. Where *would* he live?"

"But I thought *you* lived in Sheffield?"

I see I was up a stump. I had to let on to get choked with a chicken bone, so as to get time to think how to get down again. Then I says:

"I mean he goes to our church regular when he's in Sheffield. That's only in the summer-time, when he comes there to take the sea baths."

"Why, how you talk—Sheffield ain't on the sea."

"Well, who said it was?"

"Why, you did."

"I *didn't*, nuther."

"You did!"

"I didn't."

"You did."

"I never said nothing of the kind."

"Well, what *did* you say, then?"

"Said he come to take the sea *baths*—that's what I said."

"Well, then! how's he going to take the sea baths if it ain't on the sea?"

"Looky here," I says; "did you ever see any Congress water?"

"Yes."

"Well, did you have to go to Congress to get it?"

"Why, no."

"Well, neither does William Fourth have to go to the sea to get a sea bath."

"How does he get it, then?"

"Gets it the way people down here gets Congress-water—

in barrels. There in the palace at Sheffield they've got furnaces, and he wants his water hot. They can't bile that
amount of water away off there at the sea. They haven't got
no conveniences for it."

"Oh, I see, now. You might a said that in the first place
and saved time."

When she said that, I see I was out of the woods again,
and so I was comfortable and glad. Next, she says:

"Do you go to church, too?"

"Yes—regular."

"Where do you set?"

"Why, in our pew."

"*Whose* pew?"

"Why, *ourn*—your Uncle Harvey's."

"His'n? What does *he* want with a pew?"

"Wants it to set in. What did you *reckon* he wanted with
it?"

"Why, I thought he'd be in the pulpit."

Rot him, I forgot he was a preacher. I see I was up a stump
again, so I played another chicken bone and got another
think. Then I says:

"Blame it, do you suppose there ain't but one preacher to
a church?"

"Why, what do they want with more?"

"What!—to preach before a king? I never see such a girl as
you. They don't have no less than seventeen."

"Seventeen! My land! Why, I wouldn't set out such a string
as that, not if I *never* got to glory. It must take 'em a week."

"Shucks, they don't *all* of 'em preach the same day—only
one of 'em."

"Well, then, what does the rest of 'em do?"

"Oh, nothing much. Loll around, pass the plate—and one
thing or another. But mainly they don't do nothing."

"Well, then, what are they *for*?"

"Why, they're for *style*. Don't you know nothing?"

"Well, I don't *want* to know no such foolishness as that.
How is servants treated in England? Do they treat 'em better
'n we treat our niggers?"

"*No!* A servant ain't nobody there. They treat them worse
than dogs."

"Don't they give 'em holidays, the way we do, Christmas and New Year's week, and Fourth of July?"

"Oh, just listen! A body could tell *you* hain't ever been to England, by that. Why, Hare-l—why, Joanna, they never see a holiday from year's end to year's end; never go to the circus, nor theatre, nor nigger shows, nor nowheres."

"Nor church?"

"Nor church."

"But *you* always went to church."

Well, I was gone up again. I forgot I was the old man's servant. But next minute I whirled in on a kind of an explanation how a valley was different from a common servant, and *had* to go to church whether he wanted to or not, and set with the family, on account of it's being the law. But I didn't do it pretty good, and when I got done I see she warn't satisfied. She says:

"Honest injun, now, hain't you been telling me a lot of lies?"

"Honest injun," says I.

"None of it at all?"

"None of it at all. Not a lie in it," says I.

"Lay your hand on this book and say it."

I see it warn't nothing but a dictionary, so I laid my hand on it and said it. So then she looked a little better satisfied, and says:

"Well, then, I'll believe some of it; but I hope to gracious if I'll believe the rest."

"What is it you won't believe, Joe?" says Mary Jane, stepping in with Susan behind her. "It ain't right nor kind for you to talk so to him, and him a stranger and so far from his people. How would you like to be treated so?"

"That's always your way, Maim—always sailing in to help somebody before they're hurt. I hain't done nothing to him. He's told some stretchers, I reckon; and I said I wouldn't swallow it all; and that's every bit and grain I *did* say. I reckon he can stand a little thing like that, can't he?"

"I don't care whether 'twas little or whether 'twas big, he's here in our house and a stranger, and it wasn't good of you to say it. If you was in his place, it would make you feel ashamed; and so you oughtn't to say a thing to another person that will make *them* feel ashamed."

"Why, Maim, he said——"

"It don't make no difference what he *said*—that ain't the thing. The thing is for you to treat him *kind*, and not be saying things to make him remember he ain't in his own country and amongst his own folks."

I says to myself, *this* is a girl that I'm letting that old reptle rob her of her money!

Then Susan *she* waltzed in; and if you'll believe me, she did give Hare-lip hark from the tomb!

Says I to myself, And this is *another* one that I'm letting him rob her of her money!

Then Mary Jane she took another inning, and went in sweet and lovely again—which was her way—but when she got done there warn't hardly anything left o' poor Hare-lip. So she hollered.

"All right, then," says the other girls, "you just ask his pardon."

She done it, too. And she done it beautiful. She done it so beautiful it was good to hear; and I wished I could tell her a thousand lies, so she could do it again.

I says to myself, this is *another* one that I'm letting him rob her of her money. And when she got through, they all jest laid theirselves out to make me feel at home and know I was amongst friends. I felt so ornery and low down and mean, that I says to myself, My mind's made up; I'll hive that money for them or bust.

So then I lit out—for bed, I said, meaning some time or another. When I got by myself, I went to thinking the thing over. I says to myself, shall I go to that doctor, private, and blow on these frauds? No—that won't do. He might tell who told him; then the king and the duke would make it warm for me. Shall I go, private, and tell Mary Jane? No—I dasn't do it. Her face would give them a hint, sure; they've got the money, and they'd slide right out and get away with it. If she was to fetch in help, I'd get mixed up in the business, before it was done with, I judge. No, there ain't no good way but one. I got to steal that money, somehow; and I got to steal it some way that they won't suspicion that I done it. They've got a good thing, here; and they ain't agoing to leave till they've played this family and this town for all they're worth, so I'll find a chance time enough. I'll steal it, and hide it; and by-and-by, when I'm away down the river, I'll write a letter and tell Mary Jane where it's hid. But I better hive it to-night, if I can, because the doctor maybe hasn't let up as much as he lets on he has; he might scare them out of here, yet.

So, thinks I, I'll go and search them rooms. Up stairs the hall was dark, but I found the duke's room, and started to paw around it with my hands; but I recollected it wouldn't be much like the king to let anybody else take care of that money but his own self; so then I went to his room and be-gun to paw around there. But I see I couldn't do nothing without a candle, and I dasn't light one, of course. So I judged I'd got to do the other thing—lay for them, and eavesdrop. About that time, I hears their footsteps coming, and was going to skip under the bed; I reached for it, but it wasn't where I thought it would be; but I touched the curtain that hid Mary Jane's frocks, so I jumped in behind that and snuggled in amongst the gowns, and stood there perfectly still.

They come in and shut the door; and the first thing the duke done was to get down and look under the bed. Then I was glad I hadn't found the bed when I wanted it. And yet, you know, it's kind of natural to hide under the bed when you are up to anything private. They sets down, then, and the king says:

"Well, what is it? and cut it middlin' short, because it's better for us to be down there a whoopin'-up the mournin', than up here givin' 'em a chance to talk us over."

"Well, this is it, Capet. I ain't easy; I ain't comfortable. That doctor lays on my mind. I wanted to know your plans. I've got a notion, and I think it's a sound one."

"What is it, duke?"

"That we better glide out of this, before three in the morn-ing, and clip it down the river with what we've got. Specially, seeing we got it so easy—*given* back to us, flung at our heads, as you may say, when of course we allowed to have to steal it back. I'm for knocking off and lighting out."

That made me feel pretty bad. About an hour or two ago,

it would a been a little different, but now it made me feel bad and disappointed. The king rips out and says:

"What! And not sell out the rest o' the property? March off like a passel o' fools and leave eight or nine thous'n' dollars' worth o' property layin' around jest sufferin' to be scooped in?—and all good salable stuff, too."

The duke he grumbled; said the bag of gold was enough, and he didn't want to go no deeper—didn't want to rob a lot of orphans of *everything* they had.

"Why, how you talk!" says the king. "We shan't rob 'em of nothing at all but jest this money. The people that *buys* the property is the suff'rers; because as soon's it's found out 'at we didn't own it—which won't be long after we've slid—the sale won't be valid, and it'll all go back to the estate. These-yer orphans 'll git their house back agin, and that's enough for *them*; they're young and spry, and k'n easy earn a livin'. *They* ain't agoing to suffer. Why, jest think—there's thous'n's and thous'n's that ain't nigh so well off. Bless you, *they* ain't got noth'n to complain of."

Well, the king he talked him blind; so at last he give in, and said all right, but said he believed it was blame foolish-ness to stay, and that doctor hanging over them. But the king says:

"Cuss the doctor! What do we k'yer for *him*? Hain't we got all the fools in town on our side? and ain't that a big enough majority in any town?"

So they got ready to go down stairs again. The duke says:

"I don't think we put that money in a good place."

That cheered me up. I'd begun to think I warn't going to get a hint of no kind to help me. The king says:

"Why?"

"Because Mary Jane 'll be in mourning from this out; and first you know the nigger that does up the rooms will get an order to box these duds up and put 'em away; and do you reckon a nigger can run across money and not borrow some of it?"

"Your head's level, agin, duke," says the king; and he come a fumbling under the curtain two or three foot from where I was. I stuck tight to the wall, and kept mighty still, though quivery; and I wondered what them fellows would say to me if they catched me; and I tried to think what I'd better do if they did catch me. But the king he got the bag before I could think more than about a half a thought, and he never suspicioned I was around. They took and shoved the bag through a rip in the straw tick that was under the feather bed, and crammed it in a foot or two amongst the straw and said it was all right, now, because a nigger only makes up the feather bed, and don't turn over the straw tick only about twice a year, and so it warn't in no danger of getting stole, now.

But I knowed better. I had it out of there before they was half-way down stairs. I groped along up to my cubby, and hid it there till I could get a chance to do better. I judged I better hide it outside of the house somewheres, because if they missed it they would give the house a good ransacking. I knowed that very well. Then I turned in, with my clothes all on; but I couldn't a gone to sleep, if I'd a wanted to, I was in such a sweat to get through with the business. By-and-by I heard the king and the duke come up; so I rolled off of my pallet and laid with my chin at the top of my ladder and waited to see if anything was going to happen. But nothing did.

So I held on till all the late sounds had quit and the early ones hadn't begun, yet; and then I slipped down the ladder.

XXVII

I CREPT to their doors and listened; they was snoring, so I tip-toed along, and got down stairs all right. There warn't a sound anywheres. I peeped through a crack of the dining-room door, and see the men that was watching the corpse all sound asleep on their chairs. The door was open into the parlor, where the corpse was laying, and there was a candle in both rooms. I passed along, and the parlor door was open; but I see there warn't nobody in there but the remainders of Peter; so I shoved on by; but the front door was locked, and the key wasn't there. Just then I heard somebody coming down the stairs, back behind me. I run in the parlor, and took a swift look around, and the only place I see to hide the bag was in the coffin. The lid was shoved along about a foot, showing the dead man's face down in there, with a wet cloth over it, and his shroud on. I tucked the money-bag in under the lid, just down beyond where his hands was crossed, which made me creep, they was so cold, and then I run back across the room and in behind the door.

The person coming was Mary Jane. She went to the coffin, very soft, and kneeled down and looked in; then she put up her handkerchief and I see she begun to cry, though I couldn't hear her, and her back was to me. I slid out, and as I passed the dining-room I thought I'd make sure them watchers hadn't seen me; so I looked through the crack and everything was all right. They hadn't stirred.

I slipped up to bed, feeling ruther blue, on accounts of the thing playing out that way after I had took so much trouble and run so much resk about it. Says I, if it could stay where it is, all right; because when we get down the river a hundred mile or two, I could write back to Mary Jane, and she could dig him up again and get it; but that ain't the thing that's going to happen; the thing that's going to happen is, the money 'll be found when they come to screw on the lid. Then the king 'll get it again, and it 'll be a long day before he gives anybody another chance to smouch it from him. Of course I *wanted* to slide down and get it out of there, but I dasn't try it. Every minute it was getting earlier, now, and pretty soon some of them watchers would begin to stir, and I might get catched—catched with six thousand dollars in my hands that nobody hadn't hired me to take care of. I don't wish to be mixed up in no such business as that, I says to myself.

When I got down stairs in the morning, the parlor was shut up, and the watchers was gone. There warn't nobody around but the family and the widow Bartley and our tribe. I watched their faces to see if anything had been happening, but I couldn't tell.

Towards the middle of the day the undertaker come, with his man, and they set the coffin in the middle of the room on a couple of chairs, and then set all our chairs in rows, and borrowed more from the neighbors till the hall and the parlor and the dining-room was full. I see the coffin lid was the way it was before, but I dasn't go to look in under it, with folks around.

Then the people begun to flock in, and the beats and the girls took seats in the front row at the head of the coffin, and for a half an hour the people filed around slow, in single rank, and looked down at the dead man's face a minute, and some dropped in a tear, and it was all very still and solemn, only the girls and the beats holding handkerchiefs to their eyes and keeping their heads bent, and sobbing a little. There warn't no other sound but the scraping of the feet on the floor, and blowing noses—because people always blows them more at a funeral than they do at other places except church.

When the place was packed full, the undertaker he slid around in his black gloves with his softy soothering ways, putting on the last touches, and getting people and things all ship-shape and comfortable, and making no more sound than a cat. He never spoke; he moved people around, he squeezed in late ones, he opened up passage-ways, and done it all with nods, and signs with his hands. Then he took his place over against the wall. He was the softest, glidingest, stealthiest man I ever see; and there warn't no more smile to him than there is to a ham.

They had borrowed a melodeum—a sick one; and when everything was ready, a young woman set down and worked it, and it was pretty skreeky and colicky, and everybody joined in and sung, and Peter was the only one that had a good thing, according to my notion. Then the Reverend Hobson opened up, slow and solemn, and begun to talk; and straight off the most outrageous row busted out in the cellar a body ever heard; it was only one dog, but he made a most powerful racket, and he kept it up, right along; the parson he had to stand there, over the coffin, and wait—you couldn't hear yourself think. It was right down awkward, and nobody didn't seem to know what to do. But pretty soon they see that long-legged undertaker make a sign to the preacher as much as to say, "Don't you worry—just depend on me." Then he stooped down and begun to glide along the wall, just his shoulders showing over the people's heads. So he glided along, and the pow-wow and racket getting more and more outrageous all the time; and at last, when he had gone around two sides of the room, he disappears down cellar. Then, in about two seconds we heard a whack, and the dog he finished up with a most amazing howl or two, and then everything was dead still, and the parson begun his solemn talk where he left off. In a minute or two here comes this undertaker's back and shoulders gliding along the wall again; and so he glided, and glided, around three sides of the room, and then rose up, and shaded his mouth with his hands, and stretched his neck out towards the preacher, over the people's heads, and says, in a kind of a coarse whisper, *"He had a rat!"* Then he drooped down and glided along the wall again to his place. You could see it was a great satisfaction to the people, because naturally they wanted to know. A little thing like that don't cost nothing, and it's just the little things that makes a man to be looked up to and liked. There warn't no more popular man in town than what that undertaker was.

Well, the funeral sermon was very good, but pison long and tiresome; and then the king he shoved in and got off some of his usual rubbage, and at last the job was through, and the undertaker begun to sneak up on the coffin with his screw-driver. I was in a sweat then, and watched him pretty keen. But he never meddled at all; just slid the lid along, as soft as mush, and screwed it down tight and fast. So there I was! I didn't know whether the money was in there, or not.

So, says I, spose somebody has hogged that bag on the sly?—now how do *I* know whether to write to Mary Jane or not? 'Spose she dug him up and didn't find nothing—what would she think of me? Blame it, I says, I might get hunted up and jailed; I'd better lay low and keep dark, and not write at all; the thing's awful mixed, now; trying to better it, I've worsened it a hundred times, and I wish to goodness I'd just let it alone, dad fetch the whole business!

They buried him, and we come back home, and I went to watching faces again—I couldn't help it, and I couldn't rest easy. But nothing come of it; the faces didn't tell me nothing.

The king he visited around, in the evening, and sweetened every body up, and made himself ever so friendly; and he give out the idea that his congregration over in England would be in a sweat about him, so he must hurry and settle up the estate right away, and leave for home. He was very sorry he was so pushed, and so was everybody; they wished he could stay longer, but they said they could see it couldn't be done. And he said of course him and William would take the girls home with them; and that pleased everybody too, because then the girls would be well fixed, and amongst their own relations; and it pleased the girls, too—tickled them so they clean forgot they ever had a trouble in the world; and told him to sell out as quick as he wanted to, they would be ready. Them poor things was that glad and happy it made my heart ache to see them getting fooled and lied to so, but I didn't see no safe way for me to chip in and change the general tune.

Well, blamed if the king didn't bill the house and the niggers and all the property for auction straight off—sale two days after the funeral; but anybody could buy private beforehand if they wanted to.

So the next day after the funeral, along about noontime, the girls' joy got the first jolt; a couple of nigger traders come along, and the king sold them the niggers reasonable, for three-day drafts as they called it, and away they went, the two sons up the river to Memphis, and their mother down the river to Orleans. I thought them poor girls and them niggers would break their hearts for grief; they cried around each

other, and took on so it most made me down sick to see it.
The girls said they hadn't ever dreamed of seeing the family
separated or sold away from the town. I can't ever get it out
of my memory, the sight of them poor miserable girls and
niggers hanging around each other's necks and crying; and I
reckon I couldn't a stood it all but would a had to bust out
and tell on our gang if I hadn't knowed the sale warn't no
account and the niggers would be back home in a week or
two.

The thing made a big stir in the town, too, and a good
many come out flat-footed and said it was scandalous to separate the mother and the children that way. It injured the
frauds some; but the old fool he bulled right along, spite of
all the duke could say or do, and I tell you the duke was
powerful uneasy.

Next day was auction day. About broad-day in the morning, the king and the duke come up in the garret and woke
me up, and I see by their look that there was trouble. The
king says:

"Was you in my room night before last?"

"No, your majesty"—which was the way I always called
him when nobody but our gang warn't around.

"Was you in there yisterday er last night?"

"No, your majesty."

"Honor bright, now—no lies."

"Honor bright, your majesty, I'm telling you the truth. I
hain't been anear your room since Miss Mary Jane took you
and the duke and showed it to you."

The duke says:

"Have you seen anybody else go in there?"

"No, your grace, not as I remember, I believe."

"Stop and think."

I studied a while, and see my chance, then I says:

"Well, I see the niggers go in there several times."

Both of them give a little jump; and looked like they hadn't
ever expected it, and then like they *had*. Then the duke says:

"What, *all* of them?"

"No—leastways not all at once. That is, I don't think I
ever see them all come *out* at once but just one time."

"Hello—when was that?"

"It was the day we had the funeral. In the morning. It warn't early, because I overslept. I was just starting down the ladder, and I see them."

"Well, go on, *go* on—what did they do? How'd they act?"

"They didn't do nothing. And they didn't act anyway, much, as fur as I see. They tip-toed away; so I seen, easy enough, that they'd shoved in there to do up your majesty's room, or something, sposing you was up; and found you *warn't* up, and so they was hoping to slide out of the way of trouble without waking you up, if they hadn't already waked you up."

"Great guns, *this* is a go!" says the king; and both of them looked pretty sick, and tolerable silly. They stood there a thinking and scratching their heads, a minute, and then the duke he bust into a kind of a little raspy chuckle, and says:

"It does beat all, how neat the niggers played their hand. They let on to be *sorry* they was going out of this region! and I believed they *was* sorry. And so did you, and so did everybody. Don't ever tell *me* any more that a nigger ain't got any histrionic talent. Why, the way they played that thing, it would fool *anybody*. In my opinion there's a fortune in 'em. If I had capital and a theatre, I wouldn't want a better lay out than that—and here we've gone and sold 'em for a song. Yes, and ain't privileged to sing the song, yet. Say, where *is* that song?—that draft."

"In the bank for to be collected. Where *would* it be?"

"Well, *that's* all right then, thank goodness."

Says I, kind of timid-like:

"Is something gone wrong?"

The king whirls on me and rips out:

"None o' your business! You keep your head shet, and mind y'r own affairs—if you got any. Long as you're in this town, don't you forget *that*, you hear?" Then he says to the duke, "We got to jest swaller it, and say noth'n: mum's the word for *us*."

As they was starting down the ladder, the duke he chuckles again, and says:

"Quick sales *and* small profits! It's a good business—yes."

The king snarls around on him and says,

"I was trying to do for the best, in sellin' 'm out so quick.

If the profits has turned out to be none, lackin' considable, and none to carry, is it my fault any more'n it's yourn?"

"Well, *they'd* be in this house yet, and we *wouldn't* if I could a got my advice listened to."

The king sassed back, as much as was safe for him, and then swapped around and lit into *me* again. He give me down the banks for not coming and *telling* him I see the niggers come out of his room acting that way—said any fool would a *knowed* something was up. And then waltzed in and cussed *himself* a while; and said it all come of him not laying late and taking his natural rest that morning, and he'd be blamed if he'd ever do it again. So they went off a jawing; and I felt dreadful glad I'd worked it all off onto the niggers and yet hadn't done the niggers no harm by it.

XXVIII

B Y-AND-BY it was getting-up time; so I come down the ladder and started for down stairs, but as I come to the girls' room, the door was open, and I see Mary Jane setting by her old hair trunk, which was open and she'd been packing things in it—getting ready to go to England. But she had stopped now, with a folded gown in her lap, and had her face in her hands, crying. I felt awful bad to see it; of course anybody would. I went in there, and says:

"Miss Mary Jane, you can't abear to see people in trouble, and *I* can't—most always. Tell me about it."

So she done it. And it was the niggers—I just expected it. She said the beautiful trip to England was most about spoiled for her; she didn't know *how* she was ever going to be happy there, knowing the mother and the children warn't ever going to see each other no more—and then busted out bitterer than ever, and flung up her hands, and says:

"Oh, dear, dear, to think they ain't *ever* going to see each other any more!"

"But they *will*—and inside of two weeks—and I *know* it!" says I.

Laws it was out before I could think!—and before I could budge, she throws her arms around my neck, and told me to say it *again*, say it *again*, say it *again*!

I see I had spoke too sudden, and said too much, and was in a close place. I asked her to let me think a minute; and she set there, very impatient and excited, and handsome, but looking kind of happy and eased-up, like a person that's had a tooth pulled out. So I went to studying it out. I says to myself, I reckon a body that ups and tells the truth when he is in a tight place, is taking considerable many resks, though I ain't had no experience, and can't say for certain; but it looks so to me, anyway; and yet here's a case where I'm blest if it don't look to me like the truth is better, and actuly *safer*, than a lie. I must lay it by in my mind, and think it over some time or other, it's so kind of strange and unregular. I never see nothing like it. Well, I says to myself at last, I'm agoing to chance it; I'll up and tell the truth this time, though it does seem most like setting down on a kag of powder and touching it off just to see where you'll go to. Then I says:

"Miss Mary Jane, is there any place out of town a little ways, where you could go and stay three or four days?"

"Yes—Mr. Lothrop's. Why?"

"Never mind why, yet. If I'll tell you how I know the niggers will see each other again—inside of two weeks—here in this house—and *prove* how I know it—will you go to Mr. Lothrop's and stay four days?"

"Four days!" she says; "I'll stay a year!"

"All right," I says, "I don't want nothing more out of *you* than just your word—I druther have it than another man's kiss-the-Bible." She smiled, and reddened up very sweet, and I says, "If you don't mind it, I'll shut the door—and bolt it."

Then I come back and set down again, and says:

"Don't you holler. Just set still, and take it like a man. I got to tell the truth, and you want to brace up, Miss Mary, because it's a bad kind, and going to be hard to take, but there ain't no help for it. These uncles of yourn ain't no uncles at all—they're a couples of frauds—regular dead-beats. There, now we're over the worst of it—you can stand the rest middling easy."

It jolted her up like everything, of course; but I was over the shoal water now, so I went right along, her eyes a blazing higher and higher all the time, and told her every blame thing, from where we first struck that young fool going up to the steamboat, clear through to where she flung herself onto the king's breast at the front door and he kissed her sixteen or seventeen times—and then up she jumps, with her face afire like sunset, and says:

"The brute! Come—don't waste a minute—not a *second*— we'll have them tarred and feathered, and flung in the river!"

Says I:

"Cert'nly. But do you mean, *before* you go to Mr. Lothrop's, or——"

"Oh," she says, "what am I *thinking* about!" she says, and set right down again. "Don't mind what I said—please don't—you *won't*, now, *will* you?" Laying her silky hand on mine in that kind of a way that I said I would die first. "I never thought, I was so stirred up," she says; "now go on, and I won't do so any more. You tell me what to do, and whatever you say, I'll do it."

"Well," I says, "it's a rough gang, them two frauds, and I'm fixed so I got to travel with them a while longer, whether I want to or not—I druther not tell you why—and if you was to blow on them this town would get me out of their claws, and I'd be all right, but there'd be another person that you don't know about who'd be in big trouble. Well, we got to save *him*, hain't we? Of course. Well, then, we won't blow on them."

Saying them words put a good idea in my head. I see how maybe I could get me and Jim rid of the frauds; get them jailed here, and then leave. But I didn't want to run the raft in day-time, without anybody aboard to answer questions but me; so I didn't want the plan to begin working till pretty late to-night. I says:

"Miss Mary Jane, I'll tell you what we'll do—and you won't have to stay at Mr. Lothrop's so long, nuther. How fur is it?"

"A little short of four miles—right out in the country, back here."

"Well, that'll answer. Now you go along out there, and lay low till nine or half-past, to-night, and then get them to fetch you home again—tell them you've thought of something. If you get here before eleven, put a candle in this window, and if I don't turn up, wait *till* eleven, and *then* if I don't turn up it means I'm gone, and out of the way, and safe. Then you come out and spread the news around, and get these beats jailed."

"Good," she says, "I'll do it."

"And if it just happens so that I don't get away, but get took up along with them, you must up and say I told you the whole thing beforehand, and you must stand by me all you can."

"Stand by you, indeed I will. They sha'n't touch a hair of your head!" she says, and I see her nostrils spread and her eyes snap when she said it, too.

"If I get away, I sha'n't be here," I says, "to prove these rapscallions ain't your uncles, and I couldn't do it if I *was* here. I could swear they was beats and bummers, that's all; though that's worth something. Well, there's others can do that better than what I can—and they're people that ain't going to be doubted as quick as I'd be. I'll tell you how to find them. Gimme a pencil and a piece of paper. There— 'Royal Nonesuch, Bricksville.' Put it away, and don't lose it. When the court wants to find out something about these two, let them send up to Bricksville and say they've got the men that played the Royal Nonesuch, and ask for some witnesses—why, you'll have that entire town down here before you can hardly wink, Miss Mary. And they'll come a-biling, too."

I judged we had got everything fixed about right, now. So I says:

"Just let the auction go right along, and don't worry. Nobody don't have to pay for the things they buy till a whole day after the auction, on accounts of the short notice, and they ain't going out of this till they get that money—and the way we've fixed it the sale ain't going to count, and they ain't going to *get* no money. It's just like the way it was with the niggers—it warn't no sale, and the niggers will be back before long. Why, they can't collect the money for the *niggers*, yet—they're in the worst kind of a fix, Miss Mary."

"Well," she says, "I'll run down to breakfast now, and then I'll start straight for Mr. Lothrop's."

" 'Deed, *that* ain't the ticket, Miss Mary Jane," I says, "by no manner of means; go *before* breakfast."

"Why?"

"What did you reckon I wanted you to go at all for, Miss Mary?"

"Well, I never thought—and come to think, I don't know. What was it?"

"Why, it's because you ain't one of these leather-face people. I don't want no better book than what your face is. A body can set down and read it off like coarse print. Do you reckon you can go and face your uncles, when they come to kiss you good-morning, and never——"

"There, there, don't! Yes, I'll go before breakfast—I'll be glad to. And leave my sisters with them?"

"Yes—never mind about them. They've got to stand it yet

a while. They might suspicion something if all of you was to
go. I don't want you to see them, nor your sisters, nor nobody in this town—if a neighbor was to ask how is your
uncles this morning, your face would tell something. No, you
go right along, Miss Mary Jane, and I'll fix it with all of them.
I'll tell Miss Susan to give your love to your uncles and say
you've went away for a few hours for to get a little rest and
change, or to see a friend, and you'll be back to-night or early
in the morning."

"Gone to see a friend is all right, but I won't have my love
given to them."

"Well, then, it sha'n't be." It was well enough to tell *her*
so—no harm in it. It was only a little thing to do, and no
trouble; and it's the little things that smoothes people's roads
the most, down here below; it would make Mary Jane comfortable, and it wouldn't cost nothing. Then I says: "There's
one more thing—that bag of money."

"Well, they've got that; and it makes me feel pretty silly to
think *how* they got it."

"No, you're out, there. They hain't got it."

"Why, who's got it?"

"I wish I knowed, but I don't. I *had* it, because I stole it
from them: and I stole it to give to you; and I know where
I hid it, but I'm afraid it ain't there no more. I'm awful sorry,
Miss Mary Jane, I'm just as sorry as I can be; but I done the
best I could; I did, honest. I come nigh getting caught, and
I had to shove it into the first place I come to, and run—and
it warn't a good place."

"Oh, stop blaming yourself—it's too bad to do it, and I
won't allow it—you couldn't help it; it wasn't your fault.
Where did you hide it?"

I didn't want to set her to thinking about her troubles
again; and I couldn't seem to get my mouth to tell her what
would make her see that corpse laying in the coffin with that
bag of of money on his stomach. So for a minute I didn't say
nothing—then I says:

"I'd ruther not *tell* you where I put it, Miss Mary Jane, if
you don't mind letting me off; but I'll write it for you on a
piece of paper, and you can read it along the road to Mr.
Lothrop's, if you want to. Do you reckon that'll do?"

"Oh, yes."

So I wrote: "I put it in the coffin. It was in there when you was crying there, away in the night. I was behind the door, and I was mighty sorry for you, Miss Mary Jane."

It made my eyes water a little, to remember her crying there all by herself in the night, and them devils laying there right under her own roof, shaming her and robbing her; and when I folded it up and give it to her, I see the water come into her eyes, too; and she shook me by the hand, hard, and says:

"*Good*-bye—I'm going to do everything just as you've told me; and if I don't ever see you again, I sha'n't ever forget you, and I'll think of you a many and a many a time, and I'll *pray* for you, too!"—and she was gone.

Pray for me! I reckoned if she knowed me she'd take a job that was more nearer her size. But I bet she done it, just the same—she was just that kind. She had the grit to pray for Judus if she took the notion—there warn't no backdown to her, I judge. You may say what you want to, but in my opinion she had more sand in her than any girl I ever see; in my opinion she was just full of sand. It sounds like flattery, but it ain't no flattery. And when it comes to beauty—and goodness too—she lays over them all. I hain't ever seen her since that time that I see her go out of that door; no, I hain't ever seen her since, but I reckon I've thought of her a many and a many a million times, and of her saying she would pray for me; and if ever I'd a thought it would do any good for me to pray for *her*, blamed if I wouldn't a done it or bust.

Well, Mary Jane she lit out the back way, I reckon; because nobody see her go. When I struck Susan and the hare-lip, I says:

"What's the name of them people over on t'other side of the river that you all goes to see sometimes?"

They says:

"There's several; but it's the Proctors, mainly."

"That's the name," I says; "I most forgot it. Well, Miss Mary Jane she told me to tell you she's gone over there in a dreadful hurry—one of them's sick."

"Which one?"

"I don't know; leastways I kinder forget; but I think it's——"

"Sakes alive, I hope it ain't *Hanner*?"

"I'm sorry to say it," I says, "but Hanner's the very one."

"My goodness—and she so well only last week! Is she took bad?"

"It ain't no name for it. They set up with her all night, Miss Mary Jane said, and they don't think she'll last many hours."

"Only think of that, now! What's the matter with her!"

I couldn't think of anything reasonable, right off that way, so I says:

"Mumps."

"Mumps your granny! They don't set up with people that's got the mumps."

"They don't, don't they? You better bet they do with *these* mumps. These mumps is different. It's a new kind, Miss Mary Jane said."

"How's it a new kind?"

"Because it's mixed up with other things."

"What other things?"

"Well, measles, and whooping-cough and erysiplas, and consumption, and yaller janders, and brain fever, and I don't know what all."

"My land! And they call it the *mumps*?"

"That's what Miss Mary Jane said."

"Well, what in the nation do they call it the *mumps* for?"

"Why, because it *is* the mumps. That's what it starts with."

"Well, ther' ain't no sense in it. A body might stump his toe, and take pison, and fall down the well, and break his neck, and bust his brains out, and somebody come along and ask what killed him, and some numskull up and say, 'Why, he stumped his *toe*.' Would ther' be any sense in that? *No.* And ther' ain't no sense in *this*, nuther. Is it ketching?"

"Is it *ketching*? Why, how you talk. Is a *harrow* catching?— in the dark? If you don't hitch onto one tooth, you're bound to on another, ain't you? And you can't get away with that tooth without fetching the whole harrow along, can you? Well, these kind of mumps is a kind of a harrow, as you may say—and it ain't no slouch of a harrow, nuther, you come to get it hitched on good."

"Well, it's awful, *I* think," says the hare-lip. "I'll go to Uncle Harvey and——"

"Oh, yes," I says, "I *would*. Of *course* I would. I wouldn't lose no time."

"Well, why wouldn't you?"

"Just look at it a minute, and maybe you can see. Hain't your uncles obleeged to get along home to England as fast as they can? And do you reckon they'd be mean enough to go off and leave you to go all that journey by yourselves? *You* know they'll wait for you. So fur, so good. Your uncle Harvey's a preacher, ain't he? Very well, then; is a *preacher* going to deceive a steamboat clerk? is he going to deceive a *ship clerk?*—so as to get them to let Miss Mary Jane go aboard? Now *you* know he ain't. What *will* he do, then? Why, he'll say, 'It's a great pity, but my church matters has got to get along the best way they can; for my niece has been exposed to the dreadful pluribus-unum mumps, and so it's my bounden duty to set down here and wait the three months it takes to show on her if she's got it.' But never mind, if you think it's best to tell your uncle Harvey——"

"Shucks, and stay fooling around here when we could all be having good times in England whilst we was waiting to find out whether Mary Jane's got it or not? Why, you talk like a muggins."

"Well, anyway, maybe you better tell some of the neighbors."

"Listen at that, now. You do beat all, for natural stupidness. Can't you *see* that *they'd* go and tell? Ther' ain't no way but just to not tell anybody at *all*."

"Well, maybe you're right—yes, I judge you *are* right."

"But I reckon we ought to tell Uncle Harvey she's gone out a while, anyway, so he wont be uneasy about her?"

"Yes, Miss Mary Jane she wanted you to do that. She says, 'Tell them to give Uncle Harvey and William my love and a kiss, and say I've run over the river to see Mr.—Mr.—what *is* the name of that rich family your uncle Peter used to think so much of?—I mean the one that——"

"Why, you must mean the Apthorps, ain't it?"

"Of course; bother them kind of names, a body can't ever seem to remember them, half the time, somehow. Yes, she

said, say she has run over for to ask the Apthorps to be sure
and come to the auction and buy this house, because she allowed her uncle Peter would ruther they had it than anybody
else; and she's going to stick to them till they say they'll
come, and then, if she ain't too tired, she's coming home; and
if she is, she'll be home in the morning anyway. She said,
don't say nothing about the Proctors, but only about the Apthorps—which'll be perfectly true, because she *is* going there
to speak about their buying the house; I know it, because she
told me so, herself."

"All right," they said, and cleared out to lay for their uncles, and give them the love and the kisses, and tell them the
message.

Everything was all right now. The girls wouldn't say nothing because they wanted to go to England; and the king and
the duke would ruther Mary Jane was off working for the
auction than around in reach of Doctor Robinson. I felt very
good; I judged I had done it pretty neat—I reckoned Tom
Sawyer couldn't a done it no neater himself. Of course he
would a throwed more style into it, but I can't do that very
handy, not being brung up to it.

Well, they held the auction in the public square, along towards the end of the afternoon, and it strung along, and
strung along, and the old man he was on hand and looking
his level pisonest, up there longside of the auctioneer, and
chipping in a little Scripture, now and then, or a little goody-
goody saying, of some kind, and the duke he was around
goo-gooing for sympathy all he knowed how, and just
spreading himself generly.

But by-and-by the thing dragged through, and everything
was sold. Everything but a little old trifling lot in the graveyard. So they'd got to work *that* off—I never see such a
girafft as the king was for wanting to swallow *everything*.
Well, whilst they was at it, a steamboat landed, and in about
two minutes up comes a crowd a whooping and yelling and
laughing and carrying on, and singing out:

"*Here's* your opposition line! here's your two sets o' heirs
to old Peter Wilks—and you pays your money and you takes
your choice!"

XXIX

THEY WAS FETCHING a very nice looking old gentleman along, and a nice looking younger one, with his right arm in a sling. And my souls, how the people yelled, and laughed, and kept it up. But I didn't see no joke about it, and I judged it would strain the duke and the king some to see any. I reckoned they'd turn pale. But no, nary a pale did *they* turn. The duke he never let on he suspicioned what was up, but just went a goo-gooing around, happy and satisfied, like a jug that's googling out buttermilk; and as for the king, he just gazed and gazed down sorrowful on them new-comers like it give him the stomach-ache in his very heart to think there could be such frauds and rascals in the world. Oh, he done it admirable. Lots of the principal people gethered around the king, to let him see they was on his side. That old gentleman that had just come looked all puzzled to death. Pretty soon he begun to speak, and I see, straight off, he pronounced *like* an Englishman, not the king's way, though the king's *was* pretty good, for an imitation. I can't give the old gent's words, nor I can't imitate him; but he turned around to the crowd, and says, about like this:

"This is a surprise to me which I wasn't looking for; and I'll acknowledge, candid and frank, I ain't very well fixed to meet it and answer it; for my brother and me has had misfortunes, he's broke his arm, and our baggage got put off at a town above here, last night in the night by a mistake. I am Peter Wilks's brother Harvey, and this is his brother William, which can't hear nor speak—and can't even make signs to amount to much, now 't he's only got one hand to work them with. We are who we say we are; and in a day or two, when I get the baggage, I can prove it. But, up till then, I won't say nothing more, but go to the hotel and wait."

So him and the new dummy started off; and the king he laughs, and blethers out:

"Broke his arm—*very* likely *ain't* it?—and very convenient, too, for a fraud that's got to make signs, and hain't learnt how. Lost their baggage! That's *mighty* good!—and mighty ingenious—under the *circumstances*!"

So he laughed again; and so did everybody else, except three or four, or maybe half a dozen. One of these was that doctor; another one was a sharp looking gentleman, with a carpet-bag of the old-fashioned kind made out of carpet-stuff, that had just come off of the steamboat and was talking to him in a low voice, and glancing towards the king now and then and nodding their heads—it was Levi Bell, the lawyer that was gone up to Louisville; and another one was a big rough husky that come along and listened to all the old gentleman said, and was listening to the king now. And when the king got done, this husky up and says:

"Say, looky here; if you are Harvey Wilks, when'd you come to this town?"

"The day before the funeral, friend," says the king.

"But what time o' day?"

"In the evenin'—'bout an hour er two before sundown."

"*How'd* you come?"

"I come down on the *Susan Powell*, from Cincinnati."

"Well, then, how'd you come to be up at the Pint in the *mornin'*—in a canoe?"

"I warn't up at the Pint in the mornin'."

"It's a lie."

Several of them jumped for him and begged him not to talk that way to an old man and a preacher.

"Preacher be hanged, he's a fraud and a liar. He was up at the Pint that mornin'. I live up there, don't I? Well, I was up there, and he was up there. I *see* him there. He come in a canoe, along with Tim Collins and a boy."

The doctor he up and says:

"Would you know the boy again if you was to see him, Hines?"

"I reckon I would, but I don't know. Why, yonder he is, now. I know him perfectly easy."

It was me he pointed at. The doctor says:

"Neighbors, I don't know whether the new couple is frauds or not; but if *these* two ain't frauds, I am an idiot, that's all. I think it's our duty to see that they don't get away from here till we've looked into this thing. Come along, Hines; come along, the rest of you. We'll take these fellows to the tavern and affront them with t'other couple, and I reckon we'll find out *something* before we get through."

It was nuts for the crowd, though maybe not for the king's friends; so we all started. It was about sundown. The doctor he led me along by the hand, and was plenty kind enough, but he never let *go* my hand.

We all got in a big room in the hotel, and lit up some candles, and fetched in the new couple. First, the doctor says:

"I don't wish to be too hard on these two men, but *I* think they're frauds, and they may have complices that we don't know nothing about. If they have, won't the complices get away with that bag of gold Peter Wilks left? It ain't unlikely. If these men ain't frauds, they won't object to sending for that money and letting us keep it till they prove they're all right—ain't that so?"

Everybody agreed to that. So I judged they had our gang in a pretty tight place, right at the outstart. But the king he only looked sorrowful, and says:

"Gentlemen, I wish the money was there, for I ain't got no disposition to throw anything in the way of a fair, open, out-and-out investigation o' this misable business; but alas, the money ain't there; you k'n send and see, if you want to."

"Where is it, then?"

"Well, when my niece give it to me to keep for her, I took and hid it inside o' the straw tick o' my bed, not wishin' to bank it for the few days we'd be here, and considerin' the bed a safe place, we not bein' used to niggers, and suppos'n' 'em honest, like servants in England. The niggers stole it the very next mornin' after I had went down stairs; and when I sold 'em, I hadn't missed the money yit, so they got clean away with it. My servant here k'n tell you 'bout it gentlemen."

The doctor and several said "Shucks!" and I see nobody didn't altogether believe him. One man asked me if I see the niggers steal it. I said no, but I see them sneaking out of the room and hustling away, and I never thought nothing, only I reckoned they was afraid they had waked up my master and was trying to get away before he made trouble with them. That was all they asked me. Then the doctor whirls on me and says:

"Are *you* English too?"

I says yes; and him and some others laughed, and said, "Stuff!"

Well, then they sailed in on the general investigation, and there we had it, up and down, hour in, hour out, and nobody never said a word about supper, nor ever seemed to think about it—and so they kept it up, and kept it up; and it *was* the worst mixed-up thing you ever see. They made the king tell his yarn, and they made the old gentleman tell his'n; and anybody but a lot of prejudiced chuckleheads would a *seen* that the old gentleman was spinning truth and t'other one lies. And by-and-by they had me up to tell what I knowed. The king he give me a left-handed look out of the corner of his eye, and so I knowed enough to talk on the right side. I begun to tell about Sheffield, and how we lived there, and all about the English Wilkses, and so on; but I didn't get pretty fur till the doctor begun to laugh; and Levi Bell, the lawyer, says:

"Set down, my boy, I wouldn't strain myself, if I was you. I reckon you ain't used to lying, it don't seem to come handy; what you want is practice. You do it pretty awkward."

I didn't care nothing for the compliment, but I was glad to be let off, anyway.

The doctor he started to say something, and turns and says:

"If you'd been in town at first, Levi Bell——"

The king broke in and reached out his hand, and says:

"Why, is this my poor dead brother's old friend that he's wrote so often about?"

The lawyer and him shook hands, and the lawyer smiled and looked pleased, and they talked right along a while, and then got to one side and talked low; and at last the lawyer speaks up and says:

"That'll fix it. I'll take the order and send it, along with your brother's, and then they'll know it's all right."

So they got some paper and a pen, and the king he set down and twisted his head to one side, and chawed his tongue, and scrawled off something; and then they give the pen to the duke—and then for the first time, the duke looked sick. But he took the pen and wrote. So then the lawyer turns to the new old gentleman and says:

"You and your brother please write a line or two and sign your names."

The old gentleman wrote, but nobody couldn't read it. The lawyer looked powerful astonished, and says:

"Well, it beats *me*"—and snaked a lot of old letters out of his pocket, and examined them, and then examined the old man's writing, and then *them* again; and then says: "These old letters is from Harvey Wilks; and here's *these* two's handwritings, and anybody can see *they* didn't write them" (the king and the duke looked sold and foolish, I tell you, to see how the lawyer had took them in), "and here's *this* old gentleman's handwriting, and anybody can tell, easy enough, *he* didn't write them—fact is, the scratches he makes ain't properly *writing*, at all. Now here's some letters from——"

The new old gentleman says:

"If you please, let me explain. Nobody can read my hand but my brother there—so he copies for me. It's *his* hand you've got there, not mine."

"*Well!*" says the lawyer, "this *is* a state of things. I've got some of William's letters too; so if you'll get him to write a line or so we can com——"

"He *can't* write with his left hand," says the old gentleman. "If he could use his right hand, you would see that he wrote his own letters and mine too. Look at both, please—they're by the same hand."

The lawyer done it, and says:

"I believe it's so—and if it ain't so, there's a heap stronger resemblance than I'd noticed before, anyway. Well, well, well! I thought we was right on the track of a slution, but it's gone to grass, partly. But anyway, *one* thing is proved—*these* two ain't either of 'em Wilkses"—and he wagged his head towards the king and the duke.

Well, what do you think?—that muleheaded old fool wouldn't give in *then*! Indeed he wouldn't. Said it warn't no fair test. Said his brother William was the cussedest joker in the world, and hadn't *tried* to write—*he* see William was going to play one of his jokes the minute he put the pen to paper. And so he warmed up and went warbling and warbling right along, till he was actuly beginning to believe what

he was saying, *himself*—but pretty soon the new old gentleman broke in, and says:

"I've thought of something. Is there anybody here that
helped to lay out my br—helped to lay out the late Peter
Wilks for burying?"

"Yes," says somebody, "me and Ab Turner done it. We're
both here."

Then the old man turns towards the king, and says:

"Peraps this gentleman can tell me what was tatooed on his
breast?"

Blamed if the king didn't have to brace up mighty quick,
or he'd a squshed down like a bluff bank that the river has
cut under, it took him so sudden—and mind you, it was a
thing that was calculated to make most *anybody* sqush to get
fetched such a solid one as that without any notice—because
how was *he* going to know what was tatooed on the man?
He whitened a little; he couldn't help it; and it was mighty
still in there, and everybody bending a little forwards and gazing at him. Says I to myself, *Now* he'll throw up the sponge—
there ain't no more use. Well, did he? A body can't hardly
believe it, but he didn't. I reckon he thought he'd keep the
thing up till he tired them people out, so they'd thin out, and
him and the duke could break loose and get away. Anyway,
he set there, and pretty soon he begun to smile, and says:

"Mf! It's a *very* tough question, *ain't* it! *Yes*, sir, I k'n tell
you what's tatooed on his breast. It's jest a small, thin, blue
arrow—that's what it is; and if you don't look clost, you
can't see it. *Now* what do you say—hey?"

Well, *I* never see anything like that old blister for clean
out-and-out cheek.

The new old gentleman turns brisk towards Ab Turner and
his pard, and his eye lights up like he judged he'd got the
king *this* time, and says:

"There—you've heard what he said! Was there any such
mark on Peter Wilks's breast?"

Both of them spoke up and says:

"We didn't see no such mark."

"Good!" says the old gentleman. "Now, what you *did* see
on his breast was a small dim P, and a B (which is an initial
he dropped when he was young), and a W, with dashes be-

tween them, so: P—B—W"—and he marked them that way on a piece of paper. "Come—ain't that what you saw?"

Both of them spoke up again, and says:

"No, we *didn't*. We never seen any marks at all."

Well, everybody *was* in a state of mind, now; and they sings out:

"The whole *bilin'* of 'm 's frauds! Le's duck 'em! le's drown 'em! le's ride 'em on a rail!" and everybody was whooping at once, and there was a rattling pow-wow. But the lawyer he jumps on the table and yells, and says:

"Gentlemen—gentle*men*! Hear me just a word—just a *single* word—if you PLEASE! There's one way yet—let's go and dig up the corpse and look."

That took them.

"Hooray!" they all shouted, and was starting right off; but the lawyer and the doctor sung out:

"Hold on, hold on! Collar all these four men and the boy, and fetch *them* along, too!"

"We'll do it!" they all shouted: "and if we don't find them marks we'll lynch the whole gang!"

I *was* scared, now, I tell you. But there warn't no getting away, you know. They gripped us all, and marched us right along, straight for the graveyard, which was a mile and a half down the river, and the whole town at our heels, for we made noise enough, and it was only nine in the evening.

As we went by our house I wished I hadn't sent Mary Jane out of town; because now if I could tip her the wink, she'd light out and save me, and blow on our dead-beats.

Well, we swarmed along down the river road, just carrying on like wild-cats; and to make it more scary, the sky was darking up, and the lightning beginning to wink and flitter, and the wind to shiver amongst the leaves. This was the most awful trouble and most dangersome I ever was in; and I was kinder stunned; everything was going so different from what I had allowed for; stead of being fixed so I could take my own time, if I wanted to, and see all the fun, and have Mary Jane at my back to save me and set me free when the close-fit come, here was nothing in the world betwixt me and sudden death but just them tatoo-marks. If they didn't find them—

I couldn't bear to think about it; and yet, somehow, I couldn't think about nothing else. It got darker and darker, and it was a beautiful time to give the crowd the slip; but that big husky had me by the wrist—Hines—and a body might as well try to give Goliar the slip. He dragged me right along, he was so excited; and I had to run to keep up.

When they got there they swarmed into the graveyard and washed over it like an overflow. And when they got to the grave, they found they had about a hundred times as many shovels as they wanted, but nobody hadn't thought to fetch a lantern. But they sailed into digging, anyway, by the flicker of the lightning, and sent a man to the nearest house a half a mile off, to borrow one.

So they dug and dug, like everything; and it got awful dark, and the rain started, and the wind swished and swushed along, and the lightning come brisker and brisker, and the thunder boomed; but them people never took no notice of it, they was so full of this business; and one minute you could see everything and every face in that big crowd, and the shovelfuls of dirt sailing up out of the grave, and the next second the dark wiped it all out, and you couldn't see nothing at all.

At last they got out the coffin, and begun to unscrew the lid, and then such another crowding, and shouldering, and shoving as there was, to scrouge in and get a sight, you never see; and in the dark, that way, it was awful. Hines he hurt my wrist dreadful, pulling and tugging so, and I reckon he clean forgot I was in the world, he was so excited and panting.

All of a sudden the lightning let go a perfect sluice of white glare, and somebody sings out:

"By the living jingo, here's the bag of gold on his breast!"

Hines let out a whoop, like everybody else, and dropped my wrist and give a big surge to bust his way in and get a look, and the way I lit out and shinned for the road in the dark, there ain't nobody can tell.

I had the road all to myself, and I fairly flew—leastways I had it all to myself except the solid dark, and the now-and-then glares, and the buzzing of the rain, and the thrashing of the wind, and the splitting of the thunder; and sure as you are born I did clip it along!

When I struck the town, I see there warn't nobody out in the storm, so I never hunted for no back streets, but humped it straight through the main one; and when I begun to get towards our house I aimed my eye and set it. No light there; the house all dark—which made me feel sorry and disappointed, I didn't know why. But at last, just as I was sailing by, *flash* comes the light in Mary Jane's window! and my heart swelled up sudden, like to bust; and the same second the house and all was behind me in the dark, and wasn't ever going to be before me no more in this world. She *was* the best girl I ever see, and had the most sand.

The minute I was far enough above the town to see I could make the towhead, I begun to look sharp for a boat to borrow; and the first time the lightning showed me one that wasn't chained, I snatched it and shoved. It was a canoe, and warn't fastened with nothing but a rope. The towhead was a rattling big distance off, away out there in the middle of the river, but I didn't lose no time; and when I struck the raft at last, I was so fagged I would a just laid down to blow and gasp if I could afforded it. But I didn't. As I sprung aboard I sung out:

"Out with you Jim, and set her loose! Glory be to goodness, we're shut of them!"

Jim lit out, and was a coming for me with both arms spread, he was so full of joy; but when I glimpsed him in the lightning, my heart shot up in my mouth, and I went overboard backwards; for I forgot he was old King Lear and a drownded A-rab all in one, and it most scared the livers and lights out of me. But Jim fished me out, and was going to hug me and bless me, and so on, he was so glad I was back and we was shut of the king and the duke, but I says:

"Not now—have it for breakfast, have it for breakfast! Cut loose and let her slide!"

So, in two seconds, away we went, a sliding down the river, and it *did* seem so good to be free again and all by ourselves on the big river and nobody to bother us. I had to skip around a bit, and jump up and crack my heels a few times, I couldn't help it; but about the third crack, I noticed a sound that I knowed mighty well—and held my breath and listened and waited—and sure enough, when the next flash busted out over the water, here they come!—and just a laying to their oars and making their skiff hum! It was the king and the duke.

So I wilted right down onto the planks, then, and give up; and it was all I could do to keep from crying.

XXX

W**HEN THEY GOT ABOARD**, the king went for me, and
shook me by the collar, and says:

"Tryin' to give us the slip, was ye, you pup! Tired of our
company—hey?"

I says:

"No, your majesty, we warn't—*please* don't, your majesty!"

"Quick, then, and tell us what *was* your idea, or I'll shake
the insides out o' you!"

"Honest, I'll tell you everything, just as it happened, your
majesty. The man that had aholt of me was very good to me,
and kept saying he had a boy about as big as me that died
last year, and he was sorry to see a boy in such a dangerous
fix; and when they was all took by surprise by finding the
gold, and made a rush for the coffin, he lets go of me and
whispers, 'Heel it, now, or they'll hang ye, sure!' and I lit
out. It didn't seem no good for *me* to stay—I couldn't do
nothing, and I didn't want to be hung if I could get away.
So I never stopped running till I found the canoe; and
when I got here I told Jim to hurry, or they'd catch me
and hang me yet, and said I was afeard you and the duke
wasn't alive, now, and I was awful sorry, and so was Jim,
and was awful glad when we see you coming, you may ask
Jim if I didn't."

Jim said it was so; and the king told him to shut up, and
said, "Oh, yes, it's *mighty* likely!" and shook me up again,
and said he reckoned he'd drownd me. But the duke says:

"Leggo the boy, you old idiot! Would *you* a done any different? Did you inquire around for *him*, when you got loose?
I don't remember it."

So the king let go of me, and begun to cuss that town and
everybody in it. But the duke says:

"You better a blame sight give *yourself* a good cussing, for
you're the one that's entitled to it most. You hain't done a
thing, from the start, that had any sense in it, except coming
out so cool and cheeky with that imaginary blue-arrow mark.
That *was* bright—it was right down bully; and it was the

thing that saved us. For if it hadn't been for that, they'd a jailed us till them Englishmen's baggage come—and then—the penitentiary, you bet! But that trick took 'em to the graveyard, and the gold done us a still bigger kindness; for if the excited fools hadn't let go all holts and made that rush to get a look, we'd a slept in our cravats to-night—cravats warranted to *wear*, too—longer than *we'd* need 'em."

They was still a minute—thinking—then the king says, kind of absent-minded like:

"Mf! And we reckoned the *niggers* stole it!"

That made me squirm!

"Yes," says the duke, kinder slow, and deliberate, and sarcastic, "*We* did."

After about a half a minute, the king drawls out:

"Leastways—*I* did."

The duke says, the same way:

"On the contrary—*I* did."

The king kind of ruffles up, and says:

"Looky here, Bilgewater, what'r you referrin' to?"

The duke says, pretty brisk:

"When it comes to that, maybe you'll let me ask, what was *you* referring to?"

"Shucks!" says the king, very sarcastic; "but *I* don't know—maybe you was asleep, and didn't know what you was about."

The duke bristles right up, now, and says:

"Oh, let *up* on this cussed nonsense—do you take me for a blame' fool? Don't you reckon *I* know who hid that money in that coffin?"

"*Yes*, sir! I know you *do* know—because you done it yourself!"

"It's a lie!"—and the duke went for him. The king sings out:

"Take y'r hands off!—leggo my throat!—I take it all back!"

The duke says:

"Well, you just own up, first, that you *did* hide that money there, intending to give me the slip one of these days, and come back and dig it up, and have it all to yourself."

"Wait jest a minute, duke—answer me this one question,

honest and fair; if you didn't put the money there, say it, and I'll b'lieve you, and take back everything I said."

"You old scoundrel, I didn't, and you know I didn't. There, now!"

"Well, then, I b'lieve you. But answer me only jest this one more—now *don't* git mad; didn't you have it in your *mind* to hook the money and hide it?"

The duke never said nothing for a little bit; then he says:

"Well—I don't care if I *did*, I didn't *do* it, anyway. But you not only had it in mind to do it, but you *done* it."

"I wisht I may never die if I done it, duke, and that's honest. I won't say I warn't *goin'* to do it, because I *was*; but you—I mean somebody—got in ahead o' me."

"It's a lie! You done it, and you got to *say* you done it, or——"

The king begun to gurgle, and then he gasps out:

"'Nough!—*I own up!*"

I was very glad to hear him say that, it made me feel much more easier than what I was feeling before. So the duke took his hands off, and says:

"If you ever deny it again, I'll drown you. It's *well* for you to set there and blubber like a baby—it's fitten for you, after the way you've acted. I never see such an old ostrich for wanting to gobble everything—and I a trusting you all the time, like you was my own father. You ought to been ashamed of yourself to stand by and hear it saddled onto a lot of poor niggers and you never say a word for 'em. It makes me feel ridiculous to think I was soft enough to *believe* that rubbage. Cuss you, I can see, now, why you was so anxious to make up the deffesit—you wanted to get what money I'd got out of the Nonesuch and one thing or another, and scoop it *all*!"

The king says, timid, and still a snuffling:

"Why, duke, it was you that said make up the deffersit, it warn't me."

"Dry up! I don't want to hear no more *out* of you!" says the duke. "And *now* you see what you *got* by it. They've got all their own money back, and all of *ourn* but a shekel or two, *besides*. G'long to bed—and don't you deffersit *me* no more deffersits, long 's *you* live!"

So the king sneaked into the wigwam, and took to his bottle for comfort; and before long the duke tackled *his* bottle; and so in about a half an hour they was as thick as thieves again, and the tighter they got, the lovinger they got; and went off a snoring in each other's arms. They both got powerful mellow, but I noticed the king didn't get mellow enough to forget to remember to not deny about hiding the money-bag again. That made me feel easy and satisfied. Of course when they got to snoring, we had a long gabble, and I told Jim everything.

XXXI

WE DASN'T stop again at any town, for days and days; kept right along down the river. We was down south in the warm weather, now, and a mighty long ways from home. We begun to come to trees with Spanish moss on them, hanging down from the limbs like long gray beards. It was the first I ever see it growing, and it made the woods look solemn and dismal. So now the frauds reckoned they was out of danger, and they begun to work the villages again.

First they done a lecture on temperance; but they didn't make enough for them both to get drunk on. Then in another village they started a dancing school; but they didn't know no more how to dance than a kangaroo does; so the first prance they made, the general public jumped in and pranced them out of town. Another time they tried a go at yellocution; but they didn't yellocute long till the audience got up and give them a solid good cussing and made them skip out. They tackled missionarying, and mesmerizering, and doctoring, and telling fortunes, and a little of everything; but they couldn't seem to have no luck. So at last they got just about dead broke, and laid around the raft, as she floated along, thinking, and thinking, and never saying nothing, by the half a day at a time, and dreadful blue and desperate.

And at last they took a change, and begun to lay their heads together in the wigwam and talk low and confidential two or three hours at a time. Jim and me got uneasy. We didn't like the look of it. We judged they was studying up some kind of worse deviltry than ever. We turned it over and over, and at last we made up our minds they was going to break into somebody's house or store, or was going into the counterfeit-money business, or something. So then we was pretty scared, and made up an agreement that we wouldn't have nothing in the world to do with such actions, and if we ever got the least show we would give them the cold shake, and clear out and leave them behind. Well, early one morning we hid the raft in a good safe place about two mile below a little bit of a shabby village, named Pikesville, and the king he

went ashore, and told us all to stay hid whilst he went up to
town and smelt around to see if anybody had got any wind
of the Royal Nonesuch there yet. ("House to rob, you
mean," says I to myself; "and when you get through robbing
it you'll come back here and wonder what's become of me
and Jim and the raft—and you'll have to take it out in wondering.") And he said if he warn't back by midday, the duke
and me would know it was all right, and we was to come
along.

So we staid where we was. The duke he fretted and
sweated around, and was in a mighty sour way. He scolded
us for everything, and we couldn't seem to do nothing right;
he found fault with every little thing. Something was a-brew-
ing, sure. I was good and glad when midday come and no
king; we could have a change, anyway—and maybe a chance
for *the* change, on top of it. So me and the duke went up to
the village, and hunted around there for the king, and by-
and-by we found him in the back room of a little low doggery, very tight, and a lot of loafers bullyragging him for
sport, and he a cussing and threatening with all his might,
and so tight he couldn't walk, and couldn't do nothing to
them. The duke he begun to abuse him for an old fool, and
the king begun to sass back; and the minute they was fairly
at it, I lit out, and shook the reefs out of my hind legs, and
spun down the river road like a deer—for I see our chance;
and I made up my mind that it would be a long day before
they ever see me and Jim again. I got down there all out of
breath but loaded up with joy, and sung out—

"Set her loose, Jim, we're all right, now!"

But there warn't no answer, and nobody come out of the
wigwam. Jim was gone! I set up a shout—and then another—and then another one; and run this way and that in
the woods, whooping and screeching; but it warn't no use—
old Jim was gone. Then I set down and cried; I couldn't help
it. But I couldn't set still long. Pretty soon I went out on the
road, trying to think what I better do, and I run across a boy
walking, and asked him if he'd seen a strange nigger, dressed
so and so, and he says:

"Yes."

"Wherebouts?" says I.

"Down to Silas Phelps's place, two mile below here. He's a runaway nigger, and they've got him. Was you looking for him?"

"You bet I ain't! I run across him in the woods about an hour or two ago, and he said if I hollered he'd cut my livers out—and told me to lay down and stay where I was; and I done it. Been there ever since; afeard to come out."

"Well," he says, "you needn't be afeard no more, becuz they've got him. He run off f'm down South, som'ers."

"It's a good job they got him."

"Well, I *reckon*! There's two hunderd dollars reward on him. It's like picking up money out'n the road."

"Yes, it is—and *I* could a had it if I'd been big enough; I see him *first*. Who nailed him?"

"It was an old fellow—a stranger—and he sold out his chance in him for forty dollars, becuz he's got to go up the river and can't wait. Think o' that, now! You bet *I'd* wait, if it was seven year."

"That's me, every time," says I. "But maybe his chance ain't worth no more than that, if he'll sell it so cheap. Maybe there's something ain't straight about it."

"But it *is*, though—straight as a string. I see the handbill myself. It tells all about him, to a dot—paints him like a picture, and tells the plantation he's frum, below Newr*leans*. No-sirree-*bob*, they ain't no trouble 'bout *that* speculation, you bet you. Say, gimme a chaw tobacker, won't ye?"

I didn't have none, so he left. I went to the raft, and set down in the wigwam to think. But I couldn't come to nothing. I thought till I wore my head sore, but I couldn't see no way out of the trouble. After all this long journey, and after all we'd done for them scoundrels, here was it all come to nothing, everything all busted up and ruined, because they could have the heart to serve Jim such a trick as that, and make him a slave again all his life, and amongst strangers, too, for forty dirty dollars.

Once I said to myself it would be a thousand times better for Jim to be a slave at home where his family was, as long as he'd *got* to be a slave, and so I'd better write a letter to Tom Sawyer and tell him to tell Miss Watson where he was. But I soon give up that notion, for two things: she'd be mad and disgusted at his rascality and ungratefulness for leaving her, and so she'd sell him straight down the river again; and if she didn't, everybody naturally despises an ungrateful nigger, and they'd make Jim feel it all the time, and so he'd feel ornery and disgraced. And then think of *me*! It would get all around, that Huck Finn helped a nigger to get his freedom; and if I was to ever see anybody from that town again, I'd be ready to get down and lick his boots for shame. That's just the way: a person does a low-down thing, and then he don't want to take no consequences of it. Thinks as long as he can hide it, it ain't no disgrace. That was my fix exactly. The more I studied about this, the more my conscience went to grinding me, and the more wicked and low-down and ornery I got to feeling. And at last, when it hit me all of a sudden that here was the plain hand of Providence slapping me in the face and letting me know my wickedness was being watched all the time from up there in heaven, whilst I was stealing a poor old woman's nigger that hadn't ever done me no harm, and now was showing me there's One that's always on the lookout, and ain't agoing to allow no such miserable doings to go only just so fur and no further, I most dropped in my tracks I was so scared. Well, I tried the best I could to kinder soften it up somehow for myself, by saying I was brung up wicked, and so I warn't so much to blame; but something inside of me kept saying, "There was the Sunday school, you could a gone to it; and if you'd a done it they'd a learnt you, there, that people that acts as I'd been acting about that nigger goes to everlasting fire."

It made me shiver. And I about made up my mind to pray; and see if I couldn't try to quit being the kind of a boy I was, and be better. So I kneeled down. But the words wouldn't come. Why wouldn't they? It warn't no use to try and hide it from Him. Nor from *me*, neither. I knowed very well why they wouldn't come. It was because my heart warn't right; it was because I warn't square; it was because I was playing double. I was letting *on* to give up sin, but away inside of me I was holding on to the biggest one of all. I was trying to make my mouth *say* I would do the right thing and the clean thing, and go and write to that nigger's owner and tell where he was; but deep down in me

I knowed it was a lie—and He knowed it. You can't pray a lie—I found that out.

So I was full of trouble, full as I could be; and didn't know what to do. At last I had an idea; and I says, I'll go and write the letter—and *then* see if I can pray. Why, it was astonishing, the way I felt as light as a feather, right straight off, and my troubles all gone. So I got a piece of paper and a pencil, all glad and excited, and set down and wrote:

> Miss Watson your runaway nigger Jim is down here two mile below Pikesville and Mr. Phelps has got him and he will give him up for the reward if you send.
>
> Huck Finn.

I felt good and all washed clean of sin for the first time I had ever felt so in my life, and I knowed I could pray now. But I didn't do it straight off, but laid the paper down and set there thinking—thinking how good it was all this happened so, and how near I come to being lost and going to hell. And went on thinking. And got to thinking over our trip down the river; and I see Jim before me, all the time, in the day, and in the night-time, sometimes moonlight, sometimes storms, and we a floating along, talking, and singing, and laughing. But somehow I couldn't seem to strike no places to harden me against him, but only the other kind. I'd see him standing my watch on top of his'n, stead of calling me, so I could go on sleeping; and see him how glad he was when I come back out of the fog; and when I come to him again in the swamp, up there where the feud was; and such-like times; and would always call me honey, and pet me, and do everything he could think of for me, and how good he always was; and at last I struck the time I saved him by telling the men we had small-pox aboard, and he was so grateful, and said I was the best friend old Jim ever had in the world, and the *only* one he's got now; and then I happened to look around, and see that paper.

It was a close place. I took it up, and held it in my hand. I was a trembling, because I'd got to decide, forever, betwixt two things, and I knowed it. I studied a minute, sort of holding my breath, and then says to myself:

"All right, then, I'll *go* to hell"—and tore it up.

It was awful thoughts, and awful words, but they was said. And I let them stay said; and never thought no more about reforming. I shoved the whole thing out of my head; and said I would take up wickedness again, which was in my line, being brung up to it, and the other warn't. And for a starter, I would go to work and steal Jim out of slavery again; and if I could think up anything worse, I would do that, too; because as long as I was in, and in for good, I might as well go the whole hog.

Then I set to thinking over how to get at it, and turned over considerable many ways in my mind; and at last fixed up a plan that suited me. So then I took the bearings of a woody island that was down the river a piece, and as soon as it was fairly dark I crept out with my raft and went for it, and hid it there, and then turned in. I slept the night through, and got up before it was light, and had my breakfast, and put on my store clothes, and tied up some others and one thing or another in a bundle, and took the canoe and cleared for shore. I landed below where I judged was Phelps's place, and hid my bundle in the woods, and then filled up the canoe with water, and loaded rocks into her and sunk her where I could find her again when I wanted her, about a quarter of a mile below a little steam sawmill that was on the bank.

Then I struck up the road, and when I passed the mill I see a sign on it, "Phelps's Sawmill," and when I come to the farm-houses, two or three hundred yards further along, I kept my eyes peeled, but didn't see nobody around, though it was good daylight, now. But I didn't mind, because I didn't want to see nobody just yet—I only wanted to get the lay of the land. According to my plan, I was going to turn up there from the village, not from below. So I just took a look, and shoved along, straight for town. Well, the very first man I see, when I got there, was the duke. He was sticking up a bill for the Royal Nonesuch—three-night performance—like that other time. *They* had the cheek, them frauds! I was right on him, before I could shirk. He looked astonished, and says:

"Hel-*lo!* Where'd *you* come from?" Then he says, kind of glad and eager, "Where's the raft?—got her in a good place?"

I says:

"Why, that's just what I was agoing to ask your grace."

Then he didn't look so joyful—and says:

"What was your idea for asking *me?*" he says.

"Well," I says, "when I see the king in that doggery yesterday, I says to myself, we can't get him home for hours, till he's soberer; so I went a loafing around town to put in the time, and wait. A man up and offered me ten cents to help him pull a skiff over the river and back to fetch a sheep, and so I went along; but when we was dragging him to the boat, and the man left me aholt of the rope and went behind him to shove him along, he was too strong for me, and jerked loose and run, and we after him. We didn't have no dog, and so we had to chase him all over the country till we tired him out. We never got him till dark, then we fetched him over, and I started down for the raft. When I got there and see it was gone, I says to myself, 'they've got into trouble and had to leave; and they've took my nigger, which is the only nigger I've got in the world, and now I'm in a strange country, and ain't got no property no more, nor nothing, and no way to make my living;' so I set down and cried. I slept in the woods all night. But what *did* become of the raft then?—and Jim, poor Jim!"

"Blamed if *I* know—that is, what's become of the raft. That old fool had made a trade and got forty dollars, and when we found him in the doggery the loafers had matched half dollars with him and got every cent but what he'd spent for whisky; and when I got him home late last night and found the raft gone, we said, 'That little rascal has stole our raft and shook us, and run off down the river.' "

"I wouldn't shake my *nigger*, would I?—the only nigger I had in the world, and the only property."

"We never thought of that. Fact is, I reckon we'd come to consider him *our* nigger; yes, we did consider him so—goodness knows we had trouble enough for him. So when we see the raft was gone, and we flat broke, there warn't anything for it but to try the Royal Nonesuch another shake. And I've pegged along ever since, dry as a powder-horn. Where's that ten cents? Give it here."

I had considerable money, so I give him ten cents, but

begged him to spend it for something to eat, and give me some, because it was all the money I had, and I hadn't had nothing to eat since yesterday. He never said nothing. The next minute he whirls on me and says:

"Do you reckon that nigger would blow on us? We'd skin him if he done that!"

"How can he blow? Hain't he run off?"

"No! That old fool sold him, and never divided with me, and the money's gone."

"*Sold* him?" I says, and begun to cry; "why, he was *my* nigger, and that was my money. Where is he?—I want my nigger."

"Well, you can't *get* your nigger, that's all—so dry up your blubbering. Looky here—do you think *you'd* venture to blow on us? Blamed if I think I'd trust you. Why, if you *was* to blow on us——"

He stopped, but I never see the duke look so ugly out of his eyes before. I went on a-whimpering, and says:

"I don't want to blow on nobody; and I ain't got no time to blow, nohow. I got to turn out and find my nigger."

He looked kinder bothered, and stood there with his bills fluttering on his arm, thinking, and wrinkling up his forehead. At last he says:

"I'll tell you something. We got to be here three days. If you'll promise you won't blow, and won't let the nigger blow, I'll tell you where to find him."

So I promised, and he says:

"A farmer by the name of Silas Ph——" and then he stopped. You see he started to tell me the truth; but when he stopped, that way, and begun to study and think again, I reckoned he was changing his mind. And so he was. He wouldn't trust me; he wanted to make sure of having me out of the way the whole three days. So pretty soon he says: "The man that bought him is named Abram Foster—Abram G. Foster—and he lives forty mile back here in the country, on the road to Lafayette."

"All right," I says, "I can walk it in three days. And I'll start this very afternoon."

"No you won't, you'll start *now*; and don't you lose any

time about it, neither, nor do any gabbling by the way. Just
keep a tight tongue in your head and move right along, and
then you won't get into trouble with *us*, d'ye hear?"

That was the order I wanted, and that was the one I played
for. I wanted to be left free to work my plans.

"So clear out," he says; "and you can tell Mr. Foster whatever you want to. Maybe you can get him to believe that Jim
is your nigger—some idiots don't require documents—leastways I've heard there's such down South here. And when you
tell him the handbill and the reward's bogus, maybe he'll believe you when you explain to him what the idea was for
getting 'em out. Go 'long, now, and tell him anything you
want to; but mind you don't work your jaw any *between* here
and there."

So I left, and struck for the back country. I didn't look
around, but I kinder felt like he was watching me. But I
knowed I could tire him out at that. I went straight out in
the country as much as a mile, before I stopped; then I doubled back through the woods towards Phelps's. I reckoned I
better start in on my plan straight off, without fooling
around, because I wanted to stop Jim's mouth till these fellows could get away. I didn't want no trouble with their kind.
I'd seen all I wanted to of them, and wanted to get entirely
shut of them.

XXXII

When I got there it was all still and Sunday-like, and hot and sunshiny—the hands was gone to the fields; and there was them kind of faint dronings of bugs and flies in the air that makes it seem so lonesome and like everybody's dead and gone; and if a breeze fans along and quivers the leaves, it makes you feel mournful, because you feel like it's spirits whispering—spirits that's been dead ever so many years—and you always think they're talking about *you*. As a general thing it makes a body wish *he* was dead, too, and done with it all.

Phelps's was one of these little one-horse cotton plantations; and they all look alike. A rail fence round a two-acre yard; a stile, made out of logs sawed off and up-ended, in steps, like barrels of a different length, to climb over the fence with, and for the women to stand on when they are going to jump onto a horse; some sickly grass-patches in the big yard, but mostly it was bare and smooth, like an old hat with the nap rubbed off; big double log house for the white folks—hewed logs, with the chinks stopped up with mud or mortar, and these mud-stripes been whitewashed some time or another; round-log kitchen, with a big broad, open but roofed passage joining it to the house; log smoke-house back of the kitchen; three little log nigger-cabins in a row t'other side the smoke-house; one little hut all by itself away down against the back fence, and some out-buildings down a piece the other side; ash-hopper, and big kettle to bile soap in, by the little hut; bench by the kitchen door, with bucket of water and a gourd; hound asleep there, in the sun; more hounds asleep, round about; about three shade-trees away off in a corner; some currant bushes and gooseberry bushes in one place by the fence; outside of the fence a garden and a water-melon patch; then the cotton fields begins; and after the fields, the woods.

I went around and clumb over the back stile by the ash-hopper, and started for the kitchen. When I got a little ways, I heard the dim hum of a spinning-wheel wailing along up

and sinking along down again; and then I knowed for certain
I wished I was dead—for that *is* the lonesomest sound in the
whole world.

I went right along, not fixing up any particular plan, but
just trusting to Providence to put the right words in my
mouth when the time come; for I'd noticed that Providence
always did put the right words in my mouth, if I left it alone.

When I got half-way, first one hound and then another got
up and went for me, and of course I stopped and faced them,
and kept still. And such another pow-wow as they made! In
a quarter of a minute I was a kind of a hub of a wheel, as you
may say—spokes made out of dogs—circle of fifteen of them
packed together around me, with their necks and noses
stretched up towards me, a barking and howling; and more a
coming; you could see them sailing over fences and around
corners from everywheres.

A nigger woman come tearing out of the kitchen with a
rolling-pin in her hand, singing out, "Begone! *you* Tige! you
Spot! begone, sah!" and she fetched first one and then another of them a clip and sent him howling, and then the rest
followed; and the next second, half of them come back, wag-
ging their tails around me and making friends with me. There
ain't no harm in a hound, nohow.

And behind the woman comes a little nigger girl and two
little nigger boys, without anything on but tow-linen shirts,
and they hung onto their mother's gown, and peeped out
from behind her at me, bashful, the way they always do. And
here comes the white woman running from the house, about
forty-five or fifty year old, bareheaded, and her spinning-stick
in her hand; and behind her comes her little white children,
acting the same way the little niggers was doing. She was
smiling all over so she could hardly stand—and says:

"It's *you*, at last!—*ain't* it?"

I out with a "Yes'm," before I thought.

She grabbed me and hugged me tight; and then gripped
me by both hands and shook and shook; and the tears come
in her eyes, and run down over; and she couldn't seem to hug
and shake enough, and kept saying, "You don't look as much
like your mother as I reckoned you would, but law sakes, I
don't care for that, I'm *so* glad to see you! Dear, dear, it does

seem like I could eat you up! Children, it's your cousin
Tom!—tell him howdy."

But they ducked their heads, and put their fingers in their
mouths, and hid behind her. So she run on:

"Lize, hurry up and get him a hot breakfast, right away—
or did you get your breakfast on the boat?"

I said I had got it on the boat. So then she started for the
house, leading me by the hand, and the children tagging after.
When we got there, she set me down in a split-bottomed
chair, and set herself down on a little low stool in front of
me, holding both of my hands, and says:

"Now I can have a *good* look at you: and laws-a-me, I've
been hungry for it a many and a many a time, all these long
years, and it's come at last! We been expecting you a couple
of days and more. What's kep' you?—boat get aground?"

"Yes'm—she——"

"Don't say yes'm—say Aunt Sally. Where'd she get
aground?"

I didn't rightly know what to say, because I didn't know
whether the boat would be coming up the river or down. But
I go a good deal on instinct; and my instinct said she would
be coming up—from down towards Orleans. That didn't
help me much, though; for I didn't know the names of bars
down that way. I see I'd got to invent a bar, or forget the
name of the one we got aground on—or— Now I struck an
idea, and fetched it out:

"It warn't the grounding—that didn't keep us back but a
little. We blowed out a cylinder-head."

"Good gracious! anybody hurt?"

"No'm. Killed a nigger."

"Well, it's lucky; because sometimes people do get hurt.
Two years ago last Christmas, your uncle Silas was coming
up from Newrleans on the old *Lally Rook*, and she blowed
out a cylinder-head and crippled a man. And I think he died
afterwards. He was a Babtist. Your uncle Silas knowed a family in Baton Rouge that knowed his people very well. Yes, I
remember, now he *did* die. Mortification set in, and they had
to amputate him. But it didn't save him. Yes, it was mortification—that was it. He turned blue all over, and died in the
hope of a glorious resurrection. They say he was a sight to

look at. Your uncle's been up to the town every day to fetch you. And he's gone again, not more'n an hour ago; he'll be back any minute, now. You must a met him on the road, didn't you?—oldish man, with a——"

"No, I didn't see nobody, Aunt Sally. The boat landed just at daylight, and I left my baggage on the wharf-boat and went looking around the town and out a piece in the country, to put in the time and not get here too soon; and so I come down the back way."

"Who'd you give the baggage to?"

"Nobody."

"Why, child, it'll be stole!"

"Not where I hid it I reckon it won't," I says.

"How'd you get your breakfast so early on the boat?"

It was kinder thin ice, but I says:

"The captain see me standing around, and told me I better have something to eat before I went ashore; so he took me in the texas to the officers' lunch, and give me all I wanted."

I was getting so uneasy I couldn't listen good. I had my mind on the children all the time; I wanted to get them out to one side, and pump them a little, and find out who I was. But I couldn't get no show, Mrs. Phelps kept it up and run on so. Pretty soon she made the cold chills streak all down my back, because she says:

"But here, we're a running on this way, and you hain't told me a word about Sis, nor any of them. Now I'll rest my works a little, and you start up yourn; just tell me *every-thing*—tell me all about 'm all—every one of 'm; and how they are, and what they're doing, and what they told you to tell me; and every last thing you can think of."

Well, I see I was up a stump—and up it good. Providence had stood by me this fur, all right, but I was hard and tight aground, now. I see it warn't a bit of use to try to go ahead— I'd *got* to throw up my hand. So I says to myself, here's another place where I got to resk the truth. I opened my mouth to begin; but she grabbed me and hustled me in behind the bed, and says:

"Here he comes! stick your head down lower—there, that'll do; you can't be seen, now. Don't you let on you're here. I'll play a joke on him. Childern, don't you say a word."

I see I was in a fix, now. But it warn't no use to worry; there warn't nothing to do but just hold still, and try and be ready to stand from under when the lightning struck.

I had just one little glimpse of the old gentleman when he come in, then the bed hid him. Mrs. Phelps she jumps for him and says:

"Has he come?"

"No," says her husband.

"Good-*ness* gracious!" she says, "what in the world *can* have become of him?"

"I can't imagine," says the old gentleman; "and I must say, it makes me dreadful uneasy."

"Uneasy!" she says, "I'm ready to go distracted! He *must* a come; and you've missed him along the road. I *know* it's so—something *tells* me so."

"Why Sally, I *couldn't* miss him along the road—*you* know that."

"But oh, dear, dear, what *will* Sis say! He must a come! You must a missed him. He——"

"Oh, don't distress me any more'n I'm already distressed. I don't know what in the world to make of it. I'm at my wit's end, and I don't mind acknowledging 't I'm right down scared. But there's no hope that he's come; for he *couldn't* come and me miss him. Sally, it's terrible—just terrible—something's happened to the boat, sure!"

"Why, Silas! Look yonder!—up the road!—ain't that somebody coming?"

He sprung to the window at the head of the bed, and that give Mrs. Phelps the chance she wanted. She stooped down quick, at the foot of the bed, and give me a pull, and out I come; and when he turned back from the window, there she stood, a-beaming and a-smiling like a house afire, and I standing pretty meek and sweaty alongside. The old gentleman stared, and says:

"Why, who's that?"

"Who do you reckon 't is?"

"I haint no idea. Who *is* it?"

"It's *Tom Sawyer*!"

By jings, I most slumped through the floor. But there warn't no time to swap knives; the old man grabbed me by

the hand and shook, and kept on shaking; and all the time,
how the woman did dance around and laugh and cry; and
then how they both did fire off questions about Sid, and
Mary, and the rest of the tribe.

But if they was joyful, it warn't nothing to what I was; for
it was like being born again, I was so glad to find out who I
was. Well, they froze to me for two hours; and at last when
my chin was so tired it couldn't hardly go, any more, I had
told them more about my family—I mean the Sawyer family—than ever happened to any six Sawyer families. And I
explained all about how we blowed out a cylinder-head at the
mouth of White River and it took us three days to fix it.
Which was all right, and worked first rate; because *they* didn't
know but what it would take three days to fix it. If I'd a called
it a bolt-head it would a done just as well.

Now I was feeling pretty comfortable all down one side,
and pretty uncomfortable all up the other. Being Tom Sawyer
was easy and comfortable; and it stayed easy and comfortable
till by-and-by I hear a steamboat coughing along down the
river—then I says to myself, spose Tom Sawyer come down
on that boat?—and spose he steps in here, any minute, and
sings out my name before I can throw him a wink to keep
quiet? Well, I couldn't *have* it that way—it wouldn't do at
all. I must go up the road and waylay him. So I told the folks
I reckoned I would go up to the town and fetch down my
baggage. The old gentleman was for going along with me,
but I said no, I could drive the horse myself, and I druther he
wouldn't take no trouble about me.

XXXIII

So I STARTED for town, in the wagon, and when I was half-way I see a wagon coming, and sure enough it was Tom Sawyer, and I stopped and waited till he come along. I says "Hold on!" and it stopped alongside, and his mouth opened up like a trunk, and staid so; and he swallowed two or three times like a person that's got a dry throat, and then says:

"I hain't ever done you no harm. You know that. So then, what you want to come back and ha'nt *me* for?"

I says:

"I hain't come back—I hain't been *gone*."

When he heard my voice, it righted him up some, but he warn't quite satisfied yet. He says:

"Don't you play nothing on me, because I wouldn't on you. Honest injun, now, you ain't a ghost?"

"Honest injun, I ain't," I says.

"Well—I—I—well, that ought to settle it, of course; but I can't somehow seem to understand it, no way. Looky here, warn't you ever murdered *at all?*"

"No. I warn't ever murdered at all—I played it on them. You come in here and feel of me if you don't believe me."

So he done it; and it satisfied him; and he was that glad to see me again, he didn't know what to do. And he wanted to know all about it right off; because it was a grand adventure, and mysterious, and so it hit him where he lived. But I said, leave it alone till by-and-by; and told his driver to wait, and we drove off a little piece, and I told him the kind of a fix I was in, and what did he reckon we better do? He said, let him alone a minute, and don't disturb him. So he thought and thought, and pretty soon he says:

"It's all right, I've got it. Take my trunk in your wagon, and let on it's your'n; and you turn back and fool along slow, so as to get to the house about the time you ought to; and I'll go towards town a piece, and take a fresh start, and get there a quarter or a half an hour after you; and you needn't let on to know me, at first."

I says:

"All right; but wait a minute. There's one more thing—a thing that *nobody* don't know but me. And that is, there's a nigger here that I'm a trying to steal out of slavery—and his name is *Jim*—old Miss Watson's Jim."

He says:

"What! Why Jim is——"

He stopped and went to studying. I says:

"*I* know what you'll say. You'll say it's dirty low-down business; but what if it is?—*I*'m low down; and I'm agoing to steal him, and I want you to keep mum and not let on. Will you?"

His eye lit up, and he says:

"I'll *help* you steal him!"

Well, I let go all holts then, like I was shot. It was the most astonishing speech I ever heard—and I'm bound to say Tom Sawyer fell, considerable, in my estimation. Only I couldn't believe it. Tom Sawyer a *nigger stealer*!

"Oh, shucks," I says, "you're joking."

"I ain't joking, either."

"Well, then," I says, "joking or no joking, if you hear anything said about a runaway nigger, don't forget to remember that *you* don't know nothing about him, and *I* don't know nothing about him."

Then we took the trunk and put it in my wagon, and he drove off his way, and I drove mine. But of course I forgot all about driving slow, on accounts of being glad and full of thinking; so I got home a heap too quick for that length of a trip. The old gentleman was at the door, and he says:

"Why, this is wonderful. Who ever would a thought it was in that mare to do it. I wish we'd a timed her. And she hain't sweated a hair—not a hair. It's wonderful. Why, I wouldn't take a hunderd dollars for that horse now; I wouldn't, honest; and yet I'd a sold her for fifteen before, and thought 'twas all she was worth."

That's all he said. He was the innocentest, best old soul I ever see. But it warn't surprising; because he warn't only just a farmer, he was a preacher, too, and had a little one-horse log church down back of the plantation, which he built it himself at his own expense, for a church and school-house, and never charged nothing for his preaching, and it was worth it, too. There was plenty other farmer-preachers like that, and done the same way, down South.

In about half an hour Tom's wagon drove up to the front stile, and Aunt Sally she see it through the window because it was only about fifty yards, and says:

"Why, there's somebody come! I wonder who 'tis? Why, I do believe it's a stranger. Jimmy" (that's one of the children), "run and tell Lize to put on another plate for dinner."

Everybody made a rush for the front door, because, of course, a stranger don't come *every* year, and so he lays over the yaller fever, for interest, when he does come. Tom was over the stile and starting for the house; the wagon was spinning up the road for the village, and we was all bunched in the front door. Tom had his store clothes on, and an audience—and that was always nuts for Tom Sawyer. In them circumstances it warn't no trouble to him to throw in an amount of style that was suitable. He warn't a boy to meeky along up that yard like a sheep; no, he come ca'm and important, like the ram. When he got afront of us, he lifts his hat ever so gracious and dainty, like it was the lid of a box that had butterflies asleep in it and he didn't want to disturb them, and says:

"Mr. Archibald Nichols, I presume?"

"No, my boy," says the old gentleman, "I'm sorry to say 't your driver has deceived you; Nichols's place is down a matter of three mile more. Come in, come in."

Tom he took a look back over his shoulder, and says, "Too late—he's out of sight."

"Yes, he's gone, my son, and you must come in and eat your dinner with us; and then we'll hitch up and take you down to Nichols's."

"Oh, I *can't* make you so much trouble; I couldn't think of it. I'll walk—I don't mind the distance."

"But we won't *let* you walk—it wouldn't be Southern hospitality to do it. Come right in."

"Oh, *do*," says Aunt Sally; "it ain't a bit of trouble to us, not a bit in the world. You *must* stay. It's a long, dusty three mile, and we *can't* let you walk. And besides, I've already told 'em to put on another plate, when I see you coming; so you mustn't disappoint us. Come right in, and make yourself at home."

So Tom he thanked them very hearty and handsome, and let himself be persuaded, and come in; and when he was in, he said he was a stranger from Hicksville, Ohio, and his name was William Thompson—and he made another bow.

Well, he run on, and on, and on, making up stuff about Hicksville and everybody in it he could invent, and I getting a little nervous, and wondering how this was going to help me out of my scrape; and at last, still talking along, he reached over and kissed Aunt Sally right on the mouth, and then settled back again in his chair, comfortable, and was going on talking; but she jumped up and wiped it off with the back of her hand, and says:

"You owdacious puppy!"

He looked kind of hurt, and says:

"I'm surprised at you, m'am."

"You're s'rp— Why, what do you reckon *I* am? I've a good notion to take and—say, what do you mean by kissing me?"

He looked kind of humble, and says:

"I didn't mean nothing, m'am. I didn't mean no harm. I—I—thought you'd like it."

"Why, you born fool!" She took up the spinning-stick, and it looked like it was all she could do to keep from giving him a crack with it. "What made you think I'd like it?"

"Well, I don't know. Only, they—they—told me you would."

"*They* told you I would. Whoever told you 's *another* lunatic. I never heard the beat of it. Who's *they*?"

"Why—everybody. They all said so, m'am."

It was all she could do to hold in; and her eyes snapped, and her fingers worked like she wanted to scratch him; and she says:

"Who's 'everybody?' Out with their names—or ther'll be an idiot short."

He got up and looked distressed, and fumbled his hat, and says:

"I'm sorry, and I warn't expecting it. They told me to. They all told me to. They all said kiss her; and said she'll like it.

They all said it—every one of them. But I'm sorry, m'am, and I won't do it no more—I won't, honest."

"You won't, won't you? Well, I sh'd *reckon* you won't!"

"No'm, I'm honest about it; I won't ever do it again. Till you ask me."

"Till I *ask* you! Well, I never see the beat of it in my born days! I lay you'll be the Methusalem-numskull of creation before ever *I* ask you—or the likes of you."

"Well," he says, "it does surprise me so. I can't make it out, somehow. They said you would, and I thought you would. But—" He stopped and looked around slow, like he wished he could run across a friendly eye, somewhere's; and fetched up on the old gentleman's, and says, "Didn't *you* think she'd like me to kiss her, sir?"

"Why, no, I—I—well, no, I b'lieve I didn't."

Then he looks on around, the same way, to me—and says:

"Tom, didn't *you* think Aunt Sally 'd open out her arms and say, 'Sid Sawyer——' "

"My land!" she says, breaking in and jumping for him, "you impudent young rascal, to fool a body so—" and was going to hug him, but he fended her off, and says:

"No, not till you've asked me, first."

So she didn't lose no time, but asked him; and hugged him and kissed him, over and over again, and then turned him over to the old man, and he took what was left. And after they got a little quiet again, she says:

"Why, dear me, I never see such a surprise. We warn't looking for *you*, at all, but only Tom. Sis never wrote to me about anybody coming but him."

"It's because it warn't *intended* for any of us to come but Tom," he says; "but I begged and begged, and at the last minute she let me come, too; so, coming down the river, me and Tom thought it would be a first-rate surprise for him to come here to the house first, and for me to by-and-by tag along and drop in and let on to be a stranger. But it was a mistake, Aunt Sally. This ain't no healthy place for a stranger to come."

"No—not impudent whelps, Sid. You ought to had your jaws boxed; I hain't been so put out since I don't know when. But I don't care, I don't mind the terms—I'd be willing to

stand a thousand such jokes to have you here. Well, to think
of that performance! I don't deny it, I was most putrified with
astonishment when you give me that smack."

We had dinner out in that broad open passage betwixt the
house and the kitchen; and there was things enough on that
table for seven families—and all hot, too; none of your flabby
tough meat that's laid in a cupboard in a damp cellar all night
and tastes like a hunk of old cold cannibal in the morning.
Uncle Silas he asked a pretty long blessing over it, but it was
worth it; and it didn't cool it a bit, neither, the way I've seen
them kind of interruptions do, lots of times.

There was a considerable good deal of talk, all the afternoon, and me and Tom was on the lookout all the time, but
it warn't no use, they didn't happen to say nothing about any
runaway nigger, and we was afraid to try to work up to it.
But at supper, at night, one of the little boys says:

"Pa, mayn't Tom and Sid and me go to the show?"

"No," says the old man, "I reckon there ain't going to be
any; and you couldn't go if there was; because the runaway
nigger told Burton and me all about that scandalous show,
and Burton said he would tell the people; so I reckon they've
drove the owdacious loafers out of town before this time."

So there it was!—but *I* couldn't help it. Tom and me was
to sleep in the same room and bed; so, being tired, we bid
good-night and went up to bed, right after supper, and clumb
out of the window and down the lightning-rod, and shoved
for the town; for I didn't believe anybody was going to give
the king and the duke a hint, and so, if I didn't hurry up and
give them one they'd get into trouble sure.

On the road Tom he told me all about how it was reckoned
I was murdered, and how pap disappeared, pretty soon, and
didn't come back no more, and what a stir there was when
Jim run away; and I told Tom all about our Royal Nonesuch
rapscallions, and as much of the raft-voyage as I had time to;
and as we struck into the town and up through the middle of
it—it was as much as half-after eight, then—here comes a
raging rush of people, with torches, and an awful whooping
and yelling, and banging tin pans and blowing horns: and we
jumped to one side to let them go by; and as they went by,
I see they had the king and the duke astraddle of a rail—that

is, I knowed it *was* the king and the duke, though they was all over tar and feathers, and didn't look like nothing in the world that was human—just looked like a couple of monstrous big soldier-plumes. Well, it made me sick to see it; and I was sorry for them poor pitiful rascals, it seemed like I couldn't ever feel any hardness against them any more in the world. It was a dreadful thing to see. Human beings *can* be awful cruel to one another.

We see we was too late—couldn't do no good. We asked some stragglers about it, and they said everybody went to the show looking very innocent; and laid low and kept dark till the poor old king was in the middle of his cavortings on the stage; then somebody give a signal, and the house rose up and went for them.

So we poked along back home, and I warn't feeling so brash as I was before, but kind of ornery, and humble, and to blame, somehow—though *I* hadn't done nothing. But that's always the way; it don't make no difference whether you do right or wrong, a person's conscience ain't got no sense, and just goes for him *anyway*. If I had a yaller dog that didn't know no more than a person's conscience does, I would pison him. It takes up more room than all the rest of a person's insides, and yet ain't no good, nohow. Tom Sawyer he says the same.

XXXIV

W E STOPPED TALKING, and got to thinking.
   By-and-by Tom says:

"Looky here, Huck, what fools we are, to not think of it before! I bet I know where Jim is."

"No! Where?"

"In that hut down by the ash-hopper. Why, looky here. When we was at dinner, didn't you see a nigger man go in there with some vittles?"

"Yes."

"What did you think the vittles was for?"

"For a dog."

"So'd I. Well, it wasn't for a dog."

"Why?"

"Because part of it was watermelon."

"So it was—I noticed it. Well, it does beat all, that I never thought about a dog not eating watermelon. It shows how a body can see and don't see at the same time."

"Well, the nigger unlocked the padlock when he went in, and he locked it again when he come out. He fetched uncle a key, about the time we got up from table—same key, I bet. Watermelon shows man, lock shows prisoner; and it ain't likely there's two prisoners on such a little plantation, and where the people's all so kind and good. Jim's the prisoner. All right—I'm glad we found it out detective fashion; I wouldn't give shucks for any other way. Now you work your mind and study out a plan to steal Jim, and I will study out one, too; and we'll take the one we like the best."

What a head for just a boy to have! If I had Tom Sawyer's head, I wouldn't trade it off to be a duke, nor mate of a steamboat, nor clown in a circus, nor nothing I can think of. I went to thinking out a plan, but only just to be doing something; I knowed very well where the right plan was going to come from. Pretty soon, Tom says:

"Ready?"

"Yes," I says.

"All right—bring it out."

"My plan is this," I says. "We can easy find out if it's Jim in there. Then get up my canoe to-morrow night, and fetch my raft over from the island. Then the first dark night that comes, steal the key out of the old man's britches, after he goes to bed, and shove off down the river on the raft, with Jim, hiding day-times and running nights, the way me and Jim used to do before. Wouldn't that plan work?"

"*Work?* Why cert'nly, it would work, like rats a fighting. But it's too blame' simple; there ain't nothing *to* it. What's the good of a plan that ain't no more trouble than that? It's as mild as goose-milk. Why, Huck, it wouldn't make no more talk than breaking into a soap factory."

I never said nothing, because I warn't expecting nothing different; but I knowed mighty well that whenever he got *his* plan ready it wouldn't have none of them objections to it.

And it didn't. He told me what it was, and I see in a minute it was worth fifteen of mine, for style, and would make Jim just as free a man as mine would, and maybe get us all killed besides. So I was satisfied, and said we would waltz in on it. I needn't tell what it was, here, because I knowed it wouldn't stay the way it was. I knowed he would be changing it around, every which way, as we went along, and heaving in new bullinesses wherever he got a chance. And that is what he done.

Well, one thing was dead sure; and that was, that Tom Sawyer was in earnest and was actuly going to help steal that nigger out of slavery. That was the thing that was too many for me. Here was a boy that was respectable, and well brung up; and had a character to lose; and folks at home that had characters; and he was bright and not leather-headed; and knowing and not ignorant; and not mean, but kind; and yet here he was, without any more pride, or rightness, or feeling, than to stoop to this business, and make himself a shame, and his family a shame, before everybody. I *couldn't* understand it, no way at all. It was outrageous, and I knowed I ought to just up and tell him so; and so be his true friend, and let him quit the thing right where he was, and save himself. And I *did* start to tell him; but he shut me up, and says:

"Don't you reckon I know what I'm about? Don't I generly know what I'm about?"

"Yes."

"Didn't I *say* I was going to help steal the nigger?"

"Yes."

"*Well* then."

That's all he said, and that's all I said. It warn't no use to say any more; because when he said he'd do a thing, he always done it. But *I* couldn't make out how he was willing to go into this thing; so I just let it go, and never bothered no more about it. If he was bound to have it so, *I* couldn't help it.

When we got home, the house was all dark and still; so we went on down to the hut by the ash-hopper, for to examine it. We went through the yard, so as to see what the hounds would do. They knowed us, and didn't make no more noise than country dogs is always doing when anything comes by in the night. When we got to the cabin, we took a look at the front and the two sides; and on the side I warn't acquainted with—which was the north side—we found a square window-hole, up tolerable high, with just one stout board nailed across it. I says:

"Here's the ticket. This hole's big enough for Jim to get through, if we wrench off the board."

Tom says:

"It's as simple as tit-tat-toe, three-in-a-row, and as easy as playing hooky. I should *hope* we can find a way that's a little more complicated than *that*, Huck Finn."

"Well then," I says, "how'll it do to saw him out, the way I done before I was murdered, that time?"

"That's more *like*," he says. "It's real mysterious, and troublesome, and good," he says; "but I bet we can find a way that's twice as long. There ain't no hurry; le's keep on looking around."

Betwixt the hut and the fence, on the back side, was a lean-to, that joined the hut at the eaves, and was made out of plank. It was as long as the hut, but narrow—only about six foot wide. The door to it was at the south end, and was padlocked. Tom he went to the soap kettle, and searched around and fetched back the iron thing they lift the lid with; so he took it and prized out one of the staples. The chain fell down, and we opened the door and went in, and shut it, and struck a match, and see the shed was only built against the cabin and hadn't no connection with it; and there warn't no floor to the shed, nor nothing in it but some old rusty played-out hoes, and spades, and picks, and a crippled plow. The match went out, and so did we, and shoved in the staple again, and the door was locked as good as ever. Tom was joyful. He says:

"Now we're all right. We'll *dig* him out. It'll take about a week!"

Then we started for the house, and I went in the back door—you only have to pull a buckskin latch-string, they don't fasten the doors—but that warn't romantical enough for Tom Sawyer: no way would do him but he must climb up the lightning-rod. But after he got up half-way about three times, and missed fire and fell every time, and the last time most busted his brains out, he thought he'd got to give it up; but after he was rested, he allowed he would give her one more turn for luck, and this time he made the trip.

In the morning we was up at break of day, and down to the nigger cabins to pet the dogs and make friends with the nigger that fed Jim—if it *was* Jim that was being fed. The niggers was just getting through breakfast and starting for the fields; and Jim's nigger was piling up a tin pan with bread and meat and things; and whilst the others was leaving, the key come from the house.

This nigger had a good-natured, chuckle-headed face, and his wool was all tied up in little bunches with thread. That was to keep witches off. He said the witches was pestering him awful, these nights, and making him see all kinds of strange things, and hear all kinds of strange words and noises, and he didn't believe he was ever witched so long, before, in his life. He got so worked up, and got to running on so about his troubles, he forgot all about what he'd been agoing to do. So Tom says:

"What's the vittles for? Going to feed the dogs?"

The nigger kind of smiled around gradully over his face, like when you heave a brickbat in a mud puddle, and he says:

"Yes, Mars Sid, *a* dog. Cur'us dog, too. Does you want to go en look at 'im?"

"Yes."

I hunched Tom, and whispers:

"You going, right here in the day-break? *That* warn't the plan."

"No, it warn't—but it's the plan *now*."

So, drat him, we went along, but I didn't like it much. When we got in, we couldn't hardly see anything, it was so dark; but Jim was there, sure enough, and could see us; and he sings out:

"Why, *Huck*! En good *lan'*! ain' dat Misto Tom?"

I just knowed how it would be; I just expected it. *I* didn't know nothing to do; and if I had, I couldn't a done it; because that nigger busted in and says:

"Why, de gracious sakes! do he know you genlmen?"

We could see pretty well, now. Tom he looked at the nigger, steady and kind of wondering, and says:

"Does *who* know us?"

"Why, dish-yer runaway nigger."

"I don't reckon he does; but what put that into your head?"

"What *put* it dar? Didn' he jis' dis minute sing out like he knowed you?"

Tom says, in a puzzled-up kind of way:

"Well, that's mighty curious. *Who* sung out? *When* did he sing out? *What* did he sing out?" And turns to me, perfectly c'am, and says, "Did *you* hear anybody sing out?"

Of course there warn't nothing to be said but the one thing; so I says:

"No; *I* ain't heard nobody say nothing."

Then he turns to Jim, and looks him over like he never see him before; and says:

"Did you sing out?"

"No, sah," says Jim; "*I* hain't said nothing, sah."

"Not a word?"

"No, sah, I hain't said a word."

"Did you ever see us before?"

"No, sah; not as *I* knows on."

So Tom turns to the nigger, which was looking wild and distressed, and says, kind of severe:

"What do you reckon's the matter with you, anyway? What made you think somebody sung out?"

"Oh, it's de dad-blame' witches, sah, en I wisht I was dead, I do. Dey's awluz at it, sah, en dey do mos' kill me, dey

sk'yers me so. Please to don't tell nobody 'bout it sah, er ole
Mars Silas he'll scole me; 'kase he say dey *ain't* no witches. I
jis' wish to goodness he was heah now—*den* what would he
say! I jis' bet he couldn' fine no way to git aroun' it *dis* time.
But it's awluz jis' so; people dat's *sot*, stays sot; dey won't
look into nothin' en fine it out f'r deyselves, en when *you* fine
it out en tell um 'bout it, dey doan' b'lieve you."

Tom give him a dime, and said we wouldn't tell nobody;
and told him to buy some more thread to tie up his wool
with; and then looks at Jim, and says:

"I wonder if Uncle Silas is going to hang this nigger. If I
was to catch a nigger that was ungrateful enough to run
away, *I* wouldn't give him up, I'd hang him." And whilst the
nigger stepped to the door to look at the dime and bite it to
see if it was good, he whispers to Jim, and says:

"Don't ever let on to know us. And if you hear any digging
going on nights, it's us: we're going to set you free."

Jim only had time to grab us by the hand and squeeze it,
then the nigger come back, and we said we'd come again
some time if the nigger wanted us to; and he said he would,
more particular if it was dark, because the witches went for
him mostly in the dark, and it was good to have folks around
then.

XXXV

I̲T WOULD BE most an hour, yet, till breakfast, so we left, and struck down into the woods; because Tom said we got to have *some* light to see how to dig by, and a lantern makes too much, and might get us into trouble; what we must have was a lot of them rotten chunks that's called fox-fire and just makes a soft kind of a glow when you lay them in a dark place. We fetched an armful and hid it in the weeds, and set down to rest, and Tom says, kind of dissatisfied:

"Blame it, this whole thing is just as easy and awkard as it can be. And so it makes it so rotten difficult to get up a difficult plan. There ain't no watchman to be drugged—now there *ought* to be a watchman. There ain't even a dog to give a sleeping-mixture to. And there's Jim chained by one leg, with a ten-foot chain, to the leg of his bed: why, all you got to do is to lift up the bedstead and slip off the chain. And Uncle Silas he trusts everybody; sends the key to the punkin-headed nigger, and don't send nobody to watch the nigger. Jim could a got out of that window hole before this, only there wouldn't be no use trying to travel with a ten-foot chain on his leg. Why, drat it, Huck, it's the stupidest arrangement I ever see. You got to invent *all* the difficulties. Well, we can't help it, we got to do the best we can with the materials we've got. Anyhow, there's one thing—there's more honor in getting him out through a lot of difficulties and dangers, where there warn't one of them furnished to you by the people who it was their duty to furnish them, and you had to contrive them all out of your own head. Now look at just that one thing of the lantern. When you come down to the cold facts, we simply got to *let on* that a lantern's resky. Why, we could work with a torchlight procession if we wanted to, *I* believe. Now, whilst I think of it, we got to hunt up something to make a saw out of, the first chance we get."

"What do we want of a saw?"

"What do we *want* of it? Hain't we got to saw the leg of Jim's bed off, so as to get the chain loose?"

"Why, you just said a body could lift up the bedstead and slip the chain off."

"Well, if that ain't just like you, Huck Finn. You *can* get up the infant-schooliest ways of going at a thing. Why, hain't you ever read any books at all?—Baron Trenck, nor Casanova, nor Benvenuto Chelleeny, nor Henri IV., nor none of them heroes? Whoever heard of getting a prisoner loose in such an old-maidy way as that? No; the way all the best authorities does, is to saw the bed-leg in two, and leave it just so, and swallow the sawdust, so it can't be found, and put some dirt and grease around the sawed place so the very keenest seneskal can't see no sign of it's being sawed, and thinks the bed-leg is perfectly sound. Then, the night you're ready, fetch the leg a kick, down she goes; slip off your chain, and there you are. Nothing to do but hitch your rope-ladder to the battlements, shin down it, break your leg in the moat—because a rope-ladder is nineteen foot too short, you know—and there's your horses and your trusty vassles, and they scoop you up and fling you across a saddle and away you go, to your native Langudoce, or Navarre, or wherever it is. It's gaudy, Huck. I wish there was a moat to this cabin. If we get time, the night of the escape, we'll dig one."

I says:

"What do we want of a moat, when we're going to snake him out from under the cabin?"

But he never heard me. He had forgot me and everything else. He had his chin in his hand, thinking. Pretty soon, he sighs, and shakes his head; then sighs again, and says:

"No, it wouldn't do—there ain't necessity enough for it."

"For what?" I says.

"Why, to saw Jim's leg off," he says.

"Good land!" I says, "why, there ain't *no* necessity for it. And what would you want to saw his leg off for, anyway?"

"Well, some of the best authorities has done it. They couldn't get the chain off, so they just cut their hand off, and shoved. And a leg would be better still. But we got to let that go. There ain't necessity enough in this case; and besides, Jim's a nigger and wouldn't understand the reasons for it, and how it's the custom in Europe; so we'll let it go. But there's one thing—he can have a rope-ladder; we can tear up our sheets and make him a rope-ladder easy enough. And we can send it to him in a pie; it's mostly done that way. And I've et worse pies."

"Why, Tom Sawyer, how you talk," I says; "Jim ain't got no use for a rope-ladder."

"He *has* got use for it. How *you* talk, you better say; you don't know nothing about it. He's *got* to have a rope ladder; they all do."

"What in the nation can he *do* with it?"

"*Do* with it? He can hide it in his bed, can't he? That's what they all do; and *he's* got to, too. Huck, you don't ever seem to want to do anything that's regular; you want to be starting something fresh all the time. Spose he *don't* do nothing with it? ain't it there in his bed, for a clew, after he's gone? and don't you reckon they'll want clews? Of course they will. And you wouldn't leave them any? That would be a *pretty* howdy-do, *wouldn't* it! I never heard of such a thing."

"Well," I says, "if it's in the regulations, and he's got to have it, all right, let him have it; because I don't wish to go back on no regulations; but there's one thing, Tom Sawyer— if we go to tearing up our sheets to make Jim a rope-ladder, we're going to get into trouble with Aunt Sally, just as sure as you're born. Now, the way I look at it, a hickry-bark ladder don't cost nothing, and don't waste nothing, and is just as good to load up a pie with, and hide in a straw tick, as any rag ladder you can start; and as for Jim, he ain't had no experience, and so *he* don't care what kind of a——"

"Oh, shucks, Huck Finn, if I was as ignorant as you, I'd keep still—that's what *I'd* do. Who ever heard of a state prisoner escaping by a hickry-bark ladder? Why, it's perfectly ridiculous."

"Well, all right, Tom, fix it your own way; but if you'll take my advice, you'll let me borrow a sheet off of the clothes-line."

He said that would do. And that give him another idea, and he says:

"Borrow a shirt, too."

"What do we want of a shirt, Tom?"

"Want it for Jim to keep a journal on."

"Journal your granny—*Jim* can't write."

"Spose he *can't* write—he can make marks on the shirt, can't he, if we make him a pen out of an old pewter spoon or a piece of an old iron barrel-hoop?"

"Why, Tom, we can pull a feather out of a goose and make him a better one; and quicker, too."

"*Prisoners* don't have geese running around the donjon-keep to pull pens out of, you muggins. They *always* make their pens out of the hardest, toughest, troublesomest piece of old brass candlestick or something like that they can get their hands on; and it takes them weeks and weeks, and months and months to file it out, too, because they've got to do it by rubbing it on the wall. *They* wouldn't use a goose-quill if they had it. It ain't regular."

"Well, then, what'll we make him the ink out of?"

"Many makes it out of iron-rust and tears; but that's the common sort and women; the best authorities uses their own blood. Jim can do that; and when he wants to send any little common ordinary mysterious message to let the world know where he's captivated, he can write it on the bottom of a tin plate with a fork and throw it out of the window. The Iron Mask always done that, and it's a blame' good way, too."

"Jim ain't got no tin plates. They feed him in a pan."

"That ain't anything; we can get him some."

"Can't nobody *read* his plates."

"That ain't got nothing to *do* with it, Huck Finn. All *he's* got to do is to write on the plate and throw it out. You don't *have* to be able to read it. Why, half the time you can't read anything a prisoner writes on a tin plate, or anywhere else."

"Well, then, what's the sense in wasting the plates?"

"Why, blame it all, it ain't the *prisoner's* plates."

"But it's *somebody's* plates, ain't it?"

"Well, spos'n it is? What does the *prisoner* care whose——"

He broke off there, because we heard the breakfast-horn blowing. So we cleared out for the house.

Along during that morning I borrowed a sheet and a white shirt off of the clothes-line; and I found an old sack and put them in it, and we went down and got the fox-fire, and put that in too. I called it borrowing, because that was what pap always called it; but Tom said it warn't borrowing, it was stealing. He said we was representing prisoners; and prisoners

don't care how they get a thing so they get it, and nobody
don't blame them for it, either. It ain't no crime in a prisoner
to steal the thing he needs to get away with, Tom said; it's
his right; and so, as long as we was representing a prisoner,
we had a perfect right to steal anything on this place we had
the least use for, to get ourselves out of prison with. He said
if we warn't prisoners it would be a very different thing, and
nobody but a mean ornery person would steal when he warn't
a prisoner. So we allowed we would steal everything there
was that come handy. And yet he made a mighty fuss, one
day, after that, when I stole a watermelon out of the nigger
patch and eat it; and he made me go and give the niggers a
dime, without telling them what it was for. Tom said that
what he meant was, we could steal anything we *needed*. Well,
I says, I needed the watermelon. But he said I didn't need it
to get out of prison with, there's where the difference was.
He said if I'd a wanted it to hide a knife in, and smuggle it
to Jim to kill the seneskal with, it would a been all right. So
I let it go at that, though I couldn't see no advantage in my
representing a prisoner, if I got to set down and chaw over a
lot of gold-leaf distinctions like that, every time I see a chance
to hog a watermelon.

Well, as I was saying, we waited that morning till everybody was settled down to business, and nobody in sight
around the yard; then Tom he carried the sack into the lean-
to whilst I stood off a piece to keep watch. By-and-by he
come out, and we went and set down on the wood-pile, to
talk. He says:

"Everything's all right, now, except tools: and that's easy
fixed."

"Tools?" I says.

"Yes."

"Tools for what?"

"Why, to dig with. We ain't agoing to *gnaw* him out, are
we?"

"Ain't them old crippled picks and things in there good
enough to dig a nigger out with?" I says.

He turns on me looking pitying enough to make a body
cry, and says:

"Huck Finn, did you *ever* hear of a prisoner having picks

and shovels, and all the modern conveniences in his wardrobe to dig himself out with? Now I want to ask you—if you got any reasonableness in you at all—what kind of a show would *that* give him to be a hero? Why, they might as well lend him the key, and done with it. Picks and shovels—why they wouldn't furnish 'em to a king."

"Well, then," I says, "if we don't want the picks and shovels, what do we want?"

"A couple of case-knives."

"To dig the foundations out from under that cabin with?"

"Yes."

"Confound it, it's foolish, Tom."

"It don't make no difference how foolish it is, it's the *right* way—and it's the regular way. And there ain't no *other* way, that ever *I* heard of, and I've read all the books that gives any information about these things. They always dig out with a case-knife—and not through dirt, mind you; generly it's through solid rock. And it takes them weeks and weeks and weeks, and for ever and ever. Why, look at one of them prisoners in the bottom dungeon of the Castle Deef, in the harbor of Marseilles, that dug himself out that way; how long was *he* at it, you reckon?"

"I don't know."

"Well, guess."

"I don't know. A month and a half?"

"*Thirty-seven year*—and he come out in China. *That's* the kind. I wish the bottom of *this* fortress was solid rock."

"*Jim* don't know nobody in China."

"What's *that* got to do with it? Neither did that other fellow. But you're always a-wandering off on a side issue. Why can't you stick to the main point?"

"All right—*I* don't care where he comes out, so he *comes* out; and Jim don't, either, I reckon. But there's one thing, anyway—Jim's too old to be dug out with a case-knife. He won't last."

"Yes he will *last*, too. You don't reckon it's going to take thirty-seven years to dig out through a *dirt* foundation, do you?"

"How long will it take, Tom?"

"Well, we can't resk being as long as we ought to, because

it mayn't take very long for Uncle Silas to hear from down
there by New Orleans. He'll hear Jim ain't from there. Then
his next move will be to advertise Jim, or something like that.
So we can't resk being as long digging him out as we ought
to. By rights I reckon we ought to be a couple of years; but
we can't. Things being so uncertain, what I recommend is
this: that we really dig right in, as quick as we can; and after
that, we can *let on*, to ourselves, that we was at it thirty-seven
years. Then we can snatch him out and rush him away the
first time there's an alarm. Yes, I reckon that'll be the best
way."

"Now, there's *sense* in that," I says. "Letting on don't cost
nothing; letting on ain't no trouble; and if it's any object, I
don't mind letting on we was at it a hundred and fifty year.
It wouldn't strain me none, after I got my hand in. So I'll
mosey along now, and smouch a couple of case-knives."

"Smouch three," he says; "we want one to make a saw out
of."

"Tom, if it ain't unregular and irreligious to sejest it," I
says, "there's an old rusty saw-blade around yonder sticking
under the weatherboarding behind the smoke-house."

He looked kind of weary and discouraged-like, and says:

"It ain't no use to try to learn you nothing, Huck. Run
along and smouch the knives—three of them." So I done it.

XXXVI

As soon as we reckoned everybody was asleep, that night, we went down the lightning-rod, and shut ourselves up in the lean-to, and got out our pile of fox-fire, and went to work. We cleared everything out of the way, about four or five foot along the middle of the bottom log. Tom said he was right behind Jim's bed now, and we'd dig in under it, and when we got through there couldn't nobody in the cabin ever know there was any hole there, because Jim's counterpin hung down most to the ground, and you'd have to raise it up and look under to see the hole. So we dug and dug, with the case-knives, till most midnight; and then we was dog-tired, and our hands was blistered, and yet you couldn't see we'd done anything, hardly. At last I says:

"This ain't no thirty-seven year job, this is a thirty-eight year job, Tom Sawyer."

He never said nothing. But he sighed, and pretty soon he stopped digging, and then for a good little while I knowed he was thinking. Then he says:

"It ain't no use, Huck, it ain't agoing to work. If we was prisoners it would, because then we'd have as many years as we wanted, and no hurry; and we wouldn't get but a few minutes to dig, every day, while they was changing watches, and so our hands wouldn't get blistered, and we could keep it up right along, year in and year out, and do it right, and the way it ought to be done. But *we* can't fool along, we got to rush; we ain't got no time to spare. If we was to put in another night this way, we'd have to knock off for a week to let our hands get well—couldn't touch a case-knife with them sooner."

"Well, then, what we going to do, Tom?"

"I'll tell you. It ain't right, and it ain't moral, and I wouldn't like it to get out—but there ain't only just the one way; we got to dig him out with the picks, and *let on* it's case-knives."

"*Now* you're *talking*!" I says; "your head gets leveler and leveler all the time, Tom Sawyer," I says. "Picks is the thing, moral or no moral; and as for me, I don't care shucks for the morality of it, nohow. When I start in to steal a nigger, or a watermelon, or a Sunday-school book, I ain't no ways particular how it's done so it's done. What I want is my nigger; or what I want is my watermelon; or what I want is my Sunday-school book; and if a pick's the handiest thing, that's the thing I'm agoing to dig that nigger or that watermelon or that Sunday-school book out with; and I don't give a dead rat what the authorities thinks about it nuther."

"Well," he says, "there's excuse for picks and letting-on in a case like this; if it warn't so, I wouldn't approve of it, nor I wouldn't stand by and see the rules broke—because right is right, and wrong is wrong, and a body ain't got no business doing wrong when he ain't ignorant and knows better. It might answer for *you* to dig Jim out with a pick, *without* any letting-on, because you don't know no better; but it wouldn't for me, because I do know better. Gimme a case-knife."

He had his own by him, but I handed him mine. He flung it down, and says:

"Gimme a *case-knife*."

I didn't know just what to do—but then I thought. I scratched around amongst the old tools, and got a pick-ax and give it to him, and he took it and went to work, and never said a word.

He was always just that particular. Full of principle.

So then I got a shovel, and then we picked and shoveled, turn about, and made the fur fly. We stuck to it about a half an hour, which was as long as we could stand up; but we had a good deal of a hole to show for it. When I got up stairs, I looked out at the window and see Tom doing his level best with the lightning-rod, but he couldn't come it, his hands was so sore. At last he says:

"It ain't no use, it can't be done. What you reckon I better do? Can't you think up no way?"

"Yes," I says, "but I reckon it ain't regular. Come up the stairs, and let on it's a lightning-rod."

So he done it.

Next day Tom stole a pewter spoon and a brass candlestick in the house, for to make some pens for Jim out of, and six tallow candles; and I hung around the nigger cabins, and laid for a chance, and stole three tin plates. Tom said it wasn't enough; but I said nobody wouldn't ever see the plates that Jim throwed out, because they'd fall in the dog-fennel and jimpson weeds under the window-hole—then we could tote them back and he could use them over again. So Tom was satisfied. Then he says:

"Now, the thing to study out is, how to get the things to Jim."

"Take them in through the hole," I says, "when we get it done."

He only just looked scornful, and said something about nobody ever heard of such an idiotic idea, and then he went to studying. By-and-by he said he had ciphered out two or three ways, but there warn't no need to decide on any of them yet. Said we'd got to post Jim first.

That night we went down the lightning-rod a little after ten, and took one of the candles along, and listened under the window-hole, and heard Jim snoring; so we pitched it in, and it didn't wake him. Then we whirled in with the pick and shovel, and in about two hours and a half the job was done. We crept in under Jim's bed and into the cabin, and pawed around and found the candle and lit it, and stood over Jim a while, and found him looking hearty and healthy, and then we woke him up gentle and gradual. He was so glad to see us he most cried; and called us honey, and all the pet names he could think of; and was for having us hunt up a cold chisel to cut the chain off of his leg with, right away, and clearing out without losing any time. But Tom he showed him how unregular it would be, and set down and told him all about our plans, and how we could alter them in a minute any time there was an alarm; and not to be the least afraid, because we would see he got away, *sure*. So Jim he said it was all right, and we set there and talked over old times a while, and then Tom asked a lot of questions, and when Jim told him Uncle Silas come in every day or two to pray with him, and Aunt Sally come in to see if he was comfortable and had plenty to eat, and both of them was kind as they could be, Tom says:

"*Now* I know how to fix it. We'll send you some things by them."

I said, "Don't do nothing of the kind; it's one of the most jackass ideas I ever struck;" but he never paid no attention to me; went right on. It was his way when he'd got his plans set.

So he told Jim how we'd have to smuggle in the rope-ladder pie, and other large things, by Nat, the nigger that fed him, and he must be on the lookout, and not be surprised, and not let Nat see him open them; and we would put small things in uncle's coat pockets and he must steal them out; and we would tie things to aunt's apron strings or put them in her apron pocket, if we got a chance; and told him what they would be and what they was for. And told him how to keep a journal on the shirt with his blood, and all that. He told him everything. Jim he couldn't see no sense in the most of it, but he allowed we was white folks and knowed better than him; so he was satisfied, and said he would do it all just as Tom said.

Jim had plenty corn-cob pipes and tobacco; so we had a right down good sociable time; then we crawled out through the hole, and so home to bed, with hands that looked like they'd been chawed. Tom was in high spirits. He said it was the best fun he ever had in his life, and the most intellectural; and said if he only could see his way to it we would keep it up all the rest of our lives and leave Jim to our children to get out; for he believed Jim would come to like it better and better the more he got used to it. He said that in that way it could be strung out to as much as eighty year, and would be the best time on record. And he said it would make us all celebrated that had a hand in it.

In the morning we went out to the wood-pile and chopped up the brass candlestick into handy sizes, and Tom put them and the pewter spoon in his pocket. Then we went to the nigger cabins, and while I got Nat's notice off, Tom shoved a piece of candlestick into the middle of a corn-pone that was in Jim's pan, and we went along with Nat to see how it would work, and it just worked noble; when Jim bit into it it most mashed all his teeth out; and there warn't ever anything could a worked better. Tom said so himself. Jim he never let on but what it was only just a piece of rock or something like that that's always getting into bread, you know; but after that he never bit into nothing but what he jabbed his fork into it in three or four places, first.

And whilst we was a standing there in the dimmish light, here comes a couple of the hounds bulging in, from under Jim's bed; and they kept on piling in till there was eleven of them, and there warn't hardly room in there to get your breath. By jings, we forgot to fasten that lean-to door. The nigger Nat he only just hollered "witches!" once, and keeled over onto the floor amongst the dogs, and begun to groan like he was dying. Tom jerked the door open and flung out a slab of Jim's meat, and the dogs went for it, and in two seconds he was out himself and back again and shut the door, and I knowed he'd fixed the other door too. Then he went to work on the nigger, coaxing him and petting him, and asking him if he'd been imagining he saw something again. He raised up, and blinked his eyes around, and says:

"Mars Sid, you'll say I's a fool, but if I didn't b'lieve I see most a million dogs, er devils, er some'n, I wisht I may die right heah in dese tracks. I did, mos' sholy. Mars Sid, I *felt* um—I *felt* um, sah; dey was all over me. Dad fetch it, I jis' wisht I could git my han's on one er dem witches jis' wunst— on'y jis' wunst—it's all I'd ast. But mos'ly I wisht dey'd lemme 'lone, I does."

Tom says:

"Well, I tell you what *I* think. What makes them come here just at this runaway nigger's breakfast-time? It's because they're hungry; that's the reason. You make them a witch pie; that's the thing for *you* to do."

"But my lan', Mars Sid, how's *I* gwyne to make 'm a witch pie? I doan' know how to make it. I hain't ever hearn er sich a thing b'fo.'"

"Well, then, I'll have to make it myself."

"Will you do it, honey?—will you? I'll wusshup de groun' und' yo' foot, I will!"

"All right, I'll do it, seeing it's you, and you've been good to us and showed us the runaway nigger. But you got to be mighty careful. When we come around, you turn your back; and then whatever we've put in the pan, don't you let on you see it at all. And don't you look, when Jim unloads the pan—

something might happen, I don't know what. And above all, don't you *handle* the witch-things."

"*Hannel* 'm Mars Sid? What *is* you a talkin' 'bout? I wouldn' lay de weight er my finger on um, not f'r ten hund'd thous'n' billion dollars, I wouldn't."

XXXVII

THAT was all fixed. So then we went away and went to the
rubbage-pile in the back yard where they keep the old
boots, and rags, and pieces of bottles, and wore-out tin
things, and all such truck, and scratched around and found an
old tin washpan and stopped up the holes as well as we could,
to bake the pie in, and took it down cellar and stole it full of
flour, and started for breakfast and found a couple of shingle-
nails that Tom said would be handy for a prisoner to scrabble
his name and sorrows on the dungeon walls with, and
dropped one of them in Aunt Sally's apron pocket which was
hanging on a chair, and t'other we stuck in the band of Uncle
Silas's hat, which was on the bureau, because we heard the
children say their pa and ma was going to the runaway nigger's house this morning, and then went to breakfast, and
Tom dropped the pewter spoon in Uncle Silas's coat pocket,
and Aunt Sally wasn't come yet, so we had to wait a little
while.

And when she come she was hot, and red, and cross, and
couldn't hardly wait for the blessing; and then she went to
sluicing out coffee with one hand and cracking the handiest
child's head with her thimble with the other, and says:

"I've hunted high, and I've hunted low, and it does beat
all, what *has* become of your other shirt."

My heart fell down amongst my lungs and livers and
things, and a hard piece of corn-crust started down my throat
after it and got met on the road with a cough and was shot
across the table and took one of the children in the eye and
curled him up like a fishing-worm, and let a cry out of him
the size of a war-whoop, and Tom he turned kinder blue
around the gills, and it all amounted to a considerable state
of things for about a quarter of a minute or as much as that,
and I would a sold out for half price if there was a bidder.
But after that we was all right again—it was the sudden surprise of it that knocked us so kind of cold. Uncle Silas he
says:

"It's most uncommon curious, I can't understand it. I know perfectly well I took it *off*, because——"

"Because you hain't got but one *on*. Just *listen* at the man! *I* know you took it off, and know it by a better way than your wool-gethering memory, too, because it was on the clo'es-line yesterday—I see it there myself. But it's gone—that's the long and the short of it, and you'll just have to change to a red flann'l one till I can get time to make a new one. And it'll be the third I've made in two years; it just keeps a body on the jump to keep you in shirts; and whatever you do manage to *do* with 'm all, is more'n *I* can make out. A body'd think you *would* learn to take some sort of care of 'em, at your time of life."

"I know it, Sally, and I do try all I can. But it oughtn't to be altogether my fault, because you know I don't see them nor have nothing to do with them except when they're on me; and I don't believe I've ever lost one of them *off* of me."

"Well, it ain't *your* fault if you haven't, Silas—you'd a done it if you could, I reckon. And the shirt ain't all that's gone, nuther. Ther's a spoon gone; and *that* ain't all. There was ten, and now ther's only nine. The calf got the shirt I reckon, but the calf never took the spoon, *that's* certain."

"Why, what else is gone, Sally?"

"Ther's six *candles* gone—that's what. The rats could a got the candles, and I reckon they did; I wonder they don't walk off with the whole place, the way you're always going to stop their holes and don't do it; and if they warn't fools they'd sleep in your hair, Silas—*you'd* never find it out; but you can't lay the *spoon* on the rats, and that I *know*."

"Well, Sally, I'm in fault, and I acknowledge it; I've been remiss; but I won't let to-morrow go by without stopping up them holes."

"Oh, I wouldn't hurry, next year'll do. Matilda Angelina Araminta *Phelps*!"

Whack comes the thimble, and the child snatches her claws out of the sugar-bowl without fooling around any. Just then, the nigger woman steps onto the passage, and says:

"Missus, dey's a sheet gone."

"A *sheet* gone! Well, for the land's sake!"

"I'll stop up them holes *to-day*," says Uncles Silas, looking sorrowful.

"Oh, *do* shet up!—spose the rats took the *sheet*? *Where's* it gone, Lize?"

"Clah to goodness I hain't no notion, Miss Sally. She wuz on de clo's-line yistiddy, but she done gone; she ain' dah no mo', now."

"I reckon the world *is* coming to an end. I *never* see the beat of it, in all my born days. A shirt, and a sheet, and a spoon, and six can——"

"Missus," comes a young yaller wench, "dey's a brass cannelstick miss'n."

"Cler out from here, you hussy, or I'll take a skillet to ye!"

Well, she was just a biling. I begun to lay for a chance; I reckoned I would sneak out and go for the woods till the weather moderated. She kept a raging right along, running her insurrection all by herself, and everybody else mighty meek and quiet; and at last Uncle Silas, looking kind of foolish, fishes up that spoon out of his pocket. She stopped, with her mouth open and her hands up; and as for me, I wished I was in Jerusalem or somewheres. But not long; because she says:

"It's *just* as I expected. So you had it in your pocket all the time; and like as not you've got the other things there, too. How'd it get there?"

"I reely don't know, Sally," he says, kind of apologizing, "or you know I would tell. I was a-studying over my text in Acts Seventeen, before breakfast, and I reckon I put it in there, not noticing, meaning to put my Testament in, and it must be so, because my Testament ain't in, but I'll go and see, and if the Testament is where I had it, I'll know I didn't put it in, and that will show that I laid the Testament down and took up the spoon, and——"

"Oh, for the land's sake! Give a body a rest! Go 'long now, the whole kit and biling of ye; and don't come nigh me again till I've got back my peace of mind."

I'd a heard her, if she'd a said it to herself, let alone speaking it out; and I'd a got up and obeyed her, if I'd a been dead. As we was passing through the setting-room, the old man he took up his hat, and the shingle-nail fell out on the floor, and he just merely picked it up and laid it on the mantel-shelf, and never said nothing, and went out. Tom see him do it, and remembered about the spoon, and says:

"Well, it ain't no use to send things by *him* no more, he ain't reliable." Then he says: "But he done us a good turn with the spoon, anyway, without knowing it, and so we'll go and do him one without *him* knowing it—stop up his rat-holes."

There was a noble good lot of them, down cellar, and it took us a whole hour, but we done the job tight and good, and ship-shape. Then we heard steps on the stairs, and blowed out our light, and hid; and here comes the old man, with a candle in one hand and a bundle of stuff in t'other, looking as absent-minded as year before last. He went a mooning around, first to one rat-hole and then another, till he'd been to them all. Then he stood about five minutes, picking tallow-drip off his candle and thinking. Then he turns off slow and dreamy towards the stairs, saying:

"Well, for the life of me I can't remember when I done it. I could show her now that I warn't to blame on account of the rats. But never mind—let it go. I reckon it wouldn't do no good."

And so he went on a mumbling up stairs, and then we left. He was a mighty nice old man. And always is.

Tom was a good deal bothered about what to do for a spoon, but he said we'd got to have it; so he took a think. When he had ciphered it out, he told me how we was to do; then we went and waited around the spoon-basket till we see Aunt Sally coming, and then Tom went to counting the spoons and laying them out to one side, and I slid one of them up my sleeve, and Tom says:

"Why, Aunt Sally, there ain't but nine spoons, *yet*."

She says:

"Go 'long to your play, and don't bother me. I know better, I counted 'm myself."

"Well, I've counted them twice, Aunty, and *I* can't make but nine."

She looked out of all patience, but of course she come to count—anybody would.

"I declare to gracious ther' *ain't* but nine!" she says. "Why, what in the world—plague *take* the things, I'll count 'm again."

So I slipped back the one I had, and when she got done counting, she says:

"Hang the troublesome rubbage, ther's *ten*, now!" and she looked huffy and bothered both. But Tom says:

"Why, Aunty, *I* don't think there's ten."

"You numskull, didn't you see me *count* 'm?"

"I know, but——"

"Well, I'll count 'm *again*."

So I smouched one, and they come out nine same as the other time. Well, she *was* in a tearing way—just a trembling all over, she was so mad. But she counted and counted, till she got that addled she'd start to count-in the *basket* for a spoon, sometimes; and so, three times they come out right, and three times they come out wrong. Then she grabbed up the basket and slammed it across the house and knocked the cat galley-west; and she said cle'r out and let her have some peace, and if we come bothering around her again betwixt that and dinner, she'd skin us. So we had the odd spoon; and dropped it in her apron pocket whilst she was a giving us our sailing-orders, and Jim got it all right, along with her shingle-nail, before noon. We was very well satisfied with this busi-ness, and Tom allowed it was worth twice the trouble it took, because he said *now* she couldn't ever count them spoons twice alike again to save her life; and wouldn't believe she'd counted them right, if she *did*; and said that after she'd about counted her head off, for the next three days, he judged she'd give it up and offer to kill anybody that wanted her to ever count them any more.

So we put the sheet back on the line, that night, and stole one out of her closet; and kept on putting it back and stealing it again, for a couple of days, till she didn't know how many sheets she had, any more, and said she didn't *care*, and warn't agoing to bullyrag the rest of her soul out about it, and wouldn't count them again not to save her life, she druther die first.

So we was all right now, as to the shirt and the sheet and the spoon and the candles, by the help of the calf and the rats and the mixed-up counting; and as to the candlestick, it warn't no consequence, it would blow over by-and-by.

But that pie was a job; we had no end of trouble with that pie. We fixed it up away down in the woods, and cooked it there; and we got it done at last, and very satisfactory, too; but not all in one day; and we had to use up three washpans full of flour, before we got through, and we got burnt pretty much all over, in places, and eyes put out with the smoke; because, you see, we didn't want nothing but a crust, and we couldn't prop it up right, and she would always cave in. But of course we thought of the right way at last; which was to cook the ladder, too, in the pie. So then we laid in with Jim, the second night, and tore up the sheet all in little strings, and twisted them together, and long before daylight we had a lovely rope, that you could a hung a person with. We let on it took nine months to make it.

And in the forenoon we took it down to the woods, but it wouldn't go in the pie. Being made of a whole sheet, that way, there was rope enough for forty pies, if we'd a wanted them, and plenty left over for soup, or sausage, or anything you choose. We could a had a whole dinner.

But we didn't need it. All we needed was just enough for the pie, and so we throwed the rest away. We didn't cook none of the pies in the washpan, afraid the solder would melt; but Uncle Silas he had a noble brass warming-pan which he thought considerable of, because it belonged to one of his ancesters with a long wooden handle that come over from England with William the Conqueror in the *Mayflower* or one of them early ships and was hid away up garret with a lot of other old pots and things that was valuable, not on account of being any account because they warn't, but on account of them being relicts, you know, and we snaked her out, private, and took her down there, but she failed on the first pies, because we didn't know how, but she come up smiling on the last one. We took and lined her with dough, and set her in the coals, and loaded her up with rag-rope, and put on a dough roof, and shut down the lid, and put hot embers on top, and stood off five foot, with the long handle, cool and comfortable, and in fifteen minutes she turned out a pie that was a satisfaction to look at. But the person that et it would want to fetch a couple of kags of toothpicks along, for if that rope-ladder wouldn't cramp him down to business, I don't know nothing what I'm talking about, and lay him in enough stomach-ache to last him till next time, too.

Nat didn't look, when we put the witch-pie in Jim's pan; and we put the three tin plates in the bottom of the pan under the vittles; and so Jim got everything all right, and as soon as he was by himself he busted into the pie and hid the rope-ladder inside of his straw tick, and scratched some marks on a tin plate and throwed it out of the window-hole.

XXXVIII

MAKING THEM PENS was a distressid-tough job, and so was the saw; and Jim allowed the inscription was going to be the toughest of all. That's the one which the prisoner has to scrabble on the wall. But we had to have it; Tom said we'd *got* to; there warn't no case of a state prisoner not scrabbling his inscription to leave behind, and his coat of arms.

"Look at Lady Jane Grey," he says; "look at Gilford Dudley; look at old Northumberland! Why, Huck, spose it *is* considerble trouble?—what you going to do?—how you going to get around it? Jim's *got* to do his inscription and coat of arms. They all do."

Jim says:

"Why, Mars Tom, I hain't got no coat o' arms; I hain't got nuffn but dish-yer ole shirt, en you knows I got to keep de journal on dat."

"Oh, you don't understand, Jim; a coat of arms is very different."

"Well," I says, "Jim's right, anyway, when he says he hain't got no coat of arms, because he hain't."

"I reckon *I* knowed that," Tom says, "but you bet he'll have one before he goes out of this—because he's going out *right*, and there ain't going to be no flaws in his record."

So whilst me and Jim filed away at the pens on a brickbat apiece, Jim a making his'n out of the brass and I making mine out of the spoon, Tom set to work to think out the coat of arms. By-and-by he said he'd struck so many good ones he didn't hardly know which to take, but there was one which he reckoned he'd decide on. He says:

"On the scutcheon we'll have a bend *or* in the dexter base, a saltire *murrey* in the fess, with a dog, couchant, for common charge, and under his foot a chain embattled, for slavery, with a chevron *vert* in a chief engrailed, and three invected lines on a field *azure*, with the nombril points rampant on a dancette indented; crest, a runaway nigger, *sable*, with his bundle over his shoulder on a bar sinister: and a couple of gules for supporters, which is you and me; motto, *Maggiore fretta, minore atto.* Got it out of a book—means, the more haste, the less speed."

"Geewhillikins," I says, "but what does the rest of it mean?"

"We ain't got no time to bother over that," he says, "we got to dig in like all git-out."

"Well, anyway," I says, "what's *some* of it? What's a fess?"

"A fess—a fess is—*you* don't need to know what a fess is. I'll show him how to make it when he gets to it."

"Shucks, Tom," I says, "I think you might tell a person. What's a bar sinister?"

"Oh, *I* don't know. But he's got to have it. All the nobility does."

That was just his way. If it didn't suit him to explain a thing to you, he wouldn't do it. You might pump at him a week, it wouldn't make no difference.

He'd got all that coat of arms business fixed, so now he started in to finish up the rest of that part of the work, which was to plan out a mournful inscription—said Jim got to have one, like they all done. He made up a lot, and wrote them out on a paper, and read them off, so:

1. *Here a captive heart busted.*

2. *Here a poor prisoner, forsook by the world and friends, fretted out his sorrowful life.*

3. *Here a lonely heart broke, and a worn spirit went to its rest, after thirty-seven years of solitary captivity.*

4. *Here, homeless and friendless, after thirty-seven years of bitter captivity, perished a noble stranger, natural son of Louis XIV.*

Tom's voice trembled, whilst he was reading them, and he most broke down. When he got done, he couldn't no way make up his mind which one for Jim to scrabble onto the wall, they was all so good; but at last he allowed he would let him scrabble them all on. Jim said it would take him a year to scrabble such a lot of truck onto the logs with a nail, and he didn't know how to make letters, besides; but Tom said he would block them out for him, and then he wouldn't have nothing to do but just follow the lines. Then pretty soon he says:

"Come to think, the logs ain't agoing to do; they don't have log walls in a dungeon: we got to dig the inscriptions into a rock. We'll fetch a rock."

Jim said the rock was worse than the logs; he said it would take him such a pison long time to dig them into a rock, he wouldn't ever get out. But Tom said he would let me help him do it. Then he took a look to see how me and Jim was getting along with the pens. It was most pesky tedious hard work and slow, and didn't give my hands no show to get well of the sores, and we didn't seem to make no headway, hardly. So Tom says:

"I know how to fix it. We got to have a rock for the coat of arms and mournful inscriptions, and we can kill two birds with that same rock. There's a gaudy big grindstone down at the mill, and we'll smouch it, and carve the things on it, and file out the pens and the saw on it, too."

It warn't no slouch of an idea; and it warn't no slouch of a grindstone nuther; but we allowed we'd tackle it. It warn't quite midnight, yet, so we cleared out for the mill, leaving Jim at work. We smouched the grindstone, and set out to roll her home, but it was a most nation tough job. Sometimes, do what we could, we couldn't keep her from falling over, and she come mighty near mashing us, every time. Tom said she was going to get one of us, sure, before we got through. We got her half way; and then we was plumb played out, and most drownded with sweat. We see it warn't no use, we got to go and fetch Jim. So he raised up his bed and slid the chain off of the bed-leg, and wrapt it round and round his neck, and we crawled out through our hole and down there, and Jim and me laid into that grindstone and walked her along like nothing; and Tom superintended. He could out-superintend any boy I ever see. He knowed how to do everything.

Our hole was pretty big, but it warn't big enough to get the grindstone through; but Jim he took the pick and soon made it big enough. Then Tom marked out them things on it with the nail, and set Jim to work on them, with the nail for a chisel and an iron bolt from the rubbage in the lean-to for a hammer, and told him to work till the rest of his candle quit on him, and then he could go to bed, and hide the grindstone under his straw tick and sleep on it. Then we helped him fix his chain back on the bed-leg, and was ready for bed ourselves. But Tom thought of something, and says:

"You got any spiders in here, Jim?"

"No, sah, thanks to goodness I hain't, Mars Tom."

"All right, we'll get you some."

"But bless you, honey, I doan' *want* none. I's afeard un um. I jis' 's soon have rattlesnakes aroun'."

Tom thought a minute or two, and says:

"It's a good idea. And I reckon it's been done. It *must* a been done; it stands to reason. Yes, it's a prime good idea. Where could you keep it?"

"Keep what, Mars Tom?"

"Why, a rattlesnake."

"De goodness gracious alive, Mars Tom! Why, if dey was a rattlesnake to come in heah, I'd take en bust right out thoo dat log wall, I would, wid my head."

"Why, Jim, you wouldn't be afraid of it, after a little. You could tame it."

"*Tame* it!"

"Yes—easy enough. Every animal is grateful for kindness and petting, and they wouldn't *think* of hurting a person that pets them. Any book will tell you that. You try— that's all I ask; just try for two or three days. Why, you can get him so, in a little while, that he'll love you; and sleep with you; and won't stay away from you a minute; and will let you wrap him round your neck and put his head in your mouth."

"*Please*, Mars Tom—*doan'* talk so! I can't *stan'* it! He'd *let* me shove his head in my mouf—fer a favor, hain't it? I lay he'd wait a pow'ful long time 'fo' I *ast* him. En mo' en dat, I doan' *want* him to sleep wid me."

"Jim, don't act so foolish. A prisoner's *got* to have some kind of a dumb pet, and if a rattlesnake hain't ever been tried, why, there's more glory to be gained in your being the first to ever try it than any other way you could ever think of to save your life."

"Why, Mars Tom, I doan' *want* no sich glory. Snake take 'n bite Jim's chin off, den *whah* is de glory? No, sah, I doan' want no sich doin's."

"Blame it, can't you *try?* I only *want* you to try—you needn't keep it up if it don't work."

"But de trouble all *done*, ef de snake bite me while I's a tryin' him. Mars Tom, I's willin' to tackle mos' anything 'at ain't onreasonable, but ef you en Huck fetches a rattlesnake in heah for me to tame, I's gwyne to *leave*, dat's *shore*."

"Well, then, let it go, let it go, if you're so bullheaded about it. We can get you some garter-snakes and you can tie some buttons on their tails, and let on they're rattlesnakes, and I reckon that'll have to do."

"I k'n stan' *dem*, Mars Tom, but blame' 'f I couldn't get along widout um, I tell you dat. I never knowed b'fo', 't was so much bother and trouble to be a prisoner."

"Well, it *always* is, when it's done right. You got any rats around here?"

"No, sah, I hain't seed none."

"Well, we'll get you some rats."

"Why, Mars Tom, I doan' *want* no rats. Dey's de dad-blamedest creturs to sturb a body, en rustle roun' over 'im, en bite his feet, when he's tryin' to sleep, I ever see. No, sah, gimme g'yarter-snakes, 'f I's got to have 'm, but doan' gimme no rats, I ain't got no use f'r um, skasely."

"But Jim, you *got* to have 'em—they all do. So don't make no more fuss about it. Prisoners ain't ever without rats. There ain't no instance of it. And they train them, and pet them, and learn them tricks, and they get to be as sociable as flies. But you got to play music to them. You got anything to play music on?"

"I ain' got nuffin but a coase comb en a piece o' paper, en a juice-harp; but I reck'n dey wouldn' take no stock in a juice-harp."

"Yes they would. *They* don't care what kind of music 'tis. A jews-harp's plenty good enough for a rat. All animals like music—in a prison they dote on it. Specially, painful music; and you can't get no other kind out of a jews-harp. It always interests them; they come out to see what's the matter with you. Yes, you're all right; you're fixed very well. You want to set on your bed, nights, before you go to sleep, and early in the mornings, and play your jews-harp; play The Last Link is Broken—that's the thing that'll scoop a rat, quicker'n anything else: and when you've played about two minutes, you'll see all the rats, and the snakes, and spiders, and things begin to feel worried about you, and come. And they'll just fairly swarm over you, and have a noble good time."

"Yes, *dey* will, I reck'n, Mars Tom, but what kine er time is *Jim* havin'? Blest if I kin see de pint. But I'll do it ef I got to. I reck'n I better keep de animals satisfied, en not have no trouble in de house."

Tom waited to think over, and see if there wasn't nothing else; and pretty soon he says:

"Oh—there's one thing I forgot. Could you raise a flower here, do you reckon?"

"I doan' know but maybe I could, Mars Tom; but it's tol'-able dark in heah, en I ain' got no use f'r no flower, nohow, en she'd be a pow'ful sight o' trouble."

"Well, you try it, anyway. Some other prisoners has done it."

"One er dem big cat-tail-lookin' mullen-stalks would grow in heah, Mars Tom, I reck'n, but she wouldn' be wuth half de trouble she'd coss."

"Don't you believe it. We'll fetch you a little one, and you plant it in the corner, over there, and raise it. And don't call it mullen, call it Pitchiola—that's its right name, when it's in a prison. And you want to water it with your tears."

"Why, I got plenty spring water, Mars Tom."

"You don't *want* spring water; you want to water it with your tears. It's the way they always do."

"Why, Mars Tom, I lay I kin raise one er dem mullen-stalks twyste wid spring water whiles another man's a *start'n* one wid tears."

"That ain't the idea. You *got* to do it with tears."

"She'll die on my han's, Mars Tom, she sholy will; kase I doan' skasely ever cry."

So Tom was stumped. But he studied it over, and then said Jim would have to worry along the best he could with an onion. He promised he would go to the nigger cabins and drop one, private, in Jim's coffee-pot, in the morning. Jim said he would "jis' 's soon have tobacker in his coffee;" and found so much fault with it, and with the work and bother of raising the mullen, and jews-harping the rats, and petting and flattering up the snakes and spiders and things, on top of all the other work he had to do on pens, and inscriptions, and journals, and things, which made it more trouble and worry and responsibility to be a prisoner than anything he ever undertook, that Tom most lost all patience with him; and said he was just loadened down with more gaudier chances than a prisoner ever had in the world to make a name for himself, and yet he didn't know enough to appreciate them, and they was just about wasted on him. So Jim he was sorry, and said he wouldn't behave so no more, and then me and Tom shoved for bed.

XXXIX

IN THE MORNING we went up to the village and bought a wire rat trap and fetched it down, and unstopped the best rat hole, and in about an hour we had fifteen of the bulliest kind of ones; and then we took it and put it in a safe place under Aunt Sally's bed. But while we was gone for spiders, little Thomas Franklin Benjamin Jefferson Elexander Phelps found it there, and opened the door of it to see if the rats would come out, and they did; and Aunt Sally she come in, and when we got back she was a standing on top of the bed raising Cain, and the rats was doing what they could to keep off the dull times for her. So she took and dusted us both with the hickry, and we was as much as two hours catching another fifteen or sixteen, drat that meddlesome cub, and they warn't the likeliest, nuther, because the first haul was the pick of the flock. I never see a likelier lot of rats than what that first haul was.

We got a splendid stock of sorted spiders, and bugs, and frogs, and caterpillars, and one thing or another; and we like-to got a hornet's nest, but we didn't. The family was at home. We didn't give it right up, but staid with them as long as we could; because we allowed we'd tire them out or they'd got to tire us out, and they done it. Then we got allycumpain and rubbed on the places, and was pretty near all right again, but couldn't set down convenient. And so we went for the snakes, and grabbed a couple of dozen garters and house-snakes, and put them in a bag, and put it in our room, and by that time it was supper time, and a rattling good honest day's work; and hungry?—oh, no, I reckon not! And there warn't a blessed snake up there, when we went back—we didn't half tie the sack, and they worked out, somehow, and left. But it didn't matter much, because they was still on the premises somewheres. So we judged we could get some of them again. No, there warn't no real scarcity of snakes about the house for a considerble spell. You'd see them dripping from the rafters and places, every now and then; and they generly landed in your plate, or down the back of your neck, and most of

the time where you didn't want them. Well, they was handsome, and striped, and there warn't no harm in a million of
them; but that never made no difference to Aunt Sally, she
despised snakes, be the breed what they might, and she
couldn't stand them no way you could fix it; and every time
one of them flopped down on her, it didn't make no difference what she was doing, she would just lay that work down
and light out. I never see such a woman. And you could hear
her whoop to Jericho. You couldn't get her to take aholt of
one of them with the tongs. And if she turned over and found
one in bed, she would scramble out and lift a howl that you
would think the house was afire. She disturbed the old man
so, that he said he could most wish there hadn't ever been no
snakes created. Why, after every last snake had been gone
clear out of the house for as much as a week, Aunt Sally
warn't over it yet; she warn't near over it; when she was setting thinking about something, you could touch her on the
back of her neck with a feather and she would jump right out
of her stockings. It was very curious. But Tom said all women
was just so. He said they was made that way; for some reason
or other.

We got a licking every time one of our snakes come in her
way; and she allowed these lickings warn't nothing to what
she would do if we ever loaded up the place again with them.
I didn't mind the lickings, because they didn't amount to
nothing; but I minded the trouble we had, to lay in another
lot. But we got them laid in, and all the other things; and
you never see a cabin as blithesome as Jim's was when they'd
all swarm out for music and go for him. Jim didn't like the
spiders, and the spiders didn't like Jim; and so they'd lay for
him and make it mighty warm for him. And he said that between the rats, and the snakes, and the grindstone, there
warn't no room in bed for him, skasely; and when there was,
a body couldn't sleep, it was so lively, and it was always lively,
he said, because *they* never all slept at one time, but took turn
about, so when the snakes was asleep the rats was on deck,
and when the rats turned in the snakes come on watch, so he
always had one gang under him, in his way, and t'other gang
having a circus over him, and if he got up to hunt a new
place, the spiders would take a chance at him as he crossed

over. He said if he ever got out, this time, he wouldn't ever be a prisoner again, not for a salary.

Well, by the end of three weeks, everything was in pretty good shape. The shirt was sent in early, in a pie, and every time a rat bit Jim he would get up and write a little in his journal whilst the ink was fresh; the pens was made, the inscriptions and so on was all carved on the grindstone; the bed-leg was sawed in two, and we had et up the sawdust, and it give us a most amazing stomach-ache. We reckoned we was all going to die, but didn't. It was the most undigestible sawdust I ever see; and Tom said the same. But as I was saying, we'd got all the work done, now, at last; and we was all pretty much fagged out, too, but mainly Jim. The old man had wrote a couple of times to the plantation below Orleans to come and get their runaway nigger, but hadn't got no answer, because there warn't no such plantation; so he allowed he would advertise Jim in the St. Louis and New Orleans papers; and when he mentioned the St. Louis ones, it give me the cold shivers, and I see we hadn't no time to lose. So Tom said, now for the nonnamous letters.

"What's them?" I says.

"Warnings to the people that something is up. Sometimes it's done one way, sometimes another. But there's always somebody spying around, that gives notice to the governor of the castle. When Louis XVI. was going to light out of the Tooleries, a servant girl done it. It's a very good way, and so is the nonnamous letters. We'll use them both. And it's usual for the prisoner's mother to change clothes with him, and she stays in, and he slides out in her clothes. We'll do that too."

"But looky here, Tom, what do we want to *warn* anybody for, that something's up? Let them find it out for themselves—it's their lookout."

"Yes, I know; but you can't depend on them. It's the way they've acted from the very start—left us to do *everything*. They're so confiding and mullet-headed they don't take notice of nothing at all. So if we don't *give* them notice, there won't be nobody nor nothing to interfere with us, and so after all our hard work and trouble this escape 'll go off perfectly flat: won't amount to nothing—won't be nothing *to* it."

"Well, as for me, Tom, that's the way I'd like."

"Shucks," he says, and looked disgusted. So I says:

"But I ain't going to make no complaint. Anyway that suits you suits me. What you going to do about the servant-girl?"

"You'll be her. You slide in, in the middle of the night, and hook that yaller girl's frock."

"Why, Tom, that'll make trouble next morning; because of course she prob'bly hain't got any but that one."

"I know; but you don't want it but fifteen minutes, to carry the nonnamous letter and shove it under the front door."

"All right, then, I'll do it; but I could carry it just as handy in my own togs."

"You wouldn't look like a servant-girl *then*, would you?"

"No, but there won't be nobody to see what I look like, *anyway*."

"That ain't got nothing to do with it. The thing for us to do, is just to do our *duty*, and not worry about whether anybody *sees* us do it or not. Hain't you got no principle at all?"

"All right, I ain't saying nothing; I'm the servant-girl. Who's Jim's mother?"

"I'm his mother. I'll hook a gown from Aunt Sally."

"Well, then, you'll have to stay in the cabin when me and Jim leaves."

"Not much. I'll stuff Jim's clothes full of straw and lay it on his bed to represent his mother in disguise, and Jim 'll take the nigger woman's gown off of me and wear it, and we'll all evade together. When a prisoner of style escapes, it's called an evasion. It's always called so when a king escapes, f'rinstance. And the same with a king's son; it don't make no difference whether he's a natural one or an unnatural one."

So Tom he wrote the nonnamous letter, and I smouched the yaller wench's frock, that night, and put it on, and shoved it under the front door, the way Tom told me to. It said:

Beware. Trouble is brewing. Keep a sharp lookout.
UNKNOWN FRIEND.

Next night we stuck a picture which Tom drawed in blood, of a skull and crossbones, on the front door; and next night another one of a coffin, on the back door. I never see a family in such a sweat. They couldn't a been worse scared if the place had a been full of ghosts laying for them behind everything and under the beds and shivering through the air. If a door banged, Aunt Sally she jumped, and said "ouch!" if anything fell, she jumped and said "ouch!" if you happened to touch her, when she warn't noticing, she done the same; she couldn't face noway and be satisfied, because she allowed there was something behind her every time—so she was always a whirling around, sudden, and saying "ouch," and before she'd get two-thirds around, she'd whirl back again, and say it again; and she was afraid to go to bed, but she dasn't set up. So the thing was working very well, Tom said; he said he never see a thing work more satisfactory. He said it showed it was done right.

So he said, now for the grand bulge! So the very next morning at the streak of dawn we got another letter ready, and was wondering what we better do with it, because we heard them say at supper they was going to have a nigger on watch at both doors all night. Tom he went down the lightning-rod to spy around; and the nigger at the back door was asleep, and he stuck it in the back of his neck and come back. This letter said:

> *Don't betray me, I wish to be your friend. There is a desprate gang of cutthroats from over in the Ingean Territory going to steal your runaway nigger to-night, and they have been trying to scare you so as you will stay in the house and not bother them. I am one of the gang, but have got religgion and wish to quit it and lead a honest life again, and will betray the helish design. They will sneak down from northards, along the fence, at midnight exact, with a false key, and go in the nigger's cabin to get him. I am to be off a piece and blow a tin horn if I see any danger; but stead of that, I will* BA *like a sheep soon as they get in and not blow at all; then whilst they are getting his chains loose, you slip there and lock them in, and can kill them at your leasure. Don't do anything but just the way I am telling you, if you do they will suspicion something and raise whoopjamboreehoo. I do not wish any reward but to know I have done the right thing.*

> UNKNOWN FRIEND.

XL

WE WAS FEELING pretty good, after breakfast, and took
my canoe and went over the river a fishing, with a
lunch, and had a good time, and took a look at the raft and
found her all right, and got home late to supper, and found
them in such a sweat and worry they didn't know which end
they was standing on, and made us go right off to bed the
minute we was done supper, and wouldn't tell us what the
trouble was, and never let on a word about the new letter,
but didn't need to, because we knowed as much about it as
anybody did, and as soon as we was half up stairs and her
back was turned, we slid for the cellar cubboard and loaded
up a good lunch and took it up to our room and went to
bed, and got up about half-past eleven, and Tom put on Aunt
Sally's dress that he stole and was going to start with the
lunch, but says:

"Where's the butter?"

"I laid out a hunk of it," I says, "on a piece of a corn-
pone."

"Well, you *left* it laid out, then—it ain't here."

"We can get along without it," I says.

"We can get along *with* it, too," he says; "just you slide
down cellar and fetch it. And then mosey right down the
lightning-rod and come along. I'll go and stuff the straw into
Jim's clothes to represent his mother in disguise, and be ready
to *ba* like a sheep and shove soon as you get there."

So out he went, and down cellar went I. The hunk of butter, big as a person's fist, was where I had left it, so I took up
the slab of corn-pone with it on, and blowed out my light,
and started up stairs, very stealthy, and got up to the main
floor all right, but here comes Aunt Sally with a candle, and
I clapped the truck in my hat, and clapped my hat on my
head, and the next second she see me; and she says:

"You been down cellar?"

"Yes'm."

"What you been doing down there?"

"Noth'n'!"

"*Noth'n!*"

"No'm."

"Well, then, what possessed you to go down there, this time of night?"

"I don't know'm."

"You don't *know*? Don't answer me that way, Tom, I want to know what you been *doing* down there?"

"I hain't been doing a single thing, Aunt Sally, I hope to gracious if I have."

I reckoned she'd let me go, now, and as a generl thing she would; but I spose there was so many strange things going on she was just in a sweat about every little thing that warn't yard-stick straight; so she says, very decided:

"You just march into that setting-room and stay there till I come. You been up to something you no business to, and I lay I'll find out what it is before *I'm* done with you."

So she went away as I opened the door and walked into the setting-room. My, but there was a crowd there! Fifteen farmers, and every one of them had a gun. I was most powerful sick, and slunk to a chair and set down. They was setting around, some of them talking a little, in a low voice, and all of them fidgety and uneasy, but trying to look like they warn't; but I knowed they was, because they was always taking off their hats, and putting them on, and scratching their heads, and changing their seats, and fumbling with their buttons. I warn't easy myself, but I didn't take my hat off, all the same.

I did wish Aunt Sally would come, and get done with me, and lick me, if she wanted to, and let me get away and tell Tom how we'd overdone this thing, and what a thundering hornet's nest we'd got ourselves into, so we could stop fooling around, straight off, and clear out with Jim before these rips got out of patience and come for us.

At last she come, and begun to ask me questions, but I *couldn't* answer them straight, I didn't know which end of me was up; because these men was in such a fidget now, that some was wanting to start right *now* and lay for them desperadoes, and saying it warn't but a few minutes to midnight; and others was trying to get them to hold on and wait for the sheep-signal; and here was aunty pegging away at the questions, and me a shaking all over and ready to sink down in my tracks I was that scared; and the place getting hotter and hotter, and the butter beginning to melt and run down my neck and behind my ears; and pretty soon, when one of them says, "*I'm* for going and getting in the cabin *first*, and right *now*, and catching them when they come," I most dropped; and a streak of butter come a trickling down my forehead, and Aunt Sally she see it, and turns white as a sheet, and says:

"For the land's sake what *is* the matter with the child!—he's got the brain fever as shore as you're born, and they're oozing out!"

And everybody runs to see, and she snatches off my hat, and out comes the bread, and what was left of the butter, and she grabbed me, and hugged me, and says:

"Oh, what a turn you did give me! and how glad and grateful I am it ain't no worse; for luck's against us, and it never rains but it pours, and when I see that truck I thought we'd lost you, for I knowed by the color and all, it was just like your brains would be if— Dear, dear, whydn't you *tell* me that was what you'd been down there for, *I* wouldn't a cared. Now cler out to bed, and don't lemme see no more of you till morning!"

I was up stairs in a second, and down the lightning-rod in another one, and shining through the dark for the lean-to. I couldn't hardly get my words out, I was so anxious; but I told Tom as quick as I could, we must jump for it, now, and not a minute to lose—the house full of men, yonder, with guns!

His eyes just blazed; and he says:

"No!—is that so? *Ain't* it bully! Why, Huck, if it was to do over again, I bet I could fetch two hundred! If we could put it off till——"

"Hurry! *hurry!*" I says. "Where's Jim?"

"Right at your elbow; if you reach out your arm you can touch him. He's dressed, and everything's ready. Now we'll slide out and give the sheep-signal."

But then we heard the tramp of men, coming to the door, and heard them begin to fumble with the padlock; and heard a man say:

"I *told* you we'd be too soon; they haven't come—the door is locked. Here, I'll lock some of you into the cabin and you lay for 'em in the dark and kill 'em when they come; and the rest scatter around a piece, and listen if you can hear 'em coming."

So in they come, but couldn't see us in the dark, and most trod on us whilst we was hustling to get under the bed. But we got under all right, and out through the hole, swift but soft—Jim first, me next, and Tom last, which was according to Tom's orders. Now we was in the lean-to, and heard trampings close by outside. So we crept to the door, and Tom stopped us there and put his eye to the crack, but couldn't make out nothing, it was so dark; and whispered and said he would listen for the steps to get further, and when he nudged us Jim must glide out first, and him last. So he set his ear to the crack and listened, and listened, and listened, and the steps a scraping around, out there, all the time; and at last he nudged us, and we slid out, and stooped down, not breathing, and not making the least noise, and slipped stealthy towards the fence, in Injun file, and got to it, all right, and me and Jim over it; but Tom's britches catched fast on a splinter on the top rail, and then he hear the steps coming, so he had to pull loose, which snapped the splinter and made a noise; and as he dropped in our tracks and started, somebody sings out:

"Who's that? Answer, or I'll shoot!"

But we didn't answer; we just unfurled our heels and shoved. Then there was a rush, and a *bang, bang, bang!* and the bullets fairly whizzed around us! We heard them sing out:

"Here they are! They've broke for the river! after 'em, boys! And turn loose the dogs!"

So here they come, full tilt. We could hear them, because they wore boots, and yelled, but we didn't wear no boots, and didn't yell. We was in the path to the mill; and when they got pretty close onto us, we dodged into the bush and let them go by, and then dropped in behind them. They'd had all the dogs shut up, so they wouldn't scare off the robbers; but by this time somebody had let them loose, and here they come, making pow-wow enough for a million; but they was our dogs; so we stopped in our tracks till they catched

up; and when they see it warn't nobody but us, and no excitement to offer them, they only just said howdy, and tore
right ahead towards the shouting and clattering; and then we
up steam again and whizzed along after them till we was
nearly to the mill, and then struck up through the bush to
where my canoe was tied, and hopped in and pulled for dear
life towards the middle of the river, but didn't make no more
noise than we was obleeged to. Then we struck out, easy and
comfortable, for the island where my raft was; and we could
hear them yelling and barking at each other all up and down
the bank, till we was so far away the sounds got dim and died
out. And when we stepped onto the raft, I says:

"*Now*, old Jim, you're a free man *again*, and I bet you
won't ever be a slave no more."

"En a mighty good job it wuz, too, Huck. It 'uz planned
beautiful, en it 'uz *done* beautiful; en dey ain't *nobody* kin git
up a plan dat's mo' mixed-up en splendid den what dat one
wuz."

We was all as glad as we could be, but Tom was the glad-
dest of all, because he had a bullet in the calf of his leg.

When me and Jim heard that, we didn't feel so brash as
what we did before. It was hurting him considerble, and
bleeding; so we laid him in the wigwam and tore up one of
the duke's shirts for to bandage him, but he says:

"Gimme the rags. I can do it myself. Don't stop, now;
don't fool around here, and the evasion booming along so
handsome; man the sweeps, and set her loose! Boys, we done
it elegant!—'deed we did. I wish *we'd* a had the handling of
Louis XVI., there wouldn't a been no 'Son of Saint Louis,
ascend to heaven!' wrote down in *his* biography: no, sir, we'd
a whooped him over the *border*—that's what we'd a done
with *him*—and done it just as slick as nothing at all, too.
Man the sweeps—man the sweeps!"

But me and Jim was consulting—and thinking. And after
we'd thought a minute, I says:

"Say it, Jim."

So he says:

"Well, den, dis is de way it look to me, Huck. Ef it wuz
him dat 'uz bein' set free, en one er de boys wuz to git shot,
would he say, 'Go on en save me, nemmine 'bout a doctor f'r

to save dis one?' Is dat like Mars Tom Sawyer? Would he say dat? You *bet* he wouldn't! *Well*, den, is *Jim* gwyne to say it? No, sah—I doan' budge a step out'n dis place, 'dout a *doctor*, not if it's forty year!"

I knowed he was white inside, and I reckoned he'd say what he did say—so it was all right, now, and I told Tom I was agoing for a doctor. He raised considerble row about it, but me and Jim stuck to it and wouldn't budge; so he was for crawling out and setting the raft loose himself; but we wouldn't let him. Then he give us a piece of his mind—but it didn't do no good.

So when he see me getting the canoe ready, he says:

"Well, then, if you're bound to go, I'll tell you the way to do, when you get to the village. Shut the door, and blindfold the doctor tight and fast, and make him swear to be silent as the grave, and put a purse full of gold in his hand, and then take and lead him all around the back alleys and everywheres, in the dark, and then fetch him here in the canoe, in a round-about way amongst the islands, and search him and take his chalk away from him, and don't give it back to him till you get him back to the village, or else he will chalk this raft so he can find it again. It's the way they all do."

So I said I would, and left, and Jim was to hide in the woods when he see the doctor coming, till he was gone again.

XLI

THE DOCTOR was an old man; a very nice, kind-looking old man, when I got him up. I told him me and my brother was over on Spanish Island hunting, yesterday after-noon, and camped on a piece of a raft we found, and about midnight he must a kicked his gun in his dreams, for it went off and shot him in the leg, and we wanted him to go over there and fix it and not say nothing about it, nor let anybody know, because we wanted to come home this evening, and surprise the folks.

"Who is your folks?" he says.

"The Phelpses, down yonder."

"Oh," he says. And after a minute, he says: "How'd you say he got shot?"

"He had a dream," I says, "and it shot him."

"Singular dream," he says.

So he lit up his lantern, and got his saddle-bags, and we started. But when he see the canoe, he didn't like the look of her—said she was big enough for one, but didn't look pretty safe for two. I says:

"Oh, you needn't be afeard, sir, she carried the three of us, easy enough."

"What three?"

"Why, me and Sid, and—and—and *the guns*; that's what I mean."

"Oh," he says.

But he put his foot on the gunnel, and rocked her; and shook his head, and said he reckoned he'd look around for a bigger one. But they was all locked and chained; so he took my canoe, and said for me to wait till he come back, or I could hunt around further, or maybe I better go down home and get them ready for the surprise, if I wanted to. But I said I didn't; so I told him just how to find the raft, and then he started.

I struck an idea, pretty soon. I says to myself, spos'n he can't fix that leg just in three shakes of a sheep's tail, as the saying is? spos'n it takes him three or four days? What are we going to do?—lay around there till he lets the cat out of the bag? No, sir, I know what *I'll* do. I'll wait, and when he comes back, if he says he's got to go any more, I'll get down there, too, if I swim; and we'll take and tie him, and keep him, and shove out down the river; and when Tom's done with him, we'll give him what it's worth, or all we got, and then let him get shore.

So then I crept into a lumber pile to get some sleep; and next time I waked up the sun was away up over my head! I shot out and went for the doctor's house, but they told me he'd gone away in the night, some time or other, and warn't back yet. Well, thinks I, that looks powerful bad for Tom, and I'll dig out for the island, right off. So away I shoved, and turned the corner, and nearly rammed my head into Uncle Silas's stomach! He says:

"Why, *Tom!* Where you been, all this time, you rascal?"

"*I* hain't been nowheres," I says, "only just hunting for the runaway nigger—me and Sid."

"Why, where ever did you go?" he says. "Your aunt's been mighty uneasy."

"She needn't," I says, "because we was all right. We followed the men and the dogs, but they out-run us, and we lost them; but we thought we heard them on the water, so we got a canoe and took out after them, and crossed over but couldn't find nothing of them; so we cruised along up-shore till we got kind of tired and beat out; and tied up the canoe and went to sleep, and never waked up till about an hour ago, then we paddled over here to hear the news, and Sid's at the post-office to see what he can hear, and I'm a branching out to get something to eat for us, and then we're going home."

So then we went to the post-office to get "Sid"; but just as I suspicioned, he warn't there; so the old man he got a letter out of the office, and we waited a while longer but Sid didn't come; so the old man said come along, let Sid foot it home, or canoe-it, when he got done fooling around—but we would ride. I couldn't get him to let me stay and wait for Sid; and he said there warn't no use in it, and I must come along, and let Aunt Sally see we was all right.

When we got home, Aunt Sally was that glad to see me she laughed and cried both, and hugged me, and give me one of them lickings of hern that don't amount to shucks, and said she'd serve Sid the same when he come.

And the place was plumb full of farmers and farmers' wives, to dinner; and such another clack a body never heard. Old Mrs. Hotchkiss was the worst; her tongue was agoing all the time. She says:

"Well, Sister Phelps, I've ransacked that-air cabin over an' I b'lieve the nigger was crazy. I says so to Sister Damrell—didn't I, Sister Damrell?—s'I, he's crazy, s'I—them's the very words I said. You all hearn me: he's crazy, s'I; everything shows it, s'I. Look at that-air grindstone, s'I; want to tell *me*'t any cretur 'ts in his right mind 's agoin' to scrabble all them crazy things onto a grindstone, s'I? Here sich 'n' sich a person busted his heart; 'n' here so 'n' so pegged along for thirty-seven year, 'n' all that—natcherl son o' Louis somebody, 'n' sich everlast'n rubbage. He's plumb crazy, s'I; it's what I says in the fust place, it's what I says in the middle, 'n' it's what I says last 'n' all the time—the nigger's crazy—crazy 's Nebo-koodneezer, s'I."

"An' look at that-air ladder made out'n rags, Sister Hotch-kiss," says old Mrs. Damrell, "what in the name o' goodness *could* he ever want of——"

"The very words I was a-sayin' no longer ago th'n this min-ute to Sister Utterback, 'n' she'll tell you so herself. Sh-she, look at that-air rag ladder, sh-she; 'n' s'I, yes, *look* at it, s'I—what *could* he a wanted of it, s'I. Sh-she, Sister Hotchkiss, sh-she——"

"But how in the nation'd they ever *git* that grindstone *in* there, *any*way? 'n' who dug that-air *hole*? 'n' who——"

"My very *words*, Brer Penrod! I was a-sayin'—pass that-air sasser o' m'lasses, won't ye?—I was a-sayin' to Sister Dunlap, jist this minute, how *did* they git that grindstone in there, s'I. Without *help*, mind you—'thout *help*! *Thar's* wher' 'tis. Don't tell *me*, s'I; there *wuz* help, s'I; 'n' ther' wuz a *plenty* help, too, s'I; ther's ben a *dozen* a-helpin' that nigger, 'n' I lay I'd skin every last nigger on this place, but *I'd* find out who done it, s'I; 'n' moreover, s'I——"

"A *dozen* says you!—*forty* couldn't a done everything that's been done. Look at them case-knife saws and things, how tedious they've been made; look at that bed-leg sawed off with 'm, a week's work for six men; look at that nigger made out'n straw on the bed; and look at——"

"You may *well* say it, Brer Hightower! It's jist as I was a-sayin' to Brer Phelps, his own self. S'e, what do *you* think of it, Sister Hotchkiss, s'e? think o' what, Brer Phelps, s'I? think o' that bed-leg sawed off that a way, s'e? *think* of it, s'I? I lay it never sawed *itself* off, s'I—somebody *sawed* it, s'I; that's my opinion, take it or leave it, it mayn't be no 'count, s'I, but sich as 't is, it's my opinion, s'I, 'n' if anybody k'n start a better one, s'I, let him *do* it, s'I, that's all. I says to Sister Dunlap, s'I——"

"Why, dog my cats, they must a ben a house-full o' niggers in there every night for four weeks, to a done all that work, Sister Phelps. Look at that shirt—every last inch of it kivered over with secret African writ'n done with blood! Must a ben a raft uv 'm at it right along, all the time, amost. Why, I'd give two dollars to have it read to me; 'n' as for the niggers that wrote it, I 'low I'd take 'n' lash 'm t'll——"

"People to *help* him, Brother Marples! Well, I reckon you'd *think* so, if you'd a been in this house for a while back. Why, they've stole everything they could lay their hands on—and we a watching, all the time, mind you. They stole that shirt right off o' the line! and as for that sheet they made the rag ladder out of ther' ain't no telling how many times they *didn't* steal that; and flour, and candles, and candlesticks, and spoons, and the old warming-pan, and most a thousand things that I disremember, now, and my new calico dress; and me, and Silas, and my Sid and Tom on the constant watch day *and* night, as I was a telling you, and not a one of us could catch hide nor hair, nor sight nor sound of them; and here at the last minute, lo and behold you, they slides right in under our noses, and fools us, and not only fools *us* but the Injun Territory robbers too, and actuly gets *away* with that nigger, safe and sound, and that with sixteen men and twenty-two dogs right on their very heels at that very time! I tell you, it just bangs anything I ever *heard* of. Why, *sperits* couldn't a done better, and been no smarter. And I reckon they must a *been* sperits—because, *you* know our dogs, and ther' ain't no better; well, them dogs never even got on the *track* of 'm, once! You explain *that* to me, if you can!—*any* of you!"

"Well, it does beat——"

"Laws alive, I never——"

"So help me, I wouldn't a be——"

"*House*-thieves as well as——"

"Goodnessgracioussakes, I'd a ben afeard to *live* in sich a——"

"'Fraid to *live*!—why, I was that scared I dasn't hardly go to bed, or get up, or lay down, or *set* down, Sister Ridgeway. Why, they'd steal the very—why, goodness sakes, you can guess what kind of a fluster *I* was in by the time midnight come, last night. I hope to gracious if I warn't afraid they'd steal some o' the family! I was just to that pass, I didn't have no reasoning faculties no more. It looks foolish enough, *now*, in the day-time; but I says to myself, there's my two poor boys asleep, 'way up stairs in that lonesome room, and I declare to goodness I was that uneasy 't I crep' up there and locked 'em in! I *did*. And anybody would. Because, you know, when you get scared, that way, and it keeps running on, and getting worse and worse, all the time, and your wits gets to addling, and you get to doing all sorts o' wild things, and by-and-by you think to yourself, spos'n *I* was a boy, and was away up there, and the door ain't locked, and you——" She stopped, looking kind of wondering, and then she turned her head around slow, and when her eye lit on me—I got up and took a walk.

Says I to myself, I can explain better how we come to not be in that room this morning, if I go out to one side and study over it a little. So I done it. But I dasn't go fur, or she'd a sent for me. And when it was late in the day, the people all went, and then I come in and told her the noise and shooting waked up me and "Sid," and the door was locked, and we wanted to see the fun, so we went down the lightning-rod, and both of us got hurt a little, and we didn't never want to try *that* no more. And then I went on and told her all what I told Uncle Silas before; and then she said she'd forgive us, and maybe it was all right enough anyway, and about what a body might expect of boys, for all boys was a pretty harum-scarum lot, as fur as she could see; and so, as long as no harm hadn't come of it, she judged she better put in her time being grateful we was alive and well and she had us still, stead of fretting over what was past and done. So then she kissed me, and patted me on the head, and dropped into a kind of a brown study; and pretty soon jumps up, and says:

"Why, lawsamercy, it's most night, and Sid not come yet! What *has* become of that boy?"

I see my chance; so I skips up and says:

"I'll run right up to town and get him," I says.

"No you won't," she says. "You'll stay right wher' you are; *one's* enough to be lost at a time. If he ain't here to supper, your uncle 'll go."

Well, he warn't there to supper; so right after supper uncle went.

He come back about ten, a little bit uneasy; hadn't run across Tom's track. Aunt Sally was a good *deal* uneasy; but Uncle Silas he said there warn't no occasion to be—boys will be boys, he said, and you'll see this one turn up in the morning, all sound and right. So she had to be satisfied. But she said she'd set up for him a while, anyway, and keep a light burning, so he could see it.

And then when I went up to bed she come up with me and fetched her candle, and tucked me in, and mothered me so good I felt mean, and like I couldn't look her in the face; and she set down on the bed and talked with me a long time, and said what a splendid boy Sid was, and didn't seem to want to ever stop talking about him; and kept asking me every now and then, if I reckoned he could a got lost, or hurt, or maybe drownded, and might be laying at this minute, somewheres, suffering or dead, and she not by him to help him, and so the tears would drip down, silent, and I would tell her that Sid was all right, and would be home in the morning, sure; and she would squeeze my hand, or maybe kiss me, and tell me to say it again, and keep on saying it, because it done her good, and she was in so much trouble. And when she was going away, she looked down in my eyes, so steady and gentle, and says:

"The door ain't going to be locked, Tom; and there's the window and the rod; but you'll be good, *won't* you? And you won't go? For *my* sake."

Laws knows I *wanted* to go, bad enough, to see about Tom, and was all intending to go; but after that, I wouldn't a went, not for kingdoms.

But she was on my mind, and Tom was on my mind; so I slept very restless. And twice I went down the rod, away in the night, and slipped around front, and see her setting there by her candle in the window with her eyes towards the road and the tears in them; and I wished I could do something for her, but I couldn't, only to swear that I wouldn't never do nothing to grieve her any more. And the third time, I waked up at dawn, and slid down, and she was there yet, and her candle was most out, and her old gray head was resting on her hand, and she was asleep.

XLII

The old man was up town again, before breakfast, but couldn't get no track of Tom; and both of them set at the table, thinking, and not saying nothing, and looking mournful, and their coffee getting cold, and not eating anything. And by-and-by the old man says:

"Did I give you the letter?"

"What letter?"

"The one I got yesterday out of the post-office."

"No, you didn't give me no letter."

"Well, I must a forgot it."

So he rummaged his pockets, and then went off somewheres where he had laid it down, and fetched it, and give it to her. She says:

"Why, it's from St. Petersburg—it's from Sis."

I allowed another walk would do me good; but I couldn't stir. But before she could break it open, she dropped it and run—for she see something. And so did I. It was Tom Sawyer on a mattress; and that old doctor; and Jim, in *her* calico dress, with his hands tied behind him; and a lot of people. I hid the letter behind the first thing that come handy, and rushed. She flung herself at Tom, crying, and says:

"Oh, he's dead, he's dead, I know he's dead!"

And Tom he turned his head a little, and muttered something or other, which showed he warn't in his right mind; then she flung up her hands, and says:

"He's alive, thank God! And that's enough!" and she snatched a kiss of him, and flew for the house to get the bed ready, and scattering orders right and left at the niggers and everybody else, as fast as her tongue could go, every jump of the way.

I followed the men to see what they was going to do with Jim; and the old doctor and Uncle Silas followed after Tom into the house. The men was very huffy, and some of them wanted to hang Jim, for an example to all the other niggers around there, so they wouldn't be trying to run away, like Jim done, and making such a raft of trouble, and keeping a whole family scared most to death for days and nights. But the others said, don't do it, it wouldn't answer at all, he ain't our nigger, and his owner would turn up and make us pay for him, sure. So that cooled them down a little, because the people that's always the most anxious for to hang a nigger that hain't done just right, is always the very ones that ain't the most anxious to pay for him when they've got their satisfaction out of him.

They cussed Jim considerble, though, and give him a cuff or two, side the head, once in a while, but Jim never said nothing, and he never let on to know me, and they took him to the same cabin, and put his own clothes on him, and chained him again, and not to no bed-leg, this time, but to a big staple drove into the bottom log, and chained his hands, too, and both legs, and said he warn't to have nothing but bread and water to eat, after this, till his owner come or he was sold at auction, because he didn't come in a certain length of time, and filled up our hole, and said a couple of farmers with guns must stand watch around about the cabin every night, and a bull-dog tied to the door in the day-time; and about this time they was through with the job and was tapering off with a kind of generl good-bye cussing, and then the old doctor comes and takes a look, and says:

"Don't be no rougher on him than you're obleeged to, because he ain't a bad nigger. When I got to where I found the boy, I see I couldn't cut the bullet out without some help, and he warn't in no condition for me to leave, to go and get help; and he got a little worse and a little worse, and after a long time he went out of his head, and wouldn't let me come anigh him, any more, and said if I chalked his raft he'd kill me, and no end of wild foolishness like that, and I see I couldn't do anything at all with him; so I says, I got to have *help*, somehow; and the minute I says it, out crawls this nigger from somewheres, and says he'll help, and he done it, too, and done it very well. Of course I judged he must be a runaway nigger, and there I *was*! and there I had to stick, right straight along all the rest of the day, and all night. It was a fix, I tell you! I had a couple of patients with the chills, and of course I'd of liked to run up to town and see them, but I dasn't, because the nigger might get away, and then I'd be to

blame; and yet never a skiff come close enough for me to hail.
So there I had to stick, plumb till daylight this morning; and
I never see a nigger that was a better nuss or faithfuller, and
yet he was resking his freedom to do it, and was all tired out,
too, and I see plain enough he'd been worked main hard,
lately. I liked the nigger for that; I tell you, gentlemen, a
nigger like that is worth a thousand dollars—and kind treatment, too. I had everything I needed, and the boy was doing
as well there as he would a done at home—better, maybe,
because it was so quiet; but there I *was*, with both of 'm on
my hands; and there I had to stick, till about dawn this morning; then some men in a skiff come by, and as good luck
would have it, the nigger was setting by the pallet with his
head propped on his knees, sound asleep; so I motioned them
in, quiet, and they slipped up on him and grabbed him and
tied him before he knowed what he was about, and we never
had no trouble. And the boy being in a kind of a flighty sleep,
too, we muffled the oars and hitched the raft on, and towed
her over very nice and quiet, and the nigger never made the
least row nor said a word, from the start. He ain't no bad
nigger, gentlemen; that's what I think about him."

Somebody says:

"Well, it sounds very good, doctor, I'm obleeged to say."

Then the others softened up a little, too, and I was mighty
thankful to that old doctor for doing Jim that good turn; and
I was glad it was according to my judgment of him, too;
because I thought he had a good heart in him and was a good
man, the first time I see him. Then they all agreed that Jim
had acted very well, and was deserving to have some notice
took of it, and reward. So every one of them promised, right
out and hearty, that they wouldn't cuss him no more.

Then they come out and locked him up. I hoped they was
going to say he could have one or two of the chains took off,
because they was rotten heavy, or could have meat and greens
with his bread and water, but they didn't think of it, and I
reckoned it warn't best for me to mix in, but I judged I'd get
the doctor's yarn to Aunt Sally, somehow or other, as soon
as I'd got through the breakers that was laying just ahead of
me. Explanations, I mean, of how I forgot to mention about
Sid being shot, when I was telling how him and me put in

that dratted night paddling around hunting the runaway nigger.

But I had plenty time. Aunt Sally she stuck to the sick-room all day and all night; and every time I see Uncle Silas mooning around, I dodged him.

Next morning I heard Tom was a good deal better, and they said Aunt Sally was gone to get a nap. So I slips to the sick-room, and if I found him awake I reckoned we could put up a yarn for the family that would wash. But he was sleeping, and sleeping very peaceful, too; and pale, not fire-faced the way he was when he come. So I set down and laid for him to wake. In about a half an hour, Aunt Sally comes gliding in, and there I was, up a stump again! She motioned me to be still, and set down by me, and begun to whisper, and said we could all be joyful now, because all the symptoms was first rate, and he'd been sleeping like that for ever so long, and looking better and peacefuller all the time, and ten to one he'd wake up in his right mind.

So we set there watching, and by-and-by he stirs a bit, and opened his eyes very natural, and takes a look, and says:

"Hello, why I'm at *home*! How's that? Where's the raft?"

"It's all right," I says.

"And *Jim*?"

"The same," I says, but couldn't say it pretty brash. But he never noticed, but says:

"Good! Splendid! *Now* we're all right and safe! Did you tell Aunty?"

I was going to say yes; but she chipped in and says:

"About what, Sid?"

"Why, about the way the whole thing was done."

"What whole thing?"

"Why, *the* whole thing. There ain't but one; how we set the runaway nigger free—me and Tom."

"Good land! Set the run— What *is* the child talking about! Dear, dear, out of his head again!"

"*No*, I ain't out of my HEAD; I know all what I'm talking about. We *did* set him free—me and Tom. We laid out to do it, and we *done* it. And we done it elegant, too." He'd got a start, and she never checked him up, just set and stared and stared, and let him clip along, and I see it warn't no use for *me* to put in. "Why, Aunty, it cost us a power of work— weeks of it—hours and hours, every night, whilst you was all asleep. And we had to steal candles, and the sheet, and the shirt, and your dress, and spoons, and tin plates, and case- knives, and the warming-pan, and the grindstone, and flour, and just no end of things, and you can't think what work it was to make the saws, and pens, and inscriptions, and one thing or another, and you can't think *half* the fun it was. And we had to make up the pictures of coffins and things, and nonnamous letters from the robbers, and get up and down the lightning-rod, and dig the hole into the cabin, and make the rope-ladder and send it in cooked up in a pie, and send in spoons and things to work with, in your apron pocket"——

"Mercy sakes!"

——"and load up the cabin with rats and snakes and so on, for company for Jim; and then you kept Tom here so long with the butter in his hat that you come near spiling the whole business, because the men come before we was out of the cabin, and we had to rush, and they heard us and let drive at us, and I got my share, and we dodged out of the path and let them go by, and when the dogs come they warn't inter- ested in us, but went for the most noise, and we got our canoe, and made for the raft, and was all safe, and Jim was a free man, and we done it all by ourselves, and *wasn't* it bully, Aunty!"

"Well, I never heard the likes of it in all my born days! So it was *you*, you little rapscallions, that's been making all this trouble, and turned everybody's wits clean inside out and scared us all most to death. I've as good a notion as ever I had in my life, to take it out o' you this very minute. To think, here I've been, night after night, a—*you* just get well once, you young scamp, and I lay I'll tan the Old Harry out o' both o' ye!"

But Tom, he *was* so proud and joyful, he just *couldn't* hold in, and his tongue just *went* it—she a-chipping in, and spit- ting fire all along, and both of them going it at once, like a cat-convention; and she says:

"*Well*, you get all the enjoyment you can out of it *now*, for mind I tell you if I catch you meddling with him again——"

"Meddling with *who*?" Tom says, dropping his smile and looking surprised.

"With *who*? Why, the runaway nigger, of course. Who'd you reckon?"

Tom looks at me very grave, and says:

"Tom, didn't you just tell me he was all right? Hasn't he got away?"

"*Him*?" says Aunt Sally; "the runaway nigger? 'Deed he hasn't. They've got him back, safe and sound, and he's in that cabin again, on bread and water, and loaded down with chains, till he's claimed or sold!"

Tom rose square up in bed, with his eye hot, and his nostrils opening and shutting like gills, and sings out to me:

"They hain't no *right* to shut him up! *Shove!*—and don't you lose a minute. Turn him loose! he ain't no slave; he's as free as any cretur that walks this earth!"

"What *does* the child mean?"

"I mean every word I *say*, Aunt Sally, and if somebody don't go, *I'll* go. I've knowed him all his life, and so has Tom, there. Old Miss Watson died two months ago, and she was ashamed she ever was going to sell him down the river, and *said* so; and she set him free in her will."

"Then what on earth did *you* want to set him free for, seeing he was already free?"

"Well, that *is* a question, I must say; and *just* like women! Why, I wanted the *adventure* of it; and I'd a waded neck-deep in blood to—goodness alive, AUNT POLLY!"

If she warn't standing right there, just inside the door, looking as sweet and contented as an angel half-full of pie, I wish I may never!

Aunt Sally jumped for her, and most hugged the head off of her, and cried over her, and I found a good enough place for me under the bed, for it was getting pretty sultry for *us*, seemed to me. And I peeped out, and in a little while Tom's Aunt Polly shook herself loose and stood there looking across at Tom over her spectacles—kind of grinding him into the earth, you know. And then she says:

"Yes, you *better* turn y'r head away—I would if I was you, Tom."

"Oh, deary me!" says Aunt Sally; "*is* he changed so? Why, that ain't *Tom* it's Sid; Tom's—Tom's—why, where is Tom? He was here a minute ago."

"You mean where's Huck *Finn*—that's what you mean! I reckon I hain't raised such a scamp as my Tom all these years, not to know him when I *see* him. That *would* be a pretty howdy-do. Come out from under that bed, Huck Finn."

So I done it. But not feeling brash.

Aunt Sally she was one of the mixed-upset looking persons I ever see; except one, and that was Uncle Silas, when he come in, and they told it all to him. It kind of made him drunk, as you may say, and he didn't know nothing at all the rest of the day, and preached a prayer-meeting sermon that night that give him a rattling reputation, because the oldest man in the world couldn't a understood it. So Tom's Aunt Polly, she told all about who I was, and what; and I had to up and tell how I was in such a tight place that when Mrs. Phelps took me for Tom Sawyer—she chipped in and says, "Oh, go on and call me Aunt Sally, I'm used to it, now, and 'tain't no need to change"—that when Aunt Sally took me for Tom Sawyer, I had to stand it—there warn't no other way, and I knowed he wouldn't mind, because it would be nuts for him, being a mystery, and he'd make an adventure out of it and be perfectly satisfied. And so it turned out, and he let on to be Sid, and made things as soft as he could for me.

And his Aunt Polly she said Tom was right about old Miss Watson setting Jim free in her will; and so, sure enough, Tom Sawyer had gone and took all that trouble and bother to set a free nigger free! and I couldn't ever understand, before, until that minute and that talk, how he *could* help a body set a nigger free, with his bringing-up.

Well, Aunt Polly she said that when Aunt Sally wrote to her that Tom and *Sid* had come, all right and safe, she says to herself:

"Look at that, now! I might have expected it, letting him go off that way without anybody to watch him. So now I got to go and trapse all the way down the river, eleven hundred mile, and find out what that creetur's up to, *this* time; as long as I couldn't seem to get any answer out of you about it."

"Why, I never heard nothing from you," says Aunt Sally.

"Well, I wonder! Why, I wrote to you twice, to ask you what you could mean by Sid being here."

"Well, I never got 'em, Sis."

Aunt Polly, she turns around slow and severe, and says:

"You, Tom!"

"Well—*what?*" he says, kind of pettish.

"Don't you what *me*, you impudent thing—hand out them letters."

"What letters?"

"*Them* letters. I be bound, if I have to take aholt of you I'll——"

"They're in the trunk. There, now. And they're just the same as they was when I got them out of the office. I hain't looked into them, I hain't touched them. But I knowed they'd make trouble, and I thought if you warn't in no hurry, I'd——"

"Well, you *do* need skinning, there ain't no mistake about it. And I wrote another one to tell you I was coming; and I spose he——"

"No, it come yesterday; I hain't read it yet, but *it's* all right, I've got that one."

I wanted to offer to bet two dollars she hadn't, but I reckoned maybe it was just as safe to not to. So I never said nothing.

Chapter the Last

THE FIRST TIME I catched Tom, private, I asked him what was his idea, time of the evasion?—what it was he'd planned to do if the evasion worked all right and he managed to set a nigger free that was already free before? And he said, what he had planned in his head, from the start, if we got Jim out all safe, was for us to run him down the river, on the raft, and have adventures plumb to the mouth of the river, and then tell him about his being free, and take him back up home on a steamboat, in style, and pay him for his lost time, and write word ahead and get out all the niggers around, and have them waltz him into town with a torch-light procession and a brass band, and then he would be a hero, and so would we. But I reckened it was about as well the way it was.

We had Jim out of the chains in no time, and when Aunt Polly and Uncle Silas and Aunt Sally found out how good he helped the doctor nurse Tom, they made a heap of fuss over him, and fixed him up prime, and give him all he wanted to eat, and a good time, and nothing to do. And we had him up to the sick-room; and had a high talk; and Tom give Jim forty dollars for being prisoner for us so patient, and doing it up so good, and Jim was pleased most to death, and busted out, and says:

"*Dah*, now, Huck, what I tell you?—what I tell you up dah on Jackson islan'? I *tole* you I got a hairy breas', en what's de sign un it; en I *tole* you I ben rich wunst, en gwineter to be rich *agin*; en it's come true; en heah she *is*! *Dah*, now! doan' talk to *me*—signs is *signs*, mine I tell you; en I knowed jis' 's well 'at I 'uz gwineter be rich agin as I's a stannin' heah dis minute!"

And then Tom he talked along, and talked along, and says, le's all three slide out of here, one of these nights, and get an outfit, and go for howling adventures amongst the Injuns, over in the Territory, for a couple of weeks or two; and I says, all right, that suits me, but I aint got no money for to buy the outfit, and I reckon I couldn't get none from home, because it's likely pap's been back before now, and got it all away from Judge Thatcher and drunk it up.

"No he hain't," Tom says; "it's all there, yet—six thousand dollars and more; and your pap hain't ever been back since. Hadn't when I come away, anyhow."

Jim says, kind of solemn:

"He ain't a comin' back no mo', Huck."

I says:

"Why, Jim?"

"Nemmine why, Huck—but he ain't comin' back no mo'."

But I kept at him; so at last he says:

"Doan' you 'member de house dat was float'n down de river, en dey wuz a man in dah, kivered up, en I went in en unkivered him and didn' let you come in? Well, den, you k'n git yo' money when you wants it; kase dat wuz him."

Tom's most well, now, and got his bullet around his neck on a watch-guard for a watch, and is always seeing what time it is, and so there ain't nothing more to write about, and I am rotten glad of it, because if I'd a knowed what a trouble it was to make a book I wouldn't a tackled it and ain't agoing to no more. But I reckon I got to light out for the Territory ahead of the rest, because Aunt Sally she's going to adopt me and sivilize me and I can't stand it. I been there before.

PUDD'NHEAD WILSON
A Tale

A Whisper to the Reader

THERE is no character, howsoever good and fine, but it can be destroyed by ridicule, howsoever poor and witless. Observe the ass, for instance: his character is about perfect, he is the choicest spirit among all the humbler animals, yet see what ridicule has brought him to. Instead of feeling complimented when we are called an ass, we are left in doubt.

—*Pudd'nhead Wilson's Calendar.*

A PERSON who is ignorant of legal matters is always liable to make mistakes when he tries to photograph a court scene with his pen; and so I was not willing to let the law chapters in this book go to press without first subjecting them to rigid and exhausting revision and correction by a trained barrister—if that is what they are called. These chapters are right, now, in every detail, for they were rewritten under the immediate eye of William Hicks, who studied law part of a while in southwest Missouri thirty-five years ago and then came over here to Florence for his health and is still helping for exercise and board in Macaroni Vermicelli's horse-feed shed which is up the back alley as you turn around the corner out of the Piazza del Duomo just beyond the house where that stone that Dante used to sit on six hundred years ago is let into the wall when he let on to be watching them build Giotto's campanile and yet always got tired looking as soon as Beatrice passed along on her way to get a chunk of chestnut cake to defend herself with in case of a Ghibelline outbreak before she got to school, at the same old stand where they sell the same old cake to this day and it is just as light and good as it was then, too, and this is not flattery, far from it. He was a little rusty on his law, but he rubbed up for this book, and those two or three legal chapters are right and straight, now. He told me so himself.

Given under my hand this second day of January, 1893, at the Villa Viviani, village of Settignano, three miles back of Florence, on the hills—the same certainly affording the most charming view to be found on this planet, and with it the most dream-like and enchanting sunsets to be found in any planet or even in any solar system—and given, too, in the swell room of the house, with the busts of Cerretani senators and other grandees of this line looking approvingly down upon me as they used to look down upon Dante, and mutely asking me to adopt them into my family, which I do with pleasure, for my remotest ancestors are but spring chickens compared with these robed and stately antiques, and it will be a great and satisfying lift for me, that six hundred years will.

Mark Twain.

I

THE SCENE of this chronicle is the town of Dawson's Landing, on the Missouri side of the Mississippi, half a day's journey, per steamboat, below St. Louis.

In 1830 it was a snug little collection of modest one- and two-story frame dwellings whose whitewashed exteriors were almost concealed from sight by climbing tangles of rose vines, honeysuckles and morning-glories. Each of these pretty homes had a garden in front fenced with white palings and opulently stocked with hollyhocks, marigolds, touch-me-nots, prince's-feathers and other old-fashioned flowers; while on the window-sills of the houses stood wooden boxes containing moss-rose plants and terra-cotta pots in which grew a breed of geranium whose spread of intensely red blossoms accented the prevailing pink tint of the rose-clad house-front like an explosion of flame. When there was room on the ledge outside of the pots and boxes for a cat, the cat was there—in sunny weather—stretched at full length, asleep and blissful, with her furry belly to the sun and a paw curved over her nose. Then that house was complete, and its contentment and peace were made manifest to the world by this symbol, whose testimony is infallible. A home without a cat—and a well-fed, well-petted and properly revered cat—may be a perfect home, perhaps, but how can it prove title?

All along the streets, on both sides, at the outer edge of the brick sidewalks, stood locust-trees with trunks protected by wooden boxing, and these furnished shade for summer and a sweet fragrance in spring when the clusters of buds came forth. The main street, one block back from the river, and running parallel with it, was the sole business street. It was six blocks long, and in each block two or three brick stores three stories high towered above interjected bunches of little frame shops. Swinging signs creaked in the wind, the street's whole length. The candy-striped pole which indicates nobility proud and ancient along the palace-bordered canals of Venice, indicated merely the humble barber-shop along the main street of Dawson's Landing. On a chief corner stood a lofty unpainted pole wreathed from top to bottom with tin pots and pans and cups, the chief tinmonger's noisy notice to the world (when the wind blew) that his shop was on hand for business at that corner.

The hamlet's front was washed by the clear waters of the great river; its body stretched itself rearward up a gentle incline; its most rearward border fringed itself out and scattered its houses about the base-line of the hills; the hills rose high, inclosing the town in a half-moon curve, clothed with forests from foot to summit.

Steamboats passed up and down every hour or so. Those belonging to the little Cairo line and the little Memphis line always stopped; the big Orleans liners stopped for hails only, or to land passengers or freight; and this was the case also with the great flotilla of "transients." These latter came out of a dozen rivers—the Illinois, the Missouri, the Upper Mississippi, the Ohio, the Monongahela, the Tennessee, the Red River, the White River, and so on; and were bound every whither and stocked with every imaginable comfort or necessity which the Mississippi's communities could want, from the frosty Falls of St. Anthony down through nine climates to torrid New Orleans.

Dawson's Landing was a slaveholding town, with a rich slave-worked grain and pork country back of it. The town was sleepy and comfortable and contented. It was fifty years old, and was growing slowly—very slowly, in fact, but still it was growing.

The chief citizen was York Leicester Driscoll, about forty years old, judge of the county court. He was very proud of his old Virginian ancestry, and in his hospitalities and his rather formal and stately manners he kept up its traditions. He was fine and just and generous. To be a gentleman—a gentleman without stain or blemish—was his only religion, and to it he was always faithful. He was respected, esteemed and beloved by all the community. He was well off, and was gradually adding to his store. He and his wife were very nearly happy, but not quite, for they had no children. The longing for the treasure of a child had grown stronger and stronger as the years slipped away, but the blessing never came—and was never to come.

With this pair lived the Judge's widowed sister, Mrs. Rachel Pratt, and she also was childless—childless, and sorrowful for that reason, and not to be comforted. The women were good and commonplace people, and did their duty and had their reward in clear consciences and the community's approbation. They were Presbyterians, the Judge was a free-thinker.

Pembroke Howard, lawyer and bachelor, aged about forty, was another old Virginian grandee with proved descent from the First Families. He was a fine, brave, majestic creature, a gentleman according to the nicest requirements of the Virginian rule, a devoted Presbyterian, an authority on the "code," and a man always courteously ready to stand up before you in the field if any act or word of his had seemed doubtful or suspicious to you, and explain it with any weapon you might prefer from brad-awls to artillery. He was very popular with the people, and was the Judge's dearest friend.

Then there was Colonel Cecil Burleigh Essex, another F. F. V. of formidable caliber—however, with him we have no concern.

Percy Northumberland Driscoll, brother to the Judge, and younger than he by five years, was a married man, and had had children around his hearthstone; but they were attacked in detail by measles, croup and scarlet fever, and this had given the doctor a chance with his effective antediluvian methods; so the cradles were empty. He was a prosperous man, with a good head for speculations, and his fortune was growing. On the 1st of February, 1830, two boy babes were born in his house: one to him, the other to one of his slave girls, Roxana by name. Roxana was twenty years old. She was up and around the same day, with her hands full, for she was tending both babies.

Mrs. Percy Driscoll died within the week. Roxy remained in charge of the children. She had her own way, for Mr. Driscoll soon absorbed himself in his speculations and left her to her own devices.

In that same month of February, Dawson's Landing gained a new citizen. This was Mr. David Wilson, a young fellow of

Scotch parentage. He had wandered to this remote region from his birthplace in the interior of the State of New York, to seek his fortune. He was twenty-five years old, college-bred, and had finished a post-college course in an Eastern law school a couple of years before.

He was a homely, freckled, sandy-haired young fellow, with an intelligent blue eye that had frankness and comradeship in it and a covert twinkle of a pleasant sort. But for an unfortunate remark of his, he would no doubt have entered at once upon a successful career at Dawson's Landing. But he made his fatal remark the first day he spent in the village, and it "gaged" him. He had just made the acquaintance of a group of citizens when an invisible dog began to yelp and snarl and howl and make himself very comprehensively disagreeable, whereupon young Wilson said, much as one who is thinking aloud—

"I wished I owned half of that dog."

"Why?" somebody asked.

"Because I would kill my half."

The group searched his face with curiosity, with anxiety even, but found no light there, no expression that they could read. They fell away from him as from something uncanny, and went into privacy to discuss him. One said:

" 'Pears to be a fool."

" 'Pears?" said another. "*Is*, I reckon you better say."

"Said he wished he owned *half* of the dog, the idiot," said a third. "What did he reckon would become of the other half if he killed his half? Do you reckon he thought it would live?"

"Why, he must have thought it, unless he *is* the downrightest fool in the world; because if he had n't thought it, he would have wanted to own the whole dog, knowing that if he killed his half and the other half died, he would be responsible for that half just the same as if he had killed that half instead of his own. Don't it look that way to you, gents?"

"Yes, it does. If he owned one half of the general dog, it would be so; if he owned one end of the dog and another person owned the other end, it would be so, just the same; particularly in the first case, because if you kill one half of a general dog, there ain't any man that can tell whose half it was, but if he owned one end of the dog, maybe he could kill his end of it and—"

"No, he could n't, either: he could n't and not be responsible if the other end died, which it would. In my opinion the man ain't in his right mind."

"In my opinion he hain't *got* any mind."

No. 3 said: "Well, he 's a lummox, anyway."

"That 's what he is," said No. 4, "he 's a labrick—just a Simon-pure labrick, if ever there was one."

"Yes, sir, he 's a dam fool, that 's the way I put him up," said No. 5. "Anybody can think different that wants to, but those are my sentiments."

"I 'm with you, gentlemen," said No. 6. "Perfect jackass—yes, and it ain't going too far to say he is a pudd'nhead. If he ain't a pudd'nhead, I ain't no judge, that 's all."

Mr. Wilson stood elected. The incident was told all over the town, and gravely discussed by everybody. Within a week he had lost his first name; Pudd'nhead took its place. In time he came to be liked, and well liked too; but by that time the nickname had got well stuck on, and it stayed. That first day's verdict made him a fool, and he was not able to get it set aside, or even modified. The nickname soon ceased to carry any harsh or unfriendly feeling with it, but it held its place, and was to continue to hold its place for twenty long years.

II

ADAM was but human—this explains it all. He did not want the apple for the apple's sake, he wanted it only because it was forbidden. The mistake was in not forbidding the serpent; then he would have eaten the serpent.

—Pudd'nhead Wilson's Calendar.

P UDD'NHEAD WILSON had a trifle of money when he arrived, and he bought a small house on the extreme western verge of the town. Between it and Judge Driscoll's house there was only a grassy yard, with a paling fence dividing the properties in the middle. He hired a small office down in the town and hung out a tin sign with these words on it:

DAVID WILSON.
ATTORNEY AND COUNSELOR-AT-LAW.
SURVEYING, CONVEYANCING, ETC.

But his deadly remark had ruined his chance—at least in the law. No clients came. He took down his sign, after a while, and put it up on his own house with the law features knocked out of it. It offered his services now in the humble capacities of land-surveyor and expert accountant. Now and then he got a job of surveying to do, and now and then a merchant got him to straighten out his books. With Scotch patience and pluck he resolved to live down his reputation and work his way into the legal field yet. Poor fellow, he could not foresee that it was going to take him such a weary long time to do it.

He had a rich abundance of idle time, but it never hung heavy on his hands, for he interested himself in every new thing that was born into the universe of ideas, and studied it and experimented upon it at his house. One of his pet fads was palmistry. To another one he gave no name, neither would he explain to anybody what its purpose was, but merely said it was an amusement. In fact he had found that his fads added to his reputation as a pudd'nhead; therefore he was growing chary of being too communicative about them.

The fad without a name was one which dealt with people's finger-marks. He carried in his coat pocket a shallow box with grooves in it, and in the grooves strips of glass five inches long and three inches wide. Along the lower edge of each strip was pasted a slip of white paper. He asked people to pass their hands through their hair (thus collecting upon them a thin coating of the natural oil) and then make a thumb-mark on a glass strip, following it with the mark of the ball of each finger in succession. Under this row of faint grease-prints he would write a record on the strip of white paper—thus:

JOHN SMITH, *right hand*—

and add the day of the month and the year, then take Smith's left hand on another glass strip, and add name and date and the words "left hand." The strips were now returned to the grooved box, and took their place among what Wilson called his "records."

He often studied his records, examining and poring over them with absorbing interest until far into the night; but what he found there—if he found anything—he revealed to no one. Sometimes he copied on paper the involved and delicate pattern left by the ball of a finger, and then vastly enlarged it with a pantograph so that he could examine its web of curving lines with ease and convenience.

One sweltering afternoon—it was the first day of July, 1830—he was at work over a set of tangled account-books in his workroom, which looked westward over a stretch of vacant lots, when a conversation outside disturbed him. It was carried on in yells, which showed that the people engaged in it were not close together:

"Say, Roxy, how does yo' baby come on?" This from the distant voice.

"Fust-rate; how does *you* come on, Jasper?" This yell was from close by.

"Oh. I 's middlin'; hain't got noth'n' to complain of. I 's gwine to come a-court'n' you bimeby, Roxy."

"*You* is, you black mud-cat! Yah—yah—yah! I got somep'n' better to do den 'sociat'n' wid niggers as black as

you is. Is ole Miss Cooper's Nancy done give you de mitten?"
Roxy followed this sally with another discharge of care-free
laughter.

"You 's jealous, Roxy, dat 's what 's de matter wid *you*, you
hussy—yah—yah—yah! Dat 's de time I got you!"

"Oh, yes, *you* got me, hain't you. 'Clah to goodness if dat
conceit o' yo'n strikes in, Jasper, it gwine to kill you sho'. If
you b'longed to me I 'd sell you down de river 'fo' you git
too fur gone. Fust time I runs acrost yo' marster, I 's gwine
to tell him so."

This idle and aimless jabber went on and on, both parties
enjoying the friendly duel and each well satisfied with his own
share of the wit exchanged—for wit they considered it.

Wilson stepped to the window to observe the combatants;
he could not work while their chatter continued. Over in the
vacant lots was Jasper, young, coal-black and of magnificent
build, sitting on a wheelbarrow in the pelting sun—at work,
supposably, whereas he was in fact only preparing for it by
taking an hour's rest before beginning. In front of Wilson's
porch stood Roxy, with a local hand-made baby-wagon, in
which sat her two charges—one at each end and facing each
other. From Roxy's manner of speech, a stranger would have
expected her to be black, but she was not. Only one sixteenth
of her was black, and that sixteenth did not show. She was of
majestic form and stature, her attitudes were imposing and
statuesque, and her gestures and movements distinguished by
a noble and stately grace. Her complexion was very fair, with
the rosy glow of vigorous health in the cheeks, her face was
full of character and expression, her eyes were brown and liq-
uid, and she had a heavy suit of fine soft hair which was also
brown, but the fact was not apparent because her head was
bound about with a checkered handkerchief and the hair was
concealed under it. Her face was shapely, intelligent and
comely—even beautiful. She had an easy, independent carriage—when she was among her own caste—and a high and
"sassy" way, withal; but of course she was meek and humble
enough where white people were.

To all intents and purposes Roxy was as white as anybody,
but the one sixteenth of her which was black outvoted the
other fifteen parts and made her a negro. She was a slave, and

salable as such. Her child was thirty-one parts white, and he, too, was a slave, and by a fiction of law and custom a negro. He had blue eyes and flaxen curls like his white comrade, but even the father of the white child was able to tell the children apart—little as he had commerce with them—by their clothes: for the white babe wore ruffled soft muslin and a coral necklace, while the other wore merely a coarse tow-linen shirt which barely reached to its knees, and no jewelry.

The white child's name was Thomas à Becket Driscoll, the other's name was Valet de Chambre: no surname—slaves had n't the privilege. Roxana had heard that phrase somewhere, the fine sound of it had pleased her ear, and as she had supposed it was a name, she loaded it on to her darling. It soon got shortened to "Chambers," of course.

Wilson knew Roxy by sight, and when the duel of wit began to play out, he stepped outside to gather in a record or two. Jasper went to work energetically, at once, perceiving that his leisure was observed. Wilson inspected the children and asked—

"How old are they, Roxy?"

"Bofe de same age, sir—five months. Bawn de fust o' Feb'uary."

"They 're handsome little chaps. One 's just as handsome as the other, too."

A delighted smile exposed the girl's white teeth, and she said:

"Bless yo' soul, Misto Wilson, it 's pow'ful nice o' you to say dat, 'ca'se one of 'em ain't on'y a nigger. Mighty prime little nigger, I al'ays says, but dat 's 'ca'se it 's mine, o' course."

"How do you tell them apart, Roxy, when they have n't any clothes on?"

Roxy laughed a laugh proportioned to her size, and said:

"Oh, I kin tell 'em 'part, Misto Wilson, but I bet Marse Percy could n't, not to save his life."

Wilson chatted along for a while, and presently got Roxy's finger-prints for his collection—right hand and left—on a couple of his glass strips; then labeled and dated them, and took the "records" of both children, and labeled and dated them also.

Two months later, on the 3d of September, he took this trio of finger-marks again. He liked to have a "series," two or three "takings" at intervals during the period of childhood, these to be followed by others at intervals of several years.

The next day—that is to say, on the 4th of September—something occurred which profoundly impressed Roxana. Mr. Driscoll missed another small sum of money—which is a way of saying that this was not a new thing, but had happened before. In truth it had happened three times before. Driscoll's patience was exhausted. He was a fairly humane man toward slaves and other animals; he was an exceedingly humane man toward the erring of his own race. Theft he could not abide, and plainly there was a thief in his house. Necessarily the thief must be one of his negroes. Sharp measures must be taken. He called his servants before him. There were three of these, besides Roxy: a man, a woman, and a boy twelve years old. They were not related. Mr. Driscoll said:

"You have all been warned before. It has done no good. This time I will teach you a lesson. I will sell the thief. Which of you is the guilty one?"

They all shuddered at the threat, for here they had a good home, and a new one was likely to be a change for the worse. The denial was general. None had stolen anything—not money, anyway—a little sugar, or cake, or honey, or something like that, that "Marse Percy would n't mind or miss," but not money—never a cent of money. They were eloquent in their protestations, but Mr. Driscoll was not moved by them. He answered each in turn with a stern "Name the thief!"

The truth was, all were guilty but Roxana; she suspected that the others were guilty, but she did not know them to be so. She was horrified to think how near she had come to being guilty herself; she had been saved in the nick of time by a revival in the colored Methodist Church, a fortnight before, at which time and place she "got religion." The very next day after that gracious experience, while her change of style was fresh upon her and she was vain of her purified condition, her master left a couple of dollars lying unprotected on his desk, and she happened upon that temptation when she was polishing around with a dust-rag. She looked at the money a while with a steadily rising resentment, then she burst out with—

"Dad blame dat revival, I wisht it had 'a' be'n put off till to-morrow!"

Then she covered the tempter with a book, and another member of the kitchen cabinet got it. She made this sacrifice as a matter of religious etiquette; as a thing necessary just now, but by no means to be wrested into a precedent; no, a week or two would limber up her piety, then she would be rational again, and the next two dollars that got left out in the cold would find a comforter—and she could name the comforter.

Was she bad? Was she worse than the general run of her race? No. They had an unfair show in the battle of life, and they held it no sin to take military advantage of the enemy—in a small way; in a small way, but not in a large one. They would smouch provisions from the pantry whenever they got a chance; or a brass thimble, or a cake of wax, or an emery bag, or a paper of needles, or a silver spoon, or a dollar bill, or small articles of clothing, or any other property of light value; and so far were they from considering such reprisals sinful, that they would go to church and shout and pray their loudest and sincerest with their plunder in their pockets. A farm smoke-house had to be kept heavily padlocked, for even the colored deacon himself could not resist a ham when Providence showed him in a dream, or otherwise, where such a thing hung lonesome and longed for some one to love. But with a hundred hanging before him the deacon would not take two—that is, on the same night. On frosty nights the humane negro prowler would warm the end of a plank and put it up under the cold claws of chickens roosting in a tree; a drowsy hen would step on to the comfortable board, softly clucking her gratitude, and the prowler would dump her into his bag, and later into his stomach, perfectly sure that in taking this trifle from the man who daily robbed him of an inestimable treasure—his liberty—he was not committing any sin that God would remember against him in the Last Great Day.

"Name the thief!"

For the fourth time Mr. Driscoll had said it, and always in the same hard tone. And now he added these words of awful import:

"I give you one minute"—he took out his watch. "If at the end of that time you have not confessed, I will not only sell all four of you, *but*—I will sell you DOWN THE RIVER!"

It was equivalent to condemning them to hell! No Missouri negro doubted this. Roxy reeled in her tracks and the color vanished out of her face; the others dropped to their knees as if they had been shot; tears gushed from their eyes, their supplicating hands went up, and three answers came in the one instant:

"I done it!"

"I done it!"

"I done it!—have mercy, marster—Lord have mercy on us po' niggers!"

"Very good," said the master, putting up his watch, "I will sell you *here*, though you don't deserve it. You ought to be sold down the river."

The culprits flung themselves prone, in an ecstasy of gratitude, and kissed his feet, declaring that they would never forget his goodness and never cease to pray for him as long as they lived. They were sincere, for like a god he had stretched forth his mighty hand and closed the gates of hell against them. He knew, himself, that he had done a noble and gracious thing, and was privately well pleased with his magnanimity; and that night he set the incident down in his diary, so that his son might read it in after years, and be thereby moved to deeds of gentleness and humanity himself.

III

WHOEVER has lived long enough to find out what life is, knows how deep a debt of gratitude we owe to Adam, the first great benefactor of our race. He brought death into the world.
—*Pudd'nhead Wilson's Calendar.*

PERCY DRISCOLL slept well the night he saved his house-minions from going down the river, but no wink of sleep visited Roxy's eyes. A profound terror had taken possession of her. Her child could grow up and be sold down the river! The thought crazed her with horror. If she dozed and lost herself for a moment, the next moment she was on her feet and flying to her child's cradle to see if it was still there. Then she would gather it to her heart and pour out her love upon it in a frenzy of kisses, moaning, crying, and saying "Dey sha'n't, oh, dey *sha'n't*!—yo' po' mammy will kill you fust!"

Once, when she was tucking it back in its cradle again, the other child nestled in its sleep and attracted her attention. She went and stood over it a long time, communing with herself: "What has my po' baby done, dat he could n't have yo' luck? He hain't done noth'n'. God was good to you; why war n't he good to him? Dey can't sell *you* down de river. I hates yo' pappy; he ain't got no heart—for niggers he hain't, any-ways. I hates him, en I could kill him!" She paused a while, thinking; then she burst into wild sobbings again, and turned away, saying, "Oh, I got to kill my chile, dey ain't no yuther way,—killin' *him* would n't save de chile fum goin' down de river. Oh, I got to do it, yo' po' mammy's got to kill you to save you, honey"—she gathered her baby to her bosom, now, and began to smother it with caresses—"Mammy 's got to kill you—how *kin* I do it! But yo' mammy ain't gwine to desert you,—no, no; *dah*, don't cry—she gwine *wid* you, she gwine to kill herself too. Come along, honey, come along wid mammy; we gwine to jump in de river, den de troubles o' dis worl' is all over—dey don't sell po' niggers down the river over *yonder*."

She started toward the door, crooning to the child and hushing it; midway she stopped, suddenly. She had caught

313

sight of her new Sunday gown—a cheap curtain-calico thing,
a conflagration of gaudy colors and fantastic figures. She surveyed it wistfully, longingly.

"Hain't ever wore it yet," she said, "en it 's jist lovely."
Then she nodded her head in response to a pleasant idea, and
added, "No, I ain't gwine to be fished out, wid everybody
lookin' at me, in dis mis'able ole linsey-woolsey."

She put down the child and made the change. She looked
in the glass and was astonished at her beauty. She resolved to
make her death-toilet perfect. She took off her handkerchief-
turban and dressed her glossy wealth of hair "like white
folks"; she added some odds and ends of rather lurid ribbon
and a spray of atrocious artificial flowers; finally she threw
over her shoulders a fluffy thing called a "cloud" in that day,
which was of a blazing red complexion. Then she was ready
for the tomb.

She gathered up her baby once more; but when her eye fell
upon its miserably short little gray tow-linen shirt and noted
the contrast between its pauper shabbiness and her own volcanic irruption of infernal splendors, her mother-heart was
touched, and she was ashamed.

"No, dolling, mammy ain't gwine to treat you so. De angels is gwine to 'mire you jist as much as dey does yo'
mammy. Ain't gwine to have 'em putt'n' dey han's up 'fo' dey
eyes en sayin' to David en Goliah en dem yuther prophets,
'Dat chile is dress' too indelicate fo' dis place.' "

By this time she had stripped off the shirt. Now she clothed
the naked little creature in one of Thomas à Becket's snowy
long baby-gowns, with its bright blue bows and dainty flum-
mery of ruffles.

"Dah—now you 's fixed." She propped the child in a chair
and stood off to inspect it. Straightway her eyes began to
widen with astonishment and admiration, and she clapped her
hands and cried out, "Why, it do beat all!—I *never* knowed
you was so lovely. Marse Tommy ain't a bit puttier—not a
single bit."

She stepped over and glanced at the other infant; she flung
a glance back at her own; then one more at the heir of the
house. Now a strange light dawned in her eyes, and in a moment she was lost in thought. She seemed in a trance; when

she came out of it she muttered, "When I 'uz a-washin' 'em in de tub, yistiddy, his own pappy asked me which of 'em was his'n."

She began to move about like one in a dream. She undressed Thomas à Becket, stripping him of everything, and put the tow-linen shirt on him. She put his coral necklace on her own child's neck. Then she placed the children side by side, and after earnest inspection she muttered—

"Now who would b'lieve clo'es could do de like o' dat? Dog my cats if it ain't all *I* kin do to tell t' other fum which, let alone his pappy."

She put her cub in Tommy's elegant cradle and said—

"You 's young Marse *Tom* fum dis out, en I got to practise and git used to 'memberin' to call you dat, honey, or I 's gwine to make a mistake some time en git us bofe into trouble. Dah—now you lay still en don't fret no mo', Marse Tom—oh, thank de good Lord in heaven, you 's saved, you 's saved!—dey ain't no man kin ever sell mammy's po' little honey down de river now!"

She put the heir of the house in her own child's unpainted pine cradle, and said, contemplating its slumbering form uneasily—

"I 's sorry for you, honey; I 's sorry, God knows I is,—but what *kin* I do, what *could* I do? Yo' pappy would sell him to somebody, some time, en den he' d go down de river, sho', en I could n't, could n't, *could n't* stan' it."

She flung herself on her bed and began to think and toss, toss and think. By and by she sat suddenly upright, for a comforting thought had flown through her worried mind—

" 'T ain't no sin—*white* folks has done it! It ain't no sin, glory to goodness it ain't no sin! *Dey 's* done it—yes, en dey was de biggest quality in de whole bilin', too—*kings!*"

She began to muse; she was trying to gather out of her memory the dim particulars of some tale she had heard some time or other. At last she said—

"Now I 's got it; now I 'member. It was dat ole nigger preacher dat tole it, de time he come over here fum Illinois en preached in de nigger church. He said dey ain't nobody kin save his own self—can't do it by faith, can't do it by works, can't do it no way at all. Free grace is de *on'y* way, en dat don't come fum nobody but jis' de Lord; en *he* kin give it to anybody he please, saint or sinner—*he* don't kyer. He do jis' as he 's a mineter. He s'lect out anybody dat suit him, en put another one in his place, en make de fust one happy forever en leave t' other one to burn wid Satan. De preacher said it was jist like dey done in Englan' one time, long time ago. De queen she lef' her baby layin' aroun' one day, en went out callin'; en one o' de niggers roun' 'bout de place dat was 'mos' white, she come in en see de chile layin' aroun', en tuck en put her own chile's clo'es on de queen's chile, en put de queen's chile's clo'es on her own chile, en den lef' her own chile layin' aroun' en tuck en toted de queen's chile home to de nigger-quarter, en nobody ever foun' it out, en her chile was de king bimeby, en sole de queen's chile down de river one time when dey had to settle up de estate. Dah, now—de preacher said it his own self, en it ain't no sin, 'ca'se white folks done it. *Dey* done it—yes, *dey* done it; en not on'y jis' common white folks nuther, but de biggest quality dey is in de whole bilin'. Oh, I 's *so* glad I 'member 'bout dat!"

She got up light-hearted and happy, and went to the cradles and spent what was left of the night "practising." She would give her own child a light pat and say humbly, "Lay still, Marse Tom," then give the real Tom a pat and say with severity, "Lay *still*, Chambers!—does you want me to take somep'n' *to* you?"

As she progressed with her practice, she was surprised to see how steadily and surely the awe which had kept her tongue reverent and her manner humble toward her young master was transferring itself to her speech and manner toward the usurper, and how similarly handy she was becoming in transferring her motherly curtness of speech and peremptoriness of manner to the unlucky heir of the ancient house of Driscoll.

She took occasional rests from practising, and absorbed herself in calculating her chances.

"Dey 'll sell dese niggers to-day fo' stealin' de money, den dey 'll buy some mo' dat don't know de chillen—so *dat 's* all right. When I takes de chillen out to git de air, de minute I 's roun' de corner I 's gwine to gaum dey mouths all roun' wid jam, den dey can't *nobody* notice dey 's changed. Yes, I gwineter do dat till I 's safe, if it 's a year.

"Dey ain't but one man dat I 's afeard of, en dat 's dat Pudd'nhead Wilson. Dey calls him a pudd'nhead, en says he 's a fool. My lan', dat man ain't no mo' fool den I is! He 's de smartes' man in dis town, less 'n it 's Jedge Driscroll or maybe Pem Howard. Blame dat man, he worries me wid dem ornery glasses o' hisn; *I* b'lieve he's a witch. But nemmine, I 's gwine to happen aroun' dah one o' dese days en let on dat I reckon he wants to print de chillen's fingers ag'in; en if *he* don't notice dey 's changed, I bound dey ain't nobody gwine to notice it, en den I 's safe, sho'. But I reckon I 'll tote along a hoss-shoe to keep off de witch-work."

The new negroes gave Roxy no trouble, of course. The master gave her none, for one of his speculations was in jeopardy, and his mind was so occupied that he hardly saw the children when he looked at them, and all Roxy had to do was to get them both into a gale of laughter when he came about; then their faces were mainly cavities exposing gums, and he was gone again before the spasm passed and the little creatures resumed a human aspect.

Within a few days the fate of the speculation became so dubious that Mr. Percy went away with his brother the Judge, to see what could be done with it. It was a land speculation as usual, and it had gotten complicated with a lawsuit. The men were gone seven weeks. Before they got back Roxy had paid her visit to Wilson, and was satisfied. Wilson took the finger-prints, labeled them with the names and with the date—October the first—put them carefully away and continued his chat with Roxy, who seemed very anxious that he should admire the great advance in flesh and beauty which the babies had made since he took their finger-prints a month before. He complimented their improvement to her contentment; and as they were without any disguise of jam or other stain, she trembled all the while and was miserably frightened lest at any moment he—

But he did n't. He discovered nothing; and she went home jubilant, and dropped all concern about the matter permanently out of her mind.

IV

ADAM and Eve had many advantages, but the principal one was, that they escaped teething.
— *Pudd'nhead Wilson's Calendar.*

THERE is this trouble about special providences—namely, there is so often a doubt as to which party was intended to be the beneficiary. In the case of the children, the bears and the prophet, the bears got more real satisfaction out of the episode than the prophet did, because they got the children.
— *Pudd'nhead Wilson's Calendar.*

THIS HISTORY must henceforth accommodate itself to the change which Roxana has consummated, and call the real heir "Chambers" and the usurping little slave "Thomas à Becket"—shortening this latter name to "Tom," for daily use, as the people about him did.

"Tom" was a bad baby, from the very beginning of his usurpation. He would cry for nothing; he would burst into storms of devilish temper without notice, and let go scream after scream and squall after squall, then climax the thing with "holding his breath"—that frightful specialty of the teething nursling, in the throes of which the creature exhausts its lungs, then is convulsed with noiseless squirmings and twistings and kickings in the effort to get its breath, while the lips turn blue and the mouth stands wide and rigid, offering for inspection one wee tooth set in the lower rim of a hoop of red gums; and when the appalling stillness has endured until one is sure the lost breath will never return, a nurse comes flying, and dashes water in the child's face, and—presto! the lungs fill, and instantly discharge a shriek, or a yell, or a howl which bursts the listening ear and surprises the owner of it into saying words which would not go well with a halo if he had one. The baby Tom would claw anybody who came within reach of his nails, and pound anybody he could reach with his rattle. He would scream for water until he got it, and then throw cup and all on the floor and scream for more. He was indulged in all his caprices, howsoever troublesome and exasperating they might be; he was allowed to eat anything he wanted, particularly things that would give him the stomach-ache.

When he got to be old enough to begin to toddle about and say broken words and get an idea of what his hands were for, he was a more consummate pest than ever. Roxy got no rest while he was awake. He would call for anything and everything he saw, simply saying "Awnt it!" (want it), which was a command. When it was brought, he said in a frenzy, and motioning it away with his hands, "Don't awnt it! don't awnt it!" and the moment it was gone he set up frantic yells of "Awnt it! awnt it! awnt it!" and Roxy had to give wings to her heels to get that thing back to him again before he could get time to carry out his intention of going into convulsions about it.

What he preferred above all other things was the tongs. This was because his "father" had forbidden him to have them lest he break windows and furniture with them. The moment Roxy's back was turned he would toddle to the presence of the tongs and say "Like it!" and cock his eye to one side to see if Roxy was observing; then, "Awnt it!" and cock his eye again; then, "Hab it!" with another furtive glance; and finally, "Take it!"—and the prize was his. The next moment the heavy implement was raised aloft; the next, there was a crash and a squall, and the cat was off on three legs to meet an engagement; Roxy would arrive just as the lamp or a window went to irremediable smash.

Tom got all the petting, Chambers got none. Tom got all the delicacies, Chambers got mush and milk, and clabber without sugar. In consequence Tom was a sickly child and Chambers was n't. Tom was "fractious," as Roxy called it, and overbearing; Chambers was meek and docile.

With all her splendid common sense and practical everyday ability, Roxy was a doting fool of a mother. She was this toward her child—and she was also more than this: by the fiction created by herself, he was become her master; the necessity of recognizing this relation outwardly and of perfecting herself in the forms required to express the recognition, had moved her to such diligence and faithfulness in practising these forms that this exercise soon concreted itself into habit; it became automatic and unconscious; then a natural result followed: deceptions intended solely for others gradually grew practically into self-deceptions as well; the mock reverence became real reverence, the mock obsequiousness real obsequiousness, the mock homage real homage; the little counterfeit rift of separation between imitation-slave and imitation-master widened and widened, and became an abyss, and a very real one—and on one side of it stood Roxy, the dupe of her own deceptions, and on the other stood her child, no longer a usurper to her, but her accepted and recognized master. He was her darling, her master, and her deity all in one, and in her worship of him she forgot who she was and what he had been.

In babyhood Tom cuffed and banged and scratched Chambers unrebuked, and Chambers early learned that between meekly bearing it and resenting it, the advantage all lay with the former policy. The few times that his persecutions had moved him beyond control and made him fight back had cost him very dear at headquarters; not at the hands of Roxy, for if she ever went beyond scolding him sharply for "forgitt'n' who his young master was," she at least never extended her punishment beyond a box on the ear. No, Percy Driscoll was the person. He told Chambers that under no provocation whatever was he privileged to lift his hand against his little master. Chambers overstepped the line three times, and got three such convincing canings from the man who was his father and did n't know it, that he took Tom's cruelties in all humility after that, and made no more experiments.

Outside of the house the two boys were together all through their boyhood. Chambers was strong beyond his years, and a good fighter; strong because he was coarsely fed and hard worked about the house, and a good fighter because Tom furnished him plenty of practice—on white boys whom he hated and was afraid of. Chambers was his constant bodyguard, to and from school; he was present on the playground at recess to protect his charge. He fought himself into such a formidable reputation, by and by, that Tom could have changed clothes with him, and "ridden in peace," like Sir Kay in Launcelot's armor.

He was good at games of skill, too. Tom staked him with marbles to play "keeps" with, and then took all the winnings away from him. In the winter season Chambers was on hand, in Tom's worn-out clothes, with "holy" red mittens, and "holy" shoes, and pants "holy" at the knees and seat, to drag a sled up the hill for Tom, warmly clad, to ride down on; but he never got a ride himself. He built snow men and snow fortifications under Tom's directions. He was Tom's patient target when Tom wanted to do some snowballing, but the target could n't fire back. Chambers carried Tom's skates to the river and strapped them on him, then trotted around after him on the ice, so as to be on hand when wanted; but he was n't ever asked to try the skates himself.

In summer the pet pastime of the boys of Dawson's Landing was to steal apples, peaches, and melons from the farmers' fruit-wagons,—mainly on account of the risk they ran of getting their head laid open with the butt of the farmer's whip. Tom was a distinguished adept at these thefts—by proxy. Chambers did his stealing, and got the peach-stones, apple-cores, and melon-rinds for his share.

Tom always made Chambers go in swimming with him, and stay by him as a protection. When Tom had had enough, he would slip out and tie knots in Chambers's shirt, dip the knots in the water to make them hard to undo, then dress himself and sit by and laugh while the naked shiverer tugged at the stubborn knots with his teeth.

Tom did his humble comrade these various ill turns partly out of native viciousness, and partly because he hated him for his superiorities of physique and pluck, and for his manifold cleverness. Tom could n't dive, for it gave him splitting headaches. Chambers could dive without inconvenience, and was fond of doing it. He excited so much admiration, one day, among a crowd of white boys, by throwing back somersaults from the stern of a canoe, that it wearied Tom's spirit, and at last he shoved the canoe underneath Chambers while he was in the air—so he came down on his head in the canoe-bottom; and while he lay unconscious, several of Tom's ancient adversaries saw that their long-desired opportunity was come, and they gave the false heir such a drubbing that with Chambers's best help he was hardly able to drag himself home afterward.

When the boys were fifteen and upward, Tom was "show-

ing off" in the river one day, when he was taken with a
cramp, and shouted for help. It was a common trick with the
boys—particularly if a stranger was present—to pretend a
cramp and howl for help; then when the stranger came tearing hand over hand to the rescue, the howler would go on
struggling and howling till he was close at hand, then replace
the howl with a sarcastic smile and swim blandly away, while
the town boys assailed the dupe with a volley of jeers and
laughter. Tom had never tried this joke as yet, but was supposed to be trying it now, so the boys held warily back; but
Chambers believed his master was in earnest, therefore he
swam out, and arrived in time, unfortunately, and saved his
life.

This was the last feather. Tom had managed to endure
everything else, but to have to remain publicly and permanently under such an obligation as this to a nigger, and to
this nigger of all niggers—this was too much. He heaped
insults upon Chambers for "pretending" to think he was in
earnest in calling for help, and said that anybody but a block-
headed nigger would have known he was funning and left
him alone.

Tom's enemies were in strong force here, so they came out
with their opinions quite freely. They laughed at him, and
called him coward, liar, sneak, and other sorts of pet names,
and told him they meant to call Chambers by a new name
after this, and make it common in the town—"Tom Driscoll's niggerpappy,"—to signify that he had had a second
birth into this life, and that Chambers was the author of his
new being. Tom grew frantic under these taunts, and
shouted—

"Knock their heads off, Chambers! knock their heads off!
What do you stand there with your hands in your pockets
for?"

Chambers expostulated, and said, "But, Marse Tom, dey 's
too many of 'em—dey 's—"

"Do you hear me?"

"Please, Marse Tom, don't make me! Dey 's so many of
'em dat—"

Tom sprang at him and drove his pocket-knife into him
two or three times before the boys could snatch him away

and give the wounded lad a chance to escape. He was considerably hurt, but not seriously. If the blade had been a little longer his career would have ended there.

Tom had long ago taught Roxy "her place." It had been many a day now since she had ventured a caress or a fondling epithet in his quarter. Such things, from a "nigger," were repulsive to him, and she had been warned to keep her distance and remember who she was. She saw her darling gradually cease from being her son, she saw *that* detail perish utterly; all that was left was master—master, pure and simple, and it was not a gentle mastership, either. She saw herself sink from the sublime height of motherhood to the somber deeps of unmodified slavery. The abyss of separation between her and her boy was complete. She was merely his chattel, now, his convenience, his dog, his cringing and helpless slave, the humble and unresisting victim of his capricious temper and vicious nature.

Sometimes she could not go to sleep, even when worn out with fatigue, because her rage boiled so high over the day's experiences with her boy. She would mumble and mutter to herself—

"He struck me, en I war n't no way to blame—struck me in de face, right before folks. En he 's al'ays callin' me nigger-wench, en hussy, en all dem mean names, when I 's doin' de very bes' I kin. Oh, Lord, I done so much for him—I lift' him away up to what he is—en dis is what I git for it."

Sometimes when some outrage of peculiar offensiveness stung her to the heart, she would plan schemes of vengeance and revel in the fancied spectacle of his exposure to the world as an impostor and a slave; but in the midst of these joys fear would strike her: she had made him too strong; she could prove nothing, and—heavens, she might get sold down the river for her pains! So her schemes always went for nothing, and she laid them aside in impotent rage against the fates, and against herself for playing the fool on that fatal September day in not providing herself with a witness for use in the day when such a thing might be needed for the appeasing of her vengeance-hungry heart.

And yet the moment Tom happened to be good to her, and kind,—and this occurred every now and then,—all her sore places were healed, and she was happy; happy and proud, for this was her son, her nigger son, lording it among the whites and securely avenging their crimes against her race.

There were two grand funerals in Dawson's Landing that fall—the fall of 1845. One was that of Colonel Cecil Burleigh Essex, the other that of Percy Driscoll.

On his death-bed Driscoll set Roxy free and delivered his idolized ostensible son solemnly into the keeping of his brother the Judge and his wife. Those childless people were glad to get him. Childless people are not difficult to please.

Judge Driscoll had gone privately to his brother, a month before, and bought Chambers. He had heard that Tom had been trying to get his father to sell the boy down the river, and he wanted to prevent the scandal—for public sentiment did not approve of that way of treating family servants for light cause or for no cause.

Percy Driscoll had worn himself out in trying to save his great speculative landed estate, and had died without succeeding. He was hardly in his grave before the boom collapsed and left his hitherto envied young devil of an heir a pauper. But that was nothing; his uncle told him he should be his heir and have all his fortune when he died; so Tom was comforted.

Roxy had no home, now; so she resolved to go around and say good-by to her friends and then clear out and see the world—that is to say, she would go chambermaiding on a steamboat, the darling ambition of her race and sex.

Her last call was on the black giant, Jasper. She found him chopping Pudd'nhead Wilson's winter provision of wood.

Wilson was chatting with him when Roxy arrived. He asked her how she could bear to go off chambermaiding and leave her boys; and chaffingly offered to copy off a series of their finger-prints, reaching up to their twelfth year, for her to remember them by; but she sobered in a moment, wondering if he suspected anything; then she said she believed she did n't want them. Wilson said to himself, "The drop of black blood in her is superstitious; she thinks there 's some devilry, some witch-business about my glass mystery somewhere; she used to come here with an old horseshoe in her hand; it could have been an accident, but I doubt it."

V

TRAINING is everything. The peach was once a bitter almond;
cauliflower is nothing but cabbage with a college education.
—*Pudd'nhead Wilson's Calendar.*

REMARK of Dr. Baldwin's, concerning up-starts: We don't care
to eat toadstools that think they are truffles.
—*Pudd'nhead Wilson's Calendar.*

MRS. YORK DRISCOLL enjoyed two years of bliss with
that prize, Tom—bliss that was troubled a little at
times, it is true, but bliss nevertheless; then she died, and her
husband and his childless sister, Mrs. Pratt, continued the
bliss-business at the old stand. Tom was petted and indulged
and spoiled to his entire content—or nearly that. This went
on till he was nineteen, then he was sent to Yale. He went
handsomely equipped with "conditions," but otherwise he
was not an object of distinction there. He remained at Yale
two years, and then threw up the struggle. He came home
with his manners a good deal improved; he had lost his sur-
liness and brusqueness, and was rather pleasantly soft and
smooth, now; he was furtively, and sometimes openly, ironical of speech, and given to gently touching people on the
raw, but he did it with a good-natured semiconscious air that
carried it off safely, and kept him from getting into trouble.
He was as indolent as ever and showed no very strenuous
desire to hunt up an occupation. People argued from this that
he preferred to be supported by his uncle until his uncle's
shoes should become vacant. He brought back one or two
new habits with him, one of which he rather openly practised—tippling—but concealed another, which was gambling. It would not do to gamble where his uncle could hear
of it; he knew that quite well.

Tom's Eastern polish was not popular among the young
people. They could have endured it, perhaps, if Tom had
stopped there; but he wore gloves, and that they could n't
stand, and would n't; so he was mainly without society. He
brought home with him a suit of clothes of such exquisite
style and cut and fashion,—Eastern fashion, city fashion,—

that it filled everybody with anguish and was regarded as a peculiarly wanton affront. He enjoyed the feeling which he was exciting, and paraded the town serene and happy all day; but the young fellows set a tailor to work that night, and when Tom started out on his parade next morning he found the old deformed negro bell-ringer straddling along in his wake tricked out in a flamboyant curtain-calico exaggeration of his finery, and imitating his fancy Eastern graces as well as he could.

Tom surrendered, and after that clothed himself in the local fashion. But the dull country town was tiresome to him, since his acquaintanceship with livelier regions, and it grew daily more and more so. He began to make little trips to St. Louis for refreshment. There he found companionship to suit him, and pleasures to his taste, along with more freedom, in some particulars, than he could have at home. So, during the next two years his visits to the city grew in frequency and his tarryings there grew steadily longer in duration.

He was getting into deep waters. He was taking chances, privately, which might get him into trouble some day—in fact, *did*.

Judge Driscoll had retired from the bench and from all business activities in 1850, and had now been comfortably idle three years. He was president of the Free-thinkers' Society, and Pudd'nhead Wilson was the other member. The society's weekly discussions were now the old lawyer's main interest in life. Pudd'nhead was still toiling in obscurity at the bottom of the ladder, under the blight of that unlucky remark which he had let fall twenty-three years before about the dog.

Judge Driscoll was his friend, and claimed that he had a mind above the average, but that was regarded as one of the Judge's whims, and it failed to modify the public opinion. Or rather, that was one of the reasons why it failed, but there was another and better one. If the judge had stopped with bare assertion, it would have had a good deal of effect; but he made the mistake of trying to prove his position. For some years Wilson had been privately at work on a whimsical almanac, for his amusement—a calendar, with a little dab of ostensible philosophy, usually in ironical form, appended to each date; and the Judge thought that these quips and fancies

of Wilson's were neatly turned and cute; so he carried a handful of them around, one day, and read them to some of the
chief citizens. But irony was not for those people; their mental vision was not focussed for it. They read those playful tri-
fles in the solidest earnest, and decided without hesitancy that
if there had ever been any doubt that Dave Wilson was a
pudd'nhead—which there had n't—this revelation removed
that doubt for good and all. That is just the way in this
world; an enemy can partly ruin a man, but it takes a good-
natured injudicious friend to complete the thing and make it
perfect. After this the Judge felt tenderer than ever toward
Wilson, and surer than ever that his calendar had merit.

Judge Driscoll could be a free-thinker and still hold his
place in society because he was the person of most consequence in the community, and therefore could venture to go
his own way and follow out his own notions. The other
member of his pet organization was allowed the like liberty
because he was a cipher in the estimation of the public, and
nobody attached any importance to what he thought or did.
He was liked, he was welcome enough all around, but he
simply did n't count for anything.

The widow Cooper—affectionately called "aunt Patsy" by
everybody—lived in a snug and comely cottage with her
daughter Rowena, who was nineteen, romantic, amiable, and
very pretty, but otherwise of no consequence. Rowena had a
couple of young brothers—also of no consequence.

The widow had a large spare room which she let to a
lodger, with board, when she could find one, but this room
had been empty for a year now, to her sorrow. Her income
was only sufficient for the family support, and she needed the
lodging-money for trifling luxuries. But now, at last, on a
flaming June day, she found herself happy; her tedious wait
was ended; her year-worn advertisement had been answered;
and not by a village applicant, oh, no!—this letter was from
away off yonder in the dim great world to the North; it was
from St. Louis. She sat on her porch gazing out with unsee-
ing eyes upon the shining reaches of the mighty Mississippi,
her thoughts steeped in her good fortune. Indeed it was specially good fortune, for she was to have two lodgers instead
of one.

She had read the letter to the family, and Rowena had danced away to see to the cleaning and airing of the room by the slave woman Nancy, and the boys had rushed abroad in the town to spread the great news, for it was matter of public interest, and the public would wonder and not be pleased if not informed. Presently Rowena returned, all ablush with joyous excitement, and begged for a re-reading of the letter. It was framed thus:

HONORED MADAM: My brother and I have seen your advertisement, by chance, and beg leave to take the room you offer. We are twenty-four years of age and twins. We are Italians by birth, but have lived long in the various countries of Europe, and several years in the United States. Our names are Luigi and Angelo Capello. You desire but one guest; but dear Madam, if you will allow us to pay for two, we will not incommode you. We shall be down Thursday.

"Italians! How romantic! Just think, ma—there 's never been one in this town, and everybody will be dying to see them, and they 're all *ours*! Think of that!"

"Yes, I reckon they 'll make a grand stir."

"Oh, indeed they will. The whole town will be on its head! Think—they 've been in Europe and everywhere! There 's never been a traveler in this town before. Ma, I should n't wonder if they 've seen kings!"

"Well, a body can't tell; but they 'll make stir enough, without that."

"Yes, that 's of course. Luigi—Angelo. They 're lovely names; and so grand and foreign—not like Jones and Robinson and such. Thursday they are coming, and this is only Tuesday; it 's a cruel long time to wait. Here comes Judge Driscoll in at the gate. He 's heard about it. I 'll go and open the door."

The judge was full of congratulations and curiosity. The letter was read and discussed. Soon Justice Robinson arrived with more congratulations, and there was a new reading and a new discussion. This was the beginning. Neighbor after neighbor, of both sexes, followed, and the procession drifted in and out all day and evening and all Wednesday and Thursday. The letter was read and re-read until it was nearly worn out; everybody admired its courtly and gracious tone, and smooth and practised style, everybody was sympathetic and excited, and the Coopers were steeped in happiness all the while.

The boats were very uncertain in low water, in these primitive times. This time the Thursday boat had not arrived at ten at night—so the people had waited at the landing all day for nothing; they were driven to their homes by a heavy storm without having had a view of the illustrious foreigners.

Eleven o'clock came; and the Cooper house was the only one in the town that still had lights burning. The rain and thunder were booming yet, and the anxious family were still waiting, still hoping. At last there was a knock at the door and the family jumped to open it. Two negro men entered, each carrying a trunk, and proceeded up-stairs toward the guest-room. Then entered the twins—the handsomest, the best dressed, the most distinguished-looking pair of young fellows the West had ever seen. One was a little fairer than the other, but otherwise they were exact duplicates.

VI

A T BREAKFAST in the morning the twins' charm of manner and easy and polished bearing made speedy conquest of the family's good graces. All constraint and formality quickly disappeared, and the friendliest feeling succeeded. Aunt Patsy called them by their Christian names almost from the beginning. She was full of the keenest curiosity about them, and showed it; they responded by talking about themselves, which pleased her greatly. It presently appeared that in their early youth they had known poverty and hardship. As the talk wandered along the old lady watched for the right place to drop in a question or two concerning that matter, and when she found it she said to the blond twin, who was now doing the biographies in his turn while the brunette one rested—

"If it ain't asking what I ought not to ask, Mr. Angelo, how did you come to be so friendless and in such trouble when you were little? Do you mind telling? But don't if you do."

"Oh, we don't mind it at all, madam; in our case it was merely misfortune, and nobody's fault. Our parents were well to do, there in Italy, and we were their only child. We were of the old Florentine nobility"—Rowena's heart gave a great bound, her nostrils expanded, and a fine light played in her eyes—"and when the war broke out my father was on the losing side and had to fly for his life. His estates were confiscated, his personal property seized, and there we were, in Germany, strangers, friendless, and in fact paupers. My brother and I were ten years old, and well educated for that age, very studious, very fond of our books, and well grounded in the German, French, Spanish, and English languages. Also, we were marvelous musical prodigies—if you will allow me to say it, it being only the truth.

"Our father survived his misfortunes only a month, our mother soon followed him, and we were alone in the world. Our parents could have made themselves comfortable by exhibiting us as a show, and they had many and large offers; but the thought revolted their pride, and they said they would starve and die first. But what they would n't consent to do we had to do without the formality of consent. We were seized for the debts occasioned by their illness and their funerals, and placed among the attractions of a cheap museum in Berlin to earn the liquidation money. It took us two years to get out of that slavery. We traveled all about Germany, receiving no wages, and not even our keep. We had to be exhibited for nothing, and beg our bread.

"Well, madam, the rest is not of much consequence. When we escaped from that slavery at twelve years of age, we were in some respects men. Experience had taught us some valuable things; among others, how to take care of ourselves, how to avoid and defeat sharks and sharpers, and how to conduct our own business for our own profit and without other people's help. We traveled everywhere—years and years—picking up smatterings of strange tongues, familiarizing ourselves with strange sights and strange customs, accumulating an education of a wide and varied and curious sort. It was a pleasant life. We went to Venice—to London, Paris, Russia, India, China, Japan—"

At this point Nancy the slave woman thrust her head in at the door and exclaimed:

"Ole Missus, de house is plum' jam full o' people, en dey 's jes a-spi'lin' to see de gen'lmen!" She indicated the twins with a nod of her head, and tucked it back out of sight again.

It was a proud occasion for the widow, and she promised herself high satisfaction in showing off her fine foreign birds before her neighbors and friends—simple folk who had hardly ever seen a foreigner of any kind, and never one of any distinction or style. Yet her feeling was moderate indeed when contrasted with Rowena's. Rowena was in the clouds, she walked on air; this was to be the greatest day, the most romantic episode, in the colorless history of that dull country town. She was to be familiarly near the source of its glory and feel the full flood of it pour over her and about her; the other girls could only gaze and envy, not partake.

The widow was ready, Rowena was ready, so also were the foreigners.

The party moved along the hall, the twins in advance, and entered the open parlor door, whence issued a low hum of conversation. The twins took a position near the door, the widow stood at Luigi's side, Rowena stood beside Angelo, and the march-past and the introductions began. The widow was all smiles and contentment. She received the procession and passed it on to Rowena.

"Good mornin', Sister Cooper"—hand-shake.

"Good morning, Brother Higgins—Count Luigi Capello, Mr. Higgins"—hand-shake, followed by a devouring stare and "I 'm glad to see ye," on the part of Higgins, and a courteous inclination of the head and a pleasant "Most happy!" on the part of Count Luigi.

"Good mornin', Roweny"—hand-shake.

"Good morning, Mr. Higgins—present you to Count Angelo Capello." Hand-shake, admiring stare, "Glad to see ye,"—courteous nod, smily "Most happy!" and Higgins passes on.

None of these visitors was at ease, but, being honest people, they did n't pretend to be. None of them had ever seen a person bearing a title of nobility before, and none had been expecting to see one now, consequently the title came upon them as a kind of pile-driving surprise and caught them unprepared. A few tried to rise to the emergency, and got out an awkward "My lord," or "Your lordship," or something of that sort, but the great majority were overwhelmed by the unaccustomed word and its dim and awful associations with gilded courts and stately ceremony and anointed kingship, so they only fumbled through the hand-shake and passed on, speechless. Now and then, as happens at all receptions everywhere, a more than ordinarily friendly soul blocked the procession and kept it waiting while he inquired how the brothers liked the village, and how long they were going to stay, and if their families were well, and dragged in the weather, and hoped it would get cooler soon, and all that sort of thing, so as to be able to say, when they got home, "I had quite a long talk with them"; but nobody did or said anything of a regrettable kind, and so the great affair went through to the end in a creditable and satisfactory fashion.

General conversation followed, and the twins drifted about from group to group, talking easily and fluently and winning approval, compelling admiration and achieving favor from all. The widow followed their conquering march with a proud eye, and every now and then Rowena said to herself with deep satisfaction, "And to think they are ours—all ours!"

There were no idle moments for mother or daughter. Eager inquiries concerning the twins were pouring into their enchanted ears all the time; each was the constant center of a group of breathless listeners; each recognized that she knew now for the first time the real meaning of that great word Glory, and perceived the stupendous value of it, and understood why men in all ages had been willing to throw away meaner happinesses, treasure, life itself, to get a taste of its sublime and supreme joy. Napoleon and all his kind stood accounted for—and justified.

When Rowena had at last done all her duty by the people in the parlor, she went up-stairs to satisfy the longings of an overflow-meeting there, for the parlor was not big enough to hold all the comers. Again she was besieged by eager questioners and again she swam in sunset seas of glory. When the forenoon was nearly gone, she recognized with a pang that this most splendid episode of her life was almost over, that nothing could prolong it, that nothing quite its equal could ever fall to her fortune again. But never mind, it was sufficient unto itself, the grand occasion had moved on an ascending scale from the start, and was a noble and memorable success. If the twins could but do some crowning act, now, to climax it, something unusual, something startling, something to concentrate upon themselves the company's loftiest admiration, something in the nature of an electric surprise—

Here a prodigious slam-banging broke out below, and everybody rushed down to see. It was the twins knocking out a classic four-handed piece on the piano, in great style. Rowena was satisfied—satisfied down to the bottom of her heart.

The young strangers were kept long at the piano. The villagers were astonished and enchanted with the magnificence of their performance, and could not bear to have them stop. All the music that they had ever heard before seemed spiritless prentice-work and barren of grace or charm when compared with these intoxicating floods of melodious sound. They realized that for once in their lives they were hearing masters.

VII

ONE of the most striking differences between a cat and a lie is
that a cat has only nine lives.

—*Pudd'nhead Wilson's Calendar.*

THE COMPANY broke up reluctantly, and drifted toward
their several homes, chatting with vivacity, and all agreeing that it would be many a long day before Dawson's Landing would see the equal of this one again. The twins had
accepted several invitations while the reception was in progress, and had also volunteered to play some duets at an amateur entertainment for the benefit of a local charity. Society
was eager to receive them to its bosom. Judge Driscoll had
the good fortune to secure them for an immediate drive, and
to be the first to display them in public. They entered his
buggy with him, and were paraded down the main street,
everybody flocking to the windows and sidewalks to see.

The Judge showed the strangers the new graveyard, and
the jail, and where the richest man lived, and the Freemasons'
hall, and the Methodist church, and the Presbyterian church,
and where the Baptist church was going to be when they got
some money to build it with, and showed them the town hall
and the slaughter-house, and got out the independent fire
company in uniform and had them put out an imaginary fire;
then he let them inspect the muskets of the militia company,
and poured out an exhaustless stream of enthusiasm over all
these splendors, and seemed very well satisfied with the responses he got, for the twins admired his admiration, and
paid him back the best they could, though they could have
done better if some fifteen or sixteen hundred thousand previous experiences of this sort in various countries had not already rubbed off a considerable part of the novelty of it.

The Judge laid himself out hospitably to make them have
a good time, and if there was a defect anywhere it was not his
fault. He told them a good many humorous anecdotes, and
always forgot the nub, but they were always able to furnish
it, for these yarns were of a pretty early vintage, and they had
had many a rejuvenating pull at them before. And he told

them all about his several dignities, and how he had held this and that and the other place of honor or profit, and had once been to the legislature, and was now president of the Society of Free-thinkers. He said the society had been in existence four years, and already had two members, and was firmly established. He would call for the brothers in the evening if they would like to attend a meeting of it.

Accordingly he called for them, and on the way he told them all about Pudd'nhead Wilson, in order that they might get a favorable impression of him in advance and be prepared to like him. This scheme succeeded—the favorable impression was achieved. Later it was confirmed and solidified when Wilson proposed that out of courtesy to the strangers the usual topics be put aside and the hour be devoted to conversation upon ordinary subjects and the cultivation of friendly relations and good-fellowship,—a proposition which was put to vote and carried.

The hour passed quickly away in lively talk, and when it was ended the lonesome and neglected Wilson was richer by two friends than he had been when it began. He invited the twins to look in at his lodgings, presently, after disposing of an intervening engagement, and they accepted with pleasure.

Toward the middle of the evening they found themselves on the road to his house. Pudd'nhead was at home waiting for them and putting in his time puzzling over a thing which had come under his notice that morning. The matter was this: He happened to be up very early—at dawn, in fact, and he crossed the hall which divided his cottage through the center, and entered a room to get something there. The window of the room had no curtains, for that side of the house had long been unoccupied, and through this window he caught sight of something which surprised and interested him. It was a young woman—a young woman where properly no young woman belonged; for she was in Judge Driscoll's house, and in the bedroom over the Judge's private study or sitting-room. This was young Tom Driscoll's bedroom. He and the Judge, the Judge's widowed sister Mrs. Pratt and three negro servants were the only people who belonged in the house. Who, then, might this young lady be? The two houses were separated by an ordinary yard, with a low fence running back through its middle from the street in front to the lane in the rear. The distance was not great, and Wilson was able to see the girl very well, the window-shades of the room she was in being up and the window also. The girl had on a neat and trim summer dress, patterned in broad stripes of pink and white, and her bonnet was equipped with a pink veil. She was practising steps, gaits and attitudes, apparently; she was doing the thing gracefully, and was very much absorbed in her work. Who could she be, and how came she to be in young Tom Driscoll's room?

Wilson had quickly chosen a position from which he could watch the girl without running much risk of being seen by her, and he remained there hoping she would raise her veil and betray her face. But she disappointed him. After a matter of twenty minutes she disappeared, and although he stayed at his post half an hour longer, she came no more.

Toward noon he dropped in at the Judge's and talked with Mrs. Pratt about the great event of the day, the levee of the distinguished foreigners at Aunt Patsy Cooper's. He asked after her nephew Tom, and she said he was on his way home, and that she was expecting him to arrive a little before night; and added that she and the Judge were gratified to gather from his letters that he was conducting himself very nicely and creditably—at which Wilson winked to himself privately. Wilson did not ask if there was a newcomer in the house, but he asked questions that would have brought light-throwing answers as to that matter if Mrs. Pratt had had any light to throw; so he went away satisfied that he knew of things that were going on in her house of which she herself was not aware.

He was now waiting for the twins, and still puzzling over the problem of who that girl might be, and how she happened to be in that young fellow's room at daybreak in the morning.

VIII

IT IS NECESSARY now, to hunt up Roxy.

At the time she was set free and went away chamber-maiding, she was thirty-five. She got a berth as second chambermaid on a Cincinnati boat in the New Orleans trade, the *Grand Mogul.* A couple of trips made her wonted and easy-going at the work, and infatuated her with the stir and adventure and independence of steamboat life. Then she was promoted and became head chambermaid. She was a favorite with the officers, and exceedingly proud of their joking and friendly ways with her.

During eight years she served three parts of the year on that boat, and the winters on a Vicksburg packet. But now for two months she had had rheumatism in her arms, and was obliged to let the wash-tub alone. So she resigned. But she was well fixed—rich, as she would have described it; for she had lived a steady life, and had banked four dollars every month in New Orleans as a provision for her old age. She said in the start that she had "put shoes on one bar'footed nigger to tromple on her with," and that one mistake like that was enough; she would be independent of the human race thenceforth forevermore if hard work and economy could accomplish it. When the boat touched the levee at New Orleans she bade good-by to her comrades on the *Grand Mogul* and moved her kit ashore.

But she was back in an hour. The bank had gone to smash and carried her four hundred dollars with it. She was a pauper, and homeless. Also disabled bodily, at least for the present. The officers were full of sympathy for her in her trouble, and made up a little purse for her. She resolved to go to her birthplace; she had friends there among the negroes, and the unfortunate always help the unfortunate, she was well aware of that; those lowly comrades of her youth would not let her starve.

She took the little local packet at Cairo, and now she was on the home-stretch. Time had worn away her bitterness against her son, and she was able to think of him with serenity. She put the vile side of him out of her mind, and dwelt only on recollections of his occasional acts of kindness to her. She gilded and otherwise decorated these, and made them very pleasant to contemplate. She began to long to see him. She would go and fawn upon him, slave-like—for this would have to be her attitude, of course—and maybe she would find that time had modified him, and that he would be glad to see his long-forgotten old nurse and treat her gently. That would be lovely; that would make her forget her woes and her poverty.

Her poverty! That thought inspired her to add another castle to her dream: maybe he would give her a trifle now and then—maybe a dollar, once a month, say; any little thing like that would help, oh, ever so much.

By the time she reached Dawson's Landing she was her old self again; her blues were gone, she was in high feather. She would get along, surely; there were many kitchens where the servants would share their meals with her, and also steal sugar and apples and other dainties for her to carry home—or give her a chance to pilfer them herself, which would answer just as well. And there was the church. She was a more rabid and devoted Methodist than ever, and her piety was no sham, but was strong and sincere. Yes, with plenty of creature comforts and her old place in the amen-corner in her possession again, she would be perfectly happy and at peace thenceforward to the end.

She went to Judge Driscoll's kitchen first of all. She was received there in great form and with vast enthusiasm. Her wonderful travels, and the strange countries she had seen and the adventures she had had, made her a marvel, and a heroine of romance. The negroes hung enchanted upon the great story of her experiences, interrupting her all along with eager questions, with laughter, exclamations of delight and expressions of applause; and she was obliged to confess to herself that if there was anything better in this world than steamboating, it was the glory to be got by telling about it. The audience loaded her stomach with their dinners and then stole the pantry bare to load up her basket.

Tom was in St. Louis. The servants said he had spent the best part of his time there during the previous two years. Roxy came every day, and had many talks about the family and its affairs. Once she asked why Tom was away so much. The ostensible "Chambers" said:

"De fac' is, ole marster kin git along better when young marster 's away den he kin when he 's in de town; yes, en he love him better, too; so he gives him fifty dollahs a month—"

"No, is dat so? Chambers, you 's a-jokin', ain't you?"

" 'Clah to goodness I ain't, mammy; Marse Tom tole me so his own self. But nemmine, 't ain't enough."

"My lan', what de reason 't ain't enough?"

"Well, I 's gwine to tell you, if you gimme a chanst, mammy. De reason it ain't enough is 'ca'se Marse Tom gambles."

Roxy threw up her hands in astonishment and Chambers went on—

"Ole marster found it out, 'ca'se he had to pay two hunderd dollahs for Marse Tom's gamblin' debts, en dat 's true, mammy, jes as dead certain as you 's bawn."

"Two—hund'd—dollahs! Why, what is you talkin' 'bout? Two—hund'd—dollahs. Sakes alive, it 's 'mos' enough to buy a tol'able good second-hand nigger wid. En you ain't lyin', honey?—you would n't lie to yo' ole mammy?"

"It 's God's own truth, jes as I tell you—two hund'd dollahs—I wisht I may never stir outen my tracks if it ain't so. En, oh, my lan', ole Marse was jes a-hoppin'! he was b'ilin' mad, I tell you! He tuck 'n' dissenhurrit him."

He licked his chops with relish after that stately word. Roxy struggled with it a moment, then gave it up and said—

"Dissen*whiched* him?"

"Dissenhurrit him."

"What 's dat? What do it mean?"

"Means he bu'sted de will."

"Bu's—ted de will! He would n't *ever* treat him so! Take it back, you mis'able imitation nigger dat I bore in sorrow en tribbilation."

Roxy's pet castle—an occasional dollar from Tom's pocket—was tumbling to ruin before her eyes. She could not abide such a disaster as that; she could n't endure the thought of it. Her remark amused Chambers:

"Yah-yah-yah! jes listen to dat! If I 's imitation, what is you? Bofe of us is imitation *white*—dat 's what we is—en pow'ful good imitation, too—yah-yah-yah!—we don't 'mount to noth'n' as imitation *niggers*; en as for—"

"Shet up yo' foolin', 'fo' I knock you side de head, en tell me 'bout de will. Tell me 't ain't bu'sted—do, honey, en I 'll never forgit you."

"Well, *'tain't*—'ca'se dey 's a new one made, en Marse Tom 's all right ag'in. But what is you in sich a sweat 'bout it for, mammy? 'T ain't none o' your business I don't reckon."

" 'T ain't none o' my business? Whose business is it den, I 'd like to know? Wuz I his mother tell he was fifteen years old, or wus n't I?—you answer me dat. En you speck I could see him turned out po' en ornery on de worl' en never care noth'n' 'bout it? I reckon if you 'd ever be'n a mother yo'self, Valet de Chambers, you would n't talk sich foolishness as dat."

"Well, den, ole Marse forgive him en fixed up de will ag'in—do dat satisfy you?"

Yes, she was satisfied now, and quite happy and sentimental over it. She kept coming daily, and at last she was told that Tom had come home. She began to tremble with emotion, and straightway sent to beg him to let his "po' ole nigger mammy have jes one sight of him en die for joy."

Tom was stretched at his lazy ease on a sofa when Chambers brought the petition. Time had not modified his ancient detestation of the humble drudge and protector of his boyhood; it was still bitter and uncompromising. He sat up and bent a severe gaze upon the fair face of the young fellow whose name he was unconsciously using and whose family rights he was enjoying. He maintained the gaze until the victim of it had become satisfactorily pallid with terror, then he said—

"What does the old rip want with me?"

The petition was meekly repeated.

"Who gave you permission to come and disturb me with the social attentions of niggers?"

Tom had risen. The other young man was trembling now, visibly. He saw what was coming, and bent his head sideways, and put up his left arm to shield it. Tom rained cuffs upon the head and its shield, saying no word; the victim received each blow with a beseeching "Please, Marse Tom!— oh, please, Marse Tom!" Seven blows—then Tom said, "Face the door—march!" He followed behind with one, two, three solid kicks. The last one helped the pure-white slave over the door-sill, and he limped away mopping his eyes with his old ragged sleeve. Tom shouted after him, "Send her in!"

Then he flung himself panting on the sofa again, and rasped out the remark, "He arrived just at the right moment; I was full to the brim with bitter thinkings, and nobody to take it out of. How refreshing it was! I feel better."

Tom's mother entered now, closing the door behind her, and approached her son with all the wheedling and supplicating servilities that fear and interest can impart to the words and attitudes of the born slave. She stopped a yard from her boy and made two or three admiring exclamations over his manly stature and general handsomeness, and Tom put an arm under his head and hoisted a leg over the sofa-back in order to look properly indifferent.

"My lan', how you is growed, honey! 'Clah to goodness, I would n't a-knowed you, Marse Tom! 'deed I would n't! Look at me good; does you 'member old Roxy?—does you know yo' old nigger mammy, honey? Well now, I kin lay down en die in peace, 'ca'se I 's seed—"

"Cut it short,——it, cut it short! What is it you want?"

"You heah dat? Jes de same old Marse Tom, al'ays so gay and funnin' wid de ole mammy. I 'uz jes as shore—"

"Cut it short, I tell you, and get along! What do you want?"

This was a bitter disappointment. Roxy had for so many days nourished and fondled and petted her notion that Tom would be glad to see his old nurse, and would make her proud and happy to the marrow with a cordial word or two, that it took two rebuffs to convince her that he was not funning, and that her beautiful dream was a fond and foolish vanity, a shabby and pitiful mistake. She was hurt to the heart, and so ashamed that for a moment she did not quite know what to do or how to act. Then her breast began to heave, the tears came, and in her forlornness she was moved to try that other dream of hers—an appeal to her boy's charity; and so, upon the impulse, and without reflection, she offered her supplication:

"Oh, Marse Tom, de po' ole mammy is in sich hard luck dese days; en she 's kinder crippled in de arms en can't work, en if you could gimme a dollah—on'y jes one little dol—"

Tom was on his feet so suddenly that the supplicant was startled into a jump herself.

"A dollar!—give you a dollar! I've a notion to strangle you! Is *that* your errand here? Clear out! and be quick about it!"

Roxy backed slowly toward the door. When she was half-way she stopped, and said mournfully:

"Marse Tom, I nussed you when you was a little baby, en I raised you all by myself tell you was 'most a young man; en now you is young en rich, en I is po' en gitt'n' ole, en I come heah b'lievin' dat you would he'p de ole mammy 'long down de little road dat 's lef' 'twix' her en de grave, en—"

Tom relished this tune less than any that had preceded it, for it began to wake up a sort of echo in his conscience; so he interrupted and said with decision, though without asperity, that he was not in a situation to help her, and was n't going to do it.

"Ain't you ever gwine to he'p me, Marse Tom?"

"No! Now go away and don't bother me any more."

Roxy's head was down, in an attitude of humility. But now the fires of her old wrongs flamed up in her breast and began to burn fiercely. She raised her head slowly, till it was well up, and at the same time her great frame unconsciously assumed an erect and masterful attitude, with all the majesty and grace of her vanished youth in it. She raised her finger and punctuated with it:

"You has said de word. You has had yo' chance, en you has trompled it under yo' foot. When you git another one, you 'll git down on yo' knees en *beg* for it!"

A cold chill went to Tom's heart, he did n't know why; for he did not reflect that such words, from such an incongruous source, and so solemnly delivered, could not easily fail of that effect. However, he did the natural thing: he replied with bluster and mockery:

"*You 'll* give me a chance—*you!* Perhaps I 'd better get down on my knees now! But in case I don't—just for argument's sake—what 's going to happen, pray?"

"Dis is what is gwine to happen. I 's gwine as straight to yo' uncle as I kin walk, en tell him every las' thing I knows 'bout you."

Tom's cheek blenched, and she saw it. Disturbing thoughts began to chase each other through his head. "How can she know? And yet she must have found out—she looks it. I 've had the will back only three months, and am already deep in debt again, and moving heaven and earth to save myself from exposure and destruction, with a reasonably fair show of getting the thing covered up if I 'm let alone, and now this fiend has gone and found me out somehow or other. I wonder how much she knows? Oh, oh, oh, it 's enough to break a body's heart! But I 've got to humor her—there 's no other way."

Then he worked up a rather sickly sample of a gay laugh and a hollow chipperness of manner, and said:

"Well, well, Roxy dear, old friends like you and me must n't quarrel. Here 's your dollar—now tell me what you know."

He held out the wild-cat bill; she stood as she was, and made no movement. It was her turn to scorn persuasive foolery, now, and she did not waste it. She said, with a grim implacability in voice and manner which made Tom almost realize that even a former slave can remember for ten minutes insults and injuries returned for compliments and flatteries received, and can also enjoy taking revenge for them when the opportunity offers:

"What does I know? I 'll tell you what I knows. I knows enough to bu'st dat will to flinders—en more, mind you, *more!*"

Tom was aghast.

"More?" he said. "What do you call more? Where 's there any room for more?"

Roxy laughed a mocking laugh, and said scoffingly, with a toss of her head, and her hands on her hips—

"Yes!—oh, I reckon! *Co'se* you 'd like to know—wid yo' po' little ole rag dollah. What you reckon I 's gwine to tell *you* for?—you ain't got no money. I 's gwine to tell yo' uncle—en I 'll do it dis minute, too—he 'll gimme *five* dollahs for de news, en mighty glad, too."

She swung herself around disdainfully, and started away. Tom was in a panic. He seized her skirts, and implored her to wait. She turned and said, loftily—

"Look-a-heah, what 'uz it I tole you?"

"You—you—I don't remember anything. What was it you told me?"

"I tole you dat de next time I give you a chance you 'd git down on yo' knees en beg for it."

Tom was stupefied for a moment. He was panting with excitement. Then he said:

"Oh, Roxy, you would n't require your young master to do such a horrible thing. You can't mean it."

"I 'll let you know mighty quick whether I means it or not! You call me names, en as good as spit on me when I comes here po' en ornery en 'umble, to praise you for bein' growed up so fine en handsome, en tell you how I used to nuss you en tend you en watch you when you 'uz sick en had n't no mother but me in de whole worl', en beg you to give de po' ole nigger a dollah for to git her sum'n' to eat, en you call me names— *names*, dad blame you! Yassir, I gives you jes one chance mo', and dat's *now*, en it las' on'y a half a second—you hear?"

Tom slumped to his knees and began to beg, saying—

"You see I 'm begging, and it 's honest begging, too! Now tell me, Roxy, tell me."

The heir of two centuries of unatoned insult and outrage looked down on him and seemed to drink in deep draughts of satisfaction. Then she said—

"Fine nice young white gen'l'man kneelin' down to a nigger-wench! I 's wanted to see dat jes once befo' I 's called. Now, Gabr'el, blow de hawn, I 's ready . . . Git up!"

Tom did it. He said, humbly—

"Now, Roxy, don't punish me any more. I deserved what I 've got, but be good and let me off with that. Don't go to uncle. Tell me—I 'll give you the five dollars."

"Yes, I bet you will; en you won't stop dah, nuther. But I ain't gwine to tell you heah—"

"Good gracious, no!"

"Is you 'feared o' de ha'nted house?"

"N-no."

"Well, den, you come to de ha'nted house 'bout ten or 'leven to-night, en climb up de ladder, 'ca'se de sta'r-steps is broke down, en you 'll fine me. I 's a-roostin' in de ha'nted house 'ca'se I can't 'ford to roos' nowher's else." She started toward the door, but stopped and said, "Gimme de dollah bill!" He gave it to her. She examined it and said, "H'm—like enough de bank 's bu'sted." She started again, but halted again. "Has you got any whisky?"

"Yes, a little."

"Fetch it!"

He ran to his room overhead and brought down a bottle which was two thirds full. She tilted it up and took a drink. Her eyes sparkled with satisfaction, and she tucked the bottle under her shawl, saying, "It 's prime. I 'll take it along."

Tom humbly held the door for her, and she marched out as grim and erect as a grenadier.

IX

TOM FLUNG HIMSELF on the sofa, and put his throbbing head in his hands, and rested his elbows on his knees. He rocked himself back and forth and moaned.

"I 've knelt to a nigger-wench!" he muttered. "I thought I had struck the deepest depths of degradation before, but oh, dear, it was nothing to this. . . . Well, there is one consolation, such as it is—I 've struck bottom this time; there 's nothing lower."

But that was a hasty conclusion.

At ten that night he climbed the ladder in the haunted house, pale, weak, and wretched. Roxy was standing in the door of one of the rooms, waiting, for she had heard him.

This was a two-story log house which had acquired the reputation a few years before of being haunted, and that was the end of its usefulness. Nobody would live in it afterward, or go near it by night, and most people even gave it a wide berth in the daytime. As it had no competition, it was called *the* haunted house. It was getting crazy and ruinous, now, from long neglect. It stood three hundred yards beyond Pudd'nhead Wilson's house, with nothing between but vacancy. It was the last house in the town at that end.

Tom followed Roxy into the room. She had a pile of clean straw in the corner for a bed, some cheap but well-kept clothing was hanging on the wall, there was a tin lantern freckling the floor with little spots of light, and there were various soap- and candle-boxes scattered about, which served for chairs. The two sat down. Roxy said—

"Now den, I 'll tell you straight off, en I 'll begin to k'leck

de money later on; I ain't in no hurry. What does you reckon
I 's gwine to tell you?"

"Well, you—you—oh, Roxy, don't make it too hard for
me! Come right out and tell me you 've found out somehow
what a shape I 'm in on account of dissipation and foolishness."

"Disposition en foolishness! *No* sir, dat ain't it. Dat jist
ain't nothin' at all, 'longside o' what *I* knows."

Tom stared at her, and said—

"Why, Roxy, what do you mean?"

She rose, and gloomed above him like a Fate.

"I means dis—en it 's de Lord's truth. You ain't no more
kin to ole Marse Driscoll den I is!—*dat 's* what I means!"
and her eyes flamed with triumph.

"What!"

"Yassir, en *dat* ain't all! You 's a *nigger*!—*bawn* a nigger
en a *slave*!—en you 's a nigger en a slave dis minute; en if I
opens my mouf ole Marse Driscoll 'll sell you down de river
befo' you is two days older den what you is now!"

"It 's a thundering lie, you miserable old blatherskite!"

"It ain't no lie, nuther. It 's jes de truth, en nothin' *but* de
truth, so he'p me. Yassir—you 's my *son*—"

"You devil!"

"En dat po' boy dat you 's be'n a-kickin' en a-cuffin' to-day
is Percy Driscoll's son en yo' *marster*—"

"You beast!"

"En *his* name 's Tom Driscoll, en *yo'* name 's Valet de
Chambers, en you ain't *got* no fambly name, beca'se niggers
don't *have* 'em!"

Tom sprang up and seized a billet of wood and raised it;
but his mother only laughed at him, and said—

"Set down, you pup! Does you think you kin skyer me? It
ain't in you, nor de likes of you. I reckon you 'd shoot me in
de back, maybe, if you got a chance, for dat 's jist yo' style—
I knows you, thoo en thoo—but I don't mind gitt'n' killed,
beca'se all dis is down in writin', en it 's in safe hands, too,
en de man dat 's got it knows whah to look for de right man
when I gits killed. Oh, bless yo' soul, if you puts yo' mother
up for as big a fool as *you* is, you 's pow'ful mistaken, I kin

tell you! Now den, you set still en behave yo'self; en don't you git up ag'in till I tell you!"

Tom fretted and chafed awhile in a whirlwind of disorganizing sensations and emotions, and finally said, with something like settled conviction—

"The whole thing is moonshine; now then, go ahead and do your worst; I 'm done with you."

Roxy made no answer. She took the lantern and started toward the door. Tom was in a cold panic in a moment.

"Come back, come back!" he wailed. "I did n't mean it, Roxy; I take it all back, and I 'll never say it again! Please come back, Roxy!"

The woman stood a moment, then she said gravely:

"Dah 's one thing you 's got to stop, Valet de Chambers. You can't call me *Roxy*, same as if you was my equal. Chillen don't speak to dey mammies like dat. You 'll call me ma or mammy, dat 's what you 'll call me—leastways when dey ain't nobody aroun'. *Say* it!"

It cost Tom a struggle, but he got it out.

"Dat 's all right. Don't you ever forgit it ag'in, if you knows what 's good for you. Now den, you has said you would n't ever call it lies en moonshine ag'in. I 'll tell you dis, for a warnin': if you ever does say it ag'in, it 's de *las'* time you 'll ever say it to me; I 'll tramp as straight to de Judge as I kin walk, en tell him who you is, en *prove* it. Does you b'lieve me when I says dat?"

"Oh," groaned Tom, "I more than believe it; I *know* it."

Roxy knew her conquest was complete. She could have proved nothing to anybody, and her threat about the writings was a lie; but she knew the person she was dealing with, and had made both statements without any doubt as to the effect they would produce.

She went and sat down on her candle-box, and the pride and pomp of her victorious attitude made it a throne. She said—

"Now den, Chambers, we 's gwine to talk business, en dey ain't gwine to be no mo' foolishness. In de fust place, you gits fifty dollahs a month; you 's gwine to han' over half of it to yo' ma. Plank it out!"

But Tom had only six dollars in the world. He gave her that, and promised to start fair on next month's pension.

"Chambers, how much is you in debt?"

Tom shuddered, and said—

"Nearly three hundred dollars."

"How is you gwine to pay it?"

Tom groaned out—

"Oh, I don't know; don't ask me such awful questions."

But she stuck to her point until she wearied a confession out of him: he had been prowling about in disguise, stealing small valuables from private houses; in fact, had made a good deal of a raid on his fellow-villagers a fortnight before, when he was supposed to be in St. Louis; but he doubted if he had sent away enough stuff to realize the required amount, and was afraid to make a further venture in the present excited state of the town. His mother approved of his conduct, and offered to help, but this frightened him. He tremblingly ventured to say that if she would retire from the town he should feel better and safer, and could hold his head higher—and was going on to make an argument, but she interrupted and surprised him pleasantly by saying she was ready; it did n't make any difference to her where she stayed, so that she got her share of the pension regularly. She said she would not go far, and would call at the haunted house once a month for her money. Then she said—

"I don't hate you so much now, but I 've hated you a many a year—and anybody would. Did n't I change you off, en give you a good fambly en a good name, en made you a white gen'l'man en rich, wid store clothes on—en what did I git for it? You despised me all de time, en was al'ays sayin' mean hard things to me befo' folks, en would n't ever let me forget I 's a nigger—en—en—"

She fell to sobbing, and broke down. Tom said—

"But you know I did n't know you were my mother; and besides—"

"Well, nemmine 'bout dat, now; let it go. I 's gwine to fo'git it." Then she added fiercely, "En don't you ever make me remember it ag'in, or you 'll be sorry, *I* tell you."

When they were parting, Tom said, in the most persuasive way he could command—

"Ma, would you mind telling me who was my father?"

He had supposed he was asking an embarrassing question. He was mistaken. Roxy drew herself up with a proud toss of her head, and said—

"Does I mine tellin' you? No, dat I don't! You ain't got no 'casion to be shame' o' yo' father, *I* kin tell you. He wuz de highest quality in dis whole town—ole Virginny stock. Fust famblies, he wuz. Jes as good stock as de Driscolls en de Howards, de bes' day dey ever seed." She put on a little prouder air, if possible, and added impressively: "Does you 'member Cunnel Cecil Burleigh Essex, dat died de same year yo' young Marse Tom Driscoll's pappy died, en all de Masons en Odd Fellers en Churches turned out en give him de bigges' funeral dis town ever seed? Dat 's de man."

Under the inspiration of her soaring complacency the departed graces of her earlier days returned to her, and her bearing took to itself a dignity and state that might have passed for queenly if her surroundings had been a little more in keeping with it.

"Dey ain't another nigger in dis town dat 's as high-bawn as you is. Now den, go 'long! En jes you hold yo' head up as high as you want to—you has de right, en dat I kin swah."

X

ALL say, "How hard it is that we have to die"—a strange complaint to come from the mouths of people who have had to live.
    —*Pudd'nhead Wilson's Calendar.*

WHEN angry, count four; when very angry, swear.
    —*Pudd'nhead Wilson's Calendar.*

EVERY NOW AND THEN, after Tom went to bed, he had sudden wakings out of his sleep, and his first thought was, "Oh, joy, it was all a dream!" Then he laid himself heavily down again, with a groan and the muttered words, "A nigger! I am a nigger! Oh, I wish I was dead!"

He woke at dawn with one more repetition of this horror, and then he resolved to meddle no more with that treacherous sleep. He began to think. Sufficiently bitter thinkings they were. They wandered along something after this fashion:

"Why were niggers *and* whites made? What crime did the uncreated first nigger commit that the curse of birth was decreed for him? And why is this awful difference made between white and black? . . . How hard the nigger's fate seems, this morning!—yet until last night such a thought never entered my head."

He sighed and groaned an hour or more away. Then "Chambers" came humbly in to say that breakfast was nearly ready. "Tom" blushed scarlet to see this aristocratic white youth cringe to him, a nigger, and call him "Young Marster." He said roughly—

"Get out of my sight!" and when the youth was gone, he muttered, "He has done me no harm, poor wretch, but he is an eyesore to me now, for he is Driscoll the young gentleman, and I am a—oh, I wish I was dead!"

A gigantic irruption, like that of Krakatoa a few years ago, with the accompanying earthquakes, tidal waves, and clouds of volcanic dust, changes the face of the surrounding landscape beyond recognition, bringing down the high lands, elevating the low, making fair lakes where deserts had been, and deserts where green prairies had smiled before. The tremendous catastrophe which had befallen Tom had changed his moral landscape in much the same way. Some of his low places he found lifted to ideals, some of his ideals had sunk to the valleys, and lay there with the sackcloth and ashes of pumice-stone and sulphur on their ruined heads.

For days he wandered in lonely places, thinking, thinking, thinking—trying to get his bearings. It was new work. If he met a friend, he found that the habit of a lifetime had in some mysterious way vanished—his arm hung limp, instead of involuntarily extending the hand for a shake. It was the "nigger" in him asserting its humility, and he blushed and was abashed. And the "nigger" in him was surprised when the white friend put out his hand for a shake with him. He found the "nigger" in him involuntarily giving the road, on the sidewalk, to the white rowdy and loafer. When Rowena, the dearest thing his heart knew, the idol of his secret worship, invited him in, the "nigger" in him made an embarrassed excuse and was afraid to enter and sit with the dread white folks on equal terms. The "nigger" in him went shrinking and skulking here and there and yonder, and fancying it saw suspicion and maybe detection in all faces, tones, and gestures. So strange and uncharacteristic was Tom's conduct that people noticed it, and turned to look after him when he passed on; and when he glanced back—as he could not help doing, in spite of his best resistance—and caught that puzzled expression in a person's face, it gave him a sick feeling, and he took himself out of view as quickly as he could. He presently came to have a hunted sense and a hunted look, and then he fled away to the hilltops and the solitudes. He said to himself that the curse of Ham was upon him.

He dreaded his meals; the "nigger" in him was ashamed to sit at the white folks' table, and feared discovery all the time; and once when Judge Driscoll said, "What's the matter with you? You look as meek as a nigger," he felt as secret murderers are said to feel when the accuser says, "Thou art the man!" Tom said he was not well, and left the table.

His ostensible "aunt's" solicitudes and endearments were become a terror to him, and he avoided them.

And all the time, hatred of his ostensible "uncle" was steadily growing in his heart; for he said to himself, "He is white;

and I am his chattel, his property, his goods, and he can sell me, just as he could his dog."

For as much as a week after this, Tom imagined that his character had undergone a pretty radical change. But that was because he did not know himself.

In several ways his opinions were totally changed, and would never go back to what they were before, but the main structure of his character was not changed, and could not be changed. One or two very important features of it were altered, and in time effects would result from this, if opportunity offered—effects of a quite serious nature, too. Under the influence of a great mental and moral upheaval his character and habits had taken on the appearance of complete change, but after a while with the subsidence of the storm both began to settle toward their former places. He dropped gradually back into his old frivolous and easy-going ways and conditions of feeling and manner of speech, and no familiar of his could have detected anything in him that differentiated him from the weak and careless Tom of other days.

The theft-raid which he had made upon the village turned out better than he had ventured to hope. It produced the sum necessary to pay his gaming-debts, and saved him from exposure to his uncle and another smashing of the will. He and his mother learned to like each other fairly well. She could n't love him, as yet, because there "war n't nothing *to* him," as she expressed it, but her nature needed something or somebody to rule over, and he was better than nothing. Her strong character and aggressive and commanding ways compelled Tom's admiration in spite of the fact that he got more illustrations of them than he needed for his comfort. However, as a rule her conversation was made up of racy tattle about the privacies of the chief families of the town (for she went harvesting among their kitchens every time she came to the village), and Tom enjoyed this. It was just in his line. She always collected her half of his pension punctually, and he was always at the haunted house to have a chat with her on these occasions. Every now and then she paid him a visit there on between-days also.

Occasionally he would run up to St. Louis for a few weeks,

and at last temptation caught him again. He won a lot of money, but lost it, and with it a deal more besides, which he promised to raise as soon as possible.

For this purpose he projected a new raid on his town. He never meddled with any other town, for he was afraid to venture into houses whose ins and outs he did not know and the habits of whose households he was not acquainted with. He arrived at the haunted house in disguise on the Wednesday before the advent of the twins—after writing his aunt Pratt that he would not arrive until two days after—and lay in hiding there with his mother until toward daylight Friday morning, when he went to his uncle's house and entered by the back way with his own key, and slipped up to his room, where he could have the use of mirror and toilet articles. He had a suit of girl's clothes with him in a bundle as a disguise for his raid, and was wearing a suit of his mother's clothing, with black gloves and veil. By dawn he was tricked out for his raid, but he caught a glimpse of Pudd'nhead Wilson through the window over the way, and knew that Pudd'nhead had caught a glimpse of him. So he entertained Wilson with some airs and graces and attitudes for a while, then stepped out of sight and resumed the other disguise, and by and by went down and out the back way and started down town to reconnoiter the scene of his intended labors.

But he was ill at ease. He had changed back to Roxy's dress, with the stoop of age added to the disguise, so that Wilson would not bother himself about a humble old woman leaving a neighbor's house by the back way in the early morning, in case he was still spying. But supposing Wilson had seen him leave, and had thought it suspicious, and had also followed him? The thought made Tom cold. He gave up the raid for the day, and hurried back to the haunted house by the obscurest route he knew. His mother was gone; but she came back, by and by, with the news of the grand reception at Patsy Cooper's, and soon persuaded him that the opportunity was like a special providence, it was so inviting and perfect. So he went raiding, after all, and made a nice success of it while everybody was gone to Patsy Cooper's. Success gave him nerve and even actual intrepidity; insomuch, indeed, that after he had conveyed his harvest to his mother in a back alley, he went to the reception himself, and added several of the valuables of that house to his takings.

After this long digression we have now arrived once more at the point where Pudd'nhead Wilson, while waiting for the arrival of the twins on that same Friday evening, sat puzzling over the strange apparition of that morning—a girl in young Tom Driscoll's bedroom; fretting, and guessing, and puzzling over it, and wondering who the shameless creature might be.

XI

THERE ARE three infallible ways of pleasing an author, and the three form a rising scale of compliment: 1, to tell him you have read one of his books; 2, to tell him you have read all of his books; 3, to ask him to let you read the manuscript of his forthcoming book. No. 1 admits you to his respect; No. 2 admits you to his admiration; No. 3 carries you clear into his heart.
—*Pudd'nhead Wilson's Calendar.*

As to the Adjective: when in doubt, strike it out.
—*Pudd'nhead Wilson's Calendar.*

THE TWINS arrived presently, and talk began. It flowed along chattily and sociably, and under its influence the new friendship gathered ease and strength. Wilson got out his Calendar, by request, and read a passage or two from it, which the twins praised quite cordially. This pleased the author so much that he complied gladly when they asked him to lend them a batch of the work to read at home. In the course of their wide travels they had found out that there are three sure ways of pleasing an author; they were now working the best of the three.

There was an interruption, now. Young Tom Driscoll appeared, and joined the party. He pretended to be seeing the distinguished strangers for the first time when they rose to shake hands; but this was only a blind, as he had already had a glimpse of them at the reception, while robbing the house. The twins made mental note that he was smooth-faced and rather handsome, and smooth and undulatory in his movements—graceful, in fact. Angelo thought he had a good eye; Luigi thought there was something veiled and sly about it. Angelo thought he had a pleasant free-and-easy way of talking; Luigi thought it was more so than was agreeable. Angelo thought he was a sufficiently nice young man; Luigi reserved his decision. Tom's first contribution to the conversation was a question which he had put to Wilson a hundred times before. It was always cheerily and good-naturedly put, and always inflicted a little pang, for it touched a secret sore; but this time the pang was sharp, since strangers were present.

357

"Well, how does the law come on? Had a case yet?"

Wilson bit his lip, but answered, "No—not yet," with as much indifference as he could assume. Judge Driscoll had generously left the law feature out of the Wilson biography which he had furnished to the twins. Young Tom laughed pleasantly, and said:

"Wilson 's a lawyer, gentlemen, but he does n't practise now."

The sarcasm bit, but Wilson kept himself under control, and said without passion:

"I don't practise, it is true. It is true that I have never had a case, and have had to earn a poor living for twenty years as an expert accountant in a town where I can't get hold of a set of books to untangle as often as I should like. But it is also true that I did fit myself well for the practice of the law. By the time I was your age, Tom, I had chosen a profession, and was soon competent to enter upon it." Tom winced. "I never got a chance to try my hand at it, and I may never get a chance; and yet if I ever do get it I shall be found ready, for I have kept up my law-studies all these years."

"That 's it; that 's good grit! I like to see it. I 've a notion to throw all my business your way. My business and your law-practice ought to make a pretty gay team, Dave," and the young fellow laughed again.

"If you will throw—" Wilson had thought of the girl in Tom's bedroom, and was going to say, "If you will throw the surreptitious and disreputable part of your business my way, it may amount to something"; but thought better of it and said, "However, this matter does n't fit well in a general conversation."

"All right, we 'll change the subject; I guess you were about to give me another dig, anyway, so I'm willing to change. How 's the Awful Mystery flourishing these days? Wilson 's got a scheme for driving plain window-glass out of the market by decorating it with greasy finger-marks, and getting rich by selling it at famine prices to the crowned heads over in Europe to outfit their palaces with. Fetch it out, Dave."

Wilson brought three of his glass strips, and said—

"I get the subject to pass the fingers of his right hand through his hair, so as to get a little coating of the natural oil on them, and then press the balls of them on the glass. A fine and delicate print of the lines in the skin results, and is permanent, if it does n't come in contact with something able to rub it off. You begin, Tom."

"Why, I think you took my finger-marks once or twice before."

"Yes; but you were a little boy the last time, only about twelve years old."

"That 's so. Of course I 've changed entirely since then, and variety is what the crowned heads want, I guess."

He passed his fingers through his crop of short hair, and pressed them one at a time on the glass. Angelo made a print of his fingers on another glass, and Luigi followed with the third. Wilson marked the glasses with names and date, and put them away. Tom gave one of his little laughs, and said—

"I thought I would n't say anything, but if variety is what you are after, you have wasted a piece of glass. The handprint of one twin is the same as the hand-print of the fellow-twin."

"Well, it 's done now, and I like to have them both, anyway," said Wilson, returning to his place.

"But look here, Dave," said Tom, "you used to tell people's fortunes, too, when you took their finger-marks. Dave 's just an all-round genius—a genius of the first water, gentlemen; a great scientist running to seed here in this village, a prophet with the kind of honor that prophets generally get at home— for here they don't give shucks for his scientifics, and they call his skull a notion-factory—hey, Dave, ain't it so? But never mind; he 'll make his mark some day—finger-mark, you know, he-he! But really, you want to let him take a shy at your palms once; it 's worth twice the price of admission or your money 's returned at the door. Why, he 'll read your wrinkles as easy as a book, and not only tell you fifty or sixty things that 's going to happen to you, but fifty or sixty thousand that ain't. Come, Dave, show the gentlemen what an inspired Jack-at-all-science we 've got in this town, and don't know it."

Wilson winced under this nagging and not very courteous chaff, and the twins suffered with him and for him. They

rightly judged, now, that the best way to relieve him would
be to take the thing in earnest and treat it with respect, ig-
noring Tom's rather overdone raillery; so Luigi said—

"We have seen something of palmistry in our wanderings,
and know very well what astonishing things it can do. If it is
n't a science, and one of the greatest of them, too, I don't
know what its other name ought to be. In the Orient—"

Tom looked surprised and incredulous. He said—

"That juggling a science? But really, you ain't serious, are
you?"

"Yes, entirely so. Four years ago we had our hands read
out to us as if our palms had been covered with print."

"Well, do you mean to say there was actually anything in
it?" asked Tom, his incredulity beginning to weaken a little.

"There was this much in it," said Angelo; "what was told
us of our characters was minutely exact—we could not have
bettered it ourselves. Next, two or three memorable things
that had happened to us were laid bare—things which no
one present but ourselves could have known about."

"Why, it 's rank sorcery!" exclaimed Tom, who was now
becoming very much interested. "And how did they make out
with what was going to happen to you in the future?"

"On the whole, quite fairly," said Luigi. "Two or three of
the most striking things foretold have happened since; much
the most striking one of all happened within that same year.
Some of the minor prophecies have come true; some of the
minor and some of the major ones have not been fulfilled yet,
and of course may never be: still, I should be more surprised
if they failed to arrive than if they did n't."

Tom was entirely sobered, and profoundly impressed. He
said, apologetically—

"Dave, I was n't meaning to belittle that science; I was only
chaffing—chattering, I reckon I 'd better say. I wish you
would look at their palms. Come, won't you?"

"Why, certainly, if you want me to; but you know I 've
had no chance to become an expert, and don't claim to be
one. When a past event is somewhat prominently recorded in
the palm I can generally detect that, but minor ones often
escape me,—not always, of course, but often,—but I have
n't much confidence in myself when it comes to reading the

future. I am talking as if palmistry was a daily study with me, but that is not so. I have n't examined half a dozen hands in the last half dozen years; you see, the people got to joking about it, and I stopped to let the talk die down. I 'll tell you what we 'll do, Count Luigi: I 'll make a try at your past, and if I have any success there—no, on the whole, I 'll let the future alone; that 's really the affair of an expert."

He took Luigi's hand. Tom said—

"Wait—don't look yet, Dave! Count Luigi, here 's paper and pencil. Set down that thing that you said was the most striking one that was foretold to you, and happened less than a year afterward, and give it to me so I can see if Dave finds it in your hand."

Luigi wrote a line privately, and folded up the piece of paper, and handed it to Tom, saying—

"I 'll tell you when to look at it, if he finds it."

Wilson began to study Luigi's palm, tracing life lines, heart lines, head lines, and so on, and noting carefully their relations with the cobweb of finer and more delicate marks and lines that enmeshed them on all sides; he felt of the fleshy cushion at the base of the thumb, and noted its shape; he felt of the fleshy side of the hand between the wrist and the base of the little finger, and noted its shape also; he painstakingly examined the fingers, observing their form, proportions, and natural manner of disposing themselves when in repose. All this process was watched by the three spectators with absorbing interest, their heads bent together over Luigi's palm, and nobody disturbing the stillness with a word. Wilson now entered upon a close survey of the palm again, and his revelations began.

He mapped out Luigi's character and disposition, his tastes, aversions, proclivities, ambitions, and eccentricities in a way which sometimes made Luigi wince and the others laugh, but both twins declared that the chart was artistically drawn and was correct.

Next, Wilson took up Luigi's history. He proceeded cautiously and with hesitation, now, moving his finger slowly along the great lines of the palm, and now and then halting it at a "star" or some such landmark, and examining that neighborhood minutely. He proclaimed one or two past events, Luigi confirmed his correctness, and the search went on. Presently Wilson glanced up suddenly with a surprised expression—

"Here is record of an incident which you would perhaps not wish me to—"

"Bring it out," said Luigi, good-naturedly; "I promise you it sha'n't embarrass me."

But Wilson still hesitated, and did not seem quite to know what to do. Then he said—

"I think it is too delicate a matter to—to—I believe I would rather write it or whisper it to you, and let you decide for yourself whether you want it talked out or not."

"That will answer," said Luigi; "write it."

Wilson wrote something on a slip of paper and handed it to Luigi, who read it to himself and said to Tom—

"Unfold your slip and read it, Mr. Driscoll."

Tom read:

"It was prophesied that I would kill a man. It came true before the year was out."

Tom added, "Great Scott!"

Luigi handed Wilson's paper to Tom, and said—

"Now read this one."

Tom read:

"You have killed some one, but whether man, woman or child, I do not make out."

"Cæsar's ghost!" commented Tom, with astonishment. "It beats anything that was ever heard of! Why, a man's own hand is his deadliest enemy! Just think of that—a man's own hand keeps a record of the deepest and fatalest secrets of his life, and is treacherously ready to expose him to any black-magic stranger that comes along. But what do you let a person look at your hand for, with that awful thing printed in it?"

"Oh," said Luigi, reposefully, "I don't mind it. I killed the man for good reasons, and I don't regret it."

"What were the reasons?"

"Well, he needed killing."

"I 'll tell you why he did it, since he won't say himself," said Angelo, warmly. "He did it to save my life, that 's what he did it for. So it was a noble act, and not a thing to be hid in the dark."

"So it was, so it was," said Wilson; "to do such a thing to save a brother's life is a great and fine action."

"Now come," said Luigi, "it is very pleasant to hear you say these things, but for unselfishness, or heroism, or magnanimity, the circumstances won't stand scrutiny. You overlook one detail: suppose I had n't saved Angelo's life, what would have become of mine? If I had let the man kill him, would n't he have killed me, too? I saved my own life, you see."

"Yes; that is your way of talking," said Angelo, "but I know you—I don't believe you thought of yourself at all. I keep that weapon yet that Luigi killed the man with, and I 'll show it to you some time. That incident makes it interesting, and it had a history before it came into Luigi's hands which adds to its interest. It was given to Luigi by a great Indian prince, the Gaikowar of Baroda, and it had been in his family two or three centuries. It killed a good many disagreeable people who troubled that hearthstone at one time and another. It is n't much to look at, except that it is n't shaped like other knives, or dirks, or whatever it may be called—here, I 'll draw it for you." He took a sheet of paper and made a rapid sketch. "There it is—a broad and murderous blade, with edges like a razor for sharpness. The devices engraved on it are the ciphers or names of its long line of possessors—I had Luigi's name added in Roman letters myself with our coat of arms, as you see. You notice what a curious handle the thing has. It is solid ivory, polished like a mirror, and is four or five inches long—round, and as thick as a large man's wrist, with the end squared off flat, for your thumb to rest on; for you grasp it, with your thumb resting on the blunt end—so—and lift it aloft and strike downward. The Gaikowar showed us how the thing was done when he gave it to Luigi, and before that night was ended Luigi had used the knife, and the Gaikowar was a man short by reason of it. The sheath is magnificently ornamented with gems of great value. You will find the sheath more worth looking at than the knife itself, of course."

Tom said to himself—

"It's lucky I came here. I would have sold that knife for a song; I supposed the jewels were glass."

"But go on; don't stop," said Wilson. "Our curiosity is up now, to hear about the homicide. Tell us about that."

"Well, briefly, the knife was to blame for that, all around. A native servant slipped into our room in the palace in the night, to kill us and steal the knife on account of the fortune incrusted on its sheath, without a doubt. Luigi had it under his pillow; we were in bed together. There was a dim night-light burning. I was asleep, but Luigi was awake, and he thought he detected a vague form nearing the bed. He slipped the knife out of the sheath and was ready, and unembarrassed by hampering bed-clothes, for the weather was hot and we had n't any. Suddenly that native rose at the bedside, and bent over me with his right hand lifted and a dirk in it aimed at my throat; but Luigi grabbed his wrist, pulled him downward, and drove his own knife into the man's neck. That is the whole story."

Wilson and Tom drew deep breaths, and after some general chat about the tragedy, Pudd'nhead said, taking Tom's hand—

"Now, Tom, I 've never had a look at your palms, as it happens; perhaps you 've got some little questionable privacies that need—hel-lo!"

Tom had snatched away his hand, and was looking a good deal confused.

"Why, he 's blushing!" said Luigi.

Tom darted an ugly look at him, and said sharply—

"Well, if I am, it ain't because I 'm a murderer!" Luigi's dark face flushed, but before he could speak or move, Tom added with anxious haste: "Oh, I beg a thousand pardons. I did n't mean that; it was out before I thought, and I 'm very, very sorry—you must forgive me!"

Wilson came to the rescue, and smoothed things down as well as he could; and in fact was entirely successful as far as the twins were concerned, for they felt sorrier for the affront put upon him by his guest's outburst of ill manners than for the insult offered to Luigi. But the success was not so pronounced with the offender. Tom tried to seem at his ease, and he went through the motions fairly well, but at bottom he felt resentful toward all the three witnesses of his exhibition; in fact, he felt so annoyed at them for having witnessed it and noticed it that he almost forgot to feel annoyed at himself for placing it before them. However, something presently happened which made him almost comfortable, and brought him nearly back to a state of charity and friendliness. This was a little spat between the twins; not much of a spat, but still a spat; and before they got far with it they were in a decided condition of irritation with each other. Tom was charmed; so pleased, indeed, that he cautiously did what he could to increase the irritation while pretending to be actuated by more respectable motives. By his help the fire got warmed up to the blazing-point, and he might have had the happiness of seeing the flames show up, in another moment, but for the interruption of a knock on the door—an interruption which fretted him as much as it gratified Wilson. Wilson opened the door.

The visitor was a good-natured, ignorant, energetic, middle-aged Irishman named John Buckstone, who was a great politician in a small way, and always took a large share in public matters of every sort. One of the town's chief excitements, just now, was over the matter of rum. There was a strong rum party and a strong anti-rum party. Buckstone was training with the rum party, and he had been sent to hunt up the twins and invite them to attend a mass-meeting of that faction. He delivered his errand, and said the clans were already gathering in the big hall over the market-house. Luigi accepted the invitation cordially, Angelo less cordially, since he disliked crowds, and did not drink the powerful intoxicants of America. In fact, he was even a teetotaler sometimes—when it was judicious to be one.

The twins left with Buckstone, and Tom Driscoll joined company with them uninvited.

In the distance one could see a long wavering line of torches drifting down the main street, and could hear the throbbing of the bass drum, the clash of cymbals, the squeaking of a fife or two, and the faint roar of remote hurrahs. The tail-end of this procession was climbing the market-house stairs when the twins arrived in its neighborhood; when they reached the hall it was full of people, torches, smoke, noise, and enthusiasm. They were conducted to the platform by Buckstone—Tom Driscoll still following—and were delivered to the chairman in the midst of a prodigious explosion of welcome. When the noise had moderated a little, the chair proposed that "our illustrious guests be at once elected, by complimentary acclamation, to membership in our ever-glorious organization, the paradise of the free and the perdition of the slave."

This eloquent discharge opened the flood-gates of enthusiasm again, and the election was carried with thundering unanimity. Then arose a storm of cries:

"Wet them down! Wet them down! Give them a drink!"

Glasses of whisky were handed to the twins. Luigi waved his aloft, then brought it to his lips; but Angelo set his down. There was another storm of cries:

"What 's the matter with the other one?" "What is the blond one going back on us for?" "Explain! Explain!"

The chairman inquired, and then reported—

"We have made an unfortunate mistake, gentlemen. I find that the Count Angelo Cappello is opposed to our creed—is a teetotaler, in fact, and was not intending to apply for membership with us. He desires that we reconsider the vote by which he was elected. What is the pleasure of the house?"

There was a general burst of laughter, plentifully accented with whistlings and cat-calls, but the energetic use of the gavel presently restored something like order. Then a man spoke from the crowd, and said that while he was very sorry that the mistake had been made, it would not be possible to rectify it at the present meeting. According to the by-laws it must go over to the next regular meeting for action. He would not offer a motion, as none was required. He desired to apologize to the gentleman in the name of the house, and begged to assure him that as far as it might lie in the power of the Sons of Liberty, his temporary membership in the order would be made pleasant to him.

This speech was received with great applause, mixed with cries of—

"That 's the talk!" "He 's a good fellow, any way, if he *is* a teetotaler!" "Drink his health!" "Give him a rouser, and no heel-taps!"

Glasses were handed around, and everybody on the platform drank Angelo's health, while the house bellowed forth in song:

> For he 's a jolly good fel-low,
> For he 's a jolly good fel-low,
> For he 's a jolly good fe-el-low,—
>   Which nobody can deny.

Tom Driscoll drank. It was his second glass, for he had drunk Angelo's the moment that Angelo had set it down. The two drinks made him very merry—almost idiotically so—and he began to take a most lively and prominent part in the proceedings, particularly in the music and cat-call and side-remarks.

The chairman was still standing at the front, the twins at his side. The extraordinarily close resemblance of the brothers to each other suggested a witticism to Tom Driscoll, and just as the chairman began a speech he skipped forward and said with an air of tipsy confidence to the audience—

"Boys, I move that he keeps still and lets this human philopena snip you out a speech."

The descriptive aptness of the phrase caught the house, and a mighty burst of laughter followed.

Luigi's southern blood leaped to the boiling-point in a moment under the sharp humiliation of this insult delivered in the presence of four hundred strangers. It was not in the young man's nature to let the matter pass, or to delay the squaring of the account. He took a couple of strides and halted behind the unsuspecting joker. Then he drew back and delivered a kick of such titanic vigor that it lifted Tom clear over the footlights and landed him on the heads of the front row of the Sons of Liberty.

Even a sober person does not like to have a human being emptied on him when he is not doing any harm; a person who is not sober cannot endure such an attention at all. The nest of Sons of Liberty that Driscoll landed in had not a sober bird in it; in fact there was probably not an entirely sober one in the auditorium. Driscoll was promptly and indignantly flung on to the heads of Sons in the next row, and these Sons passed him on toward the rear, and then immediately began to pummel the front-row Sons who had passed him to them. This course was strictly followed by bench after bench as Driscoll traveled in his tumultuous and airy flight toward the door; so he left behind him an ever lengthening wake of raging and plunging and fighting and swearing humanity. Down went group after group of torches, and presently above the deafening clatter of the gavel, roar of angry voices, and crash of succumbing benches, rose the paralyzing cry of

"FIRE!"

The fighting ceased instantly; the cursing ceased; for one distinctly defined moment there was a dead hush, a motionless calm, where the tempest had been; then with one impulse the multitude awoke to life and energy again, and went surging and struggling and swaying, this way and that, its outer edges melting away through windows and doors and gradually lessening the pressure and relieving the mass.

The fire-boys were never on hand so suddenly before; for there was no distance to go, this time, their quarters being in the rear end of the market-house. There was an engine company and a hook-and-ladder company. Half of each was composed of rummies and the other half of anti-rummies, after the moral and political share-and-share-alike fashion of the frontier town of the period. Enough anti-rummies were loafing in quarters to man the engine and the ladders. In two minutes they had their red shirts and helmets on—they never stirred officially in unofficial costume—and as the mass meeting overhead smashed through the long row of windows and poured out upon the roof of the arcade, the deliverers were ready for them with a powerful stream of water which washed some of them off the roof and nearly drowned the rest. But water was preferable to fire, and still the stampede from the windows continued, and still the pitiless drenchings assailed it until the building was empty; then the fire-boys mounted to the hall and flooded it with water enough to annihilate forty times as much fire as there was there; for a village fire-company does not often get a chance to show off, and so when it does get a chance it makes the most of it. Such citizens of that village as were of a thoughtful and judicious temperament did not insure against fire; they insured against the fire-company.

XII

COURAGE is resistance to fear, mastery of fear—not absence of fear. Except a creature be part coward it is not a compliment to say it is brave; it is merely a loose misapplication of the word. Consider the flea!—incomparably the bravest of all the creatures of God, if ignorance of fear were courage. Whether you are asleep or awake he will attack you, caring nothing for the fact that in bulk and strength you are to him as are the massed armies of the earth to a sucking child; he lives both day and night and all days and nights in the very lap of peril and the immediate presence of death, and yet is no more afraid than is the man who walks the streets of a city that was threatened by an earthquake ten centuries before. When we speak of Clive, Nelson, and Putnam as men who "did n't know what fear was," we ought always to add the flea—and put him at the head of the procession.

—*Pudd'nhead Wilson's Calendar.*

JUDGE DRISCOLL was in bed and asleep by ten o'clock on Friday night, and he was up and gone a-fishing before daylight in the morning with his friend Pembroke Howard. These two had been boys together in Virginia when that State still ranked as the chief and most imposing member of the Union, and they still coupled the proud and affectionate adjective "old" with her name when they spoke of her. In Missouri a recognized superiority attached to any person who hailed from Old Virginia; and this superiority was exalted to supremacy when a person of such nativity could also prove descent from the First Families of that great commonwealth. The Howards and Driscolls were of this aristocracy. In their eyes it was a nobility. It had its unwritten laws, and they were as clearly defined and as strict as any that could be found among the printed statutes of the land. The F. F. V. was born a gentleman; his highest duty in life was to watch over that great inheritance and keep it unsmirched. He must keep his honor spotless. Those laws were his chart; his course was marked out on it; if he swerved from it by so much as half a point of the compass it meant shipwreck to his honor; that is to say, degradation from his rank as a gentleman. These laws required certain things of him which his religion might forbid: then his religion must yield—the laws could not be relaxed to accommodate religions or anything else. Honor stood first; and the laws defined what it was and wherein it differed in certain details from honor as defined by church creeds and by the social laws and customs of some of the minor divisions of the globe that had got crowded out when the sacred boundaries of Virginia were staked out.

If Judge Driscoll was the recognized first citizen of Dawson's Landing, Pembroke Howard was easily its recognized second citizen. He was called "the great lawyer"—an earned title. He and Driscoll were of the same age—a year or two past sixty.

Although Driscoll was a free-thinker and Howard a strong and determined Presbyterian, their warm intimacy suffered no impairment in consequence. They were men whose opinions were their own property and not subject to revision and amendment, suggestion or criticism, by anybody, even their friends.

The day's fishing finished, they came floating down stream in their skiff, talking national politics and other high matters, and presently met a skiff coming up from town, with a man in it who said:

"I reckon you know one of the new twins gave your nephew a kicking last night, Judge?"

"Did *what?*"

"Gave him a kicking."

The old Judge's lips paled, and his eyes began to flame. He choked with anger for a moment, then he got out what he was trying to say—

"Well—well—go on! Give me the details."

The man did it. At the finish the Judge was silent a minute, turning over in his mind the shameful picture of Tom's flight over the footlights; then he said, as if musing aloud—

"H'm—I don't understand it. I was asleep at home. He did n't wake me. Thought he was competent to manage his affair without my help, I reckon." His face lit up with pride and pleasure at that thought, and he said with a cheery complacency, "I like that—it 's the true old blood—hey, Pembroke?"

Howard smiled an iron smile, and nodded his head approvingly. Then the news-bringer spoke again—

"But Tom beat the twin on the trial."

The Judge looked at the man wonderingly, and said—

"The trial? What trial?"

"Why, Tom had him up before Judge Robinson for assault and battery."

The old man shrank suddenly together like one who has received a death-stroke. Howard sprang for him as he sank forward in a swoon, and took him in his arms, and bedded him on his back in the boat. He sprinkled water in his face, and said to the startled visitor—

"Go, now—don't let him come to and find you here. You see what an effect your heedless speech has had; you ought to have been more considerate than to blurt out such a cruel piece of slander as that."

"I 'm right down sorry I did it now, Mr. Howard, and I would n't have done it if I had thought: but it ain't a slander; it 's perfectly true, just as I told him."

He rowed away. Presently the old Judge came out of his faint and looked up piteously into the sympathetic face that was bent over him.

"Say it ain't true, Pembroke; tell me it ain't true!" he said in a weak voice.

There was nothing weak in the deep organ-tones that responded—

"You know it 's a lie as well as I do, old friend. He is of the best blood of the Old Dominion."

"God bless you for saying it!" said the old gentleman, fervently. "Ah, Pembroke, it was such a blow!"

Howard stayed by his friend, and saw him home, and entered the house with him. It was dark, and past supper-time, but the Judge was not thinking of supper; he was eager to hear the slander refuted from headquarters, and as eager to have Howard hear it, too. Tom was sent for, and he came immediately. He was bruised and lame, and was not a happy-looking object. His uncle made him sit down, and said—

"We have been hearing about your adventure, Tom, with a handsome lie added to it for embellishment. Now pulverize that lie to dust! What measures have you taken? How does the thing stand?"

Tom answered guilelessly: "It don't stand at all; it 's all over. I had him up in court and beat him. Pudd'nhead Wilson defended him—first case he ever had, and lost it. The judge fined the miserable hound five dollars for the assault."

Howard and the Judge sprang to their feet with the opening sentence—why, neither knew; then they stood gazing vacantly at each other. Howard stood a moment, then sat mournfully down without saying anything. The Judge's wrath began to kindle, and he burst out—

"You cur! You scum! You vermin! Do you mean to tell me that blood of my race has suffered a blow and crawled to a court of law about it? Answer me!"

Tom's head drooped, and he answered with an eloquent silence. His uncle stared at him with a mixed expression of amazement and shame and incredulity that was sorrowful to see. At last he said—

"Which of the twins was it?"

"Count Luigi."

"You have challenged him?"

"N—no," hesitated Tom, turning pale.

"You will challenge him to-night. Howard will carry it."

Tom began to turn sick, and to show it. He turned his hat round and round in his hand, his uncle glowering blacker and blacker upon him as the heavy seconds drifted by; then at last he began to stammer, and said piteously—

"Oh, please don't ask me to do it, uncle! He is a murderous devil—I never could—I—I 'm afraid of him!"

Old Driscoll's mouth opened and closed three times before he could get it to perform its office; then he stormed out—

"A coward in my family! A Driscoll a coward! Oh, what have I done to deserve this infamy!" He tottered to his secretary in the corner repeating that lament again and again in heartbreaking tones, and got out of a drawer a paper, which he slowly tore to bits scattering the bits absently in his track as he walked up and down the room, still grieving and lamenting. At last he said—

"There it is, shreds and fragments once more—my will. Once more you have forced me to disinherit you, you base son of a most noble father! Leave my sight! Go—before I spit on you!"

The young man did not tarry. Then the Judge turned to Howard:

"You will be my second, old friend?"

"Of course."

"There is pen and paper. Draft the cartel, and lose no time."

"The Count shall have it in his hands in fifteen minutes," said Howard.

Tom was very heavy-hearted. His appetite was gone with his property and his self-respect. He went out the back way and wandered down the obscure lane grieving, and wondering if any course of future conduct, however discreet and carefully perfected and watched over, could win back his uncle's favor and persuade him to reconstruct once more that generous will which had just gone to ruin before his eyes. He finally concluded that it could. He said to himself that he had accomplished this sort of triumph once already, and that what had been done once could be done again. He would set about it. He would bend every energy to the task, and he would score that triumph once more, cost what it might to his convenience, limit as it might his frivolous and liberty-loving life.

"To begin," he said to himself, "I 'll square up with the proceeds of my raid, and then gambling has got to be stopped—and stopped short off. It 's the worst vice I 've got—from my standpoint, anyway, because it 's the one he can most easily find out, through the impatience of my creditors. He thought it expensive to have to pay two hundred dollars to them for me once. Expensive—*that!* Why, it cost me the whole of his fortune—but of course he never thought of that; some people can't think of any but their own side of a case. If he had known how deep I am in, now, the will would have gone to pot without waiting for a duel to help. Three hundred dollars! It 's a pile! But he 'll never hear of it, I 'm thankful to say. The minute I 've cleared it off, I 'm safe; and I 'll never touch a card again. Anyway, I won't while he lives, I make oath to that. I 'm entering on my last reform— I know it—yes, and I 'll win; but after that, if I ever slip again I 'm gone."

XIII

THUS MOURNFULLY COMMUNING with himself Tom
moped along the lane past Pudd'nhead Wilson's house,
and still on and on between fences inclosing vacant country
on each hand till he neared the haunted house, then he came
moping back again, with many sighs and heavy with trouble.
He sorely wanted cheerful company. Rowena! His heart gave
a bound at the thought, but the next thought quieted it—the
detested twins would be there.

He was on the inhabited side of Wilson's house, and now
as he approached it he noticed that the sitting-room was
lighted. This would do; others made him feel unwelcome
sometimes, but Wilson never failed in courtesy toward him,
and a kindly courtesy does at least save one's feelings, even if
it is not professing to stand for a welcome. Wilson heard
footsteps at his threshold, then the clearing of a throat.

"It's that fickle-tempered, dissipated young goose—poor
devil, he finds friends pretty scarce to-day, likely, after the
disgrace of carrying a personal-assault case into a law-court."

A dejected knock. "Come in!"

Tom entered, and drooped into a chair, without saying
anything. Wilson said kindly—

"Why, my boy, you look desolate. Don't take it so hard.
Try and forget you have been kicked."

"Oh, dear," said Tom, wretchedly, "it's not that, Pudd'n-
head—it's not that. It's a thousand times worse than that—
oh, yes, a million times worse."

"Why, Tom, what do you mean? Has Rowena—"

"Flung me? No, but the old man has."

Wilson said to himself, "Aha!" and thought of the mysterious girl in the bedroom. "The Driscolls have been making discoveries!" Then he said aloud, gravely:

"Tom, there are some kinds of dissipation which—"

"Oh, shucks, this has n't got anything to do with dissipation. He wanted me to challenge that derned Italian savage, and I would n't do it."

"Yes, of course he would do that," said Wilson in a meditative matter-of-course way; "but the thing that puzzled me was, why he did n't look to that last night, for one thing, and why he let you carry such a matter into a court of law at all, either before the duel or after it. It 's no place for it. It was not like him. I could n't understand it. How did it happen?"

"It happened because he did n't know anything about it. He was asleep when I got home last night."

"And you did n't wake him? Tom, is that possible?"

Tom was not getting much comfort here. He fidgeted a moment, then said:

"I did n't choose to tell him—that 's all. He was going a-fishing before dawn, with Pembroke Howard, and if I got the twins into the common calaboose—and I thought sure I could—I never dreamed of their slipping out on a paltry fine for such an outrageous offense—well, once in the calaboose they would be disgraced, and uncle would n't want any duels with that sort of characters, and would n't allow any."

"Tom, I am ashamed of you! I don't see how you could treat your good old uncle so. I am a better friend of his than you are; for if I had known the circumstances I would have kept that case out of court until I got word to him and let him have a gentleman's chance."

"You would?" exclaimed Tom, with lively surprise. "And it your first case! And you know perfectly well there never would have been any case if he had got that chance, don't you? And you 'd have finished your days a pauper nobody, instead of being an actually launched and recognized lawyer to-day. And you would really have done that, would you?"

"Certainly."

Tom looked at him a moment or two, then shook his head sorrowfully and said—

"I believe you—upon my word I do. I don't know why I do, but I do. Pudd'nhead Wilson, I think you're the biggest fool I ever saw."

"Thank you."

"Don't mention it."

"Well, he has been requiring you to fight the Italian and you have refused. You degenerate remnant of an honorable line! I'm thoroughly ashamed of you, Tom!"

"Oh, that's nothing! I don't care for anything, now that the will's torn up again."

"Tom, tell me squarely—did n't he find any fault with you for anything but those two things—carrying the case into court and refusing to fight?"

He watched the young fellow's face narrowly, but it was entirely reposeful, and so also was the voice that answered:

"No, he did n't find any other fault with me. If he had had any to find, he would have begun yesterday, for he was just in the humor for it. He drove that jack-pair around town and showed them the sights, and when he came home he could n't find his father's old silver watch that don't keep time and he thinks so much of, and could n't remember what he did with it three or four days ago when he saw it last; and so when I arrived he was all in a sweat about it, and when I suggested that it probably was n't lost but stolen, it put him in a regular passion and he said I was a fool—which convinced me, without any trouble, that that was just what he was afraid *had* happened, himself, but did not want to believe it, because lost things stand a better chance of being found again than stolen ones."

"Whe-ew!" whistled Wilson; "score another on the list."

"Another what?"

"Another theft!"

"Theft?"

"Yes, theft. That watch is n't lost, it's stolen. There's been another raid on the town—and just the same old mysterious sort of thing that has happened once before, as you remember."

"You don't mean it!"

"It's as sure as you are born! Have you missed anything yourself?"

"No. That is, I did miss a silver pencil-case that Aunt Mary Pratt gave me last birthday—"

"You 'll find it 's stolen—that 's what you 'll find."

"No, I sha'n't; for when I suggested theft about the watch and got such a rap, I went and examined my room, and the pencil-case was missing, but it was only mislaid, and I found it again."

"You are sure you missed nothing else?"

"Well, nothing of consequence. I missed a small plain gold ring worth two or three dollars, but that will turn up. I 'll look again."

"In my opinion you 'll not find it. There 's been a raid, I tell you. Come *in*!"

Mr. Justice Robinson entered, followed by Buckstone and the town-constable, Jim Blake. They sat down, and after some wandering and aimless weather-conversation Wilson said—

"By the way, we 've just added another to the list of thefts, maybe two. Judge Driscoll's old silver watch is gone, and Tom here has missed a gold ring."

"Well, it is a bad business," said the Justice, "and gets worse the further it goes. The Hankses, the Dobsons, the Pilligrews, the Ortons, the Grangers, the Hales, the Fullers, the Holcombs, in fact everybody that lives around about Patsy Cooper's has been robbed of little things like trinkets and teaspoons and such-like small valuables that are easily carried off. It 's perfectly plain that the thief took advantage of the reception at Patsy Cooper's, when all the neighbors were in her house and all their niggers hanging around her fence for a look at the show, to raid the vacant houses undisturbed. Patsy is miserable about it; miserable on account of the neighbors, and particularly miserable on account of her foreigners, of course; so miserable on their account that she has n't any room to worry about her own little losses."

"It 's the same old raider," said Wilson. "I suppose there is n't any doubt about that."

"Constable Blake does n't think so."

"No, you 're wrong there," said Blake; "the other times it was a man; there was plenty of signs of that, as we know, in the profession, though we never got hands on him; but this time it 's a woman."

Wilson thought of the mysterious girl straight off. She was always in his mind now. But she failed him again. Blake continued:

"She 's a stoop-shouldered old woman with a covered basket on her arm, in a black veil, dressed in mourning. I saw her going aboard the ferry-boat yesterday. Lives in Illinois, I reckon; but I don't care where she lives, I 'm going to get her—she can make herself sure of that."

"What makes you think she 's the thief?"

"Well, there ain't any other, for one thing; and for another, some of the nigger draymen that happened to be driving along saw her coming out of or going into houses, and told me so—and it just happens that they was *robbed* houses, every time."

It was granted that this was plenty good enough circumstantial evidence. A pensive silence followed, which lasted some moments, then Wilson said—

"There 's one good thing, anyway. She can't either pawn or sell Count Luigi's costly Indian dagger."

"My!" said Tom, "is *that* gone?"

"Yes."

"Well, that was a haul! But why can't she pawn it or sell it?"

"Because when the twins went home from the Sons of Liberty meeting last night, news of the raid was sifting in from everywhere, and Aunt Patsy was in distress to know if they had lost anything. They found that the dagger was gone, and they notified the police and pawnbrokers everywhere. It was a great haul, yes, but the old woman won't get anything out of it, because she 'll get caught."

"Did they offer a reward?" asked Buckstone.

"Yes; five hundred dollars for the knife, and five hundred more for the thief."

"What a leather-headed idea!" exclaimed the constable. "The thief da's n't go near them, nor send anybody. Whoever goes is going to get himself nabbed, for there ain't any pawnbroker that 's going to lose the chance to—"

If anybody had noticed Tom's face at that time, the gray-green color of it might have provoked curiosity; but nobody did. He said to himself: "I 'm gone! I never can square up;

the rest of the plunder won't pawn or sell for half of the bill. Oh, I know it—I 'm gone, I 'm gone—and this time it 's for good. Oh, this is awful—I don't know what to do, nor which way to turn!"

"Softly, softly," said Wilson to Blake. "I planned their scheme for them at midnight last night, and it was all finished up shipshape by two this morning. They 'll get their dagger back, and then I 'll explain to you how the thing was done."

There were strong signs of a general curiosity, and Buckstone said—

"Well, you have whetted us up pretty sharp, Wilson, and I 'm free to say that if you don't mind telling us in confidence—"

"Oh, I 'd as soon tell as not, Buckstone, but as long as the twins and I agreed to say nothing about it, we must let it stand so. But you can take my word for it you won't be kept waiting three days. Somebody will apply for that reward pretty promptly, and I 'll show you the thief and the dagger both very soon afterward."

The constable was disappointed, and also perplexed. He said—

"It may all be—yes, and I hope it will, but I 'm blamed if I can see my way through it. It 's too many for yours truly."

The subject seemed about talked out. Nobody seemed to have anything further to offer. After a silence the justice of the peace informed Wilson that he and Buckstone and the constable had come as a committee, on the part of the Democratic party, to ask him to run for mayor—for the little town was about to become a city and the first charter election was approaching. It was the first attention which Wilson had ever received at the hands of any party; it was a sufficiently humble one, but it was a recognition of his début into the town's life and activities at last; it was a step upward, and he was deeply gratified. He accepted, and the committee departed, followed by young Tom.

XIV

THE true Southern watermelon is a boon apart, and not to be
mentioned with commoner things. It is chief of this world's
luxuries, king by the grace of God over all the fruits of the
earth. When one has tasted it, he knows what the angels eat. It
was not a Southern watermelon that Eve took: we know it because she repented.

—Pudd'nhead Wilson's Calendar.

ABOUT THE TIME that Wilson was bowing the committee
out, Pembroke Howard was entering the next house to
report. He found the old Judge sitting grim and straight in
his chair, waiting.

"Well, Howard—the news?"

"The best in the world."

"Accepts, does he?" and the light of battle gleamed joyously
in the Judge's eye.

"Accepts? Why, he jumped at it."

"Did, did he? Now that 's fine—that 's very fine. I like that.
When is it to be?"

"Now! Straight off! To-night! An admirable fellow—
admirable!"

"Admirable? He 's a darling! Why, it 's an honor as well as
a pleasure to stand up before such a man. Come—off with
you! Go and arrange everything—and give him my heartiest
compliments. A rare fellow, indeed; an admirable fellow, as
you have said!"

Howard hurried away, saying—

"I 'll have him in the vacant stretch between Wilson's and
the haunted house within the hour, and I 'll bring my own
pistols."

Judge Driscoll began to walk the floor in a state of pleased
excitement; but presently he stopped, and began to think—
began to think of Tom. Twice he moved toward the secretary,
and twice he turned away again; but finally he said—

"This may be my last night in the world—I must not take
the chance. He is worthless and unworthy, but it is largely
my fault. He was intrusted to me by my brother on his dying

bed, and I have indulged him to his hurt, instead of training
him up severely, and making a man of him. I have violated
my trust, and I must not add the sin of desertion to that. I
have forgiven him once already, and would subject him to a
long and hard trial before forgiving him again, if I could live;
but I must not run that risk. No, I must restore the will. But
if I survive the duel, I will hide it away, and he will not know,
and I will not tell him until he reforms and I see that his
reformation is going to be permanent."

He re-drew the will, and his ostensible nephew was heir to
a fortune again. As he was finishing his task, Tom, wearied
with another brooding tramp, entered the house and went
tiptoeing past the sitting-room door. He glanced in, and hurried on, for the sight of his uncle had nothing but terrors for
him to-night. But his uncle was writing! That was unusual at
this late hour. What could he be writing? A chill of anxiety
settled down upon Tom's heart. Did that writing concern
him? He was afraid so. He reflected that when ill luck begins,
it does not come in sprinkles, but in showers. He said he
would get a glimpse of that document or know the reason
why. He heard some one coming, and stepped out of sight
and hearing. It was Pembroke Howard. What could be
hatching?

Howard said, with great satisfaction:

"Everything 's right and ready. He's gone to the battle-
ground with his second and the surgeon—also with his
brother. I 've arranged it all with Wilson—Wilson 's his second. We are to have three shots apiece."

"Good! How is the moon?"

"Bright as day, nearly. Perfect, for the distance—fifteen
yards. No wind—not a breath; hot and still."

"All good; all first-rate. Here, Pembroke, read this, and
witness it."

Pembroke read and witnessed the will, then gave the old
man's hand a hearty shake and said:

"Now that 's right, York—but I knew you would do it.
You could n't leave that poor chap to fight along without
means or profession, with certain defeat before him, and I
knew you would n't, for his father's sake if not for his own."

"For his dead father's sake I could n't, I know; for poor

Percy—but you know what Percy was to me. But mind—Tom is not to know of this unless I fall to-night."

"I understand. I 'll keep the secret."

The Judge put the will away, and the two started for the battle-ground. In another minute the will was in Tom's hands. His misery vanished, his feelings underwent a tremendous revulsion. He put the will carefully back in its place, and spread his mouth and swung his hat once, twice, three times around his head, in imitation of three rousing huzzas, no sound issuing from his lips. He fell to communing with himself excitedly and joyously, but every now and then he let off another volley of dumb hurrahs.

He said to himself: "I 've got the fortune again, but I 'll not let on that I know about it. And this time I 'm going to hang on to it. I take no more risks. I 'll gamble no more, I 'll drink no more, because—well, because I 'll not go where there is any of that sort of thing going on, again. It 's the sure way, and the only sure way; I might have thought of that sooner—well, yes, if I had wanted to. But now—dear me, I 've had a bad scare this time, and I 'll take no more chances. Not a single chance more. Land! I persuaded myself this evening that I could fetch him around without any great amount of effort, but I 've been getting more and more heavy-hearted and doubtful straight along, ever since. If he tells me about this thing, all right; but if he does n't, I sha'n't let on. I—well, I 'd like to tell Pudd'nhead Wilson, but—no, I 'll think about that; perhaps I won't." He whirled off another dead huzza, and said, "I 'm reformed, and this time I 'll stay so, sure!"

He was about to close with a final grand silent demonstration, when he suddenly recollected that Wilson had put it out of his power to pawn or sell the Indian knife, and that he was once more in awful peril of exposure by his creditors for that reason. His joy collapsed utterly, and he turned away and moped toward the door moaning and lamenting over the bitterness of his luck. He dragged himself upstairs, and brooded in his room a long time disconsolate and forlorn, with Luigi's Indian knife for a text. At last he sighed and said:

"When I supposed these stones were glass and this ivory bone, the thing had n't any interest for me because it had n't any value, and could n't help me out of my trouble. But now—why, now it is full of interest; yes, and of a sort to break a body's heart. It 's a bag of gold that has turned to dirt and ashes in my hands. It could save me, and save me so easily, and yet I 've got to go to ruin. It 's like drowning with a life-preserver in my reach. All the hard luck comes to me, and all the good luck goes to other people—Pudd'nhead Wilson, for instance; even his career has got a sort of a little start at last, and what has he done to deserve it, I should like to know? Yes, he has opened his own road, but he is n't content with that, but must block mine. It 's a sordid, selfish world, and I wish I was out of it." He allowed the light of the candle to play upon the jewels of the sheath, but the flashings and sparklings had no charm for his eye; they were only just so many pangs to his heart. "I must not say anything to Roxy about this thing," he said, "she is too daring. She would be for digging these stones out and selling them, and then—why, she would be arrested and the stones traced, and then—" The thought made him quake, and he hid the knife away, trembling all over and glancing furtively about, like a criminal who fancies that the accuser is already at hand.

Should he try to sleep? Oh, no, sleep was not for him; his trouble was too haunting, too afflicting for that. He must have somebody to mourn with. He would carry his despair to Roxy.

He had heard several distant gunshots, but that sort of thing was not uncommon, and they had made no impression upon him. He went out at the back door, and turned westward. He passed Wilson's house and proceeded along the lane, and presently saw several figures approaching Wilson's place through the vacant lots. These were the duelists returning from the fight; he thought he recognized them, but as he had no desire for white people's company, he stooped down behind the fence until they were out of his way.

Roxy was feeling fine. She said:

"Whah was you, child? Warn't you in it?"

"In what?"

"In de duel."

"Duel? Has there been a duel?"

" 'Co'se dey has. De ole Jedge has be'n havin' a duel wid one o' dem twins."

"Great Scott!" Then he added to himself: "That 's what made him re-make the will; he thought he might get killed, and it softened him toward me. And that 's what he and Howard were so busy about . . . Oh dear, if the twin had only killed him, I should be out of my—"

"What is you mumblin' 'bout, Chambers? Whah was you? Did n't you know dey was gwyne to be a duel?"

"No. I did n't. The old man tried to get me to fight one with Count Luigi, but he did n't succeed, so I reckon he concluded to patch up the family honor himself."

He laughed at the idea, and went rambling on with a detailed account of his talk with the Judge, and how shocked and ashamed the Judge was to find that he had a coward in his family. He glanced up at last, and got a shock himself. Roxana's bosom was heaving with suppressed passion, and she was glowering down upon him with measureless contempt written in her face.

"En you refuse' to fight a man dat kicked you, 'stid o' jumpin' at de chance! En you ain't got no mo' feelin' den to come en tell me, dat fetched sich a po' low-down ornery rabbit into de worl'! Pah! it make me sick! It 's de nigger in you, dat 's what it is. Thirty-one parts o' you is white, en on'y one part nigger, en dat po' little one part is yo' *soul*. Tain't wuth savin'; tain't wuth totin' out on a shovel en thowin in de gutter. You has disgraced yo' birth. What would yo' pa think o' you? It 's enough to make him turn in his grave."

The last three sentences stung Tom into a fury, and he said to himself that if his father were only alive and in reach of assassination his mother would soon find that he had a very clear notion of the size of his indebtedness to that man, and was willing to pay it up in full, and would do it too, even at risk of his life; but he kept his thought to himself; that was safest in his mother's present state.

"Whatever has come o' yo' Essex blood? Dat 's what I can't understand. En it ain't on'y jist Essex blood dat 's in you, not by a long sight—'deed it ain't. My great-great-great-gran'father en yo' great-great-great-great-gran'father was ole Cap'n John Smith, de highest blood dat Ole Virginny ever

turned out, en *his* great-great-gran'mother or somers along
back dah, was Pocahontas de Injun queen, en her husbun'
was a nigger king outen Africa—en yit here you is, a slinkin'
outen a duel en disgracin' our whole line like a ornery low-
down hound! Yes, it 's de nigger in you!"

She sat down on her candle-box and fell into a reverie.
Tom did not disturb her; he sometimes lacked prudence, but
it was not in circumstances of this kind. Roxana's storm went
gradually down, but it died hard, and even when it seemed to
be quite gone, it would now and then break out in a distant
rumble, so to speak, in the form of muttered ejaculations.
One of these was, "Ain't nigger enough in him to show in
his finger-nails, en dat takes mighty little—yit dey 's enough
to paint his soul."

Presently she muttered, "Yassir, enough to paint a whole
thimbleful of 'em." At last her ramblings ceased altogether,
and her countenance began to clear—a welcome sign to
Tom, who had learned her moods, and knew she was on the
threshold of good-humor, now. He noticed that from time to
time she unconsciously carried her finger to the end of her
nose. He looked closer and said:

"Why, mammy, the end of your nose is skinned. How did
that come?"

She sent out the sort of whole-hearted peal of laughter
which God has vouchsafed in its perfection to none but the
happy angels in heaven and the bruised and broken black
slave on the earth, and said:

"Dad fetch dat duel, I be'n in it myself."

"Gracious! did a bullet do that?"

"Yassir, you bet it did!"

"Well, I declare! Why, how did that happen?"

"Happen dis-away. I 'uz a-sett'n' here kinder dozin' in de
dark, en *che-bang!* goes a gun, right out dah. I skips along
out towards t' other end o' de house to see what 's gwyne
on, en stops by de ole winder on de side towards Pudd'nhead
Wilson's house dat ain't got no sash in it,—but dey ain't
none of 'em got any sashes, fur as dat 's concerned,—en I
stood dah in de dark en look out, en dar in de moonlight,
right down under me 'uz one o' de twins a-cussin'—not
much, but jist a-cussin' soft—it 'uz de brown one dat 'uz

cussin', 'ca'se he 'uz hit in de shoulder. En Doctor Claypool he 'uz a-workin' at him, en Pudd'nhead Wilson he 'uz a-he'pin', en ole Jedge Driscoll en Pem Howard 'uz a-standin' out yonder a little piece waitin' for 'em to git ready agin. En treckly dey squared off en give de word, en *bang-bang* went de pistols, en de twin he say, 'Ouch!'—hit him on de han' dis time,—en I hear dat same bullet go *spat!* ag'in' de logs under de winder; en de nex' time dey shoot, de twin say, 'Ouch!' ag'in, en I done it too, 'ca'se de bullet glance' on his cheek-bone en skip up here en glance on de side o' de winder en whiz right acrost my face en tuck de hide off'n my nose— why, if I 'd 'a' be'n jist a inch or a inch en a half furder 't would 'a' tuck de whole nose en disfigger me. Here 's de bul-let; I hunted her up."

"Did you stand there all the time?"

"Dat 's a question to ask, ain't it! What else would I do? Does I git a chance to see a duel every day?"

"Why, you were right in range! Were n't you afraid?"

The woman gave a sniff of scorn.

" 'Fraid! De Smith-Pocahontases ain't 'fraid o' nothin', let alone bullets."

"They 've got pluck enough, I suppose; what they lack is judgment. *I* would n't have stood there."

"Nobody 's accusin' you!"

"Did anybody else get hurt?"

"Yes, we all got hit 'cep' de blon' twin en de doctor en de seconds. De Jedge did n't git hurt, but I hear Pudd'nhead say de bullet snip some o' his ha'r off."

" 'George!" said Tom to himself, "to come so near being out of my trouble, and miss it by an inch. Oh dear, dear, he will live to find me out and sell me to some nigger-trader yet—yes, and he would do it in a minute." Then he said aloud, in a grave tone—

"Mother, we are in an awful fix."

Roxana caught her breath with a spasm, and said—

"Chile! What you hit a body so sudden for, like dat? What 's be'n en gone en happen'?"

"Well, there 's one thing I did n't tell you. When I would n't fight, he tore up the will again, and—"

Roxana's face turned a dead white, and she said—

"Now you 's *done*!—done forever! Dat 's de end. Bofe un us is gwyne to starve to—"

"Wait and hear me through, can't you! I reckon that when he resolved to fight, himself, he thought he might get killed and not have a chance to forgive me any more in this life, so he made the will again, and I 've seen it, and it 's all right. But—"

"Oh, thank goodness, den we 's safe agin!—safe! en so what did you want to come here en talk sich dreadful—"

"Hold *on*, I tell you, and let me finish. The swag I gathered won't half square me up, and the first thing we know, my creditors—well, you know what 'll happen."

Roxana dropped her chin, and told her son to leave her alone—she must think this matter out. Presently she said impressively:

"You got to go mighty keerful now, I tell you! En here 's what you got to do. He did n't git killed, en if you gives him de least reason, he 'll bust de will ag'in, en dat 's de *las'* time, now you hear me! So—you 's got to show him what you kin do in de nex' few days. You 's got to be pison good, en let him see it; you got to do everything dat 'll make him b'lieve in you, en you got to sweeten aroun' ole Aunt Pratt, too,—she 's pow'ful strong wid de Jedge, en de bes' frien' you got. Nex', you 'll go 'long away to Sent Louis, en dat 'll *keep* him in yo' favor. Den you go en make a bargain wid dem people. You tell 'em he ain't gwyne to live long—en dat 's de fac', too,—en tell 'em you 'll pay 'em intrust, en big intrust, too,—ten per—what you call it?"

"Ten per cent. a month?"

"Dat 's it. Den you take and sell yo' truck aroun', a little at a time, en pay de intrust. How long will it las'?"

"I think there 's enough to pay the interest five or six months."

"Den you 's all right. If he don't die in six months, dat don't make no diff'rence—Providence 'll provide. You 's gwyne to be safe—if you behaves." She bent an austere eye on him and added, "En you *is* gwyne to behave—does you know dat?"

He laughed and said he was going to try, anyway. She did not unbend. She said gravely:

"Tryin' ain't de thing. You 's gwyne to *do* it. You ain't
gwyne to steal a pin—'ca'se it ain't safe no mo'; en you ain't
gwyne into no bad comp'ny—not even once, you understand; en you ain't gwyne to drink a drop—nary single drop;
en you ain't gwyne to gamble one single gamble—not one!
Dis ain't what you 's gwyne to *try* to do, it 's what you 's
gwyne to *do*. En I 'll tell you how I knows it. Dis is how. I
's gwyne to foller along to Sent Louis my own self; en you
's gwyne to come to me every day o' yo' life, en I 'll look you
over; en if you fails in one single one o' dem things—jist
one—I take my oath I 'll come straight down to dis town en
tell de Jedge you 's a nigger en a slave—en *prove* it!" She
paused to let her words sink home. Then she added, "Chambers, does you b'lieve me when I says dat?"

Tom was sober enough now. There was no levity in his
voice when he answered:

"Yes, mother. I know, now, that I am reformed—and permanently. Permanently—and beyond the reach of any human
temptation."

"Den g' long home en begin!"

XV

NOTHING so needs reforming as other people's habits.
—*Pudd'nhead Wilson's Calendar.*

BEHOLD, the fool saith, "Put not all thine eggs in the one basket"—which is but a manner of saying, "Scatter your money and your attention"; but the wise man saith, "Put all your eggs in the one basket and—WATCH THAT BASKET."
—*Pudd'nhead Wilson's Calendar.*

WHAT A TIME OF IT Dawson's Landing was having! All its life it had been asleep, but now it hardly got a chance for a nod, so swiftly did big events and crashing surprises come along in one another's wake: Friday morning, first glimpse of Real Nobility, also grand reception at Aunt Patsy Cooper's, also great robber-raid; Friday evening, dramatic kicking of the heir of the chief citizen in presence of four hundred people; Saturday morning, emergence as practising lawyer of the long-submerged Pudd'nhead Wilson; Saturday night, duel between chief citizen and titled stranger.

The people took more pride in the duel than in all the other events put together, perhaps. It was a glory to their town to have such a thing happen there. In their eyes the principals had reached the summit of human honor. Everybody paid homage to their names; their praises were in all mouths. Even the duelists' subordinates came in for a handsome share of the public approbation: wherefore Pudd'nhead Wilson was suddenly become a man of consequence. When asked to run for the mayoralty Saturday night he was risking defeat, but Sunday morning found him a made man and his success assured.

The twins were prodigiously great, now; the town took them to its bosom with enthusiasm. Day after day, and night after night, they went dining and visiting from house to house, making friends, enlarging and solidifying their popularity, and charming and surprising all with their musical prodigies, and now and then heightening the effects with samples of what they could do in other directions, out of their stock of rare and curious accomplishments. They were so pleased that they gave the regulation thirty days' notice, the required preparation for citizenship, and resolved to finish their days in this pleasant place. That was the climax. The delighted community rose as one man and applauded; and when the twins were asked to stand for seats in the forthcoming aldermanic board, and consented, the public contentment was rounded and complete.

Tom Driscoll was not happy over these things; they sunk deep, and hurt all the way down. He hated the one twin for kicking him, and the other one for being the kicker's brother.

Now and then the people wondered why nothing was heard of the raider, or of the stolen knife or the other plunder, but nobody was able to throw any light on that matter. Nearly a week had drifted by, and still the thing remained a vexed mystery.

On Saturday Constable Blake and Pudd'nhead Wilson met on the street, and Tom Driscoll joined them in time to open their conversation for them. He said to Blake—

"You are not looking well, Blake; you seem to be annoyed about something. Has anything gone wrong in the detective business? I believe you fairly and justifiably claim to have a pretty good reputation in that line, is n't it so?"—which made Blake feel good, and look it; but Tom added, "for a country detective"—which made Blake feel the other way, and not only look it, but betray it in his voice—

"Yes, sir, I *have* got a reputation; and it 's as good as anybody's in the profession, too, country or no country."

"Oh, I beg pardon; I did n't mean any offense. What I started out to ask was only about the old woman that raided the town—the stoop-shouldered old woman, you know, that you said you were going to catch; and I knew you would, too, because you have the reputation of never boasting, and—well, you—you 've caught the old woman?"

"D—— the old woman!"

"Why, sho! you don't mean to say you have n't caught her?"

"No; I have n't caught her. If anybody could have caught her, I could; but nobody could n't, I don't care who he is."

"I am sorry, real sorry—for your sake; because, when it

gets around that a detective has expressed himself so confidently, and then—"

"Don't you worry, that 's all—don't you worry; and as for the town, the town need n't worry, either. She 's my meat—make yourself easy about that. I 'm on her track; I 've got clues that—"

"That 's good! Now if you could get an old veteran detective down from St. Louis to help you find out what the clues mean, and where they lead to, and then—"

"I 'm plenty veteran enough myself, and I don't need anybody's help. I 'll have her inside of a we—inside of a month. That I 'll swear to!"

Tom said carelessly—

"I suppose that will answer—yes, that will answer. But I reckon she is pretty old, and old people don't often outlive the cautious pace of the professional detective when he has got his clues together and is out on his still-hunt."

Blake's dull face flushed under this gibe, but before he could set his retort in order Tom had turned to Wilson, and was saying, with placid indifference of manner and voice—

"Who got the reward, Pudd'nhead?"

Wilson winced slightly, and saw that his own turn was come.

"What reward?"

"Why, the reward for the thief, and the other one for the knife."

Wilson answered—and rather uncomfortably, to judge by his hesitating fashion of delivering himself—

"Well, the—well, in fact, nobody has claimed it yet."

Tom seemed surprised.

"Why, is that so?"

Wilson showed a trifle of irritation when he replied—

"Yes, it 's so. And what of it?"

"Oh, nothing. Only I thought you had struck out a new idea, and invented a scheme that was going to revolutionize the time-worn and ineffectual methods of the—" He stopped, and turned to Blake, who was happy now that another had taken his place on the gridiron: "Blake, did n't you understand him to intimate that it would n't be necessary for you to hunt the old woman down?"

"B'George, he said he 'd have thief and swag both inside of three days—he did, by hokey! and that 's just about a week ago. Why, I said at the time that no thief and no thief's pal was going to try to pawn or sell a thing where he knowed the pawnbroker could get both rewards by taking *him* into camp *with* the swag. It was the blessedest idea that ever *I* struck!"

"You 'd change your mind," said Wilson, with irritated bluntness, "if you knew the entire scheme instead of only part of it."

"Well," said the constable, pensively, "I had the idea that it would n't work, and up to now I 'm right, anyway."

"Very well, then, let it stand at that, and give it a further show. It has worked at least as well as your own methods, you perceive."

The constable had n't anything handy to hit back with, so he discharged a discontented sniff, and said nothing.

After the night that Wilson had partly revealed his scheme at his house, Tom had tried for several days to guess out the secret of the rest of it, but had failed. Then it occurred to him to give Roxana's smarter head a chance at it. He made up a supposititious case, and laid it before her. She thought it over, and delivered her verdict upon it. Tom said to himself, "She 's hit it, sure!" He thought he would test that verdict, now, and watch Wilson's face; so he said reflectively—

"Wilson, you 're not a fool—a fact of recent discovery. Whatever your scheme was, it had sense in it, Blake's opinion to the contrary notwithstanding. I don't ask you to reveal it, but I will suppose a case—a case which will answer as a starting-point for the real thing I am going to come at, and that 's all I want. You offered five hundred dollars for the knife, and five hundred for the thief. We will suppose, for argument's sake, that the first reward is *advertised*, and the second offered by *private letter* to pawnbrokers and—"

Blake slapped his thigh, and cried out—

"By Jackson, he 's got you, Pudd'nhead! Now why could n't I or *any* fool have thought of that?"

Wilson said to himself, "Anybody with a reasonably good head would have thought of it. I am not surprised that Blake did n't detect it; I am only surprised that Tom did. There is more to him than I supposed." He said nothing aloud, and Tom went on:

"Very well. The thief would not suspect that there was a trap, and he would bring or send the knife, and say he bought it for a song, or found it in the road, or something like that, and try to collect the reward, and be arrested—would n't he?"

"Yes," said Wilson.

"I think so," said Tom. "There can't be any doubt of it. Have you ever seen that knife?"

"No."

"Has any friend of yours?"

"Not that I know of."

"Well, I begin to think I understand why your scheme failed."

"What do you mean, Tom? What are you driving at?" asked Wilson, with a dawning sense of discomfort.

"Why, that there *is n't* any such knife."

"Look here, Wilson," said Blake, "Tom Driscoll 's right, for a thousand dollars—if I had it."

Wilson's blood warmed a little, and he wondered if he had been played upon by those strangers; it certainly had something of that look. But what could they gain by it? He threw out that suggestion. Tom replied:

"Gain? Oh, nothing that you would value, maybe. But they are strangers making their way in a new community. Is it nothing to them to appear as pets of an Oriental prince—at no expense? Is it nothing to them to be able to dazzle this poor little town with thousand-dollar rewards—at no expense? Wilson, there is n't any such knife, or your scheme would have fetched it to light. Or if there is any such knife, they 've got it yet. I believe, myself, that they 've seen such a knife, for Angelo pictured it out with his pencil too swiftly and handily for him to have been inventing it, and of course I can't swear that they 've never had it; but this I 'll go bail for—if they had it when they came to this town, they 've got it yet."

Blake said—

"It looks mighty reasonable, the way Tom puts it; it most certainly does."

Tom responded, turning to leave—

"You find the old woman, Blake, and if she can't furnish the knife, go and search the twins!"

Tom sauntered away. Wilson felt a good deal depressed. He hardly knew what to think. He was loth to withdraw his faith from the twins, and was resolved not to do it on the present indecisive evidence; but—well, he would think, and then decide how to act.

"Blake, what do you think of this matter?"

"Well, Pudd'nhead, I 'm bound to say I put it up the way Tom does. They had n't the knife; or if they had it, they 've got it yet."

The men parted. Wilson said to himself:

"I believe they had it; if it had been stolen, the scheme would have restored it, that is certain. And so I believe they 've got it yet."

Tom had no purpose in his mind when he encountered those two men. When he began his talk he hoped to be able to gall them a little and get a trifle of malicious entertainment out of it. But when he left, he left in great spirits, for he perceived that just by pure luck and no troublesome labor he had accomplished several delightful things: he had touched both men on a raw spot and seen them squirm; he had modified Wilson's sweetness for the twins with one small bitter taste that he would n't be able to get out of his mouth right away; and, best of all, he had taken the hated twins down a peg with the community; for Blake would gossip around freely, after the manner of detectives, and within a week the town would be laughing at them in its sleeve for offering a gaudy reward for a bauble which they either never possessed or had n't lost. Tom was very well satisfied with himself.

Tom's behavior at home had been perfect during the entire week. His uncle and aunt had seen nothing like it before. They could find no fault with him anywhere.

Saturday evening he said to the Judge—

"I 've had something preying on my mind, uncle, and as I am going away, and might never see you again, I can't bear it any longer. I made you believe I was afraid to fight that Italian adventurer. I had to get out of it on some pretext or other, and maybe I chose badly, being taken unawares, but no honorable person could consent to meet him in the field, knowing what I knew about him."

"Indeed? What was that?"

"Count Luigi is a confessed assassin."

"Incredible!"

"It is perfectly true. Wilson detected it in his hand, by palmistry, and charged him with it, and cornered him up so close that he had to confess; but both twins begged us on their knees to keep the secret, and swore they would lead straight lives here; and it was all so pitiful that we gave our word of honor never to expose them while they kept that promise. You would have done it yourself, uncle."

"You are right, my boy; I would. A man's secret is still his own property, and sacred, when it has been surprised out of him like that. You did well, and I am proud of you." Then he added mournfully, "But I wish I could have been saved the shame of meeting an assassin on the field of honor."

"It could n't be helped, uncle. If I had known you were going to challenge him I should have felt obliged to sacrifice my pledged word in order to stop it, but Wilson could n't be expected to do otherwise than keep silent."

"Oh no; Wilson did right, and is in no way to blame. Tom, Tom, you have lifted a heavy load from my heart; I was stung to the very soul when I seemed to have discovered that I had a coward in my family."

"You may imagine what it cost *me* to assume such a part, uncle."

"Oh, I know it, poor boy, I know it. And I can understand how much it has cost you to remain under that unjust stigma to this time. But it is all right now, and no harm is done. You have restored my comfort of mind, and with it your own; and both of us had suffered enough."

The old man sat a while plunged in thought; then he looked up with a satisfied light in his eye, and said: "That this assassin should have put the affront upon me of letting me meet him on the field of honor as if he were a gentleman is a matter which I will presently settle—but not now. I will not shoot him until after election. I see a way to ruin them both

before; I will attend to that first. Neither of them shall be
elected, that I promise. You are sure that the fact that he is
an assassin has not got abroad?"

"Perfectly certain of it, sir."

"It will be a good card. I will fling a hint at it from the
stump on the polling-day. It will sweep the ground from under both of them."

"There 's not a doubt of it. It will finish them."

"That and outside work among the voters will, to a certainty. I want you to come down here by and by and work
privately among the rag-tag and bobtail. You shall spend
money among them; I will furnish it."

Another point scored against the detested twins! Really it
was a great day for Tom. He was encouraged to chance a
parting shot, now, at the same target, and did it.

"You know that wonderful Indian knife that the twins have
been making such a to-do about? Well, there 's no track or
trace of it yet; so the town is beginning to sneer and gossip
and laugh. Half the people believe they never had any such
knife, the other half believe they had it and have got it still. I
've heard twenty people talking like that to-day."

Yes, Tom's blemishless week had restored him to the favor
of his aunt and uncle.

His mother was satisfied with him, too. Privately, she believed she was coming to love him, but she did not say so.
She told him to go along to St. Louis, now, and she would
get ready and follow. Then she smashed her whisky bottle
and said—

"Dah now! I 's a-gwyne to make you walk as straight as a
string, Chambers, en so I 's bown' you ain't gwyne to git no
bad example out o' yo' mammy. I tole you you could n't go
into no bad comp'ny. Well, you 's gwyne into my comp'ny,
en I 's gwyne to fill de bill. Now, den, trot along, trot along!"

Tom went aboard one of the big transient boats that night
with his heavy satchel of miscellaneous plunder, and slept the
sleep of the unjust, which is serener and sounder than the
other kind, as we know by the hanging-eve history of a million rascals. But when he got up in the morning, luck was
against him again: A brother-thief had robbed him while he
slept, and gone ashore at some intermediate landing.

XVI

IF you pick up a starving dog and make him prosperous, he will not bite you. This is the principal difference between a dog and a man.

—*Pudd'nhead Wilson's Calendar.*

WE know all about the habits of the ant, we know all about the habits of the bee, but we know nothing at all about the habits of the oyster. It seems almost certain that we have been choosing the wrong time for studying the oyster.

—*Pudd'nhead Wilson's Calendar.*

WHEN ROXANA arrived, she found her son in such despair and misery that her heart was touched and her motherhood rose up strong in her. He was ruined past hope, now; his destruction would be immediate and sure, and he would be an outcast and friendless. That was reason enough for a mother to love a child; so she loved him, and told him so. It made him wince, secretly—for she was a "nigger." That he was one himself was far from reconciling him to that despised race.

Roxana poured out endearments upon him, to which he responded uncomfortably, but as well as he could. And she tried to comfort him, but that was not possible. These intimacies quickly became horrible to him, and within the hour he began to try to get up courage enough to tell her so, and require that they be discontinued or very considerably modified. But he was afraid of her; and besides, there came a lull, now, for she had begun to think. She was trying to invent a saving plan. Finally she started up, and said she had found a way out. Tom was almost suffocated by the joy of this sudden good news. Roxana said:

"Here is de plan, en she 'll win, sure. I 's a nigger, en nobody ain't gwyne to doubt it dat hears me talk. I 's wuth six hund'd dollahs. Take en sell me, en pay off dese gamblers."

Tom was dazed. He was not sure he had heard aright. He was dumb for a moment; then he said:

"Do you mean that you would be sold into slavery to save me?"

"Ain't you my chile? En does you know anything dat a mother won't do for her chile? Dey ain't nothin' a white mother won't do for her chile. Who made 'em so? De Lord done it. En who made de niggers? De Lord made 'em. In de inside, mothers is all de same. De good Lord he made 'em so. I 's gwyne to be sole into slavery, en in a year you 's gwyne to buy yo' ole mammy free ag'in. I 'll show you how. Dat 's de plan."

Tom's hopes began to rise, and his spirits along with them. He said—

"It 's lovely of you, mammy—it 's just—"

"Say it ag'in! En keep on sayin' it! It 's all de pay a body kin want in dis worl', en it 's mo' den enough. Laws bless you, honey, when I 's slavin' aroun', en dey 'buses me, if I knows you 's a-sayin' dat, 'way off yonder somers, it 'll heal up all de sore places, en I kin stan' 'em."

"I *do* say it again, mammy, and I 'll keep on saying it, too. But how am I going to sell you? You 're free, you know."

"Much diff'rence dat make! White folks ain't partic'lar. De law kin sell me now if dey tell me to leave de State in six months en I don't go. You draw up a paper—bill o' sale— en put it 'way off yonder, down in de middle 'o Kaintuck somers, en sign some names to it, en say you 'll sell me cheap 'ca'se you 's hard up; you 'll fine you ain't gwyne to have no trouble. You take me up de country a piece, en sell me on a farm; dem people ain't gwyne to ask no questions if I 's a bargain."

Tom forged a bill of sale and sold his mother to an Arkansas cotton-planter for a trifle over six hundred dollars. He did not want to commit this treachery, but luck threw the man in his way, and this saved him the necessity of going up country to hunt up a purchaser, with the added risk of having to answer a lot of questions, whereas this planter was so pleased with Roxy that he asked next to none at all. Besides, the planter insisted that Roxy would n't know where she was, at first, and that by the time she found out she would already have become contented. And Tom argued with himself that it was an immense advantage for Roxy to have a master who was so pleased with her, as this planter manifestly was. In almost no time his flowing reasonings carried him to the point of even half believing he was doing Roxy a splendid surreptitious service in selling her "down the river." And then he kept diligently saying to himself all the time: "It 's for only a year. In a year I buy her free again; she 'll keep that in mind, and it 'll reconcile her." Yes; the little deception could do no harm, and everything would come out right and pleasant in the end, any way. By agreement, the conversation in Roxy's presence was all about the man's "up-country" farm, and how pleasant a place it was, and how happy the slaves were there; so poor Roxy was entirely deceived; and easily, for she was not dreaming that her own son could be guilty of treason to a mother who, in voluntarily going into slavery— slavery of any kind, mild or severe, or of any duration, brief or long—was making a sacrifice for him compared with which death would have been a poor and commonplace one. She lavished tears and loving caresses upon him privately, and then went away with her owner—went away broken-hearted, and yet proud of what she was doing, and glad that it was in her power to do it.

Tom squared his accounts, and resolved to keep to the very letter of his reform, and never to put that will in jeopardy again. He had three hundred dollars left. According to his mother's plan, he was to put that safely away, and add her half of his pension to it monthly. In one year this fund would buy her free again.

For a whole week he was not able to sleep well, so much the villainy which he had played upon his trusting mother preyed upon his rag of a conscience; but after that he began to get comfortable again, and was presently able to sleep like any other miscreant.

The boat bore Roxy away from St. Louis at four in the afternoon, and she stood on the lower guard abaft the paddle-box and watched Tom through a blur of tears until he melted into the throng of people and disappeared; then she looked no more, but sat there on a coil of cable crying till far into the night. When she went to her foul steerage-bunk at last, between the clashing engines, it was not to sleep, but only to wait for the morning, and, waiting, grieve.

It had been imagined that she "would not know," and

would think she was traveling up stream. She! Why, she had been steamboating for years. At dawn she got up and went listlessly and sat down on the cable-coil again. She passed many a snag whose "break" could have told her a thing to break her heart, for it showed a current moving in the same direction that the boat was going; but her thoughts were elsewhere, and she did not notice. But at last the roar of a bigger and nearer break than usual brought her out of her torpor, and she looked up, and her practised eye fell upon that tell-tale rush of water. For one moment her petrified gaze fixed itself there. Then her head dropped upon her breast, and she said—

"Oh, de good Lord God have mercy on po' sinful me— *I 's sole down de river!*"

XVII

EVEN popularity can be overdone. In Rome, along at first, you are full of regrets that Michelangelo died; but by and by you only regret that you did n't see him do it.
—Pudd'nhead Wilson's Calendar.

July 4. Statistics show that we lose more fools on this day than in all the other days of the year put together. This proves, by the number left in stock, that one Fourth of July per year is now inadequate, the country has grown so.
—Pudd'nhead Wilson's Calendar.

THE SUMMER WEEKS dragged by, and then the political campaign opened—opened in pretty warm fashion, and waxed hotter and hotter daily. The twins threw themselves into it with their whole heart, for their self-love was engaged. Their popularity, so general at first, had suffered afterward; mainly because they had been *too* popular, and so a natural reaction had followed. Besides, it had been diligently whispered around that it was curious—indeed, *very* curious—that that wonderful knife of theirs did not turn up—*if* it was so valuable, or *if* it had ever existed. And with the whisperings went chucklings and nudgings and winks, and such things have an effect. The twins considered that success in the election would reinstate them, and that defeat would work them irreparable damage. Therefore they worked hard, but not harder than Judge Driscoll and Tom worked against them in the closing days of the canvass. Tom's conduct had remained so letter-perfect during two whole months, now, that his uncle not only trusted him with money with which to persuade voters, but trusted him to go and get it himself out of the safe in the private sitting-room.

The closing speech of the campaign was made by Judge Driscoll, and he made it against both of the foreigners. It was disastrously effective. He poured out rivers of ridicule upon them, and forced the big mass-meeting to laugh and applaud. He scoffed at them as adventurers, mountebanks, side-show riff-raff, dime-museum freaks; he assailed their showy titles with measureless derision; he said they were back-alley bar-bers disguised as nobilities, peanut pedlers masquerading as gentlemen, organ-grinders bereft of their brother-monkey. At last he stopped and stood still. He waited until the place had become absolutely silent and expectant, then he delivered his deadliest shot; delivered it with ice-cold seriousness and deliberation, with a significant emphasis upon the closing words: he said he believed that the reward offered for the lost knife was humbug and buncombe, and that its owner would know where to find it whenever he should have occasion *to assassinate somebody.*

Then he stepped from the stand, leaving a startled and impressive hush behind him instead of the customary explosion of cheers and party cries.

The strange remark flew far and wide over the town and made an extraordinary sensation. Everybody was asking, "What could he mean by that?" And everybody went on asking that question, but in vain; for the Judge only said he knew what he was talking about, and stopped there; Tom said he had n't any idea what his uncle meant, and Wilson, whenever he was asked what he thought it meant, parried the question by asking the questioner what *he* thought it meant.

Wilson was elected, the twins were defeated—crushed, in fact, and left forlorn and substantially friendless. Tom went back to St. Louis happy.

Dawson's Landing had a week of repose, now, and it needed it. But it was in an expectant state, for the air was full of rumors of a new duel. Judge Driscoll's election labors had prostrated him, but it was said that as soon as he was well enough to entertain a challenge he would get one from Count Luigi.

The brothers withdrew entirely from society, and nursed their humiliation in privacy. They avoided the people, and went out for exercise only late at night, when the streets were deserted.

XVIII

GRATITUDE and treachery are merely the two extremities of the same procession. You have seen all of it that is worth staying for when the band and the gaudy officials have gone by.

—Pudd'nhead Wilson's Calendar.

THANKSGIVING DAY. Let all give humble, hearty, and sincere thanks, now, but the turkeys. In the island of Fiji they do not use turkeys; they use plumbers. It does not become you and me to sneer at Fiji.

—Pudd'nhead Wilson's Calendar.

THE FRIDAY after the election was a rainy one in St. Louis. It rained all day long, and rained hard, apparently trying its best to wash that soot-blackened town white, but of course not succeeding. Toward midnight Tom Driscoll arrived at his lodgings from the theater in the heavy downpour, and closed his umbrella and let himself in; but when he would have shut the door, he found that there was another person entering—doubtless another lodger; this person closed the door and tramped up-stairs behind Tom. Tom found his door in the dark, and entered it and turned up the gas. When he faced about, lightly whistling, he saw the back of a man. The man was closing and locking his door for him. His whistle faded out and he felt uneasy. The man turned around, a wreck of shabby old clothes sodden with rain and all a-drip, and showed a black face under an old slouch hat. Tom was frightened. He tried to order the man out, but the words refused to come, and the other man got the start. He said, in a low voice—

"Keep still—I 's yo' mother!"

Tom sunk in a heap on a chair, and gasped out—

"It was mean of me, and base—I know it; but I meant it for the best, I did indeed—I can swear it."

Roxana stood awhile looking mutely down on him while he writhed in shame and went on incoherently babbling self-accusations mixed with pitiful attempts at explanation and palliation of his crime; then she seated herself and took off her hat, and her unkempt masses of long brown hair tumbled down about her shoulders.

"It ain't no fault o' yo'n dat dat ain't gray," she said sadly, noticing the hair.

"I know it, I know it! I 'm a scoundrel. But I swear I meant for the best. It was a mistake, of course, but I thought it was for the best, I truly did."

Roxy began to cry softly, and presently words began to find their way out between her sobs. They were uttered lamentingly, rather than angrily—

"Sell a pusson down de river—*down de river!*—for de bes'! I would n't treat a dog so! I is all broke down en wore out, now, en so I reckon it ain't in me to storm aroun' no mo', like I used to when I 'uz trompled on en 'bused. I don't know—but maybe it 's so. Leastways, I 's suffered so much dat mournin' seem to come mo' handy to me now den stormin'."

These words should have touched Tom Driscoll, but if they did, that effect was obliterated by a stronger one—one which removed the heavy weight of fear which lay upon him, and gave his crushed spirit a most grateful rebound, and filled all his small soul with a deep sense of relief. But he kept prudently still, and ventured no comment. There was a voiceless interval of some duration, now, in which no sounds were heard but the beating of the rain upon the panes, the sighing and complaining of the winds, and now and then a muffled sob from Roxana. The sobs became more and more infrequent, and at last ceased. Then the refugee began to talk again:

"Shet down dat light a little. More. More yit. A pusson dat is hunted don't like de light. Dah—dat 'll do. I kin see whah you is, en dat 's enough. I 's gwine to tell you de tale, en cut it jes as short as I kin, en den I 'll tell you what you 's got to do. Dat man dat bought me ain't a bad man; he 's good enough, as planters goes; en if he could 'a' had his way I 'd 'a' be'n a house servant in his fambly en be'n comfortable: but his wife she was a Yank, en not right down good lookin', en she riz up agin me straight off; so den dey sent me out to de quarter 'mongst de common fiel' han's. Dat woman war n't satisfied even wid dat, but she worked up de overseer ag'in'

me, she 'uz dat jealous en hateful; so de overseer he had me
out befo' day in de mawnin's en worked me de whole long
day as long as dey 'uz any light to see by; en many 's de
lashin's I got 'ca'se I could n't come up to de work o' de
stronges'. Dat overseer wuz a Yank, too, outen New Englan',
en anybody down South kin tell you what dat mean. *Dey*
knows how to work a nigger to death, en dey knows how to
whale 'em, too—whale 'em till dey backs is welted like a
washboard. 'Long at fust my marster say de good word for
me to de overseer, but dat 'uz bad for me; for de mistis she
fine it out, en arter dat I jist ketched it at every turn—dey
war n't no mercy for me no mo'."

Tom's heart was fired—with fury against the planter's
wife; and he said to himself, "But for that meddlesome fool,
everything would have gone all right." He added a deep and
bitter curse against her.

The expression of this sentiment was fiercely written in his
face, and stood thus revealed to Roxana by a white glare of
lightning which turned the somber dusk of the room into
dazzling day at that moment. She was pleased—pleased and
grateful; for did not that expression show that her child was
capable of grieving for his mother's wrongs and of feeling
resentment toward her persecutors?—a thing which she had
been doubting. But her flash of happiness was only a flash,
and went out again and left her spirit dark; for she said to
herself, "He sole me down de river—he can't feel for a body
long; dis 'll pass en go." Then she took up her tale again.

" 'Bout ten days ago I 'uz sayin' to myself dat I could n't
las' many mo' weeks I 'uz so wore out wid de awful work en
de lashin's, en so downhearted en misable. En I did n't care
no mo', nuther—life war n't wuth noth'n' to me if I got to
go on like dat. Well, when a body is in a frame o' mine like
dat, what do a body care what a body do? Dey was a little
sickly nigger wench 'bout ten year ole dat 'uz good to me, en
had n't no mammy, po' thing, en I loved her en she loved
me; en she come out whah I 'uz workin' en she had a roasted
tater, en tried to slip it to me,—robbin' herself, you see, 'ca'se
she knowed de overseer did n't gimme enough to eat,—en
he ketched her at it, en give her a lick acrost de back wid his
stick, which 'uz as thick as a broom-handle, en she drop'

screamin' on de groun', en squirmin' en wallerin' aroun' in de dust like a spider dat 's got crippled. I could n't stan' it. All de hell-fire dat 'uz ever in my heart flame' up, en I snatch de stick outen his han' en laid him flat. He laid dah moanin' en cussin', en all out of his head, you know, en de niggers 'uz plumb sk'yerd to death. Dey gathered roun' him to he'p him, en I jumped on his hoss en took out for de river as tight as I could go. I knowed what dey would do wid me. Soon as he got well he would start in en work me to death if marster let him; en if dey did n't do dat, they 'd sell me furder down de river, en dat 's de same thing. So I 'lowed to drown myself en git out o' my troubles. It 'uz gitt'n' towards dark. I 'uz at de river in two minutes. Den I see a canoe, en I says dey ain't no use to drown myself tell I got to; so I ties de hoss in de edge o' de timber en shove out down de river, keepin' in under de shelter o' de bluff bank en prayin' for de dark to shet down quick. I had a pow'ful good start, 'ca'se de big house 'uz three mile back f'om de river en on'y de work-mules to ride dah on, en on'y niggers to ride 'em, en *dey* war n't gwine to hurry—dey 'd gimme all de chance dey could. Befo' a body could go to de house en back it would be long pas' dark, en dey could n't track de hoss en fine out which way I went tell mawnin', en de niggers would tell 'em all de lies dey could 'bout it.

"Well, de dark come, en I went on a-spinnin' down de river. I paddled mo'n two hours, den I war n't worried no mo', so I quit paddlin', en floated down de current, considerin' what I 'uz gwine to do if I did n't have to drown myself. I made up some plans, en floated along, turnin' 'em over in my mine. Well, when it 'uz a little pas' midnight, as I reckoned, en I had come fifteen or twenty mile, I see de lights o' a steamboat layin' at de bank, whah dey war n't no town en no woodyard, en putty soon I ketched de shape o' de chimbly-tops ag'in' de stars, en de good gracious me, I 'most jumped out o' my skin for joy! It 'uz de *Gran' Mogul*—I 'uz chambermaid on her for eight seasons in de Cincinnati en Orleans trade. I slid 'long pas'—don't see nobody stirrin' no-whah—hear 'em a-hammerin' away in de engine-room, den I knowed what de matter was—some o' de machinery 's broke. I got asho' below de boat and turn' de canoe loose, den I goes 'long up, en dey 'uz jes one plank out, en I step' 'board de boat. It 'uz pow'ful hot, deckhan's en roustabouts 'uz sprawled aroun' asleep on de fo'cas'l', de second mate, Jim Bangs, he sot dah on de bitts wid his head down, asleep— 'ca'se dat 's de way de second mate stan' de cap'n's watch!— en de ole watchman, Billy Hatch, he 'uz a-noddin' on de companionway;—en I knowed 'em all; 'en, lan', but dey did look good! I says to myself, I wished old marster 'd come along *now* en try to take me—bless yo' heart, I 's 'mong frien's, I is. So I tromped right along 'mongst 'em, en went up on de b'iler deck en 'way back aft to de ladies' cabin guard, en sot down dah in de same cheer dat I 'd sot in 'mos' a hund'd million times, I reckon; en it 'uz jist home ag'in, I tell you!

"In 'bout an hour I heard de ready-bell jingle, en den de racket begin. Putty soon I hear de gong strike. 'Set her back on de outside,' I says to myself—'I reckon I knows dat music!' I hear de gong ag'in. 'Come ahead on de inside,' I says. Gong ag'in. 'Stop de outside.' Gong ag'in. 'Come ahead on de outside—now we 's pinted for Sent Louis, en I 's outer de woods en ain't got to drown myself at all.' I knowed de *Mogul* 'uz in de Sent Louis trade now, you see. It 'uz jes fair daylight when we passed our plantation, en I seed a gang o' niggers en white folks huntin' up en down de sho', en troublin' deyselves a good deal 'bout me; but I war n't troublin' myself none 'bout dem.

" 'Bout dat time Sally Jackson, dat used to be my second chambermaid en 'uz head chambermaid now, she come out on de guard, en 'uz pow'ful glad to see me, en so 'uz all de officers; en I tole 'em I 'd got kidnapped en sole down de river, en dey made me up twenty dollahs en give it to me, en Sally she rigged me out wid good clo'es, en when I got here I went straight to whah you used to wuz, en den I come to dis house, en dey say you 's away but 'spected back every day; so I did n't dast to go down de river to Dawson's, 'ca'se I might miss you.

"Well, las' Monday I 'uz pass'n' by one o' dem places in Fourth street whah dey sticks up runaway-nigger bills, en he'ps to ketch 'em, en I seed my marster! I 'mos' flopped down on de groun', I felt so gone. He had his back to me, en

'uz talkin' to de man en givin' him some bills—nigger-bills,
I reckon, en I 's de nigger. He 's offerin' a reward—dat 's it.
Ain't I right, don't you reckon?"

Tom had been gradually sinking into a state of ghastly terror, and he said to himself, now: "I 'm lost, no matter what
turn things take! This man has said to me that he thinks there
was something suspicious about that sale. He said he had a
letter from a passenger on the *Grand Mogul* saying that Roxy
came here on that boat and that everybody on board knew all
about the case; so he says that her coming here instead of
flying to a free State looks bad for me, and that if I don't find
her for him, and that pretty soon, he will make trouble for
me. I never believed that story; I could n't believe she would
be so dead to all motherly instincts as to come here, knowing
the risk she would run of getting me into irremediable trouble. And after all, here she is! And I stupidly swore I would
help him find her, thinking it was a perfectly safe thing to
promise. If I venture to deliver her up, she—she—but how
can I help myself? I 've got to do that or pay the money, and
where 's the money to come from? I—I—well, I should
think that if he would swear to treat her kindly hereafter—
and she says, herself, that he is a good man—and if he would
swear to never allow her to be overworked, or ill fed, or—"

A flash of lightning exposed Tom's pallid face, drawn and
rigid with these worrying thoughts. Roxana spoke up sharply
now, and there was apprehension in her voice—

"Turn up dat light! I want to see yo' face better. Dah
now—lemme look at you. Chambers, you 's as white as yo'
shirt! Has you seen dat man? Has he be'n to see you?"

"Ye-s."

"When?"

"Monday noon."

"Monday noon! Was he on my track?"

"He—well, he thought he was. That is, he hoped he was.
This is the bill you saw." He took it out of his pocket.

"Read it to me!"

She was panting with excitement, and there was a dusky
glow in her eyes that Tom could not translate with certainty,
but there seemed to be something threatening about it. The
handbill had the usual rude woodcut of a turbaned negro

woman running, with the customary bundle on a stick over her shoulder, and the heading in bold type, "$100 REWARD." Tom read the bill aloud—at least the part that described Roxana and named the master and his St. Louis address and the address of the Fourth-street agency; but he left out the item that applicants for the reward might also apply to Mr. Thomas Driscoll.

"Gimme de bill!"

Tom had folded it and was putting it in his pocket. He felt a chilly streak creeping down his back, but said as carelessly as he could—

"The bill? Why, it is n't any use to you; you can't read it. What do you want with it?"

"Gimme de bill!" Tom gave it to her, but with a reluctance which he could not entirely disguise. "Did you read it *all* to me?"

"Certainly I did."

"Hole up yo' han' en swah to it."

Tom did it. Roxana put the bill carefully away in her pocket, with her eyes fixed upon Tom's face all the while; then she said—

"You 's lyin'!"

"What would I want to lie about it for?"

"I don't know—but you is. Dat 's my opinion, anyways. But nemmine 'bout dat. When I seed dat man I 'uz dat sk'yerd dat I could sca'cely wobble home. Den I give a nigger man a dollar for dese clo'es, en I ain't be'n in a house sence, night ner day, till now. I blacked my face en laid hid in de cellar of a ole house dat 's burnt down, daytimes, en robbed de sugar hogsheads en grain sacks on de wharf, nights, to git somethin' to eat, en never dast to try to buy noth'n', en I 's 'mos' starved. En I never dast to come near dis place till dis rainy night, when dey ain't no people roun' sca'cely. But to-night I be'n a-stannin' in de dark alley ever sence night come, waitin' for you to go by. En here I is."

She fell to thinking. Presently she said—

"You seed dat man at noon, las' Monday?"

"Yes."

"I seed him de middle o' dat arternoon. He hunted you up, did n't he?"

"Yes."

"Did he give you de bill dat time?"

"No, he had n't got it printed yet."

Roxana darted a suspicious glance at him.

"Did you he'p him fix up de bill?"

Tom cursed himself for making that stupid blunder, and tried to rectify it by saying he remembered, now, that it *was* at noon Monday that the man gave him the bill. Roxana said—

"You 's lyin' ag'in, sho." Then she straightened up and raised her finger:

"Now den! I 's gwine to ast you a question, en I wants to know how you 's gwine to git aroun' it. You knowed he 'uz arter me; en if you run off, 'stid o' stayin' here to he'p him, he 'd know dey 'uz somethin' wrong 'bout dis business, en den he would inquire 'bout you, en dat would take him to yo' uncle, en yo' uncle would read de bill en see dat you be'n sellin' a free nigger down de river, en you know *him*, I reckon! He 'd t'ar up de will en kick you outen de house. Now, den, you answer me dis question: hain't you tole dat man dat I would be sho' to come here, en den you would fix it so he could set a trap en ketch me?"

Tom recognized that neither lies nor arguments could help him any longer—he was in a vise, with the screw turned on, and out of it there was no budging. His face began to take on an ugly look, and presently he said, with a snarl—

"Well, what could I do? You see, yourself, that I was in his grip and could n't get out."

Roxy scorched him with a scornful gaze awhile, then she said—

"What could you do? You could be Judas to yo' own mother to save yo' wuthless hide! Would anybody b'lieve it? No—a dog could n't! You is de low-downest orneriest hound dat was ever pup'd into dis worl'—en I 's 'sponsible for it!"—and she spat on him.

He made no effort to resent this. Roxy reflected a moment, then she said—

"Now I 'll tell you what you 's gwine to do. You 's gwine to give dat man de money dat you 's got laid up, en make him wait till you kin go to de Jedge en git de res' en buy me free agin."

"Thunder! what are you thinking of? Go and ask him for three hundred dollars and odd? What would I tell him I want with it, pray?"

Roxy's answer was delivered in a serene and level voice—

"You 'll tell him you 's sole me to pay yo' gamblin' debts en dat you lied to me en was a villain, en dat I 'quires you to git dat money en buy me back ag'in."

"Why, you 've gone stark mad! He would tear the will to shreds in a minute—don't you know that?"

"Yes, I does."

"Then you don't believe I 'm idiot enough to go to him, do you?"

"I don't b'lieve nothin' 'bout it—I *knows* you 's a-goin', I knows it 'ca'se you knows dat if you don't raise dat money I 'll go to him myself, en den he 'll sell *you* down de river, en you kin see how you like it!"

Tom rose, trembling and excited, and there was an evil light in his eye. He strode to the door and said he must get out of this suffocating place for a moment and clear his brain in the fresh air so that he could determine what to do. The door would n't open. Roxy smiled grimly, and said—

"I 's got de key, honey—set down. You need n't cle'r up yo' brain none to fine out what you gwine to do—*I* knows what you 's gwine to do." Tom sat down and began to pass his hands through his hair with a helpless and desperate air. Roxy said, "Is dat man in dis house?"

Tom glanced up with a surprised expression, and asked—

"What gave you such an idea?"

"You done it. Gwine out to cle'r yo' brain! In de fust place you ain't got none to cle'r, en in de second place yo' ornery eye tole on you. You 's de low-downest hound dat ever—but I done tole you dat befo'. Now den, dis is Friday. You kin fix it up wid dat man, en tell him you 's gwine away to git de res' o' de money, en dat you 'll be back wid it nex' Tuesday, or maybe Wednesday. You understan'?"

Tom answered sullenly—

"Yes."

"En when you gits de new bill o' sale dat sells me to my own self, take en send it in de mail to Mr. Pudd'nhead Wilson, en write on de back dat he 's to keep it tell I come. You understan'?"

"Yes."

"Dat 's all, den. Take yo' umbreller, en put on yo' hat."

"Why?"

"Beca'se you 's gwine to see me home to de wharf. You see dis knife? I 's toted it aroun' sence de day I seed dat man en bought dese clo'es en it. If he ketched me, I 'uz gwine to kill myself wid it. Now start along, en go sof', en lead de way; en if you gives a sign in dis house, or if anybody comes up to you in de street, I 's gwine to jam it into you. Chambers, does you b'lieve me when I says dat?"

"It 's no use to bother me with that question. I know your word 's good."

"Yes, it 's diff'rent from yo'n! Shet de light out en move along—here 's de key."

They were not followed. Tom trembled every time a late straggler brushed by them on the street, and half expected to feel the cold steel in his back. Roxy was right at his heels and always in reach. After tramping a mile they reached a wide vacancy on the deserted wharves, and in this dark and rainy desert they parted.

As Tom trudged home his mind was full of dreary thoughts and wild plans; but at last he said to himself, wearily—

"There is but the one way out. I must follow her plan. But with a variation—I will not ask for the money and ruin myself; I will *rob* the old skinflint."

XIX

D AWSON'S LANDING was comfortably finishing its season
of dull repose and waiting patiently for the duel. Count
Luigi was waiting, too; but not patiently, rumor said. Sunday
came, and Luigi insisted on having his challenge conveyed.
Wilson carried it. Judge Driscoll declined to fight with an
assassin—"that is," he added significantly, "in the field of
honor."

Elsewhere, of course, he would be ready. Wilson tried to
convince him that if he had been present himself when Angelo told about the homicide committed by Luigi, he would
not have considered the act discreditable to Luigi; but the
obstinate old man was not to be moved.

Wilson went back to his principal and reported the failure
of his mission. Luigi was incensed, and asked how it could be
that the old gentleman, who was by no means dull-witted,
held his trifling nephew's evidence and inferences to be of
more value than Wilson's. But Wilson laughed, and said—

"That is quite simple; that is easily explicable. I am not his
doll—his baby—his infatuation: his nephew is. The Judge
and his late wife never had any children. The Judge and his
wife were past middle age when this treasure fell into their
lap. One must make allowances for a parental instinct that has
been starving for twenty-five or thirty years. It is famished, it
is crazed with hunger by that time, and will be entirely satisfied with anything that comes handy; its taste is atrophied, it
can't tell mud-cat from shad. A devil born to a young couple
is measurably recognizable by them as a devil before long, but
a devil adopted by an old couple is an angel to them, and
remains so, through thick and thin. Tom is this old man's
angel; he is infatuated with him. Tom can persuade him into

things which other people can 't—not all things; I don't
mean that, but a good many—particularly one class of things:
the things that create or abolish personal partialities or prejudices in the old man's mind. The old man liked both of you.
Tom conceived a hatred for you. That was enough; it turned
the old man around at once. The oldest and strongest friendship must go to the ground when one of these late-adopted
darlings throws a brick at it."

"It 's a curious philosophy," said Luigi.

"It ain't a philosophy at all—it 's a fact. And there is something pathetic and beautiful about it, too. I think there is
nothing more pathetic than to see one of these poor old
childless couples taking a menagerie of yelping little worthless
dogs to their hearts; and then adding some cursing and
squawking parrots and a jackass-voiced macaw; and next a
couple of hundred screeching song-birds, and presently some
fetid guinea-pigs and rabbits, and a howling colony of cats. It
is all a groping and ignorant effort to construct out of base
metal and brass filings, so to speak, something to take the
place of that golden treasure denied them by Nature, a child.
But this is a digression. The unwritten law of this region requires you to kill Judge Driscoll on sight, and he and the
community will expect that attention at your hands—though
of course your own death by his bullet will answer every purpose. Look out for him! Are you heeled—that is, fixed?"

"Yes; he shall have his opportunity. If he attacks me I will
respond."

As Wilson was leaving, he said—

"The Judge is still a little used up by his campaign work,
and will not get out for a day or so; but when he does get
out, you want to be on the alert."

About eleven at night the twins went out for exercise, and
started on a long stroll in the veiled moonlight.

Tom Driscoll had landed at Hackett's Store, two miles below Dawson's, just about half an hour earlier, the only passenger for that lonely spot, and had walked up the shore road
and entered Judge Driscoll's house without having encountered any one either on the road or under the roof.

He pulled down his window-blinds and lighted his candle.
He laid off his coat and hat and began his preparations. He

unlocked his trunk and got his suit of girl's clothes out from under the male attire in it, and laid it by. Then he blacked his face with burnt cork and put the cork in his pocket. His plan was, to slip down to his uncle's private sitting-room below, pass into the bed-room, steal the safe-key from the old gentleman's clothes, and then go back and rob the safe. He took up his candle to start. His courage and confidence were high, up to this point, but both began to waver a little, now. Suppose he should make a noise, by some accident, and get caught— say, in the act of opening the safe? Perhaps it would be well to go armed. He took the Indian knife from its hiding-place, and felt a pleasant return of his waning courage. He slipped stealthily down the narrow stair, his hair rising and his pulses halting at the slightest creak. When he was half-way down, he was disturbed to perceive that the landing below was touched by a faint glow of light. What could that mean? Was his uncle still up? No, that was not likely; he must have left his nighttaper there when he went to bed. Tom crept on down, pausing at every step to listen. He found the door standing open, and glanced in. What he saw pleased him beyond measure. His uncle was asleep on the sofa; on a small table at the head of the sofa a lamp was burning low, and by it stood the old man's small tin cash-box, closed. Near the box was a pile of bank-notes and a piece of paper covered with figures in pencil. The safe-door was not open. Evidently the sleeper had wearied himself with work upon his finances, and was taking a rest.

Tom set his candle on the stairs, and began to make his way toward the pile of notes, stooping low as he went. When he was passing his uncle, the old man stirred in his sleep, and Tom stopped instantly—stopped, and softly drew the knife from its sheath, with his heart thumping, and his eyes fastened upon his benefactor's face. After a moment or two he ventured forward again—one step—reached for his prize and seized it, dropping the knife-sheath. Then he felt the old man's strong grip upon him, and a wild cry of "Help! help!" rang in his ear. Without hesitation he drove the knife home— and was free. Some of the notes escaped from his left hand and fell in the blood on the floor. He dropped the knife and snatched them up and started to fly; transferred them to his left hand, and seized the knife again, in his fright and confusion, but remembered himself and flung it from him, as being a dangerous witness to carry away with him.

He jumped for the stair-foot, and closed the door behind him; and as he snatched his candle and fled upward, the stillness of the night was broken by the sound of urgent footsteps approaching the house. In another moment he was in his room and the twins were standing aghast over the body of the murdered man!

Tom put on his coat, buttoned his hat under it, threw on his suit of girl's clothes, dropped the veil, blew out his light, locked the room door by which he had just entered, taking the key, passed through his other door into the back hall, locked that door and kept the key, then worked his way along in the dark and descended the back stairs. He was not expecting to meet anybody, for all interest was centered in the other part of the house, now; his calculation proved correct. By the time he was passing through the back yard, Mrs. Pratt, her servants, and a dozen half-dressed neighbors had joined the twins and the dead, and accessions were still arriving at the front door.

As Tom, quaking as with a palsy, passed out at the gate, three women came flying from the house on the opposite side of the lane. They rushed by him and in at the gate, asking him what the trouble was there, but not waiting for an answer. Tom said to himself, "Those old maids waited to dress—they did the same thing the night Stevens's house burned down next door." In a few minutes he was in the haunted house. He lighted a candle and took off his girl-clothes. There was blood on him all down his left side, and his right hand was red with the stains of the blood-soaked notes which he had crushed in it; but otherwise he was free from this sort of evidence. He cleansed his hand on the straw, and cleaned most of the smut from his face. Then he burned his male and female attire to ashes, scattered the ashes, and put on a disguise proper for a tramp. He blew out his light, went below, and was soon loafing down the river road with the intent to borrow and use one of Roxy's devices. He found a canoe and paddled off down-stream, setting the canoe adrift as dawn approached, and making his way by land to the next village, where he kept out of sight till a transient steamer came along, and then took deck passage for St. Louis. He was ill at ease until Dawson's Landing was behind him; then he said to himself, "All the detectives on earth could n't trace me now; there 's not a vestige of a clue left in the world; that homicide will take its place with the permanent mysteries, and people won't get done trying to guess out the secret of it for fifty years."

In St. Louis, next morning, he read this brief telegram in the papers—dated at Dawson's Landing:

Judge Driscoll, an old and respected citizen, was assassinated here about midnight by a profligate Italian nobleman or barber on account of a quarrel growing out of the recent election. The assassin will probably be lynched.

"One of the twins!" soliloquized Tom; "how lucky! It is the knife that has done him this grace. We never know when fortune is trying to favor us. I actually cursed Pudd'nhead Wilson in my heart for putting it out of my power to sell that knife. I take it back, now."

Tom was now rich and independent. He arranged with the planter, and mailed to Wilson the new bill of sale which sold Roxana to herself; then he telegraphed his Aunt Pratt:

Have seen the awful news in the papers and am almost prostrated with grief. Shall start by packet to-day. Try to bear up till I come.

When Wilson reached the house of mourning and had gathered such details as Mrs. Pratt and the rest of the crowd could tell him, he took command as mayor, and gave orders that nothing should be touched, but everything left as it was until Justice Robinson should arrive and take the proper measures as coroner. He cleared everybody out of the room but the twins and himself. The sheriff soon arrived and took the twins away to jail. Wilson told them to keep heart, and promised to do his best in their defense when the case should come to trial. Justice Robinson came presently, and with him Constable Blake. They examined the room thoroughly. They found the knife and the sheath. Wilson noticed that there were finger-prints on the knife-handle. That pleased him, for the twins had required the earliest comers to make a scrutiny of their hands and clothes, and neither these people nor Wilson himself had found any blood-stains upon them. Could there be a possibility that the twins had spoken the truth when they said they found the man dead when they ran into the house in answer to the cry for help? He thought of that mysterious girl at once. But this was not the sort of work for a girl to be engaged in. No matter; Tom Driscoll's room must be examined.

After the coroner's jury had viewed the body and its surroundings, Wilson suggested a search up-stairs, and he went along. The jury forced an entrance to Tom's room, but found nothing, of course.

The coroner's jury found that the homicide was committed by Luigi, and that Angelo was accessory to it.

The town was bitter against the unfortunates, and for the first few days after the murder they were in constant danger of being lynched. The grand jury presently indicted Luigi for murder in the first degree, and Angelo as accessory before the fact. The twins were transferred from the city jail to the county prison to await trial.

Wilson examined the finger-marks on the knife-handle and said to himself, "Neither of the twins made those marks." Then manifestly there was another person concerned, either in his own interest or as hired assassin.

But who could it be? That, he must try to find out. The safe was not open, the cash-box was closed, and had three thousand dollars in it. Then robbery was not the motive, and revenge was. Where had the murdered man an enemy except Luigi? There was but that one person in the world with a deep grudge against him.

The mysterious girl! The girl was a great trial to Wilson. If the motive had been robbery, the girl might answer; but there was n't any girl that would want to take this old man's life for revenge. He had no quarrels with girls; he was a gentleman.

Wilson had perfect tracings of the finger-marks of the knife-handle; and among his glass-records he had a great array of the finger-prints of women and girls, collected during the last fifteen or eighteen years, but he scanned them in vain, they successfully withstood every test; among them were no duplicates of the prints on the knife.

The presence of the knife on the stage of the murder was a worrying circumstance for Wilson. A week previously he had as good as admitted to himself that he believed Luigi had possessed such a knife, and that he still possessed it notwithstanding his pretense that it had been stolen. And now here was the knife, and with it the twins. Half the town had said the twins were humbugging when they claimed that they had lost their knife, and now these people were joyful, and said, "I told you so!"

If their finger-prints had been on the handle—but it was useless to bother any further about that; the finger-prints on the handle were *not* theirs—that he knew perfectly.

Wilson refused to suspect Tom; for first, Tom could n't murder anybody—he had n't character enough; secondly, if he could murder a person he would n't select his doting benefactor and nearest relative; thirdly, self-interest was in the way; for while the uncle lived, Tom was sure of a free support and a chance to get the destroyed will revived again, but with the uncle gone, that chance was gone, too. It was true the will had really been revived, as was now discovered, but Tom could not have been aware of it, or he would have spoken of it, in his native talky, unsecretive way. Finally, Tom was in St. Louis when the murder was done, and got the news out of the morning journals, as was shown by his telegram to his aunt. These speculations were unemphasized sensations rather than articulated thoughts, for Wilson would have laughed at the idea of seriously connecting Tom with the murder.

Wilson regarded the case of the twins as desperate—in fact, about hopeless. For he argued that if a confederate was not found, an enlightened Missouri jury would hang them, sure; if a confederate was found, that would not improve the matter, but simply furnish one more person for the sheriff to hang. Nothing could save the twins but the discovery of a person who did the murder on his sole personal account—an undertaking which had all the aspect of the impossible. Still, the person who made the finger-prints must be sought. The twins might have no case *with* him, but they certainly would have none without him.

So Wilson mooned around, thinking, thinking, guessing, guessing, day and night, and arriving nowhere. Whenever he ran across a girl or a woman he was not acquainted with, he got her finger-prints, on one pretext or another; and they always cost him a sigh when he got home, for they never tallied with the finger-marks on the knife-handle.

As to the mysterious girl, Tom swore he knew no such girl, and did not remember ever seeing a girl wearing a dress like the one described by Wilson. He admitted that he did not always lock his room, and that sometimes the servants forgot to lock the house doors; still, in his opinion the girl must have made but few visits or she would have been discovered. When Wilson tried to connect her with the stealing-raid, and thought she might have been the old woman's confederate, if not the very thief herself disguised as an old woman, Tom seemed struck, and also much interested, and said he would keep a sharp eye out for this person or persons, although he was afraid that she or they would be too smart to venture again into a town where everybody would now be on the watch for a good while to come.

Everybody was pitying Tom, he looked so quiet and sorrowful, and seemed to feel his great loss so deeply. He was playing a part, but it was not all a part. The picture of his alleged uncle, as he had last seen him, was before him in the dark pretty frequently, when he was awake, and called again in his dreams, when he was asleep. He would n't go into the room where the tragedy had happened. This charmed the doting Mrs. Pratt, who realized now, "as she had never done before," she said, what a sensitive and delicate nature her darling had, and how he adored his poor uncle.

XX

EVEN the clearest and most perfect circumstantial evidence is likely to be at fault, after all, and therefore ought to be received with great caution. Take the case of any pencil, sharpened by any woman: if you have witnesses, you will find she did it with a knife; but if you take simply the aspect of the pencil, you will say she did it with her teeth.

—*Pudd'nhead Wilson's Calendar.*

THE WEEKS dragged along, no friend visiting the jailed twins but their counsel and Aunt Patsy Cooper, and the day of trial came at last—the heaviest day in Wilson's life; for with all his tireless diligence he had discovered no sign or trace of the missing confederate. "Confederate" was the term he had long ago privately accepted for that person—not as being unquestionably the right term, but as being at least possibly the right one, though he was never able to understand why the twins did not vanish and escape, as the confederate had done, instead of remaining by the murdered man and getting caught there.

The court-house was crowded, of course, and would remain so to the finish, for not only in the town itself, but in the country for miles around, the trial was the one topic of conversation among the people. Mrs. Pratt, in deep mourning, and Tom with a weed on his hat, had seats near Pembroke Howard, the public prosecutor, and back of them sat a great array of friends of the family. The twins had but one friend present to keep their counsel in countenance, their poor old sorrowing landlady. She sat near Wilson, and looked her friendliest. In the "nigger corner" sat Chambers; also Roxy, with good clothes on, and her bill of sale in her pocket. It was her most precious possession, and she never parted with it, day or night. Tom had allowed her thirty-five dollars a month ever since he came into his property, and had said that he and she ought to be grateful to the twins for making them rich; but had roused such a temper in her by this speech that he did not repeat the argument afterward. She said the old Judge had treated her child a thousand times better than

he deserved, and had never done her an unkindness in his life;
so she hated these outlandish devils for killing him, and
should n't ever sleep satisfied till she saw them hanged for it.
She was here to watch the trial, now, and was going to lift
up just one "hooraw" over it if the County Judge put her in
jail a year for it. She gave her turbaned head a toss and said,
"When dat verdic' comes, I 's gwine to lif' dat *roof*, now, I
tell you."

Pembroke Howard briefly sketched the State's case. He
said he would show by a chain of circumstantial evidence
without break or fault in it anywhere, that the principal prisoner at the bar committed the murder; that the motive was
partly revenge, and partly a desire to take his own life out of
jeopardy, and that his brother, by his presence, was a con-
senting accessory to the crime; a crime which was the basest
known to the calendar of human misdeeds—assassination;
that it was conceived by the blackest of hearts and consummated by the cowardliest of hands; a crime which had broken
a loving sister's heart, blighted the happiness of a young
nephew who was as dear as a son, brought inconsolable grief
to many friends, and sorrow and loss to the whole community. The utmost penalty of the outraged law would be exacted, and upon the accused, now present at the bar, that
penalty would unquestionably be executed. He would reserve
further remark until his closing speech.

He was strongly moved, and so also was the whole house;
Mrs. Pratt and several other women were weeping when he
sat down, and many an eye that was full of hate was riveted
upon the unhappy prisoners.

Witness after witness was called by the State, and questioned at length; but the cross-questioning was brief. Wilson
knew they could furnish nothing valuable for his side. People
were sorry for Pudd'nhead; his budding career would get
hurt by this trial.

Several witnesses swore they heard Judge Driscoll say in his
public speech that the twins would be able to find their lost
knife again when they needed it to assassinate somebody
with. This was not news, but now it was seen to have been
sorrowfully prophetic, and a profound sensation quivered

through the hushed court-room when those dismal words were repeated.

The public prosecutor rose and said that it was within his knowledge, through a conversation held with Judge Driscoll on the last day of his life, that counsel for the defense had brought him a challenge from the person charged at this bar with murder; that he had refused to fight with a confessed assassin—"that is, on the field of honor," but had added significantly, that he would be ready for him elsewhere. Presumably the person here charged with murder was warned that he must kill or be killed the first time he should meet Judge Driscoll. If counsel for the defense chose to let the statement stand so, he would not call him to the witness stand. Mr. Wilson said he would offer no denial. [Murmurs in the house—"It is getting worse and worse for Wilson's case."]

Mrs. Pratt testified that she heard no outcry, and did not know what woke her up, unless it was the sound of rapid footsteps approaching the front door. She jumped up and ran out in the hall just as she was, and heard the footsteps flying up the front steps and then following behind her as she ran to the sitting-room. There she found the accused standing over her murdered brother. [Here she broke down and sobbed. Sensation in the court.] Resuming, she said the persons entering behind her were Mr. Rogers and Mr. Buckstone.

Cross-examined by Wilson, she said the twins proclaimed their innocence; declared that they had been taking a walk, and had hurried to the house in response to a cry for help which was so loud and strong that they had heard it at a considerable distance; that they begged her and the gentlemen just mentioned to examine their hands and clothes—which was done, and no blood-stains found.

Confirmatory evidence followed from Rogers and Buckstone.

The finding of the knife was verified, the advertisement minutely describing it and offering a reward for it was put in evidence, and its exact correspondence with that description proved. Then followed a few minor details, and the case for the State was closed.

Wilson said that he had three witnesses, the Misses Clarkson, who would testify that they met a veiled young woman leaving Judge Driscoll's premises by the back gate a few minutes after the cries for help were heard, and that their evidence, taken with certain circumstantial evidence which he would call the court's attention to, would in his opinion convince the court that there was still one person concerned in this crime who had not yet been found, and also that a stay of proceedings ought to be granted, in justice to his clients, until that person should be discovered. As it was late, he would ask leave to defer the examination of his three witnesses until the next morning.

The crowd poured out of the place and went flocking away in excited groups and couples, talking the events of the session over with vivacity and consuming interest, and everybody seemed to have had a satisfactory and enjoyable day except the accused, their counsel, and their old-lady friend. There was no cheer among these, and no substantial hope.

In parting with the twins Aunt Patsy did attempt a goodnight with a gay pretense of hope and cheer in it, but broke down without finishing.

Absolutely secure as Tom considered himself to be, the opening solemnities of the trial had nevertheless oppressed him with a vague uneasiness, his being a nature sensitive to even the smallest alarms; but from the moment that the poverty and weakness of Wilson's case lay exposed to the court, he was comfortable once more, even jubilant. He left the court-room sarcastically sorry for Wilson. "The Clarksons met an unknown woman in the back lane," he said to himself— "*that* is his case! I'll give him a century to find her in—a couple of them if he likes. A woman who does n't exist any longer, and the clothes that gave her her sex burnt up and the ashes thrown away—oh, certainly, he 'll find *her* easy enough!" This reflection set him to admiring, for the hundredth time, the shrewd ingenuities by which he had insured himself against detection—more, against even suspicion.

"Nearly always in cases like this there is some little detail or other overlooked, some wee little track or trace left behind, and detection follows; but here there 's not even the faintest suggestion of a trace left. No more than a bird leaves when it flies through the air—yes, through the night, you may say.

The man that can track a bird through the air in the dark and find that bird is the man to track me out and find the Judge's assassin—no other need apply. And that is the job that has been laid out for poor Pudd'nhead Wilson, of all people in the world! Lord, it will be pathetically funny to see him grubbing and groping after that woman that don't exist, and the right person sitting under his very nose all the time!" The more he thought the situation over, the more the humor of it struck him. Finally he said, "I'll never let him hear the last of that woman. Every time I catch him in company, to his dying day, I 'll ask him in the guileless affectionate way that used to gravel him so when I inquired how his unborn law-business was coming along, 'Got on her track yet—hey, Pudd'nhead?' " He wanted to laugh, but that would not have answered; there were people about, and he was mourning for his uncle. He made up his mind that it would be good entertainment to look in on Wilson that night and watch him worry over his barren law-case and goad him with an exasperating word or two of sympathy and commiseration now and then.

Wilson wanted no supper, he had no appetite. He got out all the finger-prints of girls and women in his collection of records and pored gloomily over them an hour or more, trying to convince himself that that troublesome girl's marks were there somewhere and had been overlooked. But it was not so. He drew back his chair, clasped his hands over his head, and gave himself up to dull and arid musings.

Tom Driscoll dropped in, an hour after dark, and said with a pleasant laugh as he took a seat—

"Hello, we 've gone back to the amusements of our days of neglect and obscurity for consolation, have we?" and he took up one of the glass strips and held it against the light to inspect it. "Come, cheer up, old man; there 's no use in losing your grip and going back to this child's-play merely because this big sun-spot is drifting across your shiny new disk. It 'll pass, and you 'll be all right again"—and he laid the glass down. "Did you think you could win always?"

"Oh, no," said Wilson, with a sigh, "I did n't expect that, but I can't believe Luigi killed your uncle, and I feel very sorry for him. It makes me blue. And you would feel as I do,

Tom, if you were not prejudiced against those young fellows."

"I don't know about that," and Tom's countenance darkened, for his memory reverted to his kicking; "I owe them no good will, considering the brunette one's treatment of me that night. Prejudice or no prejudice, Pudd'nhead, I don't like them, and when they get their deserts you 're not going to find me sitting on the mourner's bench."

He took up another strip of glass, and exclaimed—

"Why, here 's old Roxy's label! Are you going to ornament the royal palaces with nigger paw-marks, too? By the date here, I was seven months old when this was done, and she was nursing me and her little nigger cub. There 's a line straight across her thumb-print. How comes that?" and Tom held out the piece of glass to Wilson.

"That is common," said the bored man, wearily. "Scar of a cut or a scratch, usually"—and he took the strip of glass indifferently, and raised it toward the lamp.

All the blood sunk suddenly out of his face; his hand quaked, and he gazed at the polished surface before him with the glassy stare of a corpse.

"Great Heavens, what 's the matter with you, Wilson? Are you going to faint?"

Tom sprang for a glass of water and offered it, but Wilson shrank shuddering from him and said—

"No, no!—take it away!" His breast was rising and falling, and he moved his head about in a dull and wandering way, like a person who has been stunned. Presently he said, "I shall feel better when I get to bed; I have been overwrought to-day; yes, and overworked for many days."

"Then I 'll leave you and let you get to your rest. Good-night, old man." But as Tom went out he could n't deny himself a small parting gibe: "Don't take it so hard; a body can't win every time; you 'll hang somebody yet."

Wilson muttered to himself, "It is no lie to say I am sorry I have to begin with you, miserable dog though you are!"

He braced himself up with a glass of cold whisky, and went to work again. He did not compare the new finger-marks un-intentionally left by Tom a few minutes before on Roxy's glass with the tracings of the marks left on the knife-handle, there being no need of that (for his trained eye), but busied himself with another matter, muttering from time to time, "Idiot that I was!—Nothing but a *girl* would do me—a man in girl's clothes never occurred to me." First, he hunted out the plate containing the finger-prints made by Tom when he was twelve years old, and laid it by itself; then he brought forth the marks made by Tom's baby fingers when he was a suckling of seven months, and placed these two plates with the one containing this subject's newly (and unconsciously) made record.

"Now the series is complete," he said with satisfaction, and sat down to inspect these things and enjoy them.

But his enjoyment was brief. He stared a considerable time at the three strips, and seemed stupefied with astonishment. At last he put them down and said, "I can't make it out at all—hang it, the baby's don't tally with the others!"

He walked the floor for half an hour puzzling over his enigma, then he hunted out two other glass plates.

He sat down and puzzled over these things a good while, but kept muttering, "It 's no use; I can't understand it. They don't tally right, and yet I 'll swear the names and dates are right, and so of course they *ought* to tally. I never labeled one of these things carelessly in my life. There is a most extraordinary mystery here."

He was tired out, now, and his brains were beginning to clog. He said he would sleep himself fresh, and then see what he could do with this riddle. He slept through a troubled and unrestful hour, then unconsciousness began to shred away, and presently he rose drowsily to a sitting posture. "Now what was that dream?" he said, trying to recall it; "what was that dream?—it seemed to unravel that puz—"

He landed in the middle of the floor at a bound, without finishing the sentence, and ran and turned up his light and seized his "records." He took a single swift glance at them and cried out—

"It 's so! Heavens, what a revelation! And for twenty-three years no man has ever suspected it!"

XXI

He is useless on top of the ground; he ought to be under it, inspiring the cabbages.
—*Pudd'nhead Wilson's Calendar.*

April 1. This is the day upon which we are reminded of what we are on the other three hundred and sixty-four.
—*Pudd'nhead Wilson's Calendar.*

WILSON PUT ON enough clothes for business purposes and went to work under a high pressure of steam. He was awake all over. All sense of weariness had been swept away by the invigorating refreshment of the great and hopeful discovery which he had made. He made fine and accurate reproductions of a number of his "records," and then enlarged them on a scale of ten to one with his pantograph. He did these pantograph enlargements on sheets of white cardboard, and made each individual line of the bewildering maze of whorls or curves or loops which constituted the "pattern" of a "record" stand out bold and black by reinforcing it with ink. To the untrained eye the collection of delicate originals made by the human finger on the glass plates looked about alike; but when enlarged ten times they resembled the markings of a block of wood that has been sawed across the grain, and the dullest eye could detect at a glance, and at a distance of many feet, that no two of the patterns were alike. When Wilson had at last finished his tedious and difficult work, he arranged its results according to a plan in which a progressive order and sequence was a principal feature; then he added to the batch several pantograph enlargements which he had made from time to time in bygone years.

The night was spent and the day well advanced, now. By the time he had snatched a trifle of breakfast it was nine o'clock, and the court was ready to begin its sitting. He was in his place twelve minutes later with his "records."

Tom Driscoll caught a slight glimpse of the records, and nudged his nearest friend and said, with a wink, "Pudd'n-head's got a rare eye to business—thinks that as long as he can't win his case it's at least a noble good chance to advertise his palace-window decorations without any expense." Wilson was informed that his witnesses had been delayed, but would arrive presently; but he rose and said he should probably not have occasion to make use of their testimony. [An amused murmur ran through the room—"It 's a clean back-down! he gives up without hitting a lick!"] Wilson continued—"I have other testimony—and better. [This compelled interest, and evoked murmurs of surprise that had a detectible ingredient of disappointment in them.] If I seem to be springing this evidence upon the court, I offer as my justification for this, that I did not discover its existence until late last night, and have been engaged in examining and classifying it ever since, until half an hour ago. I shall offer it presently; but first I wish to say a few preliminary words.

"May it please the Court, the claim given the front place, the claim most persistently urged, the claim most strenuously and I may even say aggressively and defiantly insisted upon by the prosecution, is this—that the person whose hand left the blood-stained finger-prints upon the handle of the Indian knife is the person who committed the murder." Wilson paused, during several moments, to give impressiveness to what he was about to say, and then added tranquilly, *We grant that claim.*

It was an electrical surprise. No one was prepared for such an admission. A buzz of astonishment rose on all sides, and people were heard to intimate that the overworked lawyer had lost his mind. Even the veteran judge, accustomed as he was to legal ambushes and masked batteries in criminal procedure, was not sure that his ears were not deceiving him, and asked counsel what it was he had said. Howard's impassive face betrayed no sign, but his attitude and bearing lost something of their careless confidence for a moment. Wilson resumed:

"We not only grant that claim, but we welcome it and strongly endorse it. Leaving that matter for the present, we will now proceed to consider other points in the case which we propose to establish by evidence, and shall include that one in the chain in its proper place."

He had made up his mind to try a few hardy guesses, in mapping out his theory of the origin and motive of the murder—guesses designed to fill up gaps in it—guesses which could help if they hit, and would probably do no harm if they did n't.

"To my mind, certain circumstances of the case before the court seem to suggest a motive for the homicide quite different from the one insisted on by the State. It is my conviction that the motive was not revenge, but robbery. It has been urged that the presence of the accused brothers in that fatal room, just after notification that one of them must take the life of Judge Driscoll or lose his own the moment the parties should meet, clearly signifies that the natural instinct of self-preservation moved my clients to go there secretly and save Count Luigi by destroying his adversary.

"Then why did they stay there, after the deed was done? Mrs. Pratt had time, although she did not hear the cry for help, but woke up some moments later, to run to that room—and there she found these men standing, and making no effort to escape. If they were guilty, they ought to have been running out of the house at the same time that she was running to that room. If they had had such a strong instinct toward self-preservation as to move them to kill that unarmed man, what had become of it now, when it should have been more alert than ever? Would any of us have remained there? Let us not slander our intelligence to that degree.

"Much stress has been laid upon the fact that the accused offered a very large reward for the knife with which this murder was done; that no thief came forward to claim that extraordinary reward; that the latter fact was good circumstantial evidence that the claim that the knife had been stolen was a vanity and a fraud; that these details taken in connection with the memorable and apparently prophetic speech of the deceased concerning that knife, and the final discovery of that very knife in the fatal room where no living person was found present with the slaughtered man but the owner of the knife and his brother, form an indestructible chain of evidence which fixes the crime upon those unfortunate strangers.

"But I shall presently ask to be sworn, and shall testify that there was a large reward offered for the *thief*, also; that it was offered secretly and not advertised; that this fact was indiscreetly mentioned—or at least tacitly admitted—in what was supposed to be safe circumstances, but may *not* have been. The thief may have been present himself. [Tom Driscoll had been looking at the speaker, but dropped his eyes at this point.] In that case he would retain the knife in his possession, not daring to offer it for sale, or for pledge in a pawnshop. [There was a nodding of heads among the audience by way of admission that this was not a bad stroke.] I shall prove to the satisfaction of the jury that there *was* a person in Judge Driscoll's room several minutes before the accused entered it. [This produced a strong sensation; the last drowsy-head in the court-room roused up, now, and made preparation to listen.] If it shall seem necessary, I will prove by the Misses Clarkson that they met a veiled person—ostensibly a woman—coming out of the back gate a few minutes after the cry for help was heard. This person was not a woman, but a man dressed in woman's clothes." Another sensation. Wilson had his eye on Tom when he hazarded this guess, to see what effect it would produce. He was satisfied with the result, and said to himself, "It was a success—he 's hit!"

"The object of that person in that house was robbery, not murder. It is true that the safe was not open, but there was an ordinary tin cash-box on the table, with three thousand dollars in it. It is easily supposable that the thief was concealed in the house; that he knew of this box, and of its owner's habit of counting its contents and arranging his accounts at night—if he had that habit, which I do not assert, of course;—that he tried to take the box while its owner slept, but made a noise and was seized, and had to use the knife to save himself from capture; and that he fled without his booty because he heard help coming.

"I have now done with my theory, and will proceed to the evidences by which I propose to try to prove its soundness." Wilson took up several of his strips of glass. When the audience recognized these familiar mementos of Pudd'nhead's old-time childish "puttering" and folly, the tense and funereal interest vanished out of their faces, and the house burst into volleys of relieving and refreshing laughter, and Tom chirked up and joined in the fun himself; but Wilson was apparently not disturbed. He arranged his records on the table before him, and said—

"I beg the indulgence of the court while I make a few remarks in explanation of some evidence which I am about to
introduce, and which I shall presently ask to be allowed to
verify under oath on the witness stand. Every human being
carries with him from his cradle to his grave certain physical
marks which do not change their character, and by which he
can always be identified—and that without shade of doubt or
question. These marks are his signature, his physiological autograph, so to speak, and this autograph cannot be counterfeited, nor can he disguise it or hide it away, nor can it become illegible by the wear and the mutations of time. This
signature is not his face—age can change that beyond recognition; it is not his hair, for that can fall out; it is not his
height, for duplicates of that exist; it is not his form, for duplicates of that exist also, whereas this signature is each man's
very own—there is no duplicate of it among the swarming
populations of the globe! [The audience were interested once
more.]

"This autograph consists of the delicate lines or corruga-
tions with which Nature marks the insides of the hands and
the soles of the feet. If you will look at the balls of your
fingers,—you that have very sharp eyesight,—you will observe that these dainty curving lines lie close together, like
those that indicate the borders of oceans in maps, and that
they form various clearly defined patterns, such as arches, cir-
cles, long curves, whorls, etc., and that these patterns differ
on the different fingers. [Every man in the room had his hand
up to the light, now, and his head canted to one side, and
was minutely scrutinizing the balls of his fingers; there were
whispered ejaculations of "Why, it 's so—I never noticed that
before!"] The patterns on the right hand are not the same as
those on the left. [Ejaculations of "Why, that 's so, too!"]
Taken finger for finger, your patterns differ from your neighbor's. [Comparisons were made all over the house—even the
judge and jury were absorbed in this curious work.] The patterns of a twin's right hand are not the same as those on his
left. One twin's patterns are never the same as his fellow-
twin's patterns—the jury will find that the patterns upon the
finger-balls of the accused follow this rule. [An examination
of the twins' hands was begun at once.] You have often heard

of twins who were so exactly alike that when dressed alike their own parents could not tell them apart. Yet there was never a twin born into this world that did not carry from birth to death a sure identifier in this mysterious and marvelous natal autograph. That once known to you, his fellow-twin could never personate him and deceive you."

Wilson stopped and stood silent. Inattention dies a quick and sure death when a speaker does that. The stillness gives warning that something is coming. All palms and finger-balls went down, now, all slouching forms straightened, all heads came up, all eyes were fastened upon Wilson's face. He waited yet one, two, three moments, to let his pause complete and perfect its spell upon the house; then, when through the profound hush he could hear the ticking of the clock on the wall, he put out his hand and took the Indian knife by the blade and held it aloft where all could see the sinister spots upon its ivory handle; then he said, in a level and passionless voice—

"Upon this haft stands the assassin's natal autograph, written in the blood of that helpless and unoffending old man who loved you and whom you all loved. There is but one man in the whole earth whose hand can duplicate that crimson sign,"—he paused and raised his eyes to the pendulum swinging back and forth,—"and please God we will produce that man in this room before the clock strikes noon!"

Stunned, distraught, unconscious of its own movement, the house half rose, as if expecting to see the murderer appear at the door, and a breeze of muttered ejaculations swept the place. "Order in the court!—sit down!" This from the sheriff. He was obeyed, and quiet reigned again. Wilson stole a glance at Tom, and said to himself, "He is flying signals of distress, now; even people who despise him are pitying him; they think this is a hard ordeal for a young fellow who has lost his benefactor by so cruel a stroke—and they are right." He resumed his speech:

"For more than twenty years I have amused my compulsory leisure with collecting these curious physical signatures in this town. At my house I have hundreds upon hundreds of them. Each and every one is labeled with name and date; not labeled the next day or even the next hour, but in the very minute that the impression was taken. When I go upon the witness stand I will repeat under oath the things which I am now saying. I have the finger-prints of the court, the sheriff, and every member of the jury. There is hardly a person in this room, white or black, whose natal signature I cannot produce, and not one of them can so disguise himself that I cannot pick him out from a multitude of his fellow-creatures and unerringly identify him by his hands. And if he and I should live to be a hundred I could still do it! [The interest of the audience was steadily deepening, now.]

"I have studied some of these signatures so much that I know them as well as the bank cashier knows the autograph of his oldest customer. While I turn my back now, I beg that several persons will be so good as to pass their fingers through their hair, and then press them upon one of the panes of the window near the jury, and that among them the accused may set *their* finger-marks. Also, I beg that these experimenters, or others, will set their finger-marks upon another pane, and add again the marks of the accused, but not placing them in the same order or relation to the other signatures as before—for, by one chance in a million, a person might happen upon the right marks by pure guess-work *once*, therefore I wish to be tested twice."

He turned his back, and the two panes were quickly covered with delicately-lined oval spots, but visible only to such persons as could get a dark background for them—the foliage of a tree, outside, for instance. Then, upon call, Wilson went to the window, made his examination, and said—

"This is Count Luigi's right hand; this one, three signatures below, is his left. Here is Count Angelo's right; down here is his left. Now for the other pane: here and here are Count Luigi's, here and here are his brother's." He faced about. "Am I right?"

A deafening explosion of applause was the answer. The Bench said—

"This certainly approaches the miraculous!"

Wilson turned to the window again and remarked, pointing with his finger—

"This is the signature of Mr. Justice Robinson. [Applause.] This, of Constable Blake. [Applause.] This, of John Mason, juryman. [Applause.] This, of the sheriff. [Applause.] I cannot name the others, but I have them all at home, named and dated, and could identify them all by my finger-print records."

He moved to his place through a storm of applause—which the sheriff stopped, and also made the people sit down, for they were all standing and struggling to see, of course. Court, jury, sheriff, and everybody had been too absorbed in observing Wilson's performance to attend to the audience earlier.

"Now, then," said Wilson, "I have here the natal autographs of two children—thrown up to ten times the natural size by the pantograph, so that any one who can see at all can tell the markings apart at a glance. We will call the children *A* and *B*. Here are *A's* finger-marks, taken at the age of five months. Here they are again, taken at seven months. [Tom started.] They are alike, you see. Here are *B's* at five months, and also at seven months. They, too, exactly copy each other, but the patterns are quite different from *A's*, you observe. I shall refer to these again presently, but we will turn them face down, now.

"Here, thrown up ten sizes, are the natal autographs of the two persons who are here before you accused of murdering Judge Driscoll. I made these pantograph copies last night, and will so swear when I go upon the witness stand. I ask the jury to compare them with the finger-marks of the accused upon the window-panes, and tell the court if they are the same."

He passed a powerful magnifying-glass to the foreman.

One juryman after another took the cardboard and the glass and made the comparison. Then the foreman said to the judge—

"Your honor, we are all agreed that they are identical."

Wilson said to the foreman—

"Please turn that cardboard face down, and take this one, and compare it searchingly, by the magnifier, with the fatal signature upon the knife-handle, and report your findings to the court."

Again the jury made minute examination, and again reported—

"We find them to be exactly identical, your honor."

Wilson turned toward the counsel for the prosecution, and there was a clearly recognizable note of warning in his voice when he said—

"May it please the court, the State has claimed, strenuously and persistently, that the blood-stained finger-prints upon that knife-handle were left there by the assassin of Judge Driscoll. You have heard us grant that claim, and welcome it." He turned to the jury: "Compare the finger-prints of the accused with the finger-prints left by the assassin—and report."

The comparison began. As it proceeded, all movement and all sound ceased, and the deep silence of an absorbed and waiting suspense settled upon the house; and when at last the words came—

"They do not even resemble," a thunder-crash of applause followed and the house sprang to its feet, but was quickly repressed by official force and brought to order again. Tom was altering his position every few minutes, now, but none of his changes brought repose nor any small trifle of comfort. When the house's attention was become fixed once more, Wilson said gravely, indicating the twins with a gesture—

"These men are innocent—I have no further concern with them. [Another outbreak of applause began, but was promptly checked.] We will now proceed to find the guilty. [Tom's eyes were starting from their sockets—yes, it was a cruel day for the bereaved youth, everybody thought.] We will return to the infant autographs of *A* and *B*. I will ask the jury to take these large pantograph facsimiles of *A's*, marked five months and seven months. Do they tally?

The foreman responded—

"Perfectly."

"Now examine this pantograph, taken at eight months, and also marked *A*. Does it tally with the other two?"

The surprised response was—

"No—they differ widely!"

"You are quite right. Now take these two pantographs of *B's* autograph, marked five months and seven months. Do they tally with each other?"

"Yes—perfectly."

"Take this third pantograph marked *B*, eight months. Does it tally with *B's* other two?"

"*By no means!*"

"Do you know how to account for those strange discrepancies? I will tell you. For a purpose unknown to us, but probably a selfish one, somebody changed those children in the cradle."

This produced a vast sensation, naturally; Roxana was astonished at this admirable guess, but not disturbed by it. To guess the exchange was one thing, to guess who did it quite another. Pudd'nhead Wilson could do wonderful things, no doubt, but he could n't do impossible ones. Safe? She was perfectly safe. She smiled privately.

"Between the ages of seven months and eight months those children were changed in the cradle"—he made one of his effect-collecting pauses, and added—"and the person who did it is in this house!"

Roxy's pulses stood still! The house was thrilled as with an electric shock, and the people half rose as if to seek a glimpse of the person who had made that exchange. Tom was growing limp; the life seemed oozing out of him. Wilson resumed:

"*A* was put into *B's* cradle in the nursery; *B* was transferred to the kitchen and became a negro and a slave [Sensation—confusion of angry ejaculations]—but within a quarter of an hour he will stand before you white and free! [Burst of applause, checked by the officers.] From seven months onward until now, *A* has still been a usurper, and in my finger-records he bears *B's* name. Here is his pantograph at the age of twelve. Compare it with the assassin's signature upon the knife-handle. Do they tally?"

The foreman answered—

"*To the minutest detail!*"

Wilson said, solemnly—

"The murderer of your friend and mine—York Driscoll of the generous hand and the kindly spirit—sits in among you. Valet de Chambre, negro and slave,—falsely called Thomas à Becket Driscoll,—make upon the window the finger-prints that will hang you!"

Tom turned his ashen face imploringly toward the speaker,

made some impotent movements with his white lips, then slid limp and lifeless to the floor.

Wilson broke the awed silence with the words—

"There is no need. He has confessed."

Roxy flung herself upon her knees, covered her face with her hands, and out through her sobs the words struggled—

"De Lord have mercy on me, po' misable sinner dat I is!"

The clock struck twelve.

The court rose; the new prisoner, hand-cuffed, was removed.

Conclusion

THE TOWN sat up all night to discuss the amazing events of the day and swap guesses as to when Tom's trial would begin. Troop after troop of citizens came to serenade Wilson, and require a speech, and shout themselves hoarse over every sentence that fell from his lips—for all his sentences were golden, now, all were marvelous. His long fight against hard luck and prejudice was ended; he was a made man for good.

And as each of these roaring gangs of enthusiasts marched away, some remorseful member of it was quite sure to raise his voice and say—

"And this is the man the likes of us have called a pudd'nhead for more than twenty years. He has resigned from that position, friends."

"Yes, but it is n't vacant—we 're elected."

The twins were heroes of romance, now, and with rehabilitated reputations. But they were weary of Western adventure, and straightway retired to Europe.

Roxy's heart was broken. The young fellow upon whom she had inflicted twenty-three years of slavery continued the false heir's pension of thirty-five dollars a month to her, but her hurts were too deep for money to heal; the spirit in her eye was quenched, her martial bearing departed with it, and the voice of her laughter ceased in the land. In her church and its affairs she found her only solace.

The real heir suddenly found himself rich and free, but in a most embarrassing situation. He could neither read nor write, and his speech was the basest dialect of the negro quarter. His gait, his attitudes, his gestures, his bearing, his laugh—all were vulgar and uncouth; his manners were the manners of a slave. Money and fine clothes could not mend these defects or cover them up; they only made them the more glaring and the more pathetic. The poor fellow could not endure the terrors of the white man's parlor, and felt at home and at peace nowhere but in the kitchen. The family pew was a misery to him, yet he could nevermore enter into the solacing refuge of the "nigger gallery"—that was closed to him for good and all. But we cannot follow his curious fate further—that would be a long story.

The false heir made a full confession and was sentenced to imprisonment for life. But now a complication came up. The Percy Driscoll estate was in such a crippled shape when its owner died that it could pay only sixty per cent. of its great indebtedness, and was settled at that rate. But the creditors came forward, now, and complained that inasmuch as through an error for which *they* were in no way to blame the false heir was not inventoried at that time with the rest of the property, great wrong and loss had thereby been inflicted upon them. They rightly claimed that "Tom" was lawfully their property and had been so for eight years; that they had already lost sufficiently in being deprived of his services during that long period, and ought not to be required to add anything to that loss; that if he had been delivered up to them in the first place, they would have sold him and he could not have murdered Judge Driscoll; therefore it was not he that had really committed the murder, the guilt lay with the erroneous inventory. Everybody saw that there was reason in this. Everybody granted that if "Tom" were white and free it would be unquestionably right to punish him—it would be no loss to anybody; but to shut up a valuable slave for life—that was quite another matter.

As soon as the Governor understood the case, he pardoned Tom at once, and the creditors sold him down the river.

NO. 44,
THE MYSTERIOUS STRANGER

BEING AN ANCIENT TALE FOUND IN A JUG,
AND FREELY TRANSLATED FROM THE JUG

Chapter 1

I<small>T WAS</small> in 1490—winter. Austria was far away from the world, and asleep; it was still the Middle Ages in Austria, and promised to remain so forever. Some even set it away back centuries upon centuries and said that by the mental and spiritual clock it was still the Age of Faith in Austria. But they meant it as a compliment, not a slur, and it was so taken, and we were all proud of it. I remember it well, although I was only a boy; and I remember, too, the pleasure it gave me.

Yes, Austria was far from the world, and asleep, and our village was in the middle of that sleep, being in the middle of Austria. It drowsed in peace in the deep privacy of a hilly and woodsy solitude where news from the world hardly ever came to disturb its dreams, and was infinitely content. At its front flowed the tranquil river, its surface painted with cloud-forms and the reflections of drifting arks and stone-boats; behind it rose the woody steeps to the base of the lofty precipice; from the top of the precipice frowned the vast castle of Rosenfeld, its long stretch of towers and bastions mailed in vines; beyond the river, a league to the left, was a tumbled expanse of forest-clothed hills cloven by winding gorges where the sun never penetrated; and to the right, a precipice overlooked the river, and between it and the hills just spoken of lay a far-reaching plain dotted with little homesteads nested among orchards and shade-trees.

The whole region for leagues around was the hereditary property of prince Rosenfeld, whose servants kept the castle always in perfect condition for occupancy, but neither he nor his family came there oftener than once in five years. When they came it was as if the lord of the world had arrived, and had brought all the glories of its kingdoms along; and when they went they left a calm behind which was like the deep sleep which follows an orgy.

Eseldorf was a paradise for us boys. We were not overmuch pestered with schooling. Mainly we were trained to be good Catholics; to revere the Virgin, the Church and the saints above everything; to hold the Monarch in awful reverence, speak of him with bated breath, uncover before his picture, regard him as the gracious provider of our daily bread and of all our earthly blessings, and ourselves as being sent into the world with the one only mission, to labor for him, bleed for him, die for him, when necessary. Beyond these matters we were not required to know much; and in fact, not allowed to. The priests said that knowledge was not good for the common people, and could make them discontented with the lot which God had appointed for them, and God would not endure discontentment with His plans. This was true, for the priests got it of the Bishop.

It was discontentment that came so near to being the ruin of Gretel Marx the dairyman's widow, who had two horses and a cart, and carried milk to the market town. A Hussite woman named Adler came to Eseldorf and went slyly about, and began to persuade some of the ignorant and foolish to come privately by night to her house and hear "God's *real* message," as she called it. She was a cunning woman, and sought out only those few who could read—flattering them by saying it showed their intelligence, and that only the intelligent could understand her doctrine. She gradually got ten together, and these she poisoned nightly with her heresies in her house. And she gave them Hussite sermons, all written out, to keep for their own, and persuaded them that it was no sin to read them.

One day Father Adolf came along and found the widow sitting in the shade of the horse-chestnut that stood by her house, reading these iniquities. He was a very loud and zealous and strenuous priest, and was always working to get more reputation, hoping to be a Bishop some day; and he was always spying around and keeping a sharp lookout on other people's flocks as well as his own; and he was dissolute and profane and malicious, but otherwise a good enough man, it was generally thought. And he certainly had talent; he was a most fluent and chirpy speaker, and could say the cuttingest things and the wittiest, though a little coarse, maybe—however it was only his enemies who said that, and it really wasn't any truer of him than of others; but he belonged to the village council, and lorded it there, and played smart dodges that carried his projects through, and of course that nettled the others; and in their resentment they gave him nicknames privately, and called him the "Town Bull," and "Hell's Delight," and all sorts of things; which was natural, for when you are in politics you are in the wasp's nest with a short shirt-tail, as the saying is.

He was rolling along down the road, pretty full and feeling good, and braying "We'll sing the wine-cup and the lass" in his thundering bass, when he caught sight of the widow reading her book. He came to a stop before her and stood swaying there, leering down at her with his fishy eyes, and his purple fat face working and grimacing, and said—

"What is it you've got there, Frau Marx? What are you reading?"

She let him see. He bent down and took one glance, then he knocked the writings out of her hand and said angrily—

"Burn them, burn them, you fool! Don't you know it's a sin to read them? Do you want to damn your soul? Where did you get them?"

She told him, and he said—

"By God I expected it. I will attend to that woman; I will make this place sultry for her. You go to her meetings, do you? What does she teach you—to worship the Virgin?"

"No—only God."

"I thought it. You are on your road to hell. The Virgin will punish you for this—you mark my words." Frau Marx was getting frightened; and was going to try to excuse herself for her conduct, but Father Adolf shut her up and went on storming at her and telling her what the Virgin would do with her, until she was ready to swoon with fear. She went on her knees and begged him to tell her what to do to appease the Virgin. He put a heavy penance on her, scolded her some more, then took up his song where he had left off, and went rolling and zigzagging away.

But Frau Marx fell again, within the week, and went back to Frau Adler's meeting one night. Just four days afterward both of her horses died! She flew to Father Adolf, full of repentance and despair, and cried and sobbed, and said she was ruined and must starve; for how could she market her milk now? What *must* she do? tell her what to do. He said—

"I told you the Virgin would punish you—didn't I tell you

that? Hell's bells! did you think I was lying? You'll pay attention next time, I reckon."

Then he told her what to do. She must have a picture of
the horses painted, and walk on pilgrimage to the Church of
Our Lady of the Dumb Creatures, and hang it up there, and
make her offerings; then go home and sell the skins of her
horses and buy a lottery ticket bearing the number of the date
of their death, and then wait in patience for the Virgin's answer. In a week it came, when Frau Marx was almost perishing with despair—her ticket drew fifteen hundred ducats!

That is the way the Virgin rewards a real repentance. Frau
Marx did not fall again. In her gratitude she went to those
other women and told them her experience and showed them
how sinful and foolish they were and how dangerously they
were acting; and they all burned their sermons and returned
repentant to the bosom of the Church, and Frau Adler had to
carry her poisons to some other market. It was the best lesson
and the wholesomest our village ever had. It never allowed
another Hussite to come there; and for reward the Virgin
watched over it and took care of it personally, and made it
fortunate and prosperous always.

It was in conducting funerals that Father Adolf was at his
best, if he hadn't too much of a load on, but only about
enough to make him properly appreciate the sacredness of his
office. It was fine to see him march his procession through
the village, between the kneeling ranks, keeping one eye on
the candles blinking yellow in the sun to see that the acolytes
walked stiff and held them straight, and the other watching
out for any dull oaf that might forget himself and stand staring and covered when the Host was carried past. He would
snatch that oaf's broad hat from his head, hit him a staggering whack in the face with it and growl out in a low snarl—

"Where's your manners, you beast?—and the Lord God
passing by!"

Whenever there was a suicide he was active. He was on
hand to see that the government did its duty and turned the
family out into the road, and confiscated its small belongings
and didn't smouch any of the Church's share; and he was on
hand again at midnight when the corpse was buried at the
cross-roads—not to do any religious office, for of course that

was not allowable—but to see, for himself, that the stake was driven through the body in a right and permanent and workmanlike way.

It was grand to see him make procession through the village in plague-time, with our saint's relics in their jeweled casket, and trade prayers and candles to the Virgin for her help in abolishing the pest.

And he was always on hand at the bridge-head on the 9th of December, at the Assuaging of the Devil. Ours was a beautiful and massive stone bridge of five arches, and was seven hundred years old. It was built by the Devil in a single night. The prior of the monastery hired him to do it, and had trouble to persuade him, for the Devil said he had built bridges for priests all over Europe, and had always got cheated out of his wages; and this was the last time he would trust a Christian if he got cheated now. Always before, when he built a bridge, he was to have for his pay the first passenger that crossed it—everybody knowing he meant a Christian, of course. But no matter, he didn't *say* it, so they always sent a jackass or a chicken or some other undamnable passenger across first, and so got the best of him. This time he *said* Christian, and wrote it in the bond himself, so there couldn't be any misunderstanding. And that isn't tradition, it is history, for I have seen that bond myself, many a time; it is always brought out on Assuaging Day, and goes to the bridge-head with the procession; and anybody who pays ten groschen can see it and get remission of thirty-three sins besides, times being easier for every one then than they are now, and sins much cheaper; so much cheaper that all except the very poorest could afford them. Those were good days, but they are gone and will not come any more, so every one says.

Yes, he put it in the bond, and the prior said he didn't want the bridge built yet, but would soon appoint a day—perhaps in about a week. There was an old monk wavering along between life and death, and the prior told the watchers to keep a sharp eye out and let him know as soon as they saw that the monk was actually dying. Towards midnight the 9th of December the watchers brought him word, and he summoned the Devil and the bridge was begun. All the rest of the night the prior and the Brotherhood sat up and prayed that the dying one might be given strength to rise up and walk across the bridge at dawn—strength enough, but not too much. The prayer was heard, and it made great excitement in heaven; insomuch that all the heavenly host got up before dawn and came down to see; and there they were, clouds and clouds of angels filling all the air above the bridge; and the dying monk tottered across, and just had strength to get over; then he fell dead just as the Devil was reaching for him, and as his soul escaped the angels swooped down and caught it and flew up to heaven with it, laughing and jeering, and Satan found he hadn't anything but a useless carcase.

He was very angry, and charged the prior with cheating him, and said "*this* isn't a Christian," but the prior said "Yes it is, it's a *dead* one." Then the prior and all the monks went through with a great lot of mock ceremonies, pretending it was to assuage the Devil and reconcile him, but really it was only to make fun of him and stir up his bile more than ever. So at last he gave them all a solid good cursing, they laughing at him all the time. Then he raised a black storm of thunder and lightning and wind and flew away in it; and as he went the spike on the end of his tail caught on a capstone and tore it away; and there it always lay, throughout the centuries, as proof of what he had done. I have seen it myself, a thousand times. Such things speak louder than written records; for written records can lie, unless they are set down by a priest. The mock Assuaging is repeated every 9th of December, to this day, in memory of that holy thought of the prior's which rescued an imperiled Christian soul from the odious Enemy of mankind.

There have been better priests, in some ways, than Father Adolf, for he had his failings, but there was never one in our commune who was held in more solemn and awful respect. This was because he had absolutely no fear of the Devil. He was the only Christian I have ever known of whom that could be truly said. People stood in deep dread of him, on that account; for they thought there must be something supernatural about him, else he could not be so bold and so confident. All men speak in bitter disapproval of the Devil, but they do it reverently, not flippantly; but Father Adolf's way was very different; he called him by every vile and putrid name he could lay his tongue to, and it made every one shudder that heard him; and often he would even speak of him scornfully and scoffingly; then the people crossed themselves and went quickly out of his presence, fearing that something fearful might happen; and this was natural, for after all is said and done Satan is a sacred character, being mentioned in the Bible, and it cannot be proper to utter lightly the sacred names, lest heaven itself should resent it.

Father Adolf had actually met Satan face to face, more than once, and defied him. This was known to be so. Father Adolf said it himself. He never made any secret of it, but spoke it right out. And that he was speaking true, there was proof, in at least one instance; for on that occasion he quarreled with the Enemy, and intrepidly threw his bottle at him, and there, upon the wall of his study was the ruddy splotch where it struck and broke.

The priest that we all loved best and were sorriest for, was Father Peter. But the Bishop suspended him for talking around in conversation that God was all goodness and would find a way to save *all* his poor human children. It was a horrible thing to say, but there was never any absolute proof that Father Peter said it; and it was out of character for him to say it, too, for he was always good and gentle and truthful, and a good Catholic, and always teaching in the pulpit just what the Church required, and nothing else. But there it was, you see: he wasn't charged with saying it in the pulpit, where all the congregation could hear and testify, but only outside, in talk; and it is easy for enemies to manufacture *that*. Father Peter denied it; but no matter, Father Adolf wanted his place, and he told the Bishop, and swore to it, that he overheard Father Peter say it; heard Father Peter say it to his niece, when Father Adolf was behind the door listening—for he was suspicious of Father Peter's soundness, he said, and the interests of religion required that he be watched.

The niece, Gretchen, denied it, and implored the Bishop to believe her and spare her old uncle from poverty and disgrace; but Father Adolf had been poisoning the Bishop against the old man a long time privately, and he wouldn't listen; for he had a deep admiration of Father Adolf's bravery toward the Devil, and an awe of him on account of his having met the

Devil face to face; and so he was a slave to Father Adolf's influence. He suspended Father Peter, indefinitely, though he wouldn't go so far as to excommunicate him on the evidence of only one witness; and now Father Peter had been out a couple of years, and Father Adolf had his flock.

Those had been hard years for the old priest and Gretchen. They had been favorites, but of course that changed when they came under the shadow of the Bishop's frown. Many of their friends fell away entirely, and the rest became cool and distant. Gretchen was a lovely girl of eighteen, when the trouble came, and she had the best head in the village, and the most in it. She taught the harp, and earned all her clothes and pocket money by her own industry. But her scholars fell off one by one, now; she was forgotten when there were dances and parties among the youth of the village; the young fellows stopped coming to the house, all except Wilhelm Meidling— and he could have been spared; she and her uncle were sad and forlorn in their neglect and disgrace, and the sunshine was gone out of their lives. Matters went worse and worse, all through the two years. Clothes were wearing out, bread was harder and harder to get. And now at last, the very end was come. Solomon Isaacs had lent all the money he was willing to put on the house, and gave notice that to-morrow he should foreclose.

Chapter 2

I HAD BEEN familiar with that village life, but now for as much as a year I had been out of it, and was busy learning a trade. I was more curiously than pleasantly situated. I have spoken of Castle Rosenfeld; I have also mentioned a precipice which overlooked the river. Well, along this precipice stretched the towered and battlemented mass of a similar castle—prodigious, vine-clad, stately and beautiful, but mouldering to ruin. The great line that had possessed it and made it their chief home during four or five centuries was extinct, and no scion of it had lived in it now for a hundred years. It was a stanch old pile, and the greater part of it was still habitable.

Inside, the ravages of time and neglect were less evident than they were outside. As a rule the spacious chambers and the vast corridors, ballrooms, banqueting halls and rooms of state were bare and melancholy and cobwebbed, it is true, but the walls and floors were in tolerable condition, and they could have been lived in. In some of the rooms the decayed and ancient furniture still remained, but if the empty ones were pathetic to the view, these were sadder still.

This old castle was not wholly destitute of life. By grace of the Prince over the river, who owned it, my master, with his little household, had for many years been occupying a small portion of it, near the centre of the mass. The castle could have housed a thousand persons; consequently, as you may say, this handful was lost in it, like a swallow's nest in a cliff.

My master was a printer. His was a new art, being only thirty or forty years old, and almost unknown in Austria. Very few persons in our secluded region had ever seen a printed page, few had any very clear idea about the art of printing, and perhaps still fewer had any curiosity concerning it or felt any interest in it. Yet we had to conduct our business with some degree of privacy, on account of the Church. The Church was opposed to the cheapening of books and the indiscriminate dissemination of knowledge. Our villagers did not trouble themselves about our work, and had no commerce in it; we published nothing there, and printed nothing that they could have read, they being ignorant of abstruse sciences and the dead languages.

We were a mixed family. My master, Heinrich Stein, was portly, and of a grave and dignified carriage, with a large and benevolent face and calm deep eyes—a patient man whose temper could stand much before it broke. His head was bald, with a valance of silky white hair hanging around it, his face was clean shaven, his raiment was good and fine, but not rich. He was a scholar, and a dreamer or a thinker, and loved learning and study, and would have submerged his mind all the days and nights in his books and been pleasantly and peacefully unconscious of his surroundings, if God had been willing. His complexion was younger than his hair; he was four or five years short of sixty.

A large part of his surroundings consisted of his wife. She

was well along in life, and was long and lean and flat-breasted, and had an active and vicious tongue and a diligent and devilish spirit, and more religion than was good for her, considering the quality of it. She hungered for money, and believed there was a treasure hid in the black deeps of the castle somewhere; and between fretting and sweating about that and trying to bring sinners nearer to God when any fell in her way she was able to fill up her time and save her life from getting uninteresting and her soul from getting mouldy. There was old tradition for the treasure, and the word of Balthasar Hoffman thereto. He had come from a long way off, and had brought a great reputation with him, which he concealed in our family the best he could, for he had no more ambition to be burnt by the Church than another. He lived with us on light salary and board, and worked the constellations for the treasure. He had an easy berth and was not likely to lose his job if the constellations held out, for it was Frau Stein that hired him; and her faith in him, as in all things she had at heart, was of the staying kind. Inside the walls, where was safety, he clothed himself as Egyptians and magicians should, and moved stately, robed in black velvet starred and mooned and cometed and sun'd with the symbols of his trade done in silver, and on his head a conical tower with like symbols glinting from it. When he at intervals went outside he left his business suit behind, with good discretion, and went dressed like anybody else and looking the Christian with such cunning art that St. Peter would have let him in quite as a matter of course, and probably asked him to take something. Very naturally we were all afraid of him—abjectly so, I suppose I may say—though Ernest Wasserman professed that he wasn't. Not that he did it publicly; no, he didn't; for, with all his talk, Ernest Wasserman had a judgment in choosing the right place for it that never forsook him. He wasn't even afraid of ghosts, if you let him tell it; and not only that but didn't believe in them. That is to say, he *said* he didn't believe in them. The truth is, he would say any foolish thing that he thought would make him conspicuous.

To return to Frau Stein. This masterly devil was the master's second wife, and before that she had been the widow Vogel. She had brought into the family a young thing by her first marriage, and this girl was now seventeen and a blister, so to speak; for she was a second edition of her mother—just plain galley-proof, neither revised nor corrected, full of turned letters, wrong fonts, outs and doubles, as we say in the printing-shop—in a word, *pi*, if you want to put it remorselessly strong and yet not strain the facts. Yet if it ever would be fair to strain facts it would be fair in her case, for she was not loath to strain them herself when so minded. Moses Haas said that whenever she took up an en-quad fact, just watch her and you would see her try to cram it in where there wasn't breathing-room for a 4-m space; and she'd do it, too, if she had to take the sheep-foot to it. Isn't it neat! Doesn't it describe it to a dot? Well, he could say such things, Moses could—as malicious a devil as we had on the place, but as bright as a lightning-bug and as sudden, when he was in the humor. He had a talent for getting himself hated, and always had it out at usury. That daughter kept the name she was born to—Maria Vogel; it was her mother's preference and her own. Both were proud of it, without any reason, except reasons which they invented, themselves, from time to time, as a market offered. Some of the Vogels may have been distinguished, by not getting hanged, Moses thought, but no one attached much importance to what the mother and daughter claimed for them. Maria had plenty of energy and vivacity and tongue, and was shapely enough but not pretty, barring her eyes, which had all kinds of fire in them, according to the mood of the moment—opal-fire, fox-fire, hell-fire, and the rest. She hadn't any fear, broadly speaking. Perhaps she had none at all, except for Satan, and ghosts, and witches and the priest and the magician, and a sort of fear of God in the dark, and of the lightning when she had been blaspheming and hadn't time to get in *aves* enough to square up and cash-in. She despised Marget Regen, the master's niece, along with Marget's mother, Frau Regen, who was the master's sister and a dependent and bedridden widow. She loved Gustav Fischer, the big and blonde and handsome and good-hearted journeyman, and detested the rest of the tribe impartially, I think. Gustav did not reciprocate.

Marget Regen was Maria's age—seventeen. She was lithe and graceful and trim-built as a fish, and she was a blue-eyed blonde, and soft and sweet and innocent and shrinking and winning and gentle and beautiful; just a vision for the eyes, worshipful, adorable, enchanting; but that wasn't the hive for her. She was a kitten in a menagerie.

She was a second edition of what her mother had been at her age; but struck from the standing forms and needing no revising, as one says in the printing-shop. That poor meek mother! yonder she had lain, partially paralysed, ever since her brother my master had brought her eagerly there a dear and lovely young widow with her little child fifteen years before; the pair had been welcome, and had forgotten their poverty and poor-relation estate and been happy during three whole years. Then came the new wife with her five-year brat, and a change began. The new wife was never able to root out the master's love for his sister, nor to drive sister and child from under the roof, but she accomplished the rest: as soon as she had gotten her lord properly trained to harness, she shortened his visits to his sister and made them infrequent. But she made up for this by going frequently herself and roasting the widow, as the saying is.

Next was old Katrina. She was cook and housekeeper; her forbears had served the master's people and none else for three or four generations; she was sixty, and had served the master all his life, from the time when she was a little girl and he was a swaddled baby. She was erect, straight, six feet high, with the port and stride of a soldier; she was independent and masterful, and her fears were limited to the supernatural. She believed she could whip anybody on the place, and would have considered an invitation a favor. As far as her allegiance stretched, she paid it with affection and reverence, but it did not extend beyond "her family"—the master, his sister, and Marget. She regarded Frau Vogel and Maria as aliens and intruders, and was frank about saying so.

She had under her two strapping young wenches—Sara and Duffles (a nickname), and a manservant, Jacob, and a porter, Fritz.

Next, we have the printing force.

Adam Binks, sixty years old, learnèd bachelor, proof-reader, poor, disappointed, surly.

Hans Katzenyammer, 36, printer, huge, strong, freckled,

red-headed, rough. When drunk, quarrelsome. Drunk when opportunity offered.

Moses Haas, 28, printer; a looker-out for himself; liable to say acid things about people and to people; take him all around, not a pleasant character.

Barty Langbein, 15; cripple; general-utility lad; sunny spirit; affectionate; could play the fiddle.

Ernest Wasserman, 17, apprentice; braggart, malicious, hateful, coward, liar, cruel, underhanded, treacherous. He and Moses had a sort of half fondness for each other, which was natural, they having one or more traits in common, down among the lower grades of traits.

Gustav Fischer, 27, printer; large, well built, shapely and muscular; quiet, brave, kindly, a good disposition, just and fair; a slow temper to ignite, but a reliable burner when well going. He was about as much out of place as was Marget. He was the best man of them all, and deserved to be in better company.

Last of all comes August Feldner, 16, 'prentice. This is myself.

Chapter 3

OF several conveniences there was no lack; among them, fire-wood and room. There was no end of room, we had it to waste. Big or little chambers for all—suit yourself, and change when you liked. For a kitchen we used a spacious room which was high up over the massive and frowning gateway of the castle and looked down the woody steeps and southward over the receding plain.

It opened into a great room with the same outlook, and this we used as dining room, drinking room, quarreling room—in a word, family room. Above its vast fire-place, which was flanked with fluted columns, rose the wide granite mantel, heavily carved, to the high ceiling. With a cart-load of logs blazing here within and a snow-tempest howling and whirling outside, it was a heaven of a place for comfort and contentment and cosiness, and the exchange of injurious

personalities. Especially after supper, with the lamps going
and the day's work done. It was not the tribe's custom to
hurry to bed.

The apartments occupied by the Steins were beyond this
room to the east, on the same front; those occupied by Frau
Regen and Marget were on the same front also, but to the
west, beyond the kitchen. The rooms of the rest of the herd
were on the same floor, but on the other side of the principal
great interior court—away over in the north front, which rose
high in air above precipice and river.

The printing-shop was remote, and hidden in an upper section of a round tower. Visitors were not wanted there; and if
they had tried to hunt their way to it without a guide they
would have concluded to give it up and call another time before they got through.

One cold day, when the noon meal was about finished, a
most forlorn looking youth, apparently sixteen or seventeen
years old, appeared in the door, and stopped there, timid and
humble, venturing no further. His clothes were coarse and
old, ragged, and lightly powdered with snow, and for shoes
he had nothing but some old serge remnants wrapped about
his feet and ancles and tied with strings. The war of talk
stopped at once and all eyes were turned upon the apparition;
those of the master, and Marget, and Gustav Fischer, and
Barty Langbein, in pity and kindness, those of Frau Stein and
the rest in varying shades of contempt and hostility.

"What do you want here?" said the Frau, sharply.

The youth seemed to wince under that. He did not raise his
head, but with eyes still bent upon the floor and shyly fumbling his ruin of a cap which he had removed from his head,
answered meekly—

"I am friendless, gracious lady, and am so—*so* hungry!"

"*So* hungry, are you?"—mimicking him. "Who invited you?
How did you get in? Take yourself out of this!"

She half rose, as if minded to help him out with her hands.
Marget started to rise at the same moment, with her plate in
her hands and an appeal on her lips: "May I, madam?"

"No! Sit down!" commanded the Frau. The master, his
face all pity, had opened his lips—no doubt to say the kind
word—but he closed them now, discouraged. Old Katrina

emerged from the kitchen, and stood towering in the door. She took in the situation, and just as the boy was turning sorrowfully away, she hailed him:

"Come back, child, there's room in my kitchen, and plenty to eat, too!"

"Shut your mouth you hussy, and mind your own affairs and keep to your own place!" screamed the Frau, rising and turning toward Katrina, who, seeing that the boy was afraid to move, was coming to fetch him. Katrina, answering no word, came striding on. "Command her, Heinrich Stein! will you allow your own wife to be defied by a servant?"

The master said "It isn't the first time," and did not seem ungratified.

Katrina came on, undisturbed; she swung unheeding past her mistress, took the boy by the hand, and led him back to her fortress, saying, as she crossed its threshold,

"If any of you wants this boy, you come and get him, that's all!"

Apparently no one wanted him at that expense, so no one followed. The talk opened up briskly, straightway. Frau Stein wanted the boy turned out as soon as might be; she was willing he should be fed, if he was so hungry as he had said he was, which was probably a lie, for he had the look of a liar, she said, but shelter he could have none, for in her opinion he had the look of a murderer and a thief; and she asked Maria if it wasn't so. Maria confirmed it, and then the Frau asked for the general table's judgment. Opinions came freely: negatives from the master and from Marget and Fischer, affirmatives from the rest; and then war broke out. Presently, as one could easily see, the master was beginning to lose patience. He was likely to assert himself when that sign appeared. He suddenly broke in upon the wrangle, and said,

"Stop! This is a great to-do about nothing. The boy is not necessarily *bad* because he is unfortunate. And if he *is* bad, what of it? A bad person can be as hungry as a good one, and hunger is always respectable. And so is weariness. The boy is worn and tired, any one can see it. If he wants rest and shelter, *that* is no crime; let him say it and have it, be he bad or good—there's room enough."

That settled it. Frau Stein was opening her mouth to try

and unsettle it again when Katrina brought the boy in and stood him before the master and said, encouragingly,

"Don't be afraid, the master's a just man. Master, he's a plenty good enough boy, for all he looks such a singed cat. He's out of luck, there's nothing else the matter with him. Look at his face, look at his eye. He's not a beggar for love of it. He wants work."

"*Work!*" scoffed Frau Stein; "that tramp?" And "work!" sneered this and that and the other one. But the master looked interested, and not unpleased. He said,

"Work, is it? What kind of work are you willing to do, lad?"

"He's willing to do any kind, sir," interrupted Katrina, eagerly, "and he don't want any pay."

"What, no pay?"

"No sir, nothing but food to eat and shelter for his head, poor lad."

"Not even clothes?"

"He shan't go naked, sir, if you'll keep him, my wage is bail for that."

There was an affectionate light in the boy's eye as he glanced gratefully up at his majestic new friend—a light which the master noted.

"Do you think you could do rough work—rough, hard drudgery?"

"Yes, sir, I could, if you will try me; I am strong."

"Carry fire-logs up these long stairways?"

"Yes, sir."

"And scrub, like the maids; and build fires in the rooms; and carry up water to the chambers; and split wood; and help in the laundry and the kitchen; and take care of the dog?"

"Yes, sir, all those things, if you will let me try."

"All for food and shelter? Well, I don't see how a body is going to refu—"

"Heinrich Stein, wait! If you think you are going to nest this vermin in this place without ever so much as a by-your-leave to me, I can tell you you are very much mis—"

"Be quiet!" said the husband, sternly. "Now, then, you have all expressed your opinions about this boy, but there is one vote which you have not counted. I value that one above some of the others—above any of the others, in fact. On that

vote by itself I would give him a trial. That is my decision.
You can discuss some other subject, now—this one is finished.
Take him along, Katrina, and give him a room and let him get
some rest."

Katrina stiffened with pride and satisfaction in her triumph.
The boy's eyes looked his gratitude, and he said,

"I would like to go to work *now*, if I may, sir."

Before an answer could come, Frau Stein interrupted:

"I want to *know*. Whose vote was it that wasn't counted?
I'm not hard of hearing, and I don't know of any."

"The dog's."

Everybody showed surprise. But there it was: the dog had-
n't made a motion when the boy came in. Nobody but the
master had noticed it, but it was the fact. It was the first time
that that demon had ever treated a stranger with civil indifference. He was chained in the corner, and had a bone between his paws and was gnawing it; and not even growling,
which was not his usual way. Frau Stein's eyes beamed with a
vicious pleasure, and she called out,

"You want work, do you? Well, there it is, cut out for you.
Take the dog out and give him an airing!"

Even some of the hardest hearts there felt the cruelty of it,
and their horror showed in their faces when the boy stepped
innocently forward to obey.

"Stop!" shouted the master, and Katrina, flushing with
anger, sprang after the youth and halted him.

"Shame!" she said; and the master turned his indignation
loose and gave his wife a dressing down that astonished her.
Then he said to the stranger,

"You are free to rest, lad, if you like, but if you would
rather work, Katrina will see what she can find for you. What
is your name?"

The boy answered, quietly,

"Number 44, New Series 864,962."

Everybody's eyes came open in a stare. Of course. The master thought perhaps he hadn't heard aright; so he asked again,
and the boy answered the same as before,

"Number 44, New Series 864,962."

"What a hell of a name!" ejaculated Hans Katzenyammer,
piously.

"Jail-number, likely," suggested Moses Haas, searchingly examining the boy with his rat eyes, and unconsciously twisting and stroking his silky and scanty moustache with his fingers, a way he had when his cogitations were concentrated upon a thing.

"It's a strange name," said the master, with a barely noticeable touch of suspicion in his tone, "where did you get it?"

"I don't know, sir," said No. 44, tranquilly, "I've always had it."

The master forbore to pursue the matter further, probably fearing that the ice was thin, but Maria Vogel chirped up and asked,

"Have you ever been in jail?"

The master burst in with—

"There, that's enough of that! You needn't answer, my boy, unless you want to." He paused—hopeful, maybe—but 44 did not seize the opportunity to testify for himself. He stood still and said nothing. Satirical smiles flitted here and there, down the table, and the master looked annoyed and disappointed, though he tried to conceal it. "Take him along, Katrina." He said it as kindly as he could, but there was just a trifle of a chill in his manner, and it delighted those creatures.

Katrina marched out with 44.

Out of a wise respect for the temper the master was in, there was no outspoken comment, but a low buzz skimmed along down the table, whose burden was, "That silence was a confession—the chap's a Jail-Bird."

It was a bad start for 44. Everybody recognized it. Marget was troubled, and asked Gustav Fischer if he believed the boy was what these people were calling him. Fischer replied, with regret in his tone,

"Well, you know, Fräulein, he could have denied it, and he didn't do it."

"Yes, I know, but think what a good face he has. And pure, too; and beautiful."

"True, quite true. And it's astonishing. But there it is, you see—he didn't deny it. In fact he didn't even seem greatly interested in the matter."

"I know it. It is unaccountable. What do you make out of it?"

"The fact that he didn't see the gravity of the situation marks him for a fool. But it isn't the face of a fool. That he could be silent at such a time is constructive evidence that he is a Jail-Bird—with that face! which is impossible. I can't solve you that riddle, Fräulein—it's beyond my depth."

Forty-Four entered, straining under a heavy load of logs, which he dumped into a great locker and went briskly out again. He was quickly back with a similar load; and another, and still another.

"There," said the master, rising and starting away, "that will do; you are not required to kill yourself."

"One more—just one more," said the boy, as if asking a favor.

"Very well, but let that be the last," said the master, as if granting one; and he left the room.

Forty-Four brought the final load, then stood, apparently waiting for orders. None coming, he asked for them. It was Frau Stein's chance. She gave him a joyfully malicious glance out of her yellow eyes, and snapped out—

"Take the dog for an airing!"

Outraged, friend and foe alike rose at her! They surged forward to save the boy, but they were too late; he was already on his knees loosing the chain, his face and the dog's almost in contact. And now the people surged back to save themselves; but the boy rose and went, with the chain in his hand, and the dog trotted after him happy and content.

Chapter 4

DID it make a stir? Oh, on your life! For nearly two minutes the herd were speechless; and if I may judge by myself, they quaked, and felt pale; then they all broke out at once, and discussed it with animation and most of them said what an astonishing thing it was—and unbelievable, too, if they hadn't seen it with their own eyes. With Marget and Fischer and Barty the note was admiration. With Frau Stein, Maria, Katzenyammer and Binks it was wonder, but wonder mixed with maledictions—maledictions upon the devil that

possessed the Jail-Bird—they averring that no stranger unprotected by a familiar spirit could touch that dog and come
away but in fragments; and so, in their opinion the house was
in a much more serious plight, now, than it was before when
it only had a thief in it. Then there were three silent ones:
Ernest and Moses indicated by their cynical manner and
mocking smiles that they had but a small opinion of the exploit, it wasn't a matter to make such a fuss about; the other
silent one—the magician—was so massively silent, so weight-
ily silent, that it presently attracted attention. Then a light began to dawn upon some of the tribe; they turned reverent and
marveling eyes upon the great man, and Maria Vogel said
with the happy exultation of a discoverer—

"There he stands, and let him deny it if he can! He put
power upon that boy with his magic. I just suspected it, and
now I know it! Ah, you are caught, you can't escape—own
up, you wonder of the ages!"

The magician smiled a simpering smile, a detected and convicted smile, and several cried out—

"There, he *is* caught—he's trying to deny it, and he can't!
Come, be fair, be good, confess!" and Frau Stein and Maria
took hold of his great sleeves, peering worshipingly up in his
face and tried to detain him; but he gently disengaged himself
and fled from the room, apparently vastly embarrassed. So
that settled the matter. It was such a manifest confession that
not a doubter was left, every individual was convinced; and
the praises that that man got would have gone far to satisfy a
god. He was great before, he was held in awe before, but that
was as nothing to the towering repute to which he had soared
now. Frau Stein was in the clouds. She said that this was the
most astonishing exhibition of magic power Europe had ever
seen, and that the person who could doubt, after this, that he
could work any miracle he wanted to would justly take rank
as a fool. They all agreed that that was so, none denying it or
doubting; and Frau Stein, taking her departure with the other
ladies, declared that hereafter the magician should occupy her
end of the table and she would move to a humbler place at his
right, where she belonged.

All this was gall and vinegar to that jealous reptile Ernest
Wasserman, who could not endure to hear anybody praised,

and he began to cast about to turn the subject. Just then Fischer opened the way by remarking upon the Jail-Bird's
strength, as shown in the wood-carrying. He said he judged
that the Jail-Bird would be an ugly customer in a rough
stand-up fight with a youth of his own age.

"*Him!*" scoffed Ernest, "I'm of his age, and I'll bet I'd
make him sorry if he was to tackle me!"

This was Moses's chance. He said, with mock solicitude,

"Don't. Think of your mother. Don't make trouble with
him, he might hurt you badly."

"Never you mind worrying about me, Moses Haas. Let
him look out for himself if he meddles with me, that's all."

"Oh," said Moses, apparently relieved, "I was afraid you
were going to meddle with *him*. I see he is not in any danger." After a pause, "Nor you," he added carelessly.

The taunt had the intended effect.

"Do you think I'm afraid to meddle with him? I'm not
afraid of fifty of him. *I'll* show him!"

Forty-Four entered with the dog, and while he was chain-
ing him Ernest began to edge toward the door.

"Oh," simpered Moses, "good-bye, ta-ta, I thought you
were going to meddle with the Jail-Bird."

"What, to-day—and him all tired out and not at his best?
I'd be ashamed of myself."

"Haw-haw-haw!" guffawed that lumbering ox, Hans
Katzenyammer, "hear the noble-hearted poltroon!"

A whirlwind of derisive laughter and sarcastic remarks followed, and Ernest, stung to the quick, threw discretion to the
winds and marched upon the Jail-Bird, and planted himself in
front of him, crying out,

"Square off! Stand up like a man, and defend yourself."

"Defend myself?" said the boy, seeming not to understand.
"From what?"

"From me—do you hear?"

"From you? I have not injured you; why should you wish
to hurt me?"

The spectators were disgusted—and disappointed. Ernest's
courage came up with a bound. He said fiercely,

"Haven't you any sense? Don't you know anything? You've
got to fight me—do you understand that?"

"But I cannot fight you; I have nothing against you."

Ernest, mocking: "Afraid of *hurting* me, I suppose."

The Jail-Bird answered quite simply,

"No, there is no danger of that. I have nothing to hurt you for, and I shall not hurt you."

"Oh, thanks—how kind. Take that!"

But the blow did not arrive. The stranger caught both of Ernest's wrists and held them fast. Our apprentice tugged and struggled and perspired and swore, while the men stood around in a ring and laughed, and shouted, and made fun of Ernest and called him all sorts of outrageous pet names; and still the stranger held him in that grip, and did it quite easily and without puffing or blowing, whereas Ernest was gasping like a fish; and at last, when he was worn out and couldn't struggle any more, he snarled out,

"I give in—let go!" and 44 let go and said gently, "if you will let me I will stroke your arms for you and get the stiffness and the pain out;" but Ernest said "You go to hell," and went grumbling away and shaking his head and saying what he would do to the Jail-Bird one of these days, he needn't think it's over yet, he'd better look out or he'll find he's been fooling with the wrong customer; and so flourished out of the place and left the men jeering and yelling, and the Jail-Bird standing there looking as if it was all a puzzle to him and he couldn't make it out.

Chapter 5

THINGS were against that poor waif. He had maintained silence when he had had an opportunity to deny that he was a Jail-Bird, and that was bad for him. It got him that name, and he was likely to keep it. The men considered him a milksop because he spared Ernest Wasserman when it was evident that he could have whipped him. Privately my heart bled for the boy, and I wanted to be his friend, and longed to tell him so, but I had not the courage, for I was made as most people are made, and was afraid to follow my own instincts when they ran counter to other people's. The best of us would rather be popular than right. I found that out a good while ago. Katrina remained the boy's fearless friend, but she was alone in this. The master used him kindly, and protected him when he saw him ill treated, but further than this it was not in his nature to go except when he was roused, the current being so strong against him.

As to the clothes, Katrina kept her word. She sat up late, that very first night, and made him a coarse and cheap, but neat and serviceable doublet and hose with her own old hands; and she properly shod him, too. And she had her reward, for he was a graceful and beautiful creature, with the most wonderful eyes, and these facts all showed up, now, and filled her with pride. Daily he grew in her favor. Her old hungry heart was fed, she was a mother at last, with a child to love,—a child who returned her love in full measure, and to whom she was the salt of the earth.

As the days went along, everybody talked about 44, everybody observed him, everybody puzzled over him and his ways; but it was not discoverable that he ever concerned himself in the least degree about this or was in any way interested in what people thought of him or said about him. This indifference irritated the herd, but the boy did not seem aware of it.

The most ingenious and promising attempts to ruffle his temper and break up his calm went for nothing. Things flung at him struck him on the head or the back, and fell at his feet unnoticed; now and then a leg was shoved out and he tripped over it and went heavily down amid delighted laughter, but he picked himself up and went on without remark; often when he had brought a couple of twenty-pound cans of water up two long flights of stairs from the well in the court, they were seized and their winter-cold contents poured over him, but he went back unmurmuring for more; more than once, when the master was not present, Frau Stein made him share the dog's dinner in the corner, but he was content and offered no protest. The most of these persecutions were devised by Moses and Katzenyammer, but as a rule were carried out by that shabby poor coward, Ernest.

You see, now, how I was situated. I should have been despised if I had befriended him; and I should have been treated

as he was, too. It is not everybody that can be as brave as
Katrina was. More than once she caught Moses devising those
tricks and Ernest carrying them out, and gave both of them
an awful hiding; and once when Hans Katzenyammer inter-
fered she beat that big ruffian till he went on his knees and
begged.

What a devil to work the boy was! The earliest person up
found him at it by lantern-light, the latest person up found
him still at it long past midnight. It was the heaviest manual
labor, but if he was ever tired it was not perceptible. He always moved with energy, and seemed to find a high joy in
putting forth his strange and enduring strength.

He made reputation for the magician right along; no matter what unusual thing he did, the magician got the credit of
it; at first the magician was cautious, when accused, and contented himself with silences which rather confessed than denied the soft impeachment, but he soon felt safe to throw that
policy aside and frankly take the credit, and he did it. One day
44 unchained the dog and said "Now behave yourself, Felix,
and don't hurt any one," and turned him loose, to the consternation of the herd, but the magician sweetly smiled and
said,

"Do not fear. It is a little caprice of mine. My spirit is upon
him, he cannot hurt you."

They were filled with adoring wonder and admiration,
those people. They kissed the hem of the magician's robe,
and beamed unutterable things upon him. Then the boy said
to the dog,

"Go and thank your master for this great favor which he
has granted you."

Well, it was an astonishing thing that happened, then. That
ignorant and malignant vast animal, which had never been
taught language or manners or religion or any other valuable
thing, and could not be expected to understand a dandy
speech like that, went and stood straight up on its hind feet
before the magician, with its nose on a level with his face, and
curved its paws and ducked its head piously, and said

"Yap-yap!—yap-yap!—yap-yap!" most reverently, and just
as a Christian might at prayers.

Then it got down on all fours, and the boy said,

"Salute the master, and retire as from the presence of royalty."

The dog bowed very solemnly, then backed away stern-first to his corner—not with grace it is true, but well enough for a dog that hadn't had any practice of that kind and had never heard of royalty before nor its customs and etiquettes.

Did that episode take those people's breath away? You will not doubt it. They actually went on their knees to the magician, Frau Stein leading, the rest following. I know, for I was there and saw it. I was amazed at such degraded idolatry and hypocrisy—at least servility—but I knelt, too, to avert remark.

Life was become very interesting. Every few days there was a fresh novelty, some strange new thing done by the boy, something to wonder at; and so the magician's reputation was augmenting all the time. To be envied is the secret longing of pretty much all human beings—let us say *all*; to be envied makes them happy. The magician was happy, for never was a man so envied; he lived in the clouds.

I passionately longed to know 44, now. The truth is, he was being envied himself! Spite of all his shames and insults and persecutions. For, there is no denying it, it was an enviable conspicuousness and glory to be the instrument of such a dreaded and extraordinary magician as that and have people staring at you and holding their breath with awe while you did the miracles he devised. It is not for me to deny that I was one of 44's enviers. If I hadn't been, I should have been no natural boy. But I *was* a natural boy, and I longed to be conspicuous, and wondered at and talked about. Of course the case was the same with Ernest and Barty, though they did as I did—concealed it. I was always throwing myself in the magician's way whenever I could, in the hope that he would do miracles through me, too, but I could not get his attention. He never seemed to see me when he was preparing a prodigy.

At last I thought of a plan that I hoped might work. I would seek 44 privately and tell him how I was feeling and see if he would help me attain my desire. So I hunted up his room, and slipped up there clandestinely one night after the herd were in bed, and waited. After midnight an hour or two he came, and when the light of his lantern fell upon me he set it quickly down, and took me by both of my hands and beamed his gladness from his eyes, and there was no need to say a word.

Chapter 6

H E closed the door, and we sat down and began to talk, and he said it was good and generous of me to come and see him, and he hoped I would be his friend, for he was lonely and so wanted companionship. His words made me ashamed—so ashamed, and I felt so shabby and mean, that I almost had courage enough to come out and tell him how ignoble my errand was and how selfish. He smiled most kindly and winningly, and put out his hand and patted me on the knee, and said,

"Don't mind it."

I did not know what he was referring to, but the remark puzzled me, and so, in order not to let on, I thought I would throw out an observation—anything that came into my head; but nothing came but the weather, so I was dumb. He said,

"Do you care for it?"

"Care for what?"

"The weather."

I was puzzled again; in fact astonished; and said to myself "This is uncanny; I'm afraid of him."

He said cheerfully,

"Oh, you needn't be. Don't you be uneasy on my account."

I got up trembling, and said,

"I—I am not feeling well, and if you don't mind, I think I will excuse myself, and—"

"Oh, don't," he said, appealingly, "don't go. Stay with me a little. Let me do something to relieve you—I shall be so glad."

"You are so kind, so good," I said, "and I wish I could stay, but I will come another time. I—well, I—you see, it is cold, and I seem to have caught a little chill, and I think it will soon pass if I go down and cover up warm in bed—"

"Oh, a hot drink is a hundred times better, a hundred times!—that is what you really want. Now isn't it so?"

"Why yes; but in the circumstances—"

"Name it!" he said, all eager to help me. "Mulled claret, blazing hot—isn't that it?"

"Yes, indeed; but as we haven't any way to—"

"Here—take it as hot as you can bear it. You'll soon be all right."

He was holding a tumbler to me—fine, heavy cut-glass, and the steam was rising from it. I took it, and dropped into my chair again, for I was faint with fright, and the glass trembled in my hand. I drank. It was delicious; yes, and a surprise to my ignorant palate.

"Drink!" he said. "Go on—drain it. It will set you right, never fear. But this is unsociable; I'll drink with you."

A smoking glass was in his hand; I was not quick enough to see where it came from. Before my glass was empty he gave me a full one in its place and said heartily,

"Go right on, it will do you good. You are feeling better already, now aren't you?"

"Better?" said I to myself; "as to temperature, yes, but I'm scared to rags."

He laughed a pleasant little laugh and said,

"Oh, I give you my word there's no occasion for that. You couldn't be safer in my good old Mother Katrina's protection. Come, drink another."

I couldn't resist; it was nectar. I indulged myself. But I was miserably frightened and uneasy, and I couldn't stay; I didn't know what might happen next. So I said I must go. He wanted me to sleep in his bed, and said he didn't need it, he should be going to work pretty soon; but I shuddered at the idea, and got out of it by saying I should rest better in my own, because I was accustomed to it. So then he stepped outside the door with me, earnestly thanking me over and over again for coming to see him, and generously forbearing to notice how pale I was and how I was quaking; and he made me promise to come again the next night, I saying to myself that I should break that promise if I died for it. Then he said good-bye, with a most cordial shake of the hand, and I stepped feebly into the black gloom—and found myself in my own bed, with my door closed, my candle blinking on the table, and a welcome great fire flaming up the throat of the chimney!

It made me gasp! But no matter, I presently sank deliciously off to sleep, with that noble wine weltering in my head, and my last expiring effort at cerebration hit me with a cold shock:

"Did he *overhear* that thought when it passed through my mind—when I said I would break that promise if I died for it?"

Chapter 7

To my astonishment I got up thoroughly refreshed when called at sunrise. There was not a suggestion of wine or its effects in my head.

"It was all a dream," I said, gratefully. "I can get along without the mate to it."

By and by, on a stairway I met 44 coming up with a great load of wood, and he said, beseechingly,

"You *will* come again to-night, won't you?"

"Lord! I thought it was a dream," I said, startled.

"Oh, no, it was not a dream. I should be sorry, for it was a pleasant night for me, and I was *so* grateful."

There was something so pathetic in his way of saying it that a great pity rose up in me and I said impulsively,

"I'll come if I die for it!"

He looked as pleased as a child, and said,

"It's the same phrase, but I like it better this time." Then he said, with delicate consideration for me, "Treat me just as usual when others are around; it would injure you to befriend me in public, and I shall understand and not feel hurt."

"You are just lovely!" I said, "and I honor you, and would brave them all if I had been born with any spirit—which I wasn't."

He opened his big wondering eyes upon me and said,

"Why do you reproach yourself? You did not make yourself; how then are you to blame?"

How perfectly sane and sensible that was—yet I had never

thought of it before, nor had ever heard even the wisest of the professionally wise people say it—nor anything half so intelligent and unassailable, for that matter. It seemed an odd thing to get it from a boy, and he a vagabond landstreicher at that. At this juncture a proposition framed itself in my head, but I suppressed it, judging that there could be no impropriety in my acting upon it without permission if I chose. He gave me a bright glance and said,

"Ah, you couldn't if you tried!"

"Couldn't what?"

"Tell what happened last night."

"Couldn't I?"

"No. Because I don't wish it. What I don't wish, doesn't happen. I'm going to tell you various secrets by and by, one of these days. You'll keep them."

"I'm sure I'll try to."

"Oh, tell them if you think you *can*! Mind, I don't say you shan't, I only say you can't."

"Well, then, I shan't try."

Then Ernest came whistling gaily along, and when he saw 44 he cried out,

"Come, hump yourself with that wood, you lazy beggar!"

I opened my mouth to call him the hardest name in my stock, but nothing would come. I said to myself, jokingly, "Maybe it's because 44 disapproves."

Forty-Four looked back at me over his shoulder and said,

"Yes, that is it."

These things were dreadfully uncanny, but interesting. I went musing away, saying to myself, "he must have read my thoughts when I was minded to ask him if I might tell what happened last night." He called back from far up the stairs,

"I did!"

Breakfast was nearing a finish. The master had been silent all through it. There was something on his mind; all could see it. When he looked like that, it meant that he was putting the sections of an important and perhaps risky resolution together, and bracing up to pull it off and stand by it. Conversation had died out; everybody was curious, everybody was waiting for the outcome.

Forty-Four was putting a log on the fire. The master called him. The general curiosity rose higher still, now. The boy came and stood respectfully before the master, who said,

"Forty-Four, I have noticed—Forty-Four is correct, I believe?—"

The boy inclined his head and added gravely,

"New Series 864,962."

"We will not go into that," said the master with delicacy, "that is your affair and I conceive that into it charity forbids us to pry. I have noticed, as I was saying, that you are diligent and willing, and have borne a hard lot these several weeks with exemplary patience. There is much to your credit, nothing to your discredit."

The boy bent his head respectfully, the master glanced down the table, noted the displeasure along the line, then went on.

"You have earned friends, and it is not your fault that you haven't them. You haven't one in the castle, except Katrina. It is not fair. I am going to be your friend myself."

The boy's eyes glowed with happiness, Maria and her mother tossed their heads and sniffed, but there was no other applause. The master continued.

"You deserve promotion, and you shall have it. Here and now I raise you to the honorable rank of apprentice to the printer's art, which is the noblest and the most puissant of all arts, and destined in the ages to come to promote the others and preserve them."

And he rose and solemnly laid his hand upon the lad's shoulder like a king delivering the accolade. Every man jumped to his feet excited and affronted, to protest against this outrage, this admission of a pauper and tramp without name or family to the gate leading to the proud privileges and distinctions and immunities of their great order; but the master's temper was up, and he said he would turn adrift any man that opened his mouth; and he commanded them to sit down, and they obeyed, grumbling, and pretty nearly strangled with wrath. Then the master sat down himself, and began to question the new dignitary.

"This is one of the learned professions. Have you studied the Latin, Forty-Four?"

"No, sir."

Everybody laughed, but not aloud.

"The Greek?"

"No, sir."

Another clandestine laugh; and this same attention greeted all the answers, one after the other. But the boy did not blush, nor look confused or embarrassed; on the contrary he looked provokingly contented and happy and innocent. I was ashamed of him, and felt for him; and that showed me that I was liking him very deeply.

"The Hebrew?"

"No, sir."

"Any of the sciences?—the mathematics? astrology? astronomy? chemistry? medicine? geography?"

As each in turn was mentioned, the youth shook his untroubled head and answered "No, sir," and at the end said,

"None of them, sir."

The amusement of the herd was almost irrepressible by this time; and on his side the master's annoyance had risen very nearly to the bursting point. He put in a moment or two crowding it down, then asked,

"Have you ever studied *anything*?"

"No, sir," replied the boy, as innocently and idiotically as ever.

The master's project stood defeated all along the line! It was a critical moment. Everybody's mouth flew open to let go a triumphant shout; but the master, choking with rage, rose to the emergency, and it was his voice that got the innings:

"By the splendor of God I'll teach you myself!"

It was just grand! But it was a mistake. It was all I could do to keep from raising a hurrah for the generous old chief. But I held in. From the apprentices' table in the corner I could see every face, and I knew the master had made a mistake. I knew those men. They could stand a good deal, but the master had played the limit, as the saying is, and I knew it. He had struck at their order, the apple of their eye, their pride, the darling of their hearts, their dearest possession, their nobility—as they ranked it and regarded it—and had degraded it. They would not forgive that. They would seek revenge, and find it. This thing that we had witnessed, and which had

had the form and aspect of a comedy, was a tragedy. It was a turning point. There would be consequences. In ordinary cases where there was matter for contention and dispute, there had always been chatter and noise and jaw, and a general row; but now the faces were black and ugly, and not a word was said. It was an omen.

We three humble ones sat at our small table staring; and thinking thoughts. Barty looked pale and sick. Ernest searched my face with his evil eyes, and said,

"I caught you talking with the Jail-Bird on the stairs. You needn't try to lie out of it, I saw you."

All the blood seemed to sink out of my veins, and a cold terror crept through me. In my heart I cursed the luck that had brought upon me that exposure. What should I do? What could I do? What could I say in my defence? I could think of nothing; I had no words, I was dumb—and that creature's merciless eyes still boring into me. He said,

"Say—you are that animal's *friend*. Now deny it if you can."

I was in a bad scrape. He would tell the men, and I should be an outcast, and they would make my life a misery to me. I was afraid enough of the men, and wished there was a way out, but I saw there was none, and that if I did not want to complete my disaster I must pluck up some heart and not let this brute put me under his feet. I wasn't afraid of *him*, at any rate; even *my* timidity had its limitations. So I pulled myself together and said,

"It's a lie. I did talk with him, and I'll do it again if I want to, but that's no proof that I'm his friend."

"Oho, so you don't deny it! That's enough. I wouldn't be in your shoes for a good deal. When the men find it out you'll catch it, I can tell you that."

That distressed Barty, and he begged Ernest not to tell on me, and tried his best to persuade him; but it was of no use. He said he would tell if he died for it.

"Well, then," I said, "go ahead and do it; it's just like your sort, anyway. Who cares?"

"Oh, you don't care, don't you? Well, we'll see if you won't. And I'll tell them you're his friend, too."

If that should happen! The terror of it roused me up, and I said,

"Take that back, or I'll stick this dirk into you!"

He was badly scared, but pretended he wasn't, and laughed a sickly laugh and said he was only funning. That ended the discussion, for just then the master rose to go, and we had to rise, too, and look to our etiquette. I was sufficiently depressed and unhappy, for I knew there was sorrow in store for me. Still, there was one comfort: I should not be charged with being poor 44's friend, I hoped and believed; so matters were not quite so calamitous for me as they might have been.

We filed up to the printing rooms in the usual order of precedence, I following after the last man, Ernest following after me, and Barty after him. Then came 44.

Forty-Four would have to do his studying after hours. During hours he would now fill Barty's former place and put in a good deal of his time in drudgery and dirty work; and snatch such chances as he could, in the intervals, to learn the first steps of the divine art—composition, distribution and the like.

Certain ceremonies were Forty-Four's due when as an accredited apprentice he crossed the printing-shop's threshold for the first time. He should have been invested with a dagger, for he was now privileged to bear minor arms—foretaste and reminder of the future still prouder day when as a journeyman he would take the rank of a gentleman and be entitled to wear a sword. And a red chevron should have been placed upon his left sleeve to certify to the world his honorable new dignity of printer's apprentice. These courtesies were denied him, and omitted. He entered unaccosted and unwelcomed.

The youngest apprentice should now have taken him in charge and begun to instruct him in the rudimentary duties of his position. Honest little Barty was commencing this service, but Katzenyammer the foreman stopped him, and said roughly,

"Get to your case!"

So 44 was left standing alone in the middle of the place. He looked about him wistfully, mutely appealing to all faces but mine, but no one noticed him, no one glanced in his direction, or seemed aware that he was there. In the corner old Binks was bowed over a proof-slip; Katzenyammer was bending over the imposing-stone making up a form; Ernest, with ink-ball and coarse brush was proving a galley; I was overrunning a page of Haas's to correct an out; Fischer, with pastepot and brown linen, was new-covering the tympan; Moses was setting type, pulling down his guide for every line, weaving right and left, bobbing over his case with every type he picked up, fetching the box-partition a wipe with it as he brought it away, making two false motions before he put it in the stick and a third one with a click on his rule, justifying like a rail fence, spacing like an old witch's teeth—hair-spaces and m-quads turn about—just a living allegory of falseness and pretence from his green silk eye-shade down to his lifting and sinking heels, making show and bustle enough for 3,000 an hour, yet never good for 600 on a fat take and double-leaded at that. It was inscrutable that God would endure a comp like that, and lightning so cheap.

It was pitiful to see that friendless boy standing there forlorn in that hostile stillness. I did wish somebody would relent and say a kind word and tell him something to do. But it could not happen; they were all waiting to see trouble come to him, all expecting it, all tremulously alert for it, all knowing it was preparing for him, and wondering whence it would come, and in what form, and who would invent the occasion. Presently they knew. Katzenyammer had placed his pages, separated them with reglets, removed the strings from around them, arranged his bearers; the chase was on, the sheep-foot was in his hand, he was ready to lock up. He slowly turned his head and fixed an inquiring scowl upon the boy. He stood so, several seconds, then he stormed out,

"Well, are you going to fetch me some quoins, or *not*?"

Cruel! How could *he* know what the strange word meant? He begged for the needed information with his eloquent eyes—the men were watching and exulting—Katzenyammer began to move toward him with his big hand spread for cuffing—ah, my God, I mustn't venture to speak, was there no way to save him? Then I had a lightning thought; would he gather it from my brain?—"*Forty-Four, that's the quoin-box, under the stone table!*"

In an instant he had it out and on the imposing-stone! He was saved. Katzenyammer and everybody looked amazed. And deeply disappointed.

For a while Katzenyammer seemed to be puzzling over it and trying to understand it; then he turned slowly to his work and selected some quoins and drove them home. The form was ready. He set that inquiring gaze upon the boy again. Forty-Four was watching with all his eyes, but it wasn't any use; how was he to guess what was wanted of him? Katzenyammer's face began to work, and he spat dry a couple of times, spitefully; then he shouted,

"Am *I* to do it—or *who?*"

I was ready this time. I said to myself, "Forty-Four, raise it carefully on its edge, get it under your right arm, carry it to that machine yonder, which is the press, and lay it gently down flat on that stone, which is called the bed of the press."

He went tranquilly to work, and did the whole thing as right as nails—did it like an old hand! It was just astonishing. There wasn't another untaught and unpractised person in all Europe who could have carried that great and delicate feat half-way through without piing the form. I was so carried away that I wanted to shout. But I held in.

Of course the thing happened, now, that was to be expected. The men took Forty-Four for an old apprentice, a refugee flying from a hard master. They could not ask him, as to that, custom prohibiting it; but they could ask him other questions which could be awkward. They could be depended upon to do that. The men all left their work and gathered around him, and their ugly looks promised trouble. They looked him over silently—arranging their game, no doubt— he standing in the midst, waiting, with his eyes cast down. I was dreadfully sorry for him. I knew what was coming, and I saw no possibility of his getting out of the hole he was in. The very first question would be unanswerable, and quite out of range of help from me. Presently that sneering Moses Haas asked it:

"So you are an experienced apprentice to this art, and yet don't know the Latin!"

There it was! I knew it. But—oh, well, the boy was just an ever-fresh and competent mystery! He raised his innocent eyes and placidly replied,

"Who—I? Why yes, I know it."

They gazed at him puzzled—stupefied, as you might say. Then Katzenyammer said,

"Then what did you tell the master that lie for?"

"I? I didn't know I told him a lie; I didn't mean to."

"Didn't mean to? Idiot! he asked you if you knew the Latin, and you said no."

"Oh, no," said the youth, earnestly, "it was quite different. He asked me if I had *studied* it—meaning in a school or with a teacher, as I judged. Of course I said no, for I had only picked it up—from books—by myself."

"Well, upon my soul, you *are* a purist, when it comes to cast-iron exactness of statement," said Katzenyammer, exasperated. "Nobody knows how to take you or what to make of you; every time a person puts his finger on you you're not there. Can't you do *anything* but the unexpected? If you belonged to me, damned if I wouldn't drown you."

"Look here, my boy," said Fischer, not unkindly, "do you know—as required—the rudiments of all those things the master asked you about?"

"Yes, sir."

"Picked them up?"

"Yes, sir."

I wished he hadn't made that confession. Moses saw a chance straightway:

"Honest people don't get into this profession on picked-up culture; they don't get in on odds and ends, they have to *know* the initial stages of the sciences and things. You sneaked in without an examination, but you'll pass one now, or out you go."

It was a lucky idea, and they all applauded. I felt more comfortable, now, for if he could take the answers from my head I could send him through safe. Adam Binks was appointed inquisitor, but I soon saw that 44 had no use for me. He was away up. I would have shown off if I had been in his place and equipped as he was. But he didn't. In knowledge Binks was a child to him—that was soon apparent. He wasn't competent to examine 44; 44 took him out of his depth on every language and art and science, and if erudition had been water he would have been drowned. The men had to laugh, they couldn't help it; and if they had been manly men they would have softened toward their prey, but they weren't and they didn't. Their laughter made Binks ridiculous, and he lost his temper; but instead of venting it on the laughters he let drive at the boy, the shameless creature, and would have felled him if Fischer hadn't caught his arm. Fischer got no thanks for that, and the men would have resented his interference, only it was not quite safe and they didn't want to drive him from their clique, anyway. They could see that he was at best only lukewarm on their side, and they didn't want to cool his temperature any more.

The examination-scheme was a bad failure—a regular collapse, in fact,—and the men hated the boy for being the cause of it, whereas they had brought it upon themselves. That is just like human beings. The foreman spoke up sharply, now, and told them to get to work; and said that if they fooled away any more of the shop's time he would dock them. Then he ordered 44 to stop idling around and get about his business. No one watched 44 now; they all thought he knew his duties, and where to begin. But it was plain to me that he didn't; so I prompted him out of my mind, and couldn't keep my attention on my work, it was so interesting and so wonderful to see him perform.

Under my unspoken instructions he picked up all the good type and broken type from about the men's feet and put the one sort in the pi pile and the other in the hell-box; turpentined the inking-balls and cleaned them; started up the lyehopper; washed a form in the sink, and did it well; removed last week's stiff black towel from the roller and put a clean one in its place; made paste; dusted out several cases with a bellows; made glue for the bindery; oiled the platen-springs and the countersunk rails of the press; put on a paper apron and inked the form while Katzenyammer worked off a token of signature 16 of a Latin Bible, and came out of the job as black as a chimney-sweep from hair to heels; set up pi; struck galley-proofs; tied up dead matter like an artist, and set it away on the standing galley without an accident; brought the

quads when the men jeff'd for takes, and restored them
whence they came when the lucky comps were done chuckling over their fat and the others done damning their lean;
and would have gone innocently to the village saddler's after
strap-oil and *got* it—on his rear—if it had occurred to the
men to start him on the errand—a thing they didn't think of,
they supposing he knew that sell by memorable experience;
and so they lost the best chance they had in the whole day to
expose him as an impostor who had never seen a printing-
outfit before.

A marvelous creature; and he went through without a
break; but by consequence of my having to watch over him so
persistently I set a proof that had the smallpox, and the foreman made me distribute his case for him after hours as a "lesson" to me. He was not a stingy man with that kind of
tuition.

I had saved 44, unsuspected and without damage or danger
to myself, and it made me lean toward him more than ever.
That was natural.

Then, when the day was finished, and the men were washing up and I was feeling good and fine and proud, Ernest
Wasserman came out and told on me!

Chapter 8

I SLIPPED out and fled. It was wise, for in this way I escaped
the first heat of their passion, or I should have gotten not
merely insults but kicks and cuffs added. I hid deep down and
far away, in an unvisited part of the castle among a maze of
dark passages and corridors. Of course I had no thought of
keeping my promise to visit 44; but in the circumstances he
would not expect it—I knew that. I had to lose my supper,
and that was hard lines for a growing lad. And I was like to
freeze, too, in that damp and frosty place. Of sleep little was
to be had, because of the cold and the rats and the ghosts.
Not that I saw any ghosts, but I was expecting them all the
time, and quite naturally, too, for that historic old ruin was
lousy with them, so to speak, for it had had a tough career

through all the centuries of its youth and manhood—a career
filled with romance and sodden with crime—and it is my experience that between the misery of watching and listening
for ghosts and the fright of seeing them there is not much
choice. In truth I was not sorry sleep was chary, for I did not
wish to sleep. I was in trouble, and more was preparing for
me, and I wanted to pray for help, for therein lay my best
hope and my surest. I had moments of sleep now and then,
being a young creature and full of warm blood, but in the
long intervals I prayed persistently and fervently and sincerely.
But I knew I needed more powerful prayers than my own—
prayers of the pure and the holy—prayers of the consecrated—prayers certain to be heard, whereas mine might not
be. I wanted the prayers of the Sisters of Perpetual Adoration.
They could be had for 50 silver groschen. In time of threatened and imminent trouble, trouble which promised to be
continuous, one valued their championship far above that of
any priest, for his prayers would ascend at regularly appointed
times only, with nothing to protect you in the exposed intervals between, but theirs were perpetual—hence their name—
there were no intervals, night or day: when two of the Sisters
rose from before the altar two others knelt at once in their
place and the supplications went on unbroken. Their convent
was on the other side of the river, beyond the village, but Katrina would get the money to them for me. They would take
special pains for any of us in the castle, too, for our Prince had
been doing them a valuable favor lately, to appease God on
account of a murder he had done on an elder brother of his,
a great Prince in Bohemia and head of the house. He had repaired and renovated and sumptuously fitted up the ancient
chapel of our castle, to be used by them while their convent,
which had been struck by lightning again and much damaged, was undergoing reparations. They would be coming
over for Sunday, and the usual service would be greatly aug-
mented, in fact doubled: the Sacred Host would be exposed
in the monstrance, and four Sisters instead of two would hold
the hours of adoration; yet if you sent your 50 groschen in
time you would be entitled to the advantage of this, which is
getting in on the ground floor, as the saying is.

Our Prince not only did for them what I have mentioned,

but was paying for one-third of those repairs on their convent besides. Hence we were in great favor. That dear and honest old Father Peter would conduct the service for them. Father Adolf was not willing, for there was no money in it for the priest, the money all going to the support of a little house of homeless orphans whom the good Sisters took care of.

At last the rats stopped scampering over me, and I knew the long night was about at an end; so I groped my way out of my refuge. When I reached Katrina's kitchen she was at work by candle-light, and when she heard my tale she was full of pity for me and maledictions for Ernest, and promised him a piece of her mind, with foot-notes and illustrations; and she bustled around and hurried up a hot breakfast for me, and sat down and talked and gossiped, and enjoyed my voracity, as a good cook naturally would, and indeed I was fairly famished. And it was good to hear her rage at those rascals for persecuting her boy, and scoff at them for that they couldn't produce one individual manly enough to stand up for him and the master. And she burst out and said she wished to God Doangivadam was here, and I just jumped up and flung my arms around her old neck and hugged her for the thought! Then she went gently down on her knees before the little shrine of the Blessed Virgin, I doing the same of course, and she prayed for help for us all out of her fervent and faithful heart, and rose up refreshed and strengthened and gave our enemies as red-hot and competent a damning as ever came by natural gift from uncultured lips in my experience.

The dawn was breaking, now, and I told her my project concerning the Sisters of the Perpetual Adoration, and she praised me and blest me for my piety and right-heartedness, and said she would send the money for me and have it arranged. I had to ask would she lend me two groschen, for my savings lacked that much of being fifty, and she said promptly—

"Will I? and you in this trouble for being good to my boy? That I will; and I'd do it if it was five you wanted!"

And the tears came in her eyes and she gave me a hug; then I hasted to my room and shut the door and locked it, and fished my hoard out of its hiding-place and counted the coins, and there were *fifty*. I couldn't understand it. I counted them again—twice; but there was no error, there were two there that didn't belong. So I didn't have to go into debt, after all. I gave the money to Katrina and told her the marvel, and she counted it herself and was astonished, and couldn't understand it any more than I could. Then came sudden comprehension! and she sank down on her knees before the shrine and poured out her thanks to the Blessed Virgin for this swift and miraculous answer.

She rose up the proudest woman in all that region; and she was justified in feeling so. She said—and tried to say it humbly—

"To think She would do it for me, a poor lowly servant, dust of the earth: There's crowned monarchs She wouldn't do it for!" and her eyes blazed up in spite of her.

It was all over the castle in an hour, and wheresoever she went, there they made reverence and gave her honor as she passed by.

It was a bad day that had dawned for 44 and me, this wretched Tuesday. The men were sour and ugly. They snarled at me whenever they could find so much as half an occasion, they sneered at me and made jokes about me; and when Katzenyammer wittily called me by an unprintable name they shouted with laughter, and sawed their boxes with their composing-rules, which is a comp's way of expressing sarcastic applause. The laughter was praise of the foreman's wit, the sarcasm was for me. You must choose your man when you saw your box; not every man will put up with it. It is the most capable and eloquent expression of derision that human beings have ever invented. It is an urgent and strenuous and hideous sound, and when an expert makes it it shrieks out like the braying of a jackass. I have seen a comp draw his sword for that. As for that name the foreman gave me, it stung me and embittered me more than any of the other hurts and humiliations that were put upon me; and I was girl-boy enough to cry about it, which delighted the men beyond belief, and they rubbed their hands and shrieked with delight. Yet there was no point in that name when applied to a person of my shape, therefore it was entirely witless. It was the slang name (imported from England), used by printers to describe a certain kind of type. All types taper slightly, and are narrower at the letter than at the base of the shank; but in some fonts this spread is so pronounced that you can almost detect it with the eye, loose and exaggerative talkers asserting that it was exactly the taper of a leather bottle. Hence that odious name: and now they had fastened it upon me. If I knew anything about printers, it would stick. Within the hour they had added it to my slug! Think of that. Added it to my number, by initials, and there you could read it in the list above the take-file: *"Slug 4, B.-A."* It may seem a small thing; but I can tell you that not all seemingly small things are small to a boy. That one shamed me as few things have done since.

The men were persistently hard on poor unmurmuring 44. Every time he had to turn his back and cross the room they rained quoins and 3·m quads after him, which struck his head and bounded off in a kind of fountain-shower. Whenever he was bending down at any kind of work that required that attitude, the nearest man would hit him a blistering whack on his southern elevation with the flat of a galley, and then apologise and say,

"Oh, was it you? I'm sorry; I thought it was the master."

Then they would all shriek again.

And so on and so on. They insulted and afflicted him in every way they could think of—and did it far more for the master's sake than for his own. It was their purpose to provoke a retort out of 44, then they would thrash him. But they failed, and considered the day lost.

Wednesday they came loaded with new inventions, and expected to have better luck. They crept behind him and slipped cakes of ice down his back; they started a fire under the sink, and when he discovered it and ran to put it out they swarmed there in artificial excitement with buckets of water and emptied them on him instead of on the fire, and abused him for getting in the way and defeating their efforts; while he was inking for Katzenyammer, this creature continually tried to catch him on the head with the frisket before he could get out of the way, and at last fetched it down so prematurely that it failed to get home, but struck the bearers and got itself bent like a bow—and he got a cursing for it, as if it had been his fault.

They led him a dog's life all the forenoon—but they failed

again. In the afternoon they gave him a Latin Bible-take that took him till evening to set up; and after he had proved it and was carrying away the galley, Moses tripped him and he fell sprawling, galley and all. The foreman raged and fumed over his clumsiness, putting all the blame on him and none on Moses, and finished with a peculiarly mean piece of cruelty: ordering him to come back after supper and set up the take again, by candle-light, if it took him all night.

This was a little too much for Fischer's stomach, and he began to remonstrate; but Katzenyammer told him to mind his own business; and the others moved up with threatenings in their eyes, and so Fischer had to stand down and close his mouth. He had occasion to be sorry he had tried to do the boy a kindness, for it gave the foreman an excuse to double-up the punishment. He turned on Fischer and said,

"You think you've got some influence here, don't you? I'll give you a little lesson that'll teach you that the best way for you to get this Jail-Bird into trouble is to come meddling around here trying to get him out of it."

Then he told 44 he must set up the pi'd matter and distribute it before he began on the take!

An all-night job!—and that poor friendless creature hadn't done a thing to deserve it. Did the master know of these outrages? Yes, and was privately boiling over them; but he had to swallow his wrath, and not let on. The men had him in their power, and knew it. He was under heavy bonds to finish a formidable piece of work for the University of Prague—it was almost done, a few days more would finish it, to fall short of completion would mean ruin. He must see nothing, hear nothing, of these wickednesses: if his men should strike—and they only wanted an excuse and were playing for it—where would he get others? Venice? Frankfort? Paris? London? Why, these places were weeks away!

The men went to bed exultant that Wednesday night, and I sore-hearted.

But lord, how premature we were: the boy's little job was all right in the morning! Ah, he *was* the most astonishing creature!

Then the disaster fell: the men gave it up and struck! The poor master, when he heard the news, staggered to his bed, worn out with worry and wounded pride and despair, to toss there in fever and delirium and gabble distressful incoherencies to his grieving nurses, Marget and Katrina. The men struck in the forenoon of Thursday, and sent the master word. Then they discussed and discussed—trying to frame their grounds. Finally the document was ready, and they sent it to the master. He was in no condition to read it, and Marget laid it away. It was very simple and direct. It said that the Jail-Bird was a trial to them, and an unendurable aggravation; and that they would not go back to work again until he was sent away.

They knew the master couldn't send the lad away. It would break his sword and degrade him from his guild, for he could prove no offence against the apprentice. If he did not send 44 away work would stand still, he would fail to complete his costly printing-contract and be ruined.

So the men were happy; the master was their meat, as they expressed it, no matter which move he made, and he had but the two.

Chapter 9

IT was a black and mournful time, that Friday morning that the works stood idle for the first time in their history. There was no hope. As usual the men went over to early mass in the village, like the rest of us, but they did not come back for breakfast—naturally. They came an hour later, and idled about and put in the dull time the best they could, with dreary chat, and gossip, and prophecies, and cards. They were holding the fort, you see; a quite unnecessary service, since there was none to take it. It would not have been safe for any one to set a type there.

No, there was no hope. By and by Katrina was passing by a group of the strikers, when Moses, observing the sadness in her face, could not forbear a gibe:

"I wouldn't look so disconsolate, Katrina, prayer can pull off anything, you know. Toss up a hint to your friend the Virgin."

You would have thought, by the sudden and happy change

in her aspect, that he had uttered something very much pleasanter than a coarse blasphemy. She retorted,

"Thanky, dog, for the idea. I'll do it!" and she picked up
her feet and moved off briskly.

I followed her, for that remark had given me an idea, too.
It was this: to cheer up, on our side, and stop despairing and
get down to work—bring to our help every supernatural force
that could be had for love or money: the Blessed Mother,
Balthasar the magician, and the Sisters of the Perpetual Adoration. It was a splendid inspiration, and she was astonished at
my smartness in thinking of it. She was electrified with hope
and she praised me till I blushed; and indeed I was worthy of
some praise, on another count: for I told her to withdraw my
former "intention," (you have to name your desire—called
"intention"—when you apply to the P. A.,) and tell the Sisters
not to pray for my relief, but leave me quite out and throw all
their strength into praying that Doangivadam might come to
the master's rescue—an exhibition of self-sacrifice on my part
which Katrina said was noble and beautiful and God would
remember it and requite it to me; and indeed I had thought
of that already, for it would be but right and customary.

At my suggestion she said she would get 44 to implore his
overlord the magician to exert his dread powers in the master's favor. So now our spirits had a great uplift; our clouds
began to pass, and the sun to shine for us again. Nothing
could be more judicious than the arrangement we had arrived at; by it we were pooling our stock, not scattering it;
by it we had our money on three cards instead of one, and
stood to win on one turn or another. Katrina said she would
have all these great forces at work within the hour, and keep
them at it without intermission until the winner's flag went
up.

I went from Katrina's presence walking on air, as the saying
is. Privately I was afraid we had one card that was doubtful—
the magician. I was entirely certain that he could bring victory to our flag if he chose, but would he choose? He
probably would if Maria and her mother asked him, but who
was to ask them to ask him? Katrina? They would not want
the master ruined, since that would be their own ruin; but
they were in the dark, by persuasion of the strikers, who had

made them believe that no one's ruin was really going to
result except 44's. As for 44 having any influence with his
mighty master, I did not take much stock in that; one might
as well expect a poor lackey to have the ear and favor of a sov-
ereign.

I expected a good deal of Katrina's card, and as to my own
I hadn't the least doubt. It would fetch Doangivadam, let him
be where he might; of that I felt quite sure. What he might
be able to accomplish when he arrived—well, that was another matter. One thing could be depended upon, anyway—
he would take the side of the under dog in the fight, be that
dog in the right or in the wrong, and what man could do he
would do—and up to the limit, too.

He was a wandering comp. Nobody knew his name, it had
long ago sunk into oblivion under that nickname, which described him to a dot. Hamper him as you might, obstruct
him as you might, make things as desperate for him as you
pleased, he didn't give a damn, and said so. He was always
gay and breezy and cheerful, always kind and good and generous and friendly and careless and wasteful, and couldn't
keep a copper, and never tried. But let his fortune be up or
down you never could catch him other than handsomely
dressed, for he was a dandy from the cradle, and a flirt. He
was a beauty, trim and graceful as Satan, and was a born
masher and knew it. He was not afraid of anything or anybody, and was a fighter by instinct and partiality. All printers
were pretty good swordsmen, but he was a past master in the
art, and as agile as a cat and as quick. He was very learned,
and could have occupied with credit the sanctum sanctorum,
as the den of a book-editor was called, in the irreverent slang
of the profession. He had a baritone voice of great power and
richness, he had a scientific knowledge of music, was a capable player upon instruments, was possessed of a wide knowledge of the arts in general, and could swear in nine languages.
He was a good son of the Church, faithful to his religious duties, and the most pleasant and companionable friend and
comrade a person could have.

But you never could get him to stay in a place, he was always wandering, always drifting about Europe. If ever there

was a perpetual sub, he was the one. He could have had a case anywhere for the asking, but if he had ever had one, the fact had passed from the memory of man. He was sure to turn up with us several times a year, and the same in Frankfort, Venice, Paris, London, and so on, but he was as sure to flit again after a week or two or three—that is to say, as soon as he had earned enough to give the boys a rouse and have enough left over to carry him to the next front-stoop on his milk-route, as the saying is.

Here we were, standing still, and so much to do! So much to do, and so little time to do it in: it must be finished by next Monday; those commissioners from Prague would arrive then, and demand their two hundred Bibles—the sheets, that is, we were not to bind them. Half of our force had been drudging away on that great job for eight months; 30,000 ems would finish the composition; but for our trouble, we could turn on our whole strength and do it in a day of 14 hours, then print the final couple of signatures in a couple of hours more and be far within contract-time—and here we were, idle, and ruin coming on!

All Friday and Saturday I stumped nervously back and forth between the Owl Tower and the kitchen—watching from the one, in hope of seeing Doangivadam come climbing up the winding road; seeking Katrina in the other for consultation and news. But when night shut down, Saturday, nothing definite had happened, uncertainty was still our portion, and we did not know where we were at, as the saying is. The magician had treated 44 to an exceedingly prompt snub and closed out his usefulness as an ambassador; then Katrina had scared Maria and her mother into a realization of their danger and they had tried *their* hands with Balthasar. He was very gracious, very sympathetic, quite willing to oblige, but pretty non-committal. He said that these printers were not the originators of this trouble, and were acting in opposition to their own volition; they were only unwitting tools—tools of three of the most malignant and powerful demons in hell, demons whom he named, and whom he had battled with once before, overcoming them, but at cost of his life almost. They were not conspiring against the master, that was only a blind—he, the magician, was the prey they were after, and he could not as yet foresee how the struggle would come out; but he was consulting the stars, and should do his best. He believed that three other strong demons were in the conspiracy, and he was working spells to find out as to this; if it should turn out to be so, he should have to command the presence and aid of the very Prince of Darkness himself! The result would necessarily be terrible, for many innocent persons would be frightened to death by his thunders and lightnings and his awful aspect; still, if the ladies desired it—

But the ladies didn't! nor any one else, for that matter. So there it stood. If the three extra fiends didn't join the game, we might expect Balthasar to go in and win it and make everything comfortable again for the master; but if they joined, the game was blocked, of course, since no one was willing to have Lucifer go to the bat. It was a momentous uncertainty; there was nothing for it but to wait and see what those extras would elect to do.

Meantime Balthasar was doing his possible—we could see that. He was working his incantations right along, and sprinkling powders, and lizards, and newts, and human fat, and all sorts of puissant things into his caldron, and enveloping himself in clouds of smoke and raising a composite stink that made the castle next to unendurable, and could be smelt in heaven.

I clung to my hope, and stuck to the Owl Tower till night closed down and veiled the road and the valley in a silvery mist of moonlight, but Doangivadam did not come, and my heart was very heavy.

But in the morrow was promise; the service in our chapel would have double strength, because four Sisters would be on duty before the altar, whereas two was the custom. That thought lifted my hope again.

Apparently all times are meet for love, sad ones as well as bright and cheerful ones. Down on the castle roof I could see two couples doing overtime—Fischer and Marget, and Moses and Maria. I did not care for Maria, but if I had been older, and Fischer had wanted to put on a sub—but it was long ago, long ago, and such things do not interest me now. She was a beautiful girl, Marget.

Chapter 10

IT was a lovely Sunday, calm and peaceful and holy, and bright with sunshine. It seemed strange that there could be jarrings and enmities in so beautiful a world. As the forenoon advanced the household began to appear, one after another, and all in their best; the women in their comeliest gowns, the men in velvets and laces, with snug-fitting hose that gave the tendons and muscles of their legs a chance to show their quality. The master and his sister were brought to the chapel on couches, that they might have the benefit of the prayers—he pale and drowsing and not yet really at himself; then the rest of us (except 44 and the magician) followed and took our places. It was not a proper place for sorcerers and their tools. The villagers had come over, and the seats were full.

The chapel was fine and sumptuous in its new paint and gilding; and there was the organ, in full view, an invention of recent date, and hardly any in the congregation had ever seen one before. Presently it began to softly rumble and moan, and the people held their breath for wonder at the adorable sounds, and their faces were alight with ecstasy. And I—I had never heard anything so plaintive, so sweet, so charged with the deep and consoling spirit of religion. And oh, so dreamily it moaned, and wept, and sighed and sang, on and on, gently rising, gently falling, fading and fainting, retreating to dim distances and reviving and returning, healing our hurts, soothing our griefs, steeping us deeper and deeper in its unutterable peace—then suddenly it burst into breath-taking rich thunders of triumph and rejoicing, and the consecrated ones came filing in! You will believe that all worldly thoughts, all ungentle thoughts, were gone from that place, now; you will believe that these uplifted and yearning souls were as a garden thirsting for the fructifying dew of truth, and prepared to receive it and hold it precious and give it husbandry.

Father Peter's face seemed to deliver hope and blessing and grace upon us just by the benignity and love that was in it and beaming from it. It was good to look at him, that true man. He described to us the origin of the Perpetual Adoration, which was a seed planted in the heart of the Blessed Margaret

Alacoque by Our Lord himself, that time he complained to her of the neglect of his worship by the people, after all he had done for men. And Father Peter said,

"The aim of the Perpetual Adoration is to give joy to Our Lord, and to make at least some compensation by its atonement for the ingratitude of mankind. It keeps guard day and night before the Most Holy, to render to the forgotten and unknown Eucharistic God acts of praise and thanksgiving, of adoration and reparation. It is not deterred by the summer's heat nor the winter's cold. It knows no rest, no ceasing, night or day. What a sublime vocation! After the sacerdotal dignity, one more sublime can hardly be imagined. A priestly virgin should the adorer be, who raises her spotless hands and pure heart in supplication toward heaven imploring mercy, who continually prays for the welfare of her fellow creatures, and in particular for those who have recommended themselves to her prayers."

Father Peter spoke of the blessings both material and spiritual that would descend upon all who gave of their substance toward the repairing of the convent of the Sisters of the Adoration and its new chapel, and said,

"In our new chapel the Blessed Sacrament will be solemnly exposed for adoration during the greater part of the year. It is our hearts' desire to erect for Our Lord and Savior a beautiful altar, to place Him on a magnificent throne, to surround Him with splendor and a sea of light; for," continued he, "Our Lord said again to his servant Margaret Alacoque: 'I have a burning thirst to be honored by men, in the Blessed Sacrament—I wish to be treated as king in a royal palace.' You have therefore His own warrant and word: it is Our Lord's desire to dwell in a royal palace and to be treated as a king."

Many among us, recognizing the reasonableness of this ambition, rose and went forward and contributed money, and I would have done likewise, and gladly, but I had already given all I possessed. Continuing, Father Peter said, referring to testimonies of the supernatural origin and manifold endorsements of the Adoration,

"Miracles not contained in Holy Scripture are not articles of faith, and are only to be believed when proved by trustworthy witnesses."

"But," he added, "God permits such miracles from time to time, in order to strengthen our faith or to convert sinners." Then most earnestly he warned us to be on our guard against accepting miracles, or what seemed to be miracles, upon our own judgment and without the educated and penetrating help of a priest or a bishop. He said that an occurrence could be extraordinary without necessarily being miraculous; that indeed a true miracle was usually not merely extraordinary, it was also a thing likely to happen. Likely, for the reason that it happened in circumstances where it manifestly had a service to perform—circumstances which showed that it was not idly sent, but for a solemn and sufficient purpose. He illustrated this with several most interesting instances where both the likelihood of the events and their unusual nature were strikingly perceptible; and not to cultured perceptions alone perhaps, but possibly to even untrained intelligences. One of these he called "The miracle of Turin," and this he told in these words:

"In the year 1453 a church in Isiglo was robbed and among other things a precious monstrance was stolen which still contained the Sacred Host. The monstrance was put in a large sack and a beast of burden carried the booty of the robbers. On the 6th of June the thieves were passing through the streets of Turin with their spoil, when suddenly the animal became furious and no matter how much it was beaten could not be forced from the spot. At once the cords with which the burden was fastened to the ass's back broke, the sack opened of itself, the monstrance appeared, rose on high, and miraculously remained standing in the air to the astonishment of the many spectators. The news of this wonderful event was quickly spread through the city. Bishop Louis appeared with the chapter of his cathedral and the clergy of the city. But behold, a new prodigy! The Sacred Host leaves the case in which it was enclosed, the monstrance lowers itself to the ground, but the Sacred Host remains immovable and majestic in the air, shining like the sun and sending forth in all directions rays of dazzling splendor. The astonished multitude loudly expressed its joy and admiration, and prostrated itself weeping and adoring before the divine Savior, who displayed His glory here in such a visible manner. The bishop too on his knees implored our Lord to descend into the chalice which he raised up to Him. Thereupon the Sacred Host slowly descended and was carried to the church of St. John amid the inexpressible exultation of the people. The city of Turin had a grand basilica built on the spot where the miracle took place."

He observed that here we had two unchallengeable testimonies to the genuineness of the miracle: that of the bishop, who would not deceive, and that of the ass, who could not. Many in the congregation who had thitherto been able to restrain themselves, now went forward and contributed. Continuing, Father Peter said,

"But now let us hear how our dear Lord, in order to call His people to repentance, once showed something of His majesty in the city of Marseilles, in France. It was A.D. 1218 that the Blessed Sacrament was exposed for adoration in the convent church of the Cordeliers for the forty hours devotion. Many devout persons were assisting at the divine service, when suddenly the sacramental species disappeared and the people beheld the King of Glory in person. His countenance shone with brightness, His look was at once severe and mild, so that no one could bear His gaze. The faithful were motionless with fear, for they soon comprehended what this august apparition meant. Bishop Belsune had more than sixty persons witness to this fact, upon oath."

Yet notwithstanding this the people continued in sin, and had to be again admonished. As Father Peter pointed out:

"At the same time it was revealed to two saintly persons that our Lord would soon visit the city with a terrible punishment if it would not be converted. After two years a pestilence really came and carried off a great part of the inhabitants."

Father Peter told how, two centuries before, in France, Beelzebub and another devil had occupied a woman, and refused to come forth at the command of the bishop, but fled from her, blaspheming, when the Sacred Host was exposed, "this being witnessed by more than 150,000 persons;" he also told how a picture of the Sacred Host, being painted in the great window of a church that was habitually being struck by lightning, protected it afterward; then he used that opportunity to explain that churches are not struck by

lightning by accident, but for a worthy and intelligent purpose:

"Four times our chapel has been struck by lightning. Now
some might ask: why did God not turn away the lightning?
God has in all things his most wise design, and we are not permitted to search into it. But certain it is, that if our chapel had
not been visited in this way, we would not have called on the
kindness and charity of the devout lovers of the Holy Eucharist.
We would have remained hidden and would have been happy
in our obscurity. Perhaps just *this* was His loving design."

Some who had never contributed since the chapel was first
struck, on account of not understanding the idea of it before,
went forward cheerfully, now, and gave money; but others,
like the brewer Hummel, ever hard-headed and without sentiment, said it was an extravagant way to advertise, and God
the Father would do well to leave such things to persons in
the business, practical persons who had had experience; so
Hummel and his like gave nothing. Father Peter told one
more miracle, and all were sorry it was the last, for we could
have listened hours, with profit, to these moving and convincing wonders:

"On the afternoon of February 3d, 1322, the following incident took place in the Loretto Chapel at Bordeaux. The
learned priest, Dr. Delort, professor of theology in Bordeaux,
exposed the Blessed Sacrament for adoration. After the Pange
lingua had been chanted the sacristan suddenly arises, taps the
priest on the shoulder and says: 'God appears in the Sacred
Host.' Dr. Delort raises his eyes, looks at the Sacred Host and
perceives the apparition. Thinking it might be a mere effect of
the light he changes his position in order to be able to see
better. He now sees that the Sacred Host had, so to say, separated into two parts, in order to make room in the middle
for the form of a young man of wondrous beauty. The breast
of Jesus projected beyond the circle of the monstrance, and
He graciously moved His head whilst with His right hand He
blessed the assembly. His left hand rested on His heart. The
sacristan, several children, and many adults saw the apparition, which lasted during the entire time of the exposition.
With superhuman strength the priest then took the monstrance—and constantly gazing at the divine countenance—he

gave the final benediction. The commemoration of this apparition is celebrated every year in this convent."

There was not a dry eye in the house.

At this moment the lightning struck the chapel once more
and emptied it in a moment, everybody fleeing from it in a
frenzy of terror.

This was clearly another miracle, for there was not a cloud
in the sky. Proof being afterward collected and avouched by
Father Peter, it was accepted and consecrated at Rome, and
our chapel became celebrated by reason of it, and a resort for
pilgrims.

Chapter 11

To Katrina and me the miracle meant that my card had
turned up, and we were full of joy and confidence. Doangivadam was coming, we were sure of it. I hurried to the Owl
Tower and resumed my watch.

But it was another disappointment. The day wasted away,
hour by hour, the night closed down, the moon rose, and still
he did not come. At eleven I gave it up and came down heavy-
hearted and stiff with the cold. We could not understand it.
We talked it over, we turned it this way and that, it was of no
use, the thing was incomprehensible. At last Katrina had a
thought that seemed to throw light, and she uttered it, saying,

"Sometimes such things are delayed, for a wise purpose, a
purpose hidden from us, and which it is not meet for us to inquire into: to punish Marseilles and convert it, the cholera
was promised, by a revelation—but it did not come for two
years."

"Ah, dear, that is it," I said, "I see it now. He will come in
two years, but then it will be too late. The poor master! nothing can save him, he is lost. Before sunset to-morrow the
strikers will have triumphed, and he will be a ruined man. I
will go to bed; I wish I might never wake again."

About nine the next morning, Doangivadam arrived! Ah, if
he could only have come a few short days before! I was all

girl-boy again, I couldn't keep the tears back. At his leisure he had strolled over from the village inn, and he marched in among us, gay and jovial, plumed and gorgeous, and took everybody by surprise. Here he was in the midst, scattering salutations all around. He chucked old Frau Stein under the chin and said,

"Beautiful as ever, symbol of perpetual youth!" And he called Katrina his heart's desire and snatched a kiss; and fell into raptures over Maria, and said she was just dazzling and lit up the mouldy castle like the sun; then he came flourishing in where the men were at their early beer and their rascal plans, now at the threshold of success; and he started to burst out with some more cordialities there, but not a man rose nor gave him a look of welcome, for they knew him, and that as soon as he found out how things stood he would side with the under dog in the fight, from nature and habit. He glanced about him, and his face sobered. He backed against an unoccupied table, and half-sitting upon its edge, crossed his ancles, and continued his examination of the faces. Presently he said, gravely,

"There's something the matter, here; what is it?"

The men sat glum and ugly, and no one answered. He looked toward me, and said,

"Tell me about it, lad."

I was proud of his notice, and it so lifted my poor courage that although I dreaded the men and was trembling inside, I actually opened my mouth to begin; but before I could say anything 44 interposed and said, meekly,

"If you please, sir, it would get him into trouble with the men, and he is not the cause of the difficulty, but only I. If I may be allowed to explain it—"

Everybody was astonished to see poor 44 making so hardy a venture, but Katzenyammer glanced at him contemptuously and cut him short:

"Shut your mouth, if you please, and look to it that you don't open it again."

"Suppose *I* ask him to open it," said Doangivadam; "what will you do about it?"

"*Close* it for him—that's what."

A steely light began to play in Doangivadam's eyes, and he called 44 to his side and said,

"Stand there. I'll take care of you. Now go on."

The men stirred in their chairs and straightened up, their faces hardening—a sort of suggestion of preparation, of clearing for action, so to speak. There was a moment's pause, then the boy said in a level and colorless voice, like one who is not aware of the weight of his words,

"I am the new apprentice. Out of unmerited disapproval of me, and for no other or honorable reason, these cowardly men conspired to ruin the master."

The astonished men, their indignant eyes fixed upon the boy, began slowly to rise; said Doangivadam,

"They did, did they?"

"Yes," said the boy.

"The—*sons* of bitches!" and every sword was out of its sheath in an instant, and the men on their feet.

"Come on!" shouted Doangivadam, fetching his long rapier up with a whiz and falling into position.

But the men hesitated, wavered, gave back, and that was the friend of the under dog's opportunity—he was on them like a cat. They recovered, and braced up for a moment, but they could not stand against the man's impetuous assault, and had to give way before it and fall back, one sword after another parting from their hands with a wrench and flying, till only two of the enemy remained armed—Katzenyammer and Binks—then the champion slipped and fell, and they jumped for him to impale him, and I turned sick at the sight; but 44 sprang forward and gripped their necks with his small hands and they sank to the floor limp and gasping. Doangivadam was up and on guard in a moment, but the battle was over. The men formally surrendered—except the two that lay there. It was as much as ten minutes before they recovered; then they sat up, looking weak and dazed and uncertain, and maybe thinking the lightning had struck again; but the fight was all out of them and they did not need to surrender; they only felt of their necks and reflected.

We victors stood looking down upon them, the prisoners of war stood grouped apart and sullen.

"How was that done?" said Doangivadam, wondering; "what was it done with?"

"He did it with his hands," I said.

"With his hands? Let me see them, lad . . . . Why, they are soft and plump—just a girl's. Come, there's no strength in these paddies; what is the secret of this thing?"

So I explained:

"It isn't his own strength, sir; his master gives it him by magic—Balthasar the enchanter."

So then he understood it.

He noticed that the men had fallen apart and were picking up their swords, and he ordered 44 to take the swords away from them and bring them to him. And he chuckled at the thought of what the boy had done, and said,

"If they resist, try those persuaders of yours again."

But they did not resist. When 44 brought him the swords he piled them on the table and said,

"Boy, you were not in the conspiracy; with that talent of yours, why didn't you make a stand?"

"There was no one to back me, sir."

"There's something in that. But I'm here, now. It's backing enough, isn't it? You'll enlist for the war?"

"Yes, sir."

"That settles it. I'll be the right wing of the army, and you'll be the left. We will concentrate on the conspiracy here and now. What is your name?"

The boy replied with his customary simplicity,

"No. 44, New Series 864,962."

Doangivadam, who was inserting the point of his rapier into its sheath, suspended the operation where it was, and after a moment asked,

"What did I understand you to say?"

"No. 44, New Series 864,962."

"Is—is that your *name*?"

"Yes, sir."

"My—word, but it's a daisy! In the hurry of going to press, let's dock it to Forty-Four and put the rest on the standing-galley and let it go for left-over at half rates. Will that do?"

"Yes, sir."

"Come, now—range up, men, and plant yourselves! Forty-Four is going to resume his account of the conspiracy. Now go on, 44, and speak as frankly as you please."

Forty-Four told the story, and was not interrupted. When

it was finished Doangivadam was looking sober enough, for he recognized that the situation was of a seriousness beyond anything he had guessed—in fact it had a clearly hopeless look, so far as he could at the moment see. The men had the game in their hands; how could he, or any other, save the master from the ruin they had planned? That was his thought. The men read it in his face, and they looked the taunts which they judged it injudicious to put into words while their weapons were out of their reach. Doangivadam noted the looks and felt the sting of them as he sat trying to think out a course. He finished his thinkings, then spoke:

"The case stands like this. If the master dismisses 44—but he can't lawfully do it; that way out is blocked. If 44 remains, you refuse to work, and the master cannot fulfill his contract. That is ruin for him. You hold all the cards, that is evident."

Having conceded this, he began to reason upon the matter, and to plead for the master, the just master, the kind and blameless master, the generous master, now so sorely bested, a master who had never wronged any one, a master who would be compassionate if he were in their place and they in his . . . . . .

It was time to interrupt him, lest his speech begin to produce effects, presently; and Katzenyammer did it.

"That's enough of that taffy—shut it off!" he said. "We stand solid; the man that weakens—let him look to himself!"

The war-light began to rise in Doangivadam's eyes, and he said—

"You refuse to work. Very well, I can't make you, and I can't persuade you—but starvation can! I'll lock you into the shop, and put guards over you, and the man that breaks out shall have his reward."

The men realized that the tables had been turned; they knew their man—he would keep his word; he had their swords, he was master of the situation. Even Katzenyammer's face went blank with the suddenness of the checkmate, and his handy tongue found nothing at the moment to say. By order the men moved by in single file and took up their march for the shop, followed by 44 and Doangivadam, who carried swords and maintained peace and order. Presently—

"Halt!" cried the commander. "There's a man missing. Where is Ernest Wasserman?"

It was found that he had slipped out while 44 was telling his story. But all right, he was heard coming, now. He came swaying and tottering in, sank into a chair, looking snow white, and said, "O, Lord!"

Everybody forgot the march, and crowded around him, eager to find out what dreadful thing had happened. But he couldn't answer questions, he could only moan and shiver and say—

"Don't ask *me*! I've been to the shop! O, *lordy*-lord, oh, *lordy*-lord!"

They couldn't get a thing out of him but that, he was that used up and gone to pieces. Then there was a break for the shop, Doangivadam in the lead, and the rest clattering after him through the dim and musty corridors. When we arrived we saw a sight to turn a person to stone: there before our eyes the press was whirling out printed sheets faster than a person could count them—just *snowing* them onto the pile, as you may say—yet *there wasn't a human creature in sight anywhere!*

And that wasn't all, nor the half. All the *other* printing-shop work was going briskly on—yet nobody there, not a living thing to be seen! You would see a sponge get up and dip itself in a basin of water; see it sail along through the air; see it halt an inch above a galley of dead matter and squeeze itself and drench the galley, then toss itself aside; then an invisible expert would flirt the leads out of that matter so fast they fairly seemed to rain onto the imposing-stone, and you would see the matter contract and shrink together under the process; next you would see as much as five inches of that matter separate itself from the mass and rise in the air and stand upright; see it settle itself upon that invisible expert's ring-finger as upon a seat; see it move across the room and pause above a case and go to scattering itself like lightning into the boxes—raining again? yes, it was like that. And in half or three-quarters of no time you would see that five inches of matter scatter itself out and another five come and take its place; and in another minute or two there would be a mountain of wet type in every box and the job finished.

At other cases you would see "sticks" hovering in the air above the space-box; see a line set, spaced, justified and the rule slipped over in the time it takes a person to snap his fingers; next minute the stick is full! next moment it is emptied into the galley! and in ten minutes the *galley's* full and the case empty! It made you dizzy to see these incredible things, these impossible things.

Yes, all the different kinds of work were racing along like Sam Hill—*and all in a sepulchral stillness.* The way the press was carrying on, you would think it was making noise enough for an insurrection, but in a minute you would find it was only your fancy, it wasn't producing a sound—then you would have that sick and chilly feeling a person always has when he recognizes that he is in the presence of creatures and forces not of this world. The invisibles were making up forms, locking up forms, unlocking forms, carrying new signatures to the press and removing the old: abundance of movement, you see, plenty of tramping to and fro, yet you couldn't hear a footfall; there wasn't a spoken word, there wasn't a whisper, there wasn't a sigh—oh, the saddest, uncanniest silence that ever was.

But at last I noticed that there really was one industry lacking—a couple of them: no proofs were taken, no proofs were read! Oh, these *were* experts, sure enough! When *they* did a thing, they did it right, apparently, and it hadn't any occasion to be corrected.

Frightened? We were paralyzed; we couldn't move a limb to get away, we couldn't even cross ourselves, we were so nerveless. And we couldn't look away, the spectacle of those familiar objects drifting about in the air unsupported, and doing their complex and beautiful work without visible help, was so terrifyingly fascinating that we had to look and keep on looking, we couldn't help it.

At the end of half an hour the distribution stopped, and the composing. In turn, one industry after another ceased. Last of all, the churning and fluttering press's tremendous energies came to a stand-still; invisible hands removed the form and washed it, invisible hands scraped the bed and oiled it, invisible hands hung the frisket on its hook. Not anywhere in the place was any motion, any movement, now; there was

nothing there but a soundless emptiness, a ghostly hush. This
lasted during a few clammy moments, then came a sound
from the furthest case—soft, subdued, but harsh, gritty,
mocking, sarcastic: the scraping of a rule on a box-partition!
and with it came half a dozen dim and muffled spectral
chuckles, the dry and crackly laughter of the dead, as it
seemed to me.

In about a minute something cold passed by. Not wind,
just cold. I felt it on my cheek. It was one of those ghosts; I
did not need any one to tell me that; it had that damp, tomby
feel which you do not get from any live person. We all shrank
together, so as not to obstruct the others. They straggled
along by at their leisure, and we counted the frosts as they
passed: eight.

Chapter 12

WE arrived back to our beer-and-chess room troubled
and miserable. Our adventure went the rounds of the
castle, and soon the ladies and the servants came, pale and
frightened, and when they heard the facts it knocked them
dumb for one while, which was not a bad thing.

But the men were not dumb. They boldly proposed to denounce the magician to the Church and get him burnt, for
this thing was a little *too* much, they said. And just then the
magician appeared, and when he heard those awful words, fire
and the Church, he was that scared he couldn't stand; the
bones fairly melted in his legs and he squshed down in a chair
alongside of Frau Stein and Maria, and began to beg and beseech. His airy pride and self-sufficiency had all gone out of
him, and he pretended with all his might that he hadn't
brought those spectres and hadn't had anything to do with it.
He seemed so earnest that a body could hardly keep from believing him, and so distressed that I had to pity him though I
had no love for him, but only admiration.

But Katzenyammer pressed him hard, and so did Binks and
Moses Haas, and when Maria and her mother tried to put in
a word for him they convinced nobody and did him no good.

Doangivadam put the climax to the poor man's trouble and
hit the nail on the head with a remark which everybody recognized as the wisest and tellingest thing that had been said
yet. He said—

"Balthasar Hoffman, such things don't happen by accident—you know that very well, and we all do. You are the
only person in the castle that has the power to do a miracle
like that. Now then—firstly, it *happened*; secondly, it didn't
happen by itself; thirdly, *you are here*. What would anybody
but a fool conclude?"

Several shouted—

"He's *got* him! got him where he can't budge!"

Another shouted—

"He doesn't answer, and he can't—the stake's the place for
him!"

The poor old thing began to cry. The men rose against him
in a fury; they were going to seize him and hale him before
the authorities, but Doangivadam interposed some more wisdom, good and sound. He said—

"Wait. It isn't the best way. He will leave the enchantment
on, for revenge. We want it taken off, don't we?"

Everybody agreed, by acclamation. Doangivadam certainly
had a wonderful head, and full of talent.

"Very well, then. Now Balthasar Hoffman, you've got a
chance for your life. It has suited you to deny, in the most
barefaced way, that you put that enchantment on—let that
pass, it doesn't signify. What we want to know now, is, if we
let you alone, do you promise it shan't happen again?"

It brought up his spirits like raising the dead, he was so
glad and grateful.

"I do, I do!" he said; "on my honor it shan't happen
again."

It made the greatest change. Everybody was pleased, and
the awful shadow of that fear vanished from all faces, and they
were as doomed men that had been saved. Doangivadam
made the magician give his honor that he would not try to
leave the castle, but would stand by, and be a safeguard; and
went on to say—

"That enchantment had malice back of it. It is my opinion
that those invisible creatures have been setting up and printing

mere rubbish, in order to use up the paper-supply and defeat the master's contract and ruin him. I want somebody to go and see. Who will volunteer?"

There was a large silence; enough of it to spread a foot deep over four acres. It spread further and further, and got thicker and thicker. Finally Moses Haas said, in his mean way—

"Why don't *you* go?"

They all had to smile at that, for it was a good hit. Doangivadam managed to work up a smile, too, but you could see it didn't taste good; then he said—

"I'll be frank about it. I don't go because I am afraid to. Who is the bravest person here?"

Nearly everybody nominated Ernest Wasserman, and laughed, and Doangivadam ordered him to go and see, but he spoke out with disgust and indignation and said—

"See you in hell, first, and *then* I wouldn't!"

Then old Katrina spoke up proud and high, and said—

"There's my boy, there. I lay he's not afraid. Go 'long and look, child."

They thought 44 wouldn't, but I thought he would, and I was right, for he started right along, and Doangivadam patted him on the head and praised his pluck as he went by. It annoyed Ernest Wasserman and made him jealous, and he pursed up his lips and said—

"I wasn't *afraid* to go, but I'm no slave and I wasn't going to do it on any random unclassified Tom-Dick-and-Harry's orders."

Not a person laughed or said a word, but every man got out his composing rule and scraped wood, and the noise of it was like a concert of jackasses. That is a thing that will take the stiffening out of the conceitedest donkey you can start, and it squelched Ernest Wasserman, and he didn't pipe up any more. Forty-Four came back with an astonisher. He said—

"The invisibles have finished the job, and it's perfect. The contract is saved."

"Carry that news to the master!" shouted Doangivadam, and Marget got right up and started on that mission; and when she delivered it and her uncle saw he was saved in purse and honor and everything, it was medicine for him, and he was a well man again or next to it before he was an hour older.

Well, the men looked that disgusted, you can't think—at least those that had gotten up the strike. It was a good deal of a pill, and Katzenyammer said so; and said—

"We've got to take it—but there'll be sugar on it. We've lost the game, but I'll not call off the strike nor let a man go to work till we've been paid *waiting*-wages."

The men applauded.

"What's waiting-wages?" inquired Doangivadam.

"Full wages for the time we've lost during the strike."

"M-y—word! Well, if that isn't cheek! You're to be paid for time lost in trying to ruin the master! Meantime, where does *he* come in? Who pays him *his* waiting-time?"

The leaders tossed their heads contemptuously, and Binks said he wasn't interested in irrelevances.

So there we were, you see—at a stand-still. There was plenty of work on hand, and the "takes" were on the hooks in the shop, but the men stood out; they said they wouldn't go near the place till their waiting-wages had been paid and the shop spiritually disinfected by the priest. The master was as firm; he said he would never submit to that extortion.

It seemed to be a sort of drawn battle, after all. The master had won the biggest end of the game, but the rest of it remained in the men's hands. This was exasperating and humiliating, but it was a fact just the same, and the men did a proper amount of crowing over it.

About this time Katzenyammer had a thought which perhaps had occurred to others, but he was the first to utter it. He said, with a sneer—

"A lot is being taken for granted—on not even respectable *evidence*, let alone proof. How do *we* know the contract has been completed and saved?"

It certainly was a hit, everybody recognized that; in fact you could call it a sockdolajer, and not be any out of the way. The prejudice against 44 was pretty strong, you know. Doangivadam was jostled—you could see it. He didn't know what to say—you could see that, too. Everybody had an expression on his face, now—a very exultant one on the rebel side, a very uncomfortable one on the other—with two exceptions: Katrina and 44; 44 hadn't any expression at all—his face was wood; but Katrina's eyes were snapping. She said—

"*I* know what you mean, you ornery beer-jug, you Katzenyammer; you mean he's a liar. Well, then, why don't you go and see for yourself? Answer me that—why *don't* you?"

"I don't *need* to, if you want to know. It's nothing to me—*I* don't care what becomes of the contract."

"Well, then, keep your mouth shut and mind your own business. You *dasn't* go, and you know it. Why, you great big mean coward, to call a poor friendless boy a liar, and then ain't man enough to go and prove it!"

"Look here, woman, if you—"

"Don't you call *me* woman, you scum of the earth!" and she strode to him and stood over him; "say it again and I'll tear you to rags!"

The bully murmured—

"I take it back," which made many laugh.

Katrina faced about and challenged the house to go and see. There was a visible shrinkage all around. No answer. Katrina looked at Doangivadam. He slowly shook his head, and said—

"I'll not deny it—I lack the grit."

Then Katrina stretched herself away up in the air and said—

"I'm under the protection of the Queen of Heaven, and I'll go myself! Come along, 44."

They were gone a considerable time. When they returned Katrina said—

"He showed me everything and explained it all, and it's just exactly as he told you." She searched the house, face by face, with her eyes, then settled them upon Katzenyammer and finished: "Is there any polecat here that's got the sand to doubt it *now*?"

Nobody showed up. Several of our side laughed, and Doangivadam he laughed too, and fetched his fist down with a bang on the table like the Lord Chief Justice delivering an opinion, and said—

"That settles it!"

Chapter 13

NEXT day was pretty dreary. The men wouldn't go to work, but loafed around moody and sour and uncomfortable. There was not much talk; what there was was mumbled, in the main, by pairs. There was no general conversation. At meals silence was the rule. At night there was no jollity, and before ten all had disappeared to their rooms and the castle was a dim and grim solitude.

The day after, the same. Wherever 44 came he got ugly looks, threatening looks, and I was afraid for him and wanted to show sympathy but was too timid. I tried to think I avoided him for his own good, but did not succeed to my satisfaction. As usual, he did not seem to know he was being so scowled at and hated. He certainly could be inconceivably stupid at times, for all he was so capable at others. Marget pitied him and said kind things to him, and Doangivadam was cordial and handsome to him, and whenever Doangivadam saw one of those scowls he insulted the man that exhibited it and invited him to exhibit it again, which he didn't. Of course Katrina was 44's friend right along. But the friendliness was confined to those three, at least as far as any open show of it went.

So things drifted along, till the contract-gentlemen came for the goods. They brought a freight wagon along, and it waited in the great court. There was an embarrassment, now. Who would box-up the goods? Our men? Indeed, no. They refused, and said they wouldn't allow any outsider to do it, either. And Katzenyammer said to Doangivadam, while he was pleading—

"Save your breath—the contract has failed, after all!"

It made Doangivadam mad, and he said—

"It hasn't failed, either. I'll box the things myself, and Katrina and I will load them into the wagon. Rather than see you people win, I'll chance death by ghost and fright. I reckon Katrina's Virgin can protect the two of us. Perhaps you boys will interfere. I have my doubts."

The men chuckled, furtively. They knew he had spoken rashly. They knew he had not taken into account the size and weight of those boxes.

He hurried away and had a private word with the master, saying—

"It's all arranged, sir. Now if you—"

"Excellent! and most unexpected. Are the men—"

"No, but no matter, it's arranged. If you can feed and wine and otherwise sumptuously and satisfactorily entertain your guests three hours, I'll have the goods in the wagon then."

"Oh, many, many thanks—I'll make them stay all night."

Doangivadam came to the kitchen, then, and told Katrina and 44 all this, and I was there just at that time and heard it; and Katrina said all right, she would protect him to the shop, now, and leave him in the care of the Virgin while he did the packing, and in two hours and a half dinner would be down to the wine and nuts and then she would come and help carry the boxes. Then he left with her, but I stayed, for no striker would be likely to venture into the kitchen, therefore I could be in 44's company without danger. When Katrina got back, she said—

"That Doangivadam's a gem of the ocean—he's a *man*, that's what he is, not a waxwork, like that Katzenyammer. I wasn't going to discourage him, but *we* can't carry the boxes. There's five, and each of them a barrow-load; and besides, there has to be four carriers to the barrow. And then—"

Forty-Four interrupted:

"There's two of you, and I'll be the other two. You two will carry one end, and I'll carry the other. I am plenty strong enough."

"Child, you'll just stay out of sight, that's what you'll do. Do you want to provoke the men every way you can think of, you foolish little numskull? Ain't they down on you a plenty, just the way it is?"

"But you see, you two *can't* carry the boxes, and if you'll only let me help—"

"You'll not budge a step—do you hear me?" She stood stern and resolute, with her knuckles in her hips. The boy looked disappointed and grieved, and that touched her. She dropped on her knees where he sat, and took his face between her hands, and said, "Kiss your old mother, and forgive"— which he did, and the tears came into her eyes, which a moment before were so stormy. "Ain't you all I've got in the world? and don't I love the ground you walk on, and can I bear to see you getting into more and more danger all the time, and no need of it? Here, bless your heart," and she jumped up and brought a pie, "You and August sample *that*, and be good. It ain't the kind you get outside of this kitchen, that you can't tell from plate-mail when you bite it in the dark."

We began on the pie with relish, and of course conversation failed for a time. By and by 44 said, softly—

"Mother, he gave his word, you know."

Katrina was hit. She had to suspend work and think that over. She seated herself against the kitchen table, with her legs aslant and braced, and her arms folded and her chin down, and muttered several times, "Yes, that's so, he did." Finally she unlimbered and reached for the butcher-knife, which she fell to sharpening with energy on a brick. Then she lightly tested its edge with the ball of her thumb, and said—

"I know it—we've got to have two more. Doangivadam will force one, and I bet I'll persuade the other."

"*Now* I'm content," said 44, fervently, which made Katrina beam with pleasure.

We stayed there in the comfortable kitchen and chatted and played checkers, intending to be asked by Katrina to take our dinner with her, for she was the friendliest and best table-company *we* had. As time drew on, it became jolly in the master's private dining-room where it was his custom to feed guests of honor and distinction, and whenever a waiter came in or went out we could hear the distant bursts of merriment, and by and by bursts of song, also, showing that the heavy part of the feeding had been accomplished. Then we had our dinner with Katrina, and about the time we had finished, Doangivadam arrived hungry and pretty well tired out and said he had packed every box; but he wouldn't take a bite, he said, until his job was finished up and the wagon loaded. So Katrina told him her plan for securing extra help by compulsion and persuasion, and he liked it and they started. Doangivadam said he hadn't seen any of the men in sight, therefore he judged they must be lying in wait somewhere about the great court so as to interrupt any scheme of bribing the two porters of the freight wagon to help carry the boxes; so it was his idea to go there and see.

Katrina ordered us to stay behind, which we didn't do, after they were out of sight. We went down by secret passages and reached the court ahead of them, and hid. We were near the wagon. The driver and porters had been given their supper, and had been to the stalls to feed and water the horses, and now they were walking up and down chatting and waiting to receive the freight. Our two friends arrived now, and in low voices began to ask these men if they had seen any men of the castle around about there, but before they could answer, something happened: we saw some dim big bulks emerge from our side of the court about fifty yards away and come in procession in our direction. Swiftly they grew more and more distinct under the stars and by the dim lamps, and they turned out to be men, and each of them was drooping under one of our big freight boxes. The idea—carrying it all alone! And another surprising thing was, that when the first man passed us it turned out to be Katzenyammer! Doangivadam was delighted out of his senses, almost, and said some splendid words of praise about his change of heart, but Katzenyammer could only grunt and growl, he was strained so by his burden.

And the next man was Binks! and there was more praise and more grunts. And next came Moses Haas—think of it! And then Gustav Fischer! And after him, the end of the procession—Ernest Wasserman! Why, Doangivadam could hardly believe it, and said he *didn't* believe it, and *couldn't*; and said "*Is* it you, Ernest?" and Ernest told him to go to hell, and then Doangivadam was satisfied and said "that settles it."

For that was Ernest's common word, and you could know him by it in the dark.

Katrina couldn't say a word, she just stood there dazed. She saw the boxes stowed in the wagon, she saw the gang file back and disappear, and still she couldn't get her voice till then; and even then all she could say, was—

"Well, it beats the band!"

Doangivadam followed them a little way, and wanted to have a supper and a night of it, but they answered him roughly and he had to give it up.

Chapter 14

T HE freight wagon left at dawn; the honored guests had a
late breakfast, paid down the money on the contract,
then after a good-bye bottle they departed in their carriage.
About ten the master, full of happiness and forgiveness and
benevolent feeling, had the men assembled in the beer-and-
chess room, and began a speech that was full of praises of the
generous way they had thrown ill-will to the winds at the last
moment and loaded the wagon last night and saved the honor
and the life of his house—and went on and on, like that, with
the water in his eyes and his voice trembling; and there the
men sat and stared at one another, and at the master, with
their mouths open and their breath standing still; till at last
Katzenyammer burst out with—

"What in the nation *are* you mooning about? Have you lost
your mind? *We've* saved you nothing; *we've* carried no
boxes"—here he rose excited and banged the table—"and
what's more, we've arranged that nobody *else* shall carry a box
or load that wagon till our waiting-time's paid!"

Well, think of it! The master was so astonished that for a
moment or two he couldn't pull his language; then he turned
sadly and uncertainly to Doangivadam and said—

"I could not have dreamed it. Surely you told me that
they—"

"Certainly I did. I told you they brought down the
boxes—"

"*Listen* at him!" cried Binks, springing to his feet.

"—those five *there*—Katzenyammer at the head, Wasserman at the tail—"

"As sure as my name's Was—"

"—each with a box on his shoulders—"

All were on their feet, now, and they drowned out the
speaker with a perfect deluge of derisive laughter, out of the
midst of which burst Katzenyammer's bull-voice shouting—

"Oh, listen to the maniac! *Each* carrying a box weighing
five—hundred—pounds!"

Everybody took up that telling refrain and screamed it and
yelled it with all his might. Doangivadam saw the killing force

of the argument, and began to look very foolish—which the men saw, and they roared at him, challenging him to get up and purge his soul and trim his imagination. He was caught in a difficult place, and he did not try to let on that he was in easy circumstances. He got up and said, quietly, and almost humbly—

"I don't understand it, I can't explain it. I realize that no man here could carry one of those boxes; and yet as sure as I am alive I saw it done, just as I have said. Katrina saw it too. We were awake, and not dreaming. I spoke to every one of the five. I saw them load the boxes into the wagon. I—"

Moses Haas interrupted:

"Excuse me, nobody loaded any boxes into the wagon. It wouldn't have been allowed. We've kept the wagon under watch." Then he said, ironically, "Next, the gentleman will work his imagination up to saying the wagon is gone and the master paid."

It was good sarcasm, and they all laughed; but the master said, gravely, "Yes, I have been paid," and Doangivadam said, "Certainly the wagon is gone."

"Oh, come!" said Moses, leaving his seat, "this is going a little *too* far; it's a trifle *too* brazen; come out and say it to the wagon's face. If you've got the cheek to do it, follow me."

He moved ahead, and everybody swarmed after him, eager to see what would happen. I was getting worried; nearly half convinced, too; so it was a relief to me when I saw that the court was empty. Moses said—

"Now then, what do you call *that*? Is it the wagon, or isn't it?"

Doangivadam's face took on the light of a restored confidence and a great satisfaction, and he said—

"I see no wagon."

"What!" in a general chorus.

"No—I don't see any wagon."

"Oh, great guns! perhaps the master will say *he* doesn't see a wagon."

"Indeed I see none," said the master.

"Wel-l, well, *well!*" said Moses, and was plumb nonplussed. Then he had an idea, and said, "Come, Doangivadam, you seem to be near-sighted—please to follow me and *touch* the wagon, and see if you'll have the hardihood to go on with this cheap comedy."

They walked briskly out a piece, then Moses turned pale and stopped.

"By God, it's gone!" he said.

There was more than one startled face in the crowd. They crept out, silent and looking scared; then they stopped, and sort of moaned—

"It *is* gone; it was a ghost-wagon."

Then they walked right over the place where it had been, and crossed themselves and muttered prayers. Next they broke into a fury, and went storming back to the chess-room, and sent for the magician, and charged him with breaking his pledge, and swore the Church should have him now; and the more he begged the more they scared him, till at last they grabbed him to carry him off—then he broke down, and said that if they would spare his life he would confess. They told him to go ahead, and said if his confession was not satisfactory it would be the worse for him. He said—

"I hate to say it—I wish I could be spared it—oh, the shame of it, the ingratitude of it! But—pity me, pity me!—I have been nourishing a viper in my bosom. That boy, that pupil whom I have so loved—in my foolish fondness I taught him several of my enchantments, and now he is using them for your hurt and my ruin!"

It turned me sick and faint, the way the men plunged at 44, crying "Kill him, kill him!" but the master and Doangivadam jumped in and stood them off and saved him. Then Doangivadam talked some wisdom and reasonableness into the gang which had good effect. He said—

"What is the use to kill the boy? He isn't the *source*; whatever power he has, he gets from his master, this magician here. Don't you believe that if the magician wants to, he can put a spell on the boy that will abolish his power and make him harmless?"

Of course that was so, and everybody saw it and said so. So then Doangivadam worked some more wisdom: instead of letting on to know it all himself, he gave the others a chance to seem to know a little of what was left. He asked them to assist him in this difficult case and suggest some wise and practical way to meet this emergency. It flattered them, and they unloaded the suggestion that the magician be put under bond to shut off the boy's enchantments, on pain of being delivered to the Church if anything happened again.

Doangivadam said it was the very thing; and praised the idea, and let on to think it was wonderfully intelligent, whereas it was only what he had suggested himself, and what anybody would have thought of and suggested, including the cat, there being no other way with any sense in it.

So they bonded the magician, and he didn't lose any time in furnishing the pledge and getting a new lease on his hide. Then he turned on the boy and reproached him for his in-gratitude, and then he fired up on his subject and turned his tongue and his temper loose, and most certainly he did give him down the banks and roll Jordan roll! I never felt so sorry for a person, and I think others were sorry for him, too, though they would have said that as long as he deserved it he couldn't expect to be treated any gentler, and it would be a valuable lesson to him anyway, and save him future trouble, and worse. The way the magician finished, was awful; it made your blood run cold. He walked majestically across the room with his solemn professional stride, which meant that some-thing was going to happen. He stopped in the door and faced around, everybody holding their breath, and said, slow and distinct, and pointing his long finger—

"Look at him, there where he sits—and remember my words, and the doom they are laden with. I have put him un-der my spells; if he thinks he can dissolve them and do you further harm, let him try. But I make this pledge and com-pact: on the day that he succeeds I will put an enchantment upon him, here in this room, which shall slowly consume him to ashes before your eyes!"

Then he departed. Dear me, but it was a startled crowd! Their faces were that white—and they couldn't seem to say a word. But there was one good thing to see—there was pity in every face of them! That was human nature, wasn't it—when your enemy is in awful trouble, to be sorry for him, even when your pride won't let you go and say it to him before company? But the master and Doangivadam went and com-forted him and begged him to be careful and work no spells

and run no risks; and even Gustav Fischer ventured to go by,
and heave out a kindly word in passing; and pretty soon the
news had gone about the castle, and Marget and Katrina
came; *they* begged him, too, and both got to crying, and that
made him so conspicuous and heroic, that Ernest Wasserman
was bursting with jealousy, and you could see he wished *he*
was advertised for roasting, too, if this was what you get for it.

Katrina had sassed the magician more than once and had
not seemed to be afraid of him, but this time her heart was
concerned and her pluck was all gone. She went to him, with
the crowd at her heels, and went on her knees and begged
him to be good to her boy, and stay his hand from practising
enchantments, and be his guardian and protector and save
him from the fire. Everybody was moved. Except the boy. It
was one of his times to be an ass and a wooden-head. He certainly could choose them with the worst judgment I ever saw.
Katrina was alarmed; she was afraid his seeming lack of interest would have a bad effect with the magician, so she did his
manners for him and conveyed his homage and his pledges of
good behavior, and hurried him out of the presence.

Well, to my mind there is nothing that makes a person interesting like his being about to get burnt up. We had to take
44 to the sick lady's room and let her gaze at him, and shudder, and shrivel, and wonder how he would look when he was
done; she hadn't had such a stirring up for years, and it acted
on her kidneys and her spine and her livers and all those
things and her other works, and started up her flywheel and
her circulation, and she said, herself, it had done her more
good than any bucketful of medicine she had taken that week.
And begged him to come again, and he promised he would if
he could. Also said if he couldn't he would send her some of
the ashes; for he certainly was a good boy at bottom, and
thoughtful.

They all wanted to see him, even people that had taken
hardly any interest in him before—like Sara and Duffles and
the other maids, and Fritz and Jacob and the other men-
servants. And they were all tender toward him, and ever so
gentle and kind, and gave him little things out of their poverty,
and were ever so sorry, and showed it by the tears in their
eyes. But not a tear out of *him*, you might have squeezed him

in the hydraulic press and you wouldn't have got dampness enough to cloud a razor, it being one of his blamed wooden times, you know.

Why, even Frau Stein and Maria were full of interest in him, and gazed at him, and asked him how it felt—in prospect, you know—and said a lot of things to him that came nearer being kind, than anything they were used to saying, by a good deal. It was surprising how popular he was, all of a sudden, now that he was in such awful danger if he didn't behave himself. And although I was around with him I never got a sour look from the men, and so I hadn't a twinge of fear the whole time. And then the supper we had that night in the kitchen!— Katrina laid out her whole strength on it, and cried all over it, and it was wonderfully good and salty.

Katrina told us to go and pray all night that God would not lead 44 into temptation, and she would do the same. I was ready and anxious to begin, and we went to my room.

Chapter 15

B UT when we got there I saw that 44 was not minded to pray, but was full of other and temporal interests. I was shocked, and deeply concerned; for I felt rising in me with urgency a suspicion which had troubled me several times before, but which I had ungently put from me each time—that he was indifferent to religion. I questioned him—he confessed it! I leave my distress and consternation to be imagined, I cannot describe them.

In that paralysing moment my life changed, and I was a different being; I resolved to devote my life, with all the affections and forces and talents which God had given me to the rescuing of this endangered soul. Then all my spirit was invaded and suffused with a blessed feeling, a divine sensation, which I recognized as the approval of God. I knew by that sign, as surely as if He had spoken to me, that I was His appointed instrument for this great work. I knew that He would help me in it; I knew that whenever I should need light and leading I could seek it in prayer, and have it; I knew—

"I get the idea," said 44, breaking lightly in upon my thought, "it will be a Firm, with its headquarters up there and its hindquarters down here. There's a duplicate of it in every congregation—in every family, in fact. Wherever you find a warty little devotee who isn't in partnership with God—as *he* thinks—on a speculation to save some little warty soul that's no more worth saving than his own, stuff him and put him in the museum, it is where he belongs."

"Oh, don't say such things, I beseech you! They are so shocking, and so awful. And so unjust; for in the sight of God all souls are precious, there is no soul that is not worth saving."

But the words had no effect. He was in one of his frivolous moods, and when these were upon him one could not interest him in serious things. For all answer to what I had been saying, he said in a kindly but quite unconcerned way that we would discuss this trifle at another time, but not now. That was the very word he used; and plainly he used it without any sense of its gross impropriety. Then he added this strange remark—

"For the moment, I am not living in the present century, but in one which interests me more, for the time being. *You* pray, if you like—never mind me, I will amuse myself with a curious toy if it won't disturb you."

He got a little steel thing out of his pocket and set it between his teeth, remarking "it's a jew's-harp—the niggers use it"—and began to buffet out of it a most urgent and strenuous and vibrant and exceedingly gay and inspiriting kind of music, and at the same time he went violently springing and capering and swooping and swirling all up and down the room in a way to banish prayer and make a person dizzy to look at him; and now and then he would utter the excess of his joy in a wild whoop, and at other times he would leap into the air and spin there head over heels for as much as a minute like a wheel, and so frightfully fast that he was all webbed together and you could hear him buzz. And he kept perfect time to his music all the while. It was a most extravagant and stirring and heathen performance.

Instead of being fatigued by it he was only refreshed. He came and sat down by me and rested his hand on my knee in his winning way, and smiled his beautiful smile, and asked me how I liked it. It was so evident that he was expecting a compliment, that I was obliged to furnish it. I had not the heart to hurt him, and he so innocently proud of his insane exhibition. I could not expose to him how undignified it was, and how degrading, and how difficult it had been for me to stand it through; I forced myself to say it was "ideal—*more* than ideal;" which was of course a perfectly meaningless phrase, but he was just hungry enough for a compliment to make him think this was one, and also make him overlook what was going on in my mind; so his face was fairly radiant with thanks and happiness, and he impulsively hugged me and said—

"It's lovely of you to like it so. I'll do it again!"

And at it he went, God assoil him, like a tempest. I couldn't say anything, it was my own fault. Yet I was not really to blame, for I could not foresee that he would take that uninflamed compliment for an invitation to do the fiendish orgy over again. He kept it up and kept it up until my heart was broken and all my body and spirit so worn and tired and desperate that I could not hold in any longer, I *had* to speak out and beg him to stop, and not tire himself so. It was another mistake; damnation, he thought I was suffering on *his* account! so he piped out cheerily, as he whizzed by—

"Don't worry about *me*; sit right where you are and enjoy it, I can do it all night."

I thought I would go out and find a good place to die, and was starting, when he called out in a grieved and disappointed tone—

"Ah, you are not going, are you?"

"Yes."

"What for? Don't go—please don't."

"Are you going to keep still? Because I am not going to stay here and see you tire yourself to death."

"Oh, it doesn't tire me in the least, I give you my word. *Do* stay."

Of course I wanted to stay, but not unless he would sit down and act civilized, and give me a rest. For a time he could *not* seem to get the situation through his head—for he certainly could be the dullest animal that ever was, at times—

but at last he looked up with a wounded expression in his big soft eyes, and said—

"August, I believe you do not *want* any more."

Of course that broke me all down and made me ashamed of myself, and in my anxiety to heal the hurt I had given and see him happy again I came within a hair's breadth of throwing all judgment and discretion to the winds and saying I *did* want more. But I did not do it; the dread and terror of what would certainly follow, tied my tongue and saved my life. I adroitly avoided a direct answer to what he had said, by suddenly crying "ouch!" and grabbing at an imaginary spider inside my collar, whereupon he forgot his troubles at once in his concern for me. He plunged his hand in and raked it around my neck and fetched out three spiders—real ones, whereas I had supposed there was none there but imaginary ones. It was quite unusual for any but imaginary ones to be around at that time of the year, which was February.

We had a pleasant time together, but no religious conversation, for whenever I began to frame a remark of that color he saw it in my mind and squelched it with that curious power of his whereby he barred from utterance any thought of mine it happened to suit him to bar. It was an interesting time, of course, for it was the nature of 44 to be interesting. Pretty soon I noticed that we were not in my room, but in his. The change had taken place without my knowing when it happened. It was beautiful magic, but it made me feel uneasy. Forty-Four said—

"It is because you think I am traveling toward temptation."

"I am sure you are, 44. Indeed you are already arrived there, for you are doing things of a sort which the magician has prohibited."

"Oh, that's nothing! I don't obey him except when it suits me. I mean to use his enchantments whenever I can get any entertainment out of them, and whenever I can annoy him. I know every trick he knows, and some that he doesn't know. Tricks of my own—for I bought them; bought them from a bigger expert than he is. When I play my own, he is a puzzled man, for he thinks I do it by his inspiration and command, and inasmuch as he can't remember furnishing either the order or the inspiration, he is puzzled and bothered, and thinks there is something the matter with his head. He has to father everything I do, because he has begun it and can't get out of it now, and so between working his magic and my own I mean to build him up a reputation that will leave all other second-class magicians in the shade."

"It's a curious idea. Why don't you build it up for yourself?"

"I don't want it. At home we don't care for a small vanity like that, and I shouldn't value it here."

"Where is your ho—"

It got barred before I could finish. I wished in my heart I could have that gorgeous reputation which he so despised! But he paid no attention to the thought; so I sighed, and did not pursue it. Presently I got to worrying again, and said—

"Forty-Four, I foresee that before you get far with the magician's reputation you will bring a tragedy upon yourself. And you are so unprepared. You ought to prepare, 44, you ought indeed; every moment is precious. I do wish you would become a Christian; won't you try?"

He shook his head, and said—

"I should be too lonesome."

"Lonesome? How?"

"I should be the only one."

I thought it an ill jest, and said so. But he said it was not a jest—some time he would go into the matter and prove that he had spoken the truth; at present he was busy with a thing of "importance"—and added, placidly, "I must jack-up the magician's reputation, first." Then he said in his kindest manner—

"You have a quality which I do not possess—fear. You are afraid of Katzenyammer and his pals, and it keeps you from being with me as much as you would like and as I would like. That can be remedied, in a quite simple way. I will teach you how to become invisible, whenever you please. I will give you a magic word. Utter it in your mind, for you can't do it with your tongue, though I can. Say it when you wish to disappear, and say it again when you wish to be visible again."

He uttered the word, and vanished. I was so startled and so pleased and so grateful that I did not know where I was, for a moment, nor which end of me was up; then I perceived that

I was sitting by the fire in my own room, but I did not know how I got there.

Being a boy, I did what another boy would have done: as long as I could keep awake I did nothing but appear and disappear, and enjoy myself. I was very proud, and considered myself the superior of any boy in the land; and that was foolish, for I did not invent the art, it was a gift, and no merit to me that I could exercise it. Another boy with the same luck would be just as superior as I was. But these were not my thoughts, I got them later, and at second hand—where all thoughts are acquired, 44 used to say. Finally I disappeared and went to sleep happy and content, without saying one prayer for 44, and he in such danger. I never thought of it.

Chapter 16

FORTY-FOUR, by grace of his right to wear a sword, was legally a gentleman. It suited his whim, now, to come out dressed as one. He was clever, but ill balanced; and whenever he saw a particularly good chance to be a fool, pie couldn't persuade him to let it go by; he had to sample it, he couldn't seem to help it. He was as unpopular as he could be, but the hostile feeling, the intense bitterness, had been softening little by little for twenty-four hours, on account of the awful danger his life was in, so of course he must go and choose *this* time of all times, to flaunt in the faces of the comps the offensive fact that he was their social equal. And not only did he appear in the dress of a gentleman, but the quality and splendor of it surpassed even Doangivadam's best, and as for the others they were mere lilies of the valley to his Solomon. Embroidered buskins, with red heels; pink silk tights; pale blue satin trunks; cloth of gold doublet; short satin cape, of a blinding red; lace collar fit for a queen; the cunningest little blue velvet cap, with a slender long feather standing up out of a fastening of clustered diamonds; dress sword in a gold sheath, jeweled hilt. That was his outfit; and he carried himself like a princeling "doing a cake-walk," as he described it. He was as beautiful as a picture, and as satisfied with himself

as if he owned the earth. He had a lace handkerchief in his
hand, and now and then he would give his nose a dainty little dab or two with it, the way a duchess does. It was evident
that he thought he was going to be admired, and it was pitiful to see his disappointment when the men broke out on him
with insults and ridicule and called him offensive names, and
asked him where he had stolen his clothes.

He defended himself the best he could, but he was so near
to crying that he could hardly control his voice. He said he
had come by the clothes honestly, through the generosity of
his teacher the good magician, who created them instantly
out of nothing just by uttering a single magic word; and said
the magician was a far mightier enchanter than they supposed; that he hadn't shown the world the half of the wonders he could do, and he wished he was here now, he would
not like it to have his humble servant abused so when he
wasn't doing any harm; said he believed if he was here he
would do Katzenyammer a hurt for calling his servant a thief
and threatening to slap his face.

"He would, would he? Well, there he comes—let's *see* if he
loves his poor dear servant so much," said Katzenyammer,
and gave the boy a cruel slap that you could have heard a
hundred yards.

The slap spun Forty-Four around, and as soon as he saw
the magician he cried out eagerly and supplicatingly—

"Oh, noble master, oh greatest and sublimest of magicians,
I read your command in your eyes, and I must obey if it is
your will, but I pray you, I beseech you spare me the office,
do it yourself with your own just hand!"

The magician stood still and looked steadily and mutely at
Forty-Four as much as half a minute, we waiting and gazing
and holding our breath; then at last 44 made a reverent bow,
saying, "You are master, your will is law, and I obey," and
turned to Katzenyammer and said—

"In not very many hours you will discover what you have
brought upon yourself and the others. You will see that it is
not well to offend the master."

You have seen a cloud-shadow sweep along and sober a
sunlit field; just so, that darkling vague threat was a cloud-
shadow to those faces there. There is nothing that is more de-

pressing and demoralizing than the promise of an indefinite calamity when one is dealing with a powerful and malicious necromancer. It starts large, plenty large enough, but it does not stop there, the imagination goes on spreading it, till at last it covers all the space you've got, and takes away your appetite, and fills you with dreads and miseries, and you start at every noise and are afraid of your own shadow.

Old Katrina was sent by the women to beg 44 to tell what was going to happen so that they could get relieved of a part of the crushing burden of suspense, but she could not find him, nor the magician either. Neither of them was seen, the rest of the day. At supper there was but little talk, and no mention of *the* subject. In the chess-room after supper there was some private and unsociable drinking, and much deep sighing, and much getting up and walking the floor unconsciously and nervously a little while, then sitting down again unconsciously; and now and then a tortured ejaculation broke out involuntarily. At ten o'clock nobody moved to go to bed; apparently each troubled spirit found a sort of help and solace in the near presence of its kind, and dreaded to separate itself from companionship. At half past ten no one had stirred. At eleven the same. It was most melancholy to be there like this, in the dim light of unquiet and flickering candles and in a stillness that was broken by but few sounds and was all the more impressive because of the moaning of the wintry wind about the towers and battlements.

It was at half past eleven that it happened. Everybody was sitting steeped in musings, absorbed in thought, listening to that dirge the wind was chanting—Katzenyammer like the rest. A heavy step was heard, all glanced up nervously, and yonder in the door appeared a *duplicate Katzenyammer!* There was one general gasping intake of breath that nearly sucked the candles out, then the house sat paralyzed and gazing. This creature was in shop-costume, and had a "take" in its hand. It was the exact reproduction of the other Katzenyammer to the last shade and detail, a mirror couldn't have told them apart. It came marching up the room with the only gait that could be proper to it—aggressive, decided, insolent—and held out the "take" to its twin and said—

"Here! how do you want that set, leaded, or solid?"

For about a moment the original Katzenyammer was surprised out of himself; but the next moment he was all there,
and jumped up shouting—

"You bastard of black magic, I'll"—he finished with his fist,
delivering a blow on the twin's jaw that would have broken
anybody else's, but this jaw stood it uncrushed; then the pair
danced about the place hammering, banging, ramming each
other like battering machines, everybody looking on with
wonder and awe and admiration, and hoping neither of them
would survive. They fought half an hour, then sat down panting, exhausted, and streaming with blood—they hadn't
strength to go on.

The pair sat glaring at each other a while, then the original
said—

"Look here, my man, who *are* you, anyway? Answer up!"

"I'm Katzenyammer, foreman of the shop. That's who I
am, if you want to know."

"It's a lie. Have you been setting type in there?"

"Yes, I have."

"The hell you have! who told you you could?"

"I told myself. That's sufficient."

"Not on your life! Do you belong to the union?"

"No, I don't."

"Then you're a scab. Boys, up and at him!"

Which they did, with a will, fuming and cursing and swearing in a way which it was an education to listen to. In another
minute there would not have been anything left of that Duplicate, I reckon, but he promptly set up a ringing shout of
"Help, boys, help!" and in the same moment perfect Duplicates of all the *rest* of us came swarming in and plunged into
the battle!

But it was another draw. It had to be, for each Duplicate
fought his own mate and was his exact match, and neither
could whip the other. Then they tried the issue with swords,
but it was a draw once more. The parties drew apart, now,
and acrimoniously discussed the situation. The Duplicates refused to join the union, neither would they throw up their
job; they were stubbornly deaf to both threats and persuasion.
So there it was—just a deadlock! If the Duplicates remained,
the Originals were without a living—why, they couldn't even

collect their waiting-time, now! Their impregnable position, which they had been so proud of and so arrogant about had turned to air and vacancy. These were very grave and serious facts, cold and clammy ones; and the deeper they sank down into the consciousness of the ousted men the colder and clammier they became.

It was a hard situation, and pitiful. A person may say that the men had only gotten what they deserved, but when that is said is all said? I think not. They were only human beings, they had been foolish, they deserved some punishment, but to take their very bread was surely a punishment beyond the measure of their fault. But there it was—the disaster was come, the calamity had fallen, and no man could see a way out of the difficulty. The more one examined it the more perplexing and baffling and irremediable it seemed. And all so unjust, so unfair; for in the talk it came out that the Duplicates did not need to eat or drink or sleep, so long as the Originals did those things—there was enough for both; but when a *Duplicate* did them, by George, his Original got no benefit out of it! Then look at that other thing: the Originals were out of work and wageless, yet they would be supporting these intruding scabs, out of *their* food and drink, and by gracious not even a thank-you for it! It came out that the scabs got no pay for their work in the shop, and didn't care for it and wouldn't ask for it. Doangivadam finally hit upon a fair and honorable compromise, as he thought, and the boys came up a little out of their droop to listen. Doangivadam's idea was, for the Duplicates to do the work, and for the Originals to take the pay, and fairly and honorably eat and sleep enough for both. It looked bright and hopeful for a moment, but then the clouds settled down again: the plan wouldn't answer; it would not be lawful for unions and scabs to have dealings together. So that idea had to be given up, and everybody was gloomier than ever. Meantime Katzenyammer had been drinking hard, to drown his exasperations, but it was not effective, he couldn't seem to hold enough, and yet he was full. He was only half drunk; the trouble was, that his Duplicate had gotten the other half of the dividend, and was just as drunk, and as insufficiently drunk, as *he* was. When he realized this he was deeply hurt, and said reproachfully to his Duplicate, who sat there blinking and suffused with a divine contentment—

"Nobody *asked* you to partake; such conduct is grossly ill-bred; no gentleman would do such a thing."

Some were sorry for the Duplicate, for he was not to blame, but several of the Originals were evidently not sorry for him, but offended at him and ashamed of him. But the Duplicate was not affected, he did not say anything, but just blinked and looked drowsy and grateful, the same as before.

The talk went on, but it arrived nowhere, of course. The situation remained despairingly incurable and desperate. Then the talk turned upon the magician and 44, and quickly became bitter and vengeful. When it was at its sharpest, the magician came mooning in; and when he saw all those Duplicates he was either thunderstruck with amazement or he played it well. The men were vexed to see him act so, and they said, indignantly—

"It's your own fiendish work and you needn't be pretending surprise."

He was frightened at their looks and their manner, and hastened to deny, with energy and apparent earnestness, that *this* was any work of his; he said he had given a quite different command, and he only wished 44 were here, he would keep his word and burn him to ashes for misusing his enchantments; he said he would go and find him; and was starting away, but they jumped in front of him and barred his way, and Katzenyammer-original was furious, and said—

"You are trying to escape, but you'll not! You don't have to stir out of your tracks to produce that limb of perdition, and you know it and we know it. Summon him—summon him and destroy him, or I give my honor I will denounce you to the Holy Office!"

That was a plenty. The poor old man got white and shaky, and put up his hand and mumbled some strange words, and in an instant, *bang!* went a thunderclap, and there stood 44 in the midst, dainty and gay in his butterfly clothes!

All sprang up with horror in their faces to protest, for at bottom no one really wanted the boy destroyed, they only *believed* they did; there was a scream, and Katrina came flying, with her gray hair streaming behind her; for one moment a blot of black darkness fell upon the place and extinguished us all; the next moment in our midst stood that slender figure transformed to a core of dazzling white fire; in the succeeding moment it crumbled to ashes and we were blotted out in the black darkness again. Out of it rose an adoring cry—broken in the middle by a pause and a sob—

"The Lord gave, the Lord hath taken away . . . . blessed be the name of the Lord!"

It was Katrina; it was the faithful Christian parting with its all, yet still adoring the smiting hand.

Chapter 17

I WENT invisible the most of the next day, for I had no heart to talk about common matters, and had rather a shrinking from talking about the matter which was uppermost in all minds. I was full of sorrow, and also of remorse, which is the way with us in the first days of a bereavement, and at such times we wish to be alone with our trouble and our bitter recallings of failings of loyalty or love toward the comrade who is gone. There were more of these sins to my charge than I could have believed; they rose up and accused me at every turn, and kept me saying with heart-wearing iteration, "Oh, if he were only back again, how true I would be, and how differently I would act." I remembered so many times when I could perhaps have led him toward the life eternal, and had let the chance go by; and now he was lost and I to blame, and where was I to find comfort?

I always came back to that, I could not long persuade myself to other and less torturing thoughts—such, for instance, as wonderings over his yielding to the temptation to overstep the bounds of the magician's prohibition when he knew so well that it could cost him his life. Over that, of a surety, I might and did wonder in vain, quite in vain; there was no understanding it. He was volatile, and lacking in prudence, I knew that; but I had not dreamed that he was *entirely* destitute of prudence, I had not dreamed that he could actually risk his life to gratify a whim. Well, and what was I trying to get out of these reasonings? This—and I had to confess it: I was trying to excuse myself for my desertion of him in his sore need; when my promised prayers, which might have saved him, were withheld, and neglected, and even forgotten. I turned here and there and yonder for solace, but in every path stood an accusing spirit and barred the way; solace for me there was none.

No one of the household was indifferent to Katrina's grief, and the most of them went to her and tried to comfort her. I was not of these, I could not have borne it if she had asked me if I had prayed as I had said I would, or if she had thanked me for my prayers, taking for granted that I had kept my word. But I sat invisible while the others offered their comforting words; and every sob that came from her broken heart was another reproach and gave me a guilty pang. But her misery could not be abated. She moaned and wept, saying over and over again that if the magician had only shown a little mercy, which could have cost him nothing, and had granted time for a priest to come and give her boy absolution, all would have been well, and now he would be happy in heaven and she in the earth—but no! he had cruelly sent the lad unassoiled to judgment and the eternal fires of hell, and so had doomed her also to the pains of hell forevermore, for in heaven she should feel them all the days of eternity, looking down upon him suffering there and she powerless to assuage his thirst with one poor drop of water!

There was another thing which wrung her heart, and she could not speak of it without new floods of tears: her boy had died unreconciled to the Church, and his ashes could not be buried in holy ground; no priest could be present, no prayer uttered above them by consecrated lips, they were as the ashes of the beasts that perish, and fit only to lie in a dishonored grave.

And now and then, with a new outburst of love and grief she would paint the graces of his form, and the beauty of his young face, and his tenderness for her, and tell this and that and the other little thing that he had done or said, so dear and fond, so prized at the time, so sacred now forevermore!

I could not endure it; and I floated from the place upon the unrevealing air, and went wandering here and there disconsolate and finding everywhere reminders of him, and a new heartbreak with each.

By reason of the strange and uncanny tragedy, all the household were in a subdued and timorous state, and full of vague and formless and depressing apprehensions and boding terrors, and they went wandering about, aimless, comfortless and forlorn; and such talking together as there was, was of the disjointed and rambling sort that indicates preoccupation. However, if the Duplicates were properly of the household, what I have just been saying does not include them. They were not affected, they did not seem interested. They stuck industriously to their work, and one met them going to it or coming from it, but they did not speak except when spoken to. They did not go to the table, nor to the chess-room; they did not seem to avoid us, they took no pains about that, they merely did not seek us. But we avoided them, which was natural. Every time I met myself unexpectedly I got a shock and caught my breath, and was as irritated for being startled as a person is when he runs up against himself in a mirror which he didn't know was there.

Of course the destruction of a youth by supernatural flames summoned unlawfully from hell was not an event that could be hidden. The news of it went quickly all about and made a great and terrifying excitement in the village and the region, and at once a summons came for the magician to appear before a commission of the Holy Office. He could not be found. Then a second summons was posted, admonishing him to appear within twenty-four hours or remain subject to the pains and penalties attaching to contumacy. It did not seem to us likely that he would accept either of these invitations, if he could get out of it.

All day long, things went as I have described—a dreary time. Next day it was the same, with the added gloom of the preparations for the burial. This took place at midnight, in accordance with the law in such cases, and was attended by all the occupants of the castle except the sick lady and the Duplicates. We buried the ashes in waste ground half a mile from the castle, without prayer or blessing, unless the tears of Katrina and our sorrow were in some sense a blessing. It was a gusty night, with flurries of snow, and a black sky with ragged cloud-rack driving across it. We came on foot, bearing flaring and unsteady torches; and when all was over, we inverted the torches and thrust them into the soft mould of the grave and so left them, sole and perishable memorial and remembrancer of him who was gone.

Home again, it was with a burdened and desolate weight at my heart that I entered my room. There sat the corpse!

Chapter 18

MY senses forsook me and I should have fallen, but it put up its hand and flipped its fingers toward me and this brought an influence of some kind which banished my faint and restored me; yes, more than that, for I was fresher and finer now than I had been before the fatigues of the funeral. I started away at once and with such haste as I could command, for I had never seen the day that I was not afraid of a ghost or would stay where one was if there was another place convenient. But I was stopped by a word, in a voice which I knew and which was music to my ears—

"Come back! I am alive again, it is not a ghost."

I returned, but I was not comfortable, for I could not at once realize that he was really and solidly alive again, although I knew he was, for the fact was plain enough, the cat could have recognized it. As indeed the cat did; he came loafing in, waving his tail in greeting and satisfaction, and when he saw 44 he roached his back and inflated his tail and dropped a pious word and started away on urgent business; but 44 laughed, and called him back and explained to him in the cat language, and stroked him and petted him and sent him away to the other animals with the news; and in a minute here they came, padding and pattering from all directions, and they piled themselves all over him in their joy, nearly hiding him from sight, and all talking at once, each in his own tongue, and 44 answering in the language of each; and finally he fed them liberally with all sorts of palatable things from my cupboard (where there hadn't been a thing before), and sent them away convinced and happy.

By this time my tremors were gone and I was at rest, there was nothing in my mind or heart but thankfulness to have him back again, except wonder as to how it could be, and whether he had really been dead or had only seemed to perish in a magic-show and illusion; but he answered the thought while fetching a hot supper from my empty cupboard, saying—

"It wasn't an illusion, I died;" and added indifferently, "it is nothing, I have done it many a time!"

It was a hardy statement, and I did not strain myself with trying to believe it, but of course I did not say so. His supper was beyond praise for toothsomeness, but I was not acquainted with any of the dishes. He said they were all foreign, from various corners of the globe. An amazing thing, I thought, yet it seemed to me it must be true. There was a very rare-done bird that was peculiarly heavenly; it seemed to be a kind of duck.

"Canvas-back," he said, "hot from America!"

"What is America?"

"It's a country."

"A country?"

"Yes."

"Where?"

"Oh, away off. It hasn't been discovered yet. Not quite. Next fall."

"Have you—"

"Been there? Yes; in the past, in the present, in the future. You should see it four or five centuries from now! This duck is of that period. How do you like the Duplicates?"

It was his common way, the way of a boy, and most provoking: careless, capricious, unstable, never sticking to a subject, forever flitting and sampling here and there and yonder, like a bee; always, just as he was on the point of becoming interesting, he changed the subject. I was annoyed, but concealed it as well as I could, and answered—

"Oh, well, they are well enough, but they are not popular. They won't join the union, they work for nothing, the men resent their intrusion. There you have the situation: the men dislike them, and they are bitter upon the magician for sending them."

It seemed to give 44 an evil delight. He rubbed his hands vigorously together, and said—

"They were a good idea, the Duplicates; judiciously handled, they will make a lot of trouble! Do you know, those creatures are not uninteresting, all things considered, for they are not *real* persons."

"Heavens, what are they, then!"

"I will explain. Move up to the fire."

We left the table and its savory wreckage, and took comfortable seats, each at his own customary side of the fire, which blazed up briskly now, as if in a voluntary welcome of us. Then 44 reached up and took from the mantelpiece some things which I had not noticed there before: a slender reed stem with a small red-clay cup at the end of it, and a dry and dark-colored leaf, of a breed unknown to me. Chatting along,—I watching curiously—he crushed the crisp leaf in his palm, and filled that little cup with it; then he put the stem in his mouth and touched the cup with his finger, which instantly set fire to the vegetable matter and sent up a column of smoke and I dived under the bed, thinking something might happen. But nothing did, and so upon persuasion I returned to my chair but moved it a little further, for 44 was tilting his head far back and shooting ring after ring of blue smoke toward the ceiling—delicate gauzy revolving circlets, beautiful to see; and always each new ring took enlargement and 44 fired the next one through it with a good aim and happy art, and he *did* seem to enjoy it so; but not I, for I believed his entrails were on fire, and could perhaps explode and hurt some one, and most likely the wrong person, just as happens at riots and such things.

But nothing occurred, and I grew partially reconciled to the conditions, although the odor of the smoke was nauseating and a little difficult to stand. It seemed strange that he could endure it, and stranger still that he should seem to enjoy it. I turned the mystery over in my mind and concluded it was most likely a pagan religious service, and therefore I took my cap off, not in reverence but as a matter of discretion. But he said—

"No, it is only a vice, merely a vice, but not a religious one. It originated in Mexico."

"What is Mexico?"

"It's a country."

"A country?"

"Yes."

"Where is it?"

"Away off. It hasn't been discovered yet."

"Have you ever—"

"Been there? Yes, many times. In the past, in the present, and in the future. No, the Duplicates are not real, they are fictions. I will explain about them."

I sighed, but said nothing. He was always disappointing; I wanted to hear about Mexico.

"The way of it is this," he said. "You know, of course, that you are not one person, but two. One is your Workaday-Self, and 'tends to business, the other is your Dream-Self, and has no responsibilities, and cares only for romance and excursions and adventure. It sleeps when your other self is awake; when your other self sleeps, your Dream-Self has full control, and does as it pleases. It has far more imagination than has the Workaday-Self, therefore its pains and pleasures are far more real and intense than are those of the other self, and its adventures correspondingly picturesque and extraordinary. As a rule, when a party of Dream-Selves—whether comrades or strangers—get together and flit abroad in the globe, they have a tremendous time. But you understand, they have no substance, they are only spirits. The Workaday-Self has a harder lot and a duller time; it can't get away from the flesh, and is clogged and hindered by it; and also by the low grade of its own imagination."

"But 44, these Duplicates are solid enough!"

"So they are, apparently, but it is only fictitious flesh and bone, put upon them by the magician and me. We pulled them out of the Originals and gave them this independent life."

"Why, 44, they fight and bleed, like anybody!"

"Yes, and they *feel*, too. It is not a bad job, in the solidifying line, I've never seen better flesh put together by enchantment; but no matter, it is a pretty airy fabric, and if we should remove the spell they would vanish like blowing out a candle. Ah, they are a capable lot, with their measureless imaginations! If they imagine there is a mystic clog upon them and it takes them a couple of hours to set a couple of lines, that is what happens; but on the contrary, if they imagine it takes them but half a second to set a whole galleyful of matter, *that* is what happens! A dandy lot is that handful of Duplicates, and the easy match of a thousand real printers! Handled judiciously, they'll make plenty of trouble."

"But why should you *want* them to make trouble, 44?"

"Oh, merely to build up the magician's reputation. If they once get their imaginations started . . . . . oh, the consuming intensity and effectiveness of it!" He pondered a while, then said, indolently, "Those Originals are in love with these women and are not making any headway; now then, if we arrange it so that the Duplicates . . . . . lad, it's getting late—for you; time does not exist, for me. August, that is a nice table-service—you may have it. Good-night!" and he vanished.

It was heavy silver, and ornate, and on one great piece was engraved "America Cup;" on the others were chased these words, which had no meaning for me: "New York Yacht Club, 1903."

I sighed, and said to myself, "It may be that he is not honest." After some days I obliterated the words and dates, and sold the service at a good price.

Chapter 19

DAY after day went by, and Father Adolf was a busy man, for he was the head of the Commission charged with trying and punishing the magician; but he had no luck, he could come upon no trace of the necromancer. He was disappointed and exasperated, and he swore hard and drank hard, but nothing came of it, he made no progress in his hunt. So, as a vent for his wrath he turned upon the poor Duplicates, declaring them to be evil spirits, wandering devils, and condemned them to the stake on his own arbitrary authority, but 44 told me he (44,) wouldn't allow them to be hurt, they being useful in the building up of the magician's reputation.

Whether 44 was really their protector or not, no matter, they certainly had protection, for every time Father Adolf chained them to the stake they vanished and left the stake empty before the fire could be applied, and straightway they would be found at work in the shop and not in any way frightened or disturbed. After several failures Father Adolf gave it up in a rage, for he was becoming ridiculous and a butt for everybody's private laughter. To cover his chagrin he pretended that he had not really tried to burn them, he only wanted to scare them; and said he was only postponing the roasting, and that it would take place presently, when he should find that the right time had come. But not many believed him, and Doangivadam, to show how little he cared for Adolf's pretensions, took out a fire insurance policy upon his Duplicate. It was an impudent thing to do, and most irreverent, and made Father Adolf very angry, but he pretended that he did not mind it.

As 44 had expected, the Duplicates fell to making love to the young women, and in such strenuous fashion that they soon cut out the Originals and left them out in the cold; which made bad blood, and constant quarrels and fights resulted. Soon the castle was no better than a lunatic asylum. It was a cat-and-dog's life all around, but there was no helping it. The master loved peace, and he tried his best to reconcile the parties and make them friendly to each other, but it was not possible, the brawling and fighting went on in spite of all he could do. Forty-Four and I went about, visible to each other but to no one else, and we witnessed these affrays, and 44 enjoyed them and was perfectly charmed with them. Well, he had his own tastes. I was not always invisible, of course, for that would have caused remark; I showed up often enough to prevent that.

Whenever I thought I saw a good opportunity I tried to interest 44 in the life eternal, but the innate frivolity of his nature continually defeated my efforts, he could not seem to care for anything but building up the magician's reputation. He said he was interested in that, and in one other thing, *the human race*. He had nettled me more than once by seeming to speak slightingly of the human race. Finally, one day, being annoyed once more by some such remark, I said, acidly—

"You don't seem to think much of the human race; it's a pity you have to belong to it."

He looked a moment or two upon me, apparently in gentle wonder, then answered—

"What makes you think I belong to it?"

The bland audacity of it so mixed my emotions that it was a question which would get first expression, anger or mirth; but mirth got precedence, and I laughed. Expecting him to laugh, too, in response; but he did not. He looked a little hurt at my levity, and said, as in mild reproach—

"I think the human race is well enough, in its way, all things considered, but surely, August, I have never intimated that I belonged to it. Reflect. Now have I?"

It was difficult to know what to say; I seemed to be a little stunned. Presently I said, wonderingly—

"It makes me dizzy; I don't quite know where I am; it is as if I had had a knock on the head. I have had no such confusing and bewildering and catastrophical experience as this before. It is a new and strange and fearful idea: a person who is a person and yet *not a human being*. I cannot grasp it, I do not know how it can be, I have never dreamed of so tremendous a thing, so amazing a thing! Since you are not a human being, what *are* you?"

"Ah," he said, "now we have arrived at a point where words are useless; words cannot even convey *human* thought capably, and they can do nothing at all with thoughts whose realm and orbit are outside the human solar system, so to speak. I will use the language of my country, where words are not known. During half a moment my spirit shall speak to yours and tell you something about me. Not much, for it is not much of me that you would be able to understand, with your limited human mentality."

While he was speaking, my head was illuminated by a single sudden flash as of lightning, and I recognised that it had conveyed to me some knowledge of him; enough to fill me with awe. Envy, too—I do not mind confessing it. He continued—

"Now then, things which have puzzled you heretofore are not a mystery to you any more, for you are now aware that there is nothing I cannot do—and lay it on the magician and increase his reputation; and you are also now aware that the difference between a human being and me is as the difference between a drop of water and the sea, a rushlight and the sun, the difference between the infinitely trivial and the infinitely sublime! I say—we'll be comrades, and have scandalous good times!" and he slapped me on the shoulder, and his face was all alight with good-fellowship.

I said I was in awe of him, and was more moved to pay him reverence than to—

"Reverence!" he mocked; "put it away; the sun doesn't care for the rushlight's reverence, put it away. Come, we'll be boys together and comrades! Is it agreed?"

I said I was too much wounded, just now, to have any heart in levities, I must wait a little and get somewhat over this hurt; that I would rather beseech and persuade him to put all light things aside for a season and seriously and thoughtfully study my unjustly disesteemed race, whereby I was sure he would presently come to estimate it at its right and true value, and worthy of the sublime rank it had always held, undisputed, as the noblest work of God.

He was evidently touched, and said he was willing, and would do according to my desire, putting light things aside and taking up this small study in all heartiness and candor.

I was deeply pleased; so pleased that I would not allow his thoughtless characterization of it as a "small" study to greatly mar my pleasure; and to this end admonishing myself to remember that he was speaking a foreign language and must not be expected to perceive nice distinctions in the values of words. He sat musing a little while, then he said in his kindest and thoughtfulest manner—

"I am sure I can say with truth that I have no prejudices against the human race or other bugs, and no aversions, no malignities. I have known the race a long time, and out of my heart I can say that I have always felt more sorry for it than ashamed of it."

He said it with the gratified look of a person who has uttered a graceful and flattering thing. By God, I think he expected thanks! He did not get them; I said not a word. That made a pause, and was a little awkward for him for the moment; then he went on—

"I have often visited this world—often. It shows that I felt an interest in this race; it is proof, proof absolute, that I felt an interest in it." He paused, then looked up with one of those inane self-approving smiles on his face that are so trying, and added, "there is nothing just like it in any other world, it is a race by itself, and in many ways amusing."

He evidently thought he had said another handsome thing; he had the satisfied look of a person who thought he was oozing compliments at every pore. I retorted, with bitter sarcasm—I couldn't help it—

"As 'amusing' as a basket of monkeys, no doubt!"

It clean failed! He didn't know it was sarcasm.

"Yes," he said, serenely, "as amusing as those—and even more so, it may be claimed; for monkeys, in their mental and moral freaks show not so great variety, and therefore are the less entertaining."

This was too much. I asked, coldly—

But he was gone.

Chapter 20

A WEEK passed.
Meantime, where was he? what was become of him? I had gone often to his room, but had always found it vacant. I was missing him sorely. Ah, he was so interesting! there was none that could approach him for that. And there could not be a more engaging mystery than he. He was always doing and saying strange and curious things, and then leaving them but half explained or not explained at all. Who was he? what was he? where was he from? I wished I knew. Could he be converted? could he be saved? Ah, if only this could happen, and I be in some humble way a helper toward it!

While I was thus cogitating about him, he appeared—gay, of course, and even more gaily clad than he was that day that the magician burnt him. He said he had been "home." I pricked up my ears hopefully, but was disappointed: with that mere touch he left the subject, just as if because it had no interest for him it couldn't have any for others. A chuckle-headed idea, certainly. He was handy about disparaging other people's reasoning powers, but it never seemed to occur to him to look nearer home. He smacked me on the thigh and said,

"Come, you need an outing, you've been shut up here quite long enough. I'll do the handsome thing by you, now— I'll show you something creditable to your race."

That pleased me, and I said so; and said it was very kind and courteous of him to find *something* to its credit, and be good enough to mention it.

"Oh, yes," he said, lightly, and paying no attention to my sarcasm, "I'll show you a really creditable thing. At the same time I'll have to show you something discreditable, too, but that's nothing—that's merely human, you know. Make yourself invisible."

I did so, and he did the like. We were presently floating away, high in the air, over the frosty fields and hills.

"We shall go to a small town fifty miles removed," he said. "Thirty years ago Father Adolf was priest there, and was thirty years old. Johann Brinker, twenty years old, resided there, with his widowed mother and his four sisters—three younger than himself, and one a couple of years older, and marriageable. He was a rising young artist. Indeed one might say that he had already risen, for he had exhibited a picture in Vienna which had brought him great praise, and made him at once a celebrity. The family had been very poor, but now his pictures were wanted, and he sold all of his little stock at fine prices, and took orders for as many more as he could paint in two or three years. It was a happy family! and was suddenly become courted, caressed and—envied, of course, for that is human. To be envied is the human being's chiefest joy.

"Then a thing happened. On a winter's morning Johann was skating, when he heard a choking cry for help, and saw that a man had broken through the ice and was struggling; he flew to the spot, and recognised Father Adolf, who was becoming exhausted by the cold and by his unwise strugglings, for he was not a swimmer. There was but one way to do, in the circumstances, and that was, to plunge in and keep the priest's head up until further help should come—which was on the way. Both men were quickly rescued by the people.

Within the hour Father Adolf was as good as new, but it was not so with Johann. He had been perspiring freely, from energetic skating, and the icy water had consequences for him. Here is his small house, we will go in and see him."

We stood in the bedroom and looked about us. An elderly woman with a profoundly melancholy face sat at the fireside with her hands folded in her lap, and her head bowed, as with age-long weariness—that pathetic attitude which says so much! Without audible words the spirit of 44 explained to me—

"The marriageable sister. There was no marriage."

On a bed, half reclining and propped with pillows and swathed in wraps was a grizzled man of apparently great age, with hollow cheeks, and with features drawn by immemorial pains; and now and then he stirred a little, and softly moaned—whereat a faint spasm flitted across the sister's face, and it was as if that moan had carried a pain to her heart. The spirit of 44 breathed upon me again:

"Since that day it has been like this—thirty years!—"

"My God!"

"It is true. Thirty years. He has his wits—the worse for him—the cruelty of it! He cannot speak, he cannot hear, he cannot see, he is wholly helpless, the half of him is paralysed, the other half is but a house of entertainment for bodily miseries. At risk of his life he saved a fellow-being. It has cost him ten thousand deaths!"

Another sad-faced woman entered. She brought a bowl of gruel with her, and she fed it to the man with a spoon, the other woman helping.

"August, the four sisters have stood watches over this bed day and night for thirty years, ministering to this poor wreck. Marriage, and homes and families of their own was not for them; they gave up all their hopeful young dreams and suffered the ruin of their lives, in order to ameliorate as well as they might the miseries of their brother. They laid him upon this bed in the bright morning of his youth and in the golden glory of his new-born fame—and look at him now! His mother's heart broke, and she went mad. Add up the sum: one broken heart, five blighted and blasted young lives. All this it costs to save a priest for a life-long career of vice and all forms of shameless rascality! Come, come, let us go, before these enticing rewards for well-doing unbalance my judgment and persuade me to become a human being myself!"

In our flight homeward I was depressed and silent, there was a heavy weight upon my spirit; then presently came a slight uplift and a glimmer of cheer, and I said—

"Those poor people will be richly requited for all they have sacrificed and suffered."

"Oh, perhaps," he said, indifferently.

"It is my belief," I retorted. "And certainly a large mercy has been shown the poor mother, in granting her a blessed mental oblivion and thus emancipating her from miseries which the others, being younger, were better able to bear."

"The madness was a mercy, you think?"

"With the broken heart, yes; for without doubt death resulted quickly and she was at rest from her troubles."

A faint spiritual cackle fell upon my ear. After a moment 44 said—

"At dawn in the morning I will show you something."

Chapter 21

I SPENT a wearying and troubled night, for in my dreams I was a member of that ruined family and suffering with it through a dragging long stretch of years; and the infamous priest whose life had been saved at cost of these pains and sorrows seemed always present and drunk and mocking. At last I woke. In the dimmest of cold gray dawns I made out a figure sitting by my bed—an old and white-headed man in the coarse dress of a peasant.

"Ah," I said, "who are you, good man?"

It was 44. He said, in a wheezy old voice, that he was merely showing himself to me so that I would recognize him when I saw him later. Then he disappeared, and I did the same, by his order. Soon we were sailing over the village in the frosty air, and presently we came to earth in an open space behind the monastery. It was a solitude, except that a thinly and rustily clad old woman was there, sitting on the frozen ground and fastened to a post by a chain around her waist. She could hardly hold her head up for drowsiness and the chill in her bones. A pitiful spectacle she was, in the vague dawn and the stillness, with the faint winds whispering around her and the powdery snow-whorls frisking and playing and chasing each other over the black ground. Forty-Four made himself visible, and stood by, looking down upon her. She raised her old head wearily, and when she saw that it was a kindly face that was before her she said appealingly—

"Have pity on me—I am *so* tired and so cold, and the night has been so long, so long! light the fire and put me out of my misery!"

"Ah, poor soul, I am not the executioner, but tell me if I can serve you, and I will."

She pointed to a pile of fagots, and said,

"They are for me, a few can be spared to warm me, they will not be missed, there will be enough left to burn me with, oh, much more than enough, for this old body is sapless and dry. Be good to me!"

"You shall have your wish," said 44, and placed a fagot before her and lit it with a touch of his finger.

The flame flashed crackling up, and the woman stretched her lean hands over it, and out of her eyes she looked the gratitude that was too deep for words. It was weird and pathetic to see her getting comfort and happiness out of that fuel that had been provided to inflict upon her an awful death! Presently she looked up wistfully and said—

"You are good to me, you are very good to me, and I have no friends. I am not bad—you must not think I am bad, I am only poor and old, and smitten in my wits these many many years. They think I am a witch; it is the priest, Adolf, that caught me, and it is he that has condemned me. But I am not that—no, God forbid! You do not believe I am a witch?—say you do not believe that of me."

"Indeed I do not."

"Thank you for that kind word! . . . . . How long it is that I have wandered homeless—oh, many years, many! . . . . Once I had a home—I do not know where it was; and four sweet girls and a son—how dear they were! The name . . . . . the name . . . . . but I have forgotten the name. All dead, now, poor things, these many years . . . . . . If you could have seen my son! ah, so good he was, and a painter . . . . oh, such pictures he painted! . . . . Once he saved a man's life . . . . . or it could have been a woman's . . . . . . a person drowning in the ice—"

She lost her way in a tangle of vague memories, and fell to nodding her head and mumbling and muttering to herself, and I whispered anxiously in the ear of 44—

"You will save her? You will get the word to the priest, and when he knows who she is he will set her free and we will restore her to her family, God be praised!"

"No," answered 44.

"No? Why?"

"She was appointed from the beginning of time to die at the stake this day."

"How do *you* know?"

He made no reply. I waited a moment, in growing distress, then said—

"At least *I* will speak! I will tell her story. I will make myself visible, and I—"

"It is not so written," he said; "that which is not foreordained will not happen."

He was bringing a fresh fagot. A burly man suddenly appeared, from the monastery, and ran toward him and struck the fagot from his hand, saying roughly—

"You meddling old fool, mind what you are about! Pick it up and carry it back."

"And if I don't—what then?"

In his fury at being so addressed by so mean and humble a person the man struck a blow at 44's jaw with his formidable fist, but 44 caught the fist in his hand and crushed it; it was sickening to hear the bones crunch. The man staggered away, groaning and cursing, and 44 picked up the fagot and renewed the old woman's fire with it. I whispered—

"Quick—disappear, and let us get away from here; that man will soon—"

"Yes, I know," said 44, "he is summoning his underlings; they will arrest me."

"Then come—come along!"

"What good would it do? It is written. What is written

must happen. But it is of no consequence, nothing will come of it."

They came running—half a dozen—and seized him and dragged him away, cuffing him with fists and beating him with sticks till he was red with his own blood. I followed, of course, but I was merely a substanceless spirit, and there was nothing that I could do in his defence. They chained him in a dim chamber under the monastery and locked the doors and departed, promising him further attentions when they should be through with burning the witch. I was troubled beyond measure, but he was not. He said he would use this opportunity to increase the magician's reputation: he would spread the report that the aged hand-crusher was the magician in disguise.

"They will find nothing here but the prisoner's clothes when they come," he said, "then they will believe."

He vanished out of the clothes, and they slumped down in a pile. He could certainly do some wonderful things, featherheaded and frivolous as he was! There was no way of accounting for 44. We soared out through the thick walls as if they had been made of air, and followed a procession of chanting monks to the place of the burning. People were gathering, and soon they came flocking in crowds, men, women, youths, maidens; and there were even children in arms.

There was a half hour of preparation: a rope ring was widely drawn around the stake to keep the crowd at a distance; within this a platform was placed for the use of the preacher—Adolf. When all was ready he came, imposingly attended, and was escorted with proper solemnity and ceremony to this pulpit. He began his sermon at once and with business-like energy. He was very bitter upon witches, "familiars of the Fiend, enemies of God, abandoned of the angels, foredoomed to hell;" and in closing he denounced this present one unsparingly, and forbade any to pity her.

It was all lost upon the prisoner; she was warm, she was comfortable, she was worn out with fatigue and sorrow and privation, her gray head was bowed upon her breast, she was asleep. The executioners moved forward and raised her upon her feet and drew her chains tight, around her breast. She looked drowsily around upon the people while the fagots were being piled, then her head drooped again, and again she slept.

The fire was applied and the executioners stepped aside, their mission accomplished. A hush spread everywhere: there was no movement, there was not a sound, the massed people gazed, with lips apart and hardly breathing, their faces petrified in a common expression, partly of pity, mainly of horror. During more than a minute that strange and impressive absence of motion and movement continued, then it was broken in a way to make any being with a heart in his breast shudder—a man lifted his little child and sat her upon his shoulder, that she might see the better!

The blue smoke curled up about the slumberer and trailed away upon the chilly air; a red glow began to show at the base of the fagots; this increased in size and intensity and a sharp crackling sound broke upon the stillness; suddenly a sheet of flame burst upward and swept the face of the sleeper, setting her hair on fire, she uttered an agonizing shriek which was answered by a horrified groan from the crowd, then she cried out "Thou art merciful and good to Thy sinful servant, blessed be Thy holy Name—sweet Jesus receive my spirit!"

Then the flames swallowed her up and hid her from sight. Adolf stood sternly gazing upon his work. There was now a sudden movement upon the outskirts of the crowd, and a monk came plowing his way through and delivered a message to the priest—evidently a pleasant one to the receiver of it, if signs go for anything. Adolf cried out—

"Remain, everybody! It is reported to me that that arch malignant the magician, that son of Satan, is caught, and lies a chained prisoner under the monastery, disguised as an aged peasant. He is already condemned to the flames, no preliminaries are needed, his time is come. Cast the witch's ashes to the winds, clear the stake! Go—you, and you, and you—bring the sorcerer!"

The crowd woke up! this was a show to their taste. Five minutes passed—ten. What might the matter be? Adolf was growing fiercely impatient. Then the messengers returned, crestfallen. They said the magician was gone—gone, through the bolted doors and the massive walls; nothing was left of him but his peasant clothes! And they held them up for all to see.

The crowd stood amazed, wondering, speechless—and disappointed. Adolf began to storm and curse. Forty-Four whispered—

"The opportunity is come. I will personate the magician and make some more reputation for him. Oh, just watch me raise the limit!"

So the next moment there was a commotion in the midst of the crowd, which fell apart in terror exposing to view the supposed magician in his glittering oriental robes; and his face was white with fright, and he was trying to escape. But there was no escape for him, for there was one there whose boast it was that he feared neither Satan nor his servants—this being Adolf the admired. Others fell back cowed, but not he; he plunged after the sorcerer, he chased him, gained upon him, shouted, "Yield—in His Name I command!"

An awful summons! Under the blasting might of it the spurious magician reeled and fell as if he had been smitten by a bolt from the sky. I grieved for him with all my heart and in the deepest sincerity, and yet I rejoiced for that at last he had learned the power of that Name at which he had so often and so recklessly scoffed. And all too late, too late, forever and ever too late—ah, why had he not listened to me!

There were no cowards there, now! Everybody was brave, everybody was eager to help drag the victim to the stake, they swarmed about him like raging wolves; they jerked him this way and that, they beat him and reviled him, they cuffed him and kicked him, he wailing, sobbing, begging for pity, the conquering priest exulting, scoffing, boasting, laughing. Briskly they bound him to the stake and piled the fagots around him and applied the fire; and there the forlorn creature stood weeping and sniffling and pleading in his fantastic robes, a sorry contrast to that poor humble Christian who but a little while before had faced death there so bravely. Adolf lifted his hand and pronounced with impressive solemnity the words—

"Depart, damned soul, to the regions of eternal woe!"

Whereat the weeping magician laughed sardonically in his face and vanished away, leaving his robes empty and hanging collapsed in the chains! There was a whisper at my ear—

"Come, August, let us to breakfast and leave these animals to gape and stare while Adolf explains to them the unexplainable—a job just in his line. By the time I have finished with the sorcerer he will have a dandy reputation—don't you think?"

So all his pretence of being struck down by the Name was a blasphemous jest. And I had taken it so seriously, so confidingly, innocently, exultantly. I was ashamed. Ashamed of him, ashamed of myself. Oh, manifestly nothing was serious to him, levity was the blood and marrow of him, death was a joke; his ghastly fright, his moving tears, his frenzied supplications—by God, it was all just coarse and vulgar horseplay! The only thing he was capable of being interested in, was his damned magician's reputation! I was too disgusted to talk, I answered him nothing, but left him to chatter over his degraded performance unobstructed, and rehearse it and chuckle over it and glorify it up to his taste.

Chapter 22

IT was in my room. He brought it—the breakfast—dish after dish, smoking hot, from my empty cupboard, and briskly set the table, talking all the while—ah, yes, and pleasantly, fascinatingly, winningly; and not about that so-recent episode, but about these fragrant refreshments and the far countries he had summoned them from—Cathay, India, and everywhere; and as I was famishing, this talk was pleasing, indeed captivating, and under its influence my sour mood presently passed from me. Yes, and it was healing to my bruised spirit to look upon the rich and costly table-service—quaint of shape and pattern, delicate, ornate, exquisite, beautiful!—and presently quite likely to be mine, you see.

"Hot corn-pone from Arkansas—split it, butter it, close your eyes and enjoy! Fried spring chicken—milk-and-flour gravy—from Alabama. Try it, and grieve for the angels, for they have it not! Cream-smothered strawberries, with the prairie-dew still on them—let them melt in your mouth, and don't try to say what you feel! Coffee from Vienna—fluffed cream—two pellets of saccharin—drink, and have compassion for the Olympian gods that know only nectar!"

I ate, I drank, I reveled in these alien wonders; truly I was in Paradise!

"It is intoxication," I said, "it is delirium!"

"It's a jag!" he responded.

I inquired about some of the refreshments that had outlandish names. Again that weird detail: they were non-existent as yet, they were products of the unborn *future!* Understand it? How could I? Nobody could. The mere *trying* muddled the head. And yet it was a pleasure to turn those curious names over on the tongue and taste them: Corn-pone! Arkansas! Alabama! Prairie! Coffee! Saccharin! Forty-Four answered my thought with a stingy word of explanation—

"Corn-pone is made from maize. Maize is known only in America. America is not discovered yet. Arkansas and Alabama will be States, and will get their names two or three centuries hence. Prairie—a future French-American term for a meadow like an ocean. Coffee: they have it in the Orient, they will have it here in Austria two centuries from now. Saccharin—concentrated sugar, 500 to 1; as it were, the sweetness of five hundred pretty maids concentrated in a young fellow's sweetheart. Saccharin is not due yet for nearly four hundred years; I am furnishing you several advance-privileges, you see."

"Tell me a little, *little* more, 44—please! You starve me so! and I am so hungry to know how you find out these strange marvels, these impossible things."

He reflected a while, then he said he was in a mood to enlighten me, and would like to do it, but did not know how to go about it, because of my mental limitations and the general meanness and poverty of my construction and qualities. He said this in a most casual and taken-for-granted way, just as an archbishop might say it to a cat, never suspecting that the cat could have any feelings about it or take a different view of the matter. My face flushed, and I said with dignity and a touch of heat—

"I must remind you that I am made in the image of God."

"Yes," he said carelessly, but did not seem greatly impressed

by it, certainly not crushed, not overpowered. I was more indignant than ever, but remained mute, coldly rebuking him
by my silence. But it was wasted on him; he did not see it, he
was thinking. Presently he said—

"It is difficult. Perhaps impossible, unless I should make
you over again." He glanced up with a yearningly explanatory
and apologetic look in his eyes, and added, "For you are an
animal, you see—you understand that?"

I could have slapped him for it, but I austerely held my
peace, and answered with cutting indifference—

"Quite so. It happens to happen that all of us are that."

Of course I was including him, but it was only another
waste—he didn't perceive the inclusion. He said, as one
might whose way has been cleared of an embarrassing ob-
struction—

"Yes, that is just the trouble! It makes it ever so difficult.
With my race it is different; we have no limits of any kind, we
comprehend all things. You see, for your race there is such a
thing as *time*—you cut it up and measure it; to your race
there is a past, a present and a future—out of one and the
same thing you make *three*; and to your race there is also
such a thing as *distance*—and hang it, you measure *that*, too!
. . . . . Let me see: if I could only . . . . if I . . . . oh, no,
it is of no use—there is no such thing as enlightening that
kind of a mind!" He turned upon me despairingly, pathetically, adding, "If it only had *some* capacity, some depth, or
breadth, or—or—but you see it doesn't *hold* anything; one
cannot pour the starred and shoreless expanses of the universe
into a jug!"

I made no reply; I sat in frozen and insulted silence; I
would not have said a word to save his life. But again he was
not aware of what was happening—he was thinking. Presently
he said—

"Well, it is *so* difficult! If I only had a starting-point, a basis
to proceed from—but I can't find any. If—look here: *can't*
you extinguish time? *can't* you comprehend eternity? can't
you conceive of a thing like that—a thing with *no* beginning—a thing that *always* was? Try it!"

"Don't! I've tried it a hundred times," I said, "It makes my
brain whirl just to think of it!"

He was in despair again.

"Dear me—to think that there can be an ostensible Mind that cannot conceive of so simple a trifle as that! . . . . Look here, August: there are really no divisions of time—none at all. The past is always present when I want it—the *real* past, not an image of it; I can summon it, and there it *is*. The same with the future: I can summon it out of the unborn ages, and there it is, before my eyes, alive and real, not a fancy, an image, a creation of the imagination. Ah, these troublesome limitations of yours!—they hamper me. Your race cannot even conceive of something being made out of nothing—I am aware of it, your learned men and philosophers are always confessing it. They say there had to be *something* to start with—meaning a solid, a substance—to build the world out of. Man, it is perfectly simple—it was built out of *thought*. Can't you comprehend that?"

"No, I can't! *Thought!* There is no substance to thought; then how is a material thing going to be constructed out of it?"

"But August, I don't mean *your* kind of thought, I mean my kind, and the kind that the gods exercise."

"Come, what is the difference? Isn't thought just *thought*, and all said?"

"No. A man *originates* nothing in his head, he merely observes exterior things, and *combines* them in his head—puts several observed things together and draws a conclusion. His mind is merely a machine, that is all—an *automatic* one, and he has no control over it; it cannot conceive of a *new* thing, an original thing, it can only gather material from the outside and combine it into new *forms* and patterns. But it always has to have the *materials* from the *outside*, for it can't make them itself. That is to say, a man's mind cannot *create*—a god's can, and my race can. That is the difference. *We* need no contributed materials, we *create* them—out of thought. All things that exist were made out of thought—and out of nothing else."

It seemed to me charitable, also polite, to take him at his word and not require proof, and I said so. He was not offended. He only said—

"Your automatic mind has performed its function—its sole

function—and without help from you. That is to say, it has listened, it has observed, it has put this and that together, and drawn a conclusion—the conclusion that my statement was a doubtful one. It is now privately beginning to wish for a test. Is that true?"

"Well, yes," I said, "I won't deny it, though for courtesy's sake I would have concealed it if I could have had my way."

"Your mind is automatically suggesting that I offer a specific proof—that I create a dozen gold coins out of nothing; that is to say, out of *thought*. Open your hand—they are there."

And so they were! I wondered; and yet I was not very greatly astonished, for in my private heart I judged—and not for the first time—that he was using magic learned from the magician, and that he had no gifts in this line that did not come from that source. But was this so? I dearly wanted to ask this question, and I started to do it. But the words refused to leave my tongue, and I realized that he had applied that mysterious check which had so often shut off a question which I wanted to ask. He seemed to be musing. Presently he ejaculated—

"That poor old soul!"

It gave me a pang, and brought back the stake, the flames and the death-cry; and I said—

"It was a shame and a pity that she wasn't rescued."

"Why a pity?"

"*Why?* How can you ask, 44?"

"What would she have gained?"

"An extension of life, for instance; is that nothing?"

"Oh, there spoke the human! He is always pretending that the eternal bliss of heaven is such a priceless boon! Yes, and always keeping out of heaven just as long as he can! At bottom, you see, he is far from being certain about heaven."

I was annoyed at my carelessness in giving him that chance. But I allowed it to stand at that, and said nothing; it could not help the matter to go into it further. Then, to get away from it I observed that there was at least one gain that the woman could have had if she had been saved: she might have entered heaven by a less cruel death.

"She isn't going there," said 44, placidly.

It gave me a shock, and also it angered me, and I said with some heat—

"You seem to know a good deal about it—*how* do you know?"

He was not affected by my warmth, neither did he trouble to answer my question; he only said—

"The woman could have gained nothing worth considering—certainly nothing worth measuring by your curious methods. What are ten years, subtracted from ten billion years? It is the ten-thousandth part of a second—that is to say, it is nothing at all. Very well, she is in hell now, she will remain there forever. Ten years subtracted from it wouldn't count. Her bodily pain at the stake lasted six minutes—to save her from *that* would not have been worthwhile. That poor creature is in hell; see for yourself!"

Before I could beg him to spare me, the red billows were sweeping by, and she was there among the lost.

The next moment the crimson sea was gone, with its evoker, and I was alone.

Chapter 23

YOUNG as I was—I was barely seventeen—my days were now sodden with depressions, there was little or no rebound. My interest in the affairs of the castle and of its occupants faded out and disappeared; I kept to myself and took little or no note of the daily happenings; my Duplicate performed all my duties, and I had nothing to do but wander aimlessly about and be unhappy.

Thus the days wore heavily by, and meantime I was missing something; missing something, and growing more and more conscious of it. I hardly had the daring to acknowledge to myself what it was. It was the master's niece—Marget! I was a secret worshipper; I had been that a long time; I had worshipped her face and her form with my eyes, but to go further would have been quite beyond my courage. It was not for me to aspire so high; not yet, certainly; not in my timid and callow youth. Every time she had blessed me with a passing remark, the thrill of it, the bliss of it had tingled through me and swept along every nerve and fibre of me with a sort of ce-lestial ecstasy and given me a wakeful night which was better than sleep. These casual and unconsidered remarks, unvalued by her were treasures to me, and I hoarded them in my mem-ory, and knew when it was that she had uttered each of them, and the occasion and the circumstance that had produced each one, and the tone of her voice and the look of her face and the light in her eye; and there was not a night that I did not pass them through my mind caressingly, and turn them over and pet them and play with them, just as a poor girl pos-sessed of half a dozen cheap seed-pearls might do with her small hoard. But that Marget should ever give me an actual thought—any word or notice above what she might give the cat—ah, I never dreamed of it! As a rule she had never been conscious of my presence at all; as a rule she gave me merely a glance of recognition and nothing more when she passed me by in hall or corridor.

As I was saying, I had been missing her, a number of days. It was because her mother's malady was grown a trifle worse and Marget was spending all her time in the sick room. I rec-ognized, now, that I was famishing to see her, and be near that gracious presence once more. Suddenly, not twenty steps away, she rose upon my sight—a fairy vision! That sweet young face, that dainty figure, that subtle exquisite something that makes seventeen the perfect year and its bloom the per-fect bloom—oh, there it all was, and I stood transfixed and adoring! She was coming toward me, walking slowly, musing, dreaming, heeding nothing, absorbed, unconscious. As she drew near I stepped directly in her way; and as she passed through me the contact invaded my blood as with a delicious fire! She stopped, with a startled look, the rich blood rose in her face, her breath came quick and short through her parted lips, and she gazed wonderingly about her, saying twice, in a voice hardly above a whisper—

"What could it have been?"

I stood devouring her with my eyes, she remained as she was, without moving, as much as a minute, perhaps more; then she said in that same low soliloquising voice, "I was surely asleep—it was a dream—it must have been that—why did I wake?" and saying this, she moved slowly away, down the great corridor.

Nothing can describe my joy. I believed she loved me, and had been keeping her secret, as maidens will; but now I would persuade it out of her; I would be bold, brave, and speak! I made myself visible, and in a minute had overtaken her and was at her side. Excited, happy, confident, I touched her arm, and the warm words began to leap from my mouth—

"Dear Marget! oh, my own, my dar—"

She turned upon me a look of gentle but most chilly and dignified rebuke, allowed it a proper time to freeze where it struck, then moved on, without a word, and left me there. I did not feel inspired to follow.

No, I could not follow, I was petrified with astonishment. Why should she act like that? Why should she be glad to dream of me and not glad to meet me awake? It was a mystery; there was something very strange about this; I could make nothing out of it. I went on puzzling and puzzling over the enigma for a little while, still gazing after her and half crying for shame that I had been so fresh and had gotten such a blistering lesson for it, when I saw her stop. Dear me, she might turn back! I was invisible in half an instant—I wouldn't have faced her again for a province.

Sure enough, she did turn back. I stepped to the wall, and gave her the road. I wanted to fly, but I had no power to do that, the sight of her was a spell that I could not resist; I had to stay, and gaze, and worship. She came slowly along in that same absorbed and dreamy way, again; and just as she was passing by me she stopped, and stood quite still a moment—two or three moments, in fact—then moving on, she said, with a sigh, "I was mistaken, but I thought I faintly felt it again."

Was she sorry it was a mistake? It certainly sounded like that. It put me in a sort of ecstasy of hope, it filled me with a burning desire to test the hope, and I could hardly refrain from stepping out and barring her way again, to see what would happen; but that rebuff was too recent, its smart was still too fresh, and I hadn't the pluck to do it.

But I could feast my eyes upon her loveliness, at any rate,

and in safety, and I would not deny myself that delight. I followed her at a distance, I followed all her wanderings; and when at last she entered her apartment and closed the door, I went to my own place and to my solitude, desolate. But the fever born of that marvelous first contact came back upon me and there was no rest for me. Hour after hour I fought it, but still it prevailed. Night came, and dragged along, there was no abatement. At ten the castle was asleep and still, but I could not sleep. I left my room and went wandering here and there, and presently I was floating through the great corridor again. In the vague light I saw a figure standing motionless in that memorable spot. I recognized it—even less light would have answered for that. I could not help approaching it, it drew me like a magnet. I came eagerly on; but when I was within two or three steps of it I remembered, with a chill, who I was, and stopped. No matter: To be so near to Marget was happiness enough, riches enough! With a quick movement she lifted her head and poised it in the attitude of one who listens—listens with a tense and wistful and breathless interest; it was a happy and longing face that I saw in the dim light; and out of it, as through a veil, looked darkling and humid the eyes I loved so well. I caught a whisper: "I cannot hear anything—no, there is no sound—but it is near, I know it is near, and the dream is come again!" My passion rose and overpowered me and I floated to her like a breath and put my arms about her and drew her to my breast and put my lips to hers, unrebuked, and drew intoxication from them! She closed her eyes, and with a sigh which seemed born of measureless content, she said dreamily, "I love you so—and have so longed for you!"

Her body trembled with each kiss received and repaid, and by the power and volume of the emotions that surged through me I realized that the sensations I knew in my fleshly estate were cold and weak by contrast with those which a spirit feels.

I was invisible, impalpable, substanceless, I was as transparent as the air, and yet I seemed to support the girl's weight and bear it up. No, it was more than seeming, it was an actuality. This was new; I had not been aware that my spirit possessed this force. I must exploit this valuable power, I must examine it, test it, make experiments. I said—

"When I press your hand, dear, do you feel it?"

"Why, of course."

"And when I kiss you?"

"Indeed yes!" and she laughed.

"And do you *feel* my arms about you when I clasp you in them?"

"Why, certainly. What strange questions!"

"Oh, well, it's only to make talk, so that I can hear your voice. It is such music to me, Marget, that I—"

"Marget? Marget? Why do you call me that?"

"Oh, you little stickler for the conventions and proprieties! Have I got to call you Miss Regen? Dear me, I thought we were further along than that!"

She seemed puzzled, and said—

"But why should you call me *that*?"

It was my turn to be puzzled.

"Why should I? I don't know any really good reason, except that it's your name, dear."

"My name, indeed!" and she gave her comely head a toss. "I've never heard it before!"

I took her face between my hands and looked into her eyes to see if she were jesting, but there was nothing there but sweet sincerity. I did not quite know what to say, so at a venture I said—

"Any name that will be satisfactory to you will be lovely to me, you unspeakably adorable creature! Mention it! What shall I call you?"

"Oh, what a time you do have, to make talk, as you call it! What shall you *call* me? Why, call me by my own name—my *first* name—and don't put any Miss to it!"

I was still in the fog, but that was no matter—the longer it might take to work out of it the pleasanter and the better. So I made a start:

"Your first name . . . . your first name . . . . . how annoying, I've forgotten it! What is it, dear?"

The music of her laugh broke out rich and clear, like a bird-song, and she gave me a light box on the ear, and said—

"Forgotten it?—oh, no, that won't do! You are playing some kind of a game—I don't know what it is, but you are not going to catch me. You want me to say it, and then—"

then—why then you are going to spring a trap or a joke or something and make me feel foolish. Is that it? What *is* it you are going to do if I say it, dearheart?"

"*I'll* tell you," I said, sternly, "I am going to bend your head back and cradle your neck in the hollow of my left arm,—so—and squeeze you close—so—and the moment you say it I am going to kiss you on the mouth."

She gazed up from the cradling arm with the proper play-acting humility and resignation, and whispered—

"Lisabet!" and took her punishment without a protest.

"You have been a very good girl," I said, and patted her cheek approvingly. "There wasn't any trap, Lisabet—at least none but this: I pretended that forgetfulness because when the sweetest of all names comes from the sweetest of all lips it is sweeter then than ever, and I wanted to hear you say it."

"Oh, you dear thing! I'll say the rest of it at the same price!"

"Done!"

"Elisabeth von Arnim!"

"One—two—three: a kiss for each component!"

I was out of the fog, I had the name. It was a triumph of diplomacy, and I was proud of it. I repeated the name several times, partly for the pleasure of hearing it and partly to nail it in my memory, then I said I wished we had some more things to trade between us on the same delicious basis. She caught at that, and said—

"We can do *your* name, Martin."

Martin! It made me jump. Whence had she gathered this batch of thitherto unheard-of names? What was the secret of this mystery, the how of it, the why of it, the explanation of it? It was too deep for me, much too deep. However, this was no time to be puzzling over it, I ought to be resuming trade and finding out the rest of my name; so I said—

"Martin is a poor name, except when you say it. Say it again, sweetheart."

"Martin. Pay me!"

Which I did.

"Go on, Betty dear; more music—say the rest of it."

"Martin von Giesbach. I wish there was more of it. Pay!"

I did, and added interest.

Boom-m-m-m! from the solemn great bell in the main tower.

"Half-past eleven—oh, what will mother say! I did not dream it was so late, did you Martin?"

"No, it seemed only fifteen minutes."

"Come, let us hurry," she said, and we hurried—at least after a sort of fashion—with my left arm around her waist and the hollow of her right hand cupped upon my left shoulder by way of having a support. Several times she murmured dreamily, "How happy I am, how happy, happy, happy!" and seemed to lose herself in that thought and be conscious of nothing else. By and by I had a rare start—my Duplicate stepped suddenly out from a bunch of shadows, just as we were passing by! He said, reproachfully—

"Ah, Marget, I waited so long by your door, and you broke your promise! Is this kind of you? is it affectionate?"

Oh, jealousy—I felt the pang of it for the first time.

To my surprise—and joy—the girl took no more notice of him than if he had not been there. She walked right on, she did not seem to see him nor hear him. He was astonished, and stopped still and turned, following her with his eyes. He muttered something, then in a more definite voice he said—

"What a queer attitude—to be holding her hand up in the air like that! . . . . . Why, she's walking in her sleep!"

He began to follow, a few steps behind us. Arrived at Marget's door, I took her—no, Lisbet's!—peachy face between my hands and kissed the eyes and the lips, her delicate hands resting upon my shoulders the while; then she said "Goodnight—good-night and blessed dreams," and passed within. I turned toward my Duplicate. He was standing near by, staring at the vacancy where the girl had been. For a time he did only that. Then he spoke up and said joyfully—

"I've been a jealous fool! That was a kiss—and it was for me! She was dreaming of me. I understand it all, now. And that loving good-night—it was for me, too. Ah, it makes all the difference!" He went to the door and knelt down and kissed the place where she had stood.

I could not endure it. I flew at him and with all my spiritstrength I fetched him an open-handed slat on the jaw that sent him lumbering and spinning and floundering over and over along the stone floor till the wall stopped him. He was greatly surprised. He got up rubbing his bruises and looking admiringly about him for a minute or two, then went limping away, saying—

"I wonder what in hell *that* was!"

Chapter 24

I FLOATED off to my room through the unresisting air, and stirred up my fire and sat down to enjoy my happiness and study over the enigma of those names. By ferreting out of my memory certain scraps and shreds of information garnered from 44's talks I presently untangled the matter, and arrived at an explanation—which was this: the presence of my flesh-and-blood personality was not a circumstance of any interest to Marget Regen, but my presence as a spirit acted upon her hypnotically—as 44 termed it—and plunged her into the somnambulic sleep. This removed her Day-Self from command and from consciousness, and gave the command to her Dream-Self for the time being. Her Dream-Self was a quite definite and independent personality, and for reasons of its own it had chosen to name itself Elisabeth von Arnim. It was entirely unacquainted with Marget Regen, did not even know she existed, and had no knowledge of her affairs, her feelings, her opinions, her religion, her history, nor of any other matter concerning her. On the other hand, Marget was entirely unacquainted with Elisabeth and wholly ignorant of her existence and of all other matters concerning her, including her name.

Marget knew me as August Feldner, her Dream-Self knew me as Martin von Giesbach—*why*, was a matter beyond guessing. Awake, the girl cared nothing for me; steeped in the hypnotic sleep, I was the idol of her heart.

There was another thing which I had learned from 44, and that was this: each human being contains not merely two independent entities, but three—the Waking-Self, the Dream-Self, and the Soul. This last is immortal, the others are functioned by the brain and the nerves, and are physical and mortal; they are not functionable when the brain and nerves are paralysed by a temporary hurt or stupefied by narcotics; and when the man dies *they* die, since their life, their energy and their existence depend solely upon physical sustenance, and they cannot get that from dead nerves and a dead brain. When I was invisible the whole of my physical make-up was gone, nothing connected with it or depending upon it was left. My soul—my immortal spirit—alone remained. Freed from the encumbering flesh, it was able to exhibit forces, passions and emotions of a quite tremendously effective character.

It seemed to me that I had now ciphered the matter out correctly, and unpuzzled the puzzle. I was right, as I found out afterward.

And now a sorrowful thought came to me: all three of my Selves were in love with the one girl, and how could we all be happy? It made me miserable to think of it, the situation was so involved in difficulties, perplexities and unavoidable heart-burnings and resentments.

Always before, I had been tranquilly unconcerned about my Duplicate. To me he was merely a stranger, no more no less; to him I was a stranger; in all our lives we had never chanced to meet until 44 had put flesh upon him; we could not have met if we had wanted to, because whenever one of us was awake and in command of our common brain and nerves the other was of necessity asleep and unconscious. All our lives we had been what 44 called Box and Cox lodgers in the one chamber: aware of each other's existence but not interested in each other's affairs, and never encountering each other save for a dim and hazy and sleepy half-moment on the threshold, when one was coming in and the other going out, and never in any case halting to make a bow or pass a greeting.

And so it was not until my Dream-Self's fleshing that he and I met and spoke. There was no heartiness; we began as mere acquaintances, and so remained. Although we had been born together, at the same moment and of the same womb, there was no spiritual kinship between us; spiritually we were a couple of distinctly independent and unrelated individuals, with equal rights in a common fleshly property, and we cared no more for each other than we cared for any other stranger. My fleshed Duplicate did not even bear my name, but called himself Emil Schwarz.

I was always courteous to my Duplicate, but I avoided him. This was natural, perhaps, for he was my superior. My imagination, compared with his splendid dream-equipment, was as a lightning bug to the lightning; in matters of our trade he could do more with his hands in five minutes than I could do in a day; he did all my work in the shop, and found it but a trifle; in the arts and graces of beguilement and persuasion I was a pauper and he a Croesus; in passion, feeling, emotion, sensation—whether of pain or pleasure—I was phosphorus, he was fire. In a word he had all the intensities one suffers or enjoys in a dream!

This was the creature that had chosen to make love to Marget! In my coarse dull human form, what chance was there for me? Oh, none in the world, none! I knew it, I realized it, and the heartbreak of it was unbearable.

But my Soul, stripped of its vulgar flesh—what was my Duplicate in competition with *that*? Nothing, and less than nothing. The conditions were reversed, as regarded passions, emotions, sensations, and the arts and graces of persuasion. Lisbet was mine, and I could hold her against the world—but only when she was Lisbet, only when her Dream-Self was in command of her person! when she was Marget she was her Waking-Self, and the slave of that reptile! Ah, there could be no help for this, no way out of this fiendish complication. I could have only half of her; the other half, no less dear to me, must remain the possession of another. She was mine, she was his, turn-about.

These desolating thoughts kept racing and chasing and scorching and blistering through my brain without rest or halt, and I could find no peace, no comfort, no healing for the tortures they brought. Lisbet's love, so limitlessly dear and precious to me, was almost lost sight of because I couldn't have Marget's too. By this sign I perceived that I was still a human being; that is to say, a person who wants the earth, and cannot be satisfied unless he can have the whole of it. Well, we are made so; even the humblest of us has the voracity of an emperor.

At early mass the next morning my happiness came back to me, for Marget was there, and the sight of her cured all my sorrows. For a time! She took no notice of me, and I was not expecting she would, therefore I was not troubled about that, and was content to look at her, and breathe the same air with her, and note and admire everything she did and everything she didn't do, and bless myself in these privileges; but when I found she had over-many occasions to glance casually and fleetingly around to her left I was moved to glance around, myself, and see if there was anything particular there. Sure enough there was. It was Emil Schwarz. He was already become a revolting object to me, and I now so detested him that I could hardly look at anything else during the rest of the service; except, of course, Marget.

When the service was over, I lingered outside, and made myself invisible, purposing to follow Marget and resume the wooing. But she did not come. Everybody came out but two,—*those* two. After a little, Marget put her head out and looked around to see if any one was in sight, then she glanced back, with a slight nod, and moved swiftly away. That saddened me, for I interpreted it to mean that the other wooing was to have first place. Next came Schwarz, and him I followed—upward, always upward, by dim and narrow stairways seldom used; and so, to a lofty apartment in the south tower, the luxurious quarters of the departed magician. He entered, and closed the door, but I followed straight through the heavy panels, without waiting, and halted just on the inside. There was a great fire of logs at the other end of the room, and Marget was there! She came briskly to meet this odious Dream-stuff, and flung herself into his arms, and kissed him—and he her, and she him again, and he her again, and so on, and so on, and so on, till it was most unpleasant to look at. But I bore it, for I wanted to know all my misfortune, the full magnitude of it and the particulars. Next, they went arm-in-arm and sat down and cuddled up together on a sofa, and did that all over again—over and over and over and over—the most offensive spectacle I had ever seen, as it seemed to me. Then Schwarz tilted up that beautiful face, using his profane forefinger as a fulcrum under the chin that should have been sacred to me, and looked down into the luminous eyes which should have been wholly mine by rights, and said, archly—

"Little traitor!"

"Traitor? I? How, Emil?"

"You didn't keep your tryst last night."

"Why, Emil, I did!"

"Oh, not you! Come—what did we do? where did we go? For a ducat you can't tell!"

Marget looked surprised—then nonplussed—then a little frightened.

"It is very strange," she said, "very strange . . . . . unaccountable. I seem to have forgotten everything. But I know I was out; I was out till near midnight; I know it because my mother chided me, and tried her best to make me confess what had kept me out so late; and she was very uneasy, and I was cruelly afraid she would suspect the truth. I remember nothing at all of what happened before. Isn't it strange!"

Then the devil Schwarz laughed gaily and said that for a kiss he would unriddle the riddle. So he told her how he had encountered her, and how she was walking in her sleep, and how she was dreaming of him, and how happy it made him to see her kiss the air, imagining she was kissing him. And then they both laughed at the odd incident, and dropped the trifle out of their minds, and fell to trading caresses and endearments again, and thought no more about it.

They talked of the "happy day!"—a phrase that scorched me like a coal. They would win over the mother and the uncle presently—yes, they were quite sure of it. Then they built their future—built it out of sunshine and rainbows and rapture; and went on adding and adding to its golden ecstasies until they were so intoxicated with the prospect that words were no longer adequate to express what they were foreseeing and pre-enjoying, and so died upon their lips and gave place to love's true and richer language, wordless soul-communion: the heaving breast, the deep sigh, the unrelaxing embrace, the shoulder-pillowed head, the bliss-dimmed eyes, the lingering kiss . . . .

By God, my reason was leaving me! I swept forward and enveloped them as with a viewless cloud! In an instant Marget was Lisbet again; and as she sprang to her feet divinely aflame with passion for me I stepped back, and back, and back, she following, then I stopped and she fell panting in my arms, murmuring—

"Oh, my own, my idol, how wearily the time has dragged—do not leave me again!"

That Dream-mush rose astonished, and stared stupidly, his mouth working, but fetching out no words. Then he thought he understood, and started toward us, saying—

"Walking in her sleep again—how suddenly it takes her! . . . . . I wonder how she can lean over like that without falling?"

He arrived and put his arms through me and around her to support her, saying tenderly—

"Wake, dearheart, shake it off, I cannot bear to see you so!"

Lisbet freed herself from his arms and bent a stare of astonishment and wounded dignity upon him, accompanied by words to match—

"Mr. Schwarz, you forget yourself!"

It knocked the reptile stupid for a moment; then he got his bearings and said—

"Oh, please come to yourself, dear, it is so hard to see you like this. But if you can't wake, do come to the divan and sleep it off, and I will so lovingly watch over you, my darling, and protect you from intrusion and discovery. Come, Marget—do!"

"Marget!" Lisbet's eyes kindled, as at a new affront. "What Marget, please? Whom do you take me for? And why do you venture these familiarities?" She softened a little then, seeing how dazed and how pitiably distressed he looked, and added, "I have always treated you with courtesy, Mr. Schwarz, and it is very unkind of you to insult me in this wanton way."

In his miserable confusion he did not know what to say, and so he said the wrong thing—

"Oh, my poor afflicted child, shake it off, be your sweet self again, and let us steep our souls once more in dreams of our happy marriage day and—"

It was too much. She would not let him finish, but broke wrathfully into the midst of his sentence.

"Go away!" she said; "your mind is disordered, you have

been drinking. Go—go at once! I cannot bear the sight of
you!"

He crept humbly away and out at the door, mopping his
eyes with his handkerchief and muttering "Poor afflicted
thing, it breaks my heart to see her so!"

Dear Lisbet, she was just a girl—alternate sunshine and
shower, peremptory soldier one minute, crying the next. Sobbing, she took refuge on my breast, saying—

"Love me, oh my precious one, give me peace, heal my
hurts, charm away the memory of the shame this odious creature has put upon me!"

During half an hour we re-enacted that sofa-scene where it
had so lately been played before, detail by detail, kiss for kiss,
dream for dream, and the bliss of it was beyond words. But
with an important difference: in Marget's case there was a
mamma to be pacified and persuaded, but Lisbet von Arnim
had no such incumbrances; if she had a relative in the world
she was not aware of it; she was free and independent, she
could marry whom she pleased and when she pleased. And so,
with the dearest and sweetest naivety she suggested that to-
day and now was as good a time as any! The suddenness of it,
the unexpectedness of it, would have taken my breath if I had
had any. As it was, it swept through me like a delicious wind
and set my whole fabric waving and fluttering. For a moment
I was gravely embarrassed. Would it be right, would it be
honorable, would it not be treason to let this confiding young
creature marry herself to a viewless detail of the atmosphere?
I knew how to accomplish it, and was burning to do it, but
would it be fair? Ought I not to at least tell her my condition,
and let her decide for herself? Ah . . . . . She might decide
the wrong way!

No, I couldn't bring myself to it, I couldn't run the risk. I
must think—think—think. I must hunt out a good and righteous reason for the marriage without the revelation. That is
the way we are made; when we badly want a thing, we go to
hunting for good and righteous reasons for it; we give it that
fine name to comfort our consciences, whereas we privately
know we are only hunting for plausible ones.

I seemed to find what I was seeking, and I urgently pretended to myself that it hadn't a defect in it. Forty-Four was

my friend; no doubt I could persuade him to return my Dream-Self into my body and lock it up there for good. Schwarz being thus put out of the way, wouldn't my wife's Waking-Self presently lose interest in him and cease from loving him? That looked plausible. Next, by throwing *my* Waking-Self in the way of *her* Waking-Self a good deal and using tact and art, would not a time come when . . . . . oh, it was all as clear as a bell! Certainly. It wouldn't be long, it couldn't be long, before I could retire my Soul into my body, then both Lisbet and Marget being widows and longing for solace and tender companionship, would yield to the faithful beseechings and supplications of my poor inferior Waking-Self and marry *him*. Oh, the scheme was perfect, it was flawless, and my enthusiasm over it was without measure or limit. Lisbet caught that enthusiasm from my face and cried out—

"I know what it is! It is going to be *now*!"

I began to volley the necessary "suggestions" into her head as fast as I could load and fire—for by "suggestion," as 44 had told me, you make the hypnotised subject see and do and feel whatever you please: see people and things that are not there, hear words that are not spoken, eat salt for sugar, drink vinegar for wine, find the rose's sweetness in a stench, carry out all suggested acts—and forget the whole of it when he wakes, and remember the whole of it again whenever the hypnotic sleep returns!

In obedience to suggestion, Lisbet clothed herself as a bride; by suggestion she made obeisance to imaginary altar and priest, and smiled upon imaginary wedding-guests; made the solemn responses; received the ring, bent her dear little head to the benediction, put up her lips for the marriage kiss, and blushed as a new-made wife should before people!

Then, by suggestion altar and priest and friends passed away and we were alone—alone, immeasurably content, the happiest pair in the Duchy of Austria!

Ah . . . . . footsteps! some one coming! I fled to the middle of the room, to emancipate Lisbet from the embarrassment of the hypnotic sleep and be Marget again and ready for emergencies. She began to gaze around and about, surprised, wondering, also a little frightened, I thought.

"Why, where is Emil?" she said. "How strange; I did not

see him go. How could he go and I not see him? . . . . Emil!
. . . . No answer! Surely this magician's den is bewitched.
But we've been here many times, and nothing happened."

At that moment Emil slipped in, closed the door, and said,
apologetically and in a tone and manner charged with the
most respectful formality—

"Forgive me, Miss Regen, but I was afraid for you and have
stood guard—it would not do for you to be found in this
place, and asleep. Your mother is fretting about your absence—her nurse is looking for you everywhere—I have mis-
directed her . . . . . pardon, what is the matter?"

Marget was gazing at him in a sort of stupefaction, with the
tears beginning to trickle down her face. She began to sob in
her hands, and said—

"If I have been asleep it was cruel of you to leave me. Oh,
Emil, how could you desert me at such a time, if you love
me?"

The astonished and happy bullfrog had her in his arms in a
minute and was blistering her with kisses, which she paid back
as fast as she could register them, and she not cold yet from
her marriage-oath! A man—and such a man as that—hugging
my wife before my eyes, and she getting a gross and voracious
satisfaction out of it!—I could not endure the shameful sight.
I rose and winged my way thence, intending to kick a couple
of his teeth out as I passed over, but his mouth was employed
and I could not get at it.

Chapter 25

THAT night I had a terrible misfortune. The way it came
about was this. I was so unutterably happy and so unspeakably unhappy that my life was become an enchanted ecstasy and a crushing burden. I did not know what to do, and
took to drink. Merely for that evening. It was by Doangivadam's suggestion that I did this. He did not know what the
matter was, and I did not tell him; but he could see that
something *was* the matter and wanted regulating, and in his
judgment it would be well to try drink, for it might do good

and couldn't do harm. He was ready to do any kindness for me, because I had been 44's friend; and he loved to have me talk about 44, and mourn with him over his burning. I couldn't tell him 44 was alive again, for the mysterious check fell upon my tongue whenever I tried to. Very well; we were drinking and mourning together, and I took a shade too much and it biased my judgment. I was not what one could call at all far gone, but I had reached the heedless stage, the unwatchful stage, when we parted, and I forgot to make myself invisible! And so, eager and unafraid, I entered the boudoir of my bride confident of the glad welcome which would of course have been mine if I had come as Martin von Giesbach, whom she loved, instead of as August Feldner, whom she cared nothing about. The boudoir was dark, but the bedroom door was standing open, and through it I saw an enchanting picture and stopped to contemplate it and enjoy it. It was Marget. She was sitting before a pier glass, snowily arrayed in her dainty nightie, with her left side toward me; and upon her delicate profile and her shining cataract of dark red hair streaming unvexed to the floor a strong light was falling. Her maid was busily grooming her with brush and comb, and gossiping, and now and then Marget smiled up at her and she smiled back, and I smiled at both in sympathy and good-fellowship out of the dusk, and altogether it was a gracious and contenting condition of things, and my heart sang with happiness. But the picture was not quite complete, not wholly perfect—there was a pair of lovely blue eyes that persistently failed to turn my way. I thought I would go nearer and correct that defect. Supposing that I was invisible I tranquilly stepped just within the room and stood there; at the same moment Marget's mother appeared in the further door; and also at the same moment the three indignant women discovered me and began to shriek and scream in the one breath!

I fled the place. I went to my quarters, resumed my flesh, and sat mournfully down to wait for trouble. It was not long coming. I expected the master to call, and was not disappointed. He came in anger—which was natural,—but to my relief and surprise I soon found that his denunciations were not for me! What an uplift it was! No, they were all for my

Duplicate—all that the master wanted from me was a denial that I was the person who had profaned the sanctity of his niece's bedchamber. When he said *that* . . . . well, it took the most of the buoyancy out of the uplift. If he had stopped there and challenged me to testify, I—but he didn't. He went right on recounting and re-recounting the details of the exasperating episode, never suspecting that they were not news to me, and all the while he freely lashed the Duplicate and took quite for granted that he was the criminal and that my character placed me above suspicion. This was all so pleasant to my ear that I was glad to let him continue: indeed the more he abused Schwarz the better I liked it, and soon I was feeling grateful that he had neglected to ask for my testimony. He was very bitter, and when I perceived that he was minded to handle my detestable rival with severity I rejoiced exceedingly in my secret heart. Also I became evilly eager to keep him in that mind, and hoped for chances to that end.

It appeared that both the mother and the maid were positive that the Duplicate was the offender. The master kept dwelling upon that, and never referring to Marget as a witness, a thing that seemed so strange to me that at last I ventured to call his attention to the omission.

"Oh, her unsupported opinion is of no consequence!" he said, indifferently. "She says it was you—which is nonsense, in the face of the other evidence and your denial. She is only a child—how can *she* know one of you from the other? To satisfy her I said I would bring your denial; as for Emil Schwarz's testimony I don't want it and shouldn't value it. These Duplicates are ready to say anything that comes into their dreamy heads. This one is a good enough fellow, there's no deliberate harm in him, but—oh, as a witness he is not to be considered. He has made a blunder—in another person it would have been a crime—and by consequence my niece is compromised, for sure, for the maid can't keep the secret; poor thing, she's like all her kind—a secret, in a lady's-maid, is water in a basket. Oh, yes, it's true that this Duplicate has merely committed a blunder, but all the same my mind is made up as to one thing . . . . . the bell is tolling midnight, it marks a change for him . . . . . when I am through with him to-day, let him blunder as much as he likes he'll not compromise my niece again!"

I suppose it was wicked to feel such joy as I felt, but I couldn't help it. To have that hated rival put summarily out of my way and my road left free—the thought was intoxicating! The master asked me—as a formality—to deny that I was the person who had invaded Marget's chamber.

I promptly furnished the denial. It had always cost me shame to tell an injurious lie before, but I told this one without a pang, so eager was I to ruin the creature that stood between me and my worshipped little wife. The master took his leave, then, saying—

"It is sufficient. It is all I wanted. He shall marry the girl before the sun sets!"

Good heavens! in trying to ruin the Duplicate, I had only ruined myself.

Chapter 26

I WAS so miserable! A whole endless hour dragged along. Oh, why didn't he come, *why* didn't he come! wouldn't he *ever* come, and I so in need of his help and comfort!

It was awfully still and solemn and midnighty, and this made me feel creepy and shivery and afraid of ghosts; and that was natural, for the place was foggy with them, as Ernest Wasserman said, who was the most unexact person in his language in the whole castle, foggy being a noun of multitude and not applicable to ghosts, for they seldom appear in large companies, but mostly by ones and twos, and then—oh, then, when they go flitting by in the gloom like forms made of delicate smoke, and you see the furniture through them—

My, what is that! . . . . I heard it again! . . . . I was quaking like a jelly, and my heart was *so* cold and scared! Such a dry, bony noise, such a kl—lackety klackclack, kl—lackety klackclack!—dull, muffled, far away down the distant caverns and corridors—but approaching! oh, dear, approaching! It shriveled me up like a spider in a candle-flame, and I sat

scrunched together and quivering, the way the spider does in
his death-agony, and I said to myself, "skeletons a-coming,
oh, what *shall* I do!"

Do? Shut my door, of course! if I had the strength to get
to it—which I wouldn't have, on my legs, I knew it well; but
I collapsed to the floor and crawled to the door, and panted
there and listened, to see if the noise was certainly coming my
way—which it was!—and I took a look; and away down the
murky hall a long square of moonlight lay across the floor,
and a tall figure was capering across it, with both hands held
aloft and violently agitated and clacking out that clatter—and
next moment the figure was across and blotted out in the
darkness, but not the racket, which was getting loud and
sharp, now—then I pushed the door to, and crept back a
piece and lay exhausted and gasping.

It came, and came,—that dreadful noise—straight to my
door, then that figure capered in and slammed the door to,
and went on capering gaily all around me and everywhere
about the room; and it was not a skeleton; no, it was a tall
man, clothed in the loudest and most clownish and outlandish costume, with a vast white collar that stood above its
ears, and a battered hat like a bucket, tipped gallusly to one
side, and betwixt the fingers of the violent hands were curved
fragments of dry bone which smote together and made that
terrible clacking; and the man's mouth reached clear across
his face and was unnaturally red, and had extraordinarily thick
lips, and the teeth showed intensely white between them, and
the face was as black as midnight. It was a terrible and fero-
cious spectre, and would bound as high as the ceiling, and
crack its heels together, and yah-yah-yah! like a fiend, and
keep the bones going, and soon it broke into a song in a sort
of bastard English,

> "Buffalo gals can't you come out to-night,
>   Can't you come out to-night,
>   Can't you come out to-night,
>   O, Buffalo gals can't you come out to-night—
>   A-n-d *dance* by de light er de moon!"

And then it burst out with a tremendous clatter of laughter,
and flung itself furiously over and over in the air like the

wings of a windmill in a gale, and landed with a whack! on its feet alongside of me and looked down at me and shouted most cheerfully—

"*Now* den, Misto' Johnsing, how does yo' corporsosity seem to segashuate!"

I gasped out—

"Oh, dread being, have pity, oh—if—if—"

"Bress yo' soul, honey, *I* ain' no dread being, I's Cunnel Bludso's nigger fum Souf C'yarlina, en I's heah th'ee hund'd en fifty year ahead o' time, caze you's down in de mouf en I got to 'muse you wid de banjo en make you feel all right en comfy agin. So you jist lay whah you is, boss, en listen to de music; I gwineter sing to you, honey, de way de po' slave-niggers sings when dey's sol' away fum dey home en is home-sick en down in de mouf."

Then out of nowhere he got that thing that he called a banjo, and sat down and propped his left ancle on his right knee, and canted his bucket-hat a little further and more gallusly over his ear, and rested the banjo in his lap, and set the grip of his left fingers on the neck of it high up, and fetched a brisk and most thrilling rake across the strings low down, giving his head a toss of satisfaction, as much as to say "I reckon *that* gets in to where you live, oh I guess not!" Then he canted his head affectionately toward the strings, and twisted the pegs at the top and tuned the thing up with a musical plunkety-plunk or so; then he re-settled himself in his chair and lifted up his black face toward the ceiling, grave, far-away, kind of pathetic, and began to strum soft and low—and then! Why then his voice began to tremble out and float away toward heaven—such a sweet voice, such a divine voice, and so touching—

> "Way down upon de Swanee river,
>   Far, far away,
>   Dah's whah my heart is turnin' ever,
>   Dah's whah de ole folks stay."

And so on, verse after verse, sketching his humble lost home, and the joys of his childhood, and the black faces that had been dear to him, and which he would look upon no more—and there he sat lost in it, with his face lifted up that way, and there was never anything so beautiful, never anything so heart-breaking, oh, never any music like it below the skies! and by the magic of it that uncouth figure lost its uncouthness and became lovely like the song, because it so fitted the song, so belonged to it, and was such a part *of* it, so helped to body forth the feeling of it and make it visible, as it were, whereas a silken dress and a white face and white graces would have profaned it, and cheapened its noble pathos.

I closed my eyes, to try if I could picture to myself that lost home; and when the last notes were dying away, and apparently receding into the distance, I opened them again: the singer was gone, my room was gone, but afar off the home was there, a cabin of logs nestling under spreading trees, a soft vision steeped in a mellow summer twilight—and steeped in that music, too, which was dying, dying, fading, fading; and with it faded the vision, like a dream, and passed away; and as it faded and passed, my room and my furniture began to dimly reappear—spectrally, with the perishing home showing vaguely, through it, as through a veil; and when the transformation was accomplished my room was its old self again, my lights were burning, and in the black man's place sat Forty-Four beaming a self-complimenting smile. He said—

"Your eyes are wet; it's the right applause. But it's nothing, I could fetch that effect if they were glass. Glass? I could do it if they were knot-holes. Get up, and let's feed."

I *was* so glad to see him again! The very sight of him was enough to drive away my terrors and despairs and make me forget my deplorable situation. And then there was that mysterious soul-refreshment, too, that always charged the atmosphere as with wine and set one's spirits a-buzzing whenever he came about, and made you perceive that he was come, whether he was visible or not.

***When we had finished feeding, he lit his smoke-factory and we drew up to the fire to discuss my unfortunate situation and see what could be done about it. We examined it all around, and I said it seemed to me that the first and most urgent thing to be done was to stop the lady's-maid's gossiping mouth and keep her from compromising Marget; I said the master hadn't a doubt that she would spread the fact of the unpleasant incident of an hour or two ago. Next, I thought

we ought to stop that marriage, if possible. I concluded
with—

"Now, 44, the case is full of intolerable difficulties, as you
see, but do try and think of some way out of them, won't
you?"

To my grief I soon saw that he was settling down into one
of his leather-headed moods. Ah, how often they came upon
him when there was a crisis and his very brightest intelligence
was needed!

He said he saw no particular difficulties in the situation if I
was right about it: the first and main necessity was to silence
the maid and stop Schwarz from proceeding with his marriage—and then blandly proposed that we *kill* both of them!

It almost made me jump out of my clothes. I said it was a
perfectly insane idea, and if he was actually in earnest—

He stopped me there, and the argument-lust rose in his
dull eye. It always made me feel depressed to see that look,
because he loved to get a chance to show off how he could
argue, and it was so dreary to listen to him—dreary and irritating, for when he was in one of his muddy-minded moods
he couldn't argue any more than a clam. He said, big-eyed
and asinine—

"What makes you think it insane, August?"

What a hopeless question! what could a person answer to
such a foolishness as that?

"Oh, dear, me," I said, "can't you *see* that it's insane?"

He looked surprised, puzzled, pathetically mystified for a
little while, then said—

"Why, *I* don't see how you make it out, August. We don't
need those people, you know. No one needs them, so far as I
can see. There's a plenty of them around, you can get as many
as you want. Why, August, you don't seem to have any practical ideas—business ideas. You stay shut up here, and you
don't know about these things. There's dozens and dozens of
those people. I can turn out and in a couple of hours I can
fetch a whole swarm of—"

"Oh, wait, 44! Dear me, is supplying their places the whole
thing? is it the important thing? Don't you suppose *they*
would like to have something to say about it?"

That simple aspect of it did seem to work its way into his

head—after boring and tugging a moment or two—and he said, as one who had received light—

"Oh, I didn't think of that. Yes—yes, I see now." Then he brightened, and said, "but you know, they've got to die anyway, and so the *when* isn't any matter. Human beings aren't of any particular consequence; there's plenty more, plenty. Now then, after we've got them killed—"

"Damnation, we are not *going* to kill them!—now don't say another word about it; it's a perfectly atrocious idea; I should think you would be ashamed of it; and ashamed to hang to it and stick to it the way you do, and be so reluctant to give it up. Why, you act as if it was a child, and the first one you ever had."

He was crushed, and looked it. It hurt me to see him look cowed, that way; it made me feel mean, and as if I had struck a dumb animal that had been doing the best it knew how, and not meaning any harm; and at bottom I was vexed at myself for being so rough with him at such a time; for *I* know at a glance when he has a leather-headed mood on, and that he is not responsible when his brains have gone mushy; but I just *couldn't* pull myself together right off and say the gentle word and pet away the hurt I had given. I had to take time to it and work down to it gradually. But I managed it, and by and by his smiles came back, and his cheer, and then he was all right again, and as grateful as a child to see me friends with him once more.

Then he went zealously to work on the problem again, and soon evolved another scheme. The idea this time was to turn the maid into a cat, and make some *more* Schwarzes, then Marget would not be able to tell t'other from which, and couldn't choose the right one, and it wouldn't be lawful for her to marry the whole harem. That would postpone the wedding, he thought.

It certainly had the look of it! Any blind person could see that. So I gave praise, and was glad of the chance to do it and make up for bygones. He was as pleased as could be. In about ten minutes or so we heard a plaintive sound of meyow-yowing wandering around and about, away off somewhere, and 44 rubbed his hands joyfully and said—

"There she is, now!"

"Who?"

"The lady's-maid."

"No! Have you already transmuted her?"

"Yes. She was sitting up waiting for her room-mate to come, so she could tell her. Waiting for her mate to come from larking with the porter's new yunker. In a minute or two it would have been too late. Set the door ajar; she'll come when she sees the light, and we'll see what she has to say about the matter. She mustn't recognize me; I'll change to the magician. It will give him some more reputation. Would you like me to make you able to understand what she says?"

"Oh, *do*, 44, do, please!"

"All right. Here she is."

It was the magician's voice, exactly counterfeited; and there he stood, the magician's duplicate, official robes and all. I went invisible; I did not want to be seen in the condemned enchanter's company, even by a cat.

She came sauntering sadly in, a very pretty cat. But when she saw the necromancer her tail spread and her back went up and she let fly a spit or two and would have scurried away, but I flew over her head and shut the door in time. She backed into the corner and fixed her glassy eyes on 44, and said—

"It was you who did this, and it was mean of you. I never did you any harm."

"No matter, you brought it on yourself."

"How did I bring it on myself?"

"You were going to tell about Schwarz; you would have compromised your young mistress."

"It's not so; I wish I may never die if—"

"Nonsense! Don't talk so. You were waiting up to tell. I know all about it."

The cat looked convicted. She concluded not to argue the case. After thinking a moment or two she said, with a kind of sigh—

"Will they treat me well, do you think?"

"Yes."

"Do you know they will?"

"Yes, I know it."

After a pause and another sigh—

"I would rather be a cat than a servant—a slave, that has to smile, and look cheerful, and pretend to be happy, when you are scolded for every little thing, the way Frau Stein and her daughter do, and be sneered at and insulted, and they haven't any right to, *they* didn't pay my wage, I wasn't *their* slave—a hateful life, an odious life! I'd rather be a cat. Yes, I would. Will everybody treat me well?"

"Yes, everybody."

"Frau Stein, too, and the daughter?"

"Yes."

"Will *you* see that they do?"

"I will. It's a promise."

"Then I thank you. They are all afraid of you, and the most of them hate you. And it was the same with me—but not now. You seem different to me now. You have the same voice and the same clothes, but you seem different. You seem kind; I don't know why, but you do; you seem kind and good, and I trust you; I think you will protect me."

"I will keep my promise."

"I believe it. And keep me as I am. It was a bitter life. You would think those Steins would not have been harsh with me, seeing I was a poor girl, with not a friend, nor anybody that was mine, and I never did them any harm. I *was* going to tell. Yes, I was. To get revenge. Because the family said I was bribed to let Schwarz in there—and it was a lie! Even Miss Marget believed that lie—I could see it, and she—well, she tried to defend me, but she let them convince her. Yes, I was going to tell. I was hot to tell. I was angry. But I am glad I didn't get the chance, for I am not angry any more; cats do not carry anger, I see. Don't change me back, leave me as I am. Christians go—I know where they go; some to the one place some to the other; but I think cats—where do *you* think cats go?"

"Nowhere. After they die."

"Leave me as I am, then; don't change me back. Could I have these leavings?"

"And welcome—yes."

"Our supper was there, in our room, but the other maid was frightened of me because I was a strange cat, and drove me out, and I didn't get any. This is wonderful food, I wonder how it got to this room? there's never been anything like it in this castle before. Is it enchanted food?"

"Yes."

"I just guessed it was. Safe?"

"Perfectly."

"Do you have it here a good deal?"

"Always—day and night."

"How gaudy! But this isn't your room?"

"No, but I'm here a great deal, and the food is here all the time. Would you like to do your feeding here?"

"Too good to be true!"

"Well, you can. Come whenever you like, and speak at the door."

"How dear and lovely! I've had a narrow escape—I can see it now."

"From what?"

"From not getting to be a cat. It was just an accident that that idiot came blundering in there drunk; if I hadn't been there—but I *was*, and never shall I get done being thankful. This is amazing good food; there's never been anything like it in this castle before—not in my time, I can tell you. I am thankful I may come here when I'm hungry."

"Come whenever you like."

"I'll do what I can for pay. I've never caught a mouse, but I feel it in me that I could do it, and I will keep a lookout here. I'm not so sad, now; no, things look very different; but I was pretty sad when I came. Could I room here, do you think? Would you mind?"

"Not at all. Make yourself quite at home. There'll be a special bed for you. I'll see to it."

"What larks! I never knew what nuts it was to be a cat before."

"It has its advantages."

"Oh, I should smile! I'll step out, now, and browse around a little, and see if there's anything doing in my line. Au revoir, and many many thanks for all you have done for me. I'll be back before long."

And so she went out, waving her tail, which meant satisfaction.

"There, now," said 44, "that part of the plan has come out all right, and no harm done."

"No, indeed," I said, resuming my visible form, "we've done her a favor. And in her place I should feel about it just as she does. Forty-Four, it was beautiful to hear that strange language and understand it—I understood every word. Could I learn to speak it, do you think?"

"You won't have to learn it, I'll put it *into* you."

"Good. When?"

"Now. You've already got it. Try! Speak out—do The Boy Stood on the Burning Deck—in catapult, or cataplasm, or whatever one might call that tongue."

"The Boy—what was it you said?"

"It's a poem. It hasn't been written yet, but it's very pretty and stirring. It's English. But I'll empty it into you, where you stand, in cataplasm. Now you've got it. Go ahead—recite."

I did it, and never missed a wail. It was certainly beautiful in that tongue, and quaint and touching; 44 said if it was done on a back fence, by moonlight, it would make people cry—especially a quartette would. I was proud; he was not always so complimentary. I said I was glad to have the cat, particularly now that I could talk to her; and she would be happy with me, didn't he think? Yes, he said, she would. I said—

"It's a good night's work we've done for that poor little blonde-haired lady's-maid, and I believe, as you do, that quite soon she is going to be contented and happy."

"As soon as she has kittens," he said, "and it won't be long."

Then we began to think out a name for her, but he said—

"Leave that, for the present, you'd better have a nap."

He gave a wave of his hand, and that was sufficient; before the wave was completed I was asleep.

Chapter 27

I WOKE UP fresh and fine and vigorous, and found I had been asleep a little more than six minutes. The sleeps which he furnished had no dependence upon time, no connection with it, no relation to it; sometimes they did their work in one interval, sometimes in another, sometimes in half a second, sometimes in half a day, according to whether there was an interruption or wasn't; but let the interval be long or short, the result was the same: that is to say, the reinvigoration was perfect, the physical and mental refreshment complete.

There had been an interruption, a voice had spoken. I glanced up, and saw myself standing there, within the half-open door. That is to say, I saw Emil Schwarz, my Duplicate. My conscience gave me a little prod, for his face was sad. Had he found out what had been happening at midnight, and had he come at three in the morning to reproach me?

Reproach me? What for? For getting him falsely saddled with a vulgar indiscretion? What of it? Who was the loser by it? Plainly, I, myself—I had lost the girl. And who was the gainer? He himself, and none other—he had acquired her. Ah, very well, then—let him reproach me; if he was dissatisfied, let him trade places: he wouldn't find me objecting. Having reached solid ground by these logical reasonings, I advised my conscience to go take a tonic, and leave me to deal with this situation as a healthy person should.

Meantime, during these few seconds, I was looking at myself, standing there—and for once, I was admiring. Just because I had been doing a very handsome thing by this Duplicate, I was softening toward him, my prejudices were losing strength. I hadn't intended to do the handsome thing, but no matter, it had happened, and it was natural for me to take the credit of it and feel a little proud of it, for I was human. Being human accounts for a good many insanities, according to 44—upwards of a thousand a day was his estimate.

It is actually the truth that I had never looked this Duplicate over before. I never could bear the sight of him. I wouldn't look at him when I could help it; and until this moment I *couldn't* look at him dispassionately and with fairness. But now I could, for I had done him a great and creditable kindness, and it quite changed his aspects.

In those days there were several things which I didn't know. For instance I didn't know that my voice was not the same voice to me that it was to others; but when 44 made me talk into the thing which he brought in, one day, when he had arrived home from one of his plundering-raids among the unborn centuries, and then reversed the machine and allowed me to listen to my voice as other people were used to hearing it, I recognized that it had so little resemblance to the voice *I* was accustomed to hearing that I should have said it was not my voice at all if the proof had not been present that it was.

Also, I had been used to supposing that the person I saw in the mirror was the person others saw when they looked at me—whereas that was not the case. For once, when 44 had come back from robbing the future he brought a camera and made some photographs of me—those were the names which he gave the things, names which he invented out of his head for the occasion, no doubt, for that was his habit, on account of his not having any principles—and *always* the pictures which were like me as I saw myself in the glass he pronounced poor, and those which I thought exceedingly bad, he pronounced almost supernaturally good.

And here it was again. In the figure standing by the door I was now seeing myself as others saw me, but the resemblance to the self which I was familiar with in the glass was *merely* a resemblance, nothing more; not approaching the common resemblance of brother to brother, but reaching only as far as the resemblance which a person usually bears to his brother-in-law. Often one does not notice that, at all, until it is pointed out; and sometimes, even then, the resemblance owes as much to imagination as to fact. It's like a cloud which resembles a horse after some one has pointed out the resemblance. You perceive it, then, though I have often seen a cloud that didn't. Clouds often have nothing more than a brother-in-law resemblance. I wouldn't say this to everybody, but I believe it to be true, nevertheless. For I myself have seen clouds which looked like a brother-in-law, whereas I knew very well they didn't. Nearly all such are hallucinations, in my opinion.

Well, there he stood, with the strong white electric light flooding him, (more plunder,) and he hardly even reached the brother-in-law standard. I realized that I had never really seen this youth before. Of course I could recognize the general pattern, I don't deny it, but that was only because I knew who the creature was; but if I had met him in another country, the most that could have happened would have been this: that I would turn and look after him and say "I wonder if I have seen him somewhere before?" and then I would drop the matter out of my mind, as being only a fancy.

Well, there he was; that is to say, there *I* was. And I was interested; interested at last. He was distinctly handsome, distinctly trim and shapely, and his attitude was easy, and well-bred and graceful. Complexion—what it should be at seventeen, with a blonde ancestry: peachy, bloomy, fresh, wholesome. Clothes—precisely like mine, to a button—or the lack of it.

I was well satisfied with this front view. I had never seen my back; I was curious to see it. I said, very courteously—

"Would you please turn around for a moment?—only a moment? . . . Thank you."

Well, well, how little we know what our backs are like! This one was all right, I hadn't a fault to find with it, but it was all new to me, it was the back of a stranger—hair-aspects and all. If I had seen it walking up the street in front of me it would not have occurred to me that I could be in any personal way interested in it.

"Turn again, please, if you will be so good . . . . Thank you kindly."

I was to inspect the final detail, now—mentality. I had put it last, for I was reluctant, afraid, doubtful. Of course one glance was enough—I was expecting that. It saddened me: he was of a loftier world than I, he moved in regions where I could not tread, with my earth-shod feet. I wished I had left that detail alone.

"Come and sit down," I said, "and tell me what it is. You wish to speak with me about something?"

"Yes," he said, seating himself, "if you will kindly listen."

I gave a moment's thought to my defence, as regards the impending reproach, and was ready. He began, in a voice and manner which were in accord with the sadness which sat upon his young face—

"The master has been to me and has charged me with profaning the sanctity of his niece's chamber."

It was a strange place to stop, but there he stopped, and looked wistfully at me, just as a person might stop in a dream, and wait for another person to take up the matter there, without any definite text to talk to. I had to say something, and so for lack of anything better to offer, I said—

"I am truly sorry, and I hope you will be able to convince him that he is mistaken. You can, can't you?"

"Convince him?" he answered, looking at me quite vacantly, "Why should I wish to convince him?"

I felt pretty vacant myself, now. It was a most unlooked-for question. If I had guessed a week I should not have hit upon that one. I said—and it was the only thing a body would ever think of saying—

"But you do, don't you?"

The look he gave me was a look of compassion, if I know the signs. It seemed to say, gently, kindly, but clearly, "alas, this poor creature doesn't know anything." Then he uttered his answer—

"Wh-y, no, I do not see that I have that wish. It—why, you see, it isn't any matter."

"Good heavens! It isn't any matter whether you stand disgraced or not?"

He shook his head, and said quite simply—

"No, it isn't any matter, it is of no consequence."

It was difficult to believe my ears. I said—

"Well, then, if disgrace is nothing to you, consider *this* point. If the report gets around, it can mean disgrace for the young *lady*."

It had no effect that I could see! He said—

"Can it?" just as an idiot child might have said it.

"*Can* it? Why of course it can! You wouldn't want *that* to happen, would you?"

"We-ll," (reflectively), "I don't know. I don't see the bearing of it."

"Oh, great guns, this infantile stu—this—this—why, it's perfectly disheartening! You love her, and yet you don't care whether her good name is ruined or not?"

"Love her?" and he had the discouraged aspect of a person who is trying to look through a fog and is not succeeding, "why, *I* don't love her; what makes you think I do?"

"Well, I must say! Well, certainly this is too many for *me*. Why, hang it, *I* know you've been courting her."

"Yes—oh, yes, that is true."

"Oh, it is, is it! Very well, then, how is it that you were courting her and yet didn't love her?"

"No, it isn't that way. No, I loved her."

"Oh—go on, I'll take a breath or two—I don't know where I am, I'm all at sea."

He said, placidly—

"Yes, I remember about that. I loved her. It had escaped me. No—it hadn't escaped me; it was not important, and I was thinking of something else."

"Tell me," I said, "is *anything* important to you?"

"Oh, yes!" he responded, with animation and a brightening face; then the animation and the brightness passed, and he added, wearily, "but not these things."

Somehow, it touched me; it was like the moan of an exile. We were silent a while, thinking, ruminating, then I said—

"Schwarz, I'm not able to make it out. It is a sweet young girl, you certainly did love her, and—"

"Yes," he said, tranquilly, "it is quite true. I believe it was yesterday . . . . yes, I think it was yesterday."

"Oh, you *think* it was! But of course it's not important. Dear me, why should it be?—a little thing like that. Now then, something has changed it. What was it? What has happened?"

"Happened? Nothing, I think. Nothing that I know of."

"Well, then, why the devil . . . . oh, great Scott, I'll never get my wits back again! Why, look here, Schwarz, you wanted to *marry* her!"

"Yes. Quite true. I think . . . . yesterday? Yes, I think it was yesterday. I am to marry her to-day. I think it's to-day; anyway, it is pretty soon. The master requires it. He has told me so."

"Well . . . . upon my word!"

"What is the matter?"

"Why, you are as indifferent about this as you are about everything else. You show no feeling whatever, you don't even show interest. Come! surely you've got a heart hidden away somewhere; open it up; give it air; show at least some little corner of it. Land, I wish I were in your place! Don't you *care* whether you marry her or not?"

"Care? Why, *no*, of course I don't. You do ask the *strangest* questions! I wander, wander, wander! I try to make you out, I try to understand you, but it's all fog, fog, fog—you're just a riddle, nobody *can* understand you!"

Oh, the idea! the impudence of it! this to *me!*—from this frantic chaos of unimaginable incomprehensibilities, who couldn't by any chance utter so much as half a sentence that Satan himself could make head or tail of!

"Oh, I like *that!*" I cried, flying out at him. "*You* can't understand *me!* Oh, but that *is* good! It's immortal! Why, look here, when you came, I thought I knew what you came for— I thought I knew all about it—I would have said you were coming to reproach me for—for—"

I found it difficult to get it out, and so I left it in, and after a pause, added—

"Why, Schwarz, you certainly had something on your mind when you came—I could see it in your face—but if ever you've got to it I've not discovered it—oh, not even a sign of it! You *haven't* got to it, *have* you?"

"*Oh*, no!" he answered, with an outburst of very real energy. "These things were of no sort of consequence. *May* I tell it now? Oh, *will* you be good and hear me? I shall be so grateful, if you will!"

"Why, certainly, and glad to! Come, *now* you're waking up, at last! You've got a heart in you, sure enough, and plenty of feeling—why, it burns in your eye like a star! Go ahead—I'm all interest, all sympathy."

Oh, well, he was a different creature, now. All the fogs and puzzlings and perplexities were gone from his face, and had left it clear and full of life. He said—

"It was no idle errand that brought me. No, far from it! I came with my heart in my mouth, I came to beg, to plead, to pray—to beseech you, to implore you, to have mercy upon me!"

"Mercy—upon *you?*"

"Yes, mercy. Have mercy, oh, be merciful, and set me free!"

"Why, I—I—Schwarz, I don't understand. You say, yourself, that if they want you to marry, you are quite indif—"

"Oh, not *that!* I care nothing for that—it is these bonds" —stretching his arms aloft—"oh, free me from *them*; these bonds of flesh—this decaying vile matter, this foul weight, and clog, and burden, this loathsome sack of corruption in which my spirit is imprisoned, her white wings bruised and soiled—oh, be merciful and set her free! Plead for me with that malicious magic-monger—he has been here—I saw him issue from this door—he will come again—say you will be my friend, as well as brother! for brothers indeed we are; the same womb was mother to us both, I live by you, I perish when you die—brother, be my friend! plead with him to take away this rotting flesh and set my spirit free! Oh, this human life, this earthy life, this weary life! It is so groveling, and so mean; its ambitions are so paltry, its prides so trivial, its vanities so childish; and the glories that it values and applauds—lord, how empty! Oh, here I am a servant!—I who never served before; here I am a slave—slave among little mean kings and emperors made of clothes, the kings and emperors slaves themselves, to mud-built carrion that are *their* slaves!

"To think you should think I came here concerned about those other things—those inconsequentials! Why should they concern me, a spirit of air, habitant of the august Empire of Dreams? *We* have no morals; the angels have none; morals are for the impure; we have no principles, those chains are for men. We love the lovely whom we meet in dreams, we forget them the next day, and meet and love their like. They are dream-creatures—no others are real. Disgrace? We care nothing for disgrace, we do not know what it is. Crime? we commit it every night, while you sleep; it is nothing to us. We have no character, no *one* character, we have *all* characters; we are honest in one dream, dishonest in the next; we fight in one battle and flee from the next. We wear no chains, we cannot abide them; we have no home, no prison, the universe is our province; we do not know time, we do not know space— we live, and love, and labor, and enjoy, fifty years in an hour, while you are sleeping, snoring, repairing your crazy tissues; we circumnavigate your little globe while you wink; we are not tied within horizons, like a dog with cattle to mind, an emperor with human sheep to watch—we visit hell, we roam in heaven, our playgrounds are the constellations and the Milky Way. Oh, help, help! be my friend and brother in my need—beseech the magician, beg him, plead with him; he will listen, he will be moved, he will release me from this odious flesh!"

I was powerfully stirred—so moved, indeed, that in my pity for him I brushed aside unheeded or but half-heeded the scoffs and slurs which he had flung at my despised race, and jumped up and seized him by both hands and wrung them passionately, declaring that with all my heart and soul I would plead for him with the magician, and would not rest from these labors until my prayers should succeed or their continuance be peremptorily forbidden.

Chapter 28

HE could not speak, for emotion; for the same cause my voice forsook me; and so, in silence we grasped hands again; and that grip, strong and warm, said for us what our tongues could not utter. At that moment the cat entered, and stood looking at us. Under her grave gaze a shame-faced discomfort, a sense of embarrassment, began to steal over me, just as would have been the case if she had been a human being who had caught me in that gushy and sentimental situation, and I felt myself blushing. Was it because I was aware that she had lately been that kind of a being? It annoyed me to see that my brother was not similarly affected. And yet, why mind it? didn't I already know that no human intelligence could guess what occurrence would affect *him* and what event would leave him cold? With an uncomfortable feeling of being critically watched by the cat, I pressed him with clumsy courtesy into his seat again, and slumped into my own.

The cat sat down. Still looking at us in that disconcerting way, she tilted her head first to one side and then the other, inquiringly and cogitatively, the way a cat does when she has struck the unexpected and can't quite make out what she had better do about it. Next she washed one side of her face, making such an awkward and unscientific job of it that almost anybody would have seen that she was either out of practice or didn't know how. She stopped with the one side, and looked bored, and as if she had only been doing it to put in the time, and wished she could think of something else to do to put in some more time. She sat a while, blinking drowsily, then she hit an idea, and looked as if she wondered she hadn't thought of it earlier. She got up and went visiting around among the furniture and belongings, sniffing at each and every article, and elaborately examining it. If it was a chair, she examined it all around, then jumped up in it and sniffed all over its seat and its back; if it was any other thing she could examine all around, she examined it all around; if it was a chest and there was room for her between it and the wall, she crowded herself in behind there and gave it a thorough over-hauling; if it was a tall thing, like a washstand, she would stand on her hind toes and stretch up as high as she could, and reach across and paw at the toilet things and try to rake them to where she could smell them; if it was the cupboard, she stood on her toes and reached up and pawed the knob; if it was the table she would squat, and measure the distance, and make a leap, and land in the wrong place, owing to new-ness to the business; and, part of her going too far and slid-ing over the edge, she would scramble, and claw at things desperately, and save herself and make good; then she would smell everything on the table, and archly and daintily paw everything around that was movable, and finally paw some-thing off, and skip cheerfully down and paw it some more, throwing herself into the prettiest attitudes, rising on her hind feet and curving her front paws and flirting her head this way and that and glancing down cunningly at the object, then pouncing on it and spatting it half the length of the room, and chasing it up and spatting it again, and again, and racing after it and fetching it another smack—and so on and so on; and suddenly she would tire of it and try to find some way to get to the top of the cupboard or the wardrobe, and if she couldn't she would look troubled and disappointed; and to-ward the last, when you could see she was getting her bear-ings well lodged in her head and was satisfied with the place and the arrangements, she relaxed her intensities, and got to purring a little to herself, and praisefully waving her tail be-tween inspections—and at last she was done—done, and everything satisfactory and to her taste.

Being fond of cats, and acquainted with their ways, if I had been a stranger and a person had told me that this cat had spent half an hour in that room before, but hadn't happened to think to examine it until now, I should have been able to say with conviction, "Keep an eye on her, that's no orthodox cat, she's an imitation, there's a flaw in her make-up, you'll find she's born out of wedlock or some other arrested-development accident has happened, she's no true Christian cat, if *I* know the signs."

She couldn't think of anything further to do, now, so she thought she would wash the other side of her face, but she couldn't remember which one it was, so she gave it up, and sat down and went to nodding and blinking; and between nods she would jerk herself together and make remarks. I heard her say—

"One of them's the Duplicate, the other's the Original, but I can't tell t'other from which, and I don't suppose *they* can. I am sure I couldn't if I were them. The missuses said it was the Duplicate that broke in there last night, and I voted with the majority for policy's sake, which is a servant's only protection from trouble, but I would like to know how *they* knew. *I* don't believe they could tell them apart if they were stripped. Now my idea is—"

I interrupted, and intoned musingly, as if to myself,—

> "The boy stood on the burning deck,
>   Whence all but him had fled—"

and stopped there, and seemed to sink into a reverie.

It gave her a start! She muttered—

"*That's* the Duplicate. Duplicates know languages—everything, sometimes, and then again they don't know anything at all. That is what Fischer says, though of course it could have been his Duplicate that said it, there's never any telling, in this bewitched place, whether you are talking to a person himself, or only to his heathen image. And Fischer says they haven't any morals nor any principles—though of course it could have been his Duplicate that said it—one never knows. Half the time when you say to a person *he* said so-and-so, he says he didn't—so then you recognize it was the other one. As between living in such a place as this and being crazy, you don't know *which* it is, the most of the time. I would rather be a cat and not have any Duplicate, then I always know which one I am. Otherwise, not. If they haven't any principles, it was this Duplicate that broke in there, though of course, being drunk he wouldn't know which one he was, and so it could be the other without him suspecting it, which leaves the matter where it was before—not certain enough to be certain, and just uncertain enough to be *un*certain. So I don't see that anything's decided. In fact I know it isn't. Still, I think this one that wailed is the Duplicate, because sometimes they know all languages a minute, and next minute they don't know their own, if they've got one, whereas a *man* doesn't. Doesn't, and can't even *learn* it—can't learn cat-language, anyway. It's what Fischer says—Fischer or his Duplicate. So this is the one—*that's* decided. He couldn't talk cataract, nor ever learn it, either, if it was the Christian one . . . . . I'm awful tired!"

I didn't let on, but pretended to be dozing; my brother was a little further along than that—he was softly snoring. I wanted to wait and see, if I could, what was troubling the cat, for it seemed plain to me that she had something on her mind, she certainly was not at her ease. By and by she cleared her throat, and I stirred up and looked at her, as much as to say, "well, I'm listening—proceed." Then she said, with studied politeness—

"It is very late. I am sorry to disturb you gentlemen, but I am very tired, and would like to go to bed."

"Oh, dear me," I said, "don't wait up on our account I beg of you. Turn right in!"

She looked astonished.

"With you present?" she said.

So then I was astonished myself, but did not reveal it.

"Do you mind it?" I asked.

"Do I *mind* it! You will grant, I make no doubt, that so extraordinary a question is hardly entitled to the courtesy of an answer from one of my sex. You are offensive, sir; I beg that you will relieve me of your company at once, and take your friend with you."

"Remove him? I could not do that. He is my guest, and it is his place to make the first move. This is my room."

I said it with a submerged chuckle, as knowing quite well,

that soft-spoken as it was, it would knock some of the starch out of her. As indeed it did.

"*Your* room! Oh, I beg a thousand pardons, I am ashamed of my rude conduct, and will go at once. I assure you sir, I was the innocent victim of a mistake: I thought it was my room."

"And so it is. There has been no mistake. Don't you see?—there is your bed."

She looked whither I was pointing, and said with surprise—

"How strange that is! it wasn't there five seconds ago. Oh, *isn't* it a love!"

She made a spring for it—cat-like, forgetting the old interest in the new one; and feminine-like, eager to feast her native appetite for pretty things upon its elegancies and daintinesses. And really it *was* a daisy! It was a canopied four-poster, of rare wood, richly carved, with bed twenty inches wide and thirty long, sumptuously bepillowed and belaced and beruffled and besatined and all that; and when she had petted it and patted it and searched it and sniffed it all over, she cried out in an agony of delight and longing—

"Oh, I would just *love* to stretch out on that!"

The enthusiasm of it melted me, and I said heartily—

"Turn right in, Mary Florence Fortescue Baker G. Nightingale, and make yourself at home—that is the magician's own present to you, and it shows you he's no imitation-friend, but the true thing!"

"Oh, what a pretty name!" she cried; "is it mine for sure enough, and may I keep it? Where *did* you get it?"

"I don't know—the magician hooked it from somewhere, he is always at that, and it just happened to come into my mind at the psychological moment, and I'm glad it did, for your sake, for it's a dandy! Turn in, now, Baker G., and make yourself entirely at home."

"You are *so* good, dear Duplicate, and I am just as grateful as I can be, but—but—well, you see how it is. I have never roomed with any person not of my own sex, and—"

"You will be perfectly safe here, Mary, I assure you, and—"

"I should be an ingrate to doubt it, and I do not doubt it, be sure of that; but at this particular time—at this time of all others—er—well, you know, for a smaller matter than this,

Miss Marget is already compromised beyond repair, I fear, and if I—"

"Say no more, Mary Florence, you are perfectly right, perfectly. My dressing-room is large and comfortable, I can get along quite well without it, and I will carry your bed in there. Come along . . . Now then, there you are! Snug and nice and all right, isn't it? Contemplate that! Satisfactory?—yes?"

She cordially confessed that it was. So I sat down and chatted along while she went around and examined *that* place all over, and pawed everything and sampled the smell of each separate detail, like an old hand, for she was getting the hang of her trade by now; then she made a final and special examination of the button on our communicating-door, and stretched herself up on her hind-toes and fingered it till she got the trick of buttoning-out inquisitives and undesirables down fine and ship-shape, then she thanked me handsomely for fetching the bed and taking so much trouble; and gave me good-night, and when I asked if it would disturb her if I talked a while with my guest, she said no, talk as much as we pleased, she was tired enough to sleep through thunderstorms and earthquakes. So I said, right cordially—

"Good-night, Mary G., und schlafen Sie wohl!" and passed out and left her to her slumbers. As delicate-minded a cat as ever I've struck, and I've known a many of them.

Chapter 29

I STIRRED my brother up, and we talked the time away while waiting for the magician to come. I said his coming was a most uncertain thing, for he was irregular, and not at all likely to come when wanted, but Schwarz was anxious to stay and take the chances; so we did as I have said—talked and waited. He told me a great deal about his life and ways as a dream-sprite, and did it in a skipping and disconnected fashion proper to his species. He would side-track a subject right in the middle of a sentence if another subject attracted him, and he did this without apology or explanation—well, just as a dream would, you know. His talk was scatteringly seasoned with strange words and phrases, picked up in a thousand worlds, for he had been everywhere. Sometimes he could tell me their meaning and where he got them, but not always; in fact not very often, the dream-memory being pretty capricious, he said—sometimes good, oftener bad, and always flighty. "Side-track," for instance. He was not able to remember where he had picked that up, but thought it was in a star in the belt of Orion where he had spent a summer one night with some excursionists from Sirius whom he had met in space. That was as far as he could remember with anything like certainty; as to *when* it was, that was a blank with him; perhaps it was in the past, maybe it was in the future, he couldn't tell which it was, and probably didn't know, at the time it happened. *Couldn't* know, in fact, for Past and Future were human terms and not comprehendable by him, past and future being all one thing to a dream-sprite, and not distinguishable the one from the other. "And not important, anyway." How natural that sounded, coming from him! His notions of the important were just simply elementary, as you may say.

He often dropped phrases which had clear meanings to him, but which he labored in vain to make comprehensible by me. It was because they came from countries where none of the conditions resembled the conditions I had been used to; some from comets where nothing was solid, and nobody had legs; some from our sun, where nobody was comfortable except when white-hot, and where you needn't talk to people about cold and darkness, for you would not be able to explain the words so that they could understand what you were talking about; some from invisible black planets swimming in eternal midnight and thick-armored in perpetual ice, where the people have no eyes, nor any use for them, and where you might wear yourself out trying to make them understand what you meant by such words as warmth and light, you wouldn't ever succeed; and some from *general space*—that sea of ether which has no shores, and stretches on, and on, and arrives nowhere; which is a waste of black gloom and thick darkness through which you may rush forever at thought-speed, encountering at weary long intervals spirit-cheering archipelagoes of suns which rise sparkling far in front of you, and swiftly grow and swell, and burst into blinding glories of light, apparently measureless in extent, but you plunge through and in a moment they are far behind, a twinkling archipelago again, and in another moment they are blotted out in darkness; constellations, these? yes; and the earliest of them the property of your own solar system; the rest of that unending flight is through solar systems not known to men.

And he said that in that flight one came across *such* interesting dream-sprites! coming from a billion worlds, bound for a billion others; always friendly, always glad to meet up with you, always full of where they'd been and what they'd seen, and dying to tell you about it; doing it in a million foreign languages, which sometimes you understood and sometimes you didn't, and the tongue you understood to-day you forgot to-morrow, there being *nothing* permanent about a dream-sprite's character, constitution, beliefs, opinions, intentions, likes, dislikes, or anything else; all he cares for is to travel, and talk, and see wonderful things and have a good time. Schwarz said dream-sprites are well-disposed toward their fleshly brothers, and did what they could to make them partakers of the wonders of their travels, but it couldn't be managed except on a poor and not-worth-while scale, because they had to communicate through the flesh-brothers' Waking-Self imagination, and *that* medium—oh, well, it was like "emptying rainbows down a rat-hole."

His tone was not offensive. I think his tone was never that, and was never meant to be that; *it* was all right enough, but his phrasing was often hurtful, on account of the ideal frankness of it. He said he was once out on an excursion to Jupiter with some fellows about a million years ago, when—

I stopped him there, and said—

"I am only seventeen, and you said you were born with me."

"Yes," he said, "I've been with you only about two million years, I believe—counting as you count; *we* don't measure time at all. Many a time I've been abroad five or ten or twenty thousand years in a single night; I'm always abroad when you are asleep; I always leave, the moment you fall asleep, and I never return until you wake up. You are dreaming all the time I am gone, but you get little or nothing of what I see—never more than some cheap odds and ends, such as your groping Mortal Mind is competent to perceive—and sometimes there's nothing for you at all, in a whole night's adventures, covering many centuries; it's all above your dull Mortal Mind's reach."

Then he dropped into his "chances." That is to say, he went to discussing my health—as coldly as if I had been a piece of mere property that he was commercially interested in, and which ought to be thoughtfully and prudently taken care of for *his* sake. And he even went into particulars, by gracious! advising me to be very careful about my diet, and to take a good deal of exercise, and keep regular hours, and avoid dissipation and religion, and not get married, because a family brought love, and distributed it among many objects, and intensified it, and this engendered wearing cares and anxieties, and when the objects suffered or died the miseries and anxieties multiplied and broke the heart and shortened life; whereas if I took good care of myself and avoided these indiscretions, there was no reason why he should not live ten million years and be hap—

I broke in and changed the subject, so as to keep from getting inhospitable and saying language; for really I was a good deal tried. I started him on the heavens, for he had been to a good many of them and liked ours the best, on account of there not being any Sunday there. They kept Saturday, and it was very pleasant: plenty of rest for the tired, and plenty of innocent good times for the others. But no Sunday, he said; the Sunday-Sabbath was a commercial invention and quite local, having been devised by Constantine to equalize prosperities in this world between the Jews and the Christians. The government statistics of that period showed that a Jew could make as much money in five days as a Christian could in six; and so Constantine saw that at this rate the Jews would by and by have all the wealth and the Christians all the poverty. There was nothing fair nor right about this, a righteous government should have equal laws for all, and take just as much care of the incompetent as of the competent—more, if anything. So he added the Sunday-Sabbath, and it worked just right, because it equalized the prosperities. After that, the Jew had to lie idle 104 days in the year, the Christian only 52, and this enabled the Christian to catch up. But my brother said there was now talk among Constantine and other early Christians up there, of some more equalizing; because, in looking forward a few centuries they could notice that along in the twentieth century somewhere it was going to be necessary to furnish the Jews another Sabbath to keep, so as to save what might be left of Christian property at that time. Schwarz said he had been down into the first quarter of the twentieth century lately, and it looked so to him.

Then he "side-tracked" in his abrupt way, and looked avidly at my head and said he did wish he was back in my skull, he would sail out the first time I fell asleep and have a scandalous good time!—wasn't that magician *ever* coming back?

"And oh," he said, "what wouldn't I see! wonders, spectacles, splendors which your fleshly eyes couldn't endure; and what wouldn't I hear! the music of the spheres—no mortal could live through five minutes of *that* ecstasy! If he would only come! If he . . . ." He stopped, with his lips parted and his eyes fixed, like one rapt. After a moment he whispered, *"do you feel that?"*

I recognized it; it was that life-giving, refreshing, mysterious something which invaded the air when 44 was around. But I dissembled, and said—

"What is it?"

"It's the magician; he's coming. He doesn't always let that influence go out from him, and so we dream-sprites took him for an ordinary necromancer for a while; but when he burnt 44 we were all there and close by, and he let it out then, and in an instant we knew what he was! We knew he was a . . . we knew he was a . . . a . . . a . . . how curious!—my tongue won't *say* it!"

Yes, you see, 44 wouldn't let him say it—and I so near to getting that secret at last! It was a sorrowful disappointment.

Forty-Four entered, still in the disguise of the magician, and Schwarz flung himself on his knees and began to beg passionately for release, and I put in my voice and helped. Schwarz said—

"Oh, mighty one, you imprisoned me, you can set me free, and no other can. You have the power; you possess *all* the powers, all the forces that defy Nature, nothing is impossible to you, for you are a . . . a . . ."

So there it was again—he couldn't say it. I was that close to it a second time, you see; 44 wouldn't let him say that word, and I would have given anything in the world to hear it. It's the way we are made, you know: if we can get a thing, we don't want it, but if we can't get it, why—well, it changes the whole aspect of it, you see.

Forty-Four was very good about it. He said he would let this one go—Schwarz was hugging him around the knees and lifting up the hem of his robe and kissing it and kissing it before he could get any further with his remark—yes, he would let this one go, and make some fresh ones for the wedding, the family could get along very well that way. So he told Schwarz to stand up and melt. Schwarz did it, and it was very pretty. First, his clothes thinned out so you could see him through them, then they floated off like shreds of vapor, leaving him naked, then the cat looked in, but scrambled out again; next, the flesh fell to thinning, and you could see the skeleton through it, very neat and trim, a good skeleton; next the bones disappeared and nothing was left but the empty form—just a statue, perfect and beautiful, made out of the delicatest soap-bubble stuff, with rainbow-hues dreaming around over it and the furniture showing through it the same as it would through a bubble; then—poof! and it was gone!

Chapter 30

THE CAT walked in, waving her tail, then gathered it up in her right arm, as she might a train, and minced her way to the middle of the room, where she faced the magician and rose up and bent low and spread her hands wide apart, as if it was a gown she was spreading, then sank her body grandly rearward—certainly the neatest thing you ever saw, considering the limitedness of the materials. I think a curtsy is the very prettiest thing a woman ever does, and I think a lady's-maid's curtsy is prettier than any one else's; which is because they get more practice than the others, on account of being at it all the time when there's nobody looking. When she had finished her work of art she smiled quite Cheshirely (my dream-brother's word, he knew it was foreign and thought it was future, he couldn't be sure), and said, very engagingly—

"Do you think I could have a bite now, without waiting for the second table, there'll be *such* goings-on this morning, and I would just give a whole basket of rats to be in it! and if I—"

At that moment the wee-wee'est little bright-eyed mousie you ever saw went scrabbling across the floor, and Baker G. gave a skip and let out a scream and landed in the highest chair in the room and gathered up her imaginary skirts and stood there trembling. Also at that moment her breakfast came floating out of the cupboard on a silver tray, and she asked that it come to the chair, which it did, and she took a hurried bite or two to stay her stomach, then rushed away to get her share of the excitements, saying she would like the rest of her breakfast to be kept for her till she got back.

"Now then, draw up to the table," said 44. "We'll have Vienna coffee of two centuries hence—it is the best in the world—buckwheat cakes from Missouri, vintage of 1845, French eggs of last century, and deviled breakfast-whale of the post-pliocene, when he was whitebait size, and just *too* delicious!"

By now I was used to these alien meals, raked up from countries I had never heard of and out of seasons a million years apart, and was getting indifferent about their age and nationalities, seeing that they always turned out to be fresh and good. At first I couldn't stand eggs a hundred years old and canned manna of Moses's time, but that effect came from habit and prejudiced imagination, and I soon got by it, and enjoyed what came, asking few or no questions. At first I would not have touched whale, the very thought of it would have turned my stomach, but now I ate a hundred and sixty of them and never turned a hair. As we chatted along during breakfast, 44 talked reminiscently of dream-sprites, and said they used to be important in the carrying of messages where secrecy and dispatch were a desideratum. He said they took a pride in doing their work well, in old times; that they conveyed messages with perfect verbal accuracy, and that in the matter of celerity they were up to the telephone and away beyond the telegraph. He instanced the Joseph-dreams, and gave it as his opinion that if they had gone per Western Union the lean kine would all have starved to death before the telegrams arrived. He said the business went to pot in Roman times, but that was the fault of the interpreters, not of the dream-sprites, and remarked—

"You can easily see that accurate interpreting was as necessary as accurate wording. For instance, suppose the Founder sends a telegram in the Christian Silence dialect, what are you going to do? Why, there's nothing to do but *guess* the best you can, and take the chances, because there isn't anybody in heaven or earth that can understand *both* ends of it, and so, there you are, you see! Up a stump."

"Up a which?"

"Stump. American phrase. Not discovered yet. It means defeated. You are bound to misinterpret the end you do not understand, and so the matter which was to have been accomplished by the message miscarries, fails, and vast damage is done. Take a specific example, then you will get my meaning. Here is a telegram from the Founder to her disciples. Date, June 27, four hundred and thirteen years hence; it's in the paper—Boston paper—I fetched it this morning."

"What is a Boston paper?"

"It can't be described in just a mouthful of words—pictures, scare-heads and all. You wait, I'll tell you all about it another time; I want to read the telegram, now."

> "Hear, O Israel, the Lord God is one Lord.
>
> "I now request that the members of my Church cease special prayer for the peace of nations, and cease in full faith that God does not hear our prayers only because of oft speaking; but that He will bless all the inhabitants of the earth, and 'none can stay His hand nor say unto Him what doest thou.' Out of His allness He must bless all with His own truth and love.
>
> "MARY BAKER G. EDDY."
>
> "Pleasant View, Concord, N.H., June 27, 1905."

"You see? Down to the word 'nations' anybody can understand it. There's been a prodigious war going on for about

seventeen months, with destruction of whole fleets and
armies, and in seventeen words she indicates certain things,
to-wit: I believed we could squelch the war with prayer,
therefore I ordered it; it was an error of Mortal Mind,
whereas I had supposed it was an inspiration; I now order you
to cease from praying for peace and take hold of something
nearer our size, such as strikes and insurrections. The rest
seems to mean—seems to mean . . . . Let me study it a
minute. It seems to mean that He does not listen to our
prayers any more because we pester Him too much. This carries us to the phrase 'oft-speaking.' At that point the fog shuts
down, black and impenetrable, it solidifies into uninterpretable irrelevancies. Now then, you add up, and get these
results: the praying must be stopped—which is clear and definite; the reason for the stoppage is—well, uncertain. Don't
you know that the incomprehensible and uninterpretable remaining half of the message may be of *actual* importance? we
may be even sure of it, I think, because the first half wasn't;
then what are we confronted with? what is the world confronted with? Why, possible disaster—isn't it so? Possible disaster, absolutely impossible to avoid; and all because one
cannot get at the meaning of the words intended to describe
it and tell how to prevent it. You now understand how important is the interpreter's share in these matters. If you put
part of the message in school-girl and the rest in Choctaw, the
interpreter is going to be defeated, and colossal harm can
come of it."

"I am sure it is true. What is His allness?"

"I pass."

"You which?"

"Pass. Theological expression. It probably means that she
entered the game because she thought only His halfness was
in it and would need help; then perceiving that His allness
was there and playing on the other side, she considered it best
to cash-in and draw out. I think that that must be it; it looks
reasonable, you see, because in seventeen months she hadn't
put up a single chip and got it back again, and so in the circumstances it would be natural for her to want to go out and
see a friend. In Roman times the business went to pot
through bad interpreting, as I told you before. Here in Sue-

tonius is an instance. He is speaking of Atia, the mother of Augustus Caesar:

"'Before her delivery she dreamed that her bowels stretched to the stars, and expanded through the whole circuit of heaven and earth.'

"Now how would you interpret that, August?"

"Who—me? I do not think I could interpret it at all, but I do wish I could have seen it, it must have been magnificent."

"Oh, yes, like enough; but doesn't it suggest anything to you?"

"Why, n-no, I can't see that it does. What would *you* think—that there had been an accident?"

"Of course not! It wasn't real, it was only a dream. It was sent to inform her that she was going to be delivered of something remarkable. What should you think it was?"

"I—why, I don't know."

"Guess."

"Do you think—well, would it be a slaughter-house?"

"Sho, you've no talent for interpretation. But that is a striking instance of what the interpreter had to deal with, in that day. The dream-messages had become loose and rickety and indefinite, like the Founder's telegram, and soon the natural thing happened: the interpreters became loose and careless and discouraged, and got to guessing instead of interpreting, and the business went to ruin. Rome had to give up dream-messages, and the Romans took to entrails for prophetic information."

"Why, then, these ones must have come good, 44, don't you think?"

"I mean *bird* entrails—entrails of chickens."

"I would stake my money on the others; what does a chicken know about the future?"

"Sho, you don't get the idea, August. It isn't what the chicken knows; a chicken doesn't know anything, but by examining the condition of its entrails when it was slaughtered, the augurs could find out a good deal about what was going to happen to emperors, that being the way the Roman gods had invented to communicate with them when dream-transportation went out and Western Union hadn't come in yet. It was a good idea, too, because often a chicken's entrails knew more than a Roman god did, if he was drunk, and he generally was."

"Forty-Four, aren't you afraid to speak like that about a god?"

"No. Why?"

"Because it's irreverent."

"No, it isn't."

"Why isn't it? What do you *call* irreverence?"

"Irreverence is *another person's* disrespect to *your* god; there isn't any word that tells what your disrespect to *his* god is."

I studied it over and saw that it was the truth, but I hadn't ever happened to look at it in that way before.

"Now then, August, to come back to Atia's dream. It beat every soothsayer. None of them got it right. The real meaning of it was—"

The cat dashed in, excited, and said, "I heard Katzenyammer say there's hell to pay down below!" and out she dashed again. I jumped up, but 44 said—

"Sit down. Keep your head. There's no hurry. Things are working; I think we can have a good time. I have shut down the prophecy-works and prepared for it."

"The prophecy-works?"

"Yes. Where I come from, we—"

"*Where* do you co—"

It was as far as I could get. My jaw caught, there, and he gave me a look and went on as if nothing had happened:

"Where I come from we have a gift which we get tired of, now and then. We foresee everything that is going to happen, and so when it happens there's nothing *to* it, don't you see? we don't get any surprises. We can't shut down the prophecy-works there, but we can here. That is one of the main reasons that I come here so much. I do love surprises! I'm only a youth, and it's natural. I love shows and spectacles, and stunning dramatics, and I love to astonish people, and show off, and be and do all the gaudy things a boy loves to be and do; and whenever I'm here and have got matters worked up to where there is a good prospect to the fore, I shut down the works and have a time! I've shut them down now, two hours ago, and I don't know a thing that's ahead, any more than you do. That's all—now we'll go. I wanted to tell you that. I

had plans, but I've thrown them aside. I haven't any now. I
will let things go their own way, and act as circumstances suggest. Then there will be surprises. They may be small ones,
and nothing to you, because you are used to them; but even
the littlest ones are grand to me!"

The cat came racing in, greatly excited, and said—

"Oh, I'm so glad I'm in time! Shut the door—there's people everywhere—don't let them see in. Dear magician, get a
disguise, you are in greater danger now than ever before. You
have been seen, and everybody knows it, everybody is watching for you, it was most imprudent in you to show yourself.
Do put on a disguise and come with me, I know a place in the
castle where they'll never find you. Oh, please, please hurry!
don't you hear the distant noises? they're hunting for you—
do *please* hurry!"

Forty-Four was that gratified, you can't think! He said—

"There it is, you see! I hadn't any idea of it, any more than
you! And there'll be more—I just feel it."

"Oh, please don't stop to talk, but get the disguise! you
don't know what may happen any moment. Everybody is
searching for me, and for you, too, Duplicate, and for your
Original; they've been at it some time, and are coming to
think all three of us is murdered—"

"*Now* I know what I'll do!" cried 44; "oh but we'll have
the gayest time! go on with your news!"

"—and Katrina is wild to get a chance at you because you
burnt up 44, which was the idol of her heart, and she's got a
carving knife three times as long as my tail, and is ambushed
behind a marble column in the great hall, and it's awful to see
how savagely she rakes it and whets it up and down that column and makes the sparks fly, and darts her head out, with
her eyes glaring, to see if she can see you—oh, *do* get the disguise and come with me, quick! and laws bless me, there's a
conspiracy, and—"

"Oh, it's grand, August, it's just grand! and I didn't know
a thing about it, any more than you. *What* conspiracy are you
talking about, pussy?"

"It's the strikers, going to kill the Duplicates—I sat in Fischer's lap and heard them talk the whole thing in whispers;
and they've got signs and grips and passwords and all that,

so't they can tell which is themselves and which is other people, though I hope to goodness if *I* can, not if I had a thousand such; *do* get the disguise and come, I'm just ready to
cry!"

"Oh, bother the disguise, I'm going just so, and if they offer to do anything to me I will give them a piece of my
mind."

And so he opened the door and started away, Mary following him, with the tears running down, and saying—

"Oh, *they* won't care for your piece of mind—why *will* you
be so imprudent and throw your life away, and you *know*
they'll abuse me and bang me when you are gone!"

I became invisible and joined them.

Chapter 31

IT was a dark, sour, gloomy morning, and bleak and cold,
with a slanting veil of powdery snow driving along, and a
clamorous hollow wind bellowing down the chimneys and
rumbling around the battlements and towers—just the right
weather for the occasion, 44 said, nothing could improve it
but an eclipse. That gave him an idea, and he said he would
do an eclipse; not a real one, but an artificial one that nobody
but Simon Newcomb could tell from the original Jacobs—so
he started it at once, and it certainly did make those yawning
old stone tunnels pretty dim and sepulchral, and also of
course it furnished an additional uncanniness and muffledness
to way-off footfalls, taking the harshness out of them and the
edge off their echoes, because when you walk on that kind of
eclipsy gloominess on a stone floor it squshes under the foot
and makes that dull effect which is so shuddery and uncomfortable in these crumbly old castles where there has been
such ages of cruelty and captivity and murder and mystery.
And to-night would be Ghost-Night besides, and 44 did not
forget to remember that, and said he wished eclipses weren't
so much trouble after sundown, hanged if he wouldn't run
this one all night, because it could be a great help, and a lot
of ghastly effects could be gotten out of it, because all the

castle ghosts turn out then, on account of its coming only
every ten years, which makes it kind of select and distinguished, and still more so every Hundredth Year—which this
one was—because the best ghosts from many other castles
come by invitation, then, and take a hand at the great ball and
banquet at midnight, a good spectacle and full of interest, insomuch that 44 had come more than once on the Hundredth
Night to see it, he said, and it was very pathetic and interesting to meet up with shadowy friends that way that you
haven't seen for one or two centuries and hear them tell the
same mouldy things over again that they've told you several
times before; because they don't have anything fresh, the way
they are situated, poor things. And besides, he was going to
make this the swellest Hundredth Night that had been celebrated in this castle in twelve centuries, and said he was inviting A 1 ghosts from everywhere in the world and from all the
ages, past and future, and each could bring a friend if he
liked—any friend, character no object, just so he is dead—and
if I wanted to invite some I could, he hoped to accumulate a
thousand or two, and make this *the* Hundredth Night of
Hundredth Nights, and discourage competition for a thousand years.

We didn't see a soul, all the murky way from my door to
the central grand staircase and half way down it—then we began to see plenty of people, our own and men from the village—and they were armed, and stood in two ranks, waiting,
a double fence across the spacious hall—for the magician to
pass between, if it might please him to try it; and Katrina was
there, between the fences, grim and towering and soldierly,
and she was watching and waiting, with her knife. I glanced
back, by chance, and there was also a living fence *behind!* dim
forms, men who had been keeping watch in ambush, and had
silently closed in upon the magician's tracks as he passed
along. Mary G. had apparently had enough of this grisly journey—she was gone.

When the people below saw that their plans had succeeded,
and that their quarry was in the trap they had set, they set up
a loud cheer of exultation, but it didn't seem to me to ring
true; there was a doubtful note in it, and I thought likely
those folks were not as glad they had caught their bird as they

were letting on to be; and they kept crossing themselves industriously; I took that for a sign, too.

Forty-Four moved steadily down. When he was on the last
step there was turmoil down the hall, and a volley of shoutings, with cries of "make way—Father Adolf is come!" then
he burst panting through one of the ranks and threw himself
in the way, just as Katrina was plunging for the disguised 44,
and stormed out—

"Stop her, everybody! Donkeys, would you let her butcher
him, and cheat the Church's fires!"

They jumped for Katrina, and in a moment she was struggling in the jumble of swaying forms, with nothing visible
above it but her head and her long arm with the knife in it;
and her strong voice was pouring out her feelings with energy, and easily making itself heard above the general din and
the priest's commands:

"Let me at him—he burnt my child, my darling!" . . . .
"Keep her off, men, keep her off!" . . . . "He is *not* the
Church's, his blood is *mine* by rights—out of my way! I *will*
have it!" . . . . *"Back! woman, back, I tell you—force her back,
men, have you no strength? are you nothing but boys?"* . . . . "A
hundred of you shan't stay me, woman though I be!"

And sure enough, with one massy surge she wrenched herself free, and flourished her knife, and bent her head and body
forward like a foot-racer and came charging down the living
lane through the gathering darkness—

Then suddenly there was a great light! she lifted her head
and caught it full in her swarthy face, which it transfigured
with its white glory, as it did also all that place, and its marble pillars, and the frightened people, and Katrina dropped
her knife and fell to her knees, with her hands clasped, everybody doing the same; and so there they were, all kneeling,
like that, with hands thrust forward or clasped, and they and
the stately columns all awash in that unearthly splendor; and
there where the magician had stood, stood 44 now, in his su-
pernal beauty and his gracious youth; and it was from him
that that flooding light came, for all his form was clothed in
that immortal fire, and flashing like the sun; and Katrina crept
on her knees to him, and bent down her old head and kissed
his feet, and he bent down and patted her softly on the shoul-

der and touched his lips to the gray hair—*and was gone!*—and for two or three minutes you were so blinded you couldn't see your next neighbor in that submerging black darkness. Then after that it was better, and you could make out the murky forms, some still kneeling, some lying prone in a swoon, some staggering about, here and there, with their hands pressed over their eyes, as if that light had hurt them and they were in pain. Katrina was wandering off, on unsteady feet, and her knife was lying there in the midst.

It was good he thought of the eclipse, it helped out ever so much; the effects would have been fine and great in any case, but the eclipse made them grand and stunning—just letter-perfect, as it seemed to me; and he said himself it beat Barnum and Bailey hands down, and was by as much as several shades too good for the provinces—which was all Sanscrit to me, and hadn't any meaning even in Sanscrit I reckon, but was invented for the occasion, because it had a learned sound, and he liked sound better than sense as a rule. There's been others like that, but he was the worst.

I judged it would take those people several hours to get over that, and accumulate their wits again and get their bearings, for it had knocked the whole bunch dizzy; meantime there wouldn't be anything doing. I must put in the time some way until they should be in a condition to resume business at the old stand. I went to my room and put on my flesh and stretched myself out on a lounge before the fire with a book, first setting the door ajar, so that the cat could fetch news if she got hold of any, which I wished she might; but in a little while I was asleep. I did not stir again until ten at night. I woke then, and found the cat finishing her supper, and my own ready on the table and hot; and very welcome, for I hadn't eaten anything since breakfast. Mary came and occupied a chair at my board, and washed herself and delivered her news while I ate. She had witnessed the great transformation scene, and had been so astonished by it and so interested in it that she did not wait to see the end, but went up a chimney and stayed there half an hour freezing, until somebody started a fire under her, and then she was thankful and very comfortable. But it got too comfortable, and she climbed out and came down a skylight stairway and went visiting around, and a little while ago she caught a rat, and did it as easy as nothing, and would teach me how, sometime, if I cared for such things; but she didn't eat it, it wasn't a fresh rat, or was out of season or something, but it reminded her that she was hungry, so she came home. Then she said—

"If you like to be astonished, I can astonish you. The magician isn't dead!"

I threw my hands up and did the astonishment-act like an old expert, crying out—

"Mary Florence Fortescue, what *can* you mean!"

She was delighted, and exclaimed—

"There, it's just as I said! I *told* him you wouldn't ever believe it; but I can lay my paw on my heart, just so, and I wish I may never stir if I haven't *seen* him!—*seen* him, you hear?—and he's just as alive as ever he was since the day he was born!"

"Oh, go 'long, you're deceiving me!"

She was almost beside herself with joy over the success of her astonisher, and said—

"Oh, it's lovely, it's too lovely, and just as I *said* it would be—I *told* him you wouldn't, and it's come out just so!"

In her triumph and delight she tried to clap her hands, but it was a failure, they wouldn't clap any more than mushrooms. Then she said—

"Duplicate, would you believe he is alive if I should prove it?"

"Sho," I said, "come off!—what are you giving me?—as he used to say. You're talking nonsense, Mary. When a person is dead, *known* to be dead, permanently dead, demonstrably dead, you *can't* prove him alive, there isn't any *way*. Come, don't you know that?"

Well, she was just beaming, by now, and she could hardly hold her system together, she was that near to bursting with the victory she was going to spring on me. She skipped to the floor and flirted something to my foot with her paw; I picked it up, and she jumped into her chair again and said—

"There, now, he said you would know what that is; what is it?"

"It's a thing he calls a paper—Boston paper."

"That's right, that's what he said. And he said it is future

English and you know present English and can read it. Did he say right?"

"The *fact* is right, but he didn't say it, because he's dead."

"You wait—that's all. He said look at the date."

"Very well. He didn't say it, because he's dead, and of course wouldn't think of it; but here it is, all the same—June 28, 1905."

"That's right, it's what he said. Then he said ask you what was the Founder's message to her disciples, that was in the other Boston paper. What was it?"

"Well, he told me there was an immense war going on, and she got tired having her people pray for peace and never take a trick for seventeen months, so she ordered them to quit, and put their battery out of commission. And he said nobody could understand the rest of the message, and like enough that very ignorance would bring on an immense disaster."

"Aha! well, it *did*! He says the very minute she was stopping the praying, the two fleets were meeting, and the uncivilized one utterly annihilated the civilized one, and it wouldn't have happened if she had let the praying go on. Now then, you didn't know *that*, did you!"

"No, and I don't know it yet."

"Well, you soon will. The message was June 27, wasn't it?"

"Yes."

"Well, the disaster was *that very day*—right after the praying was stopped—and you'll find the news of it in the very next day's paper, which you've got in your hand—date, *June 28*."

I took a glance at the big headings, and said—

"M-y word! why it's absolutely *so*! Baker G., don't you know this is the most astounding thing that ever happened? It proves he *is* alive—nobody else could bring this paper. He certainly is alive, and back with us, after that tremendous abolishment and extinction which we witnessed; yes, he's alive, Mary, alive, and glad am I, oh, grateful beyond words!"

"Oh!" she cried, in a rapture, "it's just splendid, oh, just too lovely! I knew I could prove it; I knew it just as well! I thought he was gone, when he blazed up and went out, that way, and I *was* so scared and grieved—and isn't he a wonder! Duplicate, there isn't another necromancer in the business that can begin with him, now *is* there?"

"You can stake your tale and your ears on it, Mary, and don't you forget it—as he used to say. In my opinion he can give the whole trade ninety-nine in the hundred and go out every time, cross-eyed and left-handed."

"But he isn't, Duplicate."

"Isn't what?"

"Cross-eyed and left-handed."

"Who said he was, you little fool?"

"Why, you did."

"I never said anything of the kind; I said he could if he *was*. That isn't *saying* he was; it was a supposititious case, and literary; it was a figure, a metaphor, and its function was to augment the force of the—"

"Well, he *isn't*, anyway; because I've noticed, and—"

"Oh, shut up! don't I tell you it was only a *figure*, and I never meant—"

"I don't care, you'll never make *me* believe he's cross-eyed and left-handed, because the time he—"

"Baker G., if you open your mouth again I'll jam the boot-jack down it! you're as random and irrelevant and incoherent and mentally impenetrable as the afflicted Founder herself."

But she was under the bed by that time; and reflecting, probably, if she had the machinery for it.

Chapter 32

FORTY-FOUR, still playing Balthasar Hoffman the magician, entered briskly now, and threw himself in a chair. The cat emerged with confidence, spread herself, purring, in his lap, and said—

"This Duplicate wouldn't believe me when I told him, and when I proved it he tried to cram a boot-jack down my throat, thinking to scare me, which he didn't, *didn't* you, Duplicate?"

"Didn't I *what*?"

"Why, what I just *said*."

"*I* don't know what you just said; it was Christian Silence and untranslatable; but I'll say yes to the whole of it if that will quiet you. Now then, keep still, and let the master tell what is on his mind."

"Well, this is on my mind, August. Some of the most distinguished people can't come. Flora McFlimsey—nothing to wear; Eve, ditto; Adam, previous engagement, and so on and so on; Nero and ever so many others find the notice too short, and are urgent to have more time. Very well, we've got to accommodate them."

"But how can we do it? The show is due to begin in an hour. Listen!"

Boom-m-m—boom-m-m—boom-m-m!—

It was the great bell of the castle tolling the hour. Our American clock on the wall struck in, and simultaneously the clock of the village—faint and far, and half of the notes overtaken in their flight and strangled by the gusty wind. We sat silent and counted, to the end.

"You see?" said I.

"Yes, I see. Eleven. Now there are two ways to manage. One is, to have time stand still—which has been done before, a lot of times; and the other one is, to turn time backward for a day or two, which is comparatively new, and offers the best effects, besides.

> " 'Backward, turn backward, O Time, in thy flight—
> Make me a child again, just for to-night!'—

"—'Beautiful Snow,' you see; it hasn't been written yet. *I* vote to reverse—and that is what we will do, presently. We will make the hands of the clocks travel around in the other direction."

"But will they?"

"Sure. It will attract attention—make yourself easy, as to that. But the stunning effect is going to be the sun."

"How?"

"Well, when they see him come rising up out of the west, about half a dozen hours from now, it will secure the interest of the entire world."

"I should think as much."

"Oh, yes, depend upon it. There is going to be more early rising than the human race has seen before. In my opinion it'll be a record."

"I believe you are right about it. I mean to get up and see it myself. Or stay up."

"I think it will be a good idea to have it rise in the southwest, instead of the west. More striking, you see; and hasn't been done before."

"Master, it will be wonderful! It will be the very greatest marvel the world has ever seen. It will be talked about and written about as long as the human race endures. And there'll not be any disputing over it, because every human being that's alive will get up to look at it, and there won't be one single person to say it's a lie."

"It's so. It will be the only perfectly authenticated event in all human history. All the other happenings, big and little, have got to depend on minority-testimony, and very little of that—but not so, this time, dontcherknow. And this one's patented. There aren't going to be any encores."

"How long shall we go backwards, Balthasar?"

"Two or three days or a week; long enough to accommodate Robert Bruce, and Henry I and such, who have hearts and things scattered around here and there and yonder, and have to get a basket and go around and collect; so we will let the sun and the clocks go backwards a while, then start them ahead in time to fetch up all right at midnight to-night—then the shades will begin to arrive according to schedule."

"It grows on me! It's going to be the most prodigious thing that ever happened, and—"

"Yes," he burst out, in a rapture of eloquence, "and will round out and perfect the reputation I've been building for Balthasar Hoffman, and make him the most glorious magician that ever lived, and get him burnt, to a dead moral certainty. You know I've taken a lot of pains with that reputation; I've taken more interest in it than anything I've planned out in centuries; I've spared neither labor nor thought, and I feel a pride in it and a sense of satisfaction such as I have hardly ever felt in a mere labor of love before; and when I get it completed, now, in this magnificent way, and get him burnt, or pulverized, or something showy and picturesque, like that, I shan't mind the trouble I've had, in the least; not in the least, I give you my word."

Boom-m-m—boom-m-m—boom-m-m—

"There she goes! striking eleven again."

"Is it really?"

"Count—you'll see."

It woke the cat, and she stretched herself out about a yard and a half, and asked if time was starting back—which showed that she had heard the first part of the talk. And understood it of course, because it was in German. She was informed that time was about to start back; so she arranged herself for another nap, and said that when we got back to ten she would turn out and catch that rat again.

I was counting the clock-strokes—counting aloud—

"*Eight . . . . nine . . . . ten . . . . eleven—*"

Forty-Four shouted—

"Backward! turn backward! O Time in thy flight! Look at the clock-hands! Listen!"

Instantly I found myself counting the strokes again, aloud—

"Eleven . . . ten . . . . nine . . . eight . . . . seven . . . six . . . . five . . . . four . . . two . . . one!"

At once the cat woke and repeated her remark about recatching the rat—saying it backwards!

Then Forty-Four said—

"see you'll—Count."

Whereupon I said—

"really? it Is"

And he remarked—the booming of the great castle clock mixing with his words—

"again. eleven striking goes! she There word (here his voice began to become impressive, then to nobly rise, and swell, and grow in eloquent feeling and majestic expression), my you give I least, the in not least; the in had, I've trouble the mind shan't I that, like picturesque, and showy something or pulverized, or burnt, him get and way, magnificent this in now, completed, it get I when and before; love of labor mere a in felt ever hardly have I as such satisfaction of sense a and it in pride (here his voice was near to breaking, so deeply were his feelings stirred) a feel I and thought, nor labor neither spared I've centuries; in out planned I've anything than it in interest more taken I've reputation; that with pains of lot a taken I've know You (here his winged eloquence reached its loftiest flight, and in his deep organ-tones he thundered forth

his sublime words) certainty. moral dead a to burnt, him get
and lived, ever that magician glorious most the him make and
Hoffman, Balthasar for building been I've reputation the perfect and out round will and Yes,"——

My brain was spinning, it was audibly whizzing, I rose reeling, and was falling lifeless to the floor, when 44 caught me.
His touch restored me, and he said——

"I see it is too much for you, you cannot endure it, you
would go mad. Therefore I relieve you of your share in this
grand event. You shall look on and enjoy, taking no personal
part in the backward flight of time, nor in its return, until it
reaches the present hour again and resumes its normal march
forward. Go and come as you please, amuse yourself as you
choose."

Those were blessed words! I could not tell him how thankful I was.

A considerable blank followed—a silent one, for it represented the unrepeated conversation which he and I had had
about the turning back of time and the sun.

Then another silent blank followed; it represented the interval occupied by my dispute with the cat as to whether the
magician was come alive again or not.

I filled in these intervals not wearily nor drearily—oh, no
indeed, just the reverse; for my gaze was glued to that American clock—watching its hands creeping backward around its
face, an uncanny spectacle!

Then I fell asleep, and when I woke again the clock had
gone back seven hours, and it was mid-afternoon. Being privileged to go and come as I pleased, I threw off my flesh and
went down to see the grand transformation-spectacle repeated backwards.

It was as impressive and as magnificent as ever. In the darkness some of the people lay prone, some were kneeling, some
were wandering and tottering about with their hands over
their eyes, Katrina was walking backwards on unsteady feet;
she backed further and further, then knelt and bowed her
head—then that white glory burst upon the darkness and 44
stood clothed as with the sun; and he bent and kissed the old
head—and so on and so on, the scene repeated itself backwards, detail by detail, clear to the beginning; then the magi-

cian, the cat and I walked backward up the stairs and through the gathering eclipse to my room.

After that, as time drifted rearward, I skipped some things and took in others, according to my humor. I watched my Duplicate turn from nothing into a lovely soap-bubble statue with delicate rainbow-hues playing over it; watched its skeleton gather form and solidity; watched it put on flesh and clothes, and all that; but I skipped the interviews with the cat; I also skipped the interview with the master; and when the clock had gone back twenty-three hours and I was due to appear drunk in Marget's chamber, I took the pledge and stayed away.

Then, for amusement and to note effects, 44 and I—invisible—appeared in China, where it was noonday. The sun was just ready to turn downward on his new north-eastern track, and millions of yellow people were gazing at him, dazed and stupid, while other millions lay stretched upon the ground everywhere, exhausted with the terrors and confusions they had been through, and now blessedly unconscious. We loafed along behind the sun around the globe, tarrying in all the great cities on the route, and observing and admiring the effects. Everywhere weary people were re-chattering previous conversations backwards and not understanding each other, and oh, they did look so tuckered out and tired of it all! and always there were groups gazing miserably at the town-clocks; in every city funerals were being held again that had already been held once, and the hearses and the processions were marching solemnly backwards; where there was war, yesterday's battles were being refought, wrong-end-first; the previously killed were getting killed again, the previously wounded were getting hit again in the same place and complaining about it; there were blood-stirring and tremendous charges of masses of steel-clad knights across the field—backwards; and on the oceans the ships, with full-bellied sails were speeding backwards over the same water they had traversed the day before, and some of each crew were scared and praying, some were gazing in mute anguish at the crazy sun, and the rest were doing profanity beyond imagination.

At Rouen we saw Henry I gathering together his split skull and his other things.

Chapter 33

SURELY Forty-Four was the flightiest creature that ever was! Nothing interested him long at a time. He would contrive the most elaborate projects, and put his whole mind and heart into them, then he would suddenly drop them, in the midst of their fulfilment, and start something fresh. It was just so with his Assembly of the Dead. He summoned those forlorn wrecks from all the world and from all the epochs and ages, and then, when everything was ready for the exhibition, he wanted to flit back to Moses's time and see the Egyptians floundering around in the Dead Sea, and take me along with him. He said he had seen it twice, and it was one of the hand-somest and most exciting incidents a body ever saw. It was all I could do to persuade him to wait a while.

To me the Procession was very good indeed, and most im-pressive. First, there was an awful darkness. All visible things gloomed down gradually, losing their outlines little by little, then disappeared utterly. The thickest and solidest and black-est darkness followed, and a silence which was so still it was as if the world was holding its breath. That deep stillness contin-ued, and continued, minute after minute, and got to be so op-pressive that presently I was holding *my* breath—that is, only half-breathing. Then a wave of cold air came drifting along, damp, searching, and smelling of the grave, and was shivery and dreadful. After about ten minutes I heard a faint clicking sound coming as from a great distance. It came slowly nearer and nearer, and a little louder and a little louder, and increas-ing steadily in mass and volume, till all the place was filled with a dry sharp clacking and was right abreast of us and passing by! Then a vague twilight suffused the place and through it and drowned in it we made out the spidery dim forms of thou-sands of skeletons marching! It made me catch my breath. It was that grewsome and grisly and horrible, you can't think.

Soon the light paled to a half dawn, and we could distin-guish details fairly well. Forty-Four had enlarged the great hall of the castle, so as to get effects. It was a vast and lofty corridor, now, and stretched away for miles and miles, and the Procession drifted solemnly down it sorrowfully clacking, los-

ing definiteness gradually, and finally fading out in the far distances, and melting from sight.

Forty-Four named no end of those poor skeletons, as they
passed by, and he said the most of them had been distinguished, in their day and had cut a figure in the world. Some
of the names were familiar to me, but the most of them were
not. Which was natural, for they belonged to nations that perished from the earth ten, and twenty, and fifty, and a hundred, and three hundred, and six hundred thousand years
ago, and so of course I had never heard of them.

By force of 44's magic each skeleton had a tab on him giving his name and date, and telling all about him, in brief. It
was a good idea, and saved asking questions. Pharaoh was
there, and David and Goliah and several other of the sacred
characters; and Adam and Eve, and some of the Caesars, and
Cleopatra, and Charlemagne, and Dagobert, and kings, and
kings and kings till you couldn't count them—the most of
them from away back thousands and thousands of centuries
before Adam's time. Some of them fetched their crowns
along, and had a rotten velvet rag or two dangling about their
bones, a kind of pathetic spectacle.

And there were skeletons whom I had known, myself, and
been at their funerals, only three or four years before—men
and women, boys and girls; and they put out their poor bony
hands and shook with me, and looked so sad. Some of the
skeletons dragged the rotting ruins of their coffins after them
by a string, and seemed pitifully anxious that that poor property shouldn't come to harm.

But to think how long the pathos of a thing can last, and
still carry its touching effect, the same as if it was new and
happened yesterday! There was a slim skeleton of a young
woman, and it went by with its head bowed and its bony
hands to its eyes, crying, apparently. Well, it was a young
mother whose little child disappeared one day and was never
heard of again, and so her heart was broken, and she cried her
life away. It brought the tears to my eyes and made my heart
ache to see that poor thing's sorrow. When I looked at her
tab I saw it had happened five hundred thousand years ago! It
seemed strange that it should still affect me, but I suppose
such things never grow old, but remain always new.

King Arthur came along, by and by, with all his knights. That interested me, because we had just been printing his history, copying it from Caxton. They rode upon bony crates that had once been horses, and they looked very stately in their ancient armor, though it was rusty and lacked a piece here and there, and through those gaps you could see the bones inside. They talked together, skeletons as they were, and you could see their jawbones go up and down through the slits in their helmets. By grace of Forty-Four's magic I could understand them. They talked about Arthur's last battle, and seemed to think it happened yesterday, which shows that a thousand years in the grave is merely a night's sleep, to the dead, and counts for nothing.

It was the same with Noah and his sons and their wives. Evidently they had forgotten that they had ever left the Ark, and could not understand how they came to be wandering around on land. They talked about the weather; they did not seem to be interested in anything else.

The skeletons of Adam's predecessors outnumbered the later representatives of our race by myriads, and they rode upon undreamt-of monsters of the most extraordinary bulk and aspect. They marched ten thousand abreast, our walls receding and melting away and disappearing, to give them room, and the earth was packed with them as far as the eye could reach. Among them was the Missing Link. That is what 44 called him. He was an undersized skeleton, and he was perched on the back of a long-tailed and long-necked creature ninety feet long and thirty-three feet high; a creature that had been dead eight million years, 44 said.

For hours and hours the dead passed by in continental masses, and the bone-clacking was so deafening you could hardly hear yourself think. Then, all of a sudden 44 waved his hand and we stood in an empty and soundless world.

Chapter 34

A ND you are going away, and will not come back any more."

"Yes," he said. "We have comraded long together, and it has been pleasant—pleasant for both; but I must go now, and we shall not see each other any more."

"In this life, 44, but in another? We shall meet in another, surely, 44?"

Then all tranquilly and soberly he made the strange answer—
"There is no other."

A subtle influence blew upon my spirit from his, bringing with it a vague, dim, but blessed and hopeful feeling that the incredible words might be true—even *must* be true.

"Have you never suspected this, August?"

"No—how could I? But if it can only be true—"

"It is true."

A gush of thankfulness rose in my breast, but a doubt checked it before it could issue in words, and I said—

"But—but—we have *seen* that future life—seen it in its actuality, and so—"

"It was a vision—it had no existence."

I could hardly breathe for the great hope that was struggling in me—

"A vision?—a vi—"

"Life itself is only a vision, a dream."

It was electrical. By God I had had that very thought a thousand times in my musings!

"*Nothing* exists; all is a dream. God—man—the world,—the sun, the moon, the wilderness of stars: a dream, all a dream, they have no existence. *Nothing exists save empty space—and you!*"

"I!"

"And you are not you—you have no body, no blood, no bones, you are but a *thought*. I myself have no existence, I am but a dream—your dream, creature of your imagination. In a moment you will have realized this, then you will banish me from your visions and I shall dissolve into the nothingness out of which you made me . . . . ."

"I am perishing already—I am failing, I am passing away. In a little while you will be alone in shoreless space, to wander its limitless solitudes without friend or comrade forever—for you will remain a *Thought*, the only existent Thought, and by your nature inextinguishable, indestructible. But I your poor servant have revealed you to yourself and set you free. Dream other dreams, and better! . . . .

"Strange! that you should not have suspected, years ago, centuries, ages, aeons ago! for you have existed, companionless, through all the eternities. Strange, indeed, that you should not have suspected that your universe and its contents were only dreams, visions, fictions! Strange, because they are so frankly and hysterically insane—like all dreams: a God who could make good children as easily as bad, yet preferred to make bad ones; who could have made every one of them happy, yet never made a single happy one; who made them prize their bitter life, yet stingily cut it short; who gave his angels eternal happiness unearned, yet required his other children to earn it; who gave his angels painless lives, yet cursed his other children with biting miseries and maladies of mind and body; who mouths justice, and invented hell—mouths mercy, and invented hell—mouths Golden Rules, and foregiveness multiplied by seventy times seven, and invented hell; who mouths morals to other people, and has none himself; who frowns upon crimes, yet commits them all; who created man without invitation, then tries to shuffle the responsibility for man's acts upon man, instead of honorably placing it where it belongs, upon himself; and finally, with altogether divine obtuseness, invites this poor abused slave to worship him! . . . .

"You perceive, *now*, that these things are all impossible, except in a dream. You perceive that they are pure and puerile insanities, the silly creations of an imagination that is not conscious of its freaks—in a word, that they are a dream, and you the maker of it. The dream-marks are all present—you should have recognized them earlier . . . . .

"It is true, that which I have revealed to you: there is no God, no universe, no human race, no earthly life, no heaven, no hell. It is all a Dream, a grotesque and foolish dream. Nothing exists but You. And You are but a *Thought*—a vagrant Thought, a useless Thought, a homeless Thought, wandering forlorn among the empty eternities!"

He vanished, and left me appalled; for I knew, and realized, that all he had said was true.

THE END

SELECTED TALES
AND SKETCHES

Jim Smiley and His Jumping Frog

Mr. A. Ward,

DEAR SIR:—Well, I called on good-natured, garrulous old Simon Wheeler, and I inquired after your friend Leonidas W. Smiley, as you requested me to do, and I hereunto append the result. If you can get any information out of it you are cordially welcome to it. I have a lurking suspicion that your Leonidas W. Smiley is a myth—that you never knew such a personage, and that you only conjectured that if I asked old Wheeler about him it would remind him of his infamous *Jim* Smiley, and he would go to work and bore me nearly to death with some infernal reminiscence of him as long and tedious as it should be useless to me. If that was your design, Mr. Ward, it will gratify you to know that it succeeded.

I found Simon Wheeler dozing comfortably by the bar-room stove of the little old dilapidated tavern in the ancient mining camp of Boomerang, and I noticed that he was fat and bald-headed, and had an expression of winning gentleness and simplicity upon his tranquil countenance. He roused up and gave me good-day. I told him a friend of mine had commissioned me to make some inquiries about a cherished companion of his boyhood named Leonidas W. Smiley—Rev. Leonidas W. Smiley—a young minister of the gospel, who he had heard was at one time a resident of this village of Boomerang. I added that if Mr. Wheeler could tell me anything about this Rev. Leonidas W. Smiley, I would feel under many obligations to him.

Simon Wheeler backed me into a corner and blockaded me there with his chair—and then sat down and reeled off the monotonous narrative which follows this paragraph. He never smiled, he never frowned, he never changed his voice from the quiet, gently-flowing key to which he turned the initial sentence, he never betrayed the slightest suspicion of enthusiasm—but all through the interminable narrative there ran a vein of impressive earnestness and sincerity, which showed me plainly that so far from his imagining that there was anything ridiculous or funny about his story, he regarded it as a really important matter, and admired its two heroes as men of transcendent genius in finesse. To me, the spectacle of a man drifting serenely along through such a queer yarn without ever smiling was exquisitely absurd. As I said before, I asked him to tell me what he knew of Rev. Leonidas W. Smiley, and he replied as follows. I let him go on in his own way, and never interrupted him once:

There was a feller here once by the name of *Jim* Smiley, in the winter of '49—or maybe it was the spring of '50—I don't recollect exactly, some how, though what makes me think it was one or the other is because I remember the big flume wasn't finished when he first come to the camp; but anyway, he was the curiosest man about always betting on anything that turned up you ever see, if he could get anybody to bet on the other side, and if he couldn't he'd change sides—any way that suited the other man would suit *him*—any way just so's he got a bet, *he* was satisfied. But still, he was lucky—uncommon lucky; he most always come out winner. He was always ready and laying for a chance; there couldn't be no solitry thing mentioned but what that feller'd offer to bet on it— and take any side you please, as I was just telling you: if there was a horse race, you'd find him flush or you find him busted at the end of it; if there was a dog-fight, he'd bet on it; if there was a cat-fight, he'd bet on it; if there was a chicken-fight, he'd bet on it; why if there was two birds setting on a fence, he would bet you which one would fly first—or if there was a camp-meeting he would be there reglar to bet on parson Walker, which he judged to be the best exhorter about here, and so he was, too, and a good man; if he even see a straddle-bug start to go any wheres, he would bet you how long it would take him to get wherever he was going to, and if you took him up he would foller that straddle-bug to Mexico but what he would find out where he was bound for and how long he was on the road. Lots of the boys here has seen that Smiley and can tell you about him. Why, it never made no difference to *him*—he would bet on *anything*—the dangdest feller. Parson Walker's wife laid very sick, once, for a good while, and it seemed as if they warn't going to save her; but one morning he come in and Smiley asked him how she was, and he said she was considerable better—thank the Lord for his inf'nit mercy—and coming on so smart that with the blessing of Providence she'd get well yet—and Smiley, before he thought, says, "Well, I'll resk two-and-a-half that she don't, anyway."

Thish-yer Smiley had a mare—the boys called her the fifteen-minute nag, but that was only in fun, you know, because, of course, she was faster than that—and he used to win money on that horse, for all she was so slow and always had the asthma, or the distemper, or the consumption, or something of that kind. They used to give her two or three hundred yards' start, and then pass her under way; but always at the fag-end of the race she'd get excited and desperate-like, and come cavorting and spraddling up, and scattering her legs around limber, sometimes in the air, and sometimes out to one side amongst the fences, and kicking up m-o-r-e dust, and raising m-o-r-e racket with her coughing and sneezing and blowing her nose—and always fetch up at the stand just about a neck ahead, as near as you could cipher it down.

And he had a little small bull-pup, that to look at him you'd think he warn't worth a cent, but to set around and look ornery, and lay for a chance to steal something. But as soon as money was up on him he was a different dog—his under-jaw'd begin to stick out like the for'castle of a steamboat, and his teeth would uncover, and shine savage like the furnaces. And a dog might tackle him, and bully-rag him, and bite him, and throw him over his shoulder two or three times, and Andrew Jackson—which was the name of the pup—Andrew Jackson would never let on but what he was satisfied, and hadn't expected nothing else—and the bets being doubled and doubled on the other side all the time, till the money was all up—and then all of a sudden he would grab that other dog just by the joint of his hind legs and freeze to it—not chaw, you understand, but only just grip and hang on till they throwed up the sponge, if it was a year. Smiley always came out winner on that pup till he harnessed a dog once that didn't have no hind legs, because they'd been sawed off in a circular saw, and when the thing had gone along far enough, and the money was all up, and he came to make a snatch for his pet holt, he saw in a minute how he'd been imposed on, and how the other dog had him in the door, so to speak, and he 'peared surprised, and then he looked sorter discouraged like, and didn't try no more to win the fight, and so he got shucked out bad. He gave Smiley a look as much as to say his heart was broke, and it was *his* fault, for putting up a dog that hadn't no hind legs for him to take holt of, which was his main dependence in a fight, and then he limped off a piece, and laid down and died. It was a good pup, was that Andrew Jackson, and would have made a name for hisself if he'd lived, for the stuff was in him, and he had genius—I know it, because he hadn't had no opportunities to speak of, and it don't stand to reason that a dog could make such a fight as he could under them circumstances, if he hadn't no talent. It always makes me feel sorry when I think of that last fight of his'on, and the way it turned out.

Well, thish-yer Smiley had rat-terriers and chicken cocks, and tom-cats, and all them kind of things, till you couldn't rest, and you couldn't fetch nothing for him to bet on but he'd match you. He ketched a frog one day and took him home and said he cal'lated to educate him; and so he never done nothing for three months but set in his back yard and learn that frog to jump. And you bet you he *did* learn him, too. He'd give him a little hunch behind, and the next minute you'd see that frog whirling in the air like a doughnut—see him turn one summerset, or maybe a couple, if he got a good start, and come down flat-footed and all right, like a cat. He got him up so in the matter of ketching flies, and kept him in practice so constant, that he'd nail a fly every time as far as he could see him. Smiley said all a frog wanted was education, and he could do most anything—and I believe him. Why, I've seen him set Dan'l Webster down here on this floor— Dan'l Webster was the name of the frog—and sing out, "Flies! Dan'l, flies," and quicker'n you could wink, he'd spring straight up, and snake a fly off'n the counter there, and flop down on the floor again as solid as a gob of mud, and fall to scratching the side of his head with his hind foot as indifferent as if he hadn't no idea he'd done any more'n any frog might do. You never see a frog so modest and straightfor'ard as he was, for all he was so gifted. And when it come to fair-and-square jumping on a dead level, he could get over more ground at one straddle than any animal of his breed you ever see. Jumping on a dead level was his strong suit, you understand, and when it come to that, Smiley would ante up money on him as long as he had a red. Smiley was monstrous proud of his frog, and well he might be, for fellers that had travelled and ben everywheres all said he laid over any frog that ever *they* see.

Well, Smiley kept the beast in a little lattice box, and he used to fetch him down town sometimes and lay for a bet. One day a feller—a stranger in the camp, he was—come across him with his box, and says:

"What might it be that you've got in the box?"

And Smiley says, sorter indifferent like, "It might be a parrot, or it might be a canary, maybe, but it ain't—it's only just a frog."

And the feller took it, and looked at it careful, and turned it round this way and that, and says, "H'm—so 'tis. Well, what's *he* good for?"

"Well," Smiley says, easy and careless, "He's good enough for *one* thing I should judge—he can out-jump ary frog in Calaveras county."

The feller took the box again, and took another long, particular look, and give it back to Smiley and says, very deliberate, "Well—I don't see no points about that frog that's any better'n any other frog."

"Maybe you don't," Smiley says. "Maybe you understand frogs, and maybe you don't understand 'em; maybe you've had experience, and maybe you ain't only a amature, as it were. Anyways, I've got *my* opinion, and I'll resk forty dollars that he can outjump ary frog in Calaveras county."

And the feller studied a minute, and then says, kinder sad, like, "Well—I'm only a stranger here, and I ain't got no frog—but if I had a frog I'd bet you."

And then Smiley says, "That's all right—that's all right —if you'll hold my box a minute I'll go and get you a frog;" and so the feller took the box, and put up his forty dollars along with Smiley's, and set down to wait.

So he set there a good while thinking and thinking to hisself, and then he got the frog out and prized his mouth open and took a teaspoon and filled him full of quail-shot—filled him pretty near up to his chin—and set him on the floor. Smiley he went out to the swamp and slopped around in the mud for a long time, and finally he ketched a frog and fetched him in and give him to this feller and says:

"Now if you're ready, set him alongside of Dan'l, with his fore-paws just even with Dan'l's, and I'll give the word." Then he says, "one—two—three—jump!" and him and the feller touched up the frogs from behind, and the new frog hopped off lively, but Dan'l give a heave, and hysted up his shoulders—so—like a Frenchman, but it wasn't no use—he couldn't budge; he was planted as solid as a anvil, and he couldn't no more stir than if he was anchored out. Smiley was a good deal surprised, and he was disgusted too, but he didn't have no idea what the matter was, of course.

The feller took the money and started away, and when he was going out at the door he sorter jerked his thumb over his shoulder—this way—at Dan'l, and says again, very deliberate, "Well—I don't see no points about that frog that's any better'n any other frog."

Smiley he stood scratching his head and looking down at Dan'l a long time, and at last he says, "I do wonder what in the nation that frog throwed off for—I wonder if there ain't something the matter with him—he 'pears to look mighty baggy, somehow"—and he ketched Dan'l by the nap of the neck, and lifted him up and says, "Why blame my cats if he don't weigh five pound"—and turned him upside down, and he belched out about a double-handful of shot. And then he see how it was, and he was the maddest man—he set the frog down and took out after that feller, but he never ketched him. And——

[Here Simon Wheeler heard his name called from the front-yard, and got up to go and see what was wanted.] And turning to me as he moved away, he said: "Just sit where you are, stranger, and rest easy—I ain't going to be gone a second."

But by your leave, I did not think that a continuation of the history of the enterprising vagabond Jim Smiley would be likely to afford me much information concerning the Rev. Leonidas W. Smiley, and so I started away.

At the door I met the sociable Wheeler returning, and he buttonholed me and recommenced:

"Well, thish-yer Smiley had a yaller one-eyed cow that didn't have no tail only just a short stump like a bannanner, and——"

"O, curse Smiley and his afflicted cow!" I muttered, good-naturedly, and bidding the old gentleman good-day, I departed.

Yours, truly,
MARK TWAIN.

The Facts Concerning the Recent Carnival of Crime in Connecticut

I WAS feeling blithe, almost jocund. I put a match to my cigar, and just then the morning's mail was handed in. The first superscription I glanced at was in a handwriting that sent a thrill of pleasure through and through me. It was aunt Mary's; and she was the person I loved and honored most in all the world, outside of my own household. She had been my boyhood's idol; maturity, which is fatal to so many enchantments, had not been able to dislodge her from her pedestal; no, it had only justified her right to be there, and placed her dethronement permanently among the impossibilities. To show how strong her influence over me was, I will observe that long after everybody else's "*do*-stop-smoking" had ceased to affect me in the slightest degree, aunt Mary could still stir my torpid conscience into faint signs of life when she touched upon the matter. But all things have their limit, in this world. A happy day came at last, when even aunt Mary's words could no longer move me. I was not merely glad to see that day arrive; I was more than glad—I was grateful; for when its sun had set, the one alloy that was able to mar my enjoyment of my aunt's society was gone. The remainder of her stay with us that winter was in every way a delight. Of course she pleaded with me just as earnestly as ever, after that blessed day, to quit my pernicious habit, but to no purpose whatever; the moment she opened the subject I at once became calmly, peacefully, contentedly indifferent—absolutely, adamantinely indifferent. Consequently the closing weeks of that memorable visit melted away as pleasantly as a dream, they were so freighted, for me, with tranquil satisfaction. I could not have enjoyed my pet vice more if my gentle tormentor had been a smoker herself, and an advocate of the practice. Well, the sight of her handwriting reminded me that I was getting very hungry to see her again. I easily guessed what I should find in her letter. I opened it. Good! just as I expected; she was coming! Coming this very day, too, and by the morning train; I might expect her any moment.

I said to myself, "I am thoroughly happy and content, now.

If my most pitiless enemy could appear before me at this moment, I would freely right any wrong I may have done him."

Straightway the door opened, and a shriveled, shabby dwarf entered. He was not more than two feet high. He seemed to be about forty years old. Every feature and every inch of him was a trifle out of shape; and so, while one could not put his finger upon any particular part and say, "This is a conspicuous deformity," the spectator perceived that this little person was a deformity as a whole—a vague, general, evenly-blended, nicely-adjusted deformity. There was a fox-like cunning in the face and the sharp little eyes, and also alertness and malice. And yet, this vile bit of human rubbish seemed to bear a sort of remote and ill-defined resemblance to me! It was dully perceptible in the mean form, the countenance, and even the clothes, gestures, manner, and attitudes of the creature. He was a far-fetched, dim suggestion of a burlesque upon me, a caricature of me in little. One thing about him struck me forcibly, and most unpleasantly: he was covered all over with a fuzzy, greenish mold, such as one sometimes sees upon mildewed bread. The sight of it was nauseating.

He stepped along with a chipper air, and flung himself into a doll's chair in a very free and easy way, without waiting to be asked. He tossed his hat into the waste basket. He picked up my old chalk pipe from the floor, gave the stem a wipe or two on his knee, filled the bowl from the tobacco-box at his side, and said to me in a tone of pert command,—

"Gimme a match!"

I blushed to the roots of my hair; partly with indignation, but mainly because it somehow seemed to me that this whole performance was very like an exaggeration of conduct which I myself had sometimes been guilty of in my intercourse with familiar friends;—but never, never with strangers, I observed to myself. I wanted to kick the pygmy into the fire, but some incomprehensible sense of being legally and legitimately under his authority forced me to obey his order. He applied the match to the pipe, took a contemplative whiff or two, and remarked, in an irritatingly familiar way,—

"Seems to me it's devilish odd weather for this time of year."

I flushed again, and in anger and humiliation as before; for the language was hardly an exaggeration of some that I have uttered in my day, and moreover was delivered in a tone of voice and with an exasperating drawl that had the seeming of a deliberate travesty of my style. Now there is nothing I am quite so sensitive about as a mocking imitation of my drawling infirmity of speech. I spoke up sharply and said,—

"Look here, you miserable ash-cat! you will have to give a little more attention to your manners, or I will throw you out of the window!"

The manikin smiled a smile of malicious content and security, puffed a whiff of smoke contemptuously toward me, and said, with a still more elaborate drawl,—

"Come—go gently, now; don't put on *too* many airs with your betters."

This cool snub rasped me all over, but it seemed to subjugate me, too, for a moment. The pygmy contemplated me a while with his weasel eyes, and then said, in a peculiarly sneering way,—

"You turned a tramp away from your door this morning."

I said crustily,—

"Perhaps I did, perhaps I didn't. How do *you* know?"

"Well, I know. It isn't any matter *how* I know."

"Very well. Suppose I *did* turn a tramp away from the door—what of it?"

"Oh, nothing; nothing in particular. Only you lied to him."

"I *didn't*! That is, I"—

"Yes, but you did; you lied to him."

I felt a guilty pang,—in truth I had felt it forty times before that tramp had traveled a block from my door,—but still I resolved to make a show of feeling slandered; so I said,—

"This is a baseless impertinence. I said to the tramp"—

"There—wait. You were about to lie again. *I* know what you said to him. You said the cook was gone down town and there was nothing left from breakfast. Two lies. You knew the cook was behind the door, and plenty of provisions behind *her*."

This astonishing accuracy silenced me; and it filled me with wondering speculations, too, as to how this cub could have got his information. Of course he could have culled the conversation from the tramp, but by what sort of magic had he contrived to find out about the concealed cook? Now the dwarf spoke again:—

"It was rather pitiful, rather small, in you to refuse to read that poor young woman's manuscript the other day, and give her an opinion as to its literary value; and she had come so far, too, and *so* hopefully. Now *wasn't* it?"

I felt like a cur! And I had felt so every time the thing had recurred to my mind, I may as well confess. I flushed hotly and said,—

"Look here, have you nothing better to do than prowl around prying into other people's business? Did that girl tell you that?"

"Never mind whether she did or not. The main thing is, you did that contemptible thing. And you felt ashamed of it afterwards. Aha! you feel ashamed of it *now*!"

This with a sort of devilish glee. With fiery earnestness I responded,—

"I told that girl, in the kindest, gentlest way, that I could not consent to deliver judgment upon *any* one's manuscript, because an individual's verdict was worthless. It might under-rate a work of high merit and lose it to the world, or it might overrate a trashy production and so open the way for its in-fliction upon the world. I said that the great public was the only tribunal competent to sit in judgment upon a literary effort, and therefore it must be best to lay it before that tribunal in the outset, since in the end it must stand or fall by that mighty court's decision any way."

"Yes, you said all that. So you did, you juggling, small-souled shuffler! And yet when the happy hopefulness faded out of that poor girl's face, when you saw her furtively slip beneath her shawl the scroll she had so patiently and honestly scribbled at,—so ashamed of her darling now, so proud of it before,—when you saw the gladness go out of her eyes and the tears come there, when she crept away so humbly who had come so"—

"Oh, peace! peace! peace! Blister your merciless tongue, haven't all these thoughts tortured me enough, without *your* coming here to fetch them back again?"

Remorse! remorse! It seemed to me that it would eat the

very heart out of me! And yet that small fiend only sat there leering at me with joy and contempt, and placidly chuckling. Presently he began to speak again. Every sentence was an accusation, and every accusation a truth. Every clause was freighted with sarcasm and derision, every slow-dropping word burned like vitriol. The dwarf reminded me of times when I had flown at my children in anger and punished them for faults which a little inquiry would have taught me that others, and not they, had committed. He reminded me of how I had disloyally allowed old friends to be traduced in my hearing, and been too craven to utter a word in their defense. He reminded me of many dishonest things which I had done; of many which I had procured to be done by children and other irresponsible persons; of some which I had planned, thought upon, and longed to do, and been kept from the performance by fear of consequences only. With exquisite cruelty he recalled to my mind, item by item, wrongs and unkindnesses I had inflicted and humiliations I had put upon friends since dead, "who died thinking of those injuries, maybe, and grieving over them," he added, by way of poison to the stab.

"For instance," said he, "take the case of your younger brother, when you two were boys together, many a long year ago. He always lovingly trusted in you with a fidelity that your manifold treacheries were not able to shake. He followed you about like a dog, content to suffer wrong and abuse if he might only be with you; patient under these injuries so long as it was your hand that inflicted them. The latest picture you have of him in health and strength must be such a comfort to you! You pledged your honor that if he would let you blindfold him no harm should come to him; and then, giggling and choking over the rare fun of the joke, you led him to a brook thinly glazed with ice, and pushed him in; and how you did laugh! Man, you will never forget the gentle, reproachful look he gave you as he struggled shivering out, if you live a thousand years! Oho! you see it now, you see it *now*!"

"Beast, I have seen it a million times, and shall see it a million more! and may you rot away piecemeal, and suffer till doomsday what I suffer now, for bringing it back to me again!"

The dwarf chuckled contentedly, and went on with his accusing history of my career. I dropped into a moody, vengeful state, and suffered in silence under the merciless lash. At last this remark of his gave me a sudden rouse:—

"Two months ago, on a Tuesday, you woke up, away in the night, and fell to thinking, with shame, about a peculiarly mean and pitiful act of yours toward a poor ignorant Indian in the wilds of the Rocky Mountains in the winter of eighteen hundred and"—

"Stop a moment, devil! Stop! Do you mean to tell me that even my very *thoughts* are not hidden from you?"

"It seems to look like that. Didn't you think the thoughts I have just mentioned?"

"If I didn't, I wish I may never breathe again! Look here, friend—look me in the eye. Who *are* you?"

"Well, who do you think?"

"I think you are Satan himself. I think you are the devil."

"No."

"No? Then who *can* you be?"

"Would you really like to know?"

"*Indeed* I would."

"Well, I am your *Conscience*!"

In an instant I was in a blaze of joy and exultation. I sprang at the creature, roaring,—

"Curse you, I have wished a hundred million times that you were tangible, and that I could get my hands on your throat once! Oh, but I will wreak a deadly vengeance on"—

Folly! Lightning does not move more quickly than my Conscience did! He darted aloft so suddenly that in the moment my fingers clutched the empty air he was already perched on the top of the high book-case, with his thumb at his nose in token of derision. I flung the poker at him, and missed. I fired the boot-jack. In a blind rage I flew from place to place, and snatched and hurled any missile that came handy; the storm of books, inkstands, and chunks of coal gloomed the air and beat about the manikin's perch relentlessly, but all to no purpose; the nimble figure dodged every shot; and not only that, but burst into a cackle of sarcastic and triumphant laughter as I sat down exhausted. While I puffed and gasped with fatigue and excitement, my Conscience talked to this effect:—

"My good slave, you are curiously witless—no, I mean characteristically so. In truth, you are always consistent, always yourself, always an ass. Otherwise it must have occurred to you that if you attempted this murder with a sad heart and a heavy conscience, I would droop under the burdening influence instantly. Fool, I should have weighed a ton, and could not have budged from the floor; but instead, you are so cheerfully anxious to kill me that your conscience is as light as a feather; hence I am away up here out of your reach. I can almost respect a mere ordinary sort of fool; but *you*— pah!"

I would have given anything, then, to be heavy-hearted, so that I could get this person down from there and take his life, but I could no more be heavy-hearted over such a desire than I could have sorrowed over its accomplishment. So I could only look longingly up at my master, and rave at the ill-luck that denied me a heavy conscience the one only time that I had ever wanted such a thing in my life. By and by I got to musing over the hour's strange adventure, and of course my human curiosity began to work. I set myself to framing in my mind some questions for this fiend to answer. Just then one of my boys entered, leaving the door open behind him, and exclaimed,—

"My! what *has* been going on, here! The book-case is all one riddle of"—

I sprang up in consternation, and shouted,—

"Out of this! Hurry! Jump! Fly! Shut the door! Quick, or my Conscience will get away!"

The door slammed to, and I locked it. I glanced up and was grateful, to the bottom of my heart, to see that my owner was still my prisoner. I said,—

"Hang you, I might have lost you! Children are the heedlessest creatures. But look here, friend, the boy did not seem to notice you at all; how is that?"

"For a very good reason. I am invisible to all but you."

I made mental note of that piece of information with a

good deal of satisfaction. I could kill this miscreant now, if I got a chance, and no one would know it. But this very reflection made me so light-hearted that my Conscience could hardly keep his seat, but was like to float aloft toward the ceiling like a toy balloon. I said, presently,—

"Come, my Conscience, let us be friendly. Let us fly a flag of truce for a while. I am suffering to ask you some questions."

"Very well. Begin."

"Well, then, in the first place, why were you never visible to me before?"

"Because you never asked to see me before; that is, you never asked in the right spirit and the proper form before. You were just in the right spirit this time, and when you called for your most pitiless enemy I was that person by a very large majority, though you did not suspect it."

"Well, did that remark of mine turn you into flesh and blood?"

"No. It only made me visible to you. I am unsubstantial, just as other spirits are."

This remark prodded me with a sharp misgiving. If he was unsubstantial, how was I going to kill him? But I dissembled, and said persuasively,—

"Conscience, it isn't sociable of you to keep at such a distance. Come down and take another smoke."

This was answered with a look that was full of derision, and with this observation added:—

"Come where you can get at me and kill me? The invitation is declined with thanks."

"All right," said I to myself; "so it seems a spirit *can* be killed, after all; there will be one spirit lacking in this world, presently, or I lose my guess." Then I said aloud,—

"Friend"—

"There; wait a bit. I am not your friend, I am your enemy; I am not your equal, I am your master. Call me 'my lord,' if you please. You are too familiar."

"I don't like such titles. I am willing to call you *sir*. That is as far as"—

"We will have no argument about this. Just obey; that is all. Go on with your chatter."

"Very well, my lord,—since nothing but my lord will suit

you,—I was going to ask you how long you will be visible to me?"

"Always!"

I broke out with strong indignation: "This is simply an outrage. That is what I think of it. You have dogged, and dogged, and *dogged* me, all the days of my life, invisible. That was misery enough; now to have such a looking thing as you tagging after me like another shadow all the rest of my days is an intolerable prospect. You have my opinion, my lord; make the most of it."

"My lad, there was never so pleased a conscience in this world as I was when you made me visible. It gives me an inconceivable advantage. *Now*, I can look you straight in the eye, and call you names, and leer at you, jeer at you, sneer at you; and *you* know what eloquence there is in visible gesture and expression, more especially when the effect is heightened by audible speech. I shall always address you henceforth in your o-w-n s-n-i-v-e-l-i-n-g d-r-a-w-l—baby!"

I let fly with the coal-hod. No result. My lord said,—

"Come, come! Remember the flag of truce!"

"Ah, I forgot that. I will try to be civil; and *you* try it, too, for a novelty. The idea of a *civil* conscience! It is a good joke; an excellent joke. All the consciences *I* have ever heard of were nagging, badgering, fault-finding, execrable savages! Yes; and always in a sweat about some poor little insignificant trifle or other—destruction catch the lot of them, *I* say! I would trade mine for the small-pox and seven kinds of consumption, and be glad of the chance. Now tell me, why *is* it that a conscience can't haul a man over the coals once, for an offense, and then let him alone? Why is it that it wants to keep on pegging at him, day and night and night and day, week in and week out, forever and ever, about the same old thing? There is no sense in that, and no reason in it. I think a conscience that will act like that is meaner than the very dirt itself."

"Well, *we* like it; that suffices."

"Do you do it with the honest intent to improve a man?"

That question produced a sarcastic smile, and this reply:—

"No, sir. Excuse me. We do it simply because it is 'business.' It is our trade. The *purpose* of it *is* to improve the man, but *we* are merely disinterested agents. We are appointed by authority, and haven't anything to say in the matter. We obey orders and leave the consequences where they belong. But I am willing to admit this much: we *do* crowd the orders a trifle when we get a chance, which is most of the time. We enjoy it. We are instructed to remind a man a few times of an error; and I don't mind acknowledging that we try to give pretty good measure. And when we get hold of a man of a peculiarly sensitive nature, oh, but we do haze him! I have known consciences to come all the way from China and Russia to see a person of that kind put through his paces, on a special occasion. Why, I knew a man of that sort who had accidentally crippled a mulatto baby; the news went abroad, and I wish you may never commit another sin if the consciences didn't flock from all over the earth to enjoy the fun and help his master exercise him. That man walked the floor in torture for forty-eight hours, without eating or sleeping, and then blew his brains out. The child was perfectly well again in three weeks."

"Well, you are a precious crew, not to put it too strong. I think I begin to see, now, why you have always been a trifle inconsistent with me. In your anxiety to get all the juice you can out of a sin, you make a man repent of it in three or four different ways. For instance, you found fault with me for lying to that tramp, and I suffered over that. But it was only yesterday that I told a tramp the square truth, to wit, that, it being regarded as bad citizenship to encourage vagrancy, I would give him nothing. What did you do *then*? Why, you made me say to myself, 'Ah, it would have been so much kinder and more blameless to ease him off with a little white lie, and send him away feeling that if he could not have bread, the gentle treatment was at least something to be grateful for!' Well, I suffered all day about *that*. Three days before, I had fed a tramp, and fed him freely, supposing it a virtuous act. Straight off you said, 'O false citizen, to have fed a tramp!' and I suffered as usual. I gave a tramp work; you objected to it,—*after* the contract was made, of course; you never speak up beforehand. Next, I *refused* a tramp work; you objected to *that*. Next, I proposed to kill a tramp; you kept me awake all night, oozing remorse at every pore. Sure I was going to be right *this* time, I sent the next tramp away with my benediction; and I wish you may live as long as I do, if you did n't make me smart all night again because I did n't kill him. Is there *any* way of satisfying that malignant invention which is called a conscience?"

"Ha, ha! this is luxury! Go on!"

"But come, now, answer me that question. *Is* there any way?"

"Well, none that I propose to tell *you*, my son. Ass! I don't care *what* act you may turn your hand to, I can straightway whisper a word in your ear and make you think you have committed a dreadful meanness. It is my *business*—and my joy—to make you repent of *every*thing you do. If I have fooled away any opportunities it was not intentional; I beg to assure you it was not intentional."

"Don't worry; you haven't missed a trick that *I* know of. I never did a thing in all my life, virtuous or otherwise, that I didn't repent of within twenty-four hours. In church last Sunday I listened to a charity sermon. My first impulse was to give three hundred and fifty dollars; I repented of that and reduced it a hundred; repented of that and reduced it another hundred; repented of that and reduced it another hundred; repented of that and reduced the remaining fifty to twenty-five; repented of that and came down to fifteen; repented of that and dropped to two dollars and a half; when the plate came around at last, I repented once more and contributed ten cents. Well, when I got home, I did wish to goodness I had that ten cents back again! You never *did* let me get through a charity sermon without having something to sweat about."

"Oh, and I never shall, I never shall. You can always depend on me."

"I think so. Many and many's the restless night I've wanted to take you by the neck. If I could only get hold of you now!"

"Yes, no doubt. But I am not an ass; I am only the saddle of an ass. But go on, go on. You entertain me more than I like to confess."

"I am glad of that. (You will not mind my lying a little, to keep in practice.) Look here; not to be too personal, I think you are about the shabbiest and most contemptible little shriveled-up reptile that can be imagined. I am grateful enough that you are invisible to other people, for I should die with shame to be seen with such a mildewed monkey of a conscience as *you* are. Now if you were five or six feet high, and"—

"Oh, come! who is to blame?"

"*I* don't know."

"Why, you are; nobody else."

"Confound you, I wasn't consulted about your personal appearance."

"I don't care, you had a good deal to do with it, nevertheless. When you were eight or nine years old, I was seven feet high and as pretty as a picture."

"I wish you had died young! So you have grown the wrong way, have you?"

"Some of us grow one way and some the other. You had a large conscience once; if you've a small conscience now, I reckon there are reasons for it. However, both of us are to blame, you and I. You see, you used to be conscientious about a great many things; morbidly so, I may say. It was a great many years ago. You probably do not remember it, now. Well, I took a great interest in my work, and I so enjoyed the anguish which certain pet sins of yours afflicted you with, that I kept pelting at you until I rather overdid the matter. You began to rebel. Of course I began to lose ground, then, and shrivel a little,—diminish in stature, get moldy, and grow deformed. The more I weakened, the more stubbornly you fastened on to those particular sins; till at last the places on my person that represent those vices became as callous as shark skin. Take smoking, for instance. I played that card a little too long, and I lost. When people plead with you at this late day to quit that vice, that old callous place seems to enlarge and cover me all over like a shirt of mail. It exerts a mysterious, smothering effect; and presently I, your faithful hater, your devoted Conscience, go sound asleep! Sound? It is no name for it. I couldn't hear it thunder at such a time. You have some few other vices—perhaps eighty, or maybe ninety—that affect me in much the same way."

"This is flattering; you must be asleep a good part of your time."

"Yes, of late years. I should be asleep *all* the time, but for the help I get."

"Who helps you?"

"Other consciences. Whenever a person whose conscience I am acquainted with tries to plead with you about the vices you are callous to, I get my friend to give his client a pang concerning some villainy of his own, and that shuts off his meddling and starts him off to hunt personal consolation. My field of usefulness is about trimmed down to tramps, budding authoresses, and that line of goods, now; but don't you worry—I'll harry you on *them* while they last! Just you put your trust in me."

"I think I can. But if you had only been good enough to mention these facts some thirty years ago, I should have turned my particular attention to sin, and I think that by this time I should not only have had you pretty permanently asleep on the entire list of human vices, but reduced to the size of a homœopathic pill, at that. That is about the style of conscience *I* am pining for. If I only had you shrunk down to a homœopathic pill, and could get my hands on you, would I put you in a glass case for a keepsake? No, sir. I would give you to a yellow dog! That is where *you* ought to be—you and all your tribe. You are not fit to be in society, in my opinion. Now another question. Do you know a good many consciences in this section?"

"Plenty of them."

"I would give anything to see some of them! Could you bring them here? And would they be visible to me?"

"Certainly not."

"I suppose I ought to have known that, without asking. But no matter, you can describe them. Tell me about my neighbor Thompson's conscience, please."

"Very well. I know him intimately; have known him many years. I knew him when he was eleven feet high and of a faultless figure. But he is very rusty and tough and misshapen, now, and hardly ever interests himself about anything. As to his present size—well, he sleeps in a cigar box."

"Likely enough. There are few smaller, meaner men in this region than Hugh Thompson. Do you know Robinson's conscience?"

"Yes. He is a shade under four and a half feet high; used to be a blonde; is a brunette, now, but still shapely and comely."

"Well, Robinson is a good fellow. Do you know Tom Smith's conscience?"

"I have known him from childhood. He was thirteen inches high, and rather sluggish, when he was two years old—as nearly all of us are, at that age. He is thirty-seven feet high, now, and the stateliest figure in America. His legs are still racked with growing-pains, but he has a good time, nevertheless. Never sleeps. He is the most active and energetic member of the New England Conscience Club; is president of it. Night and day you can find him pegging away at Smith, panting with his labor, sleeves rolled up, countenance all alive with enjoyment. He has got his victim splendidly dragooned, now. He can make poor Smith imagine that the most innocent little thing he does is an odious sin; and then he sets to work and almost tortures the soul out of him about it."

"Smith is the noblest man in all this section, and the purest; and yet is always breaking his heart because he cannot be good! Only a conscience *could* find pleasure in heaping agony upon a spirit like that. Do you know my aunt Mary's conscience?"

"I have seen her at a distance, but am not acquainted with her. She lives in the open air altogether, because no door is large enough to admit her."

"I can believe that. Let me see. Do you know the conscience of that publisher who once stole some sketches of mine for a 'series' of his, and then left me to pay the law expenses I had to incur in order to choke him off?"

"Yes. He has a wide fame. He was exhibited, a month ago, with some other antiquities, for the benefit of a recent Member of the Cabinet's conscience, that was starving in exile. Tickets and fares were high, but I traveled for nothing by pretending to be the conscience of an editor, and got in for half price by representing myself to be the conscience of a clergyman. However, the publisher's conscience, which was to have been the main feature of the entertainment, was a failure—as an exhibition. He was there, but what of that? The management had provided a microscope with a magnifying power of only thirty thousand diameters, and so nobody got to see him, after all. There was great and general dissatisfaction, of course, but"—

Just here there was an eager footstep on the stair; I opened the door, and my aunt Mary burst into the room. It was a joyful meeting, and a cheery bombardment of questions and answers concerning family matters ensued. By and by my aunt said,—

"But I am going to abuse you a little now. You promised me, the day I saw you last, that you would look after the needs of the poor family around the corner as faithfully as I had done it myself. Well, I found out by accident that you failed of your promise. *Was* that right?"

In simple truth, I never had thought of that family a second time! And now such a splintering pang of guilt shot through me! I glanced up at my Conscience. Plainly, my heavy heart was affecting him. His body was drooping forward; he seemed about to fall from the book-case. My aunt continued:—

"And think how you have neglected my poor *protégée* at the almshouse, you dear, hard-hearted promise-breaker!" I blushed scarlet, and my tongue was tied. As the sense of my guilty negligence waxed sharper and stronger, my Conscience began to sway heavily back and forth; and when my aunt, after a little pause, said in a grieved tone, "Since you never once went to see her, maybe it will not distress you now to know that that poor child died, months ago, utterly friendless and forsaken!" my Conscience could no longer bear up under the weight of my sufferings, but tumbled headlong from his high perch and struck the floor with a dull, leaden thump. He lay there writhing with pain and quaking with apprehension, but straining every muscle in frantic efforts to get up. In a fever of expectancy I sprang to the door, locked it, placed my back against it, and bent a watchful gaze upon my struggling master. Already my fingers were itching to begin their murderous work.

"Oh, what *can* be the matter!" exclaimed my aunt, shrinking from me, and following with her frightened eyes the direction of mine. My breath was coming in short, quick gasps now, and my excitement was almost uncontrollable. My aunt cried out,—

"Oh, do not look so! You appall me! Oh, what can the matter be? What is it you see? Why do you stare so? Why do you work your fingers like that?"

"Peace, woman!" I said, in a hoarse whisper. "Look elsewhere; pay no attention to me; it is nothing—nothing. I am often this way. It will pass in a moment. It comes from smoking too much."

My injured lord was up, wild-eyed with terror, and trying to hobble toward the door. I could hardly breathe, I was so wrought up. My aunt wrung her hands, and said,—

"Oh, I knew how it would be; I knew it would come to this at last! Oh, I implore you to crush out that fatal habit while it may yet be time! You must not, you shall not be deaf to my supplications longer!" My struggling Conscience showed sudden signs of weariness! "Oh, promise me you will throw off this hateful slavery of tobacco!" My Conscience began to reel drowsily, and grope with his hands—enchanting spectacle! "I beg you, I beseech you, I implore you! Your reason is deserting you! There is madness in your eye! It flames with frenzy! Oh, hear me, hear me, and be saved! See, I plead with you on my very knees!" As she sank before me my Conscience reeled again, and then drooped languidly to the floor, blinking toward me a last supplication for mercy, with heavy eyes. "Oh, promise, or you are lost! Promise, and be redeemed! Promise! Promise and live!" With a long-drawn sigh my conquered Conscience closed his eyes and fell fast asleep!

With an exultant shout I sprang past my aunt, and in an instant I had my life-long foe by the throat. After so many years of waiting and longing, he was mine at last. I tore him to shreds and fragments. I rent the fragments to bits. I cast the bleeding rubbish into the fire, and drew into my nostrils the grateful incense of my burnt-offering. At last, and forever, my Conscience was dead!

I was a free man! I turned upon my poor aunt, who was almost petrified with terror, and shouted,—

"Out of this with your paupers, your charities, your reforms, your pestilent morals! You behold before you a man whose life-conflict is done, whose soul is at peace; a man whose heart is dead to sorrow, dead to suffering, dead to remorse; a man WITHOUT A CONSCIENCE! In my joy I spare you, though I could throttle you and never feel a pang! Fly!"

She fled. Since that day my life is all bliss. Bliss, unalloyed bliss. Nothing in all the world could persuade me to have a conscience again. I settled all my old outstanding scores, and began the world anew. I killed thirty-eight persons during the first two weeks—all of them on account of ancient grudges. I burned a dwelling that interrupted my view. I swindled a widow and some orphans out of their last cow, which is a very good one, though not thoroughbred, I believe. I have also committed scores of crimes, of various kinds, and have enjoyed my work exceedingly, whereas it would formerly have broken my heart and turned my hair gray, I have no doubt.

In conclusion I wish to state, by way of advertisement, that medical colleges desiring assorted tramps for scientific purposes, either by the gross, by cord measurement, or per ton, will do well to examine the lot in my cellar before purchasing elsewhere, as these were all selected and prepared by myself, and can be had at a low rate, because I wish to clear out my stock and get ready for the spring trade.

The Private History of a Campaign
That Failed

YOU have heard from a great many people who did something in the war; is it not fair and right that you listen a little moment to one who started out to do something in it, but didn't? Thousands entered the war, got just a taste of it, and then stepped out again, permanently. These, by their very numbers, are respectable, and are therefore entitled to a sort of voice,—not a loud one, but a modest one; not a boastful one, but an apologetic one. They ought not to be allowed much space among better people—people who did something—I grant that; but they ought at least to be allowed to state why they didn't do anything, and also to explain the process by which they didn't do anything. Surely this kind of light must have a sort of value.

Out West there was a good deal of confusion in men's minds during the first months of the great trouble—a good deal of unsettledness, of leaning first this way, then that, then the other way. It was hard for us to get our bearings. I call to mind an instance of this. I was piloting on the Mississippi when the news came that South Carolina had gone out of the Union on the 20th of December, 1860. My pilot-mate was a New Yorker. He was strong for the Union; so was I. But he would not listen to me with any patience; my loyalty was smirched, to his eye, because my father had owned slaves. I said, in palliation of this dark fact, that I had heard my father say, some years before he died, that slavery was a great wrong, and that he would free the solitary negro he then owned if he could think it right to give away the property of the family when he was so straitened in means. My mate retorted that a mere impulse was nothing—anybody could pretend to a good impulse; and went on decrying my Unionism and libeling my ancestry. A month later the secession atmosphere had considerably thickened on the Lower Mississippi, and I became a rebel; so did he. We were together in New Orleans, the 26th of January, when Louisiana went out of the Union. He did his full share of the rebel shouting, but was bitterly opposed to letting me do mine. He said that I came of bad stock—of a father who had been willing to set slaves free. In the following summer he was piloting a Federal gun-boat and shouting for the Union again, and I was in the Confederate army. I held his note for some borrowed money. He was one of the most upright men I ever knew; but he repudiated that note without hesitation, because I was a rebel, and the son of a man who owned slaves.

In that summer—of 1861—the first wash of the wave of war broke upon the shores of Missouri. Our State was invaded by the Union forces. They took possession of St. Louis, Jefferson Barracks, and some other points. The Governor, Claib Jackson, issued his proclamation calling out fifty thousand militia to repel the invader.

I was visiting in the small town where my boyhood had been spent—Hannibal, Marion County. Several of us got together in a secret place by night and formed ourselves into a military company. One Tom Lyman, a young fellow of a good deal of spirit but of no military experience, was made captain; I was made second lieutenant. We had no first lieutenant; I do not know why; it was long ago. There were

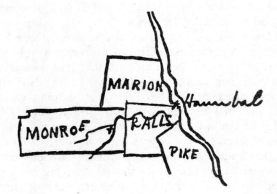

The Seat of War.

fifteen of us. By the advice of an innocent connected with the organization, we called ourselves the Marion Rangers. I do not remember that any one found fault with the name. I did not; I thought it sounded quite well. The young fellow who proposed this title was perhaps a fair sample of the kind of stuff we were made of. He was young, ignorant, good-natured, well-meaning, trivial, full of romance, and given to reading chivalric novels and singing forlorn love-ditties. He had some pathetic little nickel-plated aristocratic instincts, and detested his name, which was Dunlap; detested it, partly because it was nearly as common in that region as Smith, but mainly because it had a plebeian sound to his ear. So he tried to ennoble it by writing it in this way: *d'Unlap*. That contented his eye, but left his ear unsatisfied, for people gave the new name the same old pronunciation—emphasis on the front end of it. He then did the bravest thing that can be imagined,—a thing to make one shiver when one remembers how the world is given to resenting shams and affectations; he began to write his name so: *d'Un Lap*. And he waited patiently through the long storm of mud that was flung at this work of art, and he had his reward at last; for he lived to see that name accepted, and the emphasis put where he wanted it, by people who had known him all his life, and to whom the tribe of Dunlaps had been as familiar as the rain and the sunshine for forty years. So sure of victory at last is the courage that can wait. He said he had found, by consulting some ancient French chronicles, that the name was rightly and originally written d'Un Lap; and said that if it were translated into English it would mean Peterson: *Lap*, Latin or Greek, he said, for stone or rock, same as the French *pierre*, that is to say, Peter; *d'*, of or from; *un*, a or one; hence, d'Un Lap, of or from a stone or a Peter; that is to say, one who is the son of a stone, the son of a Peter—Peterson. Our militia company were not learned, and the explanation confused them; so they called him Peterson Dunlap. He proved useful to us in his way; he named our camps for us, and he generally struck a name that was "no slouch," as the boys said.

That is one sample of us. Another was Ed Stevens, son of the town jeweler,—trim-built, handsome, graceful, neat as a cat; bright, educated, but given over entirely to fun. There was nothing serious in life to him. As far as he was concerned, this military expedition of ours was simply a holiday. I should say that about half of us looked upon it in the same way; not consciously, perhaps, but unconsciously. We did not think; we were not capable of it. As for myself, I was full of unreasoning joy to be done with turning out of bed at midnight and four in the morning, for a while; grateful to have a change, new scenes, new occupations, a new interest. In my thoughts that was as far as I went; I did not go into the details; as a rule one doesn't at twenty-four.

Another sample was Smith, the blacksmith's apprentice. This vast donkey had some pluck, of a slow and sluggish nature, but a soft heart; at one time he would knock a horse down for some impropriety, and at another he would get homesick and cry. However, he had one ultimate credit to his account which some of us hadn't: he stuck to the war, and was killed in battle at last.

Jo Bowers, another sample, was a huge, good-natured, flax-headed lubber; lazy, sentimental, full of harmless brag, a grumbler by nature; an experienced, industrious, ambitious, and often quite picturesque liar, and yet not a successful one, for he had had no intelligent training, but was allowed to come up just any way. This life was serious enough to him, and seldom satisfactory. But he was a good fellow anyway, and the boys all liked him. He was made orderly sergeant; Stevens was made corporal.

These samples will answer—and they are quite fair ones. Well, this herd of cattle started for the war. What could you expect of them? They did as well as they knew how, but really what was justly to be expected of them? Nothing, I should say. That is what they did.

We waited for a dark night, for caution and secrecy were necessary; then, toward midnight, we stole in couples and from various directions to the Griffith place, beyond the town; from that point we set out together on foot. Hannibal lies at the extreme southeastern corner of Marion County, on the Mississippi River; our objective point was the hamlet of New London, ten miles away, in Ralls County.

The first hour was all fun, all idle nonsense and laughter. But that could not be kept up. The steady trudging came to be like work; the play had somehow oozed out of it; the still-ness of the woods and the somberness of the night began to throw a depressing influence over the spirits of the boys, and presently the talking died out and each person shut himself up in his own thoughts. During the last half of the second hour nobody said a word.

Now we approached a log farm-house where, according to report, there was a guard of five Union soldiers. Lyman called a halt; and there, in the deep gloom of the overhanging branches, he began to whisper a plan of assault upon that house, which made the gloom more depressing than it was before. It was a crucial moment; we realized, with a cold sud-denness, that here was no jest—we were standing face to face with actual war. We were equal to the occasion. In our re-sponse there was no hesitation, no indecision: we said that if Lyman wanted to meddle with those soldiers, he could go ahead and do it; but if he waited for us to follow him, he would wait a long time.

Lyman urged, pleaded, tried to shame us, but it had no effect. Our course was plain, our minds were made up: we would flank the farm-house—go out around. And that is what we did.

We struck into the woods and entered upon a rough time, stumbling over roots, getting tangled in vines, and torn by briers. At last we reached an open place in a safe region, and sat down, blown and hot, to cool off and nurse our scratches and bruises. Lyman was annoyed, but the rest of us were cheerful; we had flanked the farm-house, we had made our first military movement, and it was a success; we had nothing to fret about, we were feeling just the other way. Horse-play and laughing began again; the expedition was become a holi-day frolic once more.

Then we had two more hours of dull trudging and ultimate silence and depression; then, about dawn, we straggled into New London, soiled, heel-blistered, fagged with our little march, and all of us except Stevens in a sour and raspy humor and privately down on the war. We stacked our shabby old shot-guns in Colonel Ralls's barn, and then went in a body and breakfasted with that veteran of the Mexican war. After-wards he took us to a distant meadow, and there in the shade of a tree we listened to an old-fashioned speech from him, full of gunpowder and glory, full of that adjective-piling, mixed metaphor, and windy declamation which was regarded as eloquence in that ancient time and that remote region; and then he swore us on the Bible to be faithful to the State of Missouri and drive all invaders from her soil, no matter whence they might come or under what flag they might march. This mixed us considerably, and we could not make out just what service we were embarked in; but Colonel Ralls, the practiced politician and phrase-juggler, was not similarly in doubt; he knew quite clearly that he had invested us in the cause of the Southern Confederacy. He closed the solemnities by belting around me the sword which his neighbor, Colonel Brown, had worn at Buena Vista and Molino del Rey; and he accompanied this act with another impressive blast.

Then we formed in line of battle and marched four miles to a shady and pleasant piece of woods on the border of the far-reaching expanses of a flowery prairie. It was an enchanting region for war—our kind of war.

We pierced the forest about half a mile, and took up a strong position, with some low, rocky, and wooded hills behind us, and a purling, limpid creek in front. Straightway half the command were in swimming, and the other half fishing. The ass with the French name gave this position a romantic title, but it was too long, so the boys shortened and simplified it to Camp Ralls.

We occupied an old maple-sugar camp, whose half-rotted troughs were still propped against the trees. A long corn-crib served for sleeping quarters for the battalion. On our left, half a mile away, was Mason's farm and house; and he was a friend to the cause. Shortly after noon the farmers began to arrive from several directions, with mules and horses for our use, and these they lent us for as long as the war might last, which they judged would be about three months. The animals were of all sizes, all colors, and all breeds. They were mainly young and frisky, and nobody in the command could stay on them long at a time; for we were town boys, and ignorant of horsemanship. The creature that fell to my share was a very small mule, and yet so quick and active that it could throw me without difficulty; and it did this whenever I got on it. Then it would bray—stretching its neck out, laying its ears back, and spreading its jaws till you could see down to its works. It was a disagreeable animal, in every way. If I took it by the bridle and tried to lead it off the grounds, it would sit down and brace back, and no one could budge it. However, I was not entirely destitute of military resources, and I did presently manage to spoil this game; for I had seen many a steamboat aground in my time, and knew a trick or two which even a grounded mule would be obliged to respect. There was a well by the corn-crib; so I substituted thirty fathom of rope for the bridle, and fetched him home with the windlass.

I will anticipate here sufficiently to say that we did learn to ride, after some days' practice, but never well. We could not learn to like our animals; they were not choice ones, and most of them had annoying peculiarities of one kind or another. Stevens's horse would carry him, when he was not noticing, under the huge excrescences which form on the trunks of oak-trees, and wipe him out of the saddle; in this way Stevens got several bad hurts. Sergeant Bowers's horse was very large and tall, with slim, long legs, and looked like a railroad bridge. His size enabled him to reach all about, and as far as he wanted to, with his head; so he was always biting Bowers's legs. On the march, in the sun, Bowers slept a good deal; and as soon as the horse recognized that he was asleep he would reach around and bite him on the leg. His legs were black and blue with bites. This was the only thing that could ever make him swear, but this always did; whenever the horse bit him he always swore, and of course Stevens, who laughed at every-thing, laughed at this, and would even get into such convul-sions over it as to lose his balance and fall off his horse; and then Bowers, already irritated by the pain of the horse-bite, would resent the laughter with hard language, and there would be a quarrel; so that horse made no end of trouble and bad blood in the command.

However, I will get back to where I was—our first after-noon in the sugar-camp. The sugar-troughs came very handy as horse-troughs, and we had plenty of corn to fill them with. I ordered Sergeant Bowers to feed my mule; but he said that if I reckoned he went to war to be dry-nurse to a mule, it wouldn't take me very long to find out my mistake. I believed that this was insubordination, but I was full of uncertainties about everything military, and so I let the thing pass, and went and ordered Smith, the blacksmith's apprentice, to feed the mule; but he merely gave me a large, cold, sarcastic grin, such as an ostensibly seven-year-old horse gives you when you lift his lip and find he is fourteen, and turned his back on me. I then went to the captain, and asked if it was not right and proper and military for me to have an orderly. He said it was, but as there was only one orderly in the corps, it was but right that he himself should have Bowers on his staff. Bowers said he wouldn't serve on anybody's staff; and if anybody thought he could make him, let him try it. So, of course, the thing had to be dropped; there was no other way.

Next, nobody would cook; it was considered a degradation; so we had no dinner. We lazied the rest of the pleasant afternoon away, some dozing under the trees, some smoking cob-pipes and talking sweethearts and war, some playing games. By late supper-time all hands were famished; and to meet the difficulty all hands turned to, on an equal footing, and gathered wood, built fires, and cooked the meal. Afterward everything was smooth for a while; then trouble broke out between the corporal and the sergeant, each claiming to rank the other. Nobody knew which was the higher office; so Lyman had to settle the matter by making the rank of both officers equal. The commander of an ignorant crew like that has many troubles and vexations which probably do not occur in the regular army at all. However, with the song-singing and yarn-spinning around the camp-fire, everything presently became serene again; and by and by we raked the corn down level in one end of the crib, and all went to bed on it, tying a horse to the door, so that he would neigh if any one tried to get in.*

We had some horsemanship drill every forenoon; then,

---

*It was always my impression that that was what the horse was there for, and I know that it was also the impression of at least one other of the command, for we talked about it at the time, and admired the military ingenuity of the device; but when I was out West three years ago I was told by Mr. A. G. Fuqua, a member of our company, that the horse was his, that the leaving him tied at the door was a matter of mere forgetfulness, and that to attribute it to intelligent invention was to give him quite too much credit. In support of his position, he called my attention to the suggestive fact that the artifice was not employed again. I had not thought of that before.

afternoons, we rode off here and there in squads a few miles, and visited the farmers' girls, and had a youthful good time, and got an honest good dinner or supper, and then home again to camp, happy and content.

For a time, life was idly delicious, it was perfect; there was nothing to mar it. Then came some farmers with an alarm one day. They said it was rumored that the enemy were advancing in our direction, from over Hyde's prairie. The result was a sharp stir among us, and general consternation. It was a rude awakening from our pleasant trance. The rumor was but a rumor—nothing definite about it; so, in the confusion, we did not know which way to retreat. Lyman was for not retreating at all, in these uncertain circumstances; but he found that if he tried to maintain that attitude he would fare badly, for the command were in no humor to put up with insubordination. So he yielded the point and called a council of war—to consist of himself and the three other officers; but the privates made such a fuss about being left out, that we had to allow them to be present. I mean we had to allow them to remain, for they were already present, and doing the most of the talking too. The question was, which way to retreat; but all were so flurried that nobody seemed to have even a guess to offer. Except Lyman. He explained in a few calm words, that inasmuch as the enemy were approaching from over Hyde's prairie, our course was simple: all we had to do was not to retreat *toward* him; any other direction would answer our needs perfectly. Everybody saw in a moment how true this was, and how wise; so Lyman got a great many compliments. It was now decided that we should fall back on Mason's farm.

It was after dark by this time, and as we could not know how soon the enemy might arrive, it did not seem best to try to take the horses and things with us; so we only took the guns and ammunition, and started at once. The route was very rough and hilly and rocky, and presently the night grew very black and rain began to fall; so we had a troublesome time of it, struggling and stumbling along in the dark; and soon some person slipped and fell, and then the next person behind stumbled over him and fell, and so did the rest, one after the other; and then Bowers came with the keg of

powder in his arms, whilst the command were all mixed together, arms and legs, on the muddy slope; and so he fell, of
course, with the keg, and this started the whole detachment
down the hill in a body, and they landed in the brook at the
bottom in a pile, and each that was undermost pulling the
hair and scratching and biting those that were on top of him;
and those that were being scratched and bitten scratching and
biting the rest in their turn, and all saying they would die
before they would ever go to war again if they ever got out of
this brook this time, and the invader might rot for all they
cared, and the country along with him—and all such talk as
that, which was dismal to hear and take part in, in such
smothered, low voices, and such a grisly dark place and so
wet, and the enemy may be coming any moment.

The keg of powder was lost, and the guns too; so the
growling and complaining continued straight along whilst the
brigade pawed around the pasty hillside and slopped around
in the brook hunting for these things; consequently we lost
considerable time at this; and then we heard a sound, and
held our breath and listened, and it seemed to be the enemy
coming, though it could have been a cow, for it had a cough
like a cow; but we did not wait, but left a couple of guns
behind and struck out for Mason's again as briskly as we
could scramble along in the dark. But we got lost presently
among the rugged little ravines, and wasted a deal of time
finding the way again, so it was after nine when we reached
Mason's stile at last; and then before we could open our
mouths to give the countersign, several dogs came bounding
over the fence, with great riot and noise, and each of them
took a soldier by the slack of his trousers and began to back
away with him. We could not shoot the dogs without endan-
gering the persons they were attached to; so we had to look
on, helpless, at what was perhaps the most mortifying spectacle of the civil war. There was light enough, and to spare, for
the Masons had now run out on the porch with candles in
their hands. The old man and his son came and undid the
dogs without difficulty, all but Bowers's; but they couldn't
undo his dog, they didn't know his combination; he was of
the bull kind, and seemed to be set with a Yale time-lock; but
they got him loose at last with some scalding water, of which

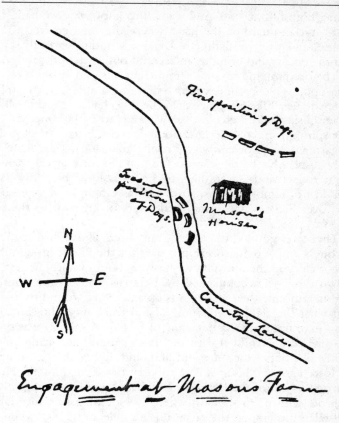

First position of Dogs.

Second position of Dogs.

Mason's House.

N
W — E
S

Country Lane.

Engagement at Mason's Farm

Bowers got his share and returned thanks. Peterson Dunlap afterwards made up a fine name for this engagement, and also for the night march which preceded it, but both have long ago faded out of my memory.

We now went into the house, and they began to ask us a world of questions, whereby it presently came out that we did not know anything concerning who or what we were running from; so the old gentleman made himself very frank, and said we were a curious breed of soldiers, and guessed we could be depended on to end up the war in time, because no government could stand the expense of the shoe-leather we should cost it trying to follow us around. "Marion *Rangers!* good name, b'gosh!" said he. And wanted to know why we hadn't had a picket-guard at the place where the road entered the prairie, and why we hadn't sent out a scouting party to spy out the enemy and bring us an account of his strength, and so on, before jumping up and stampeding out of a strong position upon a mere vague rumor—and so on and so forth, till he made us all feel shabbier than the dogs had done, not half so enthusiastically welcome. So we went to bed shamed and low-spirited; except Stevens. Soon Stevens began to devise a garment for Bowers which could be made to automatically display his battle-scars to the grateful, or conceal them from the envious, according to his occasions; but Bowers was in no humor for this, so there was a fight, and when it was over Stevens had some battle-scars of his own to think about.

Then we got a little sleep. But after all we had gone through, our activities were not over for the night; for about two o'clock in the morning we heard a shout of warning from down the lane, accompanied by a chorus from all the dogs, and in a moment everybody was up and flying around to find out what the alarm was about. The alarmist was a horseman who gave notice that a detachment of Union soldiers was on its way from Hannibal with orders to capture and hang any bands like ours which it could find, and said we had no time to lose. Farmer Mason was in a flurry this time, himself. He hurried us out of the house with all haste, and sent one of his negroes with us to show us where to hide ourselves and our tell-tale guns among the ravines half a mile away. It was raining heavily.

We struck down the lane, then across some rocky pastureland which offered good advantages for stumbling; consequently we were down in the mud most of the time, and every time a man went down he blackguarded the war, and the people that started it, and everybody connected with it, and gave himself the master dose of all for being so foolish as to go into it. At last we reached the wooded mouth of a ravine, and there we huddled ourselves under the streaming trees, and sent the negro back home. It was a dismal and heart-breaking time. We were like to be drowned with the rain, deafened with the howling wind and the booming thunder, and blinded by the lightning. It was indeed a wild night. The drenching we were getting was misery enough, but a deeper misery still was the reflection that the halter might end us before we were a day older. A death of this shameful sort had not occurred to us as being among the possibilities of war. It took the romance all out of the campaign, and turned our dreams of glory into a repulsive nightmare. As for doubting that so barbarous an order had been given, not one of us did that.

The long night wore itself out at last, and then the negro came to us with the news that the alarm had manifestly been a false one, and that breakfast would soon be ready. Straightway we were light-hearted again, and the world was bright, and life as full of hope and promise as ever—for we were young then. How long ago that was! Twenty-four years.

The mongrel child of philology named the night's refuge Camp Devastation, and no soul objected. The Masons gave us a Missouri country breakfast, in Missourian abundance, and we needed it: hot biscuits; hot "wheat bread" prettily criss-crossed in a lattice pattern on top; hot corn pone; fried chicken; bacon, coffee, eggs, milk, buttermilk, etc.;—and the world may be confidently challenged to furnish the equal to such a breakfast, as it is cooked in the South.

We staid several days at Mason's; and after all these years the memory of the dullness, the stillness and lifelessness of that slumberous farm-house still oppresses my spirit as with a sense of the presence of death and mourning. There was nothing to do, nothing to think about; there was no interest in life. The male part of the household were away in the fields all day, the women were busy and out of our sight; there was no sound but the plaintive wailing of a spinning-wheel, forever moaning out from some distant room,—the most lonesome sound in nature, a sound steeped and sodden with homesickness and the emptiness of life. The family went to bed about dark every night, and as we were not invited to intrude any new customs, we naturally followed theirs. Those nights were a hundred years long to youths accustomed to being up till twelve. We lay awake and miserable till that hour every time, and grew old and decrepit waiting through the still eternities for the clock-strikes. This was no place for town boys. So at last it was with something very like joy that we received news that the enemy were on our track again. With a new birth of the old warrior spirit, we sprang to our places in line of battle and fell back on Camp Ralls.

Captain Lyman had taken a hint from Mason's talk, and he now gave orders that our camp should be guarded against surprise by the posting of pickets. I was ordered to place a picket at the forks of the road in Hyde's prairie. Night shut down black and threatening. I told Sergeant Bowers to go out to that place and stay till midnight; and, just as I was expecting, he said he wouldn't do it. I tried to get others to go, but all refused. Some excused themselves on account of the weather; but the rest were frank enough to say they wouldn't go in any kind of weather. This kind of thing sounds odd now, and impossible, but there was no surprise in it at the time. On the contrary, it seemed a perfectly natural thing to do. There were scores of little camps scattered over Missouri where the same thing was happening. These camps were composed of young men who had been born and reared to a sturdy independence, and who did not know what it meant to be ordered around by Tom, Dick, and Harry, whom they had known familiarly all their lives, in the village or on the farm. It is quite within the probabilities that this same thing was happening all over the South. James Redpath recognized the justice of this assumption, and furnished the following instance in support of it. During a short stay in East Tennessee he was in a citizen colonel's tent one day, talking, when a big private appeared at the door, and without salute or other circumlocution said to the colonel:

"Say, Jim, I'm a-goin' home for a few days."

"What for?"

"Well, I hain't b'en there for a right smart while, and I'd like to see how things is comin' on."

"How long are you going to be gone?"

" 'Bout two weeks."

"Well, don't be gone longer than that; and get back sooner if you can."

That was all, and the citizen officer resumed his conversation where the private had broken it off. This was in the first months of the war, of course. The camps in our part of

Missouri were under Brigadier-General Thomas H. Harris. He was a townsman of ours, a first-rate fellow, and well liked; but we had all familiarly known him as the sole and modest-salaried operator in our telegraph office, where he had to send about one dispatch a week in ordinary times, and two when there was a rush of business; consequently, when he appeared in our midst one day, on the wing, and delivered a military command of some sort, in a large military fashion, nobody was surprised at the response which he got from the assembled soldiery:

"Oh, now, what'll you take to *don't*, Tom Harris!"

It was quite the natural thing. One might justly imagine that we were hopeless material for war. And so we seemed, in our ignorant state; but there were those among us who afterward learned the grim trade; learned to obey like machines; became valuable soldiers; fought all through the war, and came out at the end with excellent records. One of the very boys who refused to go out on picket duty that night, and called me an ass for thinking he would expose himself to danger in such a foolhardy way, had become distinguished for intrepidity before he was a year older.

I did secure my picket that night—not by authority, but by diplomacy. I got Bowers to go, by agreeing to exchange ranks with him for the time being, and go along and stand the watch with him as his subordinate. We staid out there a couple of dreary hours in the pitchy darkness and the rain, with nothing to modify the dreariness but Bowers's monotonous growlings at the war and the weather; then we began to nod, and presently found it next to impossible to stay in the saddle; so we gave up the tedious job, and went back to the camp without waiting for the relief guard. We rode into camp without interruption or objection from anybody, and the enemy could have done the same, for there were no sentries. Everybody was asleep; at midnight there was nobody to send out another picket, so none was sent. We never tried to establish a watch at night again, as far as I remember, but we generally kept a picket out in the daytime.

In that camp the whole command slept on the corn in the big corn-crib; and there was usually a general row before morning, for the place was full of rats, and they would scramble over the boys' bodies and faces, annoying and irritating everybody; and now and then they would bite some one's toe, and the person who owned the toe would start up and magnify his English and begin to throw corn in the dark. The ears were half as heavy as bricks, and when they struck they hurt. The persons struck would respond, and inside of five minutes every man would be locked in a death-grip with his neighbor. There was a grievous deal of blood shed in the corn-crib, but this was all that was spilt while I was in the war. No, that is not quite true. But for one circumstance it would have been all. I will come to that now.

Our scares were frequent. Every few days rumors would come that the enemy were approaching. In these cases we always fell back on some other camp of ours; we never staid where we were. But the rumors always turned out to be false; so at last even we began to grow indifferent to them. One night a negro was sent to our corn-crib with the same old warning: the enemy was hovering in our neighborhood. We all said let him hover. We resolved to stay still and be comfortable. It was a fine warlike resolution, and no doubt we all felt the stir of it in our veins—for a moment. We had been having a very jolly time, that was full of horse-play and school-boy hilarity; but that cooled down now, and presently the fast-waning fire of forced jokes and forced laughs died out altogether, and the company became silent. Silent and nervous. And soon uneasy—worried—apprehensive. We had said we would stay, and we were committed. We could have been persuaded to go, but there was nobody brave enough to suggest it. An almost noiseless movement presently began in the dark, by a general but unvoiced impulse. When the movement was completed, each man knew that he was not the only person who had crept to the front wall and had his eye at a crack between the logs. No, we were all there; all there with our hearts in our throats, and staring out toward the sugar-troughs where the forest foot-path came through. It was late, and there was a deep woodsy stillness everywhere. There was a veiled moonlight, which was only just strong enough to enable us to mark the general shape of objects. Presently a muffled sound caught our ears, and we recognized it as the hoof-beats of a horse or horses. And right away a figure appeared in the forest path; it could have been made of smoke, its mass had so little sharpness of outline. It was a man on horseback; and it seemed to me that there were others behind him. I got hold of a gun in the dark, and pushed it through a crack between the logs, hardly knowin what I was doing, I was so dazed with fright. Somebody said "Fire!" I pulled the trigger. I seemed to see a hundred flashes and hear a hundred reports, then I saw the man fall down out of the saddle. My first feeling was of surprised gratification; my first impulse was an apprentice-sportsman's impulse to run and pick up his game. Somebody said, hardly audibly, "Good—we've got him!—wait for the rest." But the rest did not come. We waited—listened—still no more came. There was not a sound, not the whisper of a leaf; just perfect stillness; an uncanny kind of stillness, which was all the more uncanny on account of the damp, earthy, late-night smells now rising and pervading it. Then, wondering, we crept stealthily out, and approached the man. When we got to him the moon revealed him distinctly. He was lying on his back, with his arms abroad; his mouth was open and his chest heaving with long gasps, and his white shirt-front was all splashed with blood. The thought shot through me that I was a murderer; that I had killed a man—a man who had never done me any harm. That was the coldest sensation that ever went through my marrow. I was down by him in a moment, helplessly stroking his forehead; and I would have given anything then—my own life freely—to make him again what he had been five minutes before. And all the boys seemed to be feeling in the same way; they hung over him, full of pitying interest, and tried all they could to help him, and said all sorts of regretful things. They had forgotten all about the enemy; they thought only of this one forlorn unit of the foe. Once my imagination persuaded me that the dying man gave me a reproachful look out of his shadowy eyes, and it seemed to me that I could rather he had stabbed me than done that. He muttered and mumbled like a dreamer in his sleep, about his wife and his child; and I thought with a new despair, "This thing that I have done does not end with him; it falls upon *them* too, and they never did me any harm, any more than he."

In a little while the man was dead. He was killed in war;

killed in fair and legitimate war; killed in battle, as you may say; and yet he was as sincerely mourned by the opposing force as if he had been their brother. The boys stood there a half hour sorrowing over him, and recalling the details of the tragedy, and wondering who he might be, and if he were a spy, and saying that if it were to do over again they would not hurt him unless he attacked them first. It soon came out that mine was not the only shot fired; there were five others,—a division of the guilt which was a grateful relief to me, since it in some degree lightened and diminished the burden I was carrying. There were six shots fired at once; but I was not in my right mind at the time, and my heated imagination had magnified my one shot into a volley.

The man was not in uniform, and was not armed. He was a stranger in the country; that was all we ever found out about him. The thought of him got to preying upon me every night; I could not get rid of it. I could not drive it away, the taking of that unoffending life seemed such a wanton thing. And it seemed an epitome of war; that all war must be just that—the killing of strangers against whom you feel no personal animosity; strangers whom, in other circumstances, you would help if you found them in trouble, and who would help you if you needed it. My campaign was spoiled. It seemed to me that I was not rightly equipped for this awful business; that war was intended for men, and I for a child's nurse. I resolved to retire from this avocation of sham soldiership while I could save some remnant of my self-respect. These morbid thoughts clung to me against reason; for at bottom I did not believe I had touched that man. The law of probabilities decreed me guiltless of his blood; for in all my small experience with guns I had never hit anything I had tried to hit, and I knew I had done my best to hit him. Yet there was no solace in the thought. Against a diseased imagination, demonstration goes for nothing.

The rest of my war experience was of a piece with what I have already told of it. We kept monotonously falling back upon one camp or another, and eating up the country. I marvel now at the patience of the farmers and their families. They ought to have shot us; on the contrary, they were as hospitably kind and courteous to us as if we had deserved it. In one of these camps we found Ab Grimes, an Upper Mississippi pilot, who afterwards became famous as a dare-devil rebel spy, whose career bristled with desperate adventures. The look and style of his comrades suggested that they had not come into the war to play, and their deeds made good the conjecture later. They were fine horsemen and good revolver-shots; but their favorite arm was the lasso. Each had one at his pommel, and could snatch a man out of the saddle with it every time, on a full gallop, at any reasonable distance.

In another camp the chief was a fierce and profane old blacksmith of sixty, and he had furnished his twenty recruits with gigantic home-made bowie-knives, to be swung with the two hands, like the *machetes* of the Isthmus. It was a grisly spectacle to see that earnest band practicing their murderous cuts and slashes under the eye of that remorseless old fanatic.

The last camp which we fell back upon was in a hollow near the village of Florida, where I was born—in Monroe County. Here we were warned, one day, that a Union colonel was sweeping down on us with a whole regiment at his heels. This looked decidedly serious. Our boys went apart and con-sulted; then we went back and told the other companies present that the war was a disappointment to us and we were going to disband. They were getting ready, themselves, to fall back on some place or other, and were only waiting for Gen-eral Tom Harris, who was expected to arrive at any moment; so they tried to persuade us to wait a little while, but the majority of us said no, we were accustomed to falling back, and didn't need any of Tom Harris's help; we could get along perfectly well without him—and save time too. So about half of our fifteen, including myself, mounted and left on the instant; the others yielded to persuasion and staid—staid through the war.

An hour later we met General Harris on the road, with two or three people in his company—his staff, probably, but we could not tell; none of them were in uniform; uniforms had not come into vogue among us yet. Harris ordered us back; but we told him there was a Union colonel coming with a whole regiment in his wake, and it looked as if there was going to be a disturbance; so we had concluded to go home. He raged a little, but it was of no use; our minds were made up. We had done our share; had killed one man, exterminated one army, such as it was; let him go and kill the rest, and that would end the war. I did not see that brisk young general again until last year; then he was wearing white hair and whiskers.

In time I came to know that Union colonel whose coming frightened me out of the war and crippled the Southern cause to that extent—General Grant. I came within a few hours of seeing him when he was as unknown as I was myself; at a time when anybody could have said, "Grant?—Ulysses S. Grant? I do not remember hearing the name before." It seems difficult to realize that there was once a time when such a remark could be rationally made; but there *was*, and I was within a few miles of the place and the occasion too, though proceeding in the other direction.

The thoughtful will not throw this war-paper of mine lightly aside as being valueless. It has this value: it is a not unfair picture of what went on in many and many a militia camp in the first months of the rebellion, when the green recruits were without discipline, without the steadying and heartening influence of trained leaders; when all their circumstances were new and strange, and charged with exaggerated terrors, and before the invaluable experience of actual collision in the field had turned them from rabbits into soldiers. If this side of the picture of that early day has not before been put into history, then history has been to that degree incomplete, for it had and has its rightful place there. There was more Bull Run material scattered through the early camps of this country than exhibited itself at Bull Run. And yet it learned its trade presently, and helped to fight the great battles later. I could have become a soldier myself, if I had waited. I had got part of it learned; I knew more about retreating than the man that invented retreating.

Fenimore Cooper's Literary Offences

The Pathfinder and *The Deerslayer* stand at the head of Cooper's novels as artistic creations. There are others of his works which contain parts as perfect as are to be found in these, and scenes even more thrilling. Not one can be compared with either of them as a finished whole.

The defects in both of these tales are comparatively slight. They were pure works of art.—*Prof. Lounsbury.*

The five tales reveal an extraordinary fulness of invention.

. . . One of the very greatest characters in fiction, "Natty Bumppo." . . .

The craft of the woodsman, the tricks of the trapper, all the delicate art of the forest, were familiar to Cooper from his youth up.
—*Prof. Brander Matthews.*

Cooper is the greatest artist in the domain of romantic fiction yet produced by America.—*Wilkie Collins.*

IT seems to me that it was far from right for the Professor of English Literature in Yale, the Professor of English Literature in Columbia, and Wilkie Collins, to deliver opinions on Cooper's literature without having read some of it. It would have been much more decorous to keep silent and let persons talk who have read Cooper.

Cooper's art has some defects. In one place in *Deerslayer*, and in the restricted space of two-thirds of a page, Cooper has scored 114 offences against literary art out of a possible 115. It breaks the record.

There are nineteen rules governing literary art in the domain of romantic fiction—some say twenty-two. In *Deerslayer* Cooper violated eighteen of them. These eighteen require:

1. That a tale shall accomplish something and arrive somewhere. But the *Deerslayer* tale accomplishes nothing and arrives in the air.

2. They require that the episodes of a tale shall be necessary parts of the tale, and shall help to develop it. But as the *Deerslayer* tale is not a tale, and accomplishes nothing and arrives nowhere, the episodes have no rightful place in the work, since there was nothing for them to develop.

3. They require that the personages in a tale shall be alive, except in the case of corpses, and that always the reader shall

be able to tell the corpses from the others. But this detail has often been overlooked in the *Deerslayer* tale.

4. They require that the personages in a tale, both dead and alive, shall exhibit a sufficient excuse for being there. But this detail also has been overlooked in the *Deerslayer* tale.

5. They require that when the personages of a tale deal in conversation, the talk shall sound like human talk, and be talk such as human beings would be likely to talk in the given circumstances, and have a discoverable meaning, also a discoverable purpose, and a show of relevancy, and remain in the neighborhood of the subject in hand, and be interesting to the reader, and help out the tale, and stop when the people cannot think of anything more to say. But this requirement has been ignored from the beginning of the *Deerslayer* tale to the end of it.

6. They require that when the author describes the character of a personage in his tale, the conduct and conversation of that personage shall justify said description. But this law gets little or no attention in the *Deerslayer* tale, as "Natty Bumppo's" case will amply prove.

7. They require that when a personage talks like an illustrated, gilt-edged, tree-calf, hand-tooled, seven-dollar Friendship's Offering in the beginning of a paragraph, he shall not talk like a negro minstrel in the end of it. But this rule is flung down and danced upon in the *Deerslayer* tale.

8. They require that crass stupidities shall not be played upon the reader as "the craft of the woodsman, the delicate art of the forest," by either the author or the people in the tale. But this rule is persistently violated in the *Deerslayer* tale.

9. They require that the personages of a tale shall confine themselves to possibilities and let miracles alone; or, if they venture a miracle, the author must so plausibly set it forth as to make it look possible and reasonable. But these rules are not respected in the *Deerslayer* tale.

10. They require that the author shall make the reader feel a deep interest in the personages of his tale and in their fate; and that he shall make the reader love the good people in the tale and hate the bad ones. But the reader of the *Deerslayer* tale dislikes the good people in it, is indifferent to the others, and wishes they would all get drowned together.

11. They require that the characters in a tale shall be so clearly defined that the reader can tell beforehand what each will do in a given emergency. But in the *Deerslayer* tale this rule is vacated.

In addition to these large rules there are some little ones. These require that the author shall

12. *Say* what he is proposing to say, not merely come near it.

13. Use the right word, not its second cousin.

14. Eschew surplusage.

15. Not omit necessary details.

16. Avoid slovenliness of form.

17. Use good grammar.

18. Employ a simple and straightforward style.

Even these seven are coldly and persistently violated in the *Deerslayer* tale.

Cooper's gift in the way of invention was not a rich endowment; but such as it was he liked to work it, he was pleased with the effects, and indeed he did some quite sweet things with it. In his little box of stage properties he kept six or eight cunning devices, tricks, artifices for his savages and woodsmen to deceive and circumvent each other with, and he was never so happy as when he was working these innocent things and seeing them go. A favorite one was to make a moccasined person tread in the tracks of the moccasined enemy, and thus hide his own trail. Cooper wore out barrels and barrels of moccasins in working that trick. Another stage-property that he pulled out of his box pretty frequently was his broken twig. He prized his broken twig above all the rest of his effects, and worked it the hardest. It is a restful chapter in any book of his when somebody doesn't step on a dry twig and alarm all the reds and whites for two hundred yards around. Every time a Cooper person is in peril, and absolute silence is worth four dollars a minute, he is sure to step on a dry twig. There may be a hundred handier things to step on, but that wouldn't satisfy Cooper. Cooper requires him to turn out and find a dry twig; and if he can't do it, go and borrow one. In fact the Leather Stocking Series ought to have been called the Broken Twig Series.

I am sorry there is not room to put in a few dozen instances of the delicate art of the forest, as practiced by Natty Bumppo and some of the other Cooperian experts. Perhaps we may venture two or three samples. Cooper was a sailor—a naval officer; yet he gravely tells us how a vessel, driving toward a lee shore in a gale, is steered for a particular spot by her skipper because he knows of an *undertow* there which will hold her back against the gale and save her. For just pure woodcraft, or sailorcraft, or whatever it is, isn't that neat? For several years Cooper was daily in the society of artillery, and he ought to have noticed that when a cannon ball strikes the ground it either buries itself or skips a hundred feet or so; skips again a hundred feet or so—and so on, till it finally gets tired and rolls. Now in one place he loses some "females"—as he always calls women—in the edge of a wood near a plain at night in a fog, on purpose to give Bumppo a chance to show off the delicate art of the forest before the reader. These mislaid people are hunting for a fort. They hear a cannon-blast, and a cannon-ball presently comes rolling into the wood and stops at their feet. To the females this suggests nothing. The case is very different with the admirable Bumppo. I wish I may never know peace again if he doesn't strike out promptly and *follow the track* of that cannon-ball across the plain through the dense fog and find the fort. Isn't it a daisy? If Cooper had any real knowledge of Nature's ways of doing things, he had a most delicate art in concealing the fact. For instance: one of his acute Indian experts, Chingachgook (pronounced Chicago, I think), has lost the trail of a person he is tracking through the forest. Apparently that trail is hopelessly lost. Neither you nor I could ever have guessed out the way to find it. It was very different with Chicago. Chicago was not stumped for long. He turned a running stream out of its course, and there, in the slush in its old bed, were that person's moccasin-tracks. The current did not wash them away, as it would have done in all other like cases—no, even the eternal laws of Nature have to vacate when Cooper wants to put up a delicate job of woodcraft on the reader.

We must be a little wary when Brander Matthews tells us that Cooper's books "reveal an extraordinary fulness of invention." As a rule, I am quite willing to accept Brander Matthews's literary judgments and applaud his lucid and graceful phrasing of them; but that particular statement needs to be taken with a few tons of salt. Bless your heart, Cooper hadn't any more invention than a horse; and I don't mean a high-class horse, either; I mean a clothes-horse. It would be very difficult to find a really clever "situation" in Cooper's books; and still more difficult to find one of any kind which he has failed to render absurd by his handling of it. Look at the episodes of "the caves;" and at the celebrated scuffle between Magua and those others on the table-land a few days later; and at Hurry Harry's queer water-transit from the castle to the ark; and at Deerslayer's half hour with his first corpse; and at the quarrel between Hurry Harry and Deerslayer later; and at—but choose for yourself; you can't go amiss.

If Cooper had been an observer, his inventive faculty would have worked better, not more interestingly, but more rationally, more plausibly. Cooper's proudest creations in the way of "situations" suffer noticeably from the absence of the observer's protecting gift. Cooper's eye was splendidly inaccurate. Cooper seldom saw anything correctly. He saw nearly all things as through a glass eye, darkly. Of course a man who cannot see the commonest little everyday matters accurately is working at a disadvantage when he is constructing a "situation." In the *Deerslayer* tale Cooper has a stream which is fifty feet wide, where it flows out of a lake; it presently narrows to twenty as it meanders along for no given reason, and yet, when a stream acts like that it ought to be required to explain itself. Fourteen pages later the width of the brook's outlet from the lake has suddenly shrunk thirty feet, and become "the narrowest part of the stream." This shrinkage is not accounted for. The stream has bends in it, a sure indication that it has alluvial banks, and cuts them; yet these bends are only thirty and fifty feet long. If Cooper had been a nice and punctilious observer he would have noticed that the bends were oftener nine hundred feet long than short of it.

Cooper made the exit of that stream fifty feet wide in the first place, for no particular reason; in the second place, he narrowed it to less than twenty to accommodate some Indians. He bends a "sapling" to the form of an arch over this narrow passage, and conceals six Indians in its foliage. They are "laying" for a settler's scow or ark which is coming up the stream on its way to the lake; it is being hauled against the stiff current by a rope whose stationary end is anchored in the lake; its rate of progress cannot be more than a mile an hour. Cooper describes the ark, but pretty obscurely. In the matter of dimensions "it was little more than a modern canal boat." Let us guess, then, that it was about 140 feet long. It was of "greater breadth than common." Let us guess, then, that it was about sixteen feet wide. This leviathan had been prowling down bends which were but a third as long as itself, and scraping between banks where it had only two feet of space to spare on each side. We cannot too much admire this miracle. A low-roofed log dwelling occupies "two-thirds of the ark's length"—a dwelling ninety feet long and sixteen feet wide, let us say—a kind of vestibule train. The dwelling has two rooms—each forty-five feet long and sixteen feet wide, let us guess. One of them is the bed-room of the Hutter girls, Judith and Hetty; the other is the parlor, in the day time, at night it is papa's bed chamber. The ark is arriving at the stream's exit, now, whose width has been reduced to less than twenty feet to accommodate the Indians—say to eighteen. There is a foot to spare on each side of the boat. Did the Indians notice that there was going to be a tight squeeze there? Did they notice that they could make money by climbing down out of that arched sapling and just stepping aboard when the ark scraped by? No; other Indians would have noticed these things, but Cooper's Indians never notice anything. Cooper thinks they are marvellous creatures for noticing, but he was almost always in error about his Indians. There was seldom a sane one among them.

The ark is 140 feet long; the dwelling is 90 feet long. The idea of the Indians is to drop softly and secretly from the arched sapling to the dwelling as the ark creeps along under it at the rate of a mile an hour, and butcher the family. It will take the ark a minute and a half to pass under. It will take the 90-foot dwelling a minute to pass under. Now, then, what did the six Indians do? It would take you thirty years to guess, and even then you would have to give it up, I believe. Therefore, I will tell you what the Indians did. Their chief, a person of quite extraordinary intellect for a

Cooper Indian, warily watched the canal boat as it squeezed along under him, and when he had got his calculations fined down to exactly the right shade, as he judged, he let go and dropped. And *missed the house!* That is actually what he did. He missed the house, and landed in the stern of the scow. It was not much of a fall, yet it knocked him silly. He lay there unconscious. If the house had been 97 feet long, he would have made the trip. The fault was Cooper's, not his. The error lay in the construction of the house. Cooper was no architect.

There still remained in the roost five Indians. The boat has passed under and is now out of their reach. Let me explain what the five did—you would not be able to reason it out for yourself. No. 1 jumped for the boat, but fell in the water astern of it. Then No. 2 jumped for the boat, but fell in the water still further astern of it. Then No. 3 jumped for the boat, and fell a good way astern of it. Then No. 4 jumped for the boat, and fell in the water *away* astern. Then even No. 5 made a jump for the boat—for he was a Cooper Indian. In the matter of intellect, the difference between a Cooper Indian and the Indian that stands in front of the cigar shop is not spacious. The scow episode is really a sublime burst of invention; but it does not thrill, because the inaccuracy of the details throws a sort of air of fictitiousness and general improbability over it. This comes of Cooper's inadequacy as an observer.

The reader will find some examples of Cooper's high talent for inaccurate observation in the account of the shooting match in *The Pathfinder*. "A common wrought nail was driven lightly into the target, its head having been first touched with paint." The color of the paint is not stated—an important omission, but Cooper deals freely in important omissions. No, after all, it was not an important omission; for this nail head is *a hundred yards* from the marksman and could not be seen by them at that distance no matter what its color might be. How far can the best eyes see a common house fly? A hundred yards? It is quite impossible. Very well, eyes that cannot see a house fly that is a hundred yards away cannot see an ordinary nail head at that distance, for the size of the two objects is the same. It takes a keen eye to see a fly or a nail head at fifty yards—one hundred and fifty feet. Can the reader do it?

The nail was lightly driven, its head painted, and game called. Then the Cooper miracles began. The bullet of the first marksman chipped an edge of the nail head; the next man's bullet drove the nail a little way into the target—and removed all the paint. Haven't the miracles gone far enough now? Not to suit Cooper; for the purpose of this whole scheme is to show off his prodigy, Deerslayer-Hawkeye-Long-Rifle-Leather-Stocking-Pathfinder-Bumppo before the ladies.

"Be all ready to clench it, boys!" cried out Pathfinder, stepping into his friend's tracks the instant they were vacant. "Never mind a new nail; I can see that, though the paint is gone, and what I can see, I can hit at a hundred yards, though it were only a mosquitoe's eye. Be ready to clench!"

The rifle cracked, the bullet sped its way and the head of the nail was buried in the wood, covered by the piece of flattened lead.

There, you see, is a man who could hunt flies with a rifle, and command a ducal salary in a Wild West show to-day, if we had him back with us.

The recorded feat is certainly surprising, just as it stands; but it is not surprising enough for Cooper. Cooper adds a touch. He has made Pathfinder do this miracle with another man's rifle, and not only that, but Pathfinder did not have even the advantage of loading it himself. He had everything against him, and yet he made that impossible shot, and not only made it, but did it with absolute confidence, saying, "Be ready to clench." Now a person like that would have undertaken that same feat with a brickbat, and with Cooper to help he would have achieved it, too.

Pathfinder showed off handsomely that day before the ladies. His very first feat was a thing which no Wild West show can touch. He was standing with the group of marksmen, observing—a hundred yards from the target, mind: one Jasper raised his rifle and drove the centre of the bull's-eye. Then the quartermaster fired. The target exhibited no result this time. There was a laugh. "It's a dead miss," said Major

Lundie. Pathfinder waited an impressive moment or two, then said in that calm, indifferent, know-it-all way of his, "No, Major—he has covered Jasper's bullet, as will be seen if any one will take the trouble to examine the target."

Wasn't it remarkable! How *could* he see that little pellet fly through the air and enter that distant bullet-hole? Yet that is what he did; for nothing is impossible to a Cooper person. Did any of those people have any deep-seated doubts about this thing? No; for that would imply sanity, and these were all Cooper people.

The respect for Pathfinder's skill and for his *quickness and accuracy of sight* (the italics are mine) was so profound and general, that the instant he made this declaration the spectators began to distrust their own opinions, and a dozen rushed to the target in order to ascertain the fact. There, sure enough, it was found that the quartermaster's bullet had gone through the hole made by Jasper's, and that, too, so accurately as to require a minute examination to be certain of the circumstance, which, however, was soon clearly established by discovering one bullet over the other in the stump against which the target was placed.

They made a "minute" examination; but never mind, how could they know that there were two bullets in that hole without digging the latest one out? for neither probe nor eyesight could prove the presence of any more than one bullet. Did they dig? No; as we shall see. It is the Pathfinder's turn now; he steps out before the ladies, takes aim, and fires.

But alas! here is a disappointment; an incredible, an unimaginable disappointment—for the target's aspect is unchanged; there is nothing there but that same old bullet hole!

"If one dared to hint at such a thing," cried Major Duncan, "I should say that the Pathfinder has also missed the target."

As nobody had missed it yet, the "also" was not necessary; but never mind about that, for the Pathfinder is going to speak.

"No, no, Major," said he, confidently, "that *would* be a risky declaration. I didn't load the piece, and can't say what was in it, but if it was lead, you will find the bullet driving down those of the Quartermaster and Jasper, else is not my name Pathfinder."

A shout from the target announced the truth of this assertion.

Is the miracle sufficient as it stands? Not for Cooper. The Pathfinder speaks again, as he "now slowly advances towards the stage occupied by the females:"

"That's not all, boys, that's not all; if you find the target touched at all, I'll own to a miss. The Quartermaster cut the wood, but you'll find no wood cut by that last messenger."

The miracle is at last complete. He knew—doubtless *saw*—at the distance of a hundred yards—that his bullet had passed into the hole *without fraying the edges*. There were now three bullets in that one hole—three bullets imbedded processionally in the body of the stump back of the target. Everybody knew this—somehow or other—and yet nobody had dug any of them out to make sure. Cooper is not a close observer, but he is interesting. He is certainly always that, no matter what happens. And he is more interesting when he is not noticing what he is about than when he is. This is a considerable merit.

The conversations in the Cooper books have a curious sound in our modern ears. To believe that such talk really ever came out of people's mouths would be to believe that there was a time when time was of no value to a person who thought he had something to say; when it was the custom to spread a two-minute remark out to ten; when a man's mouth was a rolling-mill, and busied itself all day long in turning four-foot pigs of thought into thirty-foot bars of conversational railroad iron by attenuation; when subjects were seldom faithfully stuck to, but the talk wandered all around and arrived nowhere; when conversations consisted mainly of irrelevances, with here and there a relevancy, a relevancy with an embarrassed look, as not being able to explain how it got there.

Cooper was certainly not a master in the construction of dialogue. Inaccurate observation defeated him here as it defeated him in so many other enterprises of his. He even failed to notice that the man who talks corrupt English six days in the week must and will talk it on the seventh, and can't help himself. In the *Deerslayer* story he lets Deerslayer talk the showiest kind of book talk sometimes, and at other times the basest of base dialects. For instance, when some one asks him if he has a sweetheart, and if so, where she abides, this is his majestic answer:

"She's in the forest—hanging from the boughs of the trees, in a soft rain—in the dew on the open grass—the clouds that float about in the blue heavens—the birds that sing in the woods—the sweet springs where I slake my thirst—and in all the other glorious gifts that come from God's Providence!"

And he preceded that, a little before, with this:

"It consarns me as all things that touches a fri'nd consarns a fri'nd."

And this is another of his remarks:

"If I was Injin born, now, I might tell of this, or carry in the scalp and boast of the expl'ite afore the whole tribe; or if my inimy had only been a bear"—and so on.

We cannot imagine such a thing as a veteran Scotch Commander-in-Chief comporting himself in the field like a windy melodramatic actor, but Cooper could. On one occasion Alice and Cora were being chased by the French through a fog in the neighborhood of their father's fort:

"Point de quartier aux coquins!" cried an eager pursuer, who seemed to direct the operations of the enemy.

"Stand firm and be ready, my gallant 60ths!" suddenly exclaimed a voice above them; "wait to see the enemy; fire low, and sweep the glacis."

"Father! father!" exclaimed a piercing cry from out the mist; "it is I! Alice! thy own Elsie! spare, O! save your daughters!"

"Hold!" shouted the former speaker, in the awful tones of parental agony, the sound reaching even to the woods, and rolling back in solemn echo. " 'Tis she! God has restored me my children! Throw open the sally-port; to the field, 60ths, to the field; pull not a trigger, lest ye kill my lambs! Drive off these dogs of France with your steel."

Cooper's word-sense was singularly dull. When a person has a poor ear for music he will flat and sharp right along without knowing it. He keeps near the tune, but it is *not* the tune. When a person has a poor ear for words, the result is a literary flatting and sharping; you perceive what he is intending to say, but you also perceive that he doesn't *say* it. This is Cooper. He was not a word-musician. His ear was satisfied with the *approximate* word. I will furnish some circumstantial evidence in support of this charge. My instances are gathered from half a dozen pages of the tale called *Deerslayer*. He uses "verbal," for "oral"; "precision," for "facility"; "phenomena," for "marvels"; "necessary," for "predetermined"; "unsophisticated," for "primitive"; "preparation," for "expectancy"; "rebuked," for "subdued"; "dependent on," for "resulting from"; "fact," for "condition"; "fact," for "conjecture"; "precaution," for "caution"; "explain," for "determine"; "mortified," for "disappointed"; "meretricious," for "factitious"; "materially," for "considerably"; "decreasing," for "deepening"; "increasing," for "disappearing"; "embedded," for "enclosed"; "treacherous," for "hostile"; "stood," for "stooped"; "softened," for "replaced"; "rejoined," for "remarked"; "situation," for "condition"; "different," for "differing"; "insensible," for "unsentient"; "brevity," for "celerity"; "distrusted," for "suspicious"; "mental imbecility," for "imbecility"; "eyes," for "sight"; "counteracting," for "opposing"; "funeral obsequies," for "obsequies."

There have been daring people in the world who claimed that Cooper could write English, but they are all dead now—all dead but Lounsbury. I don't remember that Lounsbury makes the claim in so many words, still he makes it, for he says that *Deerslayer* is a "pure work of art." Pure, in that connection, means faultless—faultless in all details—and language is a detail. If Mr. Lounsbury had only compared Cooper's English with the English which he writes himself—but it is plain that he didn't; and so it is likely that he imagines until this day that Cooper's is as clean and compact as his own. Now I feel sure, deep down in my heart, that Cooper wrote about the poorest English that exists in our language, and that the English of *Deerslayer* is the very worst that even Cooper ever wrote.

I may be mistaken, but it does seem to me that *Deerslayer* is not a work of art in any sense; it does seem to me that it is destitute of every detail that goes to the making of a work of art; in truth, it seems to me that *Deerslayer* is just simply a literary *delirium tremens.*

A work of art? It has no invention; it has no order, system, sequence, or result; it has no lifelikeness, no thrill, no stir, no seeming of reality; its characters are confusedly drawn, and by their acts and words they prove that they are not the sort of people the author claims that they are; its humor is pathetic; its pathos is funny; its conversations are—oh! indescribable; its love-scenes odious; its English a crime against the language.

Counting these out, what is left is Art. I think we must all admit that.

How To Tell a Story

THE HUMOROUS STORY AN AMERICAN DEVELOPMENT. — ITS DIFFERENCE FROM COMIC AND WITTY STORIES.

I DO not claim that I can tell a story as it ought to be told. I only claim to know how a story ought to be told, for I have been almost daily in the company of the most expert story-tellers for many years.

There are several kinds of stories, but only one difficult kind—the humorous. I will talk mainly about that one. The humorous story is American, the comic story is English, the witty story is French. The humorous story depends for its effect upon the *manner* of the telling; the comic story and the witty story upon the *matter.*

The humorous story may be spun out to great length, and may wander around as much as it pleases, and arrive nowhere in particular; but the comic and witty stories must be brief and end with a point. The humorous story bubbles gently along, the others burst.

The humorous story is strictly a work of art,—high and delicate art,—and only an artist can tell it; but no art is necessary in telling the comic and the witty story; anybody can do it. The art of telling a humorous story—understand, I mean by word of mouth, not print—was created in America, and has remained at home.

The humorous story is told gravely; the teller does his best to conceal the fact that he even dimly suspects that there is anything funny about it; but the teller of the comic story tells you beforehand that it is one of the funniest things he has ever heard, then tells it with eager delight, and is the first person to laugh when he gets through. And sometimes, if he has had good success, he is so glad and happy that he will repeat the "nub" of it and glance around from face to face, collecting applause, and then repeat it again. It is a pathetic thing to see.

Very often, of course, the rambling and disjointed humorous story finishes with a nub, point, snapper, or whatever you like to call it. Then the listener must be alert, for in many cases the teller will divert attention from that nub by dropping it in a carefully casual and indifferent way, with the pretence that he does not know it is a nub.

Artemus Ward used that trick a good deal; then when the belated audience presently caught the joke he would look up with innocent surprise, as if wondering what they had found to laugh at. Dan Setchell used it before him, Nye and Riley and others use it to-day.

But the teller of the comic story does not slur the nub; he shouts it at you—every time. And when he prints it, in England, France, Germany and Italy, he italicises it, puts some whooping exclamation-points after it, and sometimes explains it in a parenthesis. All of which is very depressing, and makes one want to renounce joking and lead a better life.

Let me set down an instance of the comic method, using an anecdote which has been popular all over the world for twelve or fifteen hundred years. The teller tells it in this way:

The Wounded Soldier.

In the course of a certain battle a soldier whose leg had been shot off appealed to another soldier who was hurrying by to carry him to the rear, informing him at the same time of the loss which he had sustained; whereupon the generous son of Mars, shouldering the unfortunate, proceeded to carry out his desire. The bullets and cannon-balls were flying in all directions, and presently one of the latter took the wounded man's head off—without, however, his deliverer being aware of it. In no long time he was hailed by an officer, who said:

"Where are you going with that carcass?"

"To the rear, sir—he's lost his leg!"

"His leg, forsooth?" responded the astonished officer; "you mean his head, you booby."

Whereupon the soldier dispossessed himself of his burden, and stood looking down upon it in great perplexity. At length he said:

"It is true, sir, just as you have said." Then after a pause he added, "*But he* TOLD *me* IT WAS HIS LEG!!!!!"

Here the narrator bursts into explosion after explosion of thunderous horse-laughter, repeating that nub from time to time through his gaspings and shriekings and suffocatings.

It takes only a minute and a half to tell that in its comic-story form; and isn't worth the telling, after all. Put into the humorous-story form it takes ten minutes, and is about the funniest thing I have ever listened to—as James Whitcomb Riley tells it.

He tells it in the character of a dull-witted old farmer who has just heard it for the first time, thinks it is unspeakably funny, and is trying to repeat it to a neighbor. But he can't remember it; so he gets it all mixed up and wanders helplessly round and round, putting in tedious details that don't belong in the tale and only retard it; taking them out conscientiously and putting in others that are just as useless; making minor mistakes now and then and stopping to correct them and explain how he came to make them; remembering things which he forgot to put in in their proper place and going back to put them in there; stopping his narrative a good while in order to try to recall the name of the soldier that was hurt, and finally remembering that the soldier's name was not mentioned, and remarking placidly that the name is of no real importance, any way,—better, of course, if one knew it, but not essential, after all,—and so on, and so on, and so on.

The teller is innocent and happy and pleased with himself, and has to stop every little while to hold himself in and keep from laughing outright; and does hold in, but his body quakes in a jelly-like way with interior chuckles; and at the end of the ten minutes the audience have laughed until they are exhausted, and the tears are running down their faces.

The simplicity and innocence and sincerity and unconsciousness of the old farmer are perfectly simulated, and the result is a performance which is thoroughly charming and delicious. This is art—and fine and beautiful, and only a master can compass it; but a machine could tell the other story.

To string incongruities and absurdities together in a wandering and sometimes purposeless way, and seem innocently unaware that they are absurdities, is the basis of the American art, if my position is correct. Another feature is the slurring of the point. A third is the dropping of a studied remark apparently without knowing it, as if one were thinking aloud. The fourth and last is the pause.

Artemus Ward dealt in numbers three and four a good deal. He would begin to tell with great animation something which he seemed to think was wonderful; then lose confidence, and after an apparently absent-minded pause add an incongruous remark in a soliloquizing way; and that was the remark intended to explode the mine—and it did.

For instance, he would say eagerly, excitedly, "I once knew a man in New Zealand who hadn't a tooth in his head"—here his animation would die out; a silent, reflective pause would follow, then he would say dreamily, and as if to himself, "and yet that man could beat a drum better than any man I ever saw."

The pause is an exceedingly important feature in any kind of story, and a frequently recurring feature, too. It is a dainty thing, and delicate, and also uncertain and treacherous; for it must be exactly the right length—no more and no less—or it fails of its purpose and makes trouble. If the pause is too short the impressive point is passed, and the audience have had time to divine that a surprise is intended—and then you can't surprise them, of course.

On the platform I used to tell a negro ghost story that had a pause in front of the snapper on the end, and that pause was the most important thing in the whole story. If I got it the right length precisely, I could spring the finishing ejaculation with effect enough to make some impressible girl deliver a startled little yelp and jump out of her seat—and that was what I was after. This story was called "The Golden Arm," and was told in this fashion. You can practise with it yourself—and mind you look out for the pause and get it right.

The Golden Arm.

Once 'pon a time dey wuz a monsus mean man, en he live 'way out in de prairie all 'lone by hisself, 'cep'n he had a wife. En bimeby she died, en he tuck en toted her way out dah in de prairie en buried her. Well, she had a golden arm—all solid gold, fum de shoulder down. He wuz pow'ful mean—pow'ful; en dat night he couldn't sleep, caze he want dat golden arm so bad.

When it come midnight he couldn't stan' it no mo'; so he git up, he did, en tuck his lantern en shoved out thoo de storm en dug her up en got de golden arm; en he bent his head down 'gin de win', en plowed en plowed en plowed thoo de snow. Den all on a sudden he stop (make a considerable pause here, and look startled, and take a listening attitude) en say: "My *lan'*, what's dat!"

En he listen—en listen—en de win' say (set your teeth together and imitate the wailing and wheezing singsong of the wind), "Bzzz-z-zzz"—en den, way back yonder whah de grave is, he hear a *voice!*—he hear a voice all mix' up in de win'—can't hardly tell 'em 'part—"Bzzz-zzz—W-h-o—g-o-t—m-y—g-o-l-d-e-n *arm?*—zzz—zzz—W-h-o g-o-t m-y g-o-l-d-e-n *arm?*" (You must begin to shiver violently now.)

En he begin to shiver en shake, en say, "Oh, my! *Oh*, my lan'!" en de win' blow de lantern out, en de snow en sleet blow in his face en mos' choke him, en he start a-plowin' knee-deep toward home mos' dead, he so sk'yerd—en pooty soon he hear de voice agin, en (pause) it 'us comin' *after* him! "Bzzz—zzz—zzz—W-h-o—g-o-t—m-y g-o-l-d-e-n—*arm?*"

When he git to de pasture he hear it agin—closter now, en a-*comin'!*—a-comin' back dah in de dark en de storm—(repeat the wind and the voice). When he git to de house he rush up-stairs en jump in de bed en kiver up, head and years, en lay dah shiverin' en shakin'—en den way out dah he hear it *agin!*—en a-*comin'!* En bimeby he hear (pause—awed, listening attitude)—pat—pat—pat—*hit's a-comin' up-stairs!* Den he hear de latch, en he *know* it's in de room!

Den pooty soon he know it's a-*stannin' by de bed!* (Pause.) Den—he know it's a—*bendin' down over him*—en he cain't skasely git his breath! Den—den—he seem to feel someth'n *c-o-l-d*, right down 'most agin his head! (Pause.)

Den de voice say, *right at his year*—"W-h-o—g-o-t—m-y

—g-o-l-d-e-n *arm?*" (You must wail it out very plaintively and accusingly; then you stare steadily and impressively into the face of the farthest-gone auditor,—a girl, preferably,—and let that awe-inspiring pause begin to build itself in the deep hush. When it has reached exactly the right length, jump suddenly at that girl and yell, "*You've* got it!"

If you've got the *pause* right, she'll fetch a dear little yelp and spring right out of her shoes. But you *must* get the pause right; and you will find it the most troublesome and aggravating and uncertain thing you ever undertook.)

The Man That Corrupted Hadleyburg

I.

I<small>T</small> was many years ago. Hadleyburg was the most honest and upright town in all the region round about. It had kept that reputation unsmirched during three generations, and was prouder of it than of any other of its possessions. It was so proud of it, and so anxious to insure its perpetuation, that it began to teach the principles of honest dealing to its babies in the cradle, and made the like teachings the staple of their culture thenceforward through all the years devoted to their education. Also, throughout the formative years temptations were kept out of the way of the young people, so that their honesty could have every chance to harden and solidify, and become a part of their very bone. The neighboring towns were jealous of this honorable supremacy, and affected to sneer at Hadleyburg's pride in it and call it vanity; but all the same they were obliged to acknowledge that Hadleyburg was in reality an incorruptible town; and if pressed they would also acknowledge that the mere fact that a young man hailed from Hadleyburg was all the recommendation he needed when he went forth from his natal town to seek for responsible employment.

But at last, in the drift of time, Hadleyburg had the ill luck to offend a passing stranger—possibly without knowing it, certainly without caring, for Hadleyburg was sufficient unto itself, and cared not a rap for strangers or their opinions. Still, it would have been well to make an exception in this one's case, for he was a bitter man and revengeful. All through his wanderings during a whole year he kept his injury in mind, and gave all his leisure moments to trying to invent a compensating satisfaction for it. He contrived many plans, and all of them were good, but none of them was quite sweeping enough; the poorest of them would hurt a great many individuals, but what he wanted was a plan which would comprehend the entire town, and not let so much as one person escape unhurt. At last he had a fortunate idea, and when it fell into his brain it lit up his whole head with an evil joy. He began to form a plan at once, saying to himself, "That is the thing to do—I will corrupt the town."

Six months later he went to Hadleyburg, and arrived in a buggy at the house of the old cashier of the bank about ten at night. He got a sack out of the buggy, shouldered it, and staggered with it through the cottage yard, and knocked at the door. A woman's voice said "Come in," and he entered, and set his sack behind the stove in the parlor, saying politely to the old lady who sat reading the *Missionary Herald* by the lamp:

"Pray keep your seat, madam, I will not disturb you. There—now it is pretty well concealed; one would hardly know it was there. Can I see your husband a moment, madam?"

No, he was gone to Brixton, and might not return before morning.

"Very well, madam, it is no matter. I merely wanted to leave that sack in his care, to be delivered to the rightful owner when he shall be found. I am a stranger; he does not know me; I am merely passing through the town to-night to discharge a matter which has been long in my mind. My errand is now completed, and I go pleased and a little proud, and you will never see me again. There is a paper attached to the sack which will explain everything. Good-night, madam."

The old lady was afraid of the mysterious big stranger, and was glad to see him go. But her curiosity was roused, and she went straight to the sack and brought away the paper. It began as follows:

"TO BE PUBLISHED; or, the right man sought out by private inquiry—either will answer. This sack contains gold coin weighing a hundred and sixty pounds four ounces—"

"Mercy on us, and the door not locked!"

Mrs. Richards flew to it all in a tremble and locked it, then pulled down the window-shades and stood frightened, worried, and wondering if there was anything else she could do toward making herself and the money more safe. She listened awhile for burglars, then surrendered to curiosity and went back to the lamp and finished reading the paper:

"I am a foreigner, and am presently going back to my own country, to remain there permanently. I am grateful to America for what I have received at her hands during my long stay under her flag; and to one of her citizens—a citizen of Hadleyburg—I am especially grateful for a great kindness done me a year or two ago. Two great kindnesses, in fact. I will explain. I was a gambler. I say I *was*. I was a ruined gambler. I arrived in this village at night, hungry and without a penny. I asked for help—in the dark; I was ashamed to beg in the light. I begged of the right man. He gave me twenty dollars—that is to say, he gave me life, as I considered it. He also gave me fortune; for out of that money I have made myself rich at the gaming-table. And finally, a remark which he made to me has remained with me to this day, and has at last conquered me; and in conquering has saved the remnant of my morals: I shall gamble no more. Now I have no idea who that man was, but I want him found, and I want him to have this money, to give away, throw away, or keep, as he pleases. It is merely my way of testifying my gratitude to him. If I could stay, I would find him myself; but no matter, he will be found. This is an honest town, an incorruptible town, and I know I can trust it without fear. This man can be identified by the remark which he made to me; I feel persuaded that he will remember it.

"And now my plan is this: If you prefer to conduct the inquiry privately, do so. Tell the contents of this present writing to any one who is likely to be the right man. If he shall answer, 'I am the man; the remark I made was so-and-so,' apply the test—to wit: open the sack, and in it you will find a sealed envelope containing that remark. If the remark mentioned by the candidate tallies with it, give him the money, and ask no further questions, for he is certainly the right man.

"But if you shall prefer a public inquiry, then publish this present writing in the local paper—with these instructions added, to wit: Thirty days from now, let the candidate appear at the town-hall at eight in the evening (Friday), and hand his remark, in a sealed envelope, to the Rev. Mr. Burgess (if he will be kind enough to act); and let Mr. Burgess there and then destroy the seals of the sack, open it, and see if the remark is correct; if correct, let the money be delivered, with my sincere gratitude, to my benefactor thus identified."

Mrs. Richards sat down, gently quivering with excitement, and was soon lost in thinkings—after this pattern: "What a strange thing it is! . . . . And what a fortune for that kind man who set his bread afloat upon the waters! . . . . If it had only been my husband that did it!—for we are so poor, so old and poor! . . . ." Then, with a sigh—"But it was not my Edward; no, it was not he that gave a stranger twenty dollars. It is a pity too; I see it now. . . ." Then, with a shudder— "But it is *gambler's* money! the wages of sin; we couldn't take it; we couldn't touch it. I don't like to be near it; it seems a defilement." She moved to a farther chair. . . . "I wish Edward would come, and take it to the bank; a burglar might come at any moment; it is dreadful to be here all alone with it."

At eleven Mr. Richards arrived, and while his wife was saying, "I am *so* glad you've come!" he was saying, "I'm so tired—tired clear out; it is dreadful to be poor, and have to make these dismal journeys at my time of life. Always at the grind, grind, grind, on a salary—another man's slave, and he sitting at home in his slippers, rich and comfortable."

"I am so sorry for you, Edward, you know that; but be comforted; we have our livelihood; we have our good name—"

"Yes, Mary, and that is everything. Don't mind my talk—it's just a moment's irritation and doesn't mean anything. Kiss me—there, it's all gone now, and I am not complaining any more. What have you been getting? What's in the sack?"

Then his wife told him the great secret. It dazed him for a moment; then he said:

"It weighs a hundred and sixty pounds? Why, Mary, it's for-ty thou-sand dollars—think of it—a whole fortune! Not ten men in this village are worth that much. Give me the paper."

He skimmed through it and said:

"Isn't it an adventure! Why, it's a romance; it's like the

impossible things one reads about in books, and never sees in life." He was well stirred up now; cheerful, even gleeful. He tapped his old wife on the cheek, and said, humorously, "Why, we're rich, Mary, rich; all we've got to do is to bury the money and burn the papers. If the gambler ever comes to inquire, we'll merely look coldly upon him and say: 'What is this nonsense you are talking? We have never heard of you and your sack of gold before;' and then he would look foolish, and—"

"And in the mean time, while you are running on with your jokes, the money is still here, and it is fast getting along toward burglar-time."

"True. Very well, what shall we do—make the inquiry private? No, not that; it would spoil the romance. The public method is better. Think what a noise it will make! And it will make all the other towns jealous; for no stranger would trust such a thing to any town but Hadleyburg, and they know it. It's a great card for us. I must get to the printing-office now, or I shall be too late."

"But stop—stop—don't leave me here alone with it, Edward!"

But he was gone. For only a little while, however. Not far from his own house he met the editor-proprietor of the paper, and gave him the document, and said, "Here is a good thing for you, Cox—put it in."

"It may be too late, Mr. Richards, but I'll see."

At home again he and his wife sat down to talk the charming mystery over; they were in no condition for sleep. The first question was, Who could the citizen have been who gave the stranger the twenty dollars? It seemed a simple one; both answered it in the same breath—

"Barclay Goodson."

"Yes," said Richards, "he could have done it, and it would have been like him, but there's not another in the town."

"Everybody will grant that, Edward—grant it privately, anyway. For six months, now, the village has been its own proper self once more—honest, narrow, self-righteous, and stingy."

"It is what he always called it, to the day of his death—said it right out publicly, too."

"Yes, and he was hated for it."

"Oh, of course; but he didn't care. I reckon he was the best-hated man among us, except the Reverend Burgess."

"Well, Burgess deserves it—he will never get another congregation here. Mean as the town is, it knows how to estimate *him*. Edward, doesn't it seem odd that the stranger should appoint Burgess to deliver the money?"

"Well, yes—it does. That is—that is—"

"Why so much that-*is*-ing? Would *you* select him?"

"Mary, maybe the stranger knows him better than this village does."

"Much *that* would help Burgess!"

The husband seemed perplexed for an answer; the wife kept a steady eye upon him, and waited. Finally Richards said, with the hesitancy of one who is making a statement which is likely to encounter doubt,

"Mary, Burgess is not a bad man."

His wife was certainly surprised.

"Nonsense!" she exclaimed.

"He is not a bad man. I know. The whole of his unpopularity had its foundation in that one thing—the thing that made so much noise."

"That 'one thing,' indeed! As if that 'one thing' wasn't enough, all by itself."

"Plenty. Plenty. Only he wasn't guilty of it."

"How you talk! Not guilty of it! Everybody knows he *was* guilty."

"Mary, I give you my word—he was innocent."

"I can't believe it, and I don't. How do you know?"

"It is a confession. I am ashamed, but I will make it. I was the only man who knew he was innocent. I could have saved him, and—and—well, you know how the town was wrought up—I hadn't the pluck to do it. It would have turned everybody against me. I felt mean, ever so mean; but I didn't dare; I hadn't the manliness to face that."

Mary looked troubled, and for a while was silent. Then she said, stammeringly:

"I—I don't think it would have done for you to—to— One mustn't—er—public opinion—one has to be so careful—so—" It was a difficult road, and she got mired; but

after a little she got started again. "It was a great pity, but—
Why, we couldn't afford it, Edward—we couldn't indeed.
Oh, I wouldn't have had you do it for anything!"

"It would have lost us the good-will of so many people,
Mary; and then—and then—"

"What troubles me now is, what *he* thinks of us, Edward."

"He? *He* doesn't suspect that I could have saved him."

"Oh," exclaimed the wife, in a tone of relief, "I am glad of
that. As long as he doesn't know that you could have saved
him, he—he—well, that makes it a great deal better. Why, I
might have known he didn't know, because he is always trying to be friendly with us, as little encouragement as we give
him. More than once people have twitted me with it. There's
the Wilsons, and the Wilcoxes, and the Harknesses, they take
a mean pleasure in saying, '*Your friend* Burgess,' because they
know it pesters me. I wish he wouldn't persist in liking us so;
I can't think why he keeps it up."

"I can explain it. It's another confession. When the thing
was new and hot, and the town made a plan to ride him on a
rail, my conscience hurt me so that I couldn't stand it, and I
went privately and gave him notice, and he got out of the
town and staid out till it was safe to come back."

"Edward! If the town had found it out—"

"*Don't!* It scares me yet, to think of it. I repented of it the
minute it was done; and I was even afraid to tell you, lest
your face might betray it to somebody. I didn't sleep any that
night, for worrying. But after a few days I saw that no one
was going to suspect me, and after that I got to feeling glad
I did it. And I feel glad yet, Mary—glad through and
through."

"So do I, now, for it would have been a dreadful way to
treat him. Yes, I'm glad; for really you did owe him that, you
know. But, Edward, suppose it should come out yet, some
day!"

"It won't."

"Why?"

"Because everybody thinks it was Goodson."

"Of course they would!"

"Certainly. And of course *he* didn't care. They persuaded

poor old Sawlsberry to go and charge it on him, and he went blustering over there and did it. Goodson looked him over, like as if he was hunting for a place on him that he could despise the most, then he says, 'So you are the Committee of Inquiry, are you?' Sawlsberry said that was about what he was. 'Hm. Do they require particulars, or do you reckon a kind of a *general* answer will do?' 'If they require particulars, I will come back, Mr. Goodson; I will take the general answer first.' 'Very well, then, tell them to go to hell—I reckon that's general enough. And I'll give you some advice, Sawlsberry: when you come back for the particulars, fetch a basket to carry the relics of yourself home in.' "

"Just like Goodson; it's got all the marks. He had only one vanity; he thought he could give advice better than any other person."

"It settled the business, and saved us, Mary. The subject was dropped."

"Bless you, I'm not doubting *that*."

Then they took up the gold-sack mystery again, with strong interest. Soon the conversation began to suffer breaks—interruptions caused by absorbed thinkings. The breaks grew more and more frequent. At last Richards lost himself wholly in thought. He sat long, gazing vacantly at the floor, and by-and-by he began to punctuate his thoughts with little nervous movements of his hands that seemed to indicate vexation. Meantime his wife too had relapsed into a thoughtful silence, and her movements were beginning to show a troubled discomfort. Finally Richards got up and strode aimlessly about the room, ploughing his hands through his hair, much as a somnambulist might do who was having a bad dream. Then he seemed to arrive at a definite purpose; and without a word he put on his hat and passed quickly out of the house. His wife sat brooding, with a drawn face, and did not seem to be aware that she was alone. Now and then she murmured, "Lead us not into t. . . . but—but—we are so poor, so poor! . . . . Lead us not into. . . . Ah, who would be hurt by it?—and no one would ever know. . . . Lead us. . . ." The voice died out in mumblings. After a little she glanced up and muttered in a half-frightened, half-glad way—

"He is gone! But, oh dear, he may be too late—too late.
. . . Maybe not—maybe there is still time." She rose and
stood thinking, nervously clasping and unclasping her hands.
A slight shudder shook her frame, and she said, out of a dry
throat, "God forgive me—it's awful to think such things—
but. . . . Lord, how we are made—how strangely we are
made!"

She turned the light low, and slipped stealthily over and
kneeled down by the sack and felt of its ridgy sides with her
hands, and fondled them lovingly; and there was a gloating
light in her poor old eyes. She fell into fits of absence; and
came half out of them at times to mutter, "If we had only
waited!—oh, if we had only waited a little, and not been in
such a hurry!"

Meantime Cox had gone home from his office and told his
wife all about the strange thing that had happened, and they
had talked it over eagerly, and guessed that the late Goodson
was the only man in the town who could have helped a suffering stranger with so noble a sum as twenty dollars. Then
there was a pause, and the two became thoughtful and silent.
And by-and-by nervous and fidgety. At last the wife said, as if
to herself,

"Nobody knows this secret but the Richardses . . . . and
us . . . . nobody."

The husband came out of his thinkings with a slight start,
and gazed wistfully at his wife, whose face was become very
pale; then he hesitatingly rose, and glanced furtively at his
hat, then at his wife—a sort of mute inquiry. Mrs. Cox swallowed once or twice, with her hand at her throat, then in
place of speech she nodded her head. In a moment she was
alone, and mumbling to herself.

And now Richards and Cox were hurrying through the deserted streets, from opposite directions. They met, panting, at
the foot of the printing-office stairs; by the night-light there
they read each other's face. Cox whispered,

"Nobody knows about this but us?"

The whispered answer was,

"Not a soul—on honor, not a soul!"

"If it isn't too late to—"

The men were starting up stairs; at this moment they were overtaken by a boy, and Cox asked,

"Is that you, Johnny?"

"Yes, sir."

"You needn't ship the early mail—nor *any* mail; wait till I tell you."

"It's already gone, sir."

"*Gone?*" It had the sound of an unspeakable disappointment in it.

"Yes, sir. Time-table for Brixton and all the towns beyond changed to-day, sir—had to get the papers in twenty minutes earlier than common. I had to rush; if I had been two minutes later—"

The men turned and walked slowly away, not waiting to hear the rest. Neither of them spoke during ten minutes; then Cox said, in a vexed tone,

"What possessed you to be in such a hurry, *I* can't make out."

The answer was humble enough:

"I see it now, but somehow I never thought, you know, until it was too late. But the next time—"

"Next time be hanged! It won't come in a thousand years."

Then the friends separated without a good-night, and dragged themselves home with the gait of mortally stricken men. At their homes their wives sprang up with an eager "Well?"—then saw the answer with their eyes and sank down sorrowing, without waiting for it to come in words. In both houses a discussion followed of a heated sort—a new thing; there had been discussions before, but not heated ones, not ungentle ones. The discussions to-night were a sort of seeming plagiarisms of each other. Mrs. Richards said,

"If you had only waited, Edward—if you had only stopped to think; but no, you must run straight to the printing-office and spread it all over the world."

"It *said* publish it."

"That is nothing; it also said do it privately, if you liked. There, now—is that true, or not?"

"Why, yes—yes, it is true; but when I thought what a stir

it would make, and what a compliment it was to Hadleyburg that a stranger should trust it so—"

"Oh, certainly, I know all that; but if you had only stopped to think, you would have seen that you *couldn't* find the right man, because he is in his grave, and hasn't left chick nor child nor relation behind him; and as long as the money went to somebody that awfully needed it, and nobody would be hurt by it, and—and—"

She broke down, crying. Her husband tried to think of some comforting thing to say, and presently came out with this:

"But after all, Mary, it must be for the best—it *must* be; we know that. And we must remember that it was so ordered—"

"Ordered! Oh, everything's *ordered*, when a person has to find some way out when he has been stupid. Just the same, it was *ordered* that the money should come to us in this special way, and it was you that must take it on yourself to go meddling with the designs of Providence—and who gave you the right. It was wicked, that is what it was—just blasphemous presumption, and no more becoming to a meek and humble professor of—"

"But, Mary, you know how we have been trained all our lives long, like the whole village, till it is absolutely second nature to us to stop not a single moment to think when there's an honest thing to be done—"

"Oh, I know it, I know it—it's been one everlasting training and training and training in honesty—honesty shielded, from the very cradle, against every possible temptation, and so it's *artificial* honesty, and weak as water when temptation comes, as we have seen this night. God knows I never had shade nor shadow of a doubt of my petrified and indestructible honesty until now—and now, under the very first big and real temptation, I—Edward, it is my belief that this town's honesty is as rotten as mine is; as rotten as yours is. It is a mean town, a hard, stingy town, and hasn't a virtue in the world but this honesty it is so celebrated for and so conceited about; and so help me, I do believe that if ever the day comes that its honesty falls under great temptation, its grand reputation will go to ruin like a house of cards. There, now, I've made confession, and I feel better; I am a humbug, and I've been one all my life, without knowing it. Let no man call me honest again—I will not have it."

"I— Well, Mary, I feel a good deal as you do; I certainly do. It seems strange, too, so strange. I never could have believed it—never."

A long silence followed; both were sunk in thought. At last the wife looked up and said,

"I know what you are thinking, Edward."

Richards had the embarrassed look of a person who is caught.

"I am ashamed to confess it, Mary, but—"

"It's no matter, Edward, I was thinking the same question myself."

"I hope so. State it."

"You were thinking, if a body could only guess out *what the remark was* that Goodson made to the stranger."

"It's perfectly true. I feel guilty and ashamed. And you?"

"I'm past it. Let us make a pallet here; we've got to stand watch till the bank vault opens in the morning and admits the sack. . . . Oh, dear, oh, dear—if we hadn't made the mistake!"

The pallet was made, and Mary said:

"The open sesame—what could it have been? I do wonder what that remark could have been? But come; we will get to bed now."

"And sleep?"

"No; think."

"Yes, think."

By this time the Coxes too had completed their spat and their reconciliation, and were turning in—to think, to think, and toss, and fret, and worry over what the remark could possibly have been which Goodson made to the stranded derelict: that golden remark; that remark worth forty thousand dollars, cash.

The reason that the village telegraph-office was open later than usual that night was this: The foreman of Cox's paper was the local representative of the Associated Press. One might say its honorary representative, for it wasn't four times a year that he could furnish thirty words that would be accepted. But this time it was different. His despatch stating what he had caught got an instant answer:

"*Send the whole thing—all the details—twelve hundred words.*"

A colossal order! The foreman filled the bill; and he was the proudest man in the State. By breakfast-time the next morning the name of Hadleyburg the Incorruptible was on every lip in America, from Montreal to the Gulf, from the glaciers of Alaska to the orange-groves of Florida; and millions and millions of people were discussing the stranger and his money-sack, and wondering if the right man would be found, and hoping some more news about the matter would come soon—right away.

II.

Hadleyburg village woke up world-celebrated—astonished —happy—vain. Vain beyond imagination. Its nineteen principal citizens and their wives went about shaking hands with each other, and beaming, and smiling, and congratulating, and saying *this* thing adds a new word to the dictionary— *Hadleyburg*, synonym for *incorruptible*—destined to live in dictionaries forever! And the minor and unimportant citizens and their wives went around acting in much the same way. Everybody ran to the bank to see the gold-sack; and before noon grieved and envious crowds began to flock in from Brixton and all neighboring towns; and that afternoon and next day reporters began to arrive from everywhere to verify the sack and its history and write the whole thing up anew, and make dashing free-hand pictures of the sack, and of Richards's house, and the bank, and the Presbyterian church, and the Baptist church, and the public square, and the town-hall where the test would be applied and the money delivered; and damnable portraits of the Richardses, and Pinkerton the banker, and Cox, and the foreman, and Reverend Burgess, and the postmaster—and even of Jack Halliday, who was the loafing, good-natured, no-account, irreverent fisherman, hunter, boys' friend, stray-dogs' friend, typical "Sam Lawson" of the town. The little mean, smirking, oily Pinkerton showed the sack to all comers, and rubbed his sleek palms together pleasantly, and enlarged upon the town's fine old reputation for honesty and upon this wonderful endorsement of it, and hoped and believed that the example would now spread far and wide over the American world, and be epoch-making in the matter of moral regeneration. And so on, and so on.

By the end of a week things had quieted down again; the wild intoxication of pride and joy had sobered to a soft, sweet, silent delight—a sort of deep, nameless, unutterable content. All faces bore a look of peaceful, holy happiness.

Then a change came. It was a gradual change: so gradual that its beginnings were hardly noticed; maybe were not noticed at all, except by Jack Halliday, who always noticed everything; and always made fun of it, too, no matter what it was. He began to throw out chaffing remarks about people not looking quite so happy as they did a day or two ago; and next he claimed that the new aspect was deepening to positive sadness; next, that it was taking on a sick look; and finally he said that everybody was become so moody, thoughtful, and absent-minded that he could rob the meanest man in town of a cent out of the bottom of his breeches pocket and not disturb his revery.

At this stage—or at about this stage—a saying like this was dropped at bedtime—with a sigh, usually—by the head of each of the nineteen principal households:

"Ah, what *could* have been the remark that Goodson made!"

And straightway—with a shudder—came this, from the man's wife:

"Oh, *don't!* What horrible thing are you mulling in your mind? Put it away from you, for God's sake!"

But that question was wrung from those men again the next night—and got the same retort. But weaker.

And the third night the men uttered the question yet again—with anguish, and absently. This time—and the following night—the wives fidgeted feebly, and tried to say something. But didn't.

And the night after that they found their tongues and responded—longingly,

"Oh, if we *could* only guess!"

Halliday's comments grew daily more and more sparklingly disagreeable and disparaging. He went diligently about, laughing at the town, individually and in mass. But his laugh was the only one left in the village: it fell upon a hollow and mournful vacancy and emptiness. Not even a smile was findable anywhere. Halliday carried a cigar-box around on a tripod, playing that it was a camera, and halted all passers and aimed the thing and said, "Ready!—now look pleasant, please," but not even this capital joke could surprise the dreary faces into any softening.

So three weeks passed—one week was left. It was Saturday evening—after supper. Instead of the aforetime Saturday-evening flutter and bustle and shopping and larking, the streets were empty and desolate. Richards and his old wife sat apart in their little parlor—miserable and thinking. This was become their evening habit now: the life-long habit which had preceded it, of reading, knitting, and contented chat, or receiving or paying neighborly calls, was dead and gone and forgotten, ages ago—two or three weeks ago; nobody talked now, nobody read, nobody visited—the whole village sat at home, sighing, worrying, silent. Trying to guess out that remark.

The postman left a letter. Richards glanced listlessly at the superscription and the post-mark—unfamiliar, both—and tossed the letter on the table and resumed his might-have-beens and his hopeless dull miseries where he had left them off. Two or three hours later his wife got wearily up and was going away to bed without a good-night—custom now—but she stopped near the letter and eyed it awhile with a dead interest, then broke it open, and began to skim it over. Richards, sitting there with his chair tilted back against the wall and his chin between his knees, heard something fall. It was his wife. He sprang to her side, but she cried out:

"Leave me alone, I am too happy. Read the letter—read it!"

He did. He devoured it, his brain reeling. The letter was from a distant State, and it said:

"I am a stranger to you, but no matter: I have something to tell. I have just arrived home from Mexico, and learned about that episode.

Of course you do not know who made that remark, but I know, and I am the only person living who does know. It was *Goodson*. I knew him well, many years ago. I passed through your village that very night, and was his guest till the midnight train came along. I overheard him make that remark to the stranger in the dark—it was in Hale Alley. He and I talked of it the rest of the way home, and while smoking in his house. He mentioned many of your villagers in the course of his talk—most of them in a very uncomplimentary way, but two or three favorably: among these latter yourself. I say 'favorably'—nothing stronger. I remember his saying he did not actually *like* any person in the town—not one; but that you—I *think* he said you—am almost sure—had done him a very great service once, possibly without knowing the full value of it, and he wished he had a fortune, he would leave it to you when he died, and a curse apiece for the rest of the citizens. Now, then, if it was you that did him that service, you are his legitimate heir, and entitled to the sack of gold. I know that I can trust to your honor and honesty, for in a citizen of Hadleyburg these virtues are an unfailing inheritance, and so I am going to reveal to you the remark, well satisfied that if you are not the right man you will seek and find the right one and see that poor Goodson's debt of gratitude for the service referred to is paid. This is the remark: '*You are far from being a bad man: go, and reform.*'

HOWARD L. STEPHENSON."

"Oh, Edward, the money is ours, and I am so grateful, *oh*, so grateful—kiss me, dear, it's forever since we kissed—and we needed it so—the money—and now you are free of Pinkerton and his bank, and nobody's slave any more; it seems to me I could fly for joy."

It was a happy half-hour that the couple spent there on the settee caressing each other; it was the old days come again—days that had begun with their courtship and lasted without a break till the stranger brought the deadly money. By-and-by the wife said:

"Oh, Edward, how lucky it was you did him that grand service, poor Goodson! I never liked him, but I love him now. And it was fine and beautiful of you never to mention it or brag about it." Then, with a touch of reproach, "But you ought to have told *me*, Edward, you ought to have told your wife, you know."

"Well, I—er—well, Mary, you see—"

"Now stop hemming and hawing, and tell me about it, Edward. I always loved you, and now I'm proud of you. Everybody believes there was only one good generous soul in this village, and now it turns out that you— Edward, why don't you tell me?"

"Well—er—er— Why, Mary, I can't!"

"You *can't*? *Why* can't you?"

"You see, he—well, he—he made me promise I wouldn't."

The wife looked him over, and said, very slowly,

"Made—you—promise? Edward, what do you tell me that for?"

"Mary, do you think I would lie?"

She was troubled and silent for a moment, then she laid her hand within his and said:

"No . . . . no. We have wandered far enough from our bearings—God spare us that! In all your life you have never uttered a lie. But now—now that the foundations of things seem to be crumbling from under us, we—we—" She lost her voice for a moment, then said, brokenly, "Lead us not into temptation. . . . I think you made the promise, Edward. Let it rest so. Let us keep away from that ground. Now—that is all gone by; let us be happy again; it is no time for clouds."

Edward found it something of an effort to comply, for his mind kept wandering—trying to remember what the service was that he had done Goodson.

The couple lay awake the most of the night, Mary happy and busy, Edward busy, but not so happy. Mary was planning what she would do with the money. Edward was trying to recall that service. At first his conscience was sore on account of the lie he had told Mary—if it was a lie. After much reflection—suppose it *was* a lie? What then? Was it such a great matter? Aren't we always *acting* lies? Then why not *tell* them? Look at Mary—look what she had done. While he was hurrying off on his honest errand, what was she doing? Lamenting because the papers hadn't been destroyed and the money kept! Is theft better than lying?

That point lost its sting—the lie dropped into the background and left comfort behind it. The next point came to the front: *had* he rendered that service? Well, here was Good-

son's own evidence as reported in Stephenson's letter; there
could be no better evidence than that—it was even *proof* that
he had rendered it. Of course. So that point was settled. . . .
No, not quite. He recalled with a wince that this unknown
Mr. Stephenson was just a trifle unsure as to whether the per-
former of it was Richards or some other—and, oh dear, he
had put Richards on his honor! He must himself decide
whither that money must go—and Mr. Stephenson was not
doubting that if he was the wrong man he would go honorably and find the right one. Oh, it was odious to put a man in
such a situation—ah, why couldn't Stephenson have left out
that doubt! What did he want to intrude that for?

Further reflection. How did it happen that *Richards's* name
remained in Stephenson's mind as indicating the right man,
and not some other man's name? That looked good. Yes, that
looked very good. In fact, it went on looking better and better, straight along—until by-and-by it grew into positive
proof. And then Richards put the matter at once out of his
mind, for he had a private instinct that a proof once established is better left so.

He was feeling reasonably comfortable now, but there was
still one other detail that kept pushing itself on his notice: of
course he had done that service—that was settled; but what
was that service? He must recall it—he would not go to sleep
till he had recalled it; it would make his peace of mind
perfect. And so he thought and thought. He thought of a
dozen things—possible services, even probable services—but
none of them seemed adequate, none of them seemed large
enough, none of them seemed worth the money—worth the
fortune Goodson had wished he could leave in his will. And
besides, he couldn't remember having done them, anyway.
Now, then—now, then—what *kind* of a service would it be
that would make a man so inordinately grateful? Ah—the
saving of his soul! That must be it. Yes, he could remember,
now, how he once set himself the task of converting Goodson, and labored at it as much as—he was going to say three
months; but upon closer examination it shrunk to a month,
then to a week, then to a day, then to nothing. Yes, he remembered, now, and with unwelcome vividness, that Goodson had told him to go to thunder and mind his own

business—*he* wasn't hankering to follow Hadleyburg to heaven!

So that solution was a failure—he hadn't saved Goodson's soul. Richards was discouraged. Then after a little came another idea: had he saved Goodson's property? No, that wouldn't do—he hadn't any. His life? That is it! Of course. Why, he might have thought of it before. This time he was on the right track, sure. His imagination-mill was hard at work in a minute, now.

Thereafter during a stretch of two exhausting hours he was busy saving Goodson's life. He saved it in all kinds of difficult and perilous ways. In every case he got it saved satisfactorily up to a certain point; then, just as he was beginning to get well persuaded that it had really happened, a troublesome detail would turn up which made the whole thing impossible. As in the matter of drowning, for instance. In that case he had swum out and tugged Goodson ashore in an unconscious state with a great crowd looking on and applauding, but when he had got it all thought out and was just beginning to remember all about it a whole swarm of disqualifying details arrived on the ground: the town would have known of the circumstance, Mary would have known of it, it would glare like a limelight in his own memory instead of being an inconspicuous service which he had possibly rendered "without knowing its full value." And at this point he remembered that he couldn't swim, anyway.

Ah—*there* was a point which he had been overlooking from the start: it had to be a service which he had rendered "possibly without knowing the full value of it." Why, really, that ought to be an easy hunt—much easier than those others. And sure enough, by-and-by he found it. Goodson, years and years ago, came near marrying a very sweet and pretty girl, named Nancy Hewitt, but in some way or other the match had been broken off; the girl died, Goodson remained a bachelor, and by-and-by became a soured one and a frank despiser of the human species. Soon after the girl's death the village found out, or thought it had found out, that she carried a spoonful of negro blood in her veins. Richards worked at these details a good while, and in the end he thought he remembered things concerning them which must have gotten mislaid in his memory through long neglect. He seemed to dimly remember that it was *he* that found out about the negro blood; that it was he that told the village; that the village told Goodson where they got it; that he thus saved Goodson from marrying the tainted girl; that he had done him this great service "without knowing the full value of it," in fact without knowing that he *was* doing it; but that Goodson knew the value of it, and what a narrow escape he had had, and so went to his grave grateful to his benefactor and wishing he had a fortune to leave him. It was all clear and simple now, and the more he went over it the more luminous and certain it grew; and at last, when he nestled to sleep satisfied and happy, he remembered the whole thing just as if it had been yesterday. In fact, he dimly remembered Goodson's *telling* him his gratitude once. Meantime Mary had spent six thousand dollars on a new house for herself and a pair of slippers for her pastor, and then had fallen peacefully to rest.

That same Saturday evening the postman had delivered a letter to each of the other principal citizens—nineteen letters in all. No two of the envelopes were alike, and no two of the superscriptions were in the same hand, but the letters inside were just like each other in every detail but one. They were exact copies of the letter received by Richards—handwriting and all—and were all signed by Stephenson, but in place of Richards's name each receiver's own name appeared.

All night long eighteen principal citizens did what their caste-brother Richards was doing at the same time—they put in their energies trying to remember what notable service it was that they had unconsciously done Barclay Goodson. In no case was it a holiday job; still they succeeded.

And while they were at this work, which was difficult, their wives put in the night spending the money, which was easy. During that one night the nineteen wives spent an average of seven thousand dollars each out of the forty thousand in the sack—a hundred and thirty-three thousand altogether.

Next day there was a surprise for Jack Halliday. He noticed that the faces of the nineteen chief citizens and their wives bore that expression of peaceful and holy happiness again. He could not understand it, neither was he able to invent any remarks about it that could damage it or disturb it. And so it was his turn to be dissatisfied with life. His private guesses at the reasons for the happiness failed in all instances, upon examination. When he met Mrs. Wilcox and noticed the placid ecstasy in her face, he said to himself, "Her cat has had kittens"—and went and asked the cook; it was not so; the cook had detected the happiness, but did not know the cause. When Halliday found the duplicate ecstasy in the face of "Shadbelly" Billson (village nickname), he was sure some neighbor of Billson's had broken his leg, but inquiry showed that this had not happened. The subdued ecstasy in Gregory Yates's face could mean but one thing—he was a mother-in-law short; it was another mistake. "And Pinkerton—Pinkerton—he has collected ten cents that he thought he was going to lose." And so on, and so on. In some cases the guesses had to remain in doubt, in the others they proved distinct errors. In the end Halliday said to himself, "Anyway it foots up that there's nineteen Hadleyburg families temporarily in heaven; I don't know how it happened; I only know Providence is off duty to-day."

An architect and builder from the next State had lately ventured to set up a small business in this unpromising village, and his sign had now been hanging out a week. Not a customer yet; he was a discouraged man, and sorry he had come. But his weather changed suddenly now. First one and then another chief citizen's wife said to him privately:

"Come to my house Monday week—but say nothing about it for the present. We think of building."

He got eleven invitations that day. That night he wrote his daughter and broke off her match with her student. He said she could marry a mile higher than that.

Pinkerton the banker and two or three other well-to-do men planned country-seats—but waited. That kind don't count their chickens until they are hatched.

The Wilsons devised a grand new thing—a fancy-dress ball. They made no actual promises, but told all their acquaintanceship in confidence that they were thinking the matter over and thought they should give it—"and if we do, you will be invited, of course." People were surprised, and said, one to another, "Why, they are crazy, those poor Wilsons, they can't afford it." Several among the nineteen said privately to their husbands, "It is a good idea; we will keep still till their cheap thing is over, then *we* will give one that will make it sick."

The days drifted along, and the bill of future squanderings rose higher and higher, wilder and wilder, more and more foolish and reckless. It began to look as if every member of the nineteen would not only spend his whole forty thousand dollars before receiving-day, but be actually in debt by the time he got the money. In some cases light-headed people did not stop with planning to spend, they really spent—on credit. They bought land, mortgages, farms, speculative stocks, fine clothes, horses, and various other things, paid down the bonus, and made themselves liable for the rest—at ten days. Presently the sober second thought came, and Halliday noticed that a ghastly anxiety was beginning to show up in a good many faces. Again he was puzzled, and didn't know what to make of it. "The Wilcox kittens aren't dead, for they weren't born; nobody's broken a leg; there's no shrinkage in mother-in-laws; *nothing* has happened—it is an insolvable mystery."

There was another puzzled man, too—the Rev. Mr. Burgess. For days, wherever he went, people seemed to follow him or to be watching out for him; and if he ever found himself in a retired spot, a member of the nineteen would be sure to appear, thrust an envelope privately into his hand, whisper "To be opened at the town-hall Friday evening," then vanish away like a guilty thing. He was expecting that there might be one claimant for the sack—doubtful, however, Goodson being dead—but it never occurred to him that all this crowd might be claimants. When the great Friday came at last, he found that he had nineteen envelopes.

III.

The town-hall had never looked finer. The platform at the end of it was backed by a showy draping of flags; at intervals along the walls were festoons of flags; the gallery fronts were clothed in flags; the supporting columns were swathed in flags; all this was to impress the stranger, for he would be there in considerable force, and in a large degree he would be connected with the press. The house was full. The 412 fixed seats were occupied; also the 68 extra chairs which had been packed into the aisles; the steps of the platform were occupied; some distinguished strangers were given seats on the platform; at the horseshoe of tables which fenced the front and sides of the platform sat a strong force of special correspondents who had come from everywhere. It was the best-dressed house the town had ever produced. There were some tolerably expensive toilets there, and in several cases the ladies who wore them had the look of being unfamiliar with that kind of clothes. At least the town thought they had that look, but the notion could have arisen from the town's knowledge of the fact that these ladies had never inhabited such clothes before.

The gold-sack stood on a little table at the front of the platform where all the house could see it. The bulk of the house gazed at it with a burning interest, a mouth-watering interest, a wistful and pathetic interest; a minority of nineteen couples gazed at it tenderly, lovingly, proprietarily, and the male half of this minority kept saying over to themselves the moving little impromptu speeches of thankfulness for the audience's applause and congratulations which they were presently going to get up and deliver. Every now and then one of these got a piece of paper out of his vest pocket and privately glanced at it to refresh his memory.

Of course there was a buzz of conversation going on— there always is; but at last when the Rev. Mr. Burgess rose and laid his hand on the sack he could hear his microbes gnaw, the place was so still. He related the curious history of the sack, then went on to speak in warm terms of Hadleyburg's old and well-earned reputation for spotless honesty, and of the town's just pride in this reputation. He said that this reputation was a treasure of priceless value; that under Providence its value had now become inestimably enhanced, for the recent episode had spread this fame far and wide, and thus had focussed the eyes of the American world upon this village, and made its name for all time, as he hoped and believed, a synonym for commercial incorruptibility. (*Applause.*) "And who is to be the guardian of this noble treasure—the community as a whole? No! The responsibility is individual, not communal. From this day forth each and every one of you is in his own person its special guardian, and individually responsible that no harm shall come to it. Do you—does each of you—accept this great trust? [*Tumultuous assent.*] Then all is well. Transmit it to your children and to your children's children. To-day your purity is beyond reproach—see to it that it shall remain so. To-day there is not a person in your community who could be beguiled to touch a penny not his own—see to it that you abide in this grace. [*"We will! we will!"*] This is not the place to make comparisons between ourselves and other communities—some of them ungracious toward us; they have their ways, we have ours; let us be content. [*Applause.*] I am done. Under my hand, my friends, rests a stranger's eloquent recognition of what we are; through him the world will always henceforth know what we are. We do not know who he is, but in your name I utter your gratitude, and ask you to raise your voices in indorsement."

The house rose in a body and made the walls quake with the thunders of its thankfulness for the space of a long minute. Then it sat down, and Mr. Burgess took an envelope out of his pocket. The house held its breath while he slit the envelope open and took from it a slip of paper. He read its contents—slowly and impressively—the audience listening with tranced attention to this magic document, each of whose words stood for an ingot of gold:

" 'The remark which I made to the distressed stranger was this: "You are very far from being a bad man; go, and reform." ' " Then he continued: "We shall know in a moment now whether the remark here quoted corresponds with the one concealed in the sack; and if that shall prove to be so—and it undoubtedly will—this sack of gold belongs to a fellow-citizen who will henceforth stand before the nation as the symbol of the special virtue which has made our town famous throughout the land—Mr. Billson!"

The house had gotten itself all ready to burst into the proper tornado of applause; but instead of doing it, it seemed stricken with a paralysis; there was a deep hush for a moment or two, then a wave of whispered murmurs swept the place—of about this tenor: *"Billson!* oh, come, this is *too* thin!

Twenty dollars to a stranger—or *anybody*—*Billson!* Tell it to the marines!" And now at this point the house caught its breath all of a sudden in a new access of astonishment, for it discovered that whereas in one part of the hall Deacon Billson was standing up with his head meekly bowed, in another part of it Lawyer Wilson was doing the same. There was a wondering silence now for a while. Everybody was puzzled, and nineteen couples were surprised and indignant.

Billson and Wilson turned and stared at each other. Billson asked, bitingly,

"Why do *you* rise, Mr. Wilson?"

"Because I have a right to. Perhaps you will be good enough to explain to the house why *you* rise?"

"With great pleasure. Because I wrote that paper."

"It is an impudent falsity! I wrote it myself."

It was Burgess's turn to be paralyzed. He stood looking vacantly at first one of the men and then the other, and did not seem to know what to do. The house was stupefied. Lawyer Wilson spoke up, now, and said,

"I ask the Chair to read the name signed to that paper."

That brought the Chair to itself, and it read out the name,

" 'John Wharton *Billson*.' "

"There!" shouted Billson, "what have you got to say for yourself, now? And what kind of apology are you going to make to me and to this insulted house for the imposture which you have attempted to play here?"

"No apologies are due, sir; and as for the rest of it, I publicly charge you with pilfering my note from Mr. Burgess and substituting a copy of it signed with your own name. There is no other way by which you could have gotten hold of the test-remark; I alone, of living men, possessed the secret of its wording."

There was likely to be a scandalous state of things if this went on; everybody noticed with distress that the short-hand scribes were scribbling like mad; many people were crying "Chair, Chair! Order! order!" Burgess rapped with his gavel, and said:

"Let us not forget the proprieties due. There has evidently been a mistake somewhere, but surely that is all. If Mr.

Wilson gave me an envelope—and I remember now that he did—I still have it."

He took one out of his pocket, opened it, glanced at it, looked surprised and worried, and stood silent a few moments. Then he waved his hand in a wandering and mechanical way, and made an effort or two to say something, then gave it up, despondently. Several voices cried out:

"Read it! read it! What is it?"

So he began in a dazed and sleep-walker fashion:

" '*The remark which I made to the unhappy stranger was this:* "*You are far from being a bad man.* [The house gazed at him, marvelling.] *Go, and reform.*" ' [*Murmurs:* "Amazing! what can this mean?"] This one," said the Chair, "is signed Thurlow G. Wilson."

"There!" cried Wilson, "I reckon that settles it! I knew perfectly well my note was purloined."

"Purloined!" retorted Billson. "I'll let you know that neither you nor any man of your kidney must venture to—"

The Chair. "Order, gentlemen, order! Take your seats, both of you, please."

They obeyed, shaking their heads and grumbling angrily. The house was profoundly puzzled; it did not know what to do with this curious emergency. Presently Thompson got up. Thompson was the hatter. He would have liked to be a Nineteener; but such was not for him; his stock of hats was not considerable enough for the position. He said:

"Mr. Chairman, if I may be permitted to make a suggestion, can both of these gentlemen be right? I put it to you, sir, can both have happened to say the very same words to the stranger? It seems to me—"

The tanner got up and interrupted him. The tanner was a disgruntled man; he believed himself entitled to be a Nineteener, but he couldn't get recognition. It made him a little unpleasant in his ways and speech. Said he:

"Sho, *that's* not the point! *That* could happen—twice in a hundred years—but not the other thing. *Neither* of them gave the twenty dollars!" (*A ripple of applause.*)

Billson. "*I* did!"

Wilson. "*I* did!"

Then each accused the other of pilfering.

The Chair. "Order! Sit down, if you please—both of you. Neither of the notes has been out of my possession at any moment."

A Voice. "Good—that settles *that!*"

The Tanner. "Mr. Chairman, one thing is now plain: one of these men has been eavesdropping under the other one's bed, and filching family secrets. If it is not unparliamentary to suggest it, I will remark that both are equal to it. [*The Chair.* "Order! order!"] I withdraw the remark, sir, and will confine myself to suggesting that *if* one of them has overheard the other reveal the test-remark to his wife, we shall catch him now."

A Voice. "How?"

The Tanner. "Easily. The two have not quoted the remark in exactly the same words. You would have noticed that, if there hadn't been a considerable stretch of time and an exciting quarrel inserted between the two readings."

A Voice. "Name the difference."

The Tanner. "The word *very* is in Billson's note, and not in the other."

Many Voices. "That's so—he's right!"

The Tanner. "And so, if the Chair will examine the test-remark in the sack, we shall know which of these two frauds—[*The Chair.* "Order!"]—which of these two adventures—[*The Chair.* "Order! order!"]—which of these two gentlemen—[*laughter and applause*]—is entitled to wear the belt as being the first dishonest blatherskite ever bred in this town—which he has dishonored, and which will be a sultry place for him from now out!" (*Vigorous applause.*)

Many Voices. "Open it!—open the sack!"

Mr. Burgess made a slit in the sack, slid his hand in and brought out an envelope. In it were a couple of folded notes. He said:

"One of these is marked, 'Not to be examined until all written communications which have been addressed to the Chair—if any—shall have been read.' The other is marked 'The Test.' Allow me. It is worded—to wit:

" 'I do not require that the first half of the remark which was made to me by my benefactor shall be quoted with exactness, for it was not striking, and could be forgotten; but its closing fifteen words are quite striking, and I think easily re-memberable; unless *these* shall be accurately reproduced, let the applicant be regarded as an impostor. My benefactor be-gan by saying he seldom gave advice to any one, but that it always bore the hall-mark of high value when he did give it. Then he said this—and it has never faded from my memory: *"You are far from being a bad man—"' "*

Fifty Voices. "That settles it—the money's Wilson's! Wil-son! Wilson! Speech! Speech!"

People jumped up and crowded around Wilson, wringing his hand and congratulating fervently—meantime the Chair was hammering with the gavel and shouting:

"Order, gentlemen! Order! Order! Let me finish reading, please." When quiet was restored, the reading was resumed— as follows:

" ' *"Go, and reform—or, mark my words—some day, for your sins, you will die and go to hell or Hadleyburg*—TRY AND MAKE IT THE FORMER.*"' "*

A ghastly silence followed. First an angry cloud began to settle darkly upon the faces of the citizenship; after a pause the cloud began to rise, and a tickled expression tried to take its place; tried so hard that it was only kept under with great and painful difficulty; the reporters, the Brixtonites, and other strangers bent their heads down and shielded their faces with their hands, and managed to hold in by main strength and heroic courtesy. At this most inopportune time burst upon the stillness the roar of a solitary voice—Jack Halliday's:

"*That's* got the hall-mark on it!"

Then the house let go, strangers and all. Even Mr. Bur-gess's gravity broke down presently, then the audience con-sidered itself officially absolved from all restraint, and it made the most of its privilege. It was a good long laugh, and a tempestuously whole-hearted one, but it ceased at last—long enough for Mr. Burgess to try to resume, and for the people to get their eyes partially wiped; then it broke out again; and afterward yet again; then at last Burgess was able to get out these serious words:

"It is useless to try to disguise the fact—we find ourselves in the presence of a matter of grave import. It involves the honor of your town, it strikes at the town's good name. The difference of a single word between the test-remarks offered by Mr. Wilson and Mr. Billson was itself a serious thing, since it indicated that one or the other of these gentlemen had committed a theft—"

The two men were sitting limp, nerveless, crushed; but at these words both were electrified into movement, and started to get up—

"Sit down!" said the Chair, sharply, and they obeyed. "That, as I have said, was a serious thing. And it was—but for only one of them. But the matter has become graver; for the honor of *both* is now in formidable peril. Shall I go even further, and say in inextricable peril? *Both* left out the crucial fifteen words." He paused. During several moments he allowed the pervading stillness to gather and deepen its impressive effects, then added: "There would seem to be but one way whereby this could happen. I ask these gentlemen—Was there *collusion?—agreement?*"

A low murmur sifted through the house; its import was, "He's got them both."

Billson was not used to emergencies; he sat in a helpless collapse. But Wilson was a lawyer. He struggled to his feet, pale and worried, and said:

"I ask the indulgence of the house while I explain this most painful matter. I am sorry to say what I am about to say, since it must inflict irreparable injury upon Mr. Billson, whom I have always esteemed and respected until now, and in whose invulnerability to temptation I entirely believed—as did you all. But for the preservation of my own honor I must speak—and with frankness. I confess with shame—and I now beseech your pardon for it—that I said to the ruined stranger all of the words contained in the test-remark, including the disparaging fifteen. [*Sensation.*] When the late publication was made I recalled them, and I resolved to claim the sack of coin, for by every right I was entitled to it. Now I will ask you to consider this point, and weigh it well: that stranger's gratitude to me that night knew no bounds; he said himself that he could find no words for it that were adequate, and that if he should ever be able he would repay me a thousandfold. Now, then, I ask you this: could I expect—could I believe—

could I even remotely imagine—that, feeling as he did, he would do so ungrateful a thing as to add those quite unnecessary fifteen words to his test?—set a trap for me?—expose me as a slanderer of my own town before my own people assembled in a public hall? It was preposterous; it was impossible. His test would contain only the kindly opening clause of my remark. Of that I had no shadow of doubt. You would have thought as I did. You would not have expected a base betrayal from one whom you had befriended and against whom you had committed no offence. And so, with perfect confidence, perfect trust, I wrote on a piece of paper the opening words—ending with 'Go, and reform,'—and signed it. When I was about to put it in an envelope I was called into my back office, and without thinking I left the paper lying open on my desk." He stopped, turned his head slowly toward Billson, waited a moment, then added: "I ask you to note this: when I returned, a little later, Mr. Billson was retiring by my street door." (*Sensation.*)

In a moment Billson was on his feet and shouting:

"It's a lie! It's an infamous lie!"

The Chair. "Be seated, sir! Mr. Wilson has the floor."

Billson's friends pulled him into his seat and quieted him, and Wilson went on:

"Those are the simple facts. My note was now lying in a different place on the table from where I had left it. I noticed that, but attached no importance to it, thinking a draught had blown it there. That Mr. Billson would read a private paper was a thing which could not occur to me; he was an honorable man, and he would be above that. If you will allow me to say it, I think his extra word '*very*' stands explained; it is attributable to a defect of memory. I was the only man in the world who could furnish here any detail of the test-mark—by *honorable* means. I have finished."

There is nothing in the world like a persuasive speech to fuddle the mental apparatus and upset the convictions and debauch the emotions of an audience not practised in the tricks and delusions of oratory. Wilson sat down victorious. The house submerged him in tides of approving applause; friends swarmed to him and shook him by the hand and congratulated him, and Billson was shouted down and not allowed to say a word. The Chair hammered and hammered with its gavel, and kept shouting,

"But let us proceed, gentlemen, let us proceed!"

At last there was a measurable degree of quiet, and the hatter said,

"But what is there to proceed with, sir, but to deliver the money?"

Voices. "That's it! That's it! Come forward, Wilson!"

The Hatter. "I move three cheers for Mr. Wilson, Symbol of the special virtue which——"

The cheers burst forth before he could finish; and in the midst of them—and in the midst of the clamor of the gavel also—some enthusiasts mounted Wilson on a big friend's shoulder and were going to fetch him in triumph to the platform. The Chair's voice now rose above the noise—

"Order! To your places! You forget that there is still a document to be read." When quiet had been restored he took up the document, and was going to read it, but laid it down again, saying, "I forgot; this is not to be read until all written communications received by me have first been read." He took an envelope out of his pocket, removed its enclosure, glanced at it—seemed astonished—held it out and gazed at it—stared at it.

Twenty or thirty voices cried out:

"What is it? Read it! read it!"

And he did—slowly, and wondering:

" 'The remark which I made to the stranger—[*Voices.* "Hello! how's this?"]—was this: "You are far from being a bad man. [*Voices.* "Great Scott!"] Go, and reform." ' [*Voice.* "Oh, saw my leg off!"] Signed by Mr. Pinkerton the banker."

The pandemonium of delight which turned itself loose now was of a sort to make the judicious weep. Those whose withers were unwrung laughed till the tears ran down; the reporters, in throes of laughter, set down disordered pothooks which would never in the world be decipherable; and a sleeping dog jumped up, scared out of its wits, and barked itself crazy at the turmoil. All manner of cries were scattered through the din: "We're getting rich—*two* Symbols of Incorruptibility!—without counting Billson!" "*Three!*—count

Shadbelly in—we can't have too many!" "All right—Billson's elected!" "Alas, poor Wilson—victim of *two* thieves!"

A Powerful Voice. "Silence! The Chair's fished up something more out of its pocket."

Voices. "Hurrah! Is it something fresh? Read it! read! read!"

The Chair (*reading*). " 'The remark which I made,' etc. 'You are far from being a bad man. Go,' etc. Signed, 'Gregory Yates.' "

Tornado of Voices. "Four Symbols!" " 'Rah for Yates!" "Fish again!"

The house was in a roaring humor now, and ready to get all the fun out of the occasion that might be in it. Several Nineteeners, looking pale and distressed, got up and began to work their way toward the aisles, but a score of shouts went up:

"The doors, the doors—close the doors; no Incorruptible shall leave this place! Sit down, everybody!"

The mandate was obeyed.

"Fish again! Read! read!"

The Chair fished again, and once more the familiar words began to fall from its lips—" 'You are far from being a bad man—' "

"Name! name! What's his name?"

" 'L. Ingoldsby Sargent.' "

"Five elected! Pile up the Symbols! Go on, go on!"

" 'You are far from being a bad—' "

"Name! name!"

" 'Nicholas Whitworth.' "

"Hooray! hooray! it's a symbolical day!"

Somebody wailed in, and began to sing this rhyme (leaving out "it's") to the lovely *Mikado* tune of "When a man's afraid of a beautiful maid"; the audience joined in, with joy; then, just in time, somebody contributed another line—

"And don't you this forget—"

The house roared it out. A third line was at once furnished—

"Corruptibles far from Hadleyburg are—"

The house roared that one too. As the last note died, Jack

Halliday's voice rose high and clear, freighted with a final line—

"But the Symbols are here, you bet!"

That was sung, with booming enthusiasm. Then the happy house started in at the beginning and sang the four lines through twice, with immense swing and dash, and finished up with a crashing three-times-three and a tiger for "Hadleyburg the Incorruptible and all Symbols of it which we shall find worthy to receive the hall-mark to-night."

Then the shoutings at the Chair began again, all over the place:

"Go on! go on! Read! read some more! Read all you've got!"

"That's it—go on! We are winning eternal celebrity!"

A dozen men got up now and began to protest. They said that this farce was the work of some abandoned joker, and was an insult to the whole community. Without a doubt these signatures were all forgeries—

"Sit down! sit down! Shut up! You are confessing. We'll find *your* names in the lot."

"Mr. Chairman, how many of those envelopes have you got?"

The Chair counted.

"Together with those that have been already examined, there are nineteen."

A storm of derisive applause broke out.

"Perhaps they all contain the secret. I move that you open them all and read every signature that is attached to a note of that sort—and read also the first eight words of the note."

"Second the motion!"

It was put and carried—uproariously. Then poor old Richards got up, and his wife rose and stood at his side. Her head was bent down, so that none might see that she was crying. Her husband gave her his arm, and so supporting her, he began to speak in a quavering voice:

"My friends, you have known us two—Mary and me—all our lives, and I think you have liked us and respected us—"

The Chair interrupted him:

"Allow me. It is quite true—that which you are saying,

Mr. Richards; this town *does* know you two; it *does* like you; it *does* respect you; more—it honors you and *loves* you—"

Halliday's voice rang out:

"That's the hall-marked truth, too! If the Chair is right, let the house speak up and say it. Rise! Now, then—hip! hip! hip!—all together!"

The house rose in mass, faced toward the old couple eagerly, filled the air with a snow-storm of waving handkerchiefs, and delivered the cheers with all its affectionate heart.

The Chair then continued:

"What I was going to say is this: We know your good heart, Mr. Richards, but this is not a time for the exercise of charity toward offenders. [Shouts of "Right! right!"] I see your generous purpose in your face, but I cannot allow you to plead for these men—"

"But I was going to—"

"Please take your seat, Mr. Richards. We must examine the rest of these notes—simple fairness to the men who have already been exposed requires this. As soon as that has been done—I give you my word for this—you shall be heard."

Many Voices. "Right!—the Chair is right—no interruption can be permitted at this stage! Go on!—the names! the names!—according to the terms of the motion!"

The old couple sat reluctantly down, and the husband whispered to the wife, "It is pitifully hard to have to wait; the shame will be greater than ever when they find we were only going to plead for *ourselves*."

Straightway the jollity broke loose again with the reading of the names.

" 'You are far from being a bad man—' Signature, 'Robert J. Titmarsh.'

" 'You are far from being a bad man—' Signature, 'Eliphalet Weeks.'

" 'You are far from being a bad man—' Signature, 'Oscar B. Wilder.' "

At this point the house lit upon the idea of taking the eight words out of the Chairman's hands. He was not unthankful for that. Thenceforward he held up each note in its turn, and waited. The house droned out the eight words in a massed

and measured and musical deep volume of sound (with a daringly close resemblance to a well-known church chant)—
" 'You are f-a-r from being a b-a-a-a-d man.' " Then the Chair said, "Signature, 'Archibald Wilcox.' " And so on, and so on, name after name, and everybody had an increasingly and gloriously good time except the wretched Nineteen. Now and then, when a particularly shining name was called, the house made the Chair wait while it chanted the whole of the test-remark from the beginning to the closing words, "And go to hell or Hadleyburg—try and make it the for-or-m-e-r!" and in these special cases they added a grand and agonized and imposing "A-a-a-a-*men*!"

The list dwindled, dwindled, dwindled, poor old Richards keeping tally of the count, wincing when a name resembling his own was pronounced, and waiting in miserable suspense for the time to come when it would be his humiliating privilege to rise with Mary and finish his plea, which he was intending to word thus: ". . . for until now we have never done any wrong thing, but have gone our humble way unreproached. We are very poor, we are old, and have no chick nor child to help us; we were sorely tempted, and we fell. It was my purpose when I got up before to make confession and beg that my name might not be read out in this public place, for it seemed to us that we could not bear it; but I was prevented. It was just; it was our place to suffer with the rest. It has been hard for us. It is the first time we have ever heard our name fall from any one's lips—sullied. Be merciful—for the sake of the better days; make our shame as light to bear as in your charity you can." At this point in his revery Mary nudged him, perceiving that his mind was absent. The house was chanting, "You are f-a-r," etc.

"Be ready," Mary whispered. "Your name comes now; he has read eighteen."

The chant ended.

"Next! next! next!" came volleying from all over the house.

Burgess put his hand into his pocket. The old couple, trembling, began to rise. Burgess fumbled a moment, then said,

"I find I have read them all."

Faint with joy and surprise, the couple sank into their seats, and Mary whispered,

"Oh, bless God, we are saved!—he has lost ours—I wouldn't give this for a hundred of those sacks!"

The house burst out with its *Mikado* travesty, and sang it three times with ever-increasing enthusiasm, rising to its feet when it reached for the third time the closing line—

"But the Symbols are here, you bet!"

and finishing up with cheers and a tiger for "Hadleyburg purity and our eighteen immortal representatives of it."

Then Wingate, the saddler, got up and proposed cheers "for the cleanest man in town, the one solitary important citizen in it who didn't try to steal that money—Edward Richards."

They were given with great and moving heartiness; then somebody proposed that Richards be elected sole Guardian and Symbol of the now Sacred Hadleyburg Tradition, with power and right to stand up and look the whole sarcastic world in the face.

Passed, by acclamation; then they sang the *Mikado* again, and ended it with,

"And there's *one* Symbol left, you bet!"

There was a pause; then—

A Voice. "Now, then, who's to get the sack?"

The Tanner (with bitter sarcasm). "That's easy. The money has to be divided among the eighteen Incorruptibles. They gave the suffering stranger twenty dollars apiece—and that remark—each in his turn—it took twenty-two minutes for the procession to move past. Staked the stranger—total contribution, $360. All they want is just the loan back—and interest—forty thousand dollars altogether."

Many Voices (derisively). "That's it! Divvy! divvy! Be kind to the poor—don't keep them waiting!"

The Chair. "Order! I now offer the stranger's remaining document. It says: 'If no claimant shall appear [*grand chorus of groans*], I desire that you open the sack and count out the money to the principal citizens of your town, they to take it in trust [*Cries of "Oh! Oh! Oh!"*], and use it in such ways as to them shall seem best for the propagation and preservation of your community's noble reputation for incorruptible honesty [*more cries*]—a reputation to which their names and their efforts will add a new and far-reaching lustre.' [*Enthusiastic outburst of sarcastic applause.*] That seems to be all. No—here is a postscript:

" 'P. S.—CITIZENS OF HADLEYBURG: There *is* no test-remark—nobody made one. [*Great sensation.*] There wasn't any pauper stranger, nor any twenty-dollar contribution, nor any accompanying benediction and compliment—these are all inventions. [*General buzz and hum of astonishment and delight.*] Allow me to tell my story—it will take but a word or two. I passed through your town at a certain time, and received a deep offence which I had not earned. Any other man would have been content to kill one or two of you and call it square, but to me that would have been a trivial revenge, and inadequate; for the dead do not *suffer*. Besides, I could not kill you all—and, anyway, made as I am, even that would not have satisfied me. I wanted to damage every man in the place, and every woman—and not in their bodies or in their estate, but in their vanity—the place where feeble and foolish people are most vulnerable. So I disguised myself, and came back and studied you. You were easy game. You had an old and lofty reputation for honesty, and naturally you were proud of it—it was your treasure of treasures, the very apple of your eye. As soon as I found out that you carefully and vigilantly kept yourselves and your children *out of temptation*, I knew how to proceed. Why, you simple creatures, the weakest of all weak things is a virtue which has not been tested in the fire. I laid a plan, and gathered a list of names. My project was to corrupt Hadleyburg the Incorruptible. My idea was to make liars and thieves of nearly half a hundred smirchless men and women who had never in their lives uttered a lie or stolen a penny. I was afraid of Goodson. He was neither born nor reared in Hadleyburg. I was afraid that if I started to operate my scheme by getting my letter laid before you, you would say to yourselves, "Goodson is the only man among us who would give away twenty dollars to a poor devil"—and then you might not bite at my bait. But Heaven took Goodson; then I knew I was safe, and I set my trap and baited it. It may be that I shall not catch all the men to whom I mailed the pretended test secret, but I shall catch the most of them, if I know Hadleyburg nature. [*Voices.* "Right—he got every last one of them."] I believe they will even steal ostensible *gamble-*money, rather than miss, poor, tempted, and mistrained fellows. I am hoping to eternally and everlastingly squelch your vanity and give Hadleyburg a new renown—one that will *stick*—and spread far. If I have succeeded, open the sack and summon the Committee on Propagation and Preservation of the Hadleyburg Reputation.' "

A Cyclone of Voices. "Open it! Open it! The Eighteen to the front! Committee on Propagation of the Tradition! Forward—the Incorruptibles!"

The Chair ripped the sack wide, and gathered up a handful of bright, broad, yellow coins, shook them together, then examined them—

"Friends, they are only gilded disks of lead!"

There was a crashing outbreak of delight over this news, and when the noise had subsided, the tanner called out:

"By right of apparent seniority in this business, Mr. Wilson is Chairman of the Committee on Propagation of the Tradition. I suggest that he step forward on behalf of his pals, and receive in trust the money."

A Hundred Voices. "Wilson! Wilson! Wilson! Speech! Speech!"

Wilson (*in a voice trembling with anger*). "You will allow me to say, and without apologies for my language, *damn* the money!"

A Voice. "Oh, and him a Baptist!"

A Voice. "Seventeen Symbols left! Step up, gentlemen, and assume your trust!"

There was a pause—no response.

The Saddler. "Mr. Chairman, we've got *one* clean man left, anyway, out of the late aristocracy; and he needs money, and deserves it. I move that you appoint Jack Halliday to get up there and auction off that sack of gilt twenty-dollar pieces, and give the result to the right man—the man whom Hadleyburg delights to honor—Edward Richards."

This was received with great enthusiasm, the dog taking a hand again; the saddler started the bids at a dollar, the Brixton folk and Barnum's representative fought hard for it, the people cheered every jump that the bids made, the excitement climbed moment by moment higher and higher, the bidders got on their mettle and grew steadily more and more daring, more and more determined, the jumps went from a dollar up to five, then to ten, then to twenty, then fifty, then to a hundred, then—

At the beginning of the auction Richards whispered in distress to his wife: "Oh, Mary, can we allow it? It—it—you see, it is an honor-reward, a testimonial to purity of character, and—and—can we allow it? Hadn't I better get up and—Oh, Mary, what ought we to do?—what do you think we—" (*Halliday's voice. "Fifteen I'm bid!—fifteen for the sack!—twenty!—ah, thanks!—thirty—thanks again! Thirty, thirty, thirty!—do I hear forty?—forty it is! Keep the ball rolling, gentlemen, keep it rolling!—fifty!—thanks, noble Roman!—going at fifty, fifty, fifty!—seventy!—ninety!—splendid!—a hundred!—pile it up, pile it up!—hundred and twenty—forty!—just in time!—hundred and fifty!—*TWO *hundred!—superb! Do I hear two h—thanks!—two hundred and fifty!—*")

"It is another temptation, Edward—I'm all in a tremble—but, oh, we've escaped *one* temptation, and that ought to warn us, to— [*"Six did I hear?—thanks!—six fifty, six f—*SEVEN *hundred!"*] And yet, Edward, when you think—nobody susp— [*"Eight hundred dollars!—hurrah!—make it nine!—Mr. Parsons, did I hear you say—thanks!—nine!—this noble sack of virgin lead going at only nine hundred dollars, gilding and all—come! do I hear—a thousand!—gratefully yours!—did some one say eleven?—a sack which is going to be the most celebrated in the whole Uni—"*] Oh, Edward" (beginning to sob), "we are *so* poor!—but—but—do as you think best—do as you think best."

Edward fell—that is, he sat still; sat with a conscience which was not satisfied, but which was overpowered by circumstances.

Meantime a stranger, who looked like an amateur detective gotten up as an impossible English earl, had been watching the evening's proceedings with manifest interest, and with a contented expression in his face; and he had been privately commenting to himself. He was now soliloquizing somewhat like this: "None of the Eighteen are bidding; that is not satisfactory; I must change that—the dramatic unities require it; they must buy the sack they tried to steal; they must pay a heavy price, too—some of them are rich. And another thing, when I make a mistake in Hadleyburg nature the man that puts that error upon me is entitled to a high honorarium, and some one must pay it. This poor old Richards has brought my judgment to shame; he is an honest man:—I don't understand it, but I acknowledge it. Yes, he saw my deuces-*and* with a straight flush, and by rights the pot is his. And it shall be a jack-pot, too, if I can manage it. He disappointed me, but let that pass."

He was watching the bidding. At a thousand, the market broke; the prices tumbled swiftly. He waited—and still watched. One competitor dropped out; then another, and another. He put in a bid or two, now. When the bids had sunk to ten dollars, he added a five; some one raised him a three; he waited a moment, then flung in a fifty-dollar jump, and the sack was his—at $1282. The house broke out in cheers—then stopped; for he was on his feet, and had lifted his hand. He began to speak.

"I desire to say a word, and ask a favor. I am a speculator in rarities, and I have dealings with persons interested in numismatics all over the world. I can make a profit on this purchase, just as it stands; but there is a way, if I can get your approval, whereby I can make every one of these leaden twenty-dollar pieces worth its face in gold, and perhaps more. Grant me that approval, and I will give part of my gains to your Mr. Richards, whose invulnerable probity you have so justly and so cordially recognized to-night; his share shall be ten thousand dollars, and I will hand him the money to-morrow. [*Great applause from the house*. But the "invulnerable probity" made the Richardses blush prettily; however, it went for modesty, and did no harm.] If you will pass my proposition by a good majority—I would like a two-thirds vote—I will regard that as the town's consent, and that is all I ask. Rarities are always helped by any device which will rouse curiosity and compel remark. Now if I may have your permission to stamp upon the faces of each of these ostensible coins the names of the eighteen gentlemen who—"

Nine-tenths of the audience were on their feet in a moment—dog and all—and the proposition was carried with a whirlwind of approving applause and laughter.

They sat down, and all the Symbols except "Dr." Clay Harkness got up, violently protesting against the proposed outrage, and threatening to—

"I beg you not to threaten me," said the stranger, calmly. "I know my legal rights, and am not accustomed to being frightened at bluster." (*Applause.*) He sat down. "Dr." Harkness saw an opportunity here. He was one of the two very rich men of the place, and Pinkerton was the other. Harkness was proprietor of a mint; that is to say, a popular patent medicine. He was running for the Legislature on one ticket, and Pinkerton on the other. It was a close race and a hot one, and getting hotter every day. Both had strong appetites for money; each had bought a great tract of land, with a purpose: there was going to be a new railway, and each wanted to be in the Legislature and help locate the route to his own advantage; a single vote might make the decision, and with it two or three fortunes. The stake was large, and Harkness was a daring speculator. He was sitting close to the stranger. He leaned over while one or another of the other Symbols was entertaining the house with protests and appeals, and asked, in a whisper,

"What is your price for the sack?"

"Forty thousand dollars."

"I'll give you twenty."

"No."

"Twenty-five."

"No."

"Say thirty."

"The price is forty thousand dollars; not a penny less."

"All right, I'll give it. I will come to the hotel at ten in the morning. I don't want it known; will see you privately."

"Very good." Then the stranger got up and said to the house:

"I find it late. The speeches of these gentlemen are not without merit, not without interest, not without grace; yet if I may be excused I will take my leave. I thank you for the great favor which you have shown me in granting my petition.

I ask the Chair to keep the sack for me until to-morrow, and to hand these three five-hundred dollar notes to Mr. Richards." They were passed up to the Chair. "At nine I will call for the sack, and at eleven will deliver the rest of the ten thousand to Mr. Richards in person, at his home. Good-night."

Then he slipped out, and left the audience making a vast noise, which was composed of a mixture of cheers, the *Mikado* song, dog-disapproval, and the chant, "You are f-a-r from being a b-a-a-d man—a-a-a-a-men!"

IV.

At home the Richardses had to endure congratulations and compliments until midnight. Then they were left to themselves. They looked a little sad, and they sat silent and thinking. Finally Mary sighed and said,

"Do you think we are to blame, Edward—*much* to blame?" and her eyes wandered to the accusing triplet of big bank-notes lying on the table, where the congratulators had been gloating over them and reverently fingering them. Edward did not answer at once; then he brought out a sigh and said, hesitatingly:

"We—we couldn't help it, Mary. It—well, it was ordered. *All* things are."

Mary glanced up and looked at him steadily, but he didn't return the look. Presently she said:

"I thought congratulations and praises always tasted good. But—it seems to me, now—Edward?"

"Well?"

"Are you going to stay in the bank?"

"N-no."

"Resign?"

"In the morning—by note."

"It does seem best."

Richards bowed his head in his hands and muttered:

"Before, I was not afraid to let oceans of people's money pour through my hands, but—Mary, I am so tired, so tired—"

"We will go to bed."

At nine in the morning the stranger called for the sack and took it to the hotel in a cab. At ten Harkness had a talk with him privately. The stranger asked for and got five checks on a metropolitan bank—drawn to "Bearer,"—four for $1500 each, and one for $34,000. He put one of the former in his pocket-book, and the remainder, representing $38,500, he put in an envelope, and with these he added a note, which he wrote after Harkness was gone. At eleven he called at the Richards house and knocked. Mrs. Richards peeped through the shutters, then went and received the envelope, and the stranger disappeared without a word. She came back flushed and a little unsteady on her legs, and gasped out:

"I am sure I recognized him! Last night it seemed to me that maybe I had seen him somewhere before."

"He is the man that brought the sack here?"

"I am almost sure of it."

"Then he is the ostensible Stephenson too, and sold every important citizen in this town with his bogus secret. Now if he has sent checks instead of money, we are sold too, after we thought we had escaped. I was beginning to feel fairly comfortable once more, after my night's rest, but the look of that envelope makes me sick. It isn't fat enough; $8500 in even the largest bank-notes makes more bulk than that."

"Edward, why do you object to checks?"

"Checks signed by Stephenson! I am resigned to take the $8500 if it could come in bank-notes—for it does seem that it was so ordered, Mary—but I have never had much courage, and I have not the pluck to try to market a check signed with that disastrous name. It would be a trap. That man tried to catch me; we escaped somehow or other; and now he is trying a new way. If it is checks—"

"Oh, Edward, it is *too* bad!" and she held up the checks and began to cry.

"Put them in the fire! quick! we mustn't be tempted. It is a trick to make the world laugh at *us*, along with the rest, and— Give them to *me*, since you can't do it!" He snatched them and tried to hold his grip till he could get to the stove; but he was human, he was a cashier, and he stopped a moment to make sure of the signature. Then he came near to fainting.

"Fan me, Mary, fan me! They are the same as gold!"

"Oh, how lovely, Edward! Why?"

"Signed by Harkness. What can the mystery of that be, Mary?"

"Edward, do you think——"

"Look here—look at this! Fifteen—fifteen—fifteen—thirty-four. Thirty-eight thousand five hundred! Mary, the sack isn't worth twelve dollars, and Harkness—apparently—has paid about par for it."

"And does it all come to us, do you think—instead of the ten thousand?"

"Why, it looks like it. And the checks are made to 'Bearer,' too."

"Is that good, Edward? What is it for?"

"A hint to collect them at some distant bank, I reckon. Perhaps Harkness doesn't want the matter known. What is that—a note?"

"Yes. It was with the checks."

It was in the "Stephenson" handwriting, but there was no signature. It said:

"I am a disappointed man. Your honesty is beyond the reach of temptation. I had a different idea about it, but I wronged you in that, and I beg pardon, and do it sincerely. I honor you—and that is sincere, too. This town is not worthy to kiss the hem of your garment. Dear sir, I made a square bet with myself that there were nineteen debauchable men in your self-righteous community. I have lost. Take the whole pot, you are entitled to it."

Richards drew a deep sigh, and said:

"It seems written with fire—it burns so. Mary—I am miserable again."

"I, too. Ah, dear, I wish——"

"To think, Mary—he *believes* in me."

"Oh, don't, Edward—I can't bear it."

"If those beautiful words were deserved, Mary—and God knows I believed I deserved them once—I think I could give the forty thousand dollars for them. And I would put that paper away, as representing more than gold and jewels, and keep it always. But now—— We could not live in the shadow of its accusing presence, Mary."

He put it in the fire.

A messenger arrived and delivered an envelope. Richards took from it a note and read it; it was from Burgess.

"You saved me, in a difficult time. I saved you last night. It was at cost of a lie, but I made the sacrifice freely, and out of a grateful heart. None in this village knows so well as I know how brave and good and noble you are. At bottom you cannot respect me, knowing as you do of that matter of which I am accused, and by the general voice condemned; but I beg that you will at least believe that I am a grateful man; it will help me to bear my burden.

[Signed]   BURGESS."

"Saved, once more. And on such terms!" He put the note in the fire. "I—I wish I were dead, Mary, I wish I were out of it all."

"Oh, these are bitter, bitter days, Edward. The stabs, through their very generosity, are so deep—and they come so fast!"

Three days before the election each of two thousand voters suddenly found himself in possession of a prized memento—one of the renowned bogus double-eagles. Around one of its faces was stamped these words: "THE REMARK I MADE TO THE POOR STRANGER WAS—" Around the other face was stamped these: "GO, AND REFORM. (SIGNED) PINKERTON." Thus the entire remaining refuse of the renowned joke was emptied upon a single head, and with calamitous effect. It revived the recent vast laugh and concentrated it upon Pinkerton; and Harkness's election was a walk-over.

Within twenty-four hours after the Richardses had received their checks their consciences were quieting down, discouraged; the old couple were learning to reconcile themselves to the sin which they had committed. But they were to learn, now, that a sin takes on new and real terrors when there seems a chance that it is going to be found out. This gives it a fresh and most substantial and important aspect. At church the morning sermon was of the usual pattern; it was the same old things said in the same old way; they had heard them a thousand times and found them innocuous, next to meaningless, and easy to sleep under; but now it was different: the sermon seemed to bristle with accusations; it seemed aimed straight and specially at people who were concealing deadly sins. After church they got away from the mob of congratulators as soon as they could, and hurried homeward, chilled to the bone at they did not know what— vague, shadowy, indefinite fears. And by chance they caught a glimpse of Mr. Burgess as he turned a corner. He paid no attention to their nod of recognition! He hadn't seen it; but they did not know that. What could his conduct mean? It might mean—it might mean—oh, a dozen dreadful things. Was it possible that he knew that Richards could have cleared him of guilt in that bygone time, and had been silently waiting for a chance to even up accounts? At home, in their distress they got to imagining that their servant might have been in the next room listening when Richards revealed the secret to his wife that he knew of Burgess's innocence; next, Richards began to imagine that he had heard the swish of a gown in there at that time; next, he was sure he *had* heard it. They would call Sarah in, on a pretext, and watch her face; if she had been betraying them to Mr. Burgess, it would show in her manner. They asked her some questions—questions which were so random and incoherent and seemingly purposeless that the girl felt sure that the old people's minds had been affected by their sudden good fortune; the sharp and watchful gaze which they bent upon her frightened her, and that completed the business. She blushed, she became nervous and confused, and to the old people these were plain signs of guilt—guilt of some fearful sort or other—without doubt she was a spy and a traitor. When they were alone again they began to piece many unrelated things together and get horrible results out of the combination. When things had got about to the worst, Richards was delivered of a sudden gasp, and his wife asked,

"Oh, what is it?—what is it?"

"The note—Burgess's note! Its language was sarcastic, I see it now." He quoted: " 'At bottom you cannot respect me, *knowing*, as you do, of *that matter* of which I am accused'— oh, it is perfectly plain, now, God help me! He knows that I know! You see the ingenuity of the phrasing. It was a trap—and like a fool, I walked into it. And Mary—?"

"Oh, it is dreadful—I know what you are going to say—he didn't return your transcript of the pretended test-remark."

"No—kept it to destroy us with. Mary, he has exposed us to some already. I know it—I know it well. I saw it in a dozen faces after church. Ah, he wouldn't answer our nod of recognition—*he* knew what he had been doing!"

In the night the doctor was called. The news went around in the morning that the old couple were rather seriously ill—prostrated by the exhausting excitement growing out of their great windfall, the congratulations, and the late hours, the doctor said. The town was sincerely distressed; for these old people were about all it had left to be proud of, now.

Two days later the news was worse. The old couple were delirious, and were doing strange things. By witness of the nurses, Richards had exhibited checks—for $8500? No—for an amazing sum—$38,500! What could be the explanation of this gigantic piece of luck?

The following day the nurses had more news—and wonderful. They had concluded to hide the checks, lest harm come to them; but when they searched they were gone from under the patient's pillow—vanished away. The patient said:

"Let the pillow alone; what do you want?"

"We thought it best that the checks—"

"You will never see them again—they are destroyed. They came from Satan. I saw the hell-brand on them, and I knew they were sent to betray me to sin." Then he fell to gabbling strange and dreadful things which were not clearly understandable, and which the doctor admonished them to keep to themselves.

Richards was right; the checks were never seen again.

A nurse must have talked in her sleep, for within two days the forbidden gabblings were the property of the town; and they were of a surprising sort. They seemed to indicate that Richards had been a claimant for the sack himself, and that Burgess had concealed that fact and then maliciously betrayed it.

Burgess was taxed with this and stoutly denied it. And he

said it was not fair to attach weight to the chatter of a sick old man who was out of his mind. Still, suspicion was in the air, and there was much talk.

After a day or two it was reported that Mrs. Richards's delirious deliveries were getting to be duplicates of her husband's. Suspicion flamed up into conviction, now, and the town's pride in the purity of its one undiscredited important citizen began to dim down and flicker toward extinction.

Six days passed, then came more news. The old couple were dying. Richards's mind cleared in his latest hour, and he sent for Burgess. Burgess said:

"Let the room be cleared. I think he wishes to say something in privacy."

"No!" said Richards; "I want witnesses. I want you all to hear my confession, so that I may die a man, and not a dog. I was clean—artificially—like the rest; and like the rest I fell when temptation came. I signed a lie, and claimed the miserable sack. Mr. Burgess remembered that I had done him a service, and in gratitude (and ignorance) he suppressed my claim and saved me. You know the thing that was charged against Burgess years ago. My testimony, and mine alone, could have cleared him, and I was a coward, and left him to suffer disgrace—"

"No—no—Mr. Richards, you—"

"My servant betrayed my secret to him—"

"No one has betrayed anything to me—"

—"and then he did a natural and justifiable thing; he repented of the saving kindness which he had done me, and he *exposed* me—as I deserved—"

"Never!—I make oath—"

"Out of my heart I forgive him."

Burgess's impassioned protestations fell upon deaf ears; the dying man passed away without knowing that once more he had done poor Burgess a wrong. The old wife died that night.

The last of the sacred Nineteen had fallen a prey to the fiendish sack; the town was stripped of the last rag of its ancient glory. Its mourning was not showy, but it was deep.

By act of the Legislature—upon prayer and petition—Hadleyburg was allowed to change its name to (never mind what—I will not give it away), and leave one word out of the motto that for many generations had graced the town's official seal.

It is an honest town once more, and the man will have to rise early that catches it napping again.

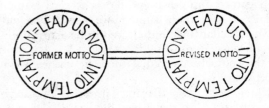

To the Person Sitting in Darkness

"Christmas will dawn in the United States over a people full of hope and aspiration and good cheer. Such a condition means contentment and happiness. The carping grumbler who may here and there go forth will find few to listen to him. The majority will wonder what is the matter with him and pass on."—*New York Tribune*, on Christmas Eve.

From *The Sun*, of New York:

"The purpose of this article is not to describe the terrible offences against humanity committed in the name of Politics in some of the most notorious East Side districts. *They could not be described, even verbally.* But it is the intention to let the great mass of more or less careless citizens of this beautiful metropolis of the New World get some conception of the havoc and ruin wrought to man, woman and child in the most densely populated and least known section of the city. Name, date and place can be supplied to those of little faith—or to any man who feels himself aggrieved. It is a plain statement of record and observation, written without license and without garnish.

"Imagine, if you can, a section of the city territory completely dominated by one man, without whose permission neither legitimate nor illegitimate business can be conducted; *where illegitimate business is encouraged and legitimate business discouraged;* where the respectable residents have to fasten their doors and windows summer nights and sit in their rooms with asphyxiating air and 100-degree temperature, rather than try to catch the faint whiff of breeze in their natural breathing places, the stoops of their homes; *where naked women dance by night in the streets, and unsexed men prowl like vultures through the darkness on 'business'* not only permitted but encouraged by the police; *where the education of infants begins with the knowledge of prostitution* and the training of little girls is training in the arts of Phryne; where *American* girls brought up with the refinements of *American* homes are imported from small towns up-State, Massachusetts, Connecticut and New Jersey, and kept as virtually prisoners as if they were locked up behind jail bars until they have lost all semblance of womanhood; *where small boys are taught to solicit for the women of disorderly houses;* where there is an organized society of young men *whose sole business in life is to corrupt young girls and turn them over to bawdy houses;* where men walking with their wives along the street are openly insulted; *where children that have adult diseases are the chief patrons of the hospitals and dispensaries;* where it is the rule, rather than the exception, that *murder, rape, robbery and theft go unpunished*—in short where the Premium of the most awful forms of Vice is the Profit of the politicians."

The following news from China appeared in *The Sun*, of New York, on Christmas Eve. The italics are mine:

"The Rev. Mr. Ament, of the American Board of Foreign Missions, has returned from a trip which he made for the purpose of collecting indemnities for damages done by Boxers. *Everywhere he went he compelled the Chinese to pay.* He says that all his native Christians are now provided for. He had 700 of them under his charge, and 300 were killed. He has *collected* 300 *taels for each* of these murders, and has *compelled full payment for all the property belonging to Christians* that was destroyed. He also assessed *fines* amounting to THIRTEEN TIMES the amount of the indemnity. *This money will be used for the propagation of the Gospel.*

"Mr. Ament declares that the compensation he has collected is *moderate*, when compared with the amount secured by the Catholics, who demand, in addition to money, *head for head.* They collect 500 taels for each murder of a Catholic. In the Wenchiu country, 680 Catholics were killed, and for this the European Catholics here demand 750,000 strings of cash and 680 *heads*.

"In the course of a conversation, Mr. Ament referred to the attitude of the missionaries toward the Chinese. He said:

" 'I deny emphatically that the missionaries are *vindictive*, that they *generally* looted, or that they have done anything *since* the siege that *the circumstances did not demand.* I criticise the Americans. *The soft hand of the Americans is not as good as the mailed fist of the Germans.* If you deal with the Chinese with a soft hand they will take advantage of it.'

"The statement that the French Government will return the loot taken by the French soldiers, is the source of the greatest amusement here. The French soldiers were more systematic looters than the Germans, and it is a fact that to-day *Catholic Christians*, carrying French flags and armed with modern guns, *are looting villages* in the Province of Chili."

By happy luck, we get all these glad tidings on Christmas Eve—just in time to enable us to celebrate the day with proper gaiety and enthusiasm. Our spirits soar, and we find we can even make jokes: Taels I win, Heads you lose.

Our Reverend Ament is the right man in the right place.

What we want of our missionaries out there is, not that they shall merely represent in their acts and persons the grace and gentleness and charity and loving kindness of our religion, but that they shall also represent the American spirit. The oldest Americans are the Pawnees. Macallum's History says:

"When a white Boxer kills a Pawnee and destroys his property, the other Pawnees do not trouble to seek *him* out, they kill any white person that comes along; also, they make some white village pay deceased's heirs the full cash value of deceased, together with full cash value of the property destroyed; they also make the village pay, in addition, *thirteen times* the value of that property into a fund for the dissemination of the Pawnee religion, which they regard as the best of all religions for the softening and humanizing of the heart of man. It is their idea that it is only fair and right that the innocent should be made to suffer for the guilty, and that it is better that ninety and nine innocent should suffer than that one guilty person should escape."

Our Reverend Ament is justifiably jealous of those enterprising Catholics, who not only get big money for each lost convert, but get "head for head" besides. But he should soothe himself with the reflection that the entirety of their exactions are for their own pockets, whereas he, less selfishly, devotes only 300 taels per head to that service, and gives the whole vast thirteen repetitions of the property-indemnity to the service of propagating the Gospel. His magnanimity has won him the approval of his nation, and will get him a monument. Let him be content with these rewards. We all hold him dear for manfully defending his fellow missionaries from exaggerated charges which were beginning to distress us, but which his testimony has so considerably modified that we can now contemplate them without noticeable pain. For now we know that, even before the siege, the missionaries were not "generally" out looting, and that, "since the siege," they have acted quite handsomely, except when "circumstances" crowded them. I am arranging for the monument. Subscriptions for it can be sent to the American Board; designs for it can be sent to me. Designs must allegorically set forth the Thirteen Reduplications of the Indemnity, and the Object for which they were exacted; as Ornaments, the designs must exhibit 680 Heads, so disposed as to give a pleasing and pretty effect; for the Catholics have done nicely, and are entitled to notice in the monument. Mottoes may be suggested, if any shall be discovered that will satisfactorily cover the ground.

Mr. Ament's financial feat of squeezing a thirteen-fold indemnity out of the pauper peasants to square other people's offenses, thus condemning them and their women and innocent little children to inevitable starvation and lingering death, in order that the blood-money so acquired might be *"used for the propagation of the Gospel,"* does not flutter my serenity; although the act and the words, taken together, concrete a blasphemy so hideous and so colossal that, without doubt, its mate is not findable in the history of this or of any other age. Yet, if a layman had done that thing and justified it with those words, I should have shuddered, I know. Or, if I had done the thing and said the words myself—however, the thought is unthinkable, irreverent as some imperfectly informed people think me. Sometimes an ordained minister sets out to be blasphemous. When this happens, the layman is out of the running; he stands no chance.

We have Mr. Ament's impassioned assurance that the missionaries are not "vindictive." Let us hope and pray that they will never become so, but will remain in the almost morbidly fair and just and gentle temper which is affording so much satisfaction to their brother and champion to-day.

The following is from the *New York Tribune* of Christmas Eve. It comes from that journal's Tokio correspondent. It has a strange and impudent sound, but the Japanese are but partially civilized as yet. When they become wholly civilized they will not talk so:

"The missionary question, of course, occupies a foremost place in the discussion. It is now felt as essential that the Western Powers take cognizance of the sentiment here, that religious invasions of Oriental countries by powerful Western organizations are tantamount to filibustering expeditions, and should not only be discountenanced, but that stern measures should be adopted for their suppression. The feeling here is that the missionary organizations constitute a constant menace to peaceful international relations."

Shall we? That is, shall we go on conferring our Civilization upon the peoples that sit in darkness, or shall we give those poor things a rest? Shall we bang right ahead in our old-time, loud, pious way, and commit the new century to the game; or shall we sober up and sit down and think it over first? Would it not be prudent to get our Civilization-tools together, and see how much stock is left on hand in the way of Glass Beads and Theology, and Maxim Guns and Hymn Books, and Trade-Gin and Torches of Progress and Enlightenment (patent adjustable ones, good to fire villages with, upon occasion), and balance the books, and arrive at the profit and loss, so that we may intelligently decide whether to continue the business or sell out the property and start a new Civilization Scheme on the proceeds?

Extending the Blessings of Civilization to our Brother who Sits in Darkness has been a good trade and has paid well, on the whole; and there is money in it yet, if carefully worked— but not enough, in my judgment, to make any considerable risk advisable. The People that Sit in Darkness are getting to be too scarce—too scarce and too shy. And such darkness as is now left is really of but an indifferent quality, and not dark enough for the game. The most of those People that Sit in Darkness have been furnished with more light than was good for them or profitable for us. We have been injudicious.

The Blessings-of-Civilization Trust, wisely and cautiously administered, is a Daisy. There is more money in it, more territory, more sovereignty, and other kinds of emolument, than there is in any other game that is played. But Christendom has been playing it badly of late years, and must certainly suffer by it, in my opinion. She has been so eager to get every stake that appeared on the green cloth, that the People who Sit in Darkness have noticed it—they have noticed it, and have begun to show alarm. They have become suspicious of the Blessings of Civilization. More—they have begun to examine them. This is not well. The Blessings of Civilization are all right, and a good commercial property; there could not be a better, in a dim light. In the right kind of a light, and at a proper distance, with the goods a little out of focus, they furnish this desirable exhibit to the Gentlemen who Sit in Darkness:

LOVE,	LAW AND ORDER,
JUSTICE,	LIBERTY,
GENTLENESS,	EQUALITY,
CHRISTIANITY,	HONORABLE DEALING,
PROTECTION TO THE WEAK,	MERCY,
TEMPERANCE,	EDUCATION,
—and so on.	

There. Is it good? Sir, it is pie. It will bring into camp any idiot that sits in darkness anywhere. But not if we adulterate it. It is proper to be emphatic upon that point. This brand is strictly for Export—apparently. *Apparently.* Privately and confidentially, it is nothing of the kind. Privately and confidentially, it is merely an outside cover, gay and pretty and attractive, displaying the special patterns of our Civilization which we reserve for Home Consumption, while *inside* the bale is the Actual Thing that the Customer Sitting in Darkness buys with his blood and tears and land and liberty. That Actual Thing is, indeed, Civilization, but it is only for Export. Is there a difference between the two brands? In some of the details, yes.

We all know that the Business is being ruined. The reason is not far to seek. It is because our Mr. McKinley, and Mr. Chamberlain, and the Kaiser, and the Czar and the French have been exporting the Actual Thing *with the outside cover left off.* This is bad for the Game. It shows that these new players of it are not sufficiently acquainted with it.

It is a distress to look on and note the mismoves, they are so strange and so awkward. Mr. Chamberlain manufactures a war out of materials so inadequate and so fanciful that they make the boxes grieve and the gallery laugh, and he tries hard to persuade himself that it isn't purely a private raid for cash, but has a sort of dim, vague respectability about it somewhere, if he could only find the spot; and that, by and by, he can scour the flag clean again after he has finished dragging it through the mud, and make it shine and flash in the vault of heaven once more as it had shone and flashed there a thousand years in the world's respect until he laid his unfaithful hand upon it. It is bad play—bad. For it exposes the Actual Thing to Them that Sit in Darkness, and they say: "What!

Christian against Christian? And only for money? Is *this* a case of magnanimity, forbearance, love, gentleness, mercy, protection of the weak—this strange and over-showy onslaught of an elephant upon a nest of field-mice, on the pretext that the mice had squeaked an insolence at him—conduct which 'no self-respecting government could allow to pass unavenged?' as Mr. Chamberlain said. Was that a good pretext in a small case, when it had not been a good pretext in a large one?—for only recently Russia had affronted the elephant three times and survived alive and unsmitten. Is this Civilization and Progress? Is it something better than we already possess? These harryings and burnings and desert-makings in the Transvaal—is this an improvement on our darkness? Is it, perhaps, possible that there are two kinds of Civilization—one for home consumption and one for the heathen market?"

Then They that Sit in Darkness are troubled, and shake their heads; and they read this extract from a letter of a British private, recounting his exploits in one of Methuen's victories, some days before the affair of Magersfontein, and they are troubled again:

"We tore up the hill and into the intrenchments, and the Boers saw we had them; so they dropped their guns and went down on their knees and put up their hands clasped, and begged for mercy. And we gave it them—*with the long spoon.*"

The long spoon is the bayonet. See *Lloyd's Weekly*, London, of those days. The same number—and the same column—contained some quite unconscious satire in the form of shocked and bitter upbraidings of the Boers for their brutalities and inhumanities!

Next, to our heavy damage, the Kaiser went to playing the game without first mastering it. He lost a couple of missionaries in a riot in Shantung, and in his account he made an overcharge for them. China had to pay a hundred thousand dollars apiece for them, in money; twelve miles of territory, containing several millions of inhabitants and worth twenty million dollars; and to build a monument, and also a Christian church; whereas the people of China could have been depended upon to remember the missionaries without the help of these expensive memorials. This was all bad play. Bad, because it would not, and could not, and will not now or ever, deceive the Person Sitting in Darkness. He knows that it was an overcharge. He knows that a missionary is like any other man: he is worth merely what you can supply his place for, and no more. He is useful, but so is a doctor, so is a sheriff, so is an editor; but a just Emperor does not charge war-prices for such. A diligent, intelligent, but obscure missionary, and a diligent, intelligent country editor are worth much, and we know it; but they are not worth the earth. We esteem such an editor, and we are sorry to see him go; but, when he goes, we should consider twelve miles of territory, and a church, and a fortune, over-compensation for his loss. I mean, if he was a Chinese editor, and we had to settle for him. It is no proper figure for an editor or a missionary; one can get shop-worn kings for less. It was bad play on the Kaiser's part. It got this property, true; but it *produced the Chinese revolt*, the indignant uprising of China's traduced patriots, the Boxers. The results have been expensive to Germany, and to the other Disseminators of Progress and the Blessings of Civilization.

The Kaiser's claim was paid, yet it was bad play, for it could not fail to have an evil effect upon Persons Sitting in Darkness in China. They would muse upon the event, and be likely to say: "Civilization is gracious and beautiful, for such is its reputation; but can we afford it? There are rich Chinamen, perhaps they could afford it; but this tax is not laid upon them, it is laid upon the peasants of Shantung; it is they that must pay this mighty sum, and their wages are but four cents a day. Is this a better civilization than ours, and holier and higher and nobler? Is not this rapacity? Is not this extortion? Would Germany charge America two hundred thousand dollars for two missionaries, and shake the mailed fist in her face, and send warships, and send soldiers, and say: 'Seize twelve miles of territory, worth twenty millions of dollars, as additional pay for the missionaries; and make those peasants build a monument to the missionaries, and a costly Christian church to remember them by?' And later would Germany say to her soldiers: 'March through America and slay, *giving no quarter*; make the German face there, as has been our Hun-face here, a terror for a thousand years; march through the

Great Republic and slay, slay, slay, carving a road for our offended religion through its heart and bowels?' Would Germany do like this to America, to England, to France, to Russia? Or only to China the helpless—imitating the elephant's assault upon the field-mice? Had we better invest in this Civilization—this Civilization which called Napoleon a buccaneer for carrying off Venice's bronze horses, but which steals our ancient astronomical instruments from our walls, and goes looting like common bandits—that is, all the alien soldiers except America's; and (Americans again excepted) storms frightened villages and cables the result to glad journals at home every day: 'Chinese losses, 450 killed; ours, *one officer and two men wounded*. Shall proceed against neighboring village to-morrow, where a *massacre* is reported.' Can we afford Civilization?"

And, next, Russia must go and play the game injudiciously. She affronts England once or twice—with the Person Sitting in Darkness observing and noting; by moral assistance of France and Germany, she robs Japan of her hard-earned spoil, all swimming in Chinese blood—Port Arthur—with the Person again observing and noting; then she seizes Manchuria, raids its villages, and chokes its great river with the swollen corpses of countless massacred peasants—that astonished Person still observing and noting. And perhaps he is saying to himself: "It is yet *another* Civilized Power, with its banner of the Prince of Peace in one hand and its loot-basket and its butcher-knife in the other. Is there no salvation for us but to adopt Civilization and lift ourselves down to its level?"

And by and by comes America, and our Master of the Game plays it badly—plays it as Mr. Chamberlain was playing it in South Africa. It was a mistake to do that; also, it was one which was quite unlooked for in a Master who was playing it so well in Cuba. In Cuba, he was playing the usual and regular *American* game, and it was winning, for there is no way to beat it. The Master, contemplating Cuba, said: "Here is an oppressed and friendless little nation which is willing to fight to be free; we go partners, and put up the strength of seventy million sympathizers and the resources of the United States: play!" Nothing but Europe combined could call that hand: and Europe cannot combine on anything. There, in

Cuba, he was following our great traditions in a way which made us very proud of him, and proud of the deep dissatisfaction which his play was provoking in Continental Europe. Moved by a high inspiration, he threw out those stirring words which proclaimed that forcible annexation would be "criminal aggression;" and in that utterance fired another "shot heard round the world." The memory of that fine saying will be outlived by the remembrance of no act of his but one—that he forgot it within the twelvemonth, and its honorable gospel along with it.

For, presently, came the Philippine temptation. It was strong; it was too strong, and he made that bad mistake: he played the European game, the Chamberlain game. It was a pity; it was a great pity, that error; that one grievous error, that irrevocable error. For it was the very place and time to play the American game again. And at no cost. Rich winnings to be gathered in, too; rich and permanent; indestructible; a fortune transmissible forever to the children of the flag. Not land, not money, not dominion—no, something worth many times more than that dross: our share, the spectacle of a nation of long harassed and persecuted slaves set free through our influence; our posterity's share, the golden memory of that fair deed. The game was in our hands. If it had been played according to the American rules, Dewey would have sailed away from Manila as soon as he had destroyed the Spanish fleet—after putting up a sign on shore guaranteeing foreign property and life against damage by the Filipinos, and warning the Powers that interference with the emancipated patriots would be regarded as an act unfriendly to the United States. The Powers cannot combine, in even a bad cause, and the sign would not have been molested.

Dewey could have gone about his affairs elsewhere, and left the competent Filipino army to starve out the little Spanish garrison and send it home, and the Filipino citizens to set up the form of government they might prefer, and deal with the friars and their doubtful acquisitions according to Filipino ideas of fairness and justice—ideas which have since been tested and found to be of as high an order as any that prevail in Europe or America.

But we played the Chamberlain game, and lost the chance

to add another Cuba and another honorable deed to our good record.

The more we examine the mistake, the more clearly we perceive that it is going to be bad for the Business. The Person Sitting in Darkness is almost sure to say: "There is something curious about this—curious and unaccountable. There must be two Americas: one that sets the captive free, and one that takes a once-captive's new freedom away from him, and picks a quarrel with him with nothing to found it on; then kills him to get his land."

The truth is, the Person Sitting in Darkness *is* saying things like that; and for the sake of the Business we must persuade him to look at the Philippine matter in another and healthier way. We must arrange his opinions for him. I believe it can be done; for Mr. Chamberlain has arranged England's opinion of the South African matter, and done it most cleverly and successfully. He presented the facts—some of the facts—and showed those confiding people what the facts meant. He did it statistically, which is a good way. He used the formula: "Twice 2 are 14, and 2 from 9 leaves 35." Figures are effective; figures will convince the elect.

Now, my plan is a still bolder one than Mr. Chamberlain's, though apparently a copy of it. Let us be franker than Mr. Chamberlain; let us audaciously present the whole of the facts, shirking none, then explain them according to Mr. Chamberlain's formula. This daring truthfulness will astonish and dazzle the Person Sitting in Darkness, and he will take the Explanation down before his mental vision has had time to get back into focus. Let us say to him:

"Our case is simple. On the 1st of May, Dewey destroyed the Spanish fleet. This left the Archipelago in the hands of its proper and rightful owners, the Filipino nation. Their army numbered 30,000 men, and they were competent to whip out or starve out the little Spanish garrison; then the people could set up a government of their own devising. Our traditions required that Dewey should now set up his warning sign, and go away. But the Master of the Game happened to think of another plan—the European plan. He acted upon it. This was, to send out an army—ostensibly to help the native patriots put the finishing touch upon their long and plucky struggle for independence, but really to take their land away from them and keep it. That is, in the interest of Progress and Civilization. The plan developed, stage by stage, and quite satisfactorily. We entered into a military alliance with the trusting Filipinos, and they hemmed in Manila on the land side, and by their valuable help the place, with its garrison of 8,000 or 10,000 Spaniards, was captured—a thing which we could not have accomplished unaided at that time. We got their help by—by ingenuity. We knew they were fighting for their independence, and that they had been at it for two years. We knew they supposed that we also were fighting in their worthy cause—just as we had helped the Cubans fight for Cuban independence—and we allowed them to go on thinking so. *Until Manila was ours and we could get along without them.* Then we showed our hand. Of course, they were surprised—that was natural; surprised and disappointed; disappointed and grieved. To them it looked un-American; uncharacteristic; foreign to our established traditions. And this was natural, too; for we were only playing the American Game in public—in private it was the European. It was neatly done, very neatly, and it bewildered them. They could not understand it; for we had been so friendly—so affectionate, even—with those simple-minded patriots! We, our own selves, had brought back out of exile their leader, their hero, their hope, their Washington—Aguinaldo; brought him in a warship, in high honor, under the sacred shelter and hospitality of the flag; brought him back and restored him to his people, and got their moving and eloquent gratitude for it. Yes, we had been so friendly to them, and had heartened them up in so many ways! We had lent them guns and ammunition; advised with them; exchanged pleasant courtesies with them; placed our sick and wounded in their kindly care; entrusted our Spanish prisoners to their humane and honest hands; fought shoulder to shoulder with them against 'the common enemy' (our own phrase); praised their courage, praised their gallantry, praised their mercifulness, praised their fine and honorable conduct; borrowed their trenches, borrowed strong positions which they had previously captured from the Spaniard; petted them, lied to them—officially proclaiming that our land and naval forces came to give them their freedom and displace the bad Spanish Government—fooled them, used them until we needed them no longer; then derided the sucked orange and threw it away. We kept the positions which we had beguiled them of; by and by, we moved a force forward and overlapped patriot ground—a clever thought, for we needed trouble, and this would produce it. A Filipino soldier, crossing the ground, where no one had a right to forbid him, was shot by our sentry. The badgered patriots resented this with arms, without waiting to know whether Aguinaldo, who was absent, would approve or not. Aguinaldo did not approve; but that availed nothing. What we wanted, in the interest of Progress and Civilization, was the Archipelago, unencumbered by patriots struggling for independence; and War was what we needed. We clinched our opportunity. It is Mr. Chamberlain's case over again—at least in its motive and intention; and we played the game as adroitly as he played it himself."

At this point in our frank statement of fact to the Person Sitting in Darkness, we should throw in a little trade-taffy about the Blessings of Civilization—for a change, and for the refreshment of his spirit—then go on with our tale:

"We and the patriots having captured Manila, Spain's ownership of the Archipelago and her sovereignty over it were at an end—obliterated—annihilated—not a rag or shred of either remaining behind. It was then that we conceived the divinely humorous idea of *buying* both of these spectres from Spain! [It is quite safe to confess this to the Person Sitting in Darkness, since neither he nor any other sane person will believe it.] In buying those ghosts for twenty millions, we also contracted to take care of the friars and their accumulations. I think we also agreed to propagate leprosy and smallpox, but as to this there is doubt. But it is not important; persons afflicted with the friars do not mind other diseases.

"With our Treaty ratified, Manila subdued, and our Ghosts secured, we had no further use for Aguinaldo and the owners of the Archipelago. We forced a war, and we have been hunting America's guest and ally through the woods and swamps ever since."

At this point in the tale, it will be well to boast a little of our war-work and our heroisms in the field, so as to make our performance look as fine as England's in South Africa; but I believe it will not be best to emphasize this too much. We must be cautious. Of course, we must read the war-telegrams to the Person, in order to keep up our frankness; but we can throw an air of humorousness over them, and that will modify their grim eloquence a little, and their rather indiscreet exhibitions of gory exultation. Before reading to him the following display heads of the dispatches of November 18, 1900, it will be well to practice on them in private first, so as to get the right tang of lightness and gaiety into them:

> "ADMINISTRATION WEARY OF PROTRACTED HOSTILITIES!"
> "REAL WAR AHEAD FOR FILIPINO REBELS!"*
> "WILL SHOW NO MERCY!"
> "KITCHENER'S PLAN ADOPTED!"

Kitchener knows how to handle disagreeable people who are fighting for their homes and their liberties, and we must let on that we are merely imitating Kitchener, and have no national interest in the matter, further than to get ourselves admired by the Great Family of Nations, in which august company our Master of the Game has bought a place for us in the back row.

Of course, we must not venture to ignore our General MacArthur's reports—oh, why do they keep on printing those embarrassing things?—we must drop them trippingly from the tongue and take the chances:

> "During the last ten months our losses have been 268 killed and 750 wounded; Filipino loss, *three thousand two hundred and twenty-seven killed*, and 694 wounded."

We must stand ready to grab the Person Sitting in Darkness, for he will swoon away at this confession, saying: "Good God, those 'niggers' spare their wounded, and the Americans massacre theirs!"

We must bring him to, and coax him and coddle him, and assure him that the ways of Providence are best, and that it

---

*"Rebels!" Mumble that funny word—don't let the Person catch it distinctly.

would not become us to find fault with them; and then, to show him that we are only imitators, not originators, we must read the following passage from the letter of an American soldier-lad in the Philippines to his mother, published in *Public Opinion*, of Decorah, Iowa, describing the finish of a victorious battle:

"WE NEVER LEFT ONE ALIVE. IF ONE WAS WOUNDED, WE WOULD RUN OUR BAYONETS THROUGH HIM."

Having now laid all the historical facts before the Person Sitting in Darkness, we should bring him to again, and explain them to him. We should say to him:

"They look doubtful, but in reality they are not. There have been lies; yes, but they were told in a good cause. We have been treacherous; but that was only in order that real good might come out of apparent evil. True, we have crushed a deceived and confiding people; we have turned against the weak and the friendless who trusted us; we have stamped out a just and intelligent and well-ordered republic; we have stabbed an ally in the back and slapped the face of a guest; we have bought a Shadow from an enemy that hadn't it to sell; we have robbed a trusting friend of his land and his liberty; we have invited our clean young men to shoulder a discredited musket and do bandit's work under a flag which bandits have been accustomed to fear, not to follow; we have debauched America's honor and blackened her face before the world; but each detail was for the best. We know this. The Head of every State and Sovereignty in Christendom and ninety per cent. of every legislative body in Christendom, including our Congress and our fifty State Legislatures, are members not only of the church, but also of the Blessings-of-Civilization Trust. This world-girdling accumulation of trained morals, high principles, and justice, cannot do an unright thing, an unfair thing, an ungenerous thing, an unclean thing. It knows what it is about. Give yourself no uneasiness; it is all right."

Now then, that will convince the Person. You will see. It will restore the Business. Also, it will elect the Master of the Game to the vacant place in the Trinity of our national gods; and there on their high thrones the Three will sit, age after age, in the people's sight, each bearing the Emblem of his service: Washington, the Sword of the Liberator; Lincoln, the Slave's Broken Chains; the Master, the Chains Repaired.

It will give the Business a splendid new start. You will see.

Everything is prosperous, now; everything is just as we should wish it. We have got the Archipelago, and we shall never give it up. Also, we have every reason to hope that we shall have an opportunity before very long to slip out of our Congressional contract with Cuba and give her something better in the place of it. It is a rich country, and many of us are already beginning to see that the contract was a sentimental mistake. But now—right now—is the best time to do some profitable rehabilitating work—work that will set us up and make us comfortable, and discourage gossip. We cannot conceal from ourselves that, privately, we are a little troubled about our uniform. It is one of our prides; it is acquainted with honor; it is familiar with great deeds and noble; we love it, we revere it; and so this errand it is on makes us uneasy. And our flag—another pride of ours, our chiefest! We have worshipped it so; and when we have seen it in far lands—glimpsing it unexpectedly in that strange sky, waving its welcome and benediction to us—we have caught our breath, and uncovered our heads, and couldn't speak, for a moment, for the thought of what it was to us and the great ideals it stood for. Indeed, we *must* do something about these things; we must not have the flag out there, and the uniform. They are not needed there; we can manage in some other way. England manages, as regards the uniform, and so can we. We have to send soldiers—we can't get out of that—but we can disguise them. It is the way England does in South Africa. Even Mr. Chamberlain himself takes pride in England's honorable uniform, and makes the army down there wear an ugly and odious and appropriate disguise, of yellow stuff such as quarantine flags are made of, and which are hoisted to warn the healthy away from unclean disease and repulsive death. This cloth is called khaki. We could adopt it. It is light, comfortable, grotesque, and deceives the enemy, for he cannot conceive of a soldier being concealed in it.

And as for a flag for the Philippine Province, it is easily managed. We can have a special one—our States do it: we can have just our usual flag, with the white stripes painted black and the stars replaced by the skull and cross-bones.

And we do not need that Civil Commission out there. Having no powers, it has to invent them, and that kind of work cannot be effectively done by just anybody; an expert is required. Mr. Croker can be spared. We do not want the United States represented there, but only the Game.

By help of these suggested amendments, Progress and Civilization in that country can have a boom, and it will take in the Persons who are Sitting in Darkness, and we can resume Business at the old stand.

The United States of Lyncherdom

I

AND so Missouri has fallen, that great state! Certain of her children have joined the lynchers, and the smirch is upon the rest of us. That handful of her children have given us a character and labeled us with a name, and to the dwellers in the four quarters of the earth we are "lynchers," now, and ever shall be. For the world will not stop and think—it never does, it is not its way; its way is to generalize from a single sample. It will not say, "Those Missourians have been busy eighty years in building an honorable good name for themselves; these hundred lynchers down in the corner of the state are not real Missourians, they are renegades." No, that truth will not enter its mind; it will generalize from the one or two misleading samples and say, "The Missourians are lynchers." It has no reflection, no logic, no sense of proportion. With it, figures go for nothing; to it, figures reveal nothing, it cannot reason upon them rationally; it would say, for instance, that China is being swiftly and surely Christianized, since nine Chinese Christians are being made every day; and it would fail, with him, to notice that the fact that 33,000 pagans are *born* there every day, damages the argument. It would say, "There are a hundred lynchers there, therefore the Missourians are lynchers"; the considerable fact that there are two and a half million Missourians who are *not* lynchers would not affect their verdict.

II

Oh, Missouri!

The tragedy occurred near Pierce City, down in the southwestern corner of the state. On a Sunday afternoon a young white woman who had started alone from church was found murdered. For there are churches there; in my time religion was more general, more pervasive, in the South than it was in the North, and more virile and earnest, too, I think; I have some reason to believe that this is still the case. The young

754

woman was found murdered. Although it was a region of churches and schools the people rose, lynched three negroes—two of them very aged ones—burned out five negro households, and drove thirty negro families into the woods.

I do not dwell upon the provocation which moved the people to these crimes, for that has nothing to do with the matter; the only question is, does the assassin *take the law into his own hands*? It is very simple, and very just. If the assassin be proved to have usurped the law's prerogative in righting his wrongs, that ends the matter; a thousand provocations are no defense. The Pierce City people had bitter provocation— indeed, as revealed by certain of the particulars, the bitterest of all provocations—but no matter, they took the law into their own hands, when by the terms of their statutes their victim would certainly hang if the law had been allowed to take its course, for there are but few negroes in that region and they are without authority and without influence in overawing juries.

Why has lynching, with various barbaric accompaniments, become a favorite regulator in cases of "the usual crime" in several parts of the country? Is it because men think a lurid and terrible punishment a more forcible object lesson and a more effective deterrent than a sober and colorless hanging done privately in a jail would be? Surely sane men do not think that. Even the average child should know better. It should know that any strange and much-talked-of event is always followed by imitations, the world being so well supplied with excitable people who only need a little stirring up to make them lose what is left of their heads and do mad things which they would not have thought of ordinarily. It should know that if a man jump off Brooklyn Bridge another will imitate him; that if a person venture down Niagara Whirlpool in a barrel another will imitate him; that if a Jack the Ripper make notoriety by slaughtering women in dark alleys he will be imitated; that if a man attempt a king's life and the newspapers carry the noise of it around the globe, regicides will crop up all around. The child should know that one much-talked-of outrage and murder committed by a negro will upset the disturbed intellects of several other negroes and produce a series of the very tragedies the community would so strenuously wish to prevent; that each of these crimes will produce another series, and year by year steadily increase the tale of these disasters instead of diminishing it; that, in a word, the lynchers are themselves the worst enemies of their women. The child should also know that by a law of our make, communities, as well as individuals, are imitators; and that a much-talked-of lynching will infallibly produce other lynchings here and there and yonder, and that in time these will breed a mania, a fashion; a fashion which will spread wide and wider, year by year, covering state after state, as with an advancing disease. Lynching has reached Colorado, it has reached California, it has reached Indiana—and now Missouri! I may live to see a negro burned in Union Square, New York, with fifty thousand people present, and not a sheriff visible, not a governor, not a constable, not a colonel, not a clergyman, not a law-and-order representative of any sort.

Increase in Lynching.—In 1900 there were eight more cases than in 1899, and probably this year there will be more than there were last year. The year is little more than half gone, and yet there are eighty-eight cases as compared with one hundred and fifteen for all of last year. The four Southern states, Alabama, Georgia, Louisiana, and Mississippi are the worst offenders. Last year there were eight cases in Alabama, sixteen in Georgia, twenty in Louisiana, and twenty in Mississippi—over one-half the total. This year to date there have been nine in Alabama, twelve in Georgia, eleven in Louisiana, and thirteen in Mississippi—again more than one-half the total number in the whole United States.—Chicago *Tribune*.

It must be that the increase comes of the inborn human instinct to imitate—that and man's commonest weakness, his aversion to being unpleasantly conspicuous, pointed at, shunned, as being on the unpopular side. Its other name is Moral Cowardice, and is the commanding feature of the make-up of 9,999 men in the 10,000. I am not offering this as a discovery; privately the dullest of us knows it to be true. History will not allow us to forget or ignore this supreme trait of our character. It persistently and sardonically reminds us that from the beginning of the world no revolt against a public infamy or oppression has ever been begun but by the one daring man in the 10,000, the rest timidly waiting, and slowly and reluctantly joining, under the influence of that

man and his fellows from the other ten thousands. The aboli-
tionists remember. Privately the public feeling was with them
early, but each man was afraid to speak out until he got some
hint that his neighbor was privately feeling as he privately felt
himself. Then the boom followed. It always does. It will
occur in New York, some day; and even in Pennsylvania.

It has been supposed—and said—that the people at a
lynching enjoy the spectacle and are glad of a chance to see it.
It cannot be true; all experience is against it. The people in
the South are made like the people in the North—the vast
majority of whom are right-hearted and compassionate, and
would be cruelly pained by such a spectacle—and *would attend it*, and let on to be pleased with it, if the public approval
seemed to require it. We are made like that, and we cannot
help it. The other animals are not so, but we cannot help that,
either. They lack the Moral Sense; we have no way of trading
ours off, for a nickel or some other thing above its value. The
Moral Sense teaches us what is right, and how to avoid it—
when unpopular.

It is thought, as I have said, that a lynching crowd enjoys a
lynching. It certainly is not true; it is impossible of belief. It is
freely asserted—you have seen it in print many times of
late—that the lynching impulse has been misinterpreted; that
it is *not* the outcome of a spirit of revenge, but of a "mere
atrocious hunger *to look upon human suffering*." If that were
so, the crowds that saw the Windsor Hotel burn down would
have enjoyed the horrors that fell under their eyes. Did they?
No one will think that of them, no one will make that charge.
Many risked their lives to save the men and women who were
in peril. Why did they do that? Because *none would disapprove*.
There was no restraint; they could follow their natural impulse. Why does a crowd of the same kind of people in Texas,
Colorado, Indiana, stand by, smitten to the heart and miserable, and by ostentatious outward signs pretend to enjoy a
lynching? Why does it lift no hand or voice in protest? Only
because it would be unpopular to do it, I think; each man is
afraid of his neighbor's disapproval—a thing which, to the
general run of the race, is more dreaded than wounds and
death. When there is to be a lynching the people hitch up and
come miles to see it, bringing their wives and children. Really

to see it? No—they come only because they are afraid to stay at home, lest it be noticed and offensively commented upon. We may believe this, for we all know how *we* feel about such spectacles—also, how we would act under the like pressure. We are not any better nor any braver than anybody else, and we must not try to creep out of it.

A Savonarola can quell and scatter a mob of lynchers with a mere glance of his eye: so can a Merrill* or a Beloat.[†] For no mob has any sand in the presence of a man known to be splendidly brave. Besides, a lynching mob would *like* to be scattered, for of a certainty there are never ten men in it who would not prefer to be somewhere else—and would be, if they but had the courage to go. When I was a boy I saw a brave gentleman deride and insult a mob and drive it away; and afterward, in Nevada, I saw a noted desperado make two hundred men sit still, with the house burning under them, until he gave them permission to retire. A plucky man can rob a whole passenger train by himself; and the half of a brave man can hold up a stagecoach and strip its occupants.

Then perhaps the remedy for lynchings comes to this: station a brave man in each affected community to encourage, support, and bring to light the deep disapproval of lynching hidden in the secret places of its heart—for it is there, beyond question. Then those communities will find something better to imitate—of course, being human, they must imitate something. Where shall these brave men be found? That is indeed a difficulty; there are not three hundred of them in the earth. If merely *physically* brave men would do, then it were easy; they could be furnished by the cargo. When Hobson called for seven volunteers to go with him to what promised to be certain death, four thousand men responded—the whole fleet, in fact. Because *all the world would approve.* They knew that; but if Hobson's project had been charged with the scoffs and jeers of the friends and associates, whose good opinion and approval the sailors valued, he could not have got his seven.

---

*Sheriff of Carroll County, Georgia.

[†]Sheriff, Princeton, Indiana. By that formidable power which lies in an established reputation for cold pluck they faced lynching mobs and securely held the field against them.

No, upon reflection, the scheme will not work. There are not enough morally brave men in stock. We are out of moral-courage material; we are in a condition of profound poverty. We have those two sheriffs down South who—but never mind, it is not enough to go around; they have to stay and take care of their own communities.

But if we only *could* have three or four more sheriffs of that great breed! Would it help? I think so. For we are all imitators: other brave sheriffs would follow; to be a dauntless sheriff would come to be recognized as the correct and only thing, and the dreaded disapproval would fall to the share of the other kind; courage in this office would become custom, the absence of it a dishonor, just as courage presently replaces the timidity of the new soldier; then the mobs and the lynchings would disappear, and——

However. It can never be done without some starters, and where are we to get the starters? Advertise? Very well, then, let us advertise.

In the meantime, there is another plan. Let us import American missionaries from China, and send them into the lynching field. With 1,511 of them out there converting two Chinamen apiece per annum against an uphill birth rate of 33,000 pagans per day,* it will take upward of a million years to make the conversions balance the output and bring the Christianizing of the country in sight to the naked eye; therefore, if we can offer our missionaries as rich a field at home at lighter expense and quite satisfactory in the matter of danger, why shouldn't they find it fair and right to come back and give us a trial? The Chinese are universally conceded to be excellent people, honest, honorable, industrious, trustworthy, kind-hearted, and all that—leave them alone, they are plenty good enough just as they are; and besides, almost every convert runs a risk of catching our civilization. We ought to be careful. We ought to think twice before we encourage a risk like that; for, *once civilized, China can never*

---

*These figures are not fanciful; all of them are genuine and authentic. They are from official missionary records in China. See Doctor Morrison's book on his pedestrian journey across China; he quotes them and gives his authorities. For several years he has been the London *Times's* representative in Peking, and was there through the siege.

be uncivilized again. We have not been thinking of that. Very well, we ought to think of it now. Our missionaries will find that we have a field for them—and not only for the 1,511, but for 15,011. Let them look at the following telegram and see if they have anything in China that is more appetizing. It is from Texas:

The negro was taken to a tree and swung in the air. Wood and fodder were piled beneath his body and a hot fire was made. *Then it was suggested that the man ought not to die too quickly, and he was let down to the ground while a party went to Dexter, about two miles distant, to procure coal oil.* This was thrown on the flames and the work completed.

We implore them to come back and help us in our need. Patriotism imposes this duty on them. Our country is worse off than China; they are our countrymen, their motherland supplicates their aid in this her hour of deep distress. They are competent; our people are not. They are used to scoffs, sneers, revilings, danger; our people are not. They have the martyr spirit; nothing but the martyr spirit can brave a lynching mob, and cow it and scatter it. They can save their country, we beseech them to come home and do it. We ask them to read that telegram again, and yet again, and picture the scene in their minds, and soberly ponder it; then multiply it by 115, add 88; place the 203 in a row, allowing 600 feet of space for each human torch, so that there may be viewing room around it for 5,000 Christian American men, women, and children, youths and maidens; make it night, for grim effect; have the show in a gradually rising plain, and let the course of the stakes be uphill; the eye can then take in the whole line of twenty-four miles of blood-and-flesh bonfires unbroken, whereas if it occupied level ground the ends of the line would bend down and be hidden from view by the curvature of the earth. All being ready, now, and the darkness opaque, the stillness impressive—for there should be no sound but the soft moaning of the night wind and the muffled sobbing of the sacrifices—let all the far stretch of kerosened pyres be touched off simultaneously and the glare and the shrieks and the agonies burst heavenward to the Throne. There are more than a million persons present; the light from the fires flushes into vague outline against the night the spires of five thousand churches. O kind missionary, O compassionate missionary, leave China! come home and convert these Christians!

I believe that if anything can stop this epidemic of bloody insanities it is martial personalities that can face mobs without flinching; and as such personalities are developed only by familiarity with danger and by the training and seasoning which come of resisting it, the likeliest place to find them must be among the missionaries who have been under tuition in China during the past year or two. We have abundance of work for them, and for hundreds and thousands more, and the field is daily growing and spreading. Shall we find them? We can try. In 75,000,000 there must be other Merrills and Beloats; and it is the law of our make that each example shall wake up drowsing chevaliers of the same great knighthood and bring them to the front.

Corn-Pone Opinions

FIFTY years ago, when I was a boy of fifteen and helping to inhabit a Missourian village on the banks of the Mississippi, I had a friend whose society was very dear to me because I was forbidden by my mother to partake of it. He was a gay and impudent and satirical and delightful young black man—a slave—who daily preached sermons from the top of his master's woodpile, with me for sole audience. He imitated the pulpit style of the several clergymen of the village, and did it well, and with fine passion and energy. To me he was a wonder. I believed he was the greatest orator in the United States, and would some day be heard from. But it did not happen; in the distribution of rewards he was overlooked. It is the way, in this world.

He interrupted his preaching, now and then, to saw a stick of wood; but the sawing was a pretence—he did it with his mouth; exactly imitating the sound the buck-saw makes in shrieking its way through the wood. But it served its purpose: it kept his master from coming out to see how the work was getting along. I listened to the sermons from the open window of a lumber-room at the back of our house. One of his texts was this:

"You tell me whar a man gits his corn-pone, en I'll tell you what his 'pinions is."

I can never forget it. It was deeply impressed upon me. By my mother. Not upon my memory, but elsewhere. She had slipped in upon me while I was absorbed and not watching. The black philosopher's idea was, that a man is not independent, and cannot afford views which might interfere with his bread and butter. If he would prosper, he must train with the majority; in matters of large moment, like politics and religion, he must think and feel with the bulk of his neighbors, or suffer damage in his social standing and in his business prosperities. He must restrict himself to corn-pone opinions —at least on the surface. He must get his opinions from other people; he must reason out none for himself; he must have no first-hand views.

I think Jerry was right, in the main, but I think he did not go far enough.

1. It was his idea that a man conforms to the majority-view of his locality by calculation and intention. This happens, but I think it is not the rule.

2. It was his idea that there is such a thing as a first-hand opinion; an original opinion; an opinion which is coldly reasoned-out in a man's head, by a searching analysis of the facts involved, with the heart unconsulted, and the jury-room closed against outside influences. It may be that such an opinion has been born somewhere, at some time or other, but I suppose it got away before they could catch it and stuff it and put it in the museum.

I am persuaded that a coldly thought-out and independent verdict upon a fashion in clothes, or manners, or literature, or politics, or religion, or any other matter that is projected into the field of our notice and interest, is a most rare thing—if it has indeed ever existed.

A new thing in costume appears—the flaring hoop-skirt, for example—and the passers-by are shocked, and the irreverent laugh. Six months later everybody is reconciled; the fashion has established itself; it is admired, now, and no one laughs. Public opinion resented it before, public opinion accepts it now, and is happy in it. Why? Was the resentment reasoned out? Was the acceptance reasoned out? No. The instinct that moves to conformity did the work. It is our nature to conform; it is a force which not many can successfully resist. What is its seat? The inborn requirement of Self-Approval. We all have to bow to that; there are no exceptions. Even the woman who refuses from first to last to wear the hoop-skirt comes under that law and is its slave; she could not wear the skirt and have her own approval; and that she *must* have, she cannot help herself. But as a rule our self-approval has its source in but one place and not elsewhere—the approval of other people. A person of vast consequence can introduce any kind of novelty in dress and the general world will presently adopt it—moved to do it, in the first place, by the natural instinct to passively yield to that vague something recognized as authority, and in the second place by the human instinct to train with the multitude and have its approval. An Empress introduced the hoop-skirt, and we know the result. A nobody introduced the Bloomer, and we know the result. If Eve should come again, in her ripe renown, and reintroduce her quaint styles—well, we know what would happen. And we should be cruelly embarrassed, along at first.

The hoop-skirt runs its course, and disappears. Nobody reasons about it. One woman abandons the fashion; her neighbor notices this and follows her lead; this influences the next woman; and so on and so on, and presently the skirt has vanished out of the world, no one knows how nor why; nor cares, for that matter. It will come again, by and by; and in due course will go again.

Twenty-five years ago, in England, six or eight wine glasses stood grouped by each person's plate at a dinner party, and they were used, not left idle and empty; to-day there are but three or four in the group, and the average guest sparingly uses about two of them. We have not adopted this new fashion yet, but we shall do it presently. We shall not think it out, we shall merely conform, and let it go at that. We get our notions and habits and opinions from outside influences, we do not have to study them out.

Our table manners, and company manners, and street manners change from time to time, but the changes are not reasoned out; we merely notice and conform. We are creatures of outside influences; as a rule we do not think, we only imitate. We cannot invent standards that will stick; what we mistake for standards are only fashions, and perishable. We may continue to admire them, but we drop the use of them. We notice this in literature. Shakspeare is a standard, and fifty years ago we used to write tragedies which he couldn't tell from—from somebody else's; but we don't do it any more, now. Our prose standard, three-quarters of a century ago, was ornate and diffuse; some authority or other changed it in the direction of compactness and simplicity, and conformity followed, without argument. The historical novel starts up suddenly, and sweeps the land. Everybody writes one, and the nation is glad. We had historical novels before; but nobody read them, and the rest of us conformed—without reasoning it out. We are conforming in the other way, now, because it is another case of everybody.

The outside influences are always pouring in upon us, and we are always obeying their orders and accepting their verdicts. The Smiths like the new play; the Joneses go to see it, and they copy the Smith verdict. Morals, religions, politics, get their following from surrounding influences and atmospheres, almost entirely; not from study, not from thinking. A man must and will have his own approval first of all, in each and every moment and circumstance of his life—even if he must repent of a self-approved act the moment after its commission, in order to get his self-approval *again*; but, speaking in general terms, a man's self-approval, in the large concerns of life, has its source in the approval of the people about him, and not in a searching personal examination of the matter. Mohammedans are Mohammedans because they are born and reared among that sect, not because they have thought it out and can furnish sound reasons for being Mohammedans; we know why Catholics are Catholics; why Presbyterians are Presbyterians; why Baptists are Baptists; why Mormons are Mormons; why thieves are thieves; why monarchists are monarchists; why republicans are republicans, and democrats democrats. We know it is a matter of association and sympathy, not reasoning and examination; that hardly a man in the world has an opinion upon morals, politics or religion which he got otherwise than through his associations and sympathies. Broadly speaking, there are none but corn-pone opinions. And broadly speaking, Corn-Pone stands for Self-Approval. Self-approval is acquired mainly from the approval of other people. The result is Conformity. Sometimes Conformity has a sordid business interest—the bread-and-butter interest—but not in most cases, I think. I think that in the majority of cases it is unconscious and not calculated; that it is born of the human being's natural yearning to stand well with his fellows, and have their inspiring approval and praise —a yearning which is commonly so strong and so insistent that it cannot be effectually resisted, and must have its way.

A political emergency brings out the corn-pone opinion in fine force in its two chief varieties—the pocket-book variety, which has its origin in self-interest, and the bigger variety, the sentimental variety—the one which can't bear to be outside the pale; can't bear to be in disfavor; can't endure the averted face and the cold shoulder; wants to stand well with the friends, wants to be smiled upon, wants to be welcome, wants to hear the precious words "*he's* on the right track!" Uttered, perhaps, by an ass, but still an ass of high degree, an ass whose approval is gold and diamonds to a smaller ass, and confers glory, and honor and happiness, and membership in the herd. For these gauds many a man will dump his life-long principles into the street, and his conscience along with them. We have seen it happen. In some millions of instances.

Men think they think upon great political questions, and they do; but they think with their party, not independently; they read its literature, but not that of the other side; they arrive at convictions, but they are drawn from a partial view of the matter in hand and are of no particular value. They swarm with their party, they feel with their party, they are happy in their party's approval; and where the party leads they will follow, whether for right and honor, or through blood and dirt and a mush of mutilated morals.

In our late canvas half of the nation passionately believed that in silver lay salvation, the other half as passionately believed that that way lay destruction. Do you believe that a tenth part of the people, on either side, had any rational excuse for having an opinion about the matter at all? I studied that mighty question to the bottom—and came out empty. Half of our people passionately believe in high tariff, the other half believe otherwise. Does this mean study and examination, or only feeling? The latter, I think. I have deeply studied that question, too—and didn't arrive. We all do no end of feeling, and we mistake it for thinking. And out of it we get an aggregation which we consider a Boon. Its name is Public Opinion. It is held in reverence. It settles everything. Some think it the Voice of God. Pr'aps.

I suppose that in more cases than we should like to admit, we have two sets of opinions: one private, the other public; one secret and sincere, the other corn-pone, and more or less tainted.

The War Prayer

IT was a time of great and exalting excitement. The country was up in arms, the war was on, in every breast burned the holy fire of patriotism; the drums were beating, the bands playing, the toy pistols popping, the bunched firecrackers hissing and spluttering; on every hand and far down the receding and fading spread of roofs and balconies a fluttering wilderness of flags flashed in the sun; daily the young volunteers marched down the wide avenue gay and fine in their new uniforms, the proud fathers and mothers and sisters and sweethearts cheering them with voices choked with happy emotion as they swung by; nightly the packed mass-meetings listened, panting, to patriot oratory which stirred the deepest deeps of their hearts, and which they interrupted at briefest intervals with cyclones of applause, the tears running down their cheeks the while; in the churches the pastors preached devotion to flag and country, and invoked the God of Battles, beseeching His aid in our good cause in outpourings of fervid eloquence which moved every listener. It was indeed a glad and gracious time, and the half dozen rash spirits that ventured to disapprove of the war and cast a doubt upon its righteousness straightway got such a stern and angry warning that for their personal safety's sake they quickly shrank out of sight and offended no more in that way.

Sunday morning came—next day the battalions would leave for the front; the church was filled; the volunteers were there, their young faces alight with martial dreams—visions of the stern advance, the gathering momentum, the rushing charge, the flashing sabres, the flight of the foe, the tumult, the enveloping smoke, the fierce pursuit, the surrender!— then home from the war, bronzed heroes, welcomed, adored, submerged in golden seas of glory! With the volunteers sat their dear ones, proud, happy, and envied by the neighbors and friends who had no sons and brothers to send forth to the field of honor, there to win for the flag, or, failing, die the noblest of noble deaths. The service proceeded; a war-chapter from the Old Testament was read; the first prayer was said; it was followed by an organ-burst that shook the building, and with one impulse the house rose, with glowing eyes and beating hearts and poured out that tremendous invocation—

> God the all-terrible! Thou who ordainest,
> Thunder thy clarion and lightning thy sword!

Then came the "long" prayer. None could remember the like of it for passionate pleading and moving and beautiful language. The burden of its supplication was, that the ever-merciful and benignant Father of us all would watch over our noble young soldiers, and aid, comfort, and encourage them in their patriotic work; bless them, shield them in the day of battle and the hour of peril, bear them in His mighty hand, make them strong and confident, invincible in the bloody onset, help them to crush the foe, grant to them and to their flag and country imperishable honor and glory—

An aged stranger entered, and moved with slow and noiseless step up the main aisle, his eyes fixed upon the minister, his long body clothed in a robe that reached to his feet, his head bare, his white hair descending in a frothy cataract to his shoulders, his seamy face unnaturally pale, pale even to ghastliness. With all eyes following him and wondering, he made his silent way; without pausing, he ascended to the preacher's side and stood there, waiting. With shut lids the preacher, unconscious of his presence, continued his moving prayer, and at last finished it with the words, uttered in fervent appeal, "Bless our arms, grant us the victory, O Lord our God, Father and Protector of our land and flag!"

The stranger touched his arm, motioned him to step aside—which the startled minister did—and took his place. During some moments he surveyed the spell-bound audience with solemn eyes, in which burned an uncanny light; then in a deep voice he said—

"I come from the Throne—bearing a message from Almighty God!" The words smote the house with a shock; if the stranger perceived it he gave it no attention. "He has heard the prayer of His servant your shepherd, and will grant it if such shall be your desire after I, His messenger, shall have explained to you its import—that is to say, its full import. For it is like unto many of the prayers of men, in that it asks for more than he who utters it is aware of—except he pause and think.

"God's servant and yours has prayed his prayer. Has he paused, and taken thought? Is it one prayer? No, it is two— one uttered, the other not. Both have reached the ear of Him who heareth all supplications, the spoken and the unspoken. Ponder this—keep it in mind. If you would beseech a blessing upon yourself, beware! lest without intent you invoke a curse upon a neighbor at the same time. If you pray for the blessing of rain upon your crop which needs it, by that act you are possibly praying for a curse upon some neighbor's crop which may not need rain and can be injured by it.

"You have heard your servant's prayer—the uttered part of it. I am commissioned of God to put into words the other part of it—that part which the pastor—and also you in your hearts—fervently prayed silently. And ignorantly and unthinkingly? God grant that it was so! You heard these words: 'Grant us the victory, O Lord our God!' That is sufficient. The *whole* of the uttered prayer is compacted into those pregnant words. Elaborations were not necessary. When you have prayed for victory you have prayed for many unmentioned results which follow victory—*must* follow it, cannot help but follow it. Upon the listening spirit of God the Father fell also the unspoken part of the prayer. He commandeth me to put it into words. Listen!

"O Lord, our Father, our young patriots, idols of our hearts, go forth to battle—be Thou near them! With them —in spirit—we also go forth from the sweet peace of our beloved firesides to smite the foe. O Lord, our God, help us to tear their soldiers to bloody shreds with our shells; help us to cover their smiling fields with the pale forms of their patriot dead; help us to drown the thunder of the guns with the shrieks of their wounded, writhing in pain; help us to lay waste their humble homes with a hurricane of fire; help us to wring the hearts of their unoffending widows with unavailing grief; help us to turn them out roofless with their little children to wander unfriended the wastes of their desolated land in rags and hunger and thirst, sport of the sun-flames of summer and the icy winds of winter, broken in spirit, worn with travail, imploring Thee for the refuge of the grave and

denied it—for our sakes who adore Thee, Lord, blast their
hopes, blight their lives, protract their bitter pilgrimage, make
heavy their steps, water their way with their tears, stain the
white snow with the blood of their wounded feet! We ask it,
in the spirit of love, of Him Who is the Source of Love, and
Who is the ever-faithful refuge and friend of all that are sore
beset and seek His aid with humble and contrite hearts.
Amen."

[*After a pause.*] "Ye have prayed it; if ye still desire it,
speak!—The messenger of the Most High waits."

It was believed afterwards, that the man was a lunatic, because there was no sense in what he said.

"The Turning Point of My Life"

IF I understand the idea, the *Bazar* invites several of us to write upon the above text. It means the change in my life's course which introduced what must be regarded by me as the most *important* condition of my career. But it also implies— without intention, perhaps—that that turning point was *it- self*, individually, the creator of the new condition. This gives it too much distinction, too much prominence, too much credit. It is only the *last* link in a very long chain of turning points commissioned to produce the weighty result; it is not any more important than the humblest of its ten thousand predecessors. Each of the ten thousand did its appointed share, on its appointed date, in forwarding the scheme, and they were all necessary; to have left out any one of them would have defeated the scheme and brought about *some other* result. I know we have a fashion of saying "such and such an event was *the* turning point in my life," but we shouldn't say it. We should merely grant that its place as *last* link in the chain makes it the most *conspicuous* link; in real importance it has no advantage over any one of its predecessors.

Perhaps the most celebrated turning point recorded in history was the crossing of the Rubicon. Suetonius says:

Coming up with his troops on the banks of the Rubicon, he halted for a while, and, revolving in his mind the importance of the step he was on the point of taking, he turned to those about him and said, "We may still retreat; but if we pass this little bridge, nothing is left for us but to fight it out in arms."

This was a stupendously important moment. And all the incidents, big and little, of Caesar's previous life had been leading up to it, stage by stage, link by link. This was the *last* link—merely the last one, and no bigger than the others; but as we gaze back at it through the inflating mists of our imagination, it looks as big as the orbit of Neptune.

You, the reader, have a *personal* interest in that link, and so have I; so has the rest of the human race. It was one of the links in your life-chain, and it was one of the links in mine. We may wait, now, with bated breath, while Caesar reflects. Your fate and mine are involved in his decision.

While he was thus hesitating, the following incident occurred. A person remarkable for his noble mien and graceful aspect, appeared close at hand, sitting and playing upon a pipe. When not only the shepherds, but a number of soldiers also, flocked to listen to him, and some trumpeters among them, he snatched a trumpet from one of them, ran to the river with it, and sounding the advance with a piercing blast, crossed to the other side. Upon this, Caesar exclaimed, "Let us go whither the omens of the gods and the iniquity of our enemies call us. *The die is cast.*"

So he crossed—and changed the future of the whole human race, for all time. But that stranger was a link in Caesar's life-chain, too; and a necessary one. We don't know his name, we never hear of him again, he was very casual, he acts like an accident; but he was no accident, he was there by compulsion of *his* life-chain, to blow the electrifying blast that was to make up Caesar's mind for him, and thence go piping down the aisles of history forever.

If the stranger hadn't been there! But he *was*. And Caesar crossed. With such results! Such vast events—each a link in the *human race's* life-chain; each event producing the next one, and that one the next one, and so on: the destruction of the republic; the founding of the empire; the breaking up of the empire; the rise of Christianity upon its ruins; the spread of the religion to other lands—and so on: link by link took its appointed place at its appointed time, the discovery of America being one of them; our Revolution another; the inflow of English and other immigrants another; their drift westward (my ancestors among them) another; the settlement of certain of them in Missouri—which resulted in *me*. For I was one of the unavoidable results of the crossing of the Rubicon. If the stranger, with his trumpet blast, had stayed away (which he *couldn't*, for he was an appointed link), Caesar would not have crossed. What would have happened, in that case, we can never guess. We only know that the things that did happen would not have happened. They might have been replaced by equally prodigious things, of course, but their nature and results are beyond our guessing. But the matter that interests me personally is, that I would not be *here*, now, but somewhere else; and probably black—there is no telling. Very well, I am glad he crossed. And very really and thankfully glad, too, though I never cared anything about it before.

II

To me, the most important feature of my life is its literary feature. I have been professionally literary something more than forty years. There have been many turning points in my life, but the one that was the last link in the chain appointed to conduct me to the literary guild is the most *conspicuous* link in that chain. *Because* it was the last one. It was not any more important than its predecessors. All the other links have an inconspicuous look, except the crossing of the Rubicon; but as factors in making me literary they are all of the one size, the crossing of the Rubicon included.

I know how I came to be literary, and I will tell the steps that led up to it and brought it about.

The crossing of the Rubicon was not the first one, it was hardly even a recent one; I should have to go back ages before Caesar's day to find the first one. To save space I will go back only a couple of generations, and start with an incident of my boyhood. When I was twelve and a half years old, my father died. It was in the spring. The summer came, and brought with it an epidemic of measles. For a time, a child died almost every day. The village was paralysed with fright, distress, despair. Children that were not smitten with the disease were imprisoned in their homes to save them from the infection. In the homes there were no cheerful faces, there was no music, there was no singing but of solemn hymns, no voice but of prayer, no romping was allowed, no noise, no laughter, the family moved spectrally about on tiptoe, in a ghostly hush. I was a prisoner. My soul was steeped in this awful dreariness—and in fear. At some time or other every day and every night a sudden shiver shook me to the marrow, and I said to myself, "There, I've got it! and I shall die." Life on these miserable terms was not worth living, and at last I made up my mind to get the disease and have it over, one way or the other. I escaped from the house and went to the house of a neighbor where a playmate of mine was very ill with the malady. When the chance offered I crept into his room and got into bed with him. I was discovered by his mother and sent back into captivity. But I had the disease; they could not take that from me. I came near to dying. The whole village was interested, and anxious, and sent for news of me every day; and not only once a day, but several times. Everybody believed I would die; but on the fourteenth day a change came for the worse and they were disappointed.

This was a turning point of my life. (Link number one.) For when I got well my mother closed my school career and apprenticed me to a printer. She was tired of trying to keep me out of mischief, and the adventure of the measles decided her to put me into more masterful hands than hers.

I became a printer, and began to add one link after another to the chain which was to lead me into the literary profession. A long road, but I could not know that; and as I did not know what its goal was, or even that it had one, I was indifferent. Also contented.

A young printer wanders around a good deal, seeking and finding work; and seeking again, when necessity commands. N. B. Necessity is a *Circumstance*; Circumstance is man's master—and when Circumstance commands, he must obey; he may argue the matter—that is his privilege, just as it is the honorable privilege of a falling body to argue with the attraction of gravitation—but it won't do any good, he must *obey*. I wandered for ten years, under the guidance and dictatorship of Circumstance, and finally arrived in a city of Iowa, where I worked several months. Among the books that interested me in those days was one about the Amazon. The traveler told an alluring tale of his long voyage up the great river from Para to the sources of the Madeira, through the heart of an enchanted land, a land wastefully rich in tropical wonders, a romantic land where all the birds and flowers and animals were of the museum varieties, and where the alligator and the crocodile and the monkey seemed as much at home as if they were in the Zoo. Also, he told an astonishing tale about *coca*, a vegetable product of miraculous powers; asserting that it was so nourishing and so strength-giving that the native of the mountains of the Madeira region would tramp up-hill and down all day on a pinch of powdered coca and require no other sustenance.

I was fired with a longing to ascend the Amazon. Also with a longing to open up a trade in coca with all the world. During months I dreamed that dream, and tried to contrive ways to get to Para and spring that splendid enterprise upon an unsuspecting planet. But all in vain. A person may *plan* as much as he wants to, but nothing of consequence is likely to come of it until the magician *Circumstance* steps in and takes the matter off his hands. At last Circumstance came to my help. It was in this way. Circumstance, to help or hurt another man, made him lose a fifty-dollar bill in the street; and to help or hurt me, made me find it. I advertised the find, and left for the Amazon the same day. This was another turning point, another link.

Could Circumstance have ordered another dweller in that town to go to the Amazon and open up a world-trade in coca on a fifty-dollar basis and been obeyed? No, I was the only one. There were other fools there—shoals and shoals of them—but they were not of my kind. I was the only one of my kind.

Circumstance is powerful, but it cannot work alone, it has to have a partner. Its partner is man's *temperament*—his natural disposition. His temperament is not his invention, it is *born* in him, and he has no authority over it, neither is he responsible for its acts. He cannot change it, nothing can change it, nothing can modify it,—except temporarily. But it won't stay modified. It is permanent; like the color of the man's eyes and the shape of his ears. Blue eyes are gray, in certain unusual lights; but they resume their natural color when that stress is removed.

A Circumstance that will coerce one man, will have no effect upon a man of a different temperament. If Circumstance had thrown the bank note in Caesar's way, his temperament would not have made him start for the Amazon. His temperament would have compelled him to do something with the money, but not that. It might have made him advertise the note—and *wait*. We can't tell. Also, it might have made him go to New York and buy into the government; with results that would leave Tweed nothing to learn when it came his turn.

Very well, Circumstance furnished the capital, and my temperament told me what to do with it. Sometimes a temperament is an ass. When that is the case the owner of it is an ass, too, and is going to remain one. Training, experience, association, can temporarily so elevate him that people will think he is a mule, but they will be mistaken. Artificially he *is* a mule, for the time being, but at bottom he is an ass yet, and will remain one.

By temperament I was the kind of person that *does* things. Does them, and reflects afterwards. So I started for the Amazon, without reflecting, and without asking any questions. That was more than fifty years ago. In all that time my temperament has not changed, by even a shade. I have been punished many and many a time, and bitterly, for doing things first and reflecting afterward, but these tortures have been of no value to me; I still do the thing commanded by Circumstance and Temperament, and reflect afterward. Always violently. When I am reflecting, on those occasions, even deaf persons can hear me think.

I went by the way of Cincinnati, and down the Ohio and Mississippi. My idea was to take ship, at New Orleans, for Para. In New Orleans I inquired, and found there was no ship leaving for Para. Also, that there never had *been* one leaving for Para. I reflected. A policeman came and asked me what I was doing, and I told him. He made me move on; and said if he caught me reflecting in the public street again he would run me in.

After a few days I was out of money. Then Circumstance arrived, with another turning point of my life—a new link. On my way down, I had made the acquaintance of a pilot; I begged him to teach me the river, and he consented. I became a pilot.

By and by Circumstance came again—introducing the Civil War, this time, in order to push me ahead a stage or two toward the literary profession. The boats stopped running, my livelihood was gone.

Circumstance came to the rescue with a new turning point and a fresh link. My brother was appointed secretary to the new Territory of Nevada, and he invited me to go with him and help him in his office. I accepted.

In Nevada, Circumstance furnished me the silver fever and I went into the mines to make a fortune and enter the ministry. As I supposed; but that was not the idea. The idea was, to move me another step toward literature. For amusement I scribbled things for the Virginia City *Enterprise*. One isn't a printer ten years without setting up acres of good and bad literature, and learning—unconsciously at first, consciously later—to discriminate between the two, within his mental limitations; and meantime he is unconsciously acquiring what is called a "style." One of my efforts attracted attention, and the *Enterprise* sent for me, and put me on its staff.

And so I became a journalist—another link. By and by Circumstance and the Sacramento *Union* sent me to the Sandwich Islands for five or six months, to write up sugar. I did it; and threw in a good deal of extraneous matter that hadn't anything to do with sugar. But it was this extraneous matter that helped me to another link.

It made me notorious, and San Francisco invited me to lecture. Which I did. And profitably. I had long had a desire to travel and see the world, and now the platform had furnished me the means. So I joined the "Quaker City Excursion."

When I returned to America, Circumstance was waiting on the pier—with the *last* link: I was asked to *write a book*, and I did it, and called it *The Innocents Abroad*. Thus at last I became a member of the literary guild. That was forty-two years ago, and I have been a member ever since. Leaving the Rubicon incident away back where it belongs, I can say with truth that the reason I am in the literary profession is because I had the measles when I was twelve years old.

III

Now what interests me, as regards these details, is not the details themselves, but the fact that none of them was foreseen by me, none of them was planned by me, I was the author of none of them. Circumstance, working in harness with my temperament, created them all and compelled them all. I often offered help, and with the best intentions, but it was rejected: as a rule, uncourteously. I could never plan a thing and get it to come out the way I planned it. It came out some other way—some way I had not counted upon.

And so I do not admire the human being—as an intellectual marvel—as much as I did when I was young, and got him out of books, and did not know him personally. When I used to read that such and such a general did a certain brilliant thing, I believed it. Whereas it was not so. Circumstance did it, by help of his temperament. The circumstances would have failed of effect with a general of another temperament: he might see the chance, but lose the advantage by being by nature too slow or too quick or too doubtful. Once General Grant was asked a question about a matter which had been much debated by the public and the newspapers; he answered the question without any hesitancy: "General, who planned the march through Georgia?" "The enemy!" He added that the enemy usually makes your plans for you. He meant that the enemy, by neglect or through force of circumstances, leaves an opening for you, and you see your chance and take advantage of it.

Circumstances do the planning for us all, no doubt, by help of our temperaments. I see no great difference between a man and a watch, except that the man is conscious and the watch isn't, and the man *tries* to plan things and the watch doesn't. The watch doesn't wind itself, and doesn't regulate itself— these things are done exteriorly. Outside influences, outside circumstances, wind the *man* and regulate him. Left to himself he wouldn't get regulated at all, and the sort of time he would keep would not be valuable. Some rare men are wonderful watches, with gold case, compensation balance, and all those things, and some men are only simple and sweet and humble Waterburys. I am a Waterbury. A Waterbury of that kind, some say.

A nation is only an individual, multiplied. It makes plans, and Circumstance comes and upsets them—or enlarges them.

A gang of patriots throws the tea overboard; it destroys a Bastile. The plans stop there; then Circumstance comes in, quite unexpectedly, and turns these modest riots into a revolution.

And there was poor Columbus. He elaborated a deep plan to find a new route to an old country. Circumstance revised his plan for him, and he found a new *world*. And *he* gets the credit of it, to this day. He hadn't anything to do with it.

Necessarily the scene of the real turning point of my life (and of yours) was the Garden of Eden. It was there that the first link was forged of the chain that was ultimately to lead to the emptying of me into the literary guild. Adam's *temperament* was the first command the Deity ever issued to a human being on this planet. And it was the only command Adam would *never* be able to disobey. It said, "Be weak, be water, be characterless, be cheaply persuadable." The later command, to let the fruit alone, was certain to be disobeyed. Not by Adam himself, but by his *temperament*—which he did not create and had no authority over. For the *temperament* is the man; the thing tricked out with clothes and named Man, is merely its Shadow, nothing more. The law of the tiger's temperament is, Thou shalt kill; the law of the sheep's temperament is, Thou shalt not kill. To issue later commands requiring the tiger to let the fat stranger alone, and requiring the sheep to imbue its hands in the blood of the lion is not worth while, for those commands *can't* be obeyed. They would invite to violations of the law of *temperament*, which is supreme, and takes precedence of all other authorities. I cannot help feeling disappointed in Adam and Eve. That is, in their temperaments. Not in *them*, poor helpless young creatures—afflicted with temperaments made out of butter; which butter was commanded to get into contact with fire and *be melted*. What I cannot help wishing is, that Adam and Eve had been postponed, and Martin Luther and Joan of Arc put in their place—that splendid pair equipped with temperaments not made of butter, but of asbestos. By neither sugary persuasions nor by hellfire could Satan have beguiled *them* to eat the apple.

There would have been results! Indeed yes. The apple

would be intact to-day: there would be no human race; there would be no *you*; there would be no *me*. And the old, old creation-dawn scheme of ultimately launching me into the literary guild would have been defeated.

CHRONOLOGY

NOTE ON THE TEXTS

NOTES

Chronology

1835   Samuel Langhorne Clemens born November 30 in Flor-
        ida, Missouri, third of the four children of John Marshall
        Clemens (1798–1847) and Jane Lampton Clemens
        (1803–90) who survived into adulthood. The other chil-
        dren were: Orion (1825–97); Pamela (1827–1904); and
        Henry (1838–58). The Clemenses, of slaveholding but
        struggling Virginia farming stock, arrived about June 1 in
        Florida after unsuccessful efforts to establish themselves in
        Kentucky and Tennessee. Martha Ann Quarles, sister of
        Jane Clemens, and her husband, John Quarles, were al-
        ready in Florida.

1839   John Clemens—austere, industrious, luckless—moves his
        family thirty miles from inland Florida to Hannibal, a port
        village about 116 miles by road (or about 130 miles by wa-
        ter) north of St. Louis.

1847   Unsuccessful as storekeeper, farmer, lawyer, and land-
        owner, John Clemens dies on March 24. A few months
        later, Sam begins part-time work but probably receives in-
        termittent schooling for two additional years. During the
        autumn is employed in the printshop of Joseph P. Ament.

1848   Works in the office of Ament's *Missouri Courier* and lives
        meagerly in Ament's house as an apprentice.

1851   On January 16 publishes first known sketch, the humorous
        anecdote "A Gallant Fireman," in the Hannibal *Western
        Union*. The newspaper is owned and edited by his brother
        Orion. Receives little or no pay as printer and editorial
        assistant.

1852   Writes squibs for Orion's new paper, the *Journal*, and
        publishes a brief example of Southwestern humor, "The
        Dandy Frightening the Squatter," in the Boston *Carpet
        Bag*, May 1. On September 9 signs a sketch "W. Epami-
        nondas Adrastus Perkins," probably the first of his many
        pseudonyms.

1853–57   Leaves Hannibal at the end of May, 1853, to work as a
            printer in St. Louis, New York, Philadelphia, Keokuk,
            and Cincinnati. Publishes humorous travel letters in the
            Muscatine, Iowa, *Journal.*

1857–61   About April, 1857, becomes a cub pilot on the Mississippi
            under tutelage of Horace Bixby. Henry Clemens, a much-
            loved brother, dies (1858) as a result of an explosion on
            the steamboat *Pennsylvania.* Publishes May 17, 1859, in the
            New Orleans *Crescent* a widely read lampoon of Captain
            Isaiah Sellers, a senior pilot, from whom Clemens later
            claimed (though unconvincingly) he borrowed the pseu-
            donym "Mark Twain." License as a pilot granted him on
            September 9, 1859. Continues on the river until approxi-
            mately April 25, 1861, when river traffic is disrupted.

1861   Member of the Marion Rangers, a small Confederate mi-
            litia group, for perhaps two weeks. Through the influence
            of Edward Bates of St. Louis, attorney general under
            Lincoln, Orion is appointed Secretary to the Nevada Ter-
            ritory. Sam accompanies Orion with some prospect of
            assisting him. They arrive in Carson City by stage on Au-
            gust 14. Sam is clerk of the Territorial Legislature October
            1 through November 29. Enters timber claims, speculates
            in mining stock, and prospects for silver.

1862   Contributes letters and sketches to the Keokuk, Iowa,
            Gate City; the Carson City, Nevada, *Silver Age*; the Vir-
            ginia City, Nevada, *Territorial Enterprise*; and the Sacra-
            mento, California, *Union.* Probably late in September
            joins the staff of the *Enterprise* as local reporter and re-
            ports on the proceedings of the legislature when it is in
            session. Quickly masters such popular forms of newspaper
            comedy as the satirical sketch, the tall tale, the hoax, and
            the burlesque; gains a reputation with Western readers.

1863   On February 3, in a letter from Carson City to the *Enter-
            prise* reporting legislative proceedings, signs himself for
            the first time as "Mark Twain." Vacations in San Fran-
            cisco during May and June. Becomes a correspondent for
            the San Francisco *Morning Call.* Contributes to the
            Golden Era, a literary weekly.

1864   Leaves Virginia City on May 29, 1864, for San Francisco. Works about four months as a local reporter for the *Morning Call* but dislikes the restraints of straight reporting. Contributes to the *Californian*, a literary weekly edited by Bret Harte. Joins storytelling prospectors in the Tuolumne hills and hears, perhaps from Ben Coon of Angel's Camp, a tale about a jumping frog.

1865   Returns to San Francisco on February 25 and remains for a year writing for newspapers and literary periodicals. Publishes "Jim Smiley and His Jumping Frog"—often called his earliest masterpiece—in the New York *Saturday Press* for November 18, 1865.

1866   Leaves San Francisco for Sacramento at the end of February, then takes five-month journey to the Sandwich Islands (Hawaii) to report in letters to the Sacramento *Union* on prospects for industry and trade. October 2 enters the lucrative business of public lecturing and reading by delivering first of many lectures on the Islands. Already he is taking on the attributes of a charismatic public figure and metaphoric Western hero. Publicized as the best of the Western humorists, he sails, with conquest in mind, for New York on December 15 as roving correspondent for the San Francisco *Alta California*.

1867   Is commissioned by the *Alta* to sail June 10 on the first cruise ship, the *Quaker City*, for Europe and the Holy Land in order to send back entertaining travel letters. Dislikes most of his affluent, religiously minded fellow passengers, but accepts from Mrs. Abel W. Fairbanks ("Mother Fairbanks") correction of his manners and purification of his prose. Young Charles Jervis Langdon (born 1849), another passenger, is said to have shown him a miniature of his sister, Olivia Lewis Langdon (born 1845). Returns to United States on November 19. Meets Olivia (Livy) in New York on December 27. Her parents, the Jervis Langdons of Elmira, New York, are newly rich from mining and marketing coal. Serves briefly in Washington as private secretary to Senator William M. Stewart of Nevada. In collaboration with Charles Henry Webb publishes *The Celebrated Jumping Frog of Calaveras County and Other Sketches*.

1868   Lectures widely. Assists in support of his mother, sister, and his always aspiring, always indigent brother, Orion. Begins courtship of the semi-invalid Livy Langdon. Reworks and expands his *Quaker City* letters. At his insistence, Livy begins her career as chief among his many editors and censors. Livy's influence, like that of the East in general, is toward the serious and genteel, away from the vulgar and comic.

1869   With a loan from Livy's father, buys a one-third interest in the Buffalo *Express*. The thoroughly reworked *Quaker City* travel letters, published as *The Innocents Abroad*, are a great financial success and set patterns for a number of his later books.

1870   Marries Livy on February 2. The next day goes with members of the bridal party by private train to Buffalo, where he and Livy are installed in the handsome house Jervis Langdon has bought and furnished for them. Langdon dies on August 16. Son, Langdon, born to Livy November 7.

1871   Hating the tedium of newspaper work, sells house and interest in the *Express*, both at losses. Begins residence of twenty-one years in Hartford, Connecticut, interspersed with periods abroad and working summers at Quarry Farm, near Elmira, home of Susan Crane (Mrs. Theodore Crane), Livy's sister-by-adoption.

1872   Susan Olivia Clemens (Susy), born March 19. First-born, sickly Langdon dies in June. Clemens publishes *Roughing It*.

1873   Takes family for the first of several stays in Europe, some of long duration. Economy in living is often the chief object, as speculations and lavish expenditures consume his and Livy's income and a substantial portion of Livy's inheritance. Publishes *The Gilded Age* with co-author Charles Dudley Warner, friend and Hartford neighbor.

1874   Clara Langdon Clemens born June 8 in Elmira. In September the family moves into their not-quite-complete, architecturally bizarre, extremely costly, luxuriously furnished mansion in the "Nook Farm" area of Hartford. Clemens increasingly in demand as a speaker at breakfasts, lunches, dinners, political rallies, reunions, fund raisings, and celebrations of all kinds.

1875   Publishes "Old Times on the Mississippi" (later part of *Life on the Mississippi*) in the *Atlantic Monthly*, then edited by his friend, admirer, and sometimes literary adviser and censor, William Dean Howells.

1876   In summer receives proofs of *The Adventures of Tom Sawyer* and begins writing *Adventures of Huckleberry Finn*. Is becoming deeply engaged in exploiting boyhood and the vernacular in a partly remembered, partly imagined Mississippi River Valley, the post-frontier. Publishes *The Adventures of Tom Sawyer*.

1877   On December 17 delivers the "Whittier Birthday Speech," a burlesque treating the New Englanders Longfellow, Emerson, and Holmes in a way that shocks a number of listeners and is at times to be deeply regretted by Clemens.

1878–79   Travels in Europe, turns again to the writing of *Huckleberry Finn*.

1880   In this or the following year begins "investing" in the Paige typesetter, the most monetarily and psychically costly of his many speculations. Expends approximately $190,000 and untold hours before abandoning hope for this machine in January 1895. Between late 1880 and early 1883 works once more on *Huckleberry Finn*. Publishes *A Tramp Abroad* and permits the private publication of the best known and most reprinted of his scatological writings, *1601: Conversation, as It Was by the Social Fireside, in the Time of the Tudors*. Jane Lampton Clemens (called Jean) born July 26.

1882   Makes trip on the Mississippi with James R. Osgood (at this time his publisher) and a stenographer to refresh his recollections, form new impressions, and collect information useful in completing *Life on the Mississippi*. Leaves New York on April 18, returns to Hartford on May 24. Publishes *The Prince and the Pauper*, a favorite with Livy and the children.

1883   Once again returns to writing *Huckleberry Finn*. Publishes *Life on the Mississippi*.

1884–85   Makes successful reading tour with George W. Cable,
            Louisiana writer and civil rights advocate (November 5–
            February 28). On December 10, 1884, publishes *Adven-
            tures of Huckleberry Finn* in England; on February 18, 1885,
            through his own publishing house, Charles L. Webster
            & Company, in the United States.

1889   Publishes *A Connecticut Yankee in King Arthur's Court*.
            Annoyed by its mixed reception in England.

1890   Jane Clemens (his mother) and Olivia L. Langdon (Livy's
            mother) both die.

1891   Sails for Europe in June and lives there for most of the
            next decade.

1894   Charles L. Webster & Company declares itself bankrupt
            in April. Clemens loses roughly $110,000 of his own
            money and $60,000 of Livy's. With the encouragement
            of Livy and the shrewd assistance of Henry H. Rogers, a
            vice-president of the Standard Oil Company, begins the
            difficult task of setting his tangled affairs in order, making
            his copyrights secure, and paying off his creditors. His in-
            clination toward pessimism and determinism is height-
            ened. Publishes *Pudd'nhead Wilson, A Tale* in the *Century
            Magazine*. (In book form the novel is entitled *The Tragedy
            of Pudd'nhead Wilson*.)

1895   In August begins a lecture trip around the world to raise
            money to repay creditors. Has become a public figure
            worldwide. Tour ends in Europe in July 1896.

1896   Publishes *Personal Recollections of Joan of Arc*. Daughter
            Susy dies in Hartford of meningitis, August 18, while Cle-
            mens is in London, Livy and Clara are en route home.
            Clemens characteristically blames himself, then inveighs
            against fate and a God whom he increasingly depicts as
            malevolent. Jean Clemens diagnosed as epileptic; there-
            after often in rest homes and clinics.

1897   Publishes *Following the Equator*.

1898   In March Henry Rogers notifies Clemens in Vienna that his undisputed creditors have been repaid. Within days Clemens attempts to engage in new, grandiose speculative ventures. During these last years he places increased emphasis on the monetary value of his writings, which he has always treated as marketable products. At the same time he is strongly moved to write "seriously," to set down what he deems unprintable truths about God, religious institutions, man, politicians, tycoons, business associates, friends, and relatives.

1900   Returns to New York in October. Makes anti-missionary and anti-imperialist statements in connection with actions of the United States in China and the Philippines.

1901   Receives honorary degree from Yale.

1902   Receives honorary degree from the University of Missouri. Isabel Lyon, who comes into the household to be secretary to Livy, becomes Clemens' secretary and general family factotum until forced out, April 1909, following bitter quarrels, especially with Clara. Their fortunes partly restored, the Clemenses' combined incomes for the year amount to more than $100,000.

1903   Takes a villa in Florence for the benefit of Livy's health.

1904   Olivia Clemens dies in Florence on June 5, and her body is taken to Elmira for burial. Clara enters a sanitarium in July; later undergoes a number of restorative treatments.

1906   Publishes *What Is Man?* privately and anonymously. In January accepts as his biographer Albert Bigelow Paine. A close association begins that lasts until Clemens' death and results in the publication of a massive biography and miscellaneous additional volumes.

1907   Receives honorary degree from Oxford University; enjoys displaying himself then and later in his crimson gown.

1908   John Howells (architect son of William Dean Howells) and Isabel Lyon supervise the building of a mansion called Stormfield near Redding, Connecticut. Clemens moves there from New York.

1909   Clara marries Ossip Gabrilowitsch, pianist and conductor, at Stormfield on October 6. Jean dies in bathtub, apparently during a seizure, on the morning of Christmas Eve.

1910   Clemens dies at Stormfield on April 21. Joseph Twichell of Hartford, one of Clemens' oldest friends, and Henry Van Dyck conduct services at the Presbyterian Brick Church in New York. Buried in Elmira on April 24 in the Langdon family plot, where little Langdon, Susy, Livy, and Jean had been interred before him. Left behind an enormous quantity of unpublished papers: autobiographical dictations, notebooks, letters, finished and unfinished sketches, essays, stories, polemics, and incomplete drafts of "The Mysterious Stranger," generally considered even in its unfinished state to be the most powerful of his later writings. For literary executors and editors, sifting and publishing these literary remains becomes almost at once a major, long-continuing enterprise.

Note on the Texts

This volume contains three of Mark Twain's novels, *Adventures of Huckleberry Finn*, *Pudd'nhead Wilson*, and *No. 44, The Mysterious Stranger*, the tale "Jim Smiley and His Jumping Frog," and a selection of ten sketches.

Adventures of Huckleberry Finn was probably begun early in July 1876, for on August 9 Clemens wrote to tell William Dean Howells that he had started another boys' book. Soon afterward, however, he set aside the approximately 400 pages of manuscript that he had composed. He may have taken it up again in the winter of 1879–80; probably he prepared some working notes in 1882, and he went seriously to work in 1883. On August 22, 1883, he informed Howells that he had almost finished; on April 8, 1884, he thanked Howells for offering to read proof for him, and on August 7 he mailed proofs to Howells.

The first American edition of February 18, 1885, is at present the best available text. A holograph manuscript of about 700 sheets of octavo-size paper representing approximately three-fifths of the book, preserved in the Buffalo Public Library, is fragmentary and in important respects unlike the finished book. It begins in the middle of chapter XII, continues through chapter XIV, resumes again with chapter XXII, and continues to the end. (Most of the missing manuscript was recently discovered.) Howells had part of a manuscript retyped in May 1884, and somewhat more than one-fourth of the book, much edited by Richard Watson Gilder, appeared in *Century Magazine*. Existing proof sheets for the book (preserved among the Mark Twain Papers in the Bancroft Library at the University of California, Berkeley) cover a part of the text that is missing from the manuscript. Following editing of a typescript by Howells, the novel was printed by Clemens' own publishing house under the eye of his manager, Charles L. Webster. Some printer's proofs were read by Howells; Clemens wrote, "I cursed my way through the rest and survived." The text printed here is that of the first American edition.

Clemens once commented that writing *Pudd'nhead Wilson* cost him little effort but that revising it almost killed him. The novel that he published was indeed radically different from the one that he began to write some time after December 1891, when conjoined Italian twins began to tour the United States. He worked on the story in Europe early in 1892. An incomplete manuscript of perhaps 10,000

words called "Those Extraordinary Twins," now preserved in the
Berg Collection of the New York Public Library, records this early
stage in the work's development. During the summer of 1892 he
continued revising, ending in December with a long, mainly holograph, partly typescript text that was commented on unfavorably by
his wife and by readers in New York. This extended version is now
preserved in the J. Pierpont Morgan Library.

During June and July of 1893, Clemens again substantially revised
his work, separating the twins, subordinating nonessential characters,
and centering the story, he said, on the murder and the trial. The resulting text, probably mainly typescript, was ready on August 14 to
send to *Century Magazine*, which bought the serial rights in September 1893, and published the story, from December 1893 through
June 1894, under the title "Pudd'nhead Wilson, A Tale." Clemens
himself read at least part of the proof of the *Century* text.

For book publication Clemens turned to the American Publishing
Company, from which he had parted in anger a dozen years earlier,
and to Chatto & Windus, in England. The American publisher used
the *Century* text for printer's copy of *Pudd'nhead Wilson* and added
what Clemens called "refuse matter," a patched-together version of
the excluded story of Siamese twins, to enlarge the volume. This edition was almost surely not proofread by Clemens, nor was the English first edition (which does not include the "refuse matter," *Those
Extraordinary Twins*). Readers who wish to examine lists of variants
between the different versions of Clemens' work may consult the
text established by Sidney E. Berger, *Pudd'nhead Wilson and Those
Extraordinary Twins* (New York: W. W. Norton & Co., 1980). This
volume reprints the 1893–94 *Century* text.

The first published version of *No. 44, The Mysterious Stranger*
was issued posthumously in an edition prepared by Albert Bigelow
Paine, Clemens' biographer and literary executor, and Frederick A.
Duneka, an editor at Harper and Brothers. This version, entitled *The
Mysterious Stranger, A Romance*, was published as a Christmas gift-
book in 1916. Although Paine claimed that they had printed the "final complete work," their edition was in fact assembled from three
manuscripts: "The Chronicle of Young Satan," written between 1897
and 1900, and left incomplete; "Schoolhouse Hill," written in 1898
and also left incomplete; and "No. 44, The Mysterious Stranger,"
written mostly between 1902 and 1905, and last worked on in 1908.
The liberties taken by Paine and Duneka's edition, based primarily
on the "Young Satan" manuscript, were extreme and resulted in a
work that Clemens would not have recognized. His language was
bowdlerized; one-fourth of the "Young Satan" manuscript was cut;

an astrologer, who did not appear in the manuscript, was introduced into the story; the concluding chapter Clemens had written for his latest and longest version, "No. 44, The Mysterious Stranger," was grafted onto the end of the book, with alterations of the characters' names in order to make the ending consistent with "The Chronicle of Young Satan." These alterations were first discussed in John S. Tuckey's *Mark Twain and Little Satan* in 1963.

The three manuscripts relating to *No. 44, The Mysterious Stranger* are in the Mark Twain Papers in the Bancroft Library at the University of California, Berkeley. They were published in an edition prepared by William M. Gibson in *Mark Twain's Mysterious Stranger Manuscripts*. Those texts were carefully established from the manuscripts, and the typesetting meticulously checked by Professor Gibson and the staff of the Mark Twain Project in accord with the standards of the Center for Editions of American Authors. This volume's text of *No. 44, The Mysterious Stranger* is taken from the 1982 paperback edition based on Gibson's text as it appeared in *Mark Twain's Mysterious Stranger Manuscripts*. The paperback edition differs from the original 1969 typesetting only in its adoption of the full title and subtitle preserved in Clemens' manuscript. For more information about the composition of this novel and about related matters, see William M. Gibson, *Mark Twain's Mysterious Stranger Manuscripts* (Berkeley: University of California Press, 1969); John S. Tuckey, *Mark Twain and Little Satan: The Writing of "The Mysterious Stranger"* (West Lafayette: Purdue University Studies, 1963); John S. Tuckey, *The Mysterious Stranger and the Critics* (Belmont: Wadsworth Publishing Co., 1968); Sholom J. Kahn, *Mark Twain's Mysterious Stranger: A Study of the Manuscript Texts* (Columbia: University of Missouri Press, 1978).

"Jim Smiley and His Jumping Frog" first appeared in the New York *Saturday Press* of November 18, 1865. Manuscripts of two earlier versions survive in the Jean Webster McKinney Family Papers at Vassar. The story was later reprinted in many collections. The text in this volume is the one printed in *Early Tales & Sketches: Volume 2, 1864–1865* (Berkeley: University of California Press, 1981), edited by Edgar Marquess Branch and Robert H. Hirst with the assistance of Harriet Elinor Smith.

For six of the ten sketches printed in this volume, the texts are taken from their first periodical appearances, listed below:

"The Facts Concerning the Recent Carnival of Crime in Connecticut." *Atlantic Monthly*, June 1876, pp. 641–50. Clemens read this speech before the Hartford Monday Evening Club on January 24, 1876.

"The Private History of a Campaign That Failed." *Centur*
azine, December 1885, pp. 193–204.

"Fenimore Cooper's Literary Offences." *North A*
July 1895, pp. 1–12.

"How To Tell a Story." *Youth's Companion,* O
p. 464.

"The Man That Corrupted Hadleyburg." *Harper*
cember 1899, pp. 29–54.

"To the Person Sitting in Darkness." *North Ame*
February 1901, pp. 161–76.

"The United States of Lyncherdom" was compose
1901 but not published in Clemens' lifetime. The text p
volume is that of Albert Bigelow Paine (ed.), *Europe a*
(New York: Harper & Bros., 1923), pp. 239–49.

"Corn-Pone Opinions" was written sometime in 190
book entry for January 31, 1901, and an annotated clippin
New York *Herald* of February 18, 1901, make reference to
opinions" and "Corn-pone," respectively. A holograph m
and a typescript survive, but the typescript contains no corr
revisions by Clemens. Deletions and cancellations on the ma
in pencil by another hand (possibly Albert Bigelow Paine's
flected in the typescript and in the first published appearance
in *Europe and Elsewhere,* edited by Paine. The text in this vo
taken from *What Is Man? And Other Philosophical Writings (*
ley: University of California Press, 1973), edited by Paul Baend
92–97. Baender's edition of the text is based on the manuscrip
includes portions omitted in earlier published versions.

"The War Prayer" was written on or before March 10, 1905,
Isabel Lyon recorded in her diary that Clemens had read it to some
friends. It was not published during his life, and it first appeared in
1923 in *Europe and Elsewhere,* edited by Albert Bigelow Paine. The
text in this volume is taken from *A Pen Warmed-up in Hell: Mark
Twain in Protest* (New York: Harper & Row, 1972), edited by Frederick Anderson, pp. 88–91, which was prepared from the surviving
typescript in the Mark Twain Papers bearing Clemens' final revisions.

"'The Turning Point of My Life'" first appeared in *Harper's
Bazar* for February 1910. It was rewritten late in 1909, after Albert
Bigelow Paine and Jean Clemens disapproved of an earlier version.
The text in this volume is taken from *What Is Man? And Other
Philosophical Writings* (Berkeley: University of California Press,
1973), edited by Paul Baender, pp. 455–64. Baender examined the
surviving manuscript, typescript, and proof as well as the first pub-
lished appearance, and prepared a critical edition based upon

Notes

In the notes below, the reference numbers denote pa
the present volume (the line count includes standard desk
note is made for material included in *Collegiate, Biographical,* and G
such as Webster's *Collegiate,* are keyed to the King J
naries. Biblical references are keyed to *The Riv*
tations from Shakespeare are keyed to Houghton Mi
G. Blakemore Evans (Boston: Houghton Mi
in the texts are Mark Twain's own. For mo
about the printing terms used in No. 44
475–80) in a standard diction
Stranger Manuscripts (Berkeley: U
1969), and Herbert Simon and He
(Leicester, 1931).

For further biographical
Chronology, see *Mark Twain's*
Brothers, 1917), ed. Albert Big
Twain to Mrs. Fairb
Mark Twain to Mrs. Fairb
1949), ed. Dixon Wecter;
bridge: Harvard Universi
William M. Gibson; M
(Berkeley: University
Mark Twain's Corre
(Berkeley: Univer
Mark Twain's Vol
1988–1997), Vol
B. Frank, and
riet Elinor S
cher, Mich
Victor Fi
ed. Lin
The S
Univ
No
P

1877–1883, ed. Frederick Anderson, Lin Salamo, and Bernard L. Stein, *Volume III, 1883–1891*, ed. Robert Pack Browning, Michael B. Frank, and Lin Salamo; Albert Bigelow Paine, *Mark Twain: A Biography* (New York: Harper & Brothers, 1912); Bernard DeVoto, *Mark Twain's America* (Boston: Little Brown and Company, 1932); *Mark Twain, Business Man* (Boston: Little, Brown and Company, 1946), ed. Samuel Charles Webster; and Dixon Wecter, *Sam Clemens of Hannibal* (Boston: Houghton Mifflin Company, 1952).

ADVENTURES OF HUCKLEBERRY FINN

3.7 PER G. G.] Probably a joking reference to General Ulysses S. Grant, whom Clemens greatly admired. Early in 1885, Charles L. Webster & Co., which belonged to Clemens, contracted to publish Grant's memoirs.

4.2–12 IN . . . succeeding.] Although Clemens did make numerous revisions directed toward some kind of accuracy, his use of dialect was not as systematic as he claimed.

10.4 Moses . . . Bulrushers] Exodus 2:3.

19.6 took . . . closet] Matthew 6:6: "But thou, when thou prayest, enter into thy closet."

20.28 hived] Here means "captured."

20.33 slogan] One of many mistaken or garbled words, phrases, names, and episodes, usually drawn from Tom Sawyer's reading as remembered by Huck. "Slogan," which means a battle-cry in Sir Walter Scott's "The Lay of the Last Minstrel," Canto IV, is confused with the fiery cross sent about to call the clans together in *The Lady of the Lake*, Canto III.

34.31 a free nigger] There were free Negroes in Hannibal during the 1840's, but Missouri passed increasingly strict laws intended to exclude them.

36.37–38 Angel of Death] Azrael, from Mohammedan iconology and mythology. The phrase appears in *The Arabian Nights* and in Byron's "The Destruction of Sennacherib," both of which were well known to Clemens. Clemens quoted often from Byron's poem.

44.21–22 firing . . . water] A folk belief held that the concussion would bring the body to the surface.

44.30 quicksilver in loaves] That the loaves would seek out the corpse of a drowned person was widely believed.

45.25–26 Bessie Thatcher] Clemens forgot repeatedly what names he had given to characters or, for that matter, to books. Here he means "Becky Thatcher."

47.26–37   By the . . . around."]   This passage, like several others, may be a fragment from a plot sequence which was deleted before the novel was published.

85.30   dolphin]   The Dauphin, Louis Charles (1785–95?), almost certainly died in prison, but legends of his escape persisted, and imposters appeared in Europe and in America. In early English usage "dolphin" was one of several alternative variants of "dauphin," in France the name of the cetacean and also, from the fourteenth century to 1830, the appellation of the eldest son of the King of France.

88.5–6   up . . . trouble]   In August 1876, Clemens seems to have completed this chapter and most of the following one before running into difficulties and setting the manuscript aside. The book was developing into something more than an episodic, lighthearted tale for boys, and, besides, he knew nothing of the Ohio River country that Jim should have turned toward. In October 1879, he took up the manuscript again and began to introduce new themes, new characters, and somewhat casual explanations for not taking Huck and Jim up the Ohio toward freedom but on down the Mississippi into territory where slavery existed in some of its worst aspects.

94.26   waited.]   Clemens was asked in a letter of April 21, 1884, by Charles L. Webster, husband of his niece and manager of his publishing company, whether it would not be better to omit from *Huckleberry Finn* "the raft passage," which began at this point but had already been removed from the manuscript and published in Chapter III of *Life on the Mississippi*. The book was, he complained, "so much larger than *Tom Sawyer*." Clemens readily agreed. For the "raft passage," see Chapter III of *Life on the Mississippi*.

100.10–11   clear . . . Muddy!]   The Missouri River is frequently called "the Muddy" because the Mississippi is the clearer of the two at their juncture just above St. Louis. Clemens has the Mississippi become "the Muddy," because at Cairo, where the Ohio and the Mississippi come together, the Ohio is the clearer.

101.21   raft.]   Clemens set his manuscript aside at about this point in the summer of 1876.

108.14   Highland Marys]   Pictures of Mary Campbell, briefly before her death the sweetheart of Robert Burns, about whom Burns wrote several poems, best known of which is "Highland Mary."

117.27   coarse-hand]   Apparently a rare Americanism meaning written in capital letters.

120.22–23   wood-rank]   Usually means about half a cord of neatly laid-up wood.

134.34   Garrick the Younger]   The duke confuses David Garrick and Charles John Kean, son of Edmund Kean and called "the Younger." Clemens introduces similar blunders later.

an astrologer, who did not appear in the manuscript, was introduced into the story; the concluding chapter Clemens had written for his latest and longest version, "No. 44, The Mysterious Stranger," was grafted onto the end of the book, with alterations of the characters' names in order to make the ending consistent with "The Chronicle of Young Satan." These alterations were first discussed in John S. Tuckey's *Mark Twain and Little Satan* in 1963.

The three manuscripts relating to *No. 44, The Mysterious Stranger* are in the Mark Twain Papers in the Bancroft Library at the University of California, Berkeley. They were published in an edition prepared by William M. Gibson in *Mark Twain's Mysterious Stranger Manuscripts*. Those texts were carefully established from the manuscripts, and the typesetting meticulously checked by Professor Gibson and the staff of the Mark Twain Project in accord with the standards of the Center for Editions of American Authors. This volume's text of *No. 44, The Mysterious Stranger* is taken from the 1982 paperback edition based on Gibson's text as it appeared in *Mark Twain's Mysterious Stranger Manuscripts*. The paperback edition differs from the original 1969 typesetting only in its adoption of the full title and subtitle preserved in Clemens' manuscript. For more information about the composition of this novel and about related matters, see William M. Gibson, *Mark Twain's Mysterious Stranger Manuscripts* (Berkeley: University of California Press, 1969); John S. Tuckey, *Mark Twain and Little Satan: The Writing of "The Mysterious Stranger"* (West Lafayette: Purdue University Studies, 1963); John S. Tuckey, *The Mysterious Stranger and the Critics* (Belmont: Wadsworth Publishing Co., 1968); Sholom J. Kahn, *Mark Twain's Mysterious Stranger: A Study of the Manuscript Texts* (Columbia: University of Missouri Press, 1978).

"Jim Smiley and His Jumping Frog" first appeared in the New York *Saturday Press* of November 18, 1865. Manuscripts of two earlier versions survive in the Jean Webster McKinney Family Papers at Vassar. The story was later reprinted in many collections. The text in this volume is the one printed in *Early Tales & Sketches: Volume 2, 1864–1865* (Berkeley: University of California Press, 1981), edited by Edgar Marquess Branch and Robert H. Hirst with the assistance of Harriet Elinor Smith.

For six of the ten sketches printed in this volume, the texts are taken from their first periodical appearances, listed below:

"The Facts Concerning the Recent Carnival of Crime in Connecticut." *Atlantic Monthly*, June 1876, pp. 641–50. Clemens read this speech before the Hartford Monday Evening Club on January 24, 1876.

"The Private History of a Campaign That Failed." *Century Magazine*, December 1885, pp. 193–204.

"Fenimore Cooper's Literary Offences." *North American Review*, July 1895, pp. 1–12.

"How To Tell a Story." *Youth's Companion*, October 3, 1895, p. 464.

"The Man That Corrupted Hadleyburg." *Harper's Monthly*, December 1899, pp. 29–54.

"To the Person Sitting in Darkness." *North American Review*, February 1901, pp. 161–76.

"The United States of Lyncherdom" was composed in August 1901 but not published in Clemens' lifetime. The text printed in this volume is that of Albert Bigelow Paine (ed.), *Europe and Elsewhere* (New York: Harper & Bros., 1923), pp. 239–49.

"Corn-Pone Opinions" was written sometime in 1901. A notebook entry for January 31, 1901, and an annotated clipping from the New York *Herald* of February 18, 1901, make reference to "Hoecake opinions" and "Corn-pone," respectively. A holograph manuscript and a typescript survive, but the typescript contains no corrections or revisions by Clemens. Deletions and cancellations on the manuscript in pencil by another hand (possibly Albert Bigelow Paine's) are reflected in the typescript and in the first published appearance in 1923 in *Europe and Elsewhere*, edited by Paine. The text in this volume is taken from *What Is Man? And Other Philosophical Writings* (Berkeley: University of California Press, 1973), edited by Paul Baender, pp. 92–97. Baender's edition of the text is based on the manuscript and includes portions omitted in earlier published versions.

"The War Prayer" was written on or before March 10, 1905, when Isabel Lyon recorded in her diary that Clemens had read it to some friends. It was not published during his life, and it first appeared in 1923 in *Europe and Elsewhere*, edited by Albert Bigelow Paine. The text in this volume is taken from *A Pen Warmed-up in Hell: Mark Twain in Protest* (New York: Harper & Row, 1972), edited by Frederick Anderson, pp. 88–91, which was prepared from the surviving typescript in the Mark Twain Papers bearing Clemens' final revisions.

"'The Turning Point of My Life'" first appeared in *Harper's Bazar* for February 1910. It was rewritten late in 1909, after Albert Bigelow Paine and Jean Clemens disapproved of an earlier version. The text in this volume is taken from *What Is Man? And Other Philosophical Writings* (Berkeley: University of California Press, 1973), edited by Paul Baender, pp. 455–64. Baender examined the surviving manuscript, typescript, and proof as well as the first published appearance, and prepared a critical edition based upon

Clemens' final holographic text, with the exception of the last two paragraphs, which are not in manuscript, typescript, or proof, and so are based on the first publication in *Harper's Bazar*.

This volume presents the texts of the printings chosen for inclusion here, but does not attempt to reproduce features of their typographic design. Spelling, punctuation, and capitalization are often expressive features and they are not altered, even when inconsistent or irregular. The following is a list of typographical errors corrected, cited by page and line number: 25.19, I I; 41.17, was; 53.7, agin; 54.7, po,'; 68.3, Goshen."; 74.12, wrack.'; 79.3, didn'; 86.30, age; 90.25, then; 112.5, Douglass; 113.21, twenty; 128.37, its; 151.35, you re; 159.20, By-and by; 161.32, "Shet; 165.4, says'; 166.24, get's; 174.2, orgiess h'd; 175.28, invest for; 191.17, says; 192.40, mind; 194.34, that; 217.35, is; 225.22, did'nt; 239.31, runinng; 248.11, way"; 257.7, mo,'; 266.33, jew-sharp's; 279.1, one?; 284.9, das'nt; 296.20, aint't; 358.1, yet?; 369.32, F.F.V.; 479.30, ley-hopper; 492.1, what; 500.15, evident.; 661.13, lighted-hearted; 673.9, Maqua; 674.12, two-third's; 676.15, mosquitos's; 680.32, than; 711.28, *reform."* '; 713.12, *reform.*' "; 723.17, face."; 748.34, "the; 748.35, enemy".

Notes

In the notes below, the reference numbers denote page and line of the present volume (the line count includes chapter headings). No note is made for material included in standard desk-reference books such as Webster's *Collegiate*, *Biographical*, and *Geographical* dictionaries. Biblical references are keyed to the King James Version. Quotations from Shakespeare are keyed to *The Riverside Shakespeare*, ed. G. Blakemore Evans (Boston: Houghton Mifflin, 1974). Footnotes in the texts are Mark Twain's own. For more detailed information about the printing terms used in *No. 44, The Mysterious Stranger* than is provided in a standard dictionary, see the glossary (pp. 475–80) in William M. Gibson (ed.), *Mark Twain's Mysterious Stranger Manuscripts* (Berkeley: University of California Press, 1969), and Herbert Simon and Henry Carter, *Printing Explained* (Leicester, 1931).

For further biographical background than is provided in the Chronology, see *Mark Twain's Letters*, 2 vols. (New York: Harper & Brothers, 1917), ed. Albert Bigelow Paine; *The Love Letters of Mark Twain* (New York: Harper & Brothers, 1949), ed. Dixon Wecter; *Mark Twain to Mrs. Fairbanks* (San Marino: Huntington Library, 1949), ed. Dixon Wecter; *Mark Twain–Howells Letters*, 2 vols. (Cambridge: Harvard University Press, 1960), ed. Henry Nash Smith and William M. Gibson; *Mark Twain's Letters to His Publishers 1867–1894* (Berkeley: University of California Press, 1967), ed. Hamlin Hill; *Mark Twain's Correspondence with Henry Huttleston Rogers 1893–1909* (Berkeley: University of California Press, 1969), ed. Lewis Leary; *Mark Twain's Letters* (Berkeley: University of California Press, 1988–1997), *Volume 1, 1853–1866*, ed. Edgar Marquess Branch, Michael B. Frank, and Kenneth M. Sanderson, *Volume 2, 1867–1868*, ed. Harriet Elinor Smith and Richard Bucci, *Volume 3, 1869*, ed. Victor Fischer, Michael B. Frank, and Dahlia Armon *Volume 4, 1870–1871*, ed. Victor Fischer, Michael B. Frank, and Lin Salmo, *Volume 5, 1872–1873*, ed. Lin Salmo and Harriet Elinor Smith; *Mark Twain's Aquarium: The Samuel Clemens Angelfish Correspondence, 1905–1910* (Athens: University of Georgia Press, 1991), ed. John Cooley; *Mark Twain's Notebook* (New York: Harper & Brothers, 1935), ed. Albert Bigelow Paine; *Mark Twain's Notebooks & Journals* (Berkeley: University of California Press, 1975–1979), *Volume I, 1855–1873*, ed. Frederick Anderson, Michael B. Frank, and Kenneth M. Sanderson, *Volume II,*

1877–1883, ed. Frederick Anderson, Lin Salamo, and Bernard L. Stein, *Volume III, 1883–1891*, ed. Robert Pack Browning, Michael B. Frank, and Lin Salamo; Albert Bigelow Paine, *Mark Twain: A Biography* (New York: Harper & Brothers, 1912); Bernard DeVoto, *Mark Twain's America* (Boston: Little Brown and Company, 1932); *Mark Twain, Business Man* (Boston: Little, Brown and Company, 1946), ed. Samuel Charles Webster; and Dixon Wecter, *Sam Clemens of Hannibal* (Boston: Houghton Mifflin Company, 1952).

ADVENTURES OF HUCKLEBERRY FINN

3.7   PER G. G.]   Probably a joking reference to General Ulysses S. Grant, whom Clemens greatly admired. Early in 1885, Charles L. Webster & Co., which belonged to Clemens, contracted to publish Grant's memoirs.

4.2–12   IN . . . succeeding.]   Although Clemens did make numerous revisions directed toward some kind of accuracy, his use of dialect was not as systematic as he claimed.

10.4   Moses . . . Bulrushers]   Exodus 2:3.

19.6   took . . . closet]   Matthew 6:6: "But thou, when thou prayest, enter into thy closet."

20.28   hived]   Here means "captured."

20.33   slogan]   One of many mistaken or garbled words, phrases, names, and episodes, usually drawn from Tom Sawyer's reading as remembered by Huck. "Slogan," which means a battle-cry in Sir Walter Scott's "The Lay of the Last Minstrel," Canto IV, is confused with the fiery cross sent about to call the clans together in *The Lady of the Lake*, Canto III.

34.31   a free nigger]   There were free Negroes in Hannibal during the 1840's, but Missouri passed increasingly strict laws intended to exclude them.

36.37–38   Angel of Death]   Azrael, from Mohammedan iconology and mythology. The phrase appears in *The Arabian Nights* and in Byron's "The Destruction of Sennacherib," both of which were well known to Clemens. Clemens quoted often from Byron's poem.

44.21–22   firing . . . water]   A folk belief held that the concussion would bring the body to the surface.

44.30   quicksilver in loaves]   That the loaves would seek out the corpse of a drowned person was widely believed.

45.25–26   Bessie Thatcher]   Clemens forgot repeatedly what names he had given to characters or, for that matter, to books. Here he means "Becky Thatcher."

47.26–37   By the . . . around."] This passage, like several others, may be a fragment from a plot sequence which was deleted before the novel was published.

85.30   dolphin] The Dauphin, Louis Charles (1785–95?), almost certainly died in prison, but legends of his escape persisted, and imposters appeared in Europe and in America. In early English usage "dolphin" was one of several alternative variants of "dauphin," in France the name of the cetacean and also, from the fourteenth century to 1830, the appellation of the eldest son of the King of France.

88.5–6   up . . . trouble] In August 1876, Clemens seems to have completed this chapter and most of the following one before running into difficulties and setting the manuscript aside. The book was developing into something more than an episodic, lighthearted tale for boys, and, besides, he knew nothing of the Ohio River country that Jim should have turned toward. In October 1879, he took up the manuscript again and began to introduce new themes, new characters, and somewhat casual explanations for not taking Huck and Jim up the Ohio toward freedom but on down the Mississippi into territory where slavery existed in some of its worst aspects.

94.26   waited.] Clemens was asked in a letter of April 21, 1884, by Charles L. Webster, husband of his niece and manager of his publishing company, whether it would not be better to omit from *Huckleberry Finn* "the raft passage," which began at this point but had already been removed from the manuscript and published in Chapter III of *Life on the Mississippi*. The book was, he complained, "so much larger than *Tom Sawyer*." Clemens readily agreed. For the "raft passage," see Chapter III of *Life on the Mississippi*.

100.10–11   clear . . . Muddy!] The Missouri River is frequently called "the Muddy" because the Mississippi is the clearer of the two at their juncture just above St. Louis. Clemens has the Mississippi become "the Muddy," because at Cairo, where the Ohio and the Mississippi come together, the Ohio is the clearer.

101.21   raft.] Clemens set his manuscript aside at about this point in the summer of 1876.

108.14   Highland Marys] Pictures of Mary Campbell, briefly before her death the sweetheart of Robert Burns, about whom Burns wrote several poems, best known of which is "Highland Mary."

117.27   coarse-hand] Apparently a rare Americanism meaning written in capital letters.

120.22–23   wood-rank] Usually means about half a cord of neatly laid-up wood.

134.34   Garrick the Younger] The duke confuses David Garrick and Charles John Kean, son of Edmund Kean and called "the Younger." Clemens introduces similar blunders later.

142.19–143.10   To . . . go!] Extraneous passages from *Macbeth* and *Richard III* are jumbled together with lines from *Hamlet*, mainly from the soliloquy, III, ii. Comparable literary burlesques written by American humorists were familiar to Clemens.

143.22   little one-horse town] Clemens has in mind Napoleon, Arkansas. Arkansas was notoriously given to violence.

148.32–149.13   I . . . off.] John Marshall Clemens, J. P., took depositions in 1845 relative to the shooting on January 24, of Samuel Smarr, a farmer, by William Owsley of Hannibal. The shooting of Boggs by Sherburn follows closely the details of the actual killing as recorded in these depositions. Owsley was tried and acquitted on March 14, 1846, in Palmyra, Missouri.

155.37   THE KING'S CAMELOPARD] The dramatic hoax introduced under this title was called "The Burning Shame" in the manuscript of *Huckleberry Finn* and was probably based on a story told to Clemens by Dick Stoker, a miner, in a cabin at Jackass Gulch, Calaveras County, California, where Clemens spent part of the winter of 1864–65. A reviewer of *Huckleberry Finn* called "The King's Camelopard" a polite version of the "Giascutus" (usually spelled "gyascutus") story, a hoaxing story of a fabulous animal which was circulated in multiple versions in oral tradition and in newspapers and was presumably given various portrayals on the stage. It has usually been supposed that the part of the king's outfit which Huck refers to as "just wild" was a false phallus. An alternative explanation suggests that, as in comic scenes over the centuries, the king, during his prancing and capering, has a lighted candle protruding from his anus. The candle would account for the original title, "The Burning Shame," or, as Clemens says it was called by its narrator at Jackass Gulch, "The Tragedy of the Burning Shame." "The Burning Shame" could be a version of the gyascutus story, as Clemens' use of the word "Camelopard" may indicate.

180.11   hark . . . tomb!] "Hark from the tombs, a doleful sound," from Isaac Watts, bk. ii, Hymn 63, used as a socially acceptable substitute for an obscene or profane expression.

190.6–7   down the banks] A substitute expression analogous to "down the country," meaning a chiding.

231.18   meeky] To skulk or sneak along. Cf. meach, meech, miche.

245.20–21   Iron Mask] The masked prisoner in Alexandre Dumas' romance, *Dix ans plus, ou le Vicomte de Bragelonne* (1845–50), part of which was translated as *The Man in the Iron Mask*. The prisoner is said to have died in the Bastille in 1703.

247.20   Castle Deef] The Château d'If, a state prison where the hero of Dumas' *Le Comte de Monte Cristo* (1844) was imprisoned.

267.23   Pitchiola] In the romance *Picciola* (1836) by Joseph-Xavier Boniface ("Xavier Saintine") a plant enables a noble prisoner to survive.

269.23   allycumpain] Elecampane, a perennial composite with large yellow radiate flowers; formerly used as a tonic and stimulant; here used to relieve pain.

273.22   *Ingean Territory*] The federal land grant to Indians in what became Oklahoma; also a base for desperadoes.

278.29–30   'Son . . . heaven!'] The quotation is from Thomas Carlyle's *The French Revolution*, III, 2, viii.

282.18–19   Nebokoodneezer] Nebuchadnezzar, Chaldean King of Babylon (reigned ca. 605–562 B.C.), is represented in Daniel 4:33 as becoming insane.

PUDD'NHEAD WILSON

299.8   *Pudd'nhead Wilson's Calendar.*] Clemens set down in notes and notebooks perhaps three hundred examples—most of them written during the 1890's and some in two or more versions—of aphoristic expressions such as were popularly used in calendars and almanacs. In *Pudd'nhead Wilson*'s serial publication, *Century Magazine* printed a miniature calendar with maxims from among those used as epigraphs at the head of each chapter. Early in 1894, after entering into an agreement, soon canceled, with L. Prang & Co., an almanac maker, permitting the use of appropriate passages from his writings, Clemens spent several days composing compact witticisms, writing "special squibs for 10 of the months & all the national holidays." He later made use of previously unprinted maxims—over the inscription "Pudd'nhead Wilson's New Calendar"—at the heads of chapters in *Following the Equator* (1897).

299.34   the Villa Viviani] Although much concerned about approaching bankruptcy, beginning on September 26, 1892, the Clemenses settled for a prolonged stay in this handsome, twenty-eight-room villa approximately three miles outside of the center of Florence.

301.4–5   Dawson's Landing] The name is taken from J. D. Dawson, master of one of the schools that Clemens attended.

302.23   Falls . . . St. Anthony] At Minneapolis, Minnesota, supplying the water power which determined the development of that city as a manufacturing center.

303.8–9   the Judge . . . free-thinker] In his working notes Clemens made Judge Driscoll the father of the slave woman Roxy's child.

303.14   the "code,"] Meaning not the legal code but the "code duello."

303.23   Percy Northumberland Driscoll] Percy Driscoll is more exemplary of the dehumanizing effect of slavery on slaveholders in the J. Pierpont

Morgan Library manuscript version of *Pudd'nhead Wilson* than he is in the published text. In the earlier version Percy Driscoll travels miles to collect a debt but lets it go uncollected because the debtor is in unfortunate circumstances. On the other hand, Driscoll sells a slave because the slave is a nuisance to travel with. This omitted episode parallels closely at key points an episode in the life of John Clemens, who, when virtually bankrupt, made a long, expensive trip during the winter of 1841–42 trying to collect an old debt.

303.32   Roxana]   The name may come from Daniel Defoe's *Roxana, or the Fortunate Mistress* (1724), a novel urgently recommended to Clemens by William Dean Howells in 1885.

304.17   "I . . . dog."]   The witticism appears in many versions, including the story of Solomon as told in Chapter XIV of *Huckleberry Finn* and the story of an elephant with two proprietors as recounted in *The Life of P. T. Barnum, Written by Himself* (1854), a book that Clemens read with pleasure.

305.8   labrick]   U.S. (Missouri) slang: a fool, an ass.

307.2   finger-marks]   Clemens used the device of fingerprinting for the discovery of identity in Chapter XXXI of *Life on the Mississippi* (1883), but at that time little was accurately known about the regularity of these markings. In an earlier version of *Pudd'nhead Wilson*, he planned to use footprints as a means for establishing identity; then in 1892 Sir Francis Galton published *Finger Prints*, the first book on the subject, and Clemens requested a copy from his London publishers. Galton, he later declared, changed the whole plot and plan of his book. The use by Clemens of fingerprints for identification in 1830 has been questioned as an anachronism, but Galton refers to a university thesis on the subject at Breslau in 1823.

318.7–9   In . . . children.]   How two she bears "tare forty and two" of the children who mocked Elisha. Cf. II Kings 2:23–25.

320.37–38   Sir . . . armor]   Clemens knew Sir Thomas Malory's *Le Morte d'Arthur* in a printing of the Globe edition and in the version for boys edited by Sidney Lanier. Sir Lancelot takes the armor, shield, and horse of Sir Kay while Kay sleeps, leaving his own in their place. Upon waking, Kay says that knights will be bold against Lancelot, whereas because of Lancelot's armor and shield, he will ride in peace. (In the Globe text, London, 1868, bk. 6, chap. 11; in *The Boy's King Arthur*, New York, 1880, bk. 2, chap. 8.)

325.15   "conditions,"]   Courses or subjects in which Tom did not satisfy the entrance requirements of the college.

325.35–326.9   He . . . could.]   The passage is transcribed from memory of life in Hannibal. In "Villagers of 1840–3," written around 1897, Clemens describes an envied rich boy, Neil Moss: "Was sent to Yale—a mighty journey and an incomparable distinction. Came back in swell eastern clothes, and the

young men dressed up the warped negro bell ringer in a travesty of him—
which made him descend to village fashions."

328.6   ablush]   Manuscript reading here is "aflush."

328.11   twins]   Clemens was acquainted with twins and doubles in litera-
ture ranging from Shakespeare to Charlotte M. Yonge and Sarah Grand.
Clemens' interest in Siamese twins was not new. Chang and Eng (1811–74),
born in Siam of mainly Chinese extraction, were exhibited in the United
States, settled in North Carolina, and married sisters. In August 1869,
Clemens published "Personal Habits of the Siamese Twins" in *Packard's
Monthly*, and on September 2, 1869, he published in the *Buffalo Express* a
sketch about a two-headed girl. The immediate suggestion for a tale about
Siamese twins probably came from an article (with accompanying illustration)
in the *Scientific Monthly* for December 12, 1891, on the Italian twins, Giovanni
and Giacomo Tocci, who had two heads, four arms, and one body. The
Toccis were then appearing in the United States. In early versions of what became *Pudd'nhead Wilson*, the twins Luigi and Angelo are congenitally united.
Clemens later separated them, but indications of their united origins remain
in the published text. See, for example, 330.27; 331.11; 363.9–10; and 401.35–36.

329.19   the West]   In American usage, "West" has been a relative term.
Not only could St. Louis and Cincinnati be referred to as Western cities in
this period, but parts of Georgia could be spoken of as "the West."

333.25   sunset . . . glory]   Possibly an allusion to a sonnet called
"Miracles" by Clemens' friend Thomas Bailey Aldrich, published in his *Poems*
(1865). The sonnet includes these lines (later revised): "The fading alps and
archipelagoes, / And great cloud-continents of sunset-seas."

367.19–20   human . . . speech."]   In the Morgan Library manuscript of
Pudd'nhead Wilson, Clemens wrote "human pair of scissors" because of the
visual image presented at that moment by the (still Siamese) twins. After
deleting the image and separating the twins, he revised the description to
"human philopena," referring to the twin kernels of a nut, but neglected to
change the no longer appropriate "snip."

376.18   that jack-pair]   Perhaps two meanings are intended: a pair of rascals; and (Siamese) twins, like the reversible figure of a jack, or knave, in a
deck of playing cards.

384.39–385.3   ole . . . Africa]   In an early draft Clemens wrote: "My father en yo' gran'father was ole John Randolph of Roanoke, de highes' blood
dat ole Virginny ever turned out . . ."

385.12–13   "Ain't . . . finger-nails]   It was widely believed that the appearance of the fingernails indicated black ancestry in a person who otherwise
appeared to be white. About 1884 Clemens made notes for a story about a
mixed-race character who "seeing even the best educated negro is at a disadvantage, besides always being insulted, clips his wiry hair close, wears gloves

always (to conceal his telltale nails,) & passes for a white man, in a northern city."

437.35   sits in among you]   The phrase was revised from the manuscript reading: "in your midst," and the apparently extraneous "in" was overlooked.

440.33–34   As . . . river.]   In an earlier version Tom, instead of being sold down the river, makes use of his suspenders to hang himself.

NO. 44, THE MYSTERIOUS STRANGER

453.9–11   en-quad fact . . . 4-m space]   Eight en-quads fit into a 4-em space. A quad is the basic unit of measure in printing.

453.12   sheep-foot]   Iron claw hammer used to tighten and lock up forms in printing.

454.6   the standing forms]   A form stored to use in subsequent impressions of a text.

471.4   vagabond landstreicher]   Hobo.

475.19   distribution]   Refilling the case with washed type.

476.6   proving a galley]   Making a proof-sheet from a galley.

476.18   take]   Compositor's portion of copy when several compositors were working on a single assignment. A "fat" take refers to an easily completed job—such as poetry or generously leaded prose. Compositors would sometimes play a game of chance with em-quads ("jeff for takes") to determine who received first choice of takes.

476.18   double-leaded]   Set with twice the usual space between lines of type.

476.19   comp]   Compositor.

476.30   bearers]   Strips placed in the form to allow smooth running of the ink-rollers during printing.

479.29   hell-box]   A box for damaged metal type.

479.30–31   lye-hopper]   A device for making a wood-ash lye solution used to clean type.

479.34   platen-springs]   Springs that lifted the platen off the impression.

479.35   countersunk rails of the press]   Rails for adjusting the type bed under the platen.

479.36   token]   One half-ream of paper.

479.39   dead matter]   Type, already set, no longer required for printing.

480.1   jeff'd for takes]   See note 476.18.

480.5   strap-oil] Nonexistent printing material; new apprentices were hazed when they failed to find it.

495.25–26   Pange lingua] A Gregorian chant.

561.27   Box and Cox lodgers] In John Maddison Morton's farce *Box and Cox* (1847), the journeyman printer Box works at night and the hatter Cox is employed during the day; their landlord rents the same room to both and collects double rent.

577.5   yunker] Young man.

580.6–7   The Boy Stood on the Burning Deck] "Casabianca," popular poem by Felicia Dorothea Hemans (1793–1835).

593.22   und schlafen Sie wohl] And sleep tight.

610.18   two fleets were meeting] On May 27, 1905 (a month earlier than the date cited by Clemens), the Japanese navy devastated the Russian fleet near Tsushima, in a decisive battle in the Russo-Japanese War.

612.4   Flora McFlimsey] Satirical character in "Nothing to Wear" (1857), popular poem by William Allen Butler (1825–1902).

612.23–24   Backward, turn backward . . .] First two lines of "Rock Me to Sleep," by "Florence Percy," pen name of Elizabeth Akers Allen (1832–1911). Set to music by Ernest Leslie, it became one of the hit songs of a year that was also marked by the appearance of "Dixie" and "Old Black Joe." Alexander M. W. Ball and other writers falsely claimed authorship of the poem.

SELECTED TALES AND SKETCHES

625.2   A. Ward] Artemus Ward (Charles Farrar Browne) had invited Clemens to write a sketch for Ward's book of travels in the Nevada Territory. He sent the following tale, but it arrived in New York too late to be included in Ward's book and was given to the New York *Saturday Review*, where it was first published.

653.38   Colonel Ralls's] John Ralls served as colonel of a volunteer regiment he organized for service in the Mexican War in 1847.

654.13   Colonel Brown] Hanceford Brown, an early settler in Ralls County, served as county treasurer from 1844 until 1862.

654.14   Buena Vista and Molino del Rey] In the Mexican War, General Zachary Taylor and his army defeated Santa Anna and a larger Mexican force at Buena Vista, February 22–23, 1847. At Molino del Rey, outside Mexico City, U.S. troops under General William J. Worth suffered heavy casualties while capturing Mexican fortifications on September 8, 1847.

656.36   out West . . . ago] Referring to his visit to Hannibal in 1882.

662.27   citizen colonel's]   An officer without a regular army background, sometimes elected by a local militia or volunteer regiment.

667.1   Ab Grimes]   Grimes left a memoir, published as *Absalom Grimes, Confederate Mail Runner* (1926).

668.28   Bull Run]   Unseasoned Union volunteers had fled after their defeat at the first battle of Bull Run on July 21, 1861.

669.8   *Prof. Lounsbury*]   Thomas Raynesford Lounsbury (1838–1915), author of *James Fenimore Cooper* (1882).

670.22–23   Friendship's Offering]   *Friendship's Offering: A Christmas, New Year, and Birthday Present*, published annually from 1841 to 1845, was one of the best known "gift books" or collections of belle lettres, typically given to young women by suitors.

673.20   through . . . darkly]   Cf. 1 Corinthians 13:12.

683.8   Dan Setchell]   Setchell (1831–66) was a comedian and monologuist whom Clemens had seen and admired in San Francisco in 1865.

700.37   "Sam Lawson"]   A village jack-of-all-trades and genial yarn-spinner in Harriet Beecher Stowe's *Oldtown Folks* (1869) and *Sam Lawson's Oldtown Fireside Stories* (1872).

719.31–32   "When . . . maid"]   From act II of Gilbert and Sullivan's operetta (1885).

737.1   *To . . . Darkness*]   Cf. Matthew 4:36, Isaiah 42:7, and Micah 7:8.

737.2–7   "Christmas . . . Eve.]   From the opening paragraph of "Christmas Hope and Cheer," New York *Tribune*, December 24, 1900, p. 7.

737.8   From *The Sun*]   From the New York *Evening Sun*, January 4, 1901, p. 1.

737.14   ruin wrought]   Clemens deleted the words "by Tammany methods" after the word "wrought."

738.5   *The Sun*]   The New York (morning) *Sun*, December 24, 1900, p. 1.

738.7   The Rev. Mr. Ament]   William Scott Ament (1851–1909), a Congregational missionary in China since 1877 and in Peking since 1880 and editor of *The North China News*, was maintained by the American Board of Commissioners for Foreign Missions.

738.12   *taels*]   A silver tael was worth approximately 75 cents.

738.15   THIRTEEN TIMES]   Clemens added the capitals and deleted a sentence at the end of the paragraph that read: "After paying all the damages Mr. Ament has 7,000 taels left, which will be devoted to the support of 100 Chinese widows and their children." Ament and Judson Smith, secretary of the American Board, subsequently explained that the figure "thirteen" was the result of a mistake in the cable transmission, the fraction "1/3" having been misread as "13." In an essay "To My Missionary Critics" in the *North American Review* for April 1901, Clemens accepted this correction of the amount but argued that the principles underlying his criticism remained unchanged.

738.26   the siege] During the Boxer Rebellion, the siege of the foreign community in Peking lasted from June 20 to August 14, 1900, when British and Japanese troops arrived.

738.36   Chili] Or Chihli, former province surrounding Peking.

739.5   Macallum's History] In the essay "To My Missionary Critics" in the *North American Review* for April 1901, Clemens identified this work as "imaginary."

740.32–39   "The missionary . . . relations."] In a dispatch from Yokohama, New York *Tribune*, December 24, 1900, p. 10.

741.8   Maxim Guns] Machine gun invented in 1884 by Hiram Stevens Maxim (1840–1916).

742.22–23   Mr. Chamberlain] Joseph Chamberlain (1836–1914) served as British secretary of state for the colonies from 1895 to 1903. He was accused of complicity in the Jameson Raid of December 29, 1895, in which a volunteer force, led by Leander Starr Jameson and backed by Cecil Rhodes, unsuccessfully attempted to overthrow the Boer government of the Transvaal Republic. A House of Commons inquiry cleared Chamberlain in 1897, and he continued to play a leading role in negotiations between Britain and the Transvaal until the outbreak of the South African War on October 11, 1899.

743.19   Magersfontein] British forces suffered a bloody defeat at Magersfontein in the Transvaal on December 11, 1899.

743.25   *Lloyd's Weekly*] Apparently Clemens was quoting from memory the following passage from December 10, 1899: "When we charged the Boers with our bayonets those who did not get away went on their knees for mercy, and I can tell you they got it with a long hook."

744.38–746.2   'March . . . bowels?'] Based on Kaiser William II's widely publicized remarks at Bremerhaven, July 27, 1900, to German marines departing for China. *The New York Times* of July 28, 1900, used the phrase "give no quarter" in its headline.

745.7   Venice's bronze horses] The four gilded horses standing on the gallery over the main entrance to St. Mark's Church were taken to Paris by Napoleon in 1797 but were returned to Venice in 1815.

746.5–6   words . . . aggression;"] In his message to Congress on December 6, 1897, President William McKinley wrote: "I speak not of forcible annexation, for that cannot be thought of. That by our code of morality would be criminal aggression."

746.7   "shot . . . world."]   From Emerson's "Concord Hymn" (1837).

746.36   friars and . . . acquisitions]   Under Spanish rule the Roman Catholic Church had become a major landowner and a civil power in the Philippines.

749.26   *buying*]   By the Treaty of Paris, December 10, 1898, Spain ceded the Philippines, Guam, and Puerto Rico to the United States and "relinquished" Cuba in trust for its inhabitants. Under the treaty, the United States agreed to give $20 million to Spain after the Philippines were transferred to its sovereignty, although the payment was not in the explicit form of a purchase.

750.15   KITCHENER'S PLAN]   During the Boer War, Horatio Herbert Kitchener (1850–1916) became commander in chief of British imperial forces in South Africa in November 1900. Following their defeat in a series of regular engagements earlier in the year, the Boers had adopted guerilla tactics, striking at railway lines and isolated outposts. Kitchener responded by destroying the farms of Boer soldiers, imprisoning their families in concentration camps (where at least 18,000 old men, women, and children died of disease), and building chains of blockhouses across the Transvaal and Orange Free State in order to block the movement of Boer commandos. On May 31, 1902, a peace treaty was signed in which the Boers accepted British sovereignty over all South Africa.

751.5–8   *Public Opinion* . . . HIM."]   On November 14, 1900, the Decorah, Iowa, *Public Opinion* published a letter from Will Coan to his mother that included the quoted passage (although not in capitals). The passage was preceded by the words "We killed 120 negroes," and followed by the sentence, "There was nothing but dead negroes all around us."

751.29   fifty State Legislatures]   Curiously, at the time there were only 45 states, Utah having been the last admitted in 1896.

752.8   Congressional . . . Cuba]   On April 11, 1898, President McKinley sought Congressional authority to intervene in the Cuban Revolution. Congress passed resolutions on April 19 that recognized Cuban independence, demanded Spanish withdrawal from the island, and authorized the use of force if Spain did not comply. An amendment proposed by Senator Henry M. Teller of Colorado was also adopted, disclaiming any intention to "exercise sovereignty, jurisdiction or control" over Cuba after it achieved independence. Spain severed diplomatic relations with the United States, and Congress then declared war on April 25.

753.3   Civil Commission]   Appointed by President McKinley and headed by William Howard Taft, this body was to assume civil control of the Philippines by September 1, 1900.

756.17–27   *Increase* . . . Chicago *Tribune*]   From an editorial "The Mississippi Lynchings," Chicago *Tribune*, August 3, 1901, p. 12; Twain's manuscript contains a clipping from a reprinting in the New York *Weekly Post* of August 21, 1901.

757.26   Windsor Hotel]   On the afternoon of March 17, 1899, during the St. Patrick's Day parade, a fire destroyed the Windsor Hotel on Fifth Avenue between 46th and 47th streets in New York City, killing more than 70 people and attracting a large crowd who watched many fleeing guests fall from escape ropes or jump to their deaths from windows.

758.7   Savonarola]   Girolamo Savonarola (1452–98), Florentine monk and reformer, faced down several large mobs and reportedly cowed a band of assassins sent to his prison cell.

758.8   Merrill . . . Beloat]   Joseph Merrill's actions were praised in a June 8, 1901, editorial in the New York *Evening Post*; Thomas Beloat was the subject of a June 10, 1901, article in the New York *Tribune*.

758.29   Hobson]   In June 1898, during the Spanish-American War, Lieutenant Richmond Pearson Hobson (1870–1937) and seven volunteers attempted to bottle up the Spanish fleet in the port of Santiago de Cuba by sinking the coal ship *Merrimac* at the entrance to the harbor.

759.37   Doctor Morrison's book]   *An Australian in China, Being the Narrative of a Quiet Journey across China to British Burma* (1895), by George Ernest Morrison (1862–1920).

760.7–12   The negro . . . completed.]   Dispatch carried in the Chicago *Tribune* of August 21, 1901, p. 1, and in other newspapers. Clemens apparently added the italics.

768.3–4   God . . . sword!]   "God the Omnipotent," Episcopal hymn by Henry Fothergill Chorley (1808–72), music by Alexis Lvov (1799–1870); the first line usually reads "God the Omnipotent! King, who ordainest . . ."

771.24–28   Coming . . . arms."]   Suetonius, *The Lives of the Twelve Caesars.* This and the following quotation are from the Bohn's Classical Library edition (1876), p. 22.

774.31–32   books . . . Amazon.]   William Lewis Herndon and Lardner Gibbon, *Exploration of the Valley of the Amazon* (1853–54).

Library of Congress Cataloging-in-Publication Data

Twain, Mark, 1835–1910.
  [Selections. 2000]
  Huck Finn; Pudd'nhead Wilson; No. 44, the mysterious stranger; and
other writings / Mark Twain. — 1st Library of America college ed.
    p.   cm. — (Library of America college editions)
  Includes bibliographical references.
  Contents: Adventures of Huckleberry Finn — Pudd'nhead Wilson —
No. 44, the mysterious stranger — Jim Smiley's jumping frog — The facts
concerning the recent carnival of crime in Connecticut — Private history of a
campaign that failed — Fenimore Cooper's literary offences — How to tell a
story — The man that corrupted Hadleyburg — To the person sitting in
darkness — The United States of Lyncherdom — Corn-pone opinions —
The war prayer — The turning point of my life.
  ISBN 1–883011–88–4
    I. Title.   II. Series.

PS1302 2000
813′.4—dc21   99–057964

ABOUT THE LIBRARY OF AMERICA

THE LIBRARY OF AMERICA is an award-winning, nonprofit publisher dedicated to preserving America's best and most significant writing in handsome, enduring volumes, featuring authoritative texts. Founded in 1979 with initial funding from the National Endowment for the Humanities and the Ford Foundation, the series, which now numbers over a hundred volumes, has been called "the most important book-publishing project in the nation's history."

For the first time, the full range of outstanding American writing will be permanently available in uniform, hardcover volumes, priced to reach a wide audience. Each volume contains up to 1600 pages and includes a number of works by our country's foremost novelists, historians, poets, essayists, journalists, philosophers, and statesmen. Authoritative, unabridged, scrupulously accurate texts are a hallmark of the volumes, which also feature a handsomely designed page, high-quality, acid-free paper bound in a cloth cover and sewn to lie flat when opened, a ribbon marker, and printed endpapers. The series includes acknowledged classics and neglected masterpieces, and new volumes are added each year.

Library of America hardcover volumes are available singly or by subscription. A jacketed edition, available in bookstores, is priced between $30.00 and $47.50. A slipcased edition is available by subscription at $24.95.

Library of America College Editions bring these authoritative and comprehensive editions to teachers and students for the first time in an affordable paperback format.

For more information, a complete list of titles, or to place an order, contact:

The Library of America
14 East 60th Street
New York, New York 10022
Telephone: (212) 308-3360
Fax: (212) 750-8352
E-Mail: LibAmerica@aol.com
Website: www.loa.org

LIBRARY OF AMERICA COLLEGE EDITIONS

American Poetry: The Nineteenth Century
John Hollander, editor
ISBN 1-883011-36-1 $14.95   1040 pages

Willa Cather • NOVELS AND STORIES 1905–1918
Sharon O'Brien, editor
The Troll Garden, O Pioneers!, The Song of the Lark, My Ántonia
ISBN 1-883011-74-4 $13.95   975 pages

Stephen Crane • PROSE AND POETRY
J. C. Levenson, editor
Maggie: A Girl of the Streets; The Red Badge of Courage; Stories;
Journalism; Poetry
ISBN 1-883011-39-6 $15.95   1379 pages

Frederick Douglass • AUTOBIOGRAPHIES
Henry Louis Gates, Jr., editor
Narrative of the Life; My Bondage and My Freedom; Life and Times
ISBN 1-883011-30-2 $13.95   1126 pages

W.E.B. Du Bois • WRITINGS
Nathan I. Huggins, editor
The Suppression of the African Slave-Trade; The Souls of Black Folk;
Dusk of Dawn; Essays & Articles from The Crisis
ISBN 1-883011-31-0 $15.95   1334 pages

Ralph Waldo Emerson • ESSAYS AND POEMS
Joel Porte, Harold Bloom, and Paul Kane, editors
Nature; Addresses, and Lectures; Essays: First and Second Series;
Representative Men; The Conduct of Life; Poems 1847;
May-Day and Other Poems; Uncollected Poems
ISBN 1-883011-32-9 $15.95   1360 pages

Nathaniel Hawthorne • TALES AND SKETCHES
Roy Harvey Pearce, editor
Twice-told Tales; Mosses from an Old Manse; The Snow Image
ISBN 1-883011-33-7 $13.95   1181 pages

Henry James • MAJOR STORIES AND ESSAYS
ISBN 1-883011-75-2 $11.95   705 pages

Sarah Orne Jewett • NOVELS AND STORIES
Michael Davitt Bell, editor
Deephaven; A Country Doctor; The Country of the Pointed Firs;
Stories and Sketches
ISBN 1-883011-34-5 $11.95   937 pages

Herman Melville • MOBY-DICK, BILLY BUDD, AND OTHER WRITINGS
G. Thomas Tanselle, Harrison Hayford, John Hollander, editors
*Moby-Dick, Bartleby, The Scrivener, Benito Cereno, The Encantadas,
Billy Budd, Hawthorne and His Mosses, Selected Poems*
ISBN 1-883011-89-2 $13.95   996 pages

Edgar Allan Poe • POETRY, TALES, AND SELECTED ESSAYS
Patrick F. Quinn and G. R. Thompson, editors
ISBN 1-883011-38-8 $16.95   1506 pages

Mark Twain • HUCK FINN; PUDD'NHEAD WILSON; NO. 44, THE
MYSTERIOUS STRANGER; AND OTHER WRITINGS
Guy Cardwell and Louis J. Budd, editors
ISBN 1-883011-88-4 $12.95   808 pages

Edith Wharton • FOUR NOVELS
R.W.B. Lewis and Cynthia Griffin Wolff, editors
*The House of Mirth; Ethan Frome; The Custom of the Country;
The Age of Innocence*
ISBN 1-883011-37-X $13.95   1156 pages

Walt Whitman • POETRY AND PROSE
Justin Kaplan, editor
*Leaves of Grass 1855; Leaves of Grass 1891–92; Supplementary Poems;
Complete Prose*
ISBN 1-883011-35-3 $16.95   1407 pages

Bookstore orders: Penguin Putnam Inc., Attn: Order Processing,
405 Murray Hill Parkway, East Rutherford, NJ 07073-2136;
tel: (800) 526-0275; fax: (800) 227-9604